CW00431610

Acknowledgement

I would like to dedicate this novel to my   , ~~~ friends who helped me bring this novel to fruition. There are far too many individuals to name them all here, though they all know who they are, and I am forever indebted to them for their support and patience. I would also like to thank everyone who has ever believed in me, encouraged me, and inspired me along the way. Last but not least, I would like to say a very big thank you to my late mother, Jennie Howes, who asked me to write a short supernatural tale for Christmas Eve way back in 2007. Little did she or I know what kind of a monster idea it would turn out to be.

Edited by Kimberly Huther
http://www.wordsmithproofreading.com/

The Man Behind the Glass (1860)

Written by Greg Howes

Foreword

The Victorian Age was an age unlike any other. It was a time of expansion, vision, exploration, and experiment. It was also a time of great contrasts in wealth, health and opportunities; nowhere more so than in London, England.

For the wealthy who dared to dream, all things were possible: No boundaries, no limitations; anything that could be envisaged could become manifest.

Contents

1	Daring to Dream	1
2	The Grand Opening	4
3	Accomplices	12
4	Biancas	16
5	First Clients	20
6	The Chemist	26
7	Inspirations	29
8	Formation	32
9	The Old Lady in the Window	39
10	Victim	42
11	Progress	44
12	The Model	52
13	Caught on Film	65
14	Textiles	69
15	Knowing Nonny	73
16	The Pendulum	76
17	The Plans	79
18	Pipe Dreams	84
19	Leather Bound	95
20	Into the Abyss	102
21	Going Down	107
22	Surveillance	128
23	The Italians	130
24	News	135
25	The Trouble	139
26	The Circus at Crackwillow Park	144
27	Thunderbug's Cloth Emporium	160
28	The Meeting of Minds	166
29	The Vigil	178
30	Upstairs	185
31	Dr Zeriah	189
32	An Unholy Alliance	190
33	On the Tramp	200
34	New Beginnings	207
35	The Treasure Chest	213
36	John's Plan	225

37	The Final Descent	238
38	The Ballroom	249
39	Sacred Ground	261
40	The Unkindness	291
41	Tinderbox	294
	About the Author	304

Chapter 1

Daring to Dream

John the chemist had just limped into Septimus Blackwood's photographic studio. Septimus could see that the chill of the morning did not hold John in high regard.

"Let us hope that this time, you have about your person everything we need to further our experiments," Septimus said impatiently.

"It's all here, in me bag," John said grumpily, holding up his battered brown canvas bag.

Septimus took hold of the threadbare bag and scrutinized it carefully.

"All would appear to be in order; bravo. All it needs is a little concentration, doesn't it?" Septimus patronizingly replied. He handed the bag back to John, who took one hand off the stick he was balancing on precariously, and snatched it back. "If you could see yourself fit to make a start upstairs, I shall be up presently," Septimus instructed coldly.

By this time Septimus' eyes had wandered from this shambling, broken beanpole of a man to the great outdoors.

Septimus stepped outside and dusted down his jacket and shirt, as if to dispel any form of lingering miasma left in the chemist's wake. He was greeted by a great waft of sulphurous air, but it troubled him not. He revelled in the ambiguity created by smoke … its ability to create nebulousness, a life without edges. "Ahhh, the great gift of progress," Septimus mused.

Septimus turned around and eyed his newly-acquired five-storied studio home with great pride. The studio had once been a tavern and boarding house, whose fortunes had ebbed and flowed like the Thames on which it stood. But now it was his, and he could do what he liked with it. The only way one could find the studio in Whortleberry Street was to traverse the labyrinth of dimly- lit lanes and passageways of London's East End, or alternatively by boat from the Thames.

Septimus' grand studio backed onto the great river, a mere stone's throw from the infamous Blindman's Wharf. The area was a haven for economic and religious migrants, gin sellers, and thieves of every description.

Septimus reflected on Mr Cherry, from whom he had bought the property, a portly man with a spherical face. Septimus surmised that Cherry's surname was likely due to one of his ancestors' resemblance to the fruit, and would thus be categorized and placed in the "descriptive" stable of genealogical hereditary names. "Where would we be without order and definition?" Septimus sighed.

One of Septimus' many contacts that he had put about in the area had informed him that one Jabez Cherry was heavily in debt to Hogshead Brewery, and may be only too pleased to come to some arrangement. So when Septimus made Cherry a fairly generous offer in cash, Cherry did not think twice. Indeed, after the sale was over, nothing was ever heard of the Cherry family again, much to the dismay of the bosses at the brewery and a few disgruntled customers who had to stagger a few more paces to the next watering hole.

All that was relevant to Septimus was that it was the tallest building in the vicinity, and its location was perfect for his future plans.

Many an inquisitive eye opened at the inclusion of the great glasshouse studio that Septimus had installed on top of the building. Few locals questioned it directly, but one man who did was Montague Pinner. Pinner was one of Kew Gardens' most eminent botanists, and an old university colleague of Septimus'. He arrived at the studio in Whortleberry Street, totally unannounced, much to Septimus' displeasure. Septimus was in his exhibition room when he saw Pinner from the window, waving at him. Despite Pinner's undoubted intellect, Septimus had never really taken to the man. *Much too blustery by half*, he mused. Irritated by Pinner's lack of regard for the preciousness of Septimus' day, Septimus reluctantly opened the door.

"Septimus old fellow, how the devil are you?" Pinner cordially thrust out his hand in greeting.

Septimus regarded this as yet another invasion into his space, but politely returned the gesture and replied, "Quite well Pinner; yourself?"

"Yes, never been finer, despite being knocked clean off my feet by a branch of a *Salix nigra* last week, damn whippy blighters, those black willows."

"You never could resist a challenge, could you?" Septimus replied, mockingly.

"Challenge, challenge you say!" Pinner said whilst removing his Bollinger hat and heading for a chair. "You are a fine one to talk about challenges, setting up camp in a place such as this, Blackwood. Choosing to live here, amongst the squalor, turbulence and chaos of the East End. Some would say that a madness has taken hold of you."

"I dare say," Septimus replied dryly, raising both eyebrows in resignation to the stupidity of others.

"Not me, though, you understand. I told 'em, Blackwood must have a damn good reason for such an enterprise."

"Oh, I do Pinner," retorted Septimus, who was tempted to add: *As much as you must have damn good reason to wear that ridiculously baggy suit, or grotesquely large bow tie,* but thought better of it. "Let's call it missionary work, shall we Pinner?"

Pinner scratched his ear, confused. "You what, er, aha yes old boy, good one; you wouldn't be the first. There have been a fair few brave philanthropic types who ventured into this wretched den of iniquity before you, Septimus, many of whom left with a ... how shall I call it, 'jaundiced melancholia' about their soul, so be warned."

"You need not trouble yourself Pinner. I never was, as you well know, a pious man, unlike your good self; scripture was wasted on me."

The ever-curious Montague Pinner left after less than one hour, still none the wiser as to why this brooding man of wealth and brilliant scientific mind should choose to live amongst such poverty and squalor. *Maybe he was afflicted with a yet undiagnosed form of brain fever? There always was something deeply mysterious and a little odd about the fellow,* Pinner mused.

3

Chapter 2

The Grand Opening

After the unfortunate visit of Montague Pinner, Septimus decided that the only way to avoid further intrusions into his business by curious past and present acquaintances was for him to hold a "grand opening" night.

The idea held very little appeal for Septimus, but at least in theory it would keep further interferences to a minimum by satisfying most people's curiosity in one fell swoop. Most of those who were invited were people who could potentially be of use to him: scientists, innovators, experts in their field, and his acquaintances from his exploring days, if there were *any* he could find. Septimus thought it best to invite a few artists and as many of the great and the good from the immediate locality. Not that this area was furnished with many "great," or particularly "good," though he thought it imperative to give the right impression of his studio and his work.

Septimus had hoped the unfashionable address on the top of invite would have put a substantial amount of guests off; evidently this was not to be the case.

His exhibition was literally teeming with people. One of whom was a retired customs officer and would-be explorer, a Fitzroy Woolstenhulme, "Ah Septimus, at last I have caught up with you," Fitzroy said amiably.

"Indeed you have. How are you Fitzroy?"

"Oh, somewhat frustrated… I cannot go back into the bush for a while; my good lady's been poorly, so all overseas exploration has been put on hold for a while, I am afraid."

"Sorry to hear that; what is the cause of her malady?"

"Oh it is her joints again; anyway, never mind that," Fitzroy said with a wave of his hand, as if brushing away to one side the tedious details of his wife's illness. "This is most unlike you, Septimus, if you do not mind me saying. I have seen you put on a few exhibitions in the past, but never in your own home. Don't tell me you have become a socialite after all these years?" Fitzroy enquired jovially.

4

"My dear Fitzroy, are you suggesting I have expressed anything less than a magnanimous disposition towards my fellow man over the years?" Septimus replied, with a stern, hawk-like countenance, only belied by a slightest trace of bedevilling smile.

"Would not dream of it," Fitzroy replied with an uncertain laugh; he could never quite be sure of Septimus' demeanour. "I must say you have put on a splendid display for us all, first class; the wine is not at all bad either," Fitzroy said, holding up his half-full glass in a mock toast, which Septimus suspected was not his first.

"Such attention to detail... no more than I would expect old boy. Good to see everything catalogued perfectly: family, genus, species, cultivars, country of origin; we shall teach these urbanites natural history even if it kills us, eh?"

"Well, one does try to illuminate when one can Fitzroy, though I suspect the sun has already set on some of those present."

"No doubt, quite so, ha, well put, man. Please excuse my ignorance; I know that I am a little behind the times with this photography malarkey, but even someone as ancient as myself cannot fail to notice the difference between this type of photograph and that type," Fitzroy said, while pointing at two separate likenesses. "Is there any chance of you explaining the distinction of each, in the King's English, if you will?" Fitzroy enquired while scratching his overly-long and unkempt white whiskers.

"I'd be glad to, though I feel I should warn you Fitzroy, that we have had a queen on the throne, for some twenty-three years now."

"Oh yes, ha ha, god I know that Blackwood; I am not a complete arse. You know what I mean." Fitzroy threw back his head in laughter, and waved both arms in the air in mock offence.

"This photograph here is a *Daguerreotype, named after its French inventor,* Louis Daugerre, who died about nine years ago now, there or about," *said Septimus, picking up a photograph of a middle-aged woman playing a piano.* "Notice the way the light bounces off of the glass, how it can be seen either as a positive or a negative image; black into white, or white into black, depending on the direction of the light?"

"I do see it; it is a truly remarkable science, is it not Septimus?"

"The likeness is captured on a thin copper plate," Septimus continued enthusiastically, "and finished off with a shiny reflective coating of silver. It is a science unto itself Fitzroy; it is also art too, despite what the detractors say. It captures life in a way nothing else can … such empathy. We have only just scratched the surface of its true wonder and potential; just you wait and see."

Fitzroy instinctively took a step backwards. There was something more than a little disturbing about Septimus' body language and the way Septimus' eyes had widened unnaturally as he gazed down at the image between his fingers.

"Some call it 'mirrors with a memory'," Septimus continued, eyes still asparkle, completely oblivious to Fitzroy's distaste and apprehension.

"I can see why. These are the other type I mentioned?" Fitzroy pointed somewhat nervously at a portrait of what looked to be some costermen at work in a market place.

"Ah yes, yes, quite so," Septimus spoke stutteringly, as if he had just been pulled out of trance.

"Yes, those are what are now known Calotypes. They were devised at around the same time as the Daguerreotypes, about twenty years since, using a vastly different system though. This was the work of our own Henry Fox Talbot, brilliant man, you have probably heard of him. I will not trouble you with the specifics, though Talbot's negative process method allows one to mass-produce one singular image, whereas the Daguerreotype does not. Both have uses and limitations though; it is a modernized version of the Calotype process that you will see most of nowadays, usually in the modern form of "Cartes De Visite," like those on small cards over there. This is the style, a smaller, more accessible package that Queen Victoria and Prince Albert had agreed to be photographed in last year, in so doing, bringing the art of photography to the attention of the public at large."

"Seems like the wind is blowing in your direction old boy," Fitzroy declared, congratulating Septimus modestly, before continuing, "Judging by your amount of … dare I say it, the French kind, can I conclude that to be your favourite particular method?"

"I trust that you are not inferring that I am harbouring some kind of traitorous intent Fitzroy?" Septimus replied mischievously and with wide-eyed earnestness.

"Why, I, er, no, nothing of the kind," Fitzroy replied somewhat sheepishly.

"Glad to hear it, ha ha Fitzroy."

Again the older gentleman was befuddled by Septimus' countenance.

"I would not say I favour the French method Fitzroy, though in truth, I do prefer Louis Daguerre's method."

"Very carefully put young fellow," Fitzroy replied somewhat relieved, and continued, "Can't have those Frenchies getting one up on us; I only just missed the Battle of Waterloo, you know. But getting back to the point, I can see why you find that style more agreeable; it does have certain uniqueness, vivacity one might say, to its finish. I'll bring the old girl with me next time, if she is well enough; I am sure it will be right up her street… she loves a reason to dress up."

"Please do; it would be nice to see Teresa again. Do send her my regards. I am inclined to use Talbot's method commercially, though I am happy to use Mr Daguerre's process for my own collection and for … special clients," Septimus said, with a slight hesitation.

The hesitation made Fitzroy Woolstenhulme slightly agitated about the matter; he could not quite ascertain what it was, just a slight doubt as to Septimus' motivation.

What Septimus had failed to add was that he and his assistant, John Amblewick, were actively engaged in conducting experiments in a range of cameras. One of these cameras was showing signs of possessing very special qualities indeed. Slowly but surely Septimus' plans for the future were falling into place.

Despite his misgivings about Septimus' aims, Fitzroy could not leave without complimenting Septimus on his great glass studio in the sky. "I am sure you will make a pretty penny out of your studio Septimus; people would pay you just to take a peep inside this great glass studio of yours."

"I am glad you approve of it Fitzroy. I believe they will; I do need them to come to add to my photographic portrait collection," Septimus replied politely, prudently not giving voice to his following thought which was, *One could always depend on human vanity, and the promise of immortality to pique the public's imagination.*

"Some say it is the finest rooftop glass studio in the whole of London, though I care not to immerse myself into a competition. I have little concern of what the rest of them are up to; I just know what I want to achieve, really. I had a devil of a job to find an architect to match my ambition though, let alone reliable builders. But I digress. Of course it would be prudent to make a pretty penny, though that, as you may have guessed, is not my primary aim. No, my endeavour is to achieve perfection and perhaps ... more ... the great glass studio is just a tool in the process really. Thankfully the studio is above the eye level of any of the surrounding houses; I simply cannot bear distraction when I am at my work. That said, such is the voraciousness of smog in this corner of the city, one can scarcely see in or out of it half of the time," Septimus replied with some mirth.

"I can believe that Blackwood, given your proximity to the river and all the industry over this way. However, I was not just talking about the architecture. I was referring to its contents too; all those clothes and props, and by Jupiter you must have one of the best collections of taxidermy in the country," Fitzroy proclaimed heartily.

"Thank you. Well, I have had to buy in all the outfits and most of the props. As for the taxidermy, though, I have been collecting such things since I was a small boy ... I never stop adding to my collection; wherever I go, I collect things: plants and creatures and every so often, as you know I need to feel the exhibit, see we have come full circle back to magnanimous spirit again, my good fellow," Septimus replied, opening his arms wide with acceptance and raising his brows.

"Well life is undoubtedly circular, Blackwood, dear boy, circular indeed. Now I had better be off, or else the old lady may start doubting my fidelity. Good luck in your venture," Fitzroy said with a smile and wink.

"Thank you Fitzroy, and who could blame her? She knows you too well," Septimus replied jovially.

It was true: Septimus had spent most of his adult life collecting specimens from his various explorations around the world. He had included some of his menagerie amongst the photographs, and this was causing as much of a stir as the wonderful photography on display. Though this was only part of his huge collection, the rest of it was scattered here and there around Britain. Septimus was noticing that although some of the more genteel souls among his guests were horrified at his taxidermy collection, a good deal more were in awe of it. Even the objectors could not fault the quality and quantity of exhibits and the meticulousness of its display.

To Septimus they were immaculate in every way: the eyes looked sharp and slightly moist, the stoats', foxes' and polecats' coats bristled and their teeth glistened in the gaslight. He marvelled at the falcons, hawks, and eagles behind the glass … peering down from their lofty heights, their eyes seemingly intently focused on all the life underneath them. At the far end of the exhibition room downstairs were the serpents: snakes from around the world, vividly-coloured, coiled, almost receptive. The vitality of Septimus' recent exhibits was a monument to the skill of his friend and gifted taxidermist, Professor Walter Savage, who was amongst the crowd this evening.

Whilst he was starting to enjoy the admiration of most of his guests, he hated the extra exposure he had to endure as a man, and the ceaseless puerile questioning by the less scientific-minded of his guests; a point highlighted by his engagement with the elderly Undertwill sisters.

"So you are the proprietor, are you?" asked Cecilia Undertwill haughtily.

"Yes madam, I am," Septimus said nonchalantly, assuming the lady was one of the few local shopkeepers that he felt duty-bound to invite.

"I am Celia Undertwill, milliner," she told him, as if reading his thoughts. "Can't say I am sorry to see that oaf Cherry go," said Celia.

"Nor I," said the woman next to her.

"This is my sister Frances but most call her 'Fanny'."

"Fanny, that's right," said Fanny, nodding and smiling in agreement.

"Our family have been milliners here for the last fifty years," said Cecilia.

"Yes, fifty years, nearly fifty-one," said Fanny, still nodding and still smiling inanely.

"Well, pleased to meet you both. I hope you find the displays and the food agreeable," Septimus replied politely.

"The food, yes, although the pastry a little thicker than need be in places. It's from Wrights the baker in Blue Street, isn't it? You would be better served by Birches in Salt Lane, a little further to walk, but there's a baker for you. It's true, isn't it, Fanny?"

"Yes very much so, very much a baker," Fanny replied.

"I will bear it in mind ladies. Now, if you will excuse me, I really must circulate," said Septimus wearily. He was just about to take his leave of these women, when Cecilia carried on talking.

"As for all of these stuffed animals, are they safe?"

"Safe ... I assure you, madam, they are quite dead," Septimus replied incredulously.

"Dead, you say? Did you say dead?" Cecilia replied, cocking her ear at Septimus.

"Yes, dead," Septimus replied flatly.

"Well yes, yes, I know they are dead, but isn't it unhygienic? I mean, what is the purpose of collecting all these dead things?" replied Cecilia impatiently.

Septimus sighed and then replied, almost by rote, "Everything I do is for the greater good of science, to collect and preserve specimens in their natural state. It is, I believe, a great service to mankind. Indeed I think that it is only through careful study and observation of the natural world that our species can truly progress. I trust you are now illuminated madam?" Septimus smiled politely and moved swiftly on before the frustrated Cecilia Undertwill could formulate a reply.

He could mask his obsession for his collections with clinical, carefully-worded replies for the likes of the Undertwill sisters, but keener-eyed observers noted something else, something burning deep within his eyes.

Many of the guests had arrived by horse and carriage, reluctantly creaking and clattering through Stepney's godforsaken byways. Once there, the carriages were looked after in Septimus' private coach house, across the road from his studio home. Septimus' acquaintances were not the type of people to dirty their feet along the alleyways and side streets leading up to the studio. The East End was also not the place to be seen out and about if you looked like you were worth a shilling or two.

Times were tough and life was never pretty on this side of the city. Few of these dignitaries would be coming back to this area unless invited, which suited Septimus just fine: no unwanted visitors. Some of the guests came by small boats, which Septimus had chartered in advance. Septimus had made it his business to know some of the watermen and lightermen by name; they were his eyes and ears on the Thames.

Chapter 3

Accomplices

Septimus was not the only photographer in this part of London at the time, but he was going to make himself the best and the most advanced, he was sure of that. Indeed, their numbers were multiplying month by month, two of which he knew could be very useful to him: Charlie "Melody" Kearney, or Melody, as he was known, and Algernon "Nonny" Wilding. The first was part tinker, part street entertainer. His family had travelled to London from County Mayo during the great potato dearth in the1840s. Melody had grown up making a few pennies here and there, and he was actually a gifted musician. He usually played the fiddle and penny whistle, but he could play just about anything he set his mind to.

Septimus had noticed that Melody's travelling photographic caravan booth and accompanying sideshow attracted much interest wherever it went. Melody would bang out a tune while his gaily-coloured twin daughters would dance a merry jig. Once the crowds were gathered, Melody would stand up upon his wagon and yell, "Capture your perfect likenesses, yours to keep until the end of time. Only a shilling a throw; the cheapest in the whole of London Town!"

Septimus was quick to notice, though, that Melody's problem was that the only thing not worthy of making a song and dance about was the quality of his photography.

Septimus had had his "likeness" taken two weeks earlier by Melody at a different market. He had noted that Melody's card was poor, his equipment barely adequate, and the "lifelong image" promised was gone within about a week. Septimus knew that Melody could only keep moving around London for so long; sooner or later he would be found out, and even more customers would be catching up with him and demanding refunds.

It was with this in mind that Septimus approached Melody one afternoon in February down Little George Street. Melody was nursing a black eye at the time, generously donated to him by a former customer. "Good morning to you sir," Septimus said with an outstretched arm, hand open wide in greeting.

"Would you be after a likeness or two, kind sir?" replied Melody hopefully.

"I thank you for the kind offer but I have already undergone that pleasure."

"Now listen, I have been having problems with my…"

Septimus raised his hand and interrupted, "I have not come here to complain or demand a refund, though there would be ample justification for both. No sir, I have come to make you a deal."

Melody's lips pursed a little, before he replied suspiciously, "A deal?" Melody instructed the two girls to make themselves scarce and fetch him some food.

Septimus' proposals seemed simple and generous enough to Melody. When a "specific type of client" came to Melody, he was to send them straight 'round to Septimus' studio and collect his money, if Septimus thought the client worthy of his attention. Melody felt a sense of both optimism and dread after meeting such an unusual gentleman; he wasn't sure why, but whatever it was it lingered long.

The other photographer Septimus used was Algernon "Nonny" Wilding. Nonny hoped that through Septimus he could raise his profile once more, to mix and mingle with people of high society, to be back where he deserved to be. All he needed was a little help. Septimus read both Melody and Nonny's situations well and set about taking full advantage of them.

Nonny claimed to know every actor and actress in London. He also claimed that photography was just a hobbyhorse of his, and his main source of income was treading the boards with his thespian friends. The reality, as Septimus knew very well, was somewhat different. Nonny did manage to take his travelling photography wagon around most of the theatres of London, but that was as close as got to the highlife he had once enjoyed.

Years of alcoholism and debtors' prisons had depleted his finances, and his tendency to brag and ponce off people at every given opportunity won him few friends. His overly affected camp manner was amusing but a little too bombastic for even the most broadminded of theatrical types. Whatever his faults were, he could still flatter and cajole and knew enough about people's inherent vanity to see the potential of photography.

Nonny was also technically minded enough to understand how to take and process photographs. For the most part, his acting career now consisted of the odd farce mainly in house theatres, otherwise known as "penny gaffs" up and down the East End. How he hated acting in them with their riotous audiences and their bawdy, grotesque entertainments. "Clowns and whores the lot of 'em," he told Septimus.

Nonny was a very intemperate man, slightly effeminate, with an air of the spoilt child about him. But Septimus could see some potential in Nonny: in particular he could see real ability in Nonny as a photographer. He had contemplated using him as his replacement when he went away, rather than relying on the surly chemist. He knew he had John in his pocket, but the same could not be said of Nonny.

Nonny's photographic composition and lighting were superb: he was a true artist. It was a shame he was so difficult to pin down, maybe one day... But Septimus could use Nonny's aspirations to rebuild his career, his status, his prestige, either on stage or as an agent. Nonny was by nature lazy, though his skill as an actor and desire for *a* drink had not abated one jot. Indeed Septimus had bore witness to one of his recent performances last week in Whitechapel.

Septimus had taken it upon himself to go for one of his night-time walks and he had espied Nonny walking from the Two Barrels Inn towards the entrance of the Sunflower Theatre. The show had obviously just ended and Nonny's arrival on the scene unsurprisingly coincided with the audience spilling onto the street. Just before reaching the theatre entrance, he saw Nonny reach into his pocket and place something into his mouth. When Nonny had reached the theatre door he started to totter and sway on his stick, and within seconds he had fallen to the ground.

Septimus had decided to cross the road to see the drama unfolding. By the time Septimus had crossed, Nonny was surrounded by many well-meaning theatre-goers. Of course the same would not have occurred if he had been dressed in clothes of a lower order, or, worse still, that of a beggar or tramp, but Nonny being Nonny had dressed for the occasion. Whilst on the ground,

Nonny began to shiver and convulse wildly and had started to foam at the mouth. The ensuing crowd had become very concerned about his fate and all assumed that this poor gentleman was having a fit.

More than one of the theatre-goers had reached deep into their coat pockets and produced a hip flask, keen to help revive the stricken man. Septimus watched with interest as one of the men cradled Nonny's head, whilst another unscrewed the top of his flask and gently poured what was presumably brandy into the fitful man's foaming mouth.

After about the third tilt of the flask, Nonny appeared to be making a slight recovery. The mood of the crowd lightened and some even cheered as Nonny was tenderly brought to a sitting position. He smoothed back his thinning hair and thanked the gentleman most kindly. "Thank you kind sir; I don't know how to thank you."

"Think nothing of it dear fellow; you really ought to see a doctor about it you know," said the Good Samaritan with the hip flask.

"Yes, I really think I must, and thanks again."

Septimus had heard no news of Nonny being prone to seizures such as this, and it instantly aroused his suspicion, so much so he decided to follow him for a while and see what unfolded. Sure enough, Septimus' hunch proved to be correct. The only discernable criterion in Nonny's route was that it exactly matched each individual theatre's closing time. Outside every theatre Nonny would follow the same routine, reaching into his pocket and placing what Septimus now believed to have been a small tablet of soap in his mouth. Once the small tablet of soap had become liquefied, he would duly fall to the ground, pretend to succumb to the most dreadful fits, and readily foam at the mouth. The most remarkable thing about it was that in every case it worked. Desperate, yes, but ingenious all the same.

Chapter 4

Biancas

The area around Stepney was always a place of struggle and strife but occasionally, perhaps as a consequence of that struggle, there spawned inspiration, compulsion and passion. The Bianca family had moved to London from Naples five years ago. The family consisted of Paolo Bianca, a prosperous wine merchant, his wife, Mrs Claudia Bianca, a talented semi-professional artist, and their two daughters Andrea and Sophia. Sadly Paolo died only two years after arriving on British shores, succumbing as many did to Typhus, which seeped across the city like blood on a bandage. After Paolo's death, his widow, Claudia, had fallen into a swift decline, both emotionally and financially; the effect of her husband's death had a devastating effect on her and her daughters. Claudia Bianca had decided after much thought to cut her losses and buy a lodging house and tavern.

The mother and daughters all played their part in the upkeep of the Angel Vaults Tavern and Lodging House. The tavern was about half a mile from Septimus' studio in Whortleberry Street. The family interested Septimus greatly; he delighted in their expressive, demonstrative natures. He could not help admiring the beauty of both daughters, Andrea and Sophia, but there was more there than just beauty; there was passion; an unquenchable desire to express, to create through their art.

Septimus had never witnessed such volatile natures before as seen in the two sisters (and even upon occasion their mother too). They were almost elemental, unbridled, and at times savage in their temperaments.

He had heard about the family's misfortunes and had slowly got to know all the family. He knew they could be of use to him, and he to them. They had talent and style, and threw themselves into everything they did. Septimus had befriended Andrea, the older of the sisters, first. They had met in the tavern and there was something of a connection, albeit a peculiar one, the first time they met; both outsiders in their own way, each initially as wary as the other. Septimus took Andrea to some art galleries and bought her some paints, and the friendship grew from there.

The relationship could hardly be called verbal, but it was one of mutual understanding. He treated her with respect, and in turn she admired his measured but reserved appreciation for works of art. She had great intuition, and perhaps was the only person who could see the tortured, passionate inner child within Septimus. He rarely smiled, but she could read his eyes. She suspected there was a darker side to his nature, but knew she would never see it. She trusted him and he trusted her.

Septimus decided it was time to approach the matriarch of the family, Claudia Bianca, with an idea. He had arranged to meet her in one of her rooms above the tavern. Andrea greeted him with a smile and took him up to see her mother. Upon entering the room, a seated Mrs Bianca greeted him cordially: "Ciao; welcome to my home, Mr Blackwood. Please be seated."

"Thank you; it is indeed an honour to meet you, too Mrs Bianca," Septimus replied respectfully, but not without some degree of affectation. The affectation was not lost on Claudia, but she chose to ignore it. Septimus could see that, despite her years and recent troubles, this lady still had an air of resolve and purpose about her. Her age had faded her noble beauty somewhat, and the gas lamps were throwing unflattering shadows across her aquiline face, but this lady still had presence and radiance about her.

"Please take some tea Mr Blackwood. Andrea has informed me of your passion for it."

"Indeed," Septimus replied and shifted somewhat uncomfortably in his chair, before saying, " I am well aware of both your daughters' artistic capabilities, and they inform me that you, too, possess a great deal of skill for details with a brush madam."

Claudia smiled and thought to herself how good it was to be in the company of a gentleman of society again, especially one who was as immaculately-attired as this one. She was impressed with how he wore his dark hair waxed back with a slight wave to one side of his forehead, fully dressed with Macassar oil, a moustache a little long for her taste, but its composition was nevertheless impressive.

She let out a faint sigh before replying modestly, "Bless them both; they flatter me, truly."

"I am particularly interested in getting a personalised advertising motif for the reverse side of my photographs, as well as touching up some of my slides with water colour. Would that appeal to you at all?" asked Septimus.

"*Si* Mr Blackwood; I am most intrigued by your proposal."

Mrs Bianca had not expected this from Septimus' visit at all; it had been a while since she had been approached to create any artistic works, let alone illustration, which was very much her forte. Her daughters had never stopped painting, but she had felt apathetic and uninspired since the death of her husband.

Claudia had half hoped that Septimus' visit was to ask permission for her eldest daughter's hand in marriage, but she should have known better; Andrea was far too headstrong for that ….

She had known about Septimus' involvement with her older daughter, Andrea, for some time; how close it was Claudia was never quite sure, but she was just happy to see that is was providing her most temperamental daughter with some emotional stability and distraction. There was a light tap on the door, before her younger daughter, Sophia, appeared with a dish of olives stuffed with garlic. "Ah, *grazie* Sophia; it is good to know that not all of life's pleasures have disappeared." She smiled warmly at Septimus whilst admiring Septimus' bow tie. It was the most exquisite one she had ever seen; the colour exactly matched the blood-red rose which adorned the lapel of his precisely cut dark jacket.

"I can start at the studio whenever you would like Mr Blackwood," said Sophia, cheekily.

"I see you have us all working for you now Mr Blackwood," Claudia said with a raised eyebrow.

"Don't worry about losing her from here Mrs Bianca; I will arrange help whenever you need it, and I will make sure that you and Sophia are rewarded well for your skills."

"I think I can live with that sir," Claudia replied serenely, warmed by the potential of greater financial security.

"Sophia has agreed to paint some of the backcloths and props and help me with my clients in the studio. I have seen her paintings; she has a great feeling for large works of art, and she is very agreeable with the public.

"There is truth in your words Mr Blackwood; I am sure all will be well."

Chapter 5

First Clients

Septimus' first clients at Whortleberry Street were Dr Rumbtuckle and his rather corpulent wife, Lettice. Dr Rumbtuckle was eager to be the first into the newly opened studios of the noted botanist and explorer-turned-photographer. The good doctor had spent a good while trying to convince Mrs Rumbtuckle of the wonders of photography and the joy she would have in giving copies of their likeness to their family and friends.

On entering the dimly-lit reception hall, they were greeted by Septimus' domestic servant, Angharad. She was a dour girl with chestnut-coloured hair. Her features were delicate in an elfin-type of way, though it was her eyes that people tended to notice the most; they were almost black and very deep set. It gave her an unfortunate hollowness, a sense of melancholy, which seemed to permeate far beyond her body.

"We are here to get our likenesses done young lady," said the doctor in his acute Yorkshire accent. "We have an appointment."

"Ah, yes; that is correct sir," said Angharad. "Please make yourselves comfortable while I call the master. Master!" she shouted, "Dr Rumbtuckle has arrived."

A few seconds later, Septimus appeared. He peered through the gloom of the exhibition room, greeted them cordially, and set about escorting the couple through the now-unlit exhibition room. Dr Rumbtuckle stopped to marvel at the remarkable creatures behind the glass. Mrs Rumbtuckle stood aghast at the sheer sight of this menagerie of creatures. She was a sensitive soul with unwanted mediumistic tendencies. Lettice believed in the spirit world and she frequently visited a medium's house just across the street from Septimus' studios, much to her husband's disdain. She wanted to learn how to bridle these whispers and notions that hijacked her senses.

Ernest Rumbtuckle, on the other hand, was as down to earth as it was possible to be. He was a true Darwinian through and through. He gave not one jot for the afterlife, and had little time for any form of religion of any persuasion. He had welcomed Charles Darwin's recently published book, *The Origin of Species,* embraced it fully, and felt comforted by the common sense offered. As a scientist it just reinforced his assumption that you live and you die and that was that. That said, he was a doctor of medicine and he was not short of compassion.

Dr Rumbtuckle turned around to look at his wife. Lettice had become very pale, and had had to take a seat; she felt as if the inside of her head was full of lizards and snakes all writhing around in frustration and anger. The blood drained from her cheeks and she feared she would pass out.

"Lettice," he said, "Are you feeling alright dear?"

Lettice just responded with a faint, "Yes." She tried desperately to gather herself and maintain composure. Dr Rumbtuckle grabbed her by the hand and offered her some smelling salts, which she declined fervently, though she did manage to inhale some of the contents of a rather decorative bottle hung around her neck. Dr Rumbtuckle apologised to Septimus for his wife's attack of the vapours, and proceeded to the foot of the stairs, though not before noticing a slight widening of Septimus eyes caused by his wife's dilemma. It was not an expression of sympathy that he observed, more one of intrigue and perhaps a flicker of guilt.

The stairs creaked and stirred beneath their feet as they made their way slowly to the top floor. The huge expanse of Mrs Rumbtuckle's crinoline dress and her accompanying generous girth made the ascent troublesome to say the least; she took a breather on each of the five floors. Despite her apprehension, it was her sheer determination that got her to the summit of the godforsaken building.

The long, arduous walk to the top floor had quite worn out this 60-year-old-plus couple. Mrs Rumbtuckle was fatigued and perspiring heavily as they reached the landing of the fifth floor; her heart thumped wildly, and her sense of anxiety, foreboding, and dread was immense.

Septimus smiled at the couple as he swung open the door to his great rooftop studio. The light poured into the room, making the couple shield their eyes from its glare. When their eyes finally adjusted to the light again, they could not believe what they saw.

21

The studio was incredible in every way; blue panelled sheets of glass over looking the Thames to the south and east, and a muddle of houses to the north. The drapes and backcloths were possibly the most opulent-looking items Dr Rumbtuckle had ever seen in his life. He was quite entranced also by the other occupants of the room, the living and the dead.

Mrs Rumbtuckle had noticed them too, and her eyes nervously surveyed the menagerie of glassed creatures and trophies taking stock of her every move. The huge revolving platform with chairs on top was more reminiscent of something out of the Tower of London torture chamber than an implement of capturing one's likeness. Behind the chair were clamps; Septimus used clamps for the head and back.

"Aha, I see you have noticed my little apparatus - quite harmless, I assure you. The way photography is progressing I am sure that very soon we shall not need such implements of ... restriction," Septimus said matter-of-factly, whilst adjusting the focus on one of the cameras.

"What do you mean 'restriction'?" Mrs Rumbtuckle replied in a frightened, high-pitched voice.

"I mean dear lady, that, in order to take a clear, unsullied photograph, one must be perfectly still; therefore, clamps are in order. Do not be alarmed, though; you will not see them on the finished likeness," Septimus replied, still focusing on the job in hand. Mrs Rumbtuckle looked at her husband anxiously.

"Don't fret dear; all will be well," Dr Rumbtuckle replied unconvincingly.

Septimus was not being entirely truthful; photography had moved on a little. Most of the top photographers had stop using clamps a few years back but Septimus still liked his little toys.

Septimus moved around the room, darting this way and that, in order to get the correct angle for the shot. Dr Rumbtuckle could not help but think how the man's movements resembled that of a restless dragonfly in midday sun.

He saw that Septimus left nothing to chance and that his legendary attention to detail was no myth. The positioning of furniture around the studio was carefully thought out: elaborate carvings of all shapes and sizes, balustrades of near- Grecian proportions for the more classical sets. The exotic ferns, orchids and palms made this very much a "living room."

The studio consisted of a vast array of props that would make even a theatre company weep with envy. All manner of fantastical worlds and fantasises could be conjured up within this studio, images trapped forever within a frame. A portrayal of truth or fiction? Did it really matter? This was Septimus' very own theatre of dreams and illusions, his to direct, create, capture, and preserve at will.

After they had chosen the backcloth they desired, Septimus said, "Pray, do be seated." The Rumbtuckles climbed to the top of the revolving platform and sat warily in their seats. Sophia, the raven-haired younger sister of Andrea, dropped her paintbrush and gracefully walked across the room. She had the movement and presence of a panther, Septimus thought to himself. Sophia's eyes fixed on Mrs Rumbtuckle for a second too long, and Mrs Rumbtuckle visibly shrank deeper into her chair. Sophia's eyes were emerald green and her hair as black and wild as the pit of Hades. She tightened the iron clamp securely around Lattice's head and neck, and then positioned Dr Rumbtuckle in much the same way.

The doctor had never seen such a creature as this and was mesmerised by her grace, movement, and particularly her eyes; there was something not quite human about them.

Balustrades were raised to the platform, as well as a few kentia palms, a table and a couple of free-standing falcons which stared balefully at the camera as they were set into position.

Suddenly the Rumbtuckles could feel themselves being transported. The revolving platform grinded slowly to the right, and Mrs Rumbtuckle felt as if ice was being poured down her spine. The contraption had been moved by a wheel connected to under-floor cogs by Mr Mortlake. Mortlake was a bull of a man; strong, stout, and brooding. He did most of Septimus' dirty work. The platform had been moved to avoid the sun, which had started to stream into the studio from the western side. Septimus assured the couple that the last thing they wanted was a shadow to befall them.

Septimus had arranged two cameras for the shots, one of them a standard for cartes de visites shot, and the other was a most unusual-looking camera that Septimus had sought out in a recent auction. Mrs Rumbtuckle's heart was beating faster than ever now as she braced herself for the camera.

Septimus gave a sickly smile, his eyes piercing through the couple like a hawk with its prey. A chill swept up the platform and into the bones of the unfortunate couple. Mortlake opened the door and left the room as the proceedings commenced.

As the couple sat mesmerised and securely clamped to their chairs, Septimus fired off a selection of shots from both cameras. The silence of the room filled their ears with the eternity of the grave. The creatures around them gazed on with impassiveness and nonchalance at the couples' dilemma.

Septimus nodded to Sophia, who was prowling in the background. She assailed the platform and released the clamps. The doctor let out a sigh of relief; his wife just stared vacantly at the camera with a near compulsion. The doctor waved his hand in front of her face and Lettice eventually dared to look away. Septimus helped the couple down from the platform, his face still adorned with a gloating smile whilst his eyes held fast the unblinking expression of a raptor. Lettice disembarked with due discomfort, struggling to maintain herself and her somewhat-crumpled crinoline dress.

The mood altered when Angharad bought in a tray of tea and cakes. She placed the tray on top of the mahogany table, looked at Mrs Rumbtuckle and said, "Help yourself to sugar, if you please."

"Yes, please do be seated," Septimus said, as if coming out of a trance. "It is quite an ordeal for you both, but a rewarding one nonetheless, I think you will find."

Lettice for once could not eat, but sipped lightly and deeply at her scalding-hot, semi-brewed and over-sweetened tea. Dr Rumbtuckle pulled on his whiskers in an effort to pull himself back to earth. He found himself unnerved but fascinated by the experience.

Septimus' eye wandered to the fidgety figure of Mrs Rumbtuckle; he focused on the huge expanse that was the crinoline skirt and wondered at the monster that could have invented such a preposterous device - he mused at the absurdity of it. It was only the middle and upper classes that could afford such a ridiculous item. He then considered that the only plus of the contraption would be to render the willing victim of such a style completely disabled of doing any useful practical task and therefore never to be considered part of the hoi polloi. How many fields of cotton filled the underneath of such a skirt? Though what lay beneath Mrs Rumbtuckle's bloated attire was not a thought he wanted to dwell on for long.

The two men sat and made small talk about Darwin's theories for a while. Septimus was happy to engage in such a discussion, as he, too, was fascinated by these new truths, and enjoyed the visions and possibilities they provoked in his imagination. He had often wondered about the links of certain species and agreed with Dr Rumbtuckle that this was truly a remarkable achievement.

Lettice seemed still to be in a state of some bewilderment, but did partake a little in a discussion about the various types of air and urn plants adorning the room, and which type of album she would like the prints displayed in. Septimus promised the couple that he would get to work on the photographs straight away, and that the photographs would be delivered to their door by one of his men, forthwith.

The chemist passed the somewhat-ruffled Rumbtuckles in the reception hall and limped up the dimly-lit staircase. On entering the studio he gave a brief nod to Sophia, who was vigorously painting some drapery. She begrudgingly returned his nod but with no eye contact whatsoever. The chemist had a peculiar relationship in his attitude towards women and was not at all keen on feisty ones like Sophia. He rolled his eyes at the lack of response from Sophia and disappeared off into the dark room, muttering incoherently.

Chapter 6

The Chemist

John the chemist assisted Septimus with many aspects of his photographic work; he was a knowledgeable technician and shared Septimus' love of experimentation and innovation. Septimus did not usually enjoy sharing anything with anybody, least of all his thoughts and ideas. However, he did need an assistant, one with knowledge, skill, and very few scruples. The chemist was a peculiar man in many ways: he smelt awful; indeed he had so many odours about his person that he was a walking compendium of acrid, sour, ether, sulphur, sweat, not to mention the ever-prevalent aroma of gin.

John's appearance often alarmed people and produced a combination of both pity and revulsion. He had a sallow face, fingers like claws, and what little hair he had was long and greasy and frequently stuck to his head. John's eyes were large and oval and pale grey in hue. He changed his attire rarely and often wore a bottle- green, wide-breasted jacket with what looked like burn marks on the sleeves, and blotched, beige trousers that were originally a sepia cream. His boots were black and beaten, only held together by the expensive Italian shoemaking that he could no longer afford. His shirts were grey and collarless and he frequently wore a yellow silk scarf, which was as frayed as the man's nerves. The main reasons for John's dereliction was largely due to malaise, inertia, and his penchant for gin, opium, and other vices.

John was not particularly poor; Septimus paid him adequately, and his shop should have kept him afloat by itself, as the shop was John's chief occupation. He held the chemist and druggist on the corner of Alan Road. Much of the equipment in the shop had been passed down by his father before him. John had been in the shop for at least five years and, with the help of an occasional assistant and his neighbours, Mr and Mrs Thunderbug, managed to run a viable business.

The chemist's real name was John Amblewick, though many in the past knew him as "Jack." He had been born with a bright and enquiring mind that had slowly been curdled by a veritable theatre of events throughout his life, some of which were self-inflicted. His father had also been a chemist before him, with a penchant for inventions. When he was younger, he and his father would spend much of their free time in the basement of the family shop in Deptford, experimenting with various ingenious contraptions.

John also used to help his father prepare the medicines and tonics dispensed from his shop. John showed great interest in the effects on the human body of these drugs and potions, and even started experimenting on himself, much to the disdain of his father and Uncle Dick. John's education had been erratic, though exceptional, especially for one of the lower middle-classes.

His father passed on his knowledge of chemicals as well as the uses and types of plants required for the making of medicine.

Despite the attentiveness of his father and uncle, John's childhood was not a happy one. His mother disliked John intensely and was forever telling him that it was his fault that she had had to give up her imaginary career as a singer and dancer to look after him. The fact that she was well over twenty stone and could not sing or dance seemed to have escaped her notice. The bitterness between mother and son became mutual; the older John became, the more he loathed his mother's shrill voice and flirtations with nearly every man who came into his father's shop.

When the chemist was not assisting Septimus with his work, or inebriated, he was forever testing out new contraptions and concoctions in his shop and writing down, whenever possible, his findings. His journals were full of his thoughts and references, though they were widely interspersed with confused rantings and ghoulish sketches in the margin. His latest project's scribblings were of sputum mugs, bronchial inhalers, glass nipple-shields for women, and even a possible cure for cholera. Such were the strange formulas and mathematical equations that littered John's journal. Those that saw it likened it more to that of alchemist's grimoire, rather than a modern-day apothecary.

Recently his main obsession was a hot air vapour chamber, which was to have a similar effect as a Turkish bath, if only he could get the temperature gauge to work properly.

John had recently devised his own pill-maker and was well-known throughout East London for his cure-alls. John immodestly claimed that his pills and lotions could cure everything from baldness to asthma, liver complaints, and even syphilis.

No one could accuse him or his shop of being limited. John's shop sold sauces, spiced tea, candles, lamp oils, tobacco, and scented soaps. The latter was one of his wares, which people dearly wished he would experiment more with.

At least his work with Septimus did enable John to maintain some modicum of discipline, though recently he found it difficult keeping up with the sheer volume of clients Septimus was generating, not to mention sourcing the ingredients needed for Septimus' new project. Septimus wanted too much, much too much, and one day John promised himself he would get his own back.

Chapter 7

Inspirations

Out of all the many reasons Septimus chose to make his home where he did, the most important of all had to be that this location was close to the old manor house that was destroyed by the Great Fire of Stepney in 1794.

This manor house was the ancestral home of his Blackwood family, and last owned by his grandparents Cornelius and Morwenna Blackwood. Septimus had been taken in as a small child with his Grandfather Cornelius' younger brother, Great Uncle Augustus. His great uncle had a large estate near the town of Thame in Oxfordshire, and it was here that Septimus spent most of his childhood.

Apparently Septimus' father had sought his fortune overseas and never returned home, and was so presumed dead, and Septimus' mother had died not long after, so this was where he was to stay. His Great Uncle Augustus was a reliable man, a surgeon-cum-doctor with links to the academia of Oxford; Septimus recalled his long white beard, and how it made him look like one of the ancient Greek philosophers. Although Septimus never did know Augustus' true age, he calculated that he must have been born sometime around the early to mid-1750s. He based the calculation on hearing that Cornelius, Augustus' elder brother, was aged forty-four when he and his wife died in the Great Fire.

Augustus' stubborn refusal to talk at any length about Septimus' parents and grandparents had always irked Septimus greatly. Fortunately Augustus' wife, Arianwen, was a different kettle of fish all together. She was often accused by her husband of having loose lips and being far too emotional.

Arianwen hailed from Carmarthenshire in Southwest Wales, and was always full of wondrous tales of men and women with supernatural abilities, haunted valleys, and lost villages. Her imagination knew no bounds, and young Septimus always listened most attentively to her fantastical tales. As an adult, Septimus hoped that what he had gleaned from her about his supposed ancestral manor house was not one of these fairytales too.

Arianwen only saw fit to mention the old manor house and tales of the family history when her husband was visiting a patient or on business in Oxford. But everything she did say was firmly locked away, stored away and nurtured in the back of Septimus' extensive memory banks: the deep cellars, which may or may not have survived the fire, row after row of ancient books and manuscripts, paintings, historical treasures, and even a ballroom all "possibly" entombed below-ground.

Arianwen told the young Septimus that hundreds of people died in the fire, and that large parts of Stepney and the area around it were rebuilt.

Some of the rebuilding was carried out along the original layout where houses and roads had initially stood before the fire. Other parts apparently, including where the mansion stood, were completely remodelled and their old topography changed forever.

She told Septimus of underground rivers and sewers which flowed alongside the old mansion, and about passageways and openings into the waterways below. Most of those rivers and sewers would still be there, Septimus mused, still flowing down the age-old routes back into Father Thames. But how much longer would this be the case? Presently the certainty of their passage was under threat.

Two massive projects were now underway within the capital, one of which was a consequence of what had become known as the "Great Stink" of 1858. Parliament was halted due to the noxious fumes spewing from the river Thames. Sewage had completely taken over the Thames and was leaking into the surrounding areas, virtually grinding London to a halt.

Joseph Bazalgette was the architect of this grand scheme, which he believed would transform the subterranean geography of the city and give London a sewage system that would be the envy of the world.

This new system would aid in keeping deadly diseases such as cholera and typhoid at bay, which were still thought by many to be caused by smell alone. The old system of dealing with most of the capital's waste was the use of cesspits, though some still crept its way into the old sewers. The time had come for change, and the old cesspits were now totally inadequate to deal with the burgeoning population.

The other cause of their inadequacy was that these cesspits were being flooded with water from the newly-acquired water closet toilets that many Londoners had taken so fondly to their bosom. This in turn meant that these cesspits would overflow and seep into the underground rivers, whose chief function previously was to trap rainwater and shepherd it into the Thames. But it wasn't just the overflow into the Thames that was a problem; this noxious trickle had now found its way into many of the wells and stand pumps used by Londoners for their drinking water, killing and poisoning thousands of citizens.

Another great threat to the old submerged waterways was the idea to build stations beneath the ground and create an underground railway. This was thought to be a great boon for the city, to enable people to navigate the city at speed and reduce the traffic on the roads.

Just how much traffic and how many stations there would be, only time would tell, but the potential for disturbance to Septimus' plans was huge. Time, traffic, and water were obviously not standing still, so the sooner Septimus put his subterranean plans into effect the better.

Chapter 8

Formation

Septimus peered out of one of his bedroom windows that overlooked the mighty Thames, the great gateway to the world, catalyst of so many dreams and ideas.

He never stopped marvelling how this murky, cluttered seaway was the centre of the known world. Sure, there were other great ports in Europe, but they were merely arteries to feed the great, vibrant, pumping heart of this British Empire. Septimus revelled in the empire and, moreover, the chance for exploration and endeavour. His mood was very much up with the tide this morning and his thoughts lay very much on his own explorations and endeavours.

The light breakfast Septimus had requested was served by Angharad, who also dutifully smiled at her employer. He responded with his customary nod, and a polite but quiet, "Thank you". Septimus paused and looked at the perfectly cooked scrambled eggs in front of him. *I wonder whether it would be more profitable to let Angharad process the egg-fixing paper for photographs instead of the chemist*, Septimus mused. He smiled inwardly at the thought of Angharad in the kitchen, beating the egg whites into froth, then smearing it over the thin sheets of paper. The chaos in the kitchen would be immense, eggy paper sheets hanging up to dry alongside the washing, silver nitrate splashing all over her smalls and cooking pots … perhaps not.

Septimus reached for his cape, top hat, and his trusty swordstick and set off with swift legs through Blindman's Wharf to the greater docks beyond. The early morning fog spewed forth over the river and the boatmen upon it.

Despite the fog, the water was thick with activity, a vast array of boats vying for space and the chance of open water. Watermen ferried passengers back and forth across the river in their skiffs and werries. Lightermen used their lighters with their huge steering oar to transport goods from ship to shore. Clippers effortlessly glided their way through the water despite their huge loads of tea from

China and India alike. The fog breathed its moist air into the warehouses and waterside jetties, and stole its way into the houses beyond. The heart of the empire was pumping well. A hundred different aromas seemed to crowd the air and jostle for dominance: sulphur from the chimneys, scented oils from Africa, cod from the North Sea, spices from India; every taste and every whim was sated here.

Septimus loved the hustle and bustle of dock life -- he marvelled at the great cranes toiling away: Giant insentient beasts of burden adorned with their vast chains, pulleys and wheels endlessly spinning and hauling in cask, sack and trunk, riverside warehouses greedily sucking in ton after ton of merchandise, feeding the insatiable hunger of a city without limits.

As he walked along a bit farther, Septimus noticed a Turkish clipper unloading bales to a swaying barge. Bale after bale of opium was transhipped, surely enough to sedate an entire city for a week, Septimus mused.

Septimus thought he recognised one of the crew, an acquaintance of the chemist perhaps? He walked quickly on, making sure not to make eye contact.

The shriek of a gull disrupted Septimus' train of thought, swooping down perilously close to his head, forcing him to flinch. Septimus eyed the bird malevolently, and thought, *You are a lucky gull that I can't catch you and stuff you right now, wretched creature.* Septimus tried to compose himself again -- a quick alteration to the hat and a pat down of the coat. He nearly always patted down and brushed at his coat when flustered. If not that, he would habitually stroke his hair until the agitation wore off.

As Septimus took one last look at the mayhem of the docks, he noticed that, when seen from afar, the activity of the riverside resembled a single creature, with vast tentacles coiling and uncoiling over the murky expanse of the Thames, never still, never silent. The single creature's industry was inspirational to Septimus; he hoped his forthcoming meeting would produce a similar wave of united endeavour and enterprise.

Septimus met Mr Mortlake outside the Rope and Anchor Inn, dockside. Some of the inn was landlocked, though a large proportion of the inn's bloated belly overhung the river, especially at high tide. The Thames side of the inn was supported by heavy wooden poles dotted with barnacles and sludge, which descended deep into the silt below. Rough-cut beams and even rougher- cut boarding made up the precariously slippery, splinter strewn boardwalk. Algae freckled the face of the building, so its maritime acne grew on relentlessly, despite the fact that the building's adolescence had long since subsided into its ancient timber piles countless years ago.

Mr Mortlake had frequented the inn for a fair time now. He and the landlord, a Mr Henry Ringer, had become firm acquaintances. That is to say, they formed an association which bordered on a begrudging friendship, each man slightly mistrusting the other, but realising a mutual, if malleable understanding of the other. Henry was a peculiar-looking man, wizened and worsened with age. This Scotsman in his mid-fifties had many distinguishing features: a drooping right eyelid, a lopsided ear, and a balding pate with at least eight inches of black hair carefully wrapped over the centre of his head. This careful coiffuring did little to disguise the bald pink area in between his ears.

Despite the unfortunate appearance of the landlord and his largely inclement manner, the inn had a good reputation amongst the sailors and workmen alike for its fine selection of mulled ales, porters, and whores. Mortlake had spoken to the dower Mr Ringer some days before the meeting, and mentioned that he needed a nice quiet room for a business discussion.

The landlord initially baulked at the idea and retorted, "Listen to me Jesse Mortlake, we will have no irregular goings-on here; I am not going to be peached for running a den of iniquity. This is a god-fearing, honest establishment here, you know. Do you hear me?"

Mortlake let slip a wry smile and retorted, "Perish the thought of all that iniquity-malarkey Henry; 'tis just a group of gentlemen just wanting a chat over some ideas, that's all."

"You can have the cellar, and no tampering with the barrels, do you hear me laddy?" Henry retorted gruffly.

"Loud and clear Henry, loud and clear," Mortlake said, opening his arms wide as if to deflect the mere suggestion that he would ever stoop to such a thing.

Henry Ringer nodded his head, and sighed a brow-beaten sigh, one given out for effect rather than in earnestness. He turned away, muttering to himself whilst shoving the inn's cat away with the side of his boot.

Upon entering the inn, Mortlake assured Septimus that the room, or rather the cellar, was as good and secure a place as any for a quiet chat. The inn smelt of stale tobacco and spilt beer, and the rickety façade of the building matched the blotched interior of the inn perfectly. The lopsided appearance of the landlord came as no surprise to Septimus at all; he mused as to whether it was the inn or the landlord that came out in sympathy for the other.

Henry greeted Mortlake with a cautionary, "Morning" and a slight bob of the head. After a quick glance at the cut of his cloth, he introduced himself enthusiastically to Septimus.

"Greetings to you this fine morning good sir; Henry Ringer at your service."

"And a good morning to you too sir," replied a guarded Septimus.

"The other two gentlemen are already waiting below for you both," said Ringer, with a most unnatural smile, "Do let me know if you require any refreshments at all. We do a very good eel pie, hot broth too, vegetables dug up this very morning," Ringer announced hopefully.

"From his very own garden no doubt," Mortlake's deep voice replied sarcastically. "Just look at those green fingers," he added.

Ringer unconsciously peered down at his hands, shook his head at his actions and retorted, "Don't listen to him, sir; he would not know the difference between a parsnip and the parson's nose."

The two men entered the cellar via a trap door behind the bar. The cellar was even more dimly-lit than the bar above; damp seeped down the walls and drizzled down onto the stone- slabbed floor. The room was dank and musty; the heady bouquet of hops and soggy mortar filled the air. The closer the two men got to the bottom of the stairs, another more acrid odour filled their lungs, a vile vinegar concoction indeed. The likely culprit was either the contents of a few long-since broken wine bottles shoved into the corner, or a barrel of cider that was very much "on the turn." It was in this dimly-lit and odorous environment that Septimus and Mortlake sat face-to-face with the two gentlemen already seated below.

Mortlake shifted uneasily as he introduced his two "gentleman friends" as he called them, Mr John "Jewels" Juson, and Ocky "The Snake" Blackwood.

Septimus peered at the two men and winced at the thought of sharing his surname with one of these, lower order of men, particularly a tosher; a name that referred to one of the underclass that made their living (if it was to be called a living) from sifting through and exploring the sewers of London looking for "treasure."

Septimus began to think that the acrid vinegar scent was in fact a godsend, as it probably masked the repugnant odour of these two filthy men. Septimus reluctantly shook hands with his two new acquaintances then wiped his hands under the table, so as not to cause offence.

Septimus addressed the company by saying, "I thank you for being here today. I trust this will be a fortuitous endeavour for all concerned. My business here today is to find out if you two gentlemen..." The word *gentlemen* was unwittingly drawn out by Septimus as if it were in acknowledgement to its absurdity in the present company. Septimus hastily endeavoured to carry on with his address, trying to cover up his own silent mocking. "If you two gentlemen would be interested in a little fishing..."

"Fishing?" Ocky interrupted, almost coughing the words out, brows pinched in anger.

Septimus quickly added with forced calm, "For some treasure, sir, treasure." Ocky stared coldly at Septimus for a moment, then returned very slowly back to his seat.

The atmosphere had rapidly become decidedly chilly, so Mortlake took it upon himself to intervene. "Gentlemen, let us keep this nice and relaxed now; we don't want old Ringer above setting his cat on us, now, do we?"

Jewels, the quieter of the two toshers, saw the humour and said, "Certainly not, have you seen the claws on it, not to mention the army of fleas? It would be like fighting Julius Caesar and his Roman mob all over again." Mortlake's brooding eyes released a genial smile and the two toshers said no more. The mood eased.

Septimus inhaled slightly and said, "How well do you two know the underground rivers and sewers of this city?"

"Well enough," Ocky replied as Septimus scratched his ear in quiet frustration. Septimus had known that this meeting was going to be challenging for all concerned, but this was getting ridiculous.

"Good," said Septimus. "As you gentlemen know, plans are afoot, and in some cases already in action to completely change the sewage system in this city, which is potentially a great loss to you and maybe myself as well. My interest lies within the old network of tunnels and buried rivers, which are to be found around this specific area of London. It is my belief that some of these tunnels have been there for a very long time, and that some stretch way back into antiquity, is that correct?"

The Snake looked at Jewels and grinned, "You may be right fella, but not sure if we could place, or even find the location called 'antiquity'," Ocky replied mischievously.

Septimus carried on undeterred, "I have heard reports of cemeteries, plague pits, even Roman chambers furnishing the bowels of this wondrous city, is that correct?"

"Aye, and many other things as well, such as colonies of rats, gas, and some say wild boars trapped in the northern end," said Jewels. Septimus raised an eyebrow at the mention of wild boars, and quietly mused on the potential for a new acquisition to his collection of natural wonders.

"Wild boar, you say?"

"Aye, some says a family been trapped down there for years and multiplying rapidly," replied Jewels.

"Have you ever witnessed it on your travels Jewels?"

"Erm no, not myself, mister, not my patch, you see, but know a few toshers who have." Septimus let out a small sigh of incredulity, but fought within himself to muffle any sense of losing patience.

"Is it common to find smaller openings and passageways off of these main sewers and rivers?" asked Septimus.

"Plenty," Jewels declared. "Yes, there are some smaller tunnels, covered brooks, cracks and holes, they are mainly full of rats' nests, and old rotting timber, what of it anyway?" queried Ocky.

"It is my belief, gentlemen, that beyond one of these *cracks* or *brooks,* as you call it, lays something quite…" Septimus searched for the right word - "intriguing."

"Intriguing, you say?" said Jewels. "Just how *intriguing*?"

"'Intriguing' don't pay bills," The Snake retorted gruffly, but with some interest.

Septimus replied, "Let us just say for now that you will be paid well for your time, and when, and if, we reach our goal, you would be handsomely rewarded. One thing that I do need, though, from you all, my friends," he glanced purposely at The Snake when using this expression, "We do need to keep this matter completely hush hush. The last thing we want to do is risk our little secret getting out, or, for that matter, the booty that goes with it."

Jewels and Ocky muttered amongst themselves for some while until Septimus said, "So, gentlemen, do we have a deal?"

"Count me in," said Jewels. Septimus Blackwood looked at Ocky Blackwood, each man searching the others' eyes for trust and weaknesses.

"Deal," said Ocky, with a smirk. Septimus found Ocky's smirk unsettling; he was used to being in complete control of a situation, and yet here he was making deals with glorified dung beetles, and even giving away some power to them.

"Excellent," Mortlake broke the silence. "I knew us gentlemen would see eye to eye in the end; after all we are all businessmen, ain't we?"

"Indeed we are," replied Ocky.

Septimus hoped he would be spared the formality of shaking hands with the two men, but it wasn't to be. He reluctantly accepted the hand of John Jewels, who offered his hand with the honest, open, but aged, face of a child. Ocky's handshake was different though, firmer and with a stone-faced delivery. Septimus then went on to buy his new acquaintances a tankard of porter and thanked Mr Ringer for his hospitality. He left the premises as swiftly as possible, wiping his hands and patting himself down on his way out.

Chapter 9

The Old Lady in the Window

Whortleberry Street's newest resident gazed out of her second-floor window. The view from here was excellent, though the window needed cleaning; the dust and the smut of the city were resiliently hanging on steadfastly despite the recent rains. She vowed she would tackle the landlord about it this very day. To be able to see the comings and goings of the outside was of great importance to her. She and her companion, Mrs Moon, had been making enquiries about accommodation in this street for quite some time. The thought of six months' rent paid in advance went a long way in persuading the landlord that the lady and her companion, Mrs Moon, were likely to be agreeable tenants. It was rare that anyone was keen to pay one months' rent in advance, let alone six months at one time.

Mrs Moon was a sprightly, well-organised widow of sixty-four years of age. She was a live-in assistant, companion, and friend to a much-acclaimed medium. Mrs Moon's husband had died of consumption some twenty years previously. Shortly after his death she had consulted the old lady in a bid to contact her late husband, and the two became friends. Most of her work was domestic chores, though she also helped the lady with her clients, taking bookings and making them feel at ease and welcome in the house.

The old lady would sit for hours, gazing out into the street, noting all the occurrences of one particular resident. Mrs Moon was always careful never to disturb the lady's study of the street below. The old lady found herself with much time for reflection nowadays, and at the age of ninety-six, most of her friends and family she had once known had crossed over to the other side. She had always known there was no real death as others saw it, just a release from the confines of this organic material world: a long, gentle sigh, leading to the liberty of the ethereal plain, followed in some cases by rebirth. Despite knowing all of this, she was

39

determined to prolong her own earthly existence as long as she possibly could.

She had heard voices and seen passing people dancing in and out of the shadows since she was a small girl. She often kept these apparitions to herself, fearing that others would think her troublesome or just plain mad. As she grew up, her senses seemed to grow with her. She had realised that she could, for the most part at least, control the voices, if not the shadows. One day she hoped she would be able to use them to help herself and others to explain the mystery of life. Not that she needed to look far for a mystery; for as long as she could remember, her family had been beset with intrigue and rumour.

Her family had known much wealth and prosperity and were generally seen as a family of great academics and merchants alike.

It was said that some of her ancestors were physicians of court back in the days of Queen Elizabeth. Even Sir John Dee was said to have been a family friend. Despite this, or maybe because of envy, the family had always attracted whispers and controversy. It seemed to her that people always kept a slight distance from the family. There had been friends, but very few good ones.

Many a time she had witnessed a flicker in the eyes of others when she was being introduced at a dinner or dance, a slight movement of gaze that betrayed their appearance of geniality.

She had enjoyed the great balls and social whirl of her youth; then there had always been the scent of a thousand opportunities. Her father had been one of the loveliest of men, kind to family, friends, even servants, though as a man he was not at ease with himself or the world around him. The combined weight of his ancestors, good and bad, always hung heavily on his narrow shoulders. Their brilliance, madness, respectability, and the suspicion they aroused were a heavy load indeed. How he sought to gain respect in society, to regain some of his family's former eminence in the upper echelons, and how he feared his eldest son would undo all his good work.

Money was never a problem for him: He had inherited a fortune, and the family's position as one of the chief shipping merchants was secure for the time being at least. He also saw apparitions, felt strange sensations, and heard whispers but was loath to admit to anyone but his daughter when trying to quell her fears. He was a good man and would have been turning in his grave at the reckless indulgences of his eldest son.

"Your tea is ready m'lady," Mrs Moon interrupted her thoughts.

"Oh right, yes, quite so, thank you kindly Mrs Moon." The moment and the time were gone, but not lost, never lost.

Chapter 10

Victim

Septimus' workload was increasing by the week. He was correct in his assumption that everybody wanted to grasp a little piece of perpetuity. Photography offered immortality, and many people wanted to share the liberty and vanity with their friends and neighbours, so much so that the newspapers created a name for the craze. They called it *Cartmania*, named after the small cards that the photographs were printed on. It was sweeping all over Europe and America. Some folk were acquiring vast collections of these *cartes de visits*, as they became known.

This fascination for collecting was one that Septimus knew only too well. As a child, he had started collecting insects in jars, and hunting butterflies with his Great Uncle Augustus in his Oxfordshire home. Augustus had taught young Septimus how to preserve their prey and how to stiffen the wings of butterflies.

One simple method of preservation which stuck in his mind was the cutting up of a few cherry laurel leaves, placing them in a jar with a live butterfly, and sealing the lid to let the cyanide gases seep out of the wounded leaves around the butterfly. How fascinating it was watching just how quick the wings stiffened and the preservation was complete.

Septimus smiled inwardly at the simplicity of it all. He remembered how Uncle Augustus had berated him for calling it cherry laurel and not the botanical name of *Prunus Laurecerasus*. Of course his uncle was correct; labelling, order, and discipline were all part of a serious collector's arsenal. Augustus was always singing the praises of the botanist and plant-categoriser Linnaeus, how he brought order, clarity, and definition to the otherwise-muddled masses.

Septimus' uncle did not only collect botanical specimens; he also collected books, hundreds and thousands of books. Many were about what one could call serious science, though amongst them there were some very old, dusty books on the magical uses of herbs and ointments, and even some scrolls scribed onto parchment, written in Latin.

Chapter 11

Progress

"I think we may have made some progress Septimus," the chemist said.

"Progress?" Septimus repeated the word as if asking a question.

"Yes, possibly," John replied. Septimus' eyes widened, ablaze at the possibility behind John's words, a rush of fire and anticipation coursed through his veins.

"You mean we have done it John?"

"I think so, though I cannot be sure. I saw a misting and a slight movement. At least, that is what I thought I saw," the chemist retorted.

"*Perhaps* movement, *perhaps* movement. How can there be a *perhaps* John?" Septimus snapped back hastily, starting to lose his calm demeanour.

"You know the implications of this John," Septimus said in a slow and deep voice that dared to question the very ethics of such a discovery. "We would have changed ..." Septimus started to say, but his voice and mind trailed off into the ether.

"Well, it could have been a flicker of the light or something, but I am sure there was a faint reflex though," John replied sullenly. Septimus turned on his heel with some irritation.

"Very well, I will take your word on it."

Septimus looked into the gaunt face of the chemist and searched for any flickers of emotion whilst fighting to contain his own. There was no pride, no excitement, and no recognition of the majesty of what they may have discovered. Could it be that John's apparent lack of interest meant that he was deliberately holding back? John's mind swayed in on the brink sometimes. Had the fine thread that held his mind together finally snapped? Had the distinction between reality and fantasy finally been lost to him? Septimus wanted to think not. He waved John away and sat in contemplation for a while.

It took time for Septimus to compose himself, though compose himself he had to. He wanted to share his joy, his achievement, but alas, this could never be, this was just too important to share with another. He had waited years for this development. He had dared to believe it was possible, had thought it may take decades to perfect. Now he would know for sure if it was a reality or illusion. Or perhaps both?

There was a distinct chill in the air as Septimus stepped forward on to the narrow pavement of Whortleberry Street. The street was as lively as ever, but the dampness seemed to have seeped into the very pores of the residents and costermongers alike. Even the horses seemed leadened by the heaviness of the air. But not he. Not Septimus Blackwood, not tonight. Tonight he was allowing himself a little bit of human comfort, some colour, some gratification. Sadly his hands and feet would not share the inner glow of his self-satisfaction. He warmed himself by one of the street braziers and peered into the night.

The glow of gas lamps swirled and danced into the night. They mocked the darkness, flames twisting and turning within the glass. The shouts and the laughter bounced from the taverns onto the streets. All this life behind the glass, portholes and peepholes. Confinement, amusement, yes, it was all there for him to grasp. He turned the corner onto White Monk's Lane. There was nothing white, pure, or chaste about this lane now. The cobbles beneath his feet were uneven and broken; the lane sloped in the middle to take away the rain and the filth. The gas lamps were few and the fog lay thick.

The splendour of this nebulous world excited Septimus. The paradoxes paraded like circus clowns. What secret life blossomed in these damp urban marshes?

The ragged girls with brightly-hued feathers in their bonnets, sparkling brooches, and battered bustles entertained, enthused and enticed, their giggling talk embracing the night. Hundreds of people confined to these houses night after night, restricted, entwined, and alive. The stray dogs roaming for food, the cats screaming, screeching, and running amuck. The washing lines hung low, furnished with damp sheets, like sails in the doldrums, limp and lifeless. Anyone or anything could spawn from these gin-soaked streets and be undetected for years, perhaps forever. *How comforting*, thought Septimus.

The exotic met the mundane on the window ledges. The bright parrots hung caged and cold. The upper ledges and brickwork below were stained with slops. Years and years of human waste had trickled down these walls, onto the cobbles, down the sloping gulley of the lane and into the drains below. From there it would slip into the sewers and the sunken rivers down into subterranean London, perhaps even past his inheritance.

As he walked past the bone works, he was hit by a vile miasma. The lane narrowed a little. A cart was being unloaded of sacks, their contents undefined, anonymous and best kept that way, thought he. Septimus gave the cart as wide a berth as possible and straddled the puddles with great agility.

At the end of the lane, and fortunately out of the stench of the bone yard, was a seller of hot chestnuts. How his fingers delighted at the warm fruits of these magnificent twisted trees. He shared not a moment's compassion for the consumption of the next generation of the sweet chestnut tree. He quietly mused on the paradoxical nature of this arboricultural delight: how its fruits warmed so well, yet its wood howled and spat at the mere mention of fire. Many a house fire had been started by this most treacherous of trees. His thoughts were disturbed by a drunk being tossed out of the inn across the street and this sharp reminder of his surroundings set him off with much haste. His feet were now very cold -- this was not a place to muse on trifles. This was more bear pit than museum.

Finally he came to the crossing opposite the Bianca family's inn. He could not believe it was only about half a mile from his own house in Whortleberry Street. There were so many alleyways and twists and turns on the journey that it seemed much further. He could see the Angel Vaults in front of him, but the road before him was covered in debris from the market earlier. A vast assortment of horse and donkey dung graced the cobblestones. He was not going to decorate his shiny new leather shoes with this crap. Thankfully he saw the inn's crossing sweeper half asleep in a doorway a few paces away and gave him a gentle nudge. "Oh, pardon me sir," said the crossing sweeper, as if in a daze. "It has been a long day"

"So I see," replied Septimus.

The sweeper, who was not older than his mid-thirties, hauled himself to his feet, leaning heavily on his huge battered walking stick. He smiled through the pain of the exertion. The Crimean War had left many men like this; maimed, displaced, broken. "If I knew you were coming sir, I would have been ready sharpish." He armed himself with his broom and set about clearing a safe passage through the debris. It was not easy with one arm, but he managed the task with sufficient success, enabling Septimus to cross the street unadorned with filth. Septimus tipped the man heavily and the sweeper touched his battered hat. Septimus appreciated anyone who maintained order, especially a man who enabled him to keep his shoes clean and dry.

Septimus pulled the door open with vigour and was greeted with the smoke from a hundred clay pipes, which merged briefly with the thickening fog of Father Thames, creating a noxious gateway between the inside and the outside worlds. Septimus fought his way through the sweaty huddle to the bar, smoothing down his coat all the while.

As usual there were a few curious glances his way, but he was used to that and ignored them all.

The other customers' attention was soon lost in the whirling smoke, singing, swaying, and swearing that was the language of the tavern. Septimus knew he was never going to fit in with the other clientele, but he did not need to. He knew some of the most influential and feared people in the neighbourhood. He was also companion of the tempestuous Andrea Bianca.

Andrea had started pouring out a tankard of porter for him the moment she saw him walk through the door. She greeted him with benign eyes. Septimus tried to repeat the gesture but smiling did not come easily to him. On occasion he did laugh out loud, though it was usually a laugh of incredulity when faced with the idiocy of others. Septimus knew he could never truly know this girl; she was so very deep, yet he often wondered what secrets lay beyond those mysterious hazel eyes.

Andrea appeared to contain every layer of the human condition: deep, deep emotion, which at times bordered on the edge of savagery. Contrastingly, she seemed to posses a bottomless well of empathy and sympathy for the suffering of others. He suspected that at times this girl could even penetrate his own inner depths, or at least glimpse them.

47

Her noble nose gave her face an air of pride and sensitivity; her expression and manner could be considered passive and unresponsive, but to upset her would provoke such a look that would freeze the blood of the most ferocious of opponents. Every ringlet in her coiled mane was a story of strife, passion, and devotion. Andrea's support and love for her mother and sister through difficult times was unyielding, though her deepest passion lay in her art.

Septimus peered around the bar and noticed the solid figure of Mortlake playing cards with a motley crew of assorted rogues. Mortlake had been aware of Septimus' presence as soon as he walked in, but he had discreetly held his distance.

One of the toshers was trying to engage Mortlake in a conversation; an endeavour that, by the looks of things, Mortlake was not entirely happy with. Septimus had just seen him lose his second hand of poker and more than a few coins to boot. Thankfully it was Jewels Juson, not the sneering one called The Snake. A surly fellow for sure, thought Septimus. Now there was a tricky character, too tricky by half. Septimus looked over at Mortlake and gestured with a nod that they should find a secluded corner where they could talk.

"Evening sir," Mortlake greeted quietly.

"Good evening Mr Mortlake. I trust that you are well and enjoying your card game?" Septimus replied with sardonic humour.

"Hmmm," Mortlake stuttered, "I suppose I am, if the truth be known. As for the cards, well, I have had better nights." One thing Septimus and Jesse Mortlake had in common was that neither of them was joyful even at the best of times, but Septimus' upbeat manner had quite caught Mortlake on the hop. For Jesse to admit he was okay was difficult enough, but to sit here and make small talk with Septimus was beyond the pale. It was something that he had never seen the like of before, and it made him very suspicious.

"I trust the good Lord smiles on you, too Mr Blackwood?" Mortlake continued with a hint of sarcasm.

"I suppose one could say that Mr Mortlake, though I doubt whether the good Lord's demeanour has anything to do with it. But yes, there have been one or two pleasing developments in some of my endeavours," replied Septimus smugly. "Now Mr Mortlake, has there been any advancement on our little project?"

"Aye, yes there is." Mortlake's breath was heavy with ale, and he leant a little too close to Septimus' face for his liking, but he endured and tried to remain attentive. "We, that is, Jewels, Snake and I, have had a little butchers at that old map you loaned us, and the toshers reckon that the safest access to the area in question is far from the closest. You see, some of those tunnels have not been flushed for years, you know. What's more, they are telling me that they could run into others who consider that area to be theirs, and these tosher types get very protective about their own territory." Septimus sighed but decided on letting Mortlake continue with his tale.

"One good thing is that apparently they ain't started drilling out new sewers there yet, not for the time being anyhow. So, provided we don't bump into any hostile toshers or any other residents down there, we should be okay," Mortlake said nonchalantly.

"Other residents?" queried a slightly bemused Septimus, with a raised eyebrow. "Don't tell me the wild boars have set up home there as well now Mr Mortlake," Septimus replied incredulously.

Mortlake's lazy eyes glared up at Septimus, and there was a flash of anger within them. Slowly it faded into a broad grin, exposing his erratically-toothed mouth. This ruinous sight always reminded Septimus of Highgate Cemetery.

"No wild boars, no, unless you include Jewels over there," he quipped. "By the residents, I mean the folks who live down there in the sewer. Some never come out, feels at home in there, they do."

"Well, I am sure you have ways of moving them on for a day or so Mr Mortlake. I have every confidence in your ability to be able to fix things for us."

"Yes, you are probably right, sir, always glad to help a friend I am, too kind for me own good, really," replied Mortlake, eyeing the bottom of his now-empty glass.

At that very moment Andrea appeared at the table. "A good girl, this one," Mortlake said, touching her back a little too long for Septimus. Septimus eyed Mortlake stiffly. Fortunately Andrea's intuition and experience meant that she knew exactly how to deal with the situation. She knew Mortlake could be troublesome company, but she could handle him. Septimus noticed her fingertips were slightly stained with red and yellow paint, and imagined a field of poppies exploding on the canvas.

"Refill time?" Andrea enquired with a smile. Both men nodded in agreement. Septimus relaxed a little and Mortlake removed his hand and passed her his glass. Andrea was probably the only person alive who protected Septimus. There was, she thought, something very lonely about this man, isolated and adrift from other men. She and Septimus rarely spoke to each other of their feelings, let alone their past. There was little point -- she could only speak and comprehend a little English anyway, and Septimus' Italian was scant, though he was learning fast.

As Andrea disappeared back to the bar, Jewels sauntered up to the table and pulled up a stool. Fortunately he was not too drunk, not yet anyway. "How are you, sir? Nice to see you," he announced boldly. Septimus mused that the bone factory smelt less repellent than the odour emitted from this man's mouth. He tried to edge his stool a little further away from the table and Mr Juson.

"I am hardy and well Mr Juson, thank you for asking," he replied as politely as he could muster.

"I trust you will be accompanying us on our little venture down below Mr Blackwood?" Jewels said, a little too loudly for Septimus' liking.

"Yes Mr Juson, I shall." Septimus made sure his voice was hushed, in an unlikely attempt to reduce Jewel's exuberance, and continued, "I am glad to hear progress is being made regarding our map.

"I suggest you, Ocky, and Mr Mortlake here write up a list of what we shall require for our little venture, as you put it. I also need to be furnished with a date; obviously I am aware of the tide being the greatest issue, though I mean to proceed with the upmost haste."

"Certainly sir," Jewels said loudly, before finally catching onto the idea that this was not a conversation to be overheard. "Just you leave that to Ocky, Mortlake and me, sir, we will see you alright," he said, touching his nose with his forefinger at the same time.

"Of that I am sure Mr Juson, of that I am sure," Septimus said dryly.

Andrea arrived with the drinks and asked Septimus if he could spare some time to see her mother about some design she was working on. "I will come right away," he told Andrea. "Business calls, gentlemen. Enjoy the rest of your evening and I hope to see you both soon."

"Right you are then sir," said Jewels, tipping his hat and smiling vaguely.

"Send my regards to Madam Bianca," said Mortlake with a leer.

Septimus may have heard Mortlake's final remark, but if he did, he chose not to respond to it. The pair casually dodged the swaying masses around the tavern, before vanishing up the stairs.

Chapter 12

The Model

It was a cold, autumnal morning at the Jasper's Cross market square. The hawkers and the costermongers were filling the square with the sound of their shouts and boasts. From afar, the noises blended together and sounded like a travelling menagerie of animals rather than a platform of low commerce.

One of the many folk trying to eke out a living on this very morning was Melody, the travelling photographer. Melody and his accompanying daughters had renewed their pitch on the market this morning with difficulty. Ivor, the toll man, had firstly tried to stop them accessing a pitch, shouting, "I'll have not more of your antics, good boy. Take your trade elsewhere." The blustering Welsh toll man was not for budging, so something needed to be done. In amongst the hullaballoo of the market, Bridget quickly vacated the travelling caravan and ran across the square. Temporarily the girl was lost in the mingling masses. Despite his apparent calm, Melody eyed the throbbing crowd with concern, looking for his wayward daughter.

"Go on, off with you and your travelling circus," the gruff toll man angrily bellowed.

"Now listen here, sir, we are not a circus, dear fellow. Don't you remember me? I am the best photographer in London, so I am. Photographer to Her Majesty herself," he said, mining his deep vault of Irish charm. Still the toll man persisted,

"Aye, and I suppose the queen was on the throne, sharing some plum pudding with you as well?"

"As a matter of fact, I was a guest at one of her garden parties," Melody replied, trying to inject a little humour into the altercation.

The Welshman shook his head and replied with an exasperated, "You must think I was born yesterday, good boy."

Melody was just about to say "No, sir," when Bridget burst from the crowd, clutching something in her hand. She ran as fast as her twelve-year-old legs could carry her. "Here mister," she said to the aggravated toll man. "I bought you a bowl of faggots and gravy. I know it's early, but it's mighty cold today, and I remembered it's your favourite."

The toll man opened his mouth to speak but the words had been stolen by Bridget's actions. Melody and Sally watched with fascination as Bridget stood there, her wide chestnut-brown eyes peering up through her long fringe at the befuddled old toll man.

He was completely knocked off his portly axis by the situation. Bridget had won; the poor toll man's resolve had fled along with his words. He looked up in exasperation at the heavens, let out a sigh, and shook his head. He glanced at Melody and Bridget's twin sister, Sally; he saw the same wide-eyed, guileless look. "I'll collect the tally later this morning, but if I hear one more complaint about your vanishing photographs you'll be disappearing along with 'em, do you hear me, Paddy?"

Melody tipped his hat and said, "I always said you were a gent Ivor; didn't I girls?"

Both girls nodded and said almost in unison, "A real gent, to be sure."

Ivor sighed and proclaimed, "I must be mad to allow you back here Paddy. See that you make your photos stick."

"Your mother would have been proud of you Bridget me dear. What would I do without you?" said Melody with moist eyes.

After the initial kerfuffle about securing the pitch, the punters gathered around Melody's gaily-coloured caravan and business became brisk. Crowds flocked to see Melody's daughters with their brightly-coloured smocks dance their merry jigs. In between clients Melody would grab his fiddle or tin whistle and accompany the girls with their swirling shindigs. The girls were accustomed to singing and dancing for the public, even when their feet were sore and their shoes worn through. They knew that it was entertain or go hungry.

One of the features of the Jasper's Cross market was the insatiable squabble for attention. Melody was not the only one offering cheap entertainment that day: there were snake-swallowers, sword-swallowers, clowns, rickety stilts men, weaving in and out of the crowd like oversized knitting needles, organ-grinders from Rome, singers from Paris, and pipers from Glasgow. Each and every one of them created their very own biomass:

spontaneous communities sprang up almost here, there, and everywhere. It was as if the entertainers were dazzling, coloured, pollen-filled flowers bobbing in the summer sun, waiting for the hungry swarm to extract their abundant nectar. The crowds fluttered and flew around this human garden of entertainment.

They crushed in around the centre of these enticing blooms, leaving the vulnerable outer petals to be exploited by predators. Predators in the shape of pickpockets and cutpurses, darting and hovering around like dragonflies at a pond. The ever-present opportunists and professionals alike gathered here, always ready, always prepared, anonymous and faceless parasites, forever seeking weaknesses in the swarm.

It was from one such a throng that an aspiring model-cum-actress called Anna Fountaine emerged, thankfully unscathed. She was in her early twenties, with a rich mane of strawberry blonde hair and light blue-grey eyes and blessed with a pure porcelain complexion. Anna explained at great length to Melody that she had originally come from Brittany, and how her fortunes had wavered a little in her home country, so she thought she would like to give London a try. She was in need of some photographs to make a portfolio, and in turn make her fortune by becoming a famous actress.

She would then eventually end up marrying a wealthy duke, be adorned in pretty dresses, live in a beautiful mansion, and have a large family. Melody tried very hard to keep a straight face as this wide-eyed little French girl versed, in great detail, her grand plan to him. He was just about to speak when she continued, "I would also need a garden full of camellias, roses, and most of all peonies. Oh, I love peonies *monsieur*; do you?"

"Well, young lady, to be honest I am not sure what a peony is, but I know a rose when I see one and they are mighty grand, so they are. If it is good quality photographs you are after, look no further."

"*Merci monsieur*," Anna replied. After Melody had carefully taken some shots of Anna, he looked long and hard at his equipment. His camera was second-hand when he had bought it and the card he was using was cheap and nasty. A cloud crossed the sun. Melody paused for a while.

"What is the matter *monsieur*?" Anna asked.

"Nothing, nothing at all. All is fine my young'un," replied a hesitant Melody. "I was just thinking there may be someone who could help you out more than I could, my friend."

"Oh, yes *monsieur*? Tell me their name monsieur, please."

Melody hesitated again for a while before replying. "His name is Septimus Blackwood and he lives not far from here. He has the finest photographic studio for miles around, and after me he would be the best photographer in England.

In fact, the only difference between us is that he has contacts much grander than I."

He was going to add that he thought Septimus was like a king spider waiting in a very large, very sticky web. "Oh *monsieur, merci*, thank you." She kissed Melody on the cheek and he flushed profusely. "That is *fantastique monsieur*, but he may be too expensive for a poor actress like me."

"Well, that may be true to be honest with you, missy, but given your great beauty and undoubted talent, I think he may just see his way to come to some arrangement with you."

"I'll tell you what I'll do. I will try to get word to him this very afternoon. Can you meet me outside the Tanner's Arms at around six o'clock tonight?"

"*Oui monsieur*."

"That's grand, so it is. I will take you to his studio tonight and introduce you, as he is not a man for surprises, but I will see to it he knows your intentions, missy."

"*Merci monsieur*, I shall wear my best dress and see you later." She pecked Melody on the cheek once more and then vanished back into the swarm of the square. Melody thought long and hard about what potential danger he was putting the girl in. Would he have sent his own daughters to such a man?

What was it about Septimus that made him shudder so? Septimus' words were echoing in Melody's mind: "If you come across anybody with striking physical attributes, I want to know, young man. I want the most notable of all the species for my collection. The fairest of the fair, the darkest of the dark. I want the best examples and possibly even the worst; as long as they are remarkable, my boy, send them to me. I will make them shine, glisten, and glow for all eternity and you, sir, shall be rewarded for your keen eye and generosity."

Septimus was keen to press home that moments are unique and precious, and however one tries they cannot be recaptured, no matter how strong the desire or how badly you want them. Once they have gone, they have gone for good. Surely Septimus just wanted interesting-looking subjects for his collection, thought Melody. Something to titillate his well-to-do friends; yes, that's it. What else could he possibly want these people for? She will be okay, I am sure, Melody tried to reassure himself. He watched his own two bright daughters sit down and take off their tattered shoes. Melody smiled a bittersweet smile then disappeared within the sanctuary of his caravan.

The news of Miss Fountaine had reached Septimus via a young messenger-boy-cum-mudlark, who answered to the name of 'Pigeon'. No one knew Pigeon by any other name.

There was always much speculation as to how he had come by this name. Some thought it was because he was a relayer of messages; others suggested that it was because he was "pigeon-chested" or that his surname was indeed Pigeon. Whatever the reasons for his peculiar name, it troubled Septimus not one jot. All he was interested in right now was that Pigeon wiped his feet and told him what he knew.

Although Septimus relished the news he was receiving, he was always careful that the boy, or anyone else for that matter, could only see a mild degree of enthusiasm. It would not do to lose composure, even if his enthralled mind was erupting in a thousand different directions all at once. Septimus austerely thanked the boy for his messages and rounded off with, "There you are, young man, your halfpenny. Spend it wisely, and remember ears to the ground, my boy, ears to the ground."

Anna's eyes widened as she approached Septimus' studio. "Do not tell me one man lives here by himself?" exclaimed Anna.

"He has a housekeeper, missy, but I think that is it. He's just not one of those men that people get close to, if you know what I mean." Upon reaching the entrance, Melody paused, stood up straight, and rapped timidly on the heavy ornate lion's head knocker.

The door was swiftly opened by a surly Jesse Mortlake, who appeared to be on his way out. Mortlake's width nearly filled up the whole doorway.

"Don't just stand there, come in. Septimus is on his way down. Best wipe your feet though, don't want to get his Lordship's rugs dirty, do we now?" said Mortlake gruffly while looking at Melody's boots.

Melody and Anna waited anxiously in the large and icily cold reception hall, gazing at the many animal trophy heads hanging from the walls. Septimus appeared suddenly and silently from one of the side doors and announced sharply, "Greetings to you both." The sudden appearance of Septimus and his abrupt welcome caused the two guests to flinch in surprise.

They both turned to face him, and smiled with apprehension.

"Good evening sir, I am Miss Fountaine," Anna said, trying to gather her wits.

"Sir," said Melody, with a little reservation, tilting his hat at the same time.

Septimus bowed his head a little at the young French lady, and introduced himself with courtesy.

"You have brought me a subject of fine breeding Melody Kearney, a beautiful girl to behold," said Septimus.

"Well, I said you may be interested in helping her with her ambition sir," replied Melody with some trepidation.

"Well, you know me Melody, I like to help if and when I can," replied Septimus with a hint of a smile, and continued curtly, "And now you may leave Miss Fountaine and me to it."

"Quite so sir," said Melody, whilst trying to avoid eye contact with Septimus or Anna. "Right then Mr Blackwood, sir, I'll be on my way. Good day to you Miss, as well," said Melody, walking backwards all the time.

"Thank you Mr Kearny for escorting Miss Fountaine to me. I shall see to her carriage home, never fear. I will be in touch with you soon Mr Kearney. Mind how you go," said Septimus, already turning back towards the girl.

"I look forward to it; nice meeting you again sir," Melody lied. Septimus closed the door with a little too much force for Anna's liking. "Do come through, Miss Fountaine," Septimus said as he bowed his head a little and pointed the way into his public display room.

Anna was amazed as she entered the display room: so many creatures, so many plants, and so many photographs from around the world. "Did you take all of these photographs yourself monsieur"? she asked.

"*Oui* young lady, I have developed my art over many years, and over lots of different countries. Thankfully technology has also moved on, allowing us to break new ground almost daily. With a little imagination, who knows what we can achieve next?" Septimus said with a wry smile.

"Yes, it is remarkable," said Miss Fountaine, her smile betraying a hint of anxiety.

Septimus observed Miss Fountaine's inquisitive eyes flashing around the room, taking in every adventure, every animal, and every likeness. Her eyes were full of wonderment and awe; it brought much satisfaction to see her interest in his work.

"I see you enjoy the natural world very much *monsieur*."

"Ah yes, my beautiful friends. Is it not a marvel to behold the sheer variety of life we share the planet with?"

"*Oui* sir, a true marvel," she replied politely.

"My studio is upstairs; please follow me Miss Fountaine."

"One moment *monsieur*." She had noticed the small stereoscopic viewer on a table between the encased heads of two leopards. "What is this *monsieur*?" Anna said curiously.

"Ah, that is called a stereoscopic viewer, or stereoscope," replied Septimus, quietly enjoying her curiosity.

"It is very beautiful," she said, eyeing the viewer, which looked like a small set of binoculars on a stand, set in a mother-of-pearl surround. "What is the function of such a device? What does it do?" she enquired.

"The stereoscope viewer works by having two images set side by side; you see one image with one eye and another image with the other eye. The likenesses are virtually the same. If you would care to observe young lady," Septimus said dryly.

"*Oui monsieur*, I would like that very much," Anna said eagerly.

Septimus picked up some glass slides and placed them in the viewer. The images were of fishermen and their boats from Nerja, in southern Spain, one of the vast collections of photos from Septimus' travels around the Mediterranean basin.

Anna looked into the viewer with great admiration. The photos were of tremendous clarity, and the effect on the eye gave a sense of depth and movement. The sea behind the gaily painted boats seemed to shimmer in the sunlight, the waves rippled, the eyes of the swarthy men seemed to widen for a split second as they gazed at their nets. And for a split second in time she felt utterly transported. Septimus interrupted the spell by exclaiming, "An almost living and breathing experience, would you not say Miss Fountaine?"

"Indeed sir, a quite remarkable effect," she replied."

"Ah yes young lady, a simple effect, one to build on perhaps? You have not seen one before, young lady?" Septimus enquired.

"No *monsieur*, I have not."

Septimus smiled and replied, "Well, the London Stereoscopic Society would be shocked by that. Their motto is "No home without a stereoscope."

Whether they were right or not is a matter for conjecture, but I for one would not be without one. Anyway Miss Fountaine, forgive me, I digress... Shall we proceed upstairs to the studio?"

"Yes certainly *monsieur*." Anna placed the stereoscope delicately back on the table, taking care to avoid the menacing gaze of the two stuffed leopards on either side. She quickly gathered up her dress to avoid tripping over it on the narrow winding staircase. Gas lamps fluttered in the draught and shone balefully onto the mounted trophies which decorated the walls. Flickering illumination swooped over the dimly-lit staircase, creating grotesque, agitated shadows among baleful silhouettes of mounted heads. The dark and trophy-rich staircase creaked with every new step. Anna thought that this building must be very ancient. Almost as if he had read the girl's thoughts, Septimus stopped on the stairs and turned round sharply toward the French girl. The lamplight lit up Septimus' piercing eyes, causing them to sparkle like two angry fireflies.

Septimus proclaimed, "This building is indeed very old young lady, its staircase even older. It is made from mighty oaks that would likely have been delicate saplings at the battle of Hastings, when your William the Bastard invaded this island and robbed us of our inheritance."

"*Monsieur*," Anna said with alarm. Septimus gave the smallest of winks and a trickle of a smile ran across his face.

If the gesture was supposed to put her at ease, it failed. Anna inhaled deeply, trying to regain her composure. She was no stranger to aversion, but there was something in this man's eyes that made her feel very uncomfortable. How had he known she was thinking about the age of the staircase? Septimus held his subtle but smug smile and said, "But that was all a very long time ago, young lady. Besides, where would we be without your wonderful Mr Daguerre and your delightful wines?" Anna's sense of dread lifted a little as she followed him further up the stairs, which seemed to go on forever.

"This was one of the few buildings that survived the terrible Fire of Stepney in 1794, let me see now, seventy-six years ago. The Great Fire started on the Thames. Some stupid boat builders let a drum of pitch boil over, and it quickly engulfed the barge they were working on in flames. Soon many other boats were burning and the air was full of smoke and flame. The blaze then spread onto land, and it burned and burned and burned." His voice faltered and trailed off for a little before continuing, "Many people were left homeless as building after building collapsed. There were many innocent lives lost on that day… as well as some not quite so innocent, one would imagine," he said reflectively.

"Great family fortunes were lost too. Some lost everything -- money, property and businesses." Septimus grimaced a little, as if he had witnessed the event himself. There was something personal in that anguish, thought Anna. "Who knows Miss Fountaine, maybe there are a few treasures that still remain beneath the ground, scattered in the debris just waiting to be uncovered."

When they eventually reached the top of the stairs, Septimus swung open the vast panelled door into the studio. The immense size and splendour of this huge glasshouse studio rocked Anna on her heels. This was a place of true wonder, Anna thought to herself. Her gaping grey-blue eyes looked around her in utter disbelief. The walls were draped with tapestries and painted canvases and cloths, full of romantic scenes, woodland glades, seaside glimpses and garden vistas, even classical settings from ancient Greece. Backgrounds that could be tailor-made to create your own reality, your own framed fantasy world in which to dwell forever behind the glass.

"You have some beautiful artwork here *monsieur*."

"*Oui mademoiselle*, I have some of the best and most enthusiastic painters in London working for me, and I am fortunate that their Italian passion manifests itself in my studio.

"Please be seated young lady, and tell me exactly what you would like from me." Septimus waved his hand at the lavishly upholstered settee by his side.

"Excuse me, one moment *monsieur*," Anna said as she walked hurriedly to the side of the room overlooking the Thames. Anna gazed down at the now-black, treacle-like swell of the mighty Thames; she was surprised to see so much activity still taking place at this time of the evening. "This city never rests, *monsieur*, does it?"

"Indeed it does not Miss Fountaine."

Anna was making her way over to the settee next to where Septimus was sitting, and in doing so her eyes moved upwards and she halted with a gasp. "Just look at those stars *monsieur*. Are they not sublime? Just imagine all the wishes they have heard throughout their lifetime."

Septimus smiled and said, "I see wishing on a star is not just an English pastime after all."

"No it is not *monsieur*," replied Anna.

Septimus watched her in the starlight and knew he had found a true treasure in this girl. The luxurious flames of her hair tumbled over her face, though thankfully not enough to disguise the fullest lips Septimus had ever seen: lips that exuded emotion and sensuality.

Anna eventually took up residence on the settee and explained to Septimus just how and why she was here, and about her long journey from France. Septimus smiled thinly and soaked up the story of her voyage and her ambitions as an actress and singer until he felt he could absorb no more. Losing a little patience, Septimus rose to his feet and raised his hand to stop her from saying any more, "Thank you miss. I now understand entirely why you came to this country and why you feel I can be of use to you. Mr Kearney was correct in pointing you my way. He is after all a very kind-hearted man."

"If my terms are agreeable to you, this is what I can offer you young lady." Septimus' voice suddenly became quite serious and just a little cold. "I will take some photographic likenesses of you, some of which I will keep for my exhibition. I shall furnish you with a selection of photographic likenesses on cards, which you can distribute as you see fit. I have no doubt they would be useful to show to theatre production managers, artists, and anybody else with a use for a pretty girl such as you," Septimus paused and smiled knowingly.

There was something about his tone of voice that Miss Fountaine did not like. She stood up instantly and replied without reservation, "If you are implying what I think you are *monsieur*, you are mistaken. I am going to be a great actress, and I need not such whore work to get to where I am going to."

Septimus raised an eyebrow and coolly replied. "Do excuse me young lady, I sought not to offend you. It is just that sometimes in life, particularly in the entertainment world, one would occasionally have to occupy oneself with lesser work until you are established in your chosen field. You are a beautiful girl, of that there is no doubt, and if you have the abilities that you profess to have, I am sure you will go far. But remember, one has to live, young lady, and life sadly is not born without a sacrifice or two," Septimus said whilst averting his eyes.

Anna paused for thought. Septimus regained eye contact and asked calmly but coldly, "Do we have a deal Miss Fountaine?" Anna was too shrewd to let her emotions stand in the way of this useful opportunity, despite her apprehensions.

"We have a deal *monsieur*."

Septimus nodded his head slightly and said abruptly "Good, I do hate vacillation, don't you Miss Fountaine?" and continued, "I fear hesitation reveals a lack of clarity and a slowness of wit."

"*Oui monsieur*... perhaps."

"There is perhaps one other way I could help you fulfil your ambitions," Septimus added. "I know of a gentleman who is... familiar with the theatres in London like nobody else. He could at the very least increase your physical and mental geography of the world of entertainment within this fair city of ours. His name is Mr Wilding, Algernon Wilding, to be precise, and you will find him here," said Septimus whilst handing her a calling card from out of his wallet. Anna looked at the card carefully. Algernon Wilding, actor, photographer, and theatrical agent, 12A Mermaid Street, Whitechapel.

"I feel indebted to you *monsieur*. You have been most kind," said Anna, her enthusiasm renewed.

"Ah Miss Fountaine," Septimus said without emotion, "Let's just say I appreciate your ambition and beauty, young lady. I have confidence in our ability to make something quite remarkable out of you."

"I do hope so," Anna said with a smile.

"How about we start taking some photographs? How about here tomorrow at ten o'clock sharp?" suggested Septimus.

Anna took a quick intake of breath and replied slowly and hesitantly: "So soon? *Oui, oui.* Yes, I suppose I…"

"That's settled then," said Septimus abruptly.

"*Oui*, yes, I suppose it is. Thank you, I shall be here," Anna replied hesitantly, still taken slightly aback by the pace of the situation.

Septimus nodded then sprang to his feet again and gestured to the door. "I bid you farewell then, young lady; here, let me escort you down the stairs." As they reached the reception area, Septimus rang the bell. Shortly, Angharad attended the ring. "Ah Angharad, please be kind enough to get Marmaduke to bring one of our carriages for Miss Fountaine. He should be attending the horses as we speak. Tell him to see that Miss Fountaine arrives home safely."

"There is no need sir, I am perfectly capable of …" Anna's words were halted in mid-sentence by a resolute Septimus.

"Nonsense, the streets are no place for a young woman on her own at this time of night. I have my own carriages and it would be good to give the horses some exercise. Besides, I want you as fresh as a daisy in the morning, Miss Fountaine. Fresh as a daisy, you hear?"

"*Oui, merci monsieur.* If you insist."

"Until the morning then Miss Fountaine," Septimus said with a slight nod of his head, before disappearing off to his study.

Sure enough, within a minute or two a fine black carriage appeared from a neighbouring courtyard and pulled up for her. A large coloured gentleman of possible African extraction duly jumped down from the cab, opened the door for Anna and helped her inside. She was glad to accept Septimus' generous offer of transport. The temperature had fallen quite considerably since her walk earlier to the premises, and the orange-hued fog swirling from the river had a particularly sulphurous tang now, which she found most abhorrent. Once inside the carriage, Anna took time to reflect on the wonderful navy blue furnishings and the mahogany panelling within. It was certainly all very comfortable, though Anna felt more than a little grain of apprehension about her newly-found situation.

Surely it was a very auspicious beginning to her time in London? The man's photography was awfully impressive, and to pay for a likeness of such quality would have certainly cost a pretty penny. His glasshouse studio was magnificent; such an array of outfits and props, it was just like a grand theatre in the sky. But such an odd man, such penetrating eyes.

The eyes of a hawk. Anna understood his motives for wanting to keep some of the photographs. It was only natural that he should retain some of them for his collection, but why so much interest? Anna felt no physical threat from him, nothing apparent. Not in the way she could from some men anyway. But there was something of the thief about him. She decided not to worry about it; as soon as she had the photographs she need not see the strange Mr Blackwood ever again.

Chapter 13

Caught on Film

The chemist's uneasy slumber was disturbed by Septimus' messenger boy hammering and hollering at his shop door. "Oye John, wake up, wake up!" *Thump, thump, thump!* John the Chemist crawled out of bed and winced at the light of day. He just about managed to prise open his window sash, which had swollen in the cold damp air. John stared blearily out of his window and saw the diminutive figure of Pigeon below. "What the hell do you want Pigeon boy?"

"Septimus wants to see you. Very important he says, reckons today's the day, whatever that means." The chemist raised his eyes skyward to the unforgiving daylight and shook his head in defeat.

"Oh very well, tell him I am on my way, but next time I want one of his coaches to fetch me."

"Will do John, look lively then," replied Pigeon mischievously. Pigeon loved winding the chemist up. He was just too easy to tease. Besides, he knew that John would never catch up with him to give him the caning he always said he would.

John frowned down at Pigeon and fought to shut the stubborn sash again as quickly as he could. How he hated this cold air invading his space. John shuffled over to where he had placed his clothes the night before. He could not be bothered to search around to look for something fresher. He just wanted to be warm, so he wore the same clothes he had worn yesterday and the day before that, and maybe the day before that. John had become quite oblivious to his own dilapidated appearance; never really one for mirrors, not for a long time at least, but recently he had lost even the slightest modicum of interest in how he looked.

The effects of last night's whiskey had barely left him. His head felt heavy and his boots heavier still. John administered himself a little laudanum. He had forgotten exactly when or why he had first started taking the stuff.

Whatever and whenever it was, it seemed to take the chill out of his life and pain away from his arthritic legs. John considered breakfast as he always did, and as normal he just considered it and no more. Food felt like too much of a chore this morning.

The cold seemed to seep into every pore of his being as he lurched down Crow Lane. He had forgotten his walking stick again! Septimus' early morning wakeup call had made him feel off balance and unsteady on his feet. At least, that is what he blamed it on.

Crow Lane surely had to be one of the most uncomfortable lanes in the whole of London. It was narrow and only partially paved. Horse dung and slop deposited from the jetties above decorated the ground beneath his feet. These wooden jetty houses were fast becoming a thing of the past. Many had smut-stained or boarded up windows, ill-fitting and uncomfortable.

These houses stood like avenues of weed trees tangling and jostling for light and purchase on the treacherous silt beneath them. The sun rarely shone on here, and even when it did, the billowing smoke from the factories blurred the outlines of the buildings. Each structure seemed to melt into its neighbour, like drunks at midnight struggling and spilling into one another, desperately seeking balance and stability.

John bitterly reflected on the chaos of the landscape around him and his own place within it. How very different he was to the man he was about to see. Septimus was ordered, reserved, and purposeful. How can a man deny himself at least some disorder in his life? John had always surrounded himself in disorder and erratic pleasures, how could a man not? John did, however, begrudgingly admire Septimus for his strength of purpose, if little else.

Whatever the public face of Septimus was, John knew that underneath the carefully constructed mask lay something far more curious, far more obsessive, and far more... more... John was searching his mind for a specifically fitting adjective when his thoughts were suddenly disturbed by a gust of wind blowing a rotting shutter off from one of the windows above. The decaying shutter only just missed John's head by a matter of inches, and now lay splintered unceremoniously beneath his feet.

John stared down at its ruins for a moment, for once congratulating himself on this rare display of good fortune. "That's it," John declared out loud with joy, and then again "That's the word I was looking for, Septimus is bloody *unhinged.*" John followed this revelation with a bout of near maniacal laughter. "My, my, how timely life is. The Lord does move in some mysterious ways," he carried on, muttering to himself. At that moment a washerwoman shuffled past John nervously, shielding her ragged child and desperately avoiding eye contact with this crooked madman, laughing and muttering to himself.

Septimus was arranging his notes when he caught sight of John entering the study, out of the corner of his eye. "Morning John, I hope you brought those chemicals we need."

"Yes, of course I remembered them. I did not realise I would be needed quite so soon though."

Septimus was pleased to see him. Not that he ever let John know that. It certainly wasn't because he felt any emotional tie or warmth towards him; nothing could be further from the truth. It was because John had technical vision and had a knack of getting things to work. He could grasp an idea out of thin air and set about developing that vision into a thing, an actual device. His engineering skills were second to none; the man was a practical genius, albeit a somewhat erratic one. Septimus could see huge potential in this shambling wreck of a man. He recognized him as a pioneer, a free thinker, someone who dared.

Of course Septimus knew only too well about John's past. That was how he maintained his grip on the man, though Septimus always tried not to mention it too often. Well, at least no more than he had to. No, Septimus was content to just drop the odd little hint here and there that he knew something, something that John may wish to keep secret. Of course, John knew that Septimus knew about some of his past and hated him for it. The knowledge of this festered inside John and he bitterly resented being beholden to Septimus in this way. He wished he could be free of him for good. Septimus knew there were police cases against John that had never been closed.

Indeed, Septimus had made it his business to know as much as was possible about John and the open cases relating to him. He'd carefully noted them all down, even the crimes that were very unlikely to have been anything to do with him. Unrelated or not, they were all marked to the same man by the police, the press, and the public alike. The name then was Jack, not John. "Jack the

Prankster," "Jack the Spectre of London" was now "John the Surly," "John the Sour," "John the Lame-Heeled." His athletic rooftop escapades had cost his health dearly, and his love of pyrotechnics had left parts of his body scorched and scarred.

No, Jack, or John as he was now called, was no longer the scourge of Old London Town. He was now Septimus' chief technician on one of the most pioneering scientific experiments ever conducted in the 19th century. Septimus needed John's silence almost as much as John needed his.

If this formula that they were working on and the camera could achieve all he hoped for, the possibilities were infinite – they were grasping the seed and holding the very essence of life before them. Although the experiment itself interested John, he did not share Septimus' hunger for it. As far as John was concerned, it was another interesting experiment. If it worked, it worked and if it didn't, it didn't.

Chapter 14

Textiles

Sophia was already in the studio arranging the outfits and the backdrops with much gusto when the chemist limped in, breathless from the stairs. The pair of them rarely acknowledged each other's existence. Sophia looked away, sharpish, as the chemist sneered at her and skulked off to the darkroom that lay to one side of the glasshouse studio.

The opportunity to work in Septimus' studio was too good for Sophia to miss. Sophia adored painting and arranging the props and she loved trying on the costumes magnificently made by Mrs Thunderbug and family. Sophia may not have been blessed with the same level of imagination as her older sister Andrea, but when she was instructed to create a certain image or scene for a background, she was as talented a painter as you would ever seek to find.

As an employer, Septimus paid reasonably well, though his hours were irregular and occasionally long. He demanded full commitment to a job and was a true perfectionist. Sophia had never understood her sister's affection for this strange Englishman. There again, she had always found her sister a bit of a mystery anyway. Sophia did however admire Septimus for his attention to detail, his passion for his art, and most importantly of all, the stability his employment had given to her family in these hard times.

Septimus' passion for his work was a passion that was only displayed in the eyes: an intense, unblinking, brooding gaze that missed nothing. How very different it was to the noise and physicality that her mother, her sister, and, indeed, she herself displayed when inspired. Most of the time, Septimus seemed largely devoid of any emotion at all. He rarely smiled or laughed; even a frown was as a stranger to his face. Sophia also knew though that the scarcity of words was in no way indicative of a scarcity of ideas. He was always experimenting, always trying to improve on the last photograph.

The only thing that Sophia hated about working for Septimus was having to work with the chemist. Sophia hated having to even share the same air as him. She could not think of a fouler, more repulsive creature than him. His eyes lingered too long, his humour, what little there was of it, was sadistic but thankfully rare.

Sophia recoiled at the thought of how his mouth twisted when he laughed. Never before had she met a person that she felt such an instant loathing for, and it was a loathing that *familiarity* only seemed to make worse.

Whilst Sophia was busy avoiding John and sorting out the studio, Septimus waited for Anna in the reception area, with bridled anticipation.

He was delighted when she arrived on time, and greeted her cordially, escorting her up to his lofty lair. She seemed a little nervous upon entering the glasshouse studio, especially when she caught the eyes of the prowling Sophia. Anna smiled and nodded politely at Sophia. Sophia tried to react politely back to the beautiful new client that dared to grace *her* studio. She tossed back her long black hair and her mouth forged an expression which made it perfectly clear that this was her domain and any other woman was only ever going to be a visitor here.

"I think we will start with the rustic backcloth this time Sophia, if you do not mind?" Septimus said with a little hint of sarcasm. He had picked up on the decidedly chilly atmosphere exuding from Sophia and was going to have none of it, not today of all days. Sophia lightened a little with a sigh and set about changing the backcloth. Sophia then lifted up the hairbrush and looked at Septimus. Septimus gave her the nod and Sophia walked toward Miss Fountaine.

It was with some apprehension that Anna allowed and grudgingly endured the fiery Italian to groom her in readiness for the photographs. Sophia struggled with the lush volume of Anna's beautiful mane.

Sophia had never seen such a wealth of hues before on one person's head, and she was truly envious. Despite the envy, Sophia started warming to the naïve French girl. Anna too was starting to relax and slowly starting to enjoy the pampering she was getting, when something close sparked her interest. It was a highly decorated music box. Anna looked at Septimus and he nodded

70

agreement for her to open it. Upon opening it, a very small ballerina popped up and began twirling round and around. Anna smiled. Her grandmother had had one similar, though its decoration was not so fine. The tune was different too; the melody this box had was hypnotically sedate and seemed to draw the listener into its harmony. Anna, to Septimus' pleasure, was the perfect portrait sitter. She suited every garment, every scene. She knew how to entice and enthral, her face oozed sensuality and distinction, and it all came very naturally. Her body and the backcloth became one, time and time again. She was the temptress, the lady, the cherub; her repertoire of expressions knew no bounds. She was born for the stage. The light in the studio was perfect that day; there were no shadows.

Septimus photographed Anna that day with a variety of cameras. Some shots were to be calotypes for *cartes de visite* style, and it was that type of photograph that he would give to Anna when they were developed.

The other "special photographs" were his and his alone. The finished articles would be similar too but if this new process worked, it would open up a whole new dimension in photography. It was a process that could challenge the way people viewed life and maybe even death itself.

After the photographic session, Sophia gave Septimus the hairbrush Anna had used earlier. Septimus and the chemist worked developing the photographs for the rest of the day, like crones at a cauldron. The chemist could see the maniacal look in Septimus' eyes. Septimus looked as if he were possessed by some hungry demon. It was at these times that John the Chemist kept his distance and would have preferred to leave Septimus to it.

It was deep into the night before the frames and photographs were finished. Both men were incredibly tired, though Septimus strained his inquisitive eyes at each set of new prints. He peered deeper and deeper for what seemed like an age, waiting, watching until even his unnatural zeal gave up the ghost. It was as much as Septimus could do to prise himself up out of his chair and into his bedchamber. He left the weary chemist slumped over the table, overcome with fatigue and gin.

Septimus slept fitfully in his feather bed. His body felt taut and his mind spun with peculiar images.

71

Just when he had found some semblance of serenity, he was rudely awoken by a horse whinnying close by. He cursed under his breath, and despite the lingering darkness and the distinct chill of morning, his curiosity about the prints forced him out of bed and back into the studio.

Once there he peered again at the likenesses he had created of Anna Fountaine. Most of them were *cartes de visites* for Miss Fountaine but they were of no importance now. Septimus was more interested in his "special ones." Had it worked? Does it work? Could it ever be possible? Was the chemist, who was at this point still slumped on the table, imagining things when he saw what he did? If it had worked, would it be effective on every image, or just one? Was it the adjustments to the camera or the new formulae that made it work?

His mind suddenly became full of self-doubt and cynicism, though still he looked and looked at the image, turning the glass this way and that, into the light and away from the light, hoping to entice and provoke the photograph into action. He even found himself softly whispering to the picture, willing it to react. It was shortly after this point that he shook his head in despair at the lack of movement and the condition of the comatose chemist.

Septimus filled his china jug of water and tipped it into the large bowl, which perched on a table at the side of his chamber. He washed his sore and tired eyes, dressed, and then instructed Angharad to make some eggs and tea for his breakfast and prepared for the day ahead.

Chapter 15

Knowing Nonny

Anna arrived at the Bunch of Grapes Inn on Paddle Street the day after the photo shoot at Septimus' studio. It was here she was to collect her photographs and meet this theatrical agent called Nonny, though she decided to call him Mr Wilding, at least to begin with. She dare not enter the Grapes on her own: she had seen the type of ladies who passed through the doors unescorted, and certainly did not want to be considered to be one of those, so, despite the emerging drizzle, she would desist.

Anna's attention was caught by an exotic, but rather frayed middle-aged man heading towards her. She looked up as he smiled and tilted his overly large top hat revealing a receding mop of tinselled sandy grey curls. "I take it you are Miss Fountaine?"

"*Oui*, yes, that is I sir. You are Mr Wilding?"

"I am, young lady, at your service. I am Algernon Wilding, Shakespearean actor, agent and friend to some of the finest actors and actresses in London Town." He eyed the inn door, raised his ebony stick, and pointed to the entrance. "Would such an exquisite beauty as yourself do me the pleasure of accompanying me for a drink?" Anna nodded courteously.

The inside of the inn was full of noise and hullaballoo. Anna stared 'round at the assorted human peacocks assembled herein and thought this was obviously the place to be noticed, a step in the right direction. Many tipped their hats at Mr Wilding and smiled, though others seemed less keen, and edged away slightly. Anna thought him a very curious, funny little man as she watched him waltz to the bar as if flying through the air, his whole body swaying up and down like a leaf on a breeze; he bowed and curtsied like a butterfly at every turn.

Whilst at the bar, Nonny held out the note in his right hand above his head as if he were at an auction, his other elbow resting on the bar, and his right boot perched on the foot rail, vainly attempting to look taller than he actually was. Eventually he was served and then weaved his way with affected grace to the table that Anna had secured for them overlooking the street. Nonny placed the glasses of wine on the table, smiled, then grabbed hold of his checked trousers at the thigh and pulled them up as he sat carefully onto the chair.

He then took out his clay pipe, removed his exceedingly large hat, and had one huge draw on his pipe before promptly melting into the furniture. Anna tried to stifle a laugh at this amusing little fellow, but could not help but smile as she politely thanked him for the wine. She asked if she could see the photographs Septimus had produced for her.

"Of course, there you go young lady, help yourself," Nonny said lazily. She set about thumbing her way through the likenesses. She was delighted at the results, such a beautiful finish, such clarity.

"I could have done a little better deary," said Nonny sourly, "but Blackwood does have a certain style about him, I will give him that. After all, what is life without style?" Anna tried not to smile at the absurdity of his words. Nonny smoothed back his hair and wrestled with his cravat pin, which was obviously a source of both discomfort and pride to him.

"I am sure you have a point *monsieur*. He has been very kind to me though."

"Kind, eh young lady? Hmm..." He raised his eyes to the ceiling as if searching for a suitable response.

"Yes, of course he has my pretty flower. How could one doubt his magnanimity and generosity of spirit?" Nonny uttered, not quite being able to convince himself of the truth of his words. By the end of their meeting, Anna had quite taken to this colourful eccentric and not even the murky, opaque skies of winter could dampen her optimism. She now had a magnificent set of photographs to distribute at her leisure, and her very own theatrical agent.

Anna was not totally convinced by the professionalism of the man but he was certainly well known and his experience undeniable.

Nonny lingered in the Bunch of Grapes Inn long after Anna had gone. His eyes were glazed and body slouched as he drew heartily on his long pipe, and mused at the potential of the fine young lady he had met earlier. He could tell when he met her that not only did she look the part but also she could express herself well and had real promise in the theatrical world. She could even be his grand entrance back to the high life, the Big Show Time. Nonny never aimed low, not he, not Algernon Wilding. "Always aim for the stars dear boy, for the stars," he muttered to himself. Seconds later, he and his chair became one.

Chapter 16

The Pendulum

Septimus was finding it difficult to concentrate on anything other than the photographic experiment work as he impatiently paced around his rooftop studio. The afternoon had come and gone and John had long since sloped off back to his shop. John and he had tried just about every variable version of the formulae possible. Surely one of them at least would produce the desired effect.

Septimus' only solace was watching the seductive movement of the Thames below. The lamps and the torches of the night time emblazoned upon it, it looked as if it were a living tapestry composed of fine liquid threads of amber and gold. The soft swell was interspersed with lumpy waves, the boats' tall masts swaying like bull-rushes in the weakening breeze.

After a while even the gentle swell of the Thames began to grate on Septimus. How dare it be so nonchalant on a day like today? Even the billowing smoke from the chimneys sulked in the air, the wind scarcely blew, and the whole world seemed to be drowning in apathy. The drizzle hung languid and lame; it collaborated and joined the smoke to smudge and befuddle all sense of movement, all sense of purpose.

The grandfather clock plodded and thumped as if in a dream; the pendulum swayed back and forth, getting slower and slower with a suffocating malaise. Even the chimes begrudged their hourly labour. The pregnant pause between the ringing of the hour led Septimus to believe that the clock's mechanism was silently contemplating and plotting to stop time all together. The hours wandered slowly by, slower even than the willow-strewn brooks of Oxfordshire where he had spent so much of his youth.

The photographs were as inert as his beloved collection of taxidermy. Though *they* were meant to be dead, weren't they? Septimus loved their perfection, caged, sealed, and compliant. But tonight even here he felt a strange tension as if they were harbouring ill intent. Did they mock him now? Were they silently laughing at his ambition? Did they understand ambition? No, no, absurd, he mused to himself. Was he going insane? Did they want him insane? Did the creatures ever have a will? If so, do they still have it? And was he now at the mercy of their collective malevolence? Were their eyes reflecting the life of the candle and lamp or did some lingering remnant of sentience remain? Septimus could feel his flesh crawling as his eyes swung this way and that, probing the creatures for movement. Did they recognize his fear? The room's atmosphere became unbearably heavy; the air was drying up, and he knew he must escape.

The eyes, beaks, claws, talons, teeth, and scales seeped into his brow and into his mind. The seething mass between his ears grew heavier and heavier. Septimus' hands clutched at his head as if he were squeezing out the septic spirits within. His moist, sweaty palm sought the sanctuary of the door handle. His face involuntarily swung back one last time to face his tormentors. It was then, at this precise moment, that he saw the flicker: that flicker of life… that spark, the mind-numbing realization of a dream becoming manifest. Septimus held his body very still as his head slowly turned back, so subtly so as not to destroy the illusion.

He peered down at the photographs of Anna Fountaine. He had ten photographs of her set in iron, with his special formulae added to the plate. The photographic plates were encased by glass and edged with a gold gilded. The second photograph from the right was the one that caught his attention. He picked it up tenderly and strained his eyes to gain a greater purchase of the image within. Then, sure enough, the movement happened again.

One finger started to twitch, to pulse. The photograph that featured Miss Fountaine as Cleopatra had life - her other hand pulsed too. The movements were only just about visible, but visible they were. Behind the glass Anna's eyes seemed to explore, like those of a baby, searching for focus.

The whites of her eyes seemed to moisten for a second and her mouth quivered as her chest seemed to heave with a sigh.

The draught blew through the cracks in Anna's bedroom window. Her dreams had taken her to many strange worlds over the years, but none was so strange as this one. It was as if she was peering into a world, which reflected back in on itself, one of claustrophobia and enslavement.

Septimus wiped off the film of fine mist with which his breath had tarnished the glass. He searched the photograph for more movement. It was still there, but fading with every heartbeat. Septimus hastily fetched his magnifying glass from the light room, and in a heightened state of anxiety observed the last subtle vestiges of movement trickle away from the likeness. He shook the photograph gently, blew on it once more, and buffed it up in great vigour, though nothing he could do brought back the illusion of life. Was it an illusion? Was it a spectre of the mind brought on by the inner turmoil he had felt earlier? Did his mind seek to spite him too, taunting him, enticing him with fantasies?

He was sure, wasn't he, that he had observed something? There *was* movement -- he had seen it. He sat down and peered up at the full moon through the glass roof and allowed himself to dream. If it had truly worked, it was awe-inspiring: the potential for science, for humanity, for … himself was immense.

Had he created life? Replicated life? Created a memory of life? A mirror of life? How long was that life? His eyes turned back towards the stars and he felt the power of creation.

Chapter 17

The Plans

Septimus had arranged with Andrea to hold a private meeting with the rest of the gang at the Angel Vaults Inn at nine on Monday morning to discuss his underground project once more. He had decided it was safer to alternate meetings between here and the Rope and Anchor to ward off unwanted curiosity.

Mortlake had gathered Jewels and The Snake for the early meeting, with some difficulty. Their elusiveness at times was frustrating, but find them he did. Septimus arrived on time and found the rest of them already awaiting his presence. "Good morning gentlemen, I trust you are all well?" His eyes scanned around the table, looking no one directly in the eye.

Ocky raised an eyebrow and gave a small grunt, whilst Jewels was more courteous and said, "I am well enough sir, but my old knees are…"

Mortlake cut Jewels off in midsentence and said wryly, "I am sure your knees are a complete trial to you Mr Juson, and I offer you my deepest sympathy, but for the sake of all our rapidly aging bones, I reckon we better get on with the job at hand before we all seize up." Ocky and Septimus both grinned and just for once Jewels seemed to take the hint.

"Right then gentlemen," Septimus exclaimed with some impatience, "did you bring the maps along with you?" The Snake nodded and then from his jacket pulled out a selection of rough scrolls that he had been working on. Upon these were listed many of the old underground rivers and tunnels of London, along with accompanying side notes. Mortlake's mouth opened wide. He had not expected to see such intricate detail and so neatly written too. Septimus was impressed: here was an educated man. Where on earth had this subterranean man been educated to this degree?

"Well bless me Ocky," Mortlake said with a shake of his head, "I never knew you could read, let alone write." Ocky gave a sardonic smile.

79

"Ah well Mr Mortlake, there are many things that a man can see if he looks hard enough; you should give it a try one day." Mortlake felt a sudden surge of anger.

He had never really liked the idea of working with Ocky -- he was far too slippery and far too fly. Mortlake also knew that Ocky was probably the best man for the job. No one knew below like Ocky; that's what folks said anyway.

"So, what's next on the agenda then lads?" Jewels broke the sudden silence in conversation.

Mortlake smiled through gritted teeth and proclaimed, "I am sure these maps will prove invaluable to us." Ocky nodded smugly.

"You are a man of many talents Ocky Blackwood. Shame about your tailor, but a man cannot have everything I suppose. May I enquire where you acquired such a skill with the quill, my friend?" Mortlake continued. He still doubted whether this filthy, subterranean being had produced these maps and notes with his own hands or had just robbed them from another.

"Well, you can ask Mr Mortlake, you can ask, you can ask indeed," he repeated himself, "but it does not mean you will get an honest answer, or that I should in any way feel compelled to answer you correctly, sssssirrrrr." Mortlake disliked the way Ocky prolonged the word *sir*, the faint hissing sound. Ocky had a habit of dragging out his word endings and turning them into a sneer. Mortlake was very close to standing up and throttling the daylights out of this odious serpent.

"Why Mr Mortlake sir, I meant no offence. I was just remarking on the many variable potential answers to your question, that's all," Ocky said nonchalantly.

Septimus raised his hand calmly at Mortlake, gesturing him to leave it. Mortlake flinched at Ocky, but did eventually calm down, albeit sulkily.

Mortlake decided that when they no longer needed this snake-eyed sewer rat anymore, he would personally see that next time Ocky went below he would stay there. Ocky beckoned Andrea and ordered four whiskeys as a token of good will.

It was true that few men, if any, knew the subterranean world of London as well as Ocky did. He had explored tunnel after tunnel, river after river, and had made it his own business to know as many of the nooks and crannies of that vast underground kingdom as he could. Every new cavern and bolthole he found represented a new opportunity. As a boy he had penetrated many a vent and manhole, sometimes out of necessity, but latterly out of endeavour and the spirit of exploration. The tunnels, passageways, and sewers often stank to high heaven, and it was perilous at the best of times, but to Ocky it represented freedom and sometimes treasure too.

Ocky had many a hoard of trinkets and curiosities stashed away in the underground hideaways, up in holes unbeknownst to other men. His basement flat was only reached by descending down a flight of steps and through a glorified manhole beneath them. Ocky was not alone in this type of dwelling: tens of thousands of Londoners lived in this dank, underground, claustrophobic world -- a world with no natural light, with no natural hope.

Ocky spent few daylight hours in his underground hovel, but during those that he did, he tended to his boxes of treasures. He spent hours carefully cataloguing each individual find; cleaning the detritus and filth off of his trinkets and trophies. He had brooches, clasps, daggers, brightly-coloured beads, even a small round shield, which shone proudly in the artificial light. When the weather was heavy and damp, the moist ceiling and walls glistened and twinkled like a thousand stars melting in the moonlight of moment. Moisture trickled down the walls as the room perspired, and glistened in the flame of candle and gas.

The illusion of starlight within this entombed sanctuary inspired Ocky to no end. "As above, so below," was the quotation that often floated through the mind of this most peculiar of subterranean men. He firmly believed that the underground chambers of this city were his domain, his universe and watery fields from which to reap the harvest.

Ocky's domain was approximately thirty feet long by twenty feet wide. It was furnished with a small range, one table, a battered mattress supported by wooden slats, and two rickety chairs. His clothes hung up to dry rigid on a rail near the range. His canvas trousers hung nearest the fire -- they were his working trousers and always in constant need of washing. He had chosen his subterranean dwelling well.

To the rear of the room was a doorway leading to a small underground passageway. The passageway led in one direction to a flight of steps, which came up on the edge of Soarmoor Court.

The other underground passage led to a stout oak door. The door was strong, heavy, and perched on sturdy iron hinges that age had flecked with rust. This was a sewer flusher's entrance to the sewer below. Thankfully it was rarely used by the flushers, more so by a select few who had obtained a key and used it for far more nefarious pursuits. It was the entrance to the underworld, the secret London, the ghosts of London's past, locked in an eternal shadowland of murk and murmur.

Ocky was not the only person delving deep into London's labyrinth. Many a wretch inhabited this twilight world, some of which were hardly capable of surfacing at all. Here was the sanctuary of the womb beneath the city.

Here the fluids of life and death flowed through the bowels of the metropolis, meandering far below the madness of the terrestrial order and the endless mayhem of wheels and hooves.

The stories of those who dwelt in these vast subterranean catacombs were those of hunger, neglect, and disease.

All were seeking the solace, the embrace of the mother, the cradling arms of mud, mortar, and metal within the depths of this great city; the flotsam and jetsam of society, cast adrift, washed up and clinging to life, parasitic barnacles of that place known as London.

Some of the dwellers used these tunnels as a cloak, a place to plan, hide, and misguide; others to debauch, defile, and debase. Over the years he had developed an acute awareness of the dangers within these decaying passageways. Ocky's antennae twitched and shifted at the most subtle of changes guided by experience, instinct, and the subtleties of his senses. Rats were one of the worst foes of the depths -- they could tear a man to pieces if he lost his footing and fell into the foetid, inky slime of the sewer. Gas was another killer. So were tides and deluges, and not forgetting other men -- the toshers themselves were vehemently attached to their own sewers and sunken rivers. A man must be swift and fleet of foot to escape some of the little knots of men that gripped this underwater oasis close to their bosom.

On quick inspection of the maps and scrolls, Septimus was satisfied that Ocky and Jewels were serious about the project and thanked them for their time. "Personally I think this is like looking for a thimble in Fulham, but if you think it is worth a try, I'm game," said Mortlake.

"Good, that settles it then, tomorrow we shall discuss times and dates, routes, and equipment. And I hope Mr Mortlake here can fix us up with Mr Roper at the Rope and Anchor tomorrow sometime. I trust that will be okay for you two gentlemen?" asked Septimus

Jewels nodded and Ocky said, "I'll have to check my diary, of course, but I think you may be in luck. I should by that time have also rid myself of the hangover that I'll have picked up from the Prince's Ball this evening."

Septimus ignored the petulant comment and replied, "Right then, tomorrow it is," lifting his glass to toast the agreement.

"Just one thing though, what about the cash?" hissed Ocky.

"I will pay you well for your time gentlemen, and of course for your expertise. I am sure you two gentlemen will have other pressing business to attend to today, so I shall bid you farewell until the morrow." Septimus doffed his top hat and left speedily, with the burly Mortlake in his wake. The two toshers were left to chew the fat and finish their whiskeys.

After a short pause, Jewels looked at Ocky and said, "I am sure he is kosher, Ocky. He seems like a reasonable geezer. Got money too."

"We'll just have to see, won't we Jewelsy boy?" replied Ocky thoughtfully.

Chapter 18

Pipe Dreams

The chemist had decided to have a day off today. He was feeling unwell and needed a distraction. Septimus had mentioned that he required something oriental for his collection, so he decided to leave his shop in the capable hands of Mr Thunderbug. Mr Thunderbug often helped out in John's shop, mainly when John was away at Mr Blackwood's or was too "withdrawn" to deal with the public.

Herman and Scarlet Thunderbug had the clothes and material shop next door. Both Herman and Scarlet were trained tailors and supplied many of the clothes and materials worn by people of the East End, rich and poor alike.

Their shop was something of a curiosity for many reasons -- people used to travel from far and wide just to browse and marvel. The shop was seemingly limitless in size, an endless warren of rooms, shelves, and cupboards. One door led to another, then another, then another. And in turn, one floor of the shop led to another, and another. Each room had its own specific contents and character.

There were rolls of fabric and cotton from around the world. It was a true emporium in every sense of the word. There were large bolts of material, all shapes and sizes, all colours and textures, everything a dressmaker or tailor could possible wish for.

These were situated on the top floors, so as to avoid the damp of the lower sections and cellars. Each bale of material had to be winched up by pulley and chains, and how Mr Thunderbug winced at the creaking of the timbers. The house seemed to sigh and groan at the seams as every new shipment came from the docks. How the entire shop did not crumple like an accordion or sink into the building's soggy foundations, he would never know.

But that's how Mrs Thunderbug wanted it, and no one trifled with Mrs Thunderbug. Herman had tried, but now his main strategy was avoidance and distraction. The middle floors were occupied with second-hand articles to the left and new items to the right. All of the second-hand clothes had been washed and mended, whenever necessary, by Mrs Scarlet Thunderbug or one of her many daughters.

The ground floors consisted of many fitting rooms, mixed with finery, and some second-hand wear, rags and cloth, all meticulously separated from the rest. Mrs Thunderbug simply loved her material: she loved its individual texture, scent, and colour. She was indeed a very tactile woman, and was always running her fingers through the silk and satin fabric. Scarlet was not only a fine dressmaker; she and her daughters prided themselves on their patchwork quilts, fashioned largely from offcuts and rags. One of the huge storerooms at the back of the shop contained only rags and off- cuts solely for such a purpose.

Her daughters dived into these neat piles of fabric, sorting and searching for the right material for their task. When finished, they emerged like rabbits from these multicoloured mounds, covered in fluff, laughing, coughing, and dancing around.

Even though business was good, Scarlet was always harping on about something or other. Her main beef at present was how the new-fangled sewing machines would see them all out on the street, and how there was nothing like proper stitching nowadays. That said, she had mastered the new machines well and her daughters were proving deft with the new implements. The family had made most of the exotic new costumes for Septimus' studio, a fact that she was very proud of. She admired Septimus to no end: so debonair, flawless in style and manners. He had taste and a great eye for quality. Yes, he definitely had breeding, and of course money was no object. How different life would be if she had Septimus as a husband and not hapless Herman.

Herman's role in the shop, which often resembled a pantomime, was to fetch and carry, hang up the wares on the various outside rails of the shop, and do the accounts. Indeed, it was with great relish that Herman could relinquish his duties in the shop and escape to the relative calm of the chemist's shop next door, even if it was run by the most questionable apothecary in the whole of London.

It was on such a morning that Herman relieved John at the shop. John decided it was about time to see a man about a pipe. The sun was shining brightly this morning. Even the air was surprisingly fresh and seemed to lack the sulphurous tang that made it a friend through familiarity rather than choice. He limped along the various boardwalks and side streets that criss-crossed this particularly seedy part of the city.

John was on his way to an area in London referred to, but rarely written down, as Chinatown. There were large numbers of Orientals dotted along the dockside areas of the city. Some of these were legitimate businessmen, while others were sailors, many of whom had decided to jump ship and seek their fortune within the city no matter what lengths it took.

The water sloshed and slurped against the algae-infested wooden causeways, licking the supporting timber piles that ran deep into the London silt. The tide was up: Father Thames and his tributaries held up the waste and debris of the hungry city like trophies in a tournament, proudly holding aloft the spoils of his own industry. Blissfully unaware of the worth and value of the prize, the Thames blindly displayed its wares, brazen, shameless, naïve, but ruthless in triumph.

A change of air lifted the lank coils of the chemist's hair. The narrow causeways piped the chilling east wind into John's face. The sunlight embraced the withered, tired skin that clung to his head like parchment on a scroll. His face reflected the unrequited embrace with a frown and a wince.

John's bones creaked liked the rotting woodwork beneath his feet as he climbed the timber stairway to oblivion. He gave the customary coded knock on the door of the den. He was greeted by a smiling Mr Yang and a dense wall of smoke. Bodies lay strewn around the room, comforted by soft furnishings and room to dream.

John was going to kill two birds with one stone: he was here to discuss the possibility of Mr Yang sending a couple members of his extended family across to Septimus' studio in Whortleberry Street. Septimus was very eager to expand his range of "subjects," and this was to include as great a variety of racial types and social classes as possible.

John had suggested that he may well know a Chinaman or two, to which Septimus had simply lifted an eyebrow and dryly responded, "No doubt."

Mr Yang appeared perplexed at the request when first asked, but assured John that it would be possible to send a couple of his more distant family members round for a photograph or two, if Mr Blackwood would not mind making a small donation to pay for his mother's medical fees.

John knew exactly what he meant and assured Mr Yang that the sitters would be paid upon arrival at the studio. The main reason for John's visit was his desire for the sweet oblivion of the opium pipe. John grasped the long-handled clay pipe with great delicacy and not a little affection. One of Mr Yang's assistants placed the little sticky black ball into the end of the smooth white pipe and lit up the way to dreamtime.

John inhaled as if it was his last breath and slumped onto the already used and warmed cushions beneath him. He fended off the initial instinct to vomit as the feeling of nausea swept up his body, and he fought with himself to relax. Once his head hit the pillow, the porthole was open. His senses focused on the Thames lapping outside, notions came to him in the form of distant waves, visions lapped over his mind with frustrating consistency.

Memories nudged their way back and forth into John's mind like passing clouds on a gentle breeze. John smiled as he reminisced on the expressions on the faces of the outraged public and hysterical women, the wonderful newspaper articles spreading and embellishing his legend. The mayhem he had unleashed onto the victims was embedded deep within the swirling catalogue of his mind. Flaming torches and angry voices followed his trail: he was a comet burning through the mental and physical geography of a city.

The visual embers of conquest and quest comforted and teased the stations of his psyche. The finely woven threads were unravelling, and the tapestry of his past grew dimmer each day. The fading, threadbare remnants found sanctuary in the bellow-like pipe, which rekindled and reignited the distant lighthouse in his mind.

His legs had not betrayed him then -- he could climb like a spider, pounce like a tiger, and vanish like vapour into the nefarious world of nightmare.

But that was not the only thing that he had lost. No amount of intoxication in the world could obliterate the loss of his beloved

Juliana. Her skin was soft and milky, and her auburn hair was emblazoned with hues of perpetual autumn.

They had met by chance in the Fern House at Kew Gardens on the ninth of July ... the year always escaped him but, oh, what a glorious day of sunshine that was. Juliana had accidently stepped on his toe when admiring the impressive form of one of the sword ferns in the great glasshouse, and as soon as John looked into her eyes he knew there would never be another woman who could capture his heart such as this one.

Her eyes were huge soft pools of hazel and emerald, the eyes of an ocean, an ocean that contained an endless horizon of hope and serenity. Nothing in the world could touch him as he bathed in her gaze. Incredibly, she had liked him, and took great interest in his inventions no matter how improbable they were to the rest of the world. The sun had never shone so brightly as it did that summer. She had given him a world without ceilings, a world of endless possibilities. Despite the strength of feeling between them, though, their joy was to be short-lived.

As soon as Juliana's father, an army officer, had heard of her secret meetings with this "shop-boy", he put an end to it once and for all. Juliana was taken against her will onto a ship bound for India and forced into a marriage with a man she did not love but who, her father said, had "prospects." It was not until one month after she had just disappeared from his life that he had learnt of her fate.

John had always been confused as to why exactly he still kept that letter. Was it a reminder to never allow himself to be that weak again, or just a sentimental reluctance to let go of the only love he'd ever known?

Whatever the reason, it mattered not, as it was over, all over ... such a long time ago ... John's moist and dilated eyes briefly regained a fragment of focus as he observed the knots and the grain on the rafters above him. Such strange, strange shapes, he thought to himself. His fickle attention moved once more, before his eyes were finally seduced to draw a veil over the tortured world of John Amblewick, chemist, and one-time legend of London.

Pigeon brought the news to Septimus that the chemist had been successful in his mission to entice a couple of the Orientals from what he described as Pipe Street, and that they would be coming to

88

the studio later in the day. Septimus received the news with interest, and enquired whether the chemist would be joining the Chinamen in the studio this afternoon. The boy replied, "Dunno sir, he looked a bit second-hand when I see him late last night."

"Only second-hand? He must have found a new tailor then," Septimus quipped.

"That will be the day," replied Pigeon with a grin before scurrying off to do whatever Pigeons do.

Septimus grabbed his cane, coat, and top hat, and briskly immersed himself into the morning mist. He made light work of dodging all of the vagrants with begging bowls that were languishing around the pavements like some kind of urban fungi, contagious and contaminated. Septimus had decided to take a slightly longer route to the Rope and Anchor Inn, across Deadman's Ditch and down into Rose Street, close to where he believed his ancestral home had once stood.

His route took him past the ancient church of St Anne's. Apparently it had been rebuilt by the Normans but still housed a Saxon crypt beneath it. Septimus glanced up at its impressive ivy-twined tower, one he was delighted to note that, so far at least, had not been ruined by the addition of the newly fashionable spires. Septimus decided to walk around the outside of the churchyard walls to imbue a sense of time and place. This was the church of his ancestors: it was likely that generation after generation of Blackwoods had been christened and married here, and finally buried in its hallowed soil.

One of these days he vowed to make an appointment with its vicar and search through the parish registers to see just how far back the Blackwoods' roots went down here.

The church had been built upon a mound, and its surrounding yard was reinforced by heavy stone walls slumped up against the earth above, holding its occupants firmly in place. This gave the church loftiness and held the yard well above the surrounding roadway. The churchyard area was almost one perfect circle, within which a ring of huge decaying old yews solemnly stood guard over the doleful sanctity of stone and cross. Nestled in the protective embrace of some yew trees stood the much- celebrated Ogham Stone.

There had been many attempts to decipher the strange markings inscribed onto the pitted face of the stone. True enough, the letters looked like that of the Ogham variety, but the pictures etched deep into the stone were a mystery. Many of them were of sea monsters and of strange fish. Perhaps the oddest and most unique marking of all was that of a person holding what looked like a flaming torch, walking into a cave or archway. All of these features combined gave this particular spot a feel of timelessness, of animism, a conduit between the worlds.

As Septimus made his way around the perimeter of the churchyard walls, he came across an alcove. It looked a little like a hermit's grotto but it was probably an archaic form of baptistery. The opening was about six feet high, eight feet long, and eight feet wide. The alcove sat about twenty yards away from the church.

Within the baptistery there was a finely carved stone gargoyle. It was similar to one of the strange sea creatures etched onto the Ogham Stone in the churchyard above. It was set into the wall at about a height of four feet. The water gushed freely, and when it reached the stone slabbed floor it fell straight through a rusty grid into a well below.

On the left-hand side of the baptistery there was a square-shaped opening which led to a passageway beyond. The passageway headed off towards the old church. It was blocked off to the public by six railings which were embedded into the stonework. This passageway looked dark and desolate, but clear of debris. A man could still just about get through it if he had a mind to, providing, of course, he could get through those bars.

Septimus had never seen anything quite like this before, and was intrigued. His father and grandparents must have been familiar with this spot -- shame they were not around to shed some light on its purpose and origins. Septimus made a mental note to himself that he would return here soon and find out more about the baptistery, its tunnel, and the strange stone above.

Mortlake, Ocky, and Jewels had arrived at the Rope and Anchor on time, before Septimus. Septimus was a little late due to the sudden lapse of discipline caused by his curiosity in the church and the baptistery.

But it was certainly worth keeping them waiting -- it was, after all, a reconnaissance mission. "Gentlemen, do forgive me. I was detained unexpectedly. I trust you are all well?" Before any of them could reply, Septimus said, "Shall we go below?"

The cellar was still as uninviting as it had been the last time -- more so in fact, as it was even colder this time around. "Did you bring the maps gentlemen?"

"Yes, I found a couple that may well be of use to us," Ocky replied.

"You could have been the finest cartographer in the whole of London couldn't you? I am green with envy, I am. Green with envy," said a po-faced Mortlake.

Ocky glared at Mortlake, looking for traces of sarcasm but, to his surprise, couldn't find any. He was hiding it well, thought Ocky, though he still could not resist following it up with,

"Cartographer you say? My, my, ain't that the study of market traders?"

Mortlake could feel his blood starting to rise again. Ocky was grinning at him across the table -- he was baiting him, that was for sure.

Mortlake's eyes grew cold. This was not the time to finish this little runt, though finish him he would, so he just stared through Ocky as if he were not there.

Septimus took to reading Ocky's maps with relish, though he was forever careful not to look too enthusiastic about it. He peered eagerly at the lines and text on the parchment. His eyes lifted and peered at Ocky, who sat opposite him. Ocky's eyes were expressionless, and Septimus continued to read. Septimus was impressed, more than impressed: the detail conveyed therein was extraordinary. It was written with an unpolished hand -- the presentation could be improved, but these were truly magnificent maps. These documents were utterly invaluable to him, priceless.

"I congratulate you sir," said Septimus. He could not bear to call Ocky *Mr Blackwood*. "A different scale to my documents, but nevertheless fine work."

"I am glad you approve sir," Ocky hissed with his customary sarcasm.

The time had come now for Septimus to share his knowledge with the rest of them. The air seemed a little thicker than the last time he was here. Familiarity had done little to abate Septimus' unease with the environment and company with which he now found himself. Septimus felt somewhat apprehensive, not so much for his wellbeing, but of sharing his plans and, more importantly, sharing whatever secrets were concealed in the wretched, dark, damp gloom below.

He adjusted his collar and laid out the rough copies of his maps and sketches on the table. Septimus had been careful enough to change some of the wording and a few of the important features.

Much of the information Septimus had acquired had come from what his Great-Aunt Arianwen had surreptitiously told him many years ago. The rest had come in the form of old maps of and topographical references to the area, many of which originated from the mid-to-late-18th century, the time shortly before the fire reduced much of the area to ashes. As with the Great Fire of London, many of the houses and streets were rebuilt as they were on the old original layout. Sadly, the Manor House was not one of those. It was as if the place had been deliberately erased for all time, a stain scoured from the landscape by sweat and mortar.

It had taken a while, but in his mind's eye Septimus had deduced approximately where his ancient ancestral manor house had once stood. Many of the maps also featured a huge ancient oak, which was probably the one his aunt had mentioned standing at the edge of their pleasure garden many years ago.

There was still a huge and partly-hollowed English oak standing there that now formed part of an island in the middle of the crossroads between what was now called Lime Avenue, Phoenix Lane, and Victoria Mead. The old tree was now surrounded by worn grass, and a circular seat set around its edge.

It was often used by drovers as a place of respite -- a site of shade for their cattle on the way to market.

Septimus had also heard from his aunt that the cellar to the old mansion house was accessible via an underground river that flowed underneath the road alongside the mansion's grounds. The reasons for another entrance to the cellar had always intrigued Septimus: was it to ferry goods into or out of the house? To travel by boat was a much safer way to travel than by foot or carriage, but underground…?

Whatever it was, it was a straw to clutch at and a ray of hope in the darkness. His great aunt suspected that his disreputable grandfather had kept much of the family's inheritance to himself, and had cheated his brother out of much of the estate. If his Grandfather Cornelius had had all the wealth that was accredited to him, maybe some of his fortune was still lingering below, just waiting to be rediscovered by its rightful heir.

Ocky peered at Septimus' charts -- none of the detail was lost on him. He scrutinized every square inch, and Septimus could see him making mental notes. Jewels also tried to soak in some of the details, though the text was completely lost on him.

Ocky raised his head, concerned, and said, "I know roughly how to steer myself in the right direction, but it would mean going down some very old tunnels..." Ocky's voice evaporated into the dampness of the room as if the thought was forever entombed in its own contemplation.

"They must be off from the Bleeding Brook or around the Sheppard's Crook area somewhere Ocky," Jewels said as he looked apprehensively at Ocky.

Ocky looked pensive and said, "You do realise just how dangerous a mission this could be?"

"I realise that there will be some risks which may befall us on the way sir, but needless to say we are men of initiative and enterprise, and you two gentlemen are reputed to be masters of the underworld, are you not?" enquired Septimus.

"Masters of the underworld," Jewels repeated, puffing himself up like a prize cock and smiling at Septimus' inflated words. Ocky's face twisted and furled like a leaf in autumn at his friend's naïve behaviour.

Septimus cleared his throat and said, "I am sure between us we can solve this mystery once and for all."

Ocky piped up, "Oh, we can look Septimus, but we will need to be well prepared and very, very alert when we have colonies of rats chomping at our tails and gas filling our lungs, not to mention the fact that we could be knee-deep in shit."

Septimus smirked awkwardly before saying, "Well, with an invitation like that Mr Ocky, I would be delighted to accompany you to the ball. Ultimately, the choice is yours gentlemen," continued Septimus, with a degree of impatience. Septimus knew that the men now knew too much to back out and, should they not now go through with the project, they would have to be dealt with, by hook or by crook.

"What happens if we don't find anything?" asked Ocky in a bemused tone.

"Should that be the case gentlemen, you will be paid well, regardless, though if we are successful my reward for you will be very substantial indeed. It may be that we run into some problems and fail to find it at first attempt. If that is the case, we take a leaf out of Robert the Bruce's book and we try, try, and try again. Just one thing I forgot to mention earlier -- should any of us have the notion to go it alone, think twice.

"I have withheld one piece of information that is vital in gaining access to the building, should you be lucky enough even to find it. That aside, please remember London can be a very dangerous place to be on one's own."

The chilly, pregnant pause lingered long after Septimus had finished talking. All sides knew the stakes were being raised.

"Well, perish the thought sir. I for one would never dream of going alone, especially with the chance of company as grand as yours sir," Ocky said with a sardonic twinkle.

"Quite so Mr Ocky. Now, tell me a date when the tides are favourable to our cause," Septimus continued.

After the challenging but fruitful meeting in the cellar of the Rope and Anchor, Septimus returned to his studio with much haste. Thankfully, Sophia had already prepared the room for the afternoon's photographic session with the two Chinamen. As it turned out, the photographing of the two Orientals went very well, despite John the chemist not showing up at all for it. Neither Septimus nor Sophia had ever known sitters to be so quiet before.

Of course, this may or may not have been due to the fact that it was infinitely possible that one or perhaps both of the brothers could neither speak nor understand any English. Either that, or they were both under the influence of opium.

Chapter 19

Leather-Bound

Septimus could have done with John's presence during the shoot. Though he still took his chance using one of his special cameras, he hoped John would be there later to help him prepare the fixing process. Septimus took quite a few photographs of the docile old men, both of whom looked enquiringly in and at the camera and the surrounding photographs dispersed around the studio. Both men had long, iron-grey moustaches and balding heads, and seemed to exude serenity. The only hint of emotion shown by the two Orientals was when they smiled vaguely at each other when being groomed by Sophia before the taking of the photographs. After the session was over, Septimus paid the two gentlemen for their time. Both men bowed in unison and left without asking any questions whatsoever.

After the shoot, Septimus made sure to include the curious formula into the mix that he had found in one of the old books left by his Uncle Augustus.

When Septimus had first come across this old book, he had not bothered to pay much attention to it. It was covered in must and it was clear it had not been looked at in years, maybe decades. Indeed, it was only out of sheer curiosity about its antiquity that he had made an effort to translate its handwritten words from Latin to English.

Sadly, some of the words had faded beyond recognition, but what inscriptions he could decipher had left Septimus inspired and intrigued by their content.

The old leather book housed various formulas that, so the book claimed, could help sustain life. One of the more curious contained within the book was a formula that was supposed to aid the preservation of eyes, even after a person's death. It was clear that some parts of this book were transcriptions of an earlier text, again because some of the herbs and flowers listed as ingredients could only be found on the banks of the Nile. The only use Septimus could deduce from such a formula was in the process of mummification used by the ancient priests of Egypt. There were various comments made in the margins of the book, which were clearly made by another hand than that of the writer of the book. Sadly most of them were in some strange code. Whoever's hand it was, it was certainly not that of his Uncle Augustus. His dubious brother, perhaps? Or maybe even their father, who knows? It was certainly the only book of its kind in the collection.

Septimus rarely shared any of this thoughts or ideas with anyone, but one man he did occasionally float ideas and notions with was Professor Savage, the taxidermist. Septimus had shown the formulae to Savage and watched his eyes widen at the potential.

Of course, this was followed by more than a little scepticism, which was only to be expected from a man of science like Savage. The preservation of the eyes was something that had eluded generations of taxidermists. Could it be that this parchment held the key? Savage tried not to dream too hard.

Up until now, taxidermists had been forced to use glass beads instead of living eyes. This was all well and good, but what Savage wanted as a taxidermist was vibrant, living tissue which could mirror the soul of the creature, its sentiment, and its savagery. Professor Savage was a master preserver -- his skill set him head and shoulders above the rest in his field, but even he could not save a creature's eyes. That was, until Septimus had transcribed him the formula from the book. Professor Savage could not believe the results: thankfully on this occasion, the lack of exotic ingredients had not dulled the effects, and very shortly he and Septimus became the envy of the taxidermy world. Despite the money they were offered, they shared their secret with no one. Just how long this preservation would last was anybody's guess, but the effect on the animals' eyes was truly startling.

It was sometime after, however, that Septimus had thought about using extracts from these formulae in his photographic work. At first it had been a fanciful whim, but now, maybe, just maybe … He was sure the girl had moved in the photograph that evening.

Either that or he was going insane. He had to take more and more photographs, try different blends of the formulae. Septimus wanted the most exquisite collection of human beings ever produced. He was never going to be happy with just their likeness alone -- he wanted perfection, and he wanted some ownership.

Later that afternoon, John had eventually limped into the studio far later than even he had planned. He had passed the two Chinamen at the far end of Whortleberry Street and presumed these to have been the sitters he had organised for Septimus yesterday. As John walked into the exhibition room, he heard Sophia shouting, "Ciao" to Septimus as she made her way down the stairs. At last, John thought to himself, this was the moment -- he would teach that snooty little vixen a lesson she would remember for a long time. He slid behind a door and waited. With every step Sophia made downstairs, John's anticipation grew and grew. His skin became clammy as he held his breath, his muscles tightened, and the hairs on his arms bristled.

Sophia made her way down the staircase of many creaks, and into the exhibition room. Her thoughts were filled with what to cook for supper tonight, and which grocers were best for this and that. No sooner had she passed through the open door into the exhibition room than a hand reached out and grabbed her by her waist.

Sophia swung round in horror to face the molester and saw the grotesque, gaping grin of the chemist. She instinctively shrieked at her attacker and swung her brightly shining claws at the now-flinching chemist.

The chemist ducked, but it was too late. Three ditches of blood ran freely from the chemist's haggard face. The chemist pulled her hair frantically and shouted obscenities at her by the dozen. Sophia kicked, gouged, and spat at her assailant. The adrenaline was pumping through John's veins. He had not felt such exhilaration for years, and the days of past glories came sweeping back to him. John's excitement, however, was short-lived and was abating fast. He had more than met his match with Sophia -- this swift alley- cat from Naples was not one of the cowering genteel females John had so delighted in scaring all those years ago. Here was a woman used to looking after herself, a vixen of the first degree.

John reached out blindly, but now it was more in self-defence than attack. Sophia sank her teeth into John's ear and bit with all her strength as John tore at her dress. John cried out in agony as the two of them wrestled to the floor. Suddenly there were two very

97

loud thuds on the floorboards behind them. Both John and Sophia looked up to see Septimus standing impassively, his presence filling the doorway, and his mahogany stick up high.

The two of them parted and struggled to rise to their feet. John put his hand to his cheek to try to stem the blood, and Sophia fixed John with a menacing stare. Sophia said something sharp and fast in Italian. John retorted with a faltering, "It was her Septimus -- this girl just can't take a joke. Unstable she is, unstable. Look what she's done to me." Sophia yelled back with real venom in her native Neapolitan Italian.

Septimus paused, his face still unreadable, before uttering, "I do beg your pardon Miss Bianca. You have my word that this will not happen again." He nodded at her and flashed her the most fleeting of smiles, which vanished almost as quickly as it was formed. "Thank you for your time this afternoon. I am truly sorry for this regrettable incident. Please send my regards to your sister and mother. Oh, and one more thing, tell Andrea I shall be calling on her shortly."

Sophia responded calmly, "*Si signor.*" Upon leaving the room, Sophia turned her fierce emerald eyes back onto John, followed by even more whispered curses.

"It would seem that you had a lucky escape there John. Anyway, you are too old for any of that malarkey now dear boy," said Septimus patronisingly.

"It was that Italian bitch," replied the chemist peevishly, lacking all conviction.

"Yes, I am sure in your mind she asked for it John. You do not have to justify yourself to me, but if you ever do that again here, I will make your life very difficult indeed, and I won't even have to lift a finger."

John looked at Septimus with a sour expression, but said nothing. John knew that Septimus was not joking. Septimus was always dropping hints about how much he knew about his past. How many times had Septimus mentioned the notorious Limehouse or Clapham Common incidences, knowing full well the effect it would have on him and his liberty if word got out?

Septimus could see John was starting to sulk, and decided to change tack. "The photoshoot went well by the way. Your Chinamen friends made a pretty picture. If you would be so kind as to take over where I have left off upstairs, John, it would be very helpful, but do clean yourself up first; don't want blood on the prints, now, do we? I really do need my constitutional right now, all those fumes, you know. Besides, it will be nightfall soon and we all know how dangerous it is to be walking around after dark on our own, don't we John?" Septimus looked knowingly at John before tipping his hat and leaving the building. The now-bloodied chemist seethed alone.

Septimus took his usual route across Blindman's Wharf, where he watched men and boys toiling away with great haste inspired by the fading light of the sun. Not that its glow was particularly apparent right now -- the mist was swelling up over the Thames and consuming the outlines of all things living and dead -- nothing and nobody was impervious to its greedy, grey fingers. Septimus tightened his scarf and watched a pleasure steamer dreamily plough its way affably and silently along the river. He strolled downstream along the slipways towards the leadening skies of the east.

It was there between the rickety and ramshackle piers that he observed the forlorn mudlarks scrabbling around with their buckets and rags. They were women and children for the most part, sifting through the silt and mud for trinkets of coal, rope, copper, and bones. These figures in the fog were perhaps the most anonymous of all of the life in London: always distant, always blurred, their ill-defined, coiled, and hunched silhouettes quivering like strings on a bow; creatures engulfed up to their knees by the silt and sludge, human wading birds flocking and mocking the ebbing tide.

Were these shivering shapes of life spawned by the river itself? Septimus mused, as he reflected back to tales his aunt had told him long ago about the fairy lady from the lake near Myddfai, Carmarthenshire, and how she transcended the depths of water to walk beside mankind, bestowing the gift of medical knowledge for all.

Septimus knew that the only gift that these wretches could possibly hope to hold was the merest pinprick of conscience that ran through the minds of the indolent onlooker. The fog gave wings to the sound of the mournful gulls fidgeting on the shore. The tranquillity of the moment becalmed Septimus. The infectious fog and the gentle lapping of the waves had swallowed up and seduced another victim. Time and mind were held tightly by their amorphous grasp. Septimus reflected on how the disorder of fog allows the sense of sound its greater clarity; compensation perhaps for its vague visual illusions and intrusions in the world?

An involuntary shiver shot through Septimus' side. The cold, damp air had awakened his senses once more and the intoxicating spell of the fog was lifted. Septimus shook himself vigorously, driving out the chill and the accompanying trance, which he had succumbed to. So, with the cold air tightening his muscles, he began to walk with pace and purpose once more.

When Septimus' concentration returned, it was squarely focused on increasing his photographic collection and testing his new formulae. The search for the mansion was on hold for a while. Ocky and Jewels would never find the entrance to the old cellar without the other map. *Even I know I cannot act until the tides are right*, he said to himself.

Besides, there is talk of storms coming in from the west, and even the king of the toshers would not like to be caught down a drain when that happens. I must keep testing the formula- - I must find out for sure. I need more and more people, more specimens to work with, to experiment on.

The quickest way to achieve this goal was to go and search for specimens himself, and if it should prove to be just an illusion, then he could still comfort himself with having the widest collection of human life anywhere in England. "For that, I need to find raw emotion, where life is on the precipice, somewhere I can personally select my own specimens. I will travel east and into the slums, where the streets of London are ringing with the sombre sonnets of despair and disrepair, vagabonds, violence, and vice, the forbidden and forlorn – perfect!"

Although Septimus would have loved to have gone alone, he knew he needed a crew. "I will take the boy Pigeon, for speed and reconnaissance, and Sophia to draw in the men. I will make an exhibition of living London, which will grow and grow until I capture the very soul of this city."

Thankfully, there were many types of fold-up cameras and apparatus to be found these days, far more advanced than what he had used in his travels abroad.

Septimus decided not to use one of his own carriages for the mission -- they were useful for transportation up west, fetching and delivering wealthy clients, trawling the streets looking for exhibits, but not in the abyss that was the slums of East London.

Septimus eventually decided to hire a small brewer's cart for his exploration deep into the Hangman's Hollow and beyond. It was important to draw as little attention as was humanly possible. Never was there such a dense mass of mouths feeding off the empty, broken hand of hope as in Hangman's Hollow. Septimus warmed at the potential rich seam of exhibits ahead of him.

Chapter 20

Into the Abyss

Septimus made sure he prepared his mobile photographic wagon- cum-cart well. There were vast assortments of bottles carefully bound up around the cart in boxes. There was cushioning around the base and sides of the equipment to avoid them being shattered on the cobbles and ruts of the rickety roads. There were so many boxes and bottles of all shapes and sizes needed by the travelling photographer that Septimus mused they may get mistaken for Dr Quack and his assortment of cure-alls, but that was of little concern to him.

As long as they did not know his true mission, that was fine. Septimus prepared the plates for his camera with meticulous care, making quite sure he alone could see the formulas' application and provenance. The labelled glass tubes of hair were close at hand.

Not that it mattered here, but Septimus was always very wary of prying eyes, particularly the eyes of the so-called "moral majority." Morality was never a subject Septimus gave much heed to though. Morals, he thought, were taught and instilled when one was a child; no one was born with such notions of good and bad. When one takes the overview of the anthropologist, historian, or, indeed that of the Darwinian Theory, one realises that they can be arranged and rearranged to suit one's purpose, be it a private or a public agenda.

Septimus despaired at the moral hypocrisy of the age. Not only the hypocrisy, but also the fear instilled into every aspect of modern life. It seemed that with every advance in science, there was to be a moral reaction against it, as if society were a demented, discontented pendulum swinging back and forth, demanding solace in inertia. Inertia was not for Septimus. Even photography had once been demonised for being a dark art, produced by even darker people. Small minds with small horizons, thought he.

The bitingly cold east wind challenged and confronted Septimus and his crew of Mortlake, Marmaduke, Sophia, and Pigeon as they stalked their way through the unyielding cobbled byways of decay and dereliction. The poor, the disaffected and dispossessed, their numbers hung from the doorways like rusting, broken trade signs, creaking and whistling in the wind. This was the soot-stained human clinker at the forge of the empire, the private blushes of the proud pink rash that tinted and tainted the world.

Throughout the morning, Septimus managed to gather a large repertoire of faces and forms. Sophia watched in horror as the human scavengers picked up scraps of food on the cobbles, the debris from yesterday's market. It shocked and fascinated Sophia as to why so many people were sleeping in the daytime. She gently nudged Pigeon with her boot. "Why do people sleep now?"

"Why now?" Pigeon repeated the question and looked at her incredulously. "That's simple; those that ain't legless on gin are sleeping because they ain't allowed to sleep at night."

"Not allowed to sleep?" Sophia replied, raising her eyebrows in surprise.

"No, of course they ain't! Lummy, you are green. You ain't allowed to sleep outside at night; you gotta move on see, gotta keep moving, or else the peelers will feel your collar," Pigeon replied earnestly.

"Feel your collar?" repeated a now-confused Sophia.

"Arrest you, cop you, take you in. The police say it ain't right to sleep outside at night. Baffling ain't it?" said Pigeon, shaking his head.

Many of the folk that Septimus and companions encountered were suspicious of their motives at best. Others were abusive and obstructive, although most cooperated to one extent or another when money was mentioned. All of the sitters were paid meagrely for their troubles, the only condition being that they agreed to be lightly groomed by Sophia first. Several of them were too drunk, ill, tired, or vacant to care about such a peculiar request, but one or two suspected a trick, and shied away with lingering curses.

Marmaduke and Mortlake were quite dumbfounded as to the reason that grooming was important to the entire process. Mortlake had tried to put it down to some bizarre eccentricity of the aristocracy. However, he was more than a little intrigued as to why each hairbrush was thoroughly cleaned of hair by Sophia after each individual had had their photograph taken.

Sophia would place the strands of hair into separate tubes, and a label was attached to each one.

Eventually Mortlake's curiosity got the better of him. "Septimus, what is the purpose of all this brushing, and why separate all the hair out?"

Septimus paused a little before replying, "If I decide to tint and colour the photograph, I want as accurate a likeness as possible, and having a few strands of hair enables me to get the right hair colour at least. Besides, would you not want to clean these brushes after these wretches have shared their lice and filth with the bristles?"

"Aye, you have a point there," replied Mortlake, who almost instinctively raised his cap and ran his fingers through his hair.

After dining on a lunch of eel pie and hot potatoes, the wagon and crew stalked wearily onwards into the dim side streets of Hangman's Hollow. Hangman's Hollow had once been marshland, and in many ways it still was – it was still possessed by liquid and inertia. The streets, although narrow and awry, were interspersed with line after line of irregular ditches and brooks.

Human waste mingled malevolently with the acrid wastes of tanneries and houses of slaughter. Tightly-knitted houses were roped together by rotting wooden bridges, which spanned the banks of these ditches most dire.

Decaying carcasses of animals lay half submerged, bubbling and bursting in the mire. Septimus fought desperately against the feeling of nausea that overcame him. It was then that he noticed an old woman slouched pitifully against a wall. She had a shawl pinned tightly around her shoulders, a threadbare old coat, torn dress, and boots that were only fit for a scavengers' tip.

Sophia gracefully stalked up to the old woman and tugged gently at her coat with a smile. The woman, ill of temper, stared up at her. Sophia held one of her hands and placed some money in the other. With this the old lady's eyes became focused and looked at the coins Sophia's beige hands had put in hers. The old lady looked slightly befuddled and reached for the gin bottle cradled at her side. She drank clumsily, hoping for clarity in her liquid reality.

Septimus unemotionally observed the crone from top to toe. Surely there was never a greater example of wretchedness in the whole city of London than this specimen.

He peered down at the stark, bone-bleached skin, the pox-ridden lunar surface of her face, the tattered remains of leather and cotton which clung to her body. The old girl clutched at her bottle tightly as Sophia prepared her for the photograph to be taken.

Pigeon stared at the living heap of bones and rags that furnished the pavement so despondently. Without thinking twice, he snatched up a discarded posy of flowers that must have fallen from a flower girl's bag earlier in the day, and swiftly offered them to the old lady. Septimus had been readying his camera just before this event happened and was quick to grasp the opportunity.

The camera shot the moment Pigeon offered her the blooms. Septimus knew that this was going to be a momentous photograph. Pigeon's spontaneous actions had produced an unrivalled magical moment stolen from the jaws of time. Even the curmudgeonly Mortlake was visibly moved by the lad's generosity of spirit, and Sophia's eyes welled up and let loose a trickle of tears that betrayed her proud face.

The old lady held the posy in her hand and smiled at Pigeon in disbelief and gratitude. She grasped at the partly-faded flowers, and held them tightly. It was as if the sight and fragrance had rekindled a cherished moment in time, an echo of love, a long-dead romance.

Pigeon seemed oblivious to his act of kindness, and just carried on about his business, smiling cheerfully, though he did colour a little when Sophia smiled at him. They only stopped a couple more times on their journey back to Whortleberry Street. Nothing could ever match the spectacle of Pigeon and the old lady. Septimus marvelled at Mortlake's knowledge of the route back to the studio. It seemed nothing short of an inherent awareness, the same as possessed by birds for seasonal migrations. To Septimus, all of the streets and lanes looked the same -- even the faces of the people bore the same expression. Whatever it was, he was glad of it. Twilight was upon them, and he needed to get back to his photographic plates for processing.

Once the crew were back at Whortleberry Street, they all disembarked and scuttled off to their various abodes, all except Septimus, Mortlake, and Pigeon that is. Septimus instructed Pigeon to carry the photographic plates up to the studio with the words,

"Pretend it's a baby you're carrying, and not any old baby either! Pretend it's one of Queen Victoria's finest."

It had been a worthy day's work, thought Septimus, even though his legs and back were aching and he felt all of his fifty years right now. Mortlake carried the cameras and assorted paraphernalia to the storerooms at the rear of the premises.

After what seemed like an age, sorting out the products of the day's hard work, Septimus paused briefly to fetch himself some cheese and pickles and a small tot of brandy. He wanted to at least get rid of the chore of eating before settling down to enjoy the fruits of his labour.

He picked up a photograph he had taken earlier, that of a flower girl in Mariner's Way. He noticed the various bouquets contained within her wicker baskets: roses, chrysanthemums, and gypsosphila to name but a few. Septimus' eyes moved to the smile on her face, a fleeting expression of life captured within a frame.

Behind the flower seller, in the distance, a man with a top hat glances at the camera, a moment's curiosity now caught forever. A horse and cart turns a corner, its movement blurred by the length of exposure, its motion forever constant. The mystery of the driver and destination will remain always unknown, always anonymous, always free.

The static buildings vainly try to reassure and reinforce the steadfastness of the theatre of life, though they are but fallible witnesses to its ever-changing parade.

So much for what the lens maintains, but what of the life outside the scene, just beyond the lens; edges cut away with a surgeon's precision, ruthlessly severing the world beyond? And what of the flower girl's customers, the barber's clients? The intrigues that befell before and after the shutter rose and fell -- the guillotine of time... The photographer is as a butcher and retainer, the lens as the knife, deciding what to keep and what to discard.

Two ravens croaked and fidgeted on the glass roof above. Tonight there was no performance behind the glass, but tomorrow was another day....

Chapter 21

Going Down

They day of the descent had finally arrived. Septimus felt a sense of dread and excitement. At last he was going in search of his legacy -- that is, if he had one. And if he did, would he be able to find it? These questions had both befuddled and bewitched him for many years now, and maybe, just maybe, this was going to be the day when all would be revealed.

Mortlake arrived at Septimus' residence early in the morning. He was accompanied by Septimus' sometime-coachman and all-round heavy, Marmaduke. Marmaduke had never been underground before, though Septimus did not think that would be a problem, despite his immense size. Both Septimus and Mortlake were in agreement that his strength could be invaluable.

The pair of them half-trusted oafish Jewels, but Ocky Blackwood was a different matter. "Slippery as jellied eel, that one," Mortlake said to Septimus.

"Don't worry about him; we shall all keep a close eye on him," replied Septimus reassuringly.

Whether Septimus believed that or not, he needed to believe it right now: his life was going to be in the toshers' hands, and that alone made him shudder.

He hated leaving his fortune to chance -- he had felt compelled to control the world around him, and the people in it, as far back as he could ever remember. But down below, in the stinking depths, he was going to take his chances with these others.

Mortlake, Marmaduke, and Septimus rigged themselves out in canvas trousers, knee-length boots, and jackets down to their thighs. They met the toshers at a small court just off Leather Street. Ocky and Jewels raised a questioning eyebrow at the sight of Marmaduke alongside them. "Good morning to you gentlemen," said Jewels with an almost toothless smile. Septimus touched his hat, whilst Mortlake returned the pleasantry to Jewels at least.

Ocky sneered at the sight of Septimus and company in their tosher's attire, and commented, "My, my, what a great leveller this expedition is! Don't you gentlemen look just the ticket today?"

Marmaduke took one step forward towards Ocky, but Ocky retorted with a bow and a hasty, "And it is my utmost pleasure to escort you gentlemen to my ever-fragrant domain." His smile was sickly and smug, but he did just about enough to appease Septimus and his crew.

They followed Ocky down a narrow alley and picked up the seven-foot-long wooden poles for the journey. No tosher went underground without one of these hefty staffs. Jewels had craftily stowed them away underneath some discarded canvas the night before. It was always good to be as secretive as possible about toshing, and this particular venture was no exception. In fact, secrecy was even more paramount, considering the potential rewards ahead.

"Unfortunately I have only brought along four poles, did not reckon on the big fella joining us, but we shall be alright if we stick close together. Oh, and I almost forgot, here's a sieve for you, and a shovel for you," Jewels said, handing them to Mortlake and Marmaduke respectively.

Marmaduke and Mortlake were duly baffled but thought better of asking questions for the moment at least. They picked up their poles and walked further up the alley in front of them before turning a sharp left into another squalid passageway. After a few paces, Ocky and Jewels stopped very still and became silent. Once the two men had assured themselves that there was nobody in sight, Ocky swiftly lifted up the iron manhole cover that was in front of him and slowly but surely climbed down the iron rings set into the wall as steps. Ocky hurriedly lit his lamp as Jewels and the rest of the gang made their way into the gloom and down into a red brick shaft.

Jewels was at the rear of the crew and slammed down the manhole cover behind them, causing Mortlake to jump. The sound of its slam coming down on heavy paving slabs above reverberated long and deep into the tunnel. It was the same noise a prison door must make, thought Septimus, a porthole from one life to another: they were now enclosed, incarcerated, and entombed.

One of the first noticeable things below ground was the stench. It was almost indescribable and it was all Septimus, Mortlake and Marmaduke could do not to vomit. The evil stink surrounded and suffocated them.

"Learn to breathe through your mouths gentlemen. It's kinder on the stomach," instructed Ocky.

When they reached the bottom of the shaft, all of the men descended into putrid black liquid with some trepidation. Inside this cramped tunnel there was very little natural light, save for an occasional vent overhead. Ocky and Jewels were the only two men with lamps -- Ocky had one at the front, Jewels to the rear. It took what seemed like an age to Septimus for his eyes to adjust to the scarcity of light down below.

Before the gang had reached the end of this tunnel, they were forced to wade through up to a foot and a half of foetid and detritus-strewn liquid.

To make matters worse, all of the men had to stoop down close to the vile stench sloshing around their knees. It was a great relief to one and all when they reached a main sewer through a tarnished, yellow-bricked, oval archway. At least here they could stand up straight.

"This here part of water is called Raven's Creek. It flows back to the Thames thata way and meanders up and onwards past the Shepherd's Crook," said Jewels. "It's called the Shepherd's Crook because the tunnel bends sharply round and almost doubles back on itself, like the crook of a shepherd."

"You don't say?" Mortlake responded sarcastically.

"Just off the crook there are several small inlets, and a tunnel that's called Bleeding Brook. No one goes down the Bleeding Brook, at least no one that I know of," replied Jewels, undeterred by the tone of Mortlake's response.

"Why is that then?" Mortlake replied gruffly and then answered his own question with another one. "Is it because it's too bleeding shitty even for you lot?"

"Ha, ha," rasped Jewels. "I like that, my friend; you have quite a wit sir, that you have. But no, that's not the reason."

"Well I am glad I keep you amused. Now are you or are you not going to tell me why no one goes down there and how it got its bleeding name?" Mortlake replied impatiently.

"Well it runs red with blood, it does. Runs red with blood," Jewels said.

"Oh, red with blood, does it? How on earth can you tell what colour the water is in this light?" replied Mortlake incredulously.

"Your eyes get used to it after a while, and I have got this here lamp, I have. And that's not all," Jewels continued.

"I did not think it would be," replied Mortlake curtly.

"Lots of the hidden rivers, brooks, and sewers this way are very ancient, partly blocked, and ruinous. The walls are crumbling and the vents are blocked, you see. No air, you see. No air." Jewel's voice trailed off as if to preserve the contents of his lungs for later, though he could not resist adding, "Haunted they are, too."

"Oh, don't tell me -- they are full of headless horsemen and sea serpents," replied Mortlake with unguarded cynicism.

"They are haunted; just you wait and see," said Jewels reproachfully.

"Well, I could not see any self-respecting ghosts wanting to hang around this old hole. The whole place is falling to bits, if you ask me," Mortlake said disdainfully.

"You are correct old son, many of the old sewers are giving up the ghost. Just look around you," replied Jewels with the smile of a man who's just cracked the funniest retort ever.

"Oh, ha bloody ha," replied Mortlake, who could not, despite his best efforts, contain a smile.

"That's why that Bazalgette fellow wants to make new ones -- the brickwork is crumbling in on itself. I blame the traffic -- too much movement above -- too many carriages and too many people crapping in our sewers."

"Your sewers? Anyone would think you own the things," replied Mortlake.

"Well, we care for 'em more than most folk, that's for sure," said Jewels. "Parliament seems to want to make 'em all new now, take all the fun out of 'em. It's all due to what they called the *great stink* a few years back -- they could not do the Queen's business, could they? Couldn't stand the stench," Jewels added.

"Yes, I remember it well. My heart bled for them all, it really did," Mortlake replied sardonically. "Well, come on then, out with it -- why is that brook haunted?"

"Well, I never will tell you if you are going to treat me as a fool," replied Jewels.

"Okay, okay. It's unlikely that you are going to get me to believe in any of that malarkey, but I am curious. This really ain't my world here, though I do reckon if anything unholy is going happen anywhere, it's going to happen here," said Mortlake with grudging resignation.

"Well, every tunnel has its own noises you see; they have their own rhythms, if you like. Sure you get the odd sound of the flushers, flushing the sewage out, but we generally know when they are going to flush: keeps us alive, see? Inside knowledge Mr Mortlake, inside knowledge," Jewels digressed. "Rats are another sound again. Can hear them all around us, but at least they be real, you can see 'em and touch the little bleeders."

"Yes, I have heard all this before," said Mortlake impatiently.

"Shhh now," said Jewels, "Let me continue. There are one or two tunnels that have sounds not of this earth inside them, noises that chill you to the bone. Mournful groans and scratchings the like of which you have never heard before," Jewels said with absolute awe.

True enough, Mortlake could hear plenty of muffled sounds. Sounds which seemed to echo back and forth along the tunnel, sounds which disorient and disturb, horns and cries from the distant Thames, the dull sound of hoof on stone, the grindings of wheel on cobble, and the far off sound of the water being flushed. But ghosts?

The toshers extinguished all of the lamps when they passed under the vents above. Their secrecy underground was paramount, but so was clear vision, and so once away from the vents, the lamps were reignited. Jewels tried to lighten the mood by saying, "I thought we may have seen the Scarecrow and company down here today, until a little bird told me he was thinking of making use of the tide in an inlet up west, one of Oswald's Eyes to be exact. They say a boat accidentally lost some of its goods overboard the other night and rumour has it that some of the gear made its way into one of the eyeballs."

Mortlake shook his head. "Who the hell is the Scarecrow when he's at home and where on earth is Oswald's Eyes?"

"Well, Scarecrow is another entrepreneur like us, and they call him the Scarecrow because he once lost his footing in one of the drains and the rats had him, they did. Gnawed at his face and hands, cut him to ribbons. If it wasn't for Stinking Stephen, he would not be here at all."

"And Oswald's Eyes?" enquired a curious Mortlake.

Ocky cut into the conversation before Jewels could say any more: "Oswald's Eyes are just above Oswald's nose, and that's the only place you are likely to find them, is that not right Jewels?"

Jewels could tell by the tone of Ocky's voice that he should say no more on the subject, and replied sheepishly, "Erm, that's right Ocky, just above his nose."

Mortlake rolled his eyes and said no more. The men came to the virtually-forgotten area of Raven's Creek, which had the peculiar feature called the Shepherd's Crook. Ocky assured Septimus that the ancient river did indeed bend sharply round off a straight course and doubled back on itself, before curving back outwards again.

Septimus tried to think of exactly why this strange feature occurred. Was it that this was the original, irregular path of the river? Surely a straight line would have been easier? Of course, the simpler explanation would be that it had always been two separate brooks and this was just a junction. But why let the truth get in the way of a good story?

Given the toshers' romantic fear of the place, one would be forgiven for believing that it was shying away in horror from some awful feature that lurked ahead, repelled even by the idea of lapping up against some unspeakable menace or incident that occurred in the landscape possibly centuries before.

Ocky, who was some way ahead of the rest of the gang, suddenly halted and beckoned Septimus towards him. He pointed ahead of himself and said quietly, "See that split in the tunnel ahead? That is where I reckon that this here creek separates off from the Bleeding Brook." Septimus peered into the gloom and could faintly see a small split in the waters ahead. Ocky and Septimus carefully started to bring out their maps and documents. This time Septimus pulled out one more map than before. This one contained the exact positioning of the drains to the house. Ocky looked at Septimus with knowing eyes and said, "Ah, I see you have kept the best for last my friend."

"No point in getting older unless one gets wiser dear boy," said an unmoved Septimus.

Septimus and Ocky ascertained that the most likely position for the cellar entrance was a potential tunnel somewhere off the Bleeding Brook, though neither man could be sure. The maps and drawings they both possessed were all on different scales -- Ocky's map even ended about a hundred yards into the Bleeding Brook itself. They estimated that the Bleeding Brook was not that far in front of them.

The pragmatic Ocky had thought long and hard of the potential hazards that could lie before them in the Bleeding Brook. He had explored possibly more sewers, vents, and underground rivers in London than anybody else, but the Bleeding Brook was a nebulous chasm that even his deep well of curiosity had failed to descend to, up until now at least.

"Okay lads," said Ocky, "I am sure this will come as a great delight to you all, especially to my old mucker Jewels, here -- about fifty yards ahead this scented stream bends round to the right, and my plan is to follow this bend until we see a small tunnel running straight before us. Yes Jewels, this is where, if it still exists, that is, lays the Bleeding Brook."

As soon as Ocky had hissed the words Bleeding Brook, the lantern he held beneath his eyes lit up his face grotesquely. His eyes flashed white, and Jewels winced at his very words.

"But ..." uttered Jewels.

"No buts Jewels. If we all stick close together and we use our poles, we will be fine," said Ocky, and added, "And also, let's not offer any food to the creatures behind us. Their bite is really quite painful."

Ocky was referring to the large number of rats that were now on their tail and gathering strength in numbers as they progressed further into the gloom.

Thankfully, the base of the tunnel seemed quite secure for the moment. There was the odd small hole where the heavy poles sunk in a little deeper than expected, and the odd piece of masonry underfoot, but so far so good. To lose one's balance here could be

113

fatal, not just because of the rats -- one gulp of the vile soup beneath their knees had been known to kill a man within days.

They eventually reached the low arched entrance to the Bleeding Brook. All the men gathered 'round the entrance and paused in silence. So this was the almost-mythical maw of the brook that ran with blood?

The uneven brickwork around the jaws of the entrance gave off the appearance of a sneer, a twisted lip. Its masonry looked far older and much more ragged than the creek, and it was only about half the size. Even the roof of the tunnel was lower than that of Raven's Creek, which would mean poor old Marmaduke was going to have to stoop to avoid grazing his head.

They gingerly entered the tunnel proper, ears pricked and senses raised. Septimus became aware of the crumbling brickwork and the many tiny vents coming in from both above and the sides of the tunnel. Indeed, the tunnel was so riddled with holes one could almost imagine it to be the home of a vast nest of worms grown monstrously huge on the foetid remains of human waste that oozed down this canal of filth.

Septimus was horrified that his imagination had plummeted to such outrageous notions, but down here, in the hellish depths, anything was possible. Surely nothing other than rats could survive down here for that long? Or could it? No, he was being ridiculous. Although it would not be beyond the realm of the imagination, mused Septimus, this could be the cradle for some as yet undiscovered species of life to exist. Any organism and creature fostered here may be life at its most loathsome, but it would also be tenacious, tough, and enterprising.

The peculiarities of evolution down here would offer much intrigue, and if he had the time… Gosh, what was he thinking about? It was truly a disgusting place to be, and the sooner he was out of here the better.

"How much further do you think we have to go now?" Septimus enquired of Ocky.

"You mean to tell me that you are not enjoying our little foray sir?" Ocky shrugged, put his staff to one side, and held the map up to his lantern, before continuing, "According to your map, we must be near to that inlet you mentioned earlier."

114

Ocky's voice sounded eerily deeper down here, as did all of the others' -- even the acoustics were debased in this desolate place. Septimus and Ocky made their way forward. Septimus nervously watched Ocky cautiously but continuously tap the ground as he shuffled rather than walked through the slops. Ocky was obviously not joking about the precariousness of exploring these places, especially those he did not know.

The tunnel was about six feet wide and just under six feet high, a foot of this height being made up of liquid filth beneath them.

However, Septimus' repulsion caused by the smell had somewhat been superseded by a sense of fear, foreboding, and total claustrophobia.

The sweat seeped out of Septimus' brow in defiance of the chill around him. He had overheard Jewels talking to Mortlake earlier about the unearthly sounds that could be heard below, and he had not exaggerated one little bit.

This strange place did seem home to some very odd echoes and mournful murmurs -- a place of torment and deep lament.

"Look here Ocky," Jewels shouted from the rear. He pointed at the gaps in the tunnel walls. Sure enough, the wounds and joints in the brickwork really did seep some sort of sticky red substance. "Christ Ocky, where the hell are you taking us boy?" Jewels asked with real fear in his voice.

"Calm yourself Jewelsy, there is far more things to fear down here than a bit of coloured water," Ocky said reassuringly.

Just in front of them there had been a partial collapse of the tunnel, and they were now faced with a pile of bricks and mortar blocking their passage. Roots had invaded the gaps in the wall's defences above them, and they had begun to colonise the area, teasing their way down to the inky liquid below.

"Ok, time to turn back boys," said Jewels.

"Aye," said Mortlake, seconding the motion. Even Marmaduke nodded in mute agreement.

"This tunnel is way too dangerous to go any further Ocky; it is madness," Jewels continued.

Ocky, too, looked concerned, and paused a little before looking at Septimus and saying, "Well Mr Blackwood?" Septimus could also see what a perilous state the tunnel was in, and every instinct in his body was screaming at him to agree with them and take flight … That aside, he had waited so long for this moment, surely he could not quit now? A long silence fell upon them.

Septimus knew their fate and his own rested on his decision. He must be decisive. "Fortune favours the brave. Let's just clear as much of this debris as we can to one side as quickly as possible."

Jewels opened his mouth to disagree, but Septimus raised his hand to stop him. "We all know we have a vast colony of rats on our tail. You and Ocky pointed out earlier in graphic detail what the rats will see fit to do with us if they thought we were cornered.

"Secondly, the tide will not be this low again for quite a considerable amount of time, so I say we go on, even if it is only for a little bit longer. If it gets any worse, you have my solemn word we return home immediately."

"Come on boys, you heard what the boss says. Let's not dither and give the rats a feast," Ocky said as he started to move the debris to one side.

Ocky's swift actions gained him a certain amount of respect from Septimus. In turn, Septimus' bravery, albeit inspired by greed, gained him a moderate amount of respect from Ocky. The words "give the rats a feast" seemed to inspire Mortlake and Marmaduke to join in the clearance, leaving only Jewels to shake his head and grumble.

Eventually, even Jewels joined in, grumbling all the while. The group laboured on in the stench and filth to clear the passage, while Mortlake ran to and fro, lobbing stones at the rats hovering in their wake, buying them time, or so he hoped.

Eventually they made a narrow but adequate passage through the debris. From that moment onwards the ground became increasingly unstable and unpredictable. At times the walls looked like they were made of Dutch cheese rather than bricks, stones, and mortar.

Droplets of water wept like at a funeral above their heads. This surely must be equal to the mythological River Styx, thought Septimus. Even the gateway to Hades could not have been more of a damnable place than this. He watched Ocky stride rapidly, striking his pole down firmly with each step.

Ocky had caught sight of something in front of them, and then Septimus, too, noticed a gap in the brickwork ahead. Upon reaching the opening, all of the men stood aghast at what they saw.

The gap in the brickwork turned out to be an elaborate entrance to yet another tunnel. The huge rectangular lintel above was supported by two immense pillars. The pillars themselves were perfectly fashioned like that of a cathedral, and the lintel was ornately carved with outlandish gargoyles. The gargoyles were not just of men or demons -- they seemed to represent all manner of creatures: birds, snakes, lions, and other beasts that Ocky had never set eyes on before; all of them exquisitely carved tens, hundreds, maybe even thousands of years ago by a master of his craft.

Though their finely chiselled features were stained and worn, the ravages of time had not reduced any of their splendour or grandeur. Indeed it almost seemed to give them a certain wisdom, one which only time itself could ever bestow. These stone creatures stood as guardians, peering out into the gloom, forever watchful in their warding over the subterranean lair.

Septimus had never dreamed of finding anything quite like this. None of them had. Who on earth would go to this trouble to fashion such an impressive entrance to a glorified drain? What was its true purpose? Was this truly the passageway to his grandfather's cellar? Or was it the entrance to something even more surreal?

Their attention was suddenly caught by a hideous scraping sound deep inside the mouth of the newly-discovered tunnel. They had heard it earlier, but had thought no more of it. Now it was much louder, and peculiarly abrasive.

"Look here boys, I am no coward but I am getting a really bad feeling from this place," said Jewels.

After much looking at each other, Ocky took on the mantle of leader, probably as a direct response to Septimus' boldness earlier on. "It is just a noise. It can't bite you or drag you under -- it's just a sound, albeit a very odd one. You lot can stay here while I go on ahead to find its source."

"I will go, too; wouldn't want Ocky here to have all the glory now, would I?" said Septimus with a forced smile.

"Right then Jewelsy, you stay here with Marmaduke and Mortlake, and Sir Septimus and I shall wade off ahead. If we are not back within the hour, return home without us. I know you won't let me down Jewels, will you?" said Ocky, looking Jewels straight in the eye. Jewels just nodded and let out a loud sigh.

Ocky and he had been through so many scrapes together in the past. "Yes, of course, but don't leave it longer than an hour, will ya?" said Jewels, knowing full well that to argue with Ocky when his blood was up would be futile.

"That seems like a reasonable plan to me; no doubt we will be back soon," said Septimus.

"You sure about this Septimus?" piped up the brooding Mortlake. Mortlake did not care for Septimus particularly, but he did care about being paid.

"My, my Mr Mortlake, do have a little faith in us, my friend," hissed a smiling Ocky.

"Just you make sure you bring him back ferret-face," retorted Mortlake gruffly.

"I am touched by your concern, Mr Mortlake, I really am, but on this occasion it would be better to pull together, don't you think?" Septimus said wryly, trying not to get Mortlake's dander up any more.

Mortlake replied with a grunt as both of the Blackwoods ventured forth and merged into the darkness ahead.

Although the entrance to the tunnel was no wider than that of the Bleeding Brook, it soon opened out to be nearly as wide as that of Raven's Creek. Not only did the tunnel widen, but the brickwork above their heads seemed to rise upwards into an ever-greater expanse. The roomier surroundings did little to ease the nerves of both men, who, although loathe to admit it, were both quietly terrified by the hideous scraping getting closer to them with every step.

They were now being driven by curiosity alone, hearts thumping in their chests. Neither of them wanted to show the other weakness. Both men trod warily and used their poles wisely. With only one lantern between them, they stayed close together as they inched their way onward.

Out of the blue, Septimus whispered to Ocky, "There is something I must know."

"Go on then, fire away," replied Ocky.

"Where do you get the name 'Ocky' from? What does the name stand for?"

"It is short for Octavius, given to me by my father, God rest his soul. He decided to afflict me before I was even out of the cot, I reckon. Why do you ask?"

"Curiosity is a hobby of mine," replied Septimus nonchalantly.

"It's almost as bad as Septimus, ain't it? Where on earth did you get that from?" asked Ocky.

"To be honest, I am not sure. I never enquired. May well have been my father's choice, too. I never got a chance to ask either of my parents, as they were not alive for long when I was growing up."

Ocky paused before replying, "Well, my old mum went and left me when I was about eleven years old. Ran off with the cholera, she did. Bastard cholera."

Both men decided not to continue the conversation. It did intrigue Septimus as to why Ocky's father had called him Octavius -- not really a name readily used by a member of the underclass, unless he had ambitions or pretentions above his station.

He could also see a keen intelligence in Ocky, too; not a trait inherent to his class, or indeed one that could easily be taught to any of the downtrodden masses. His knowledge of the world and peoples in it certainly did not stem from a *Penny Dreadful* magazine. Few of the underclass of London could even read, let alone write detailed plans. Sure his writing was as his speech, somewhat rough, a very deceptive veneer. Quite a mystery, Septimus mused.

The wretched scraping sound grew ever stronger and they knew now that they must be very close to its source. Whatever it was, it must be just around the next bend. The inky liquid which had been at their calves when they first entered this tunnel was now approaching knee-height as they sloshed their way cautiously around the bend. Trying to wade quietly became more and more impossible as a sense of dread clawed fervently at their spines. This was nothing compared to the hideous intermediate screeching just beyond their vision. It was as if their very core was being shredded by sound alone.

Ocky held out his lantern and peered dubiously into the murk. Much to his utter astonishment, there lay a boat -- a rowing a boat, distraught with decay. It was tethered and tamed by being chained to a huge, gnarled, wooden post. And it was here that the two men discovered the source of the scream.

Although the boat was chained up, there was still enough slack in the chains for it to be affected by the speed and motion of the filthy fluid running through the tunnel. The boat was moored to their left, at the very point where the current seemed to swirl around like water going down a sink. Some of the boat's wooden planking had rotted away, leaving the iron banding exposed to scrape back and forth against the chain with angry torment.

When Ocky and Septimus realised it was a boat, they looked at each other with relief and amazement. Neither man had had any idea at all what they were going to face, but neither of them had expected this -- a boat. Accompanying the boat were the decaying but functional remnants of a small landing area, complete with wooden decking and sturdy posts.

The tunnel had widened considerably when they reached the boat. This was now a large natural chamber, more cave than tunnel. This old landing area obviously led somewhere out of their present view. Could this lead to the cellar? Septimus dared not even hope. The decking had eroded considerably, but looking at the fact that it had survived at all must mean that it had spent far more of its existence over water rather than under it. By the side of the larger rowing boat lay two other much smaller boats, also attached to the jetty. There appeared to be a couple of punting poles, not unlike the poles the toshers used.

Coils of rope and loose lengths of chains were scattered around the decking, presumably for unloading cargo, Septimus surmised. But what cargo? And why here? "Well, well Septimus, in all my days in these fragrant bowels of the city I have never ever seen the likes of this before." The two men clambered up and onto slippery-timbered decking, which, thankfully for them, was still just about strong enough to take their weight. Ocky shone his lantern around him, and, as he did so, marvelled at how large the chamber actually was.

The further they looked, the more gargoyle-like the faces were on the walls. Some of them were carved into the surface of the cave, some were ornaments carved out of fine smooth stone and placed into the holes in the rocks. This seemed to Septimus to be a place of reverence, a shrine perhaps, a place of icons and totems.

Some of these gargoyles and figures were the same as those they had seen earlier, carved in the stone at the mouth of the tunnel. Septimus was sure he had seen one or two similar carvings elsewhere but frustratingly he could not recall where. Some of these figures looked really primitive, not only in their features but also in the stone they were carved from.

Lots of the creatures were inspired by the sea: mermaids, mermen, and serpentine nightmares of sailors' shanties. Others were of a bull similar to a Minotaur. There were also strange spirals and letters gouged in the surface of the cave.

Septimus thought that they may have been a type of Ogham Celtic script, but he could not be sure. That's where Septimus had seen some of this type of carving before! It was on the ancient standing stone in St Anne's churchyard.

Another curious feature of the place was the sheer volume of red liquid oozing out of the walls. Septimus was pretty sure it was largely made up of iron oxide, though upon closer inspection, the side of the cave was also covered with red ochre paintings.

These primitive paintings appeared to be made up of humans, stags, fish, and birds, largely disfigured by the moist surroundings. Yet despite the hostility of the environment, some were so deeply ingrained into the fabric of the wall that they stubbornly refused to relinquish their potency, power, and vigour.

Both men's eyes followed the wake of the lantern as Ocky swung it to and fro in wild curiosity. It blazed comet-like over the cave's interior. Both men were struck with awe and struggled to absorb their fantastical new surroundings. Accompanying the paintings and carvings were large amounts of candles: their waxy bodies clinging and weeping into the damp, cold walls in a final embrace. Discarded torches sat suspended in a rack on the chamber's walls: lethargic, languid, and charred.

The chamber was an emotive place indeed, primitive yet oddly refined. The air felt somehow different here, still putrid, but at times it had a mutable essence about it, as if it dare not be still. At other times it felt still and cloying. This whole area seemed to Septimus to be full of extreme emotions, unsettling yet familiar.

The two men exchanged glances and decided to venture forth to the passageway behind the landing area. Here, too, the walls were adorned with the reminders of light and flame.

The wax of hundreds of dead candles once more became fleetingly luminescent as Ocky's lantern flickered and flirted with them in the darkness, only for them to be eclipsed again by the sullen solemnity of darkness as the two men made their way further up the passageway.

After about two hundred yards they were presented with an enormous oak door straight in front of them. The door hung on huge iron hinges and had a large circular handle that, though finely made, was now covered in rust. Both men tried to unfasten the great door, without success. It was either locked or bolted on the other side; that, or the long years exposed to the damp had made it much too swollen and stubborn to oblige the whims of man.

Both men lifted up their long wooden poles and used them like battering rams to break down the door. The noise reverberated and echoed throughout the tunnel and down all the other connecting tunnels and shafts for mile after mile. It quickly reached the remaining trio at the mouth of the inlet.

"What the hell was that?" Jewels asked nervously.

"Don't ask me; you're the expert," answered Mortlake.

"I told you lot these tubes are haunted, full of strange and unearthly creatures, but you don't listen. What are we going to do now then?" asked Jewels.

The thuds kept coming like a giant heartbeat pulsating through the earth. Marmaduke looked at Mortlake anxiously. "Don't panic Jewels; let's give it another minute or two, and see what happens," said Mortlake, trying to remain calm.

"We can't wait for too much longer; the tide is on the turn now, and we have no idea how far they are up the tunnel," Jewels replied with due anxiety.

Mortlake looked at his feet. True enough, the filthy liquid was starting to flow back upstream and into the sewers again.

The Thames was reclaiming its far-flung arteries. All of a sudden, the thudding stopped and the silence was broken once more by the distant screeching sound. The boat was on the move again, invigorated by the now incoming tide.

"This ain't going to work. With all the will in the world us two are not going to break this door down," Ocky said to Septimus.

"Perhaps we should go and get the others," Septimus replied.

"It's too late for that. You will get us all drowned if we stay much longer. It took longer than I had reckoned to reach the Bleeding Brook, and then there was the rubble in our path. At least if we go now we should be fine. We'll live to find it another day. Who knows, what you are after could be behind this very door."

Septimus just stood for a little while looking at the door. What lies beyond that great door? Could this be the door? What he did know, however, was that he wanted to find out what lay beyond, regardless of whether it was his family's cellar or not. He *needed* to know.

Septimus' thoughts were broken by another screech of the boat, and something else -- a feeling that they were being watched.

The two men turned in synchronicity to look behind them. Sure enough, there gathered a great band of the children of the sewers: a plague of wet rats chattered and conspired in the gloom. Their hungry little eyes became a swarm, and the floor of the tunnel lost its solidity and became a seething, singular body of movement and breath.

Ocky took command instantly. "Here's the plan: we light a couple of these old torches and move slowly -- we move forward as one. The longer we stay here and cower, the more they will sense we are lame.

"That will lead them to become much bolder and far more dangerous. When we move forward, we do it orderly -- vermin like panic -- so don't be hasty, and no slipping and sliding -- we need to be in complete control."

The two men edged slowly forward, each thrusting their long wooden staffs together in front of them. Ocky held the lantern and struck out at the rats with his pole as Septimus thrust the flaming torches down into their eyes. Septimus' heart was in his mouth now. His breaths were short and confused. The rats reluctantly retreated, albeit gradually. Their greedy eyes were looking for the faintest lapse, the smallest of errors to exploit and enjoy.

The two reached the front of the jetty. They had purposely kept to the right-hand side, goading the rats backwards and to their left. Septimus and Ocky's way out lay to the right. Septimus lit a few more of the old torches and tossed them at the swarm. Thankfully the rats were slowly being absorbed back into the inky depths which had spawned them. The two men slid back down onto the watery base of the tunnel again, Ocky leading the way and Septimus still with torches blazing to the rear. They left the screaming boat behind them and made their way back down the tunnel to where they had left the others. As the rats fell further and further back, Septimus become suddenly aware of the height of the liquid now sloshing around his knees.

"How much time have we got before…"

"Before the incoming tide overpowers us?" Ocky said, anticipating Septimus' question.

"Something like that," replied Septimus.

"I am not particularly good with time, but I know my tides, paces, and depths. I reckon we have time enough, providing the others are waiting for us, and it does not rain."

"Why would it matter that much if the others have already gone?" Septimus asked, trying not to sound too concerned.

"Well, if the others are gone, that would be inconvenient, to put it mildly. It means that if this lantern fails, we have to rely on your already half-burnt torch. The rats will be only too aware that we are in a rush. You may not see them at the moment, but they are always present, always watching. The more of a gang we have, the less chance they will approach," Ocky replied.

"This is one of the hazards associated with going down these very old, far flung tunnels. This is very much their territory and they just keep multiplying, undeterred by man. We will just have to stick together and hope it doesn't rain.

"Worse than that even would be if one or more of the flushers forget our instructions not to flush today. If they let their drains go, we really will be in the shit. Flushers are not the most reliable people on God's earth, not by a long chalk, but fingers crossed, eh?" said Ocky with gritted optimism.

"As long as that is all," said Septimus, trying to make light of their plight.

Jewels and the others were just on the point of giving up when they heard a distant voice from within the tunnel. "Jewelsy … Jewelsy."

"They made it boys, they made it," said Jewels with relief. "Ahoy, there Ocky, get a bloody move on boy," shouted Jewels.

"You never would have believed what we have just seen Jewelsy," said Ocky when they made it to the tunnel's mouth.

"Whatever it was gentlemen, it can wait. Come on now, look sharp. This here water is rising quicker than a sailor's pecker," replied a gruff Mortlake.

"Quite so Mr Mortlake, best foot forward now," Ocky replied as he pushed his way to the front again.

The gang bravely fought every instinct in their bodies to run. Ocky had drilled them well: slow but sure, use the poles, feel your way, and stay close. When the group had reached the end of the Bleeding Brook, the foul water had risen still further. The screeching from the boat was now a distant echo, but groups of rats still hovered like rash waiting to spread.

As the liquid rose, the stench became even worse. Bits of driftwood, rope, and other jetsam seeped into this watery labyrinth. They had left it perilously late... Ocky kicked himself for spending so much time looking around the mysterious subterranean jetty. He should have known better. Both he and Septimus were two of a kind: both men had let curiosity run roughshod over rationale.

The temperature was also notably dropping, so much so that all of the men found themselves shivering to the beat of the Thames' tidal reaches. The slimy water was now around their knees, and wading became more and more difficult. Despite the falling temperatures, the men's brows were beaded with sweat, decorated with anxiety. Their backbones slithered and convulsed as the damp seeped further and further into their senses.

The trudge back to the safety of the surface was long and perilous. Even the ascent up the ladder was a good deal more arduous than the descent. Fatigue had taken its toll and the cold had numbed and stiffened their limbs.

Thankfully Septimus' ambition and Ocky's curiosity had not killed them, but it had come mighty close.

Twilight had now set in above ground, but still the men winced at its brightness. Jewels was the last of them to reach the surface. He shivered as he shut the manhole cover behind him. The dialogue between the men was muted; even Ocky had experienced moments of near panic as the incoming tide had risen and risen before them.

After a brief discussion, Jewels and Ocky gathered up their poles and sank into the misty orange dusk that was cradling the city, leaving a dishevelled Septimus, Marmaduke, and Mortlake to wearily plod their way home, all famished and bitterly cold.

Septimus kept his head bowed as he slopped through the ever-darkening streets. He would hate to have been recognised, looking as he did, but right now he was happy just to have survived the tide and the tunnel alike. There had certainly been moments earlier when he doubted whether he would see the light of day ever again. These thoughts now, though, were being replaced by a desperate need of a hot bath, dry clothing, and a warm fire. Indeed, it was agonizing for him passing all of the street vendors selling hot soup and roasted chestnuts.

But deny them he must; his saturated clothes made every step of the way home feel like a mile, so by force of will alone he carried on undeterred.

Later that night Septimus retired early, even though the adrenaline was still pumping through his veins. He was overtired and over stimulated. Tonight he felt all of his fifty years, so much so he even neglected to view his precious collection of people behind the glass. Sleep was a long time coming. He felt taut and coiled like a spring, and his mind constantly swam back up the sewers to the strange boat, the odd carvings, and the huge swollen door.

When sleep finally visited him, his mind swirled with the images on the walls of the landing place: animals mutated from one to the other, merged, then vanished completely. It was not just him and Ocky in that passageway -- he felt the presence of somebody else. The candles on the walls were lit again and muffled voices whispered incomprehensively.

Septimus awoke late the next day. His joints ached all over, and he felt as if he had been trampled by a hundred horses as he walked stiffly to the studio. Once there, he surveyed it with fresh eyes. He admired the light pouring in through the glass roof, the way it emptied itself generously over the furniture and the walls. His experience in the sewers had offered the chance to see light and space in new ways.

As a photographer, he had always been aware of the importance of light and shade. Too much light created a contrast and gave the sitter too many wrinkles. This in turn led the photograph to endure a feeling of perpetual agitation and anxiety. Not enough light, on the other hand, led to milkiness, a dullness to drown in.

This morning, Septimus felt exalted to be bathed in the light's splendour. It was far more powerful than he ever gave it credit for. Everywhere the light shone, it transformed; it had the most magical ability to give or steal colour itself.

It was as if being starved of it even for a short time had triggered off a deep appreciation for the most fundamental of energies. Septimus now felt adorned with empathy for the artist's craft, the delicate intimacy of tint, shadow, and tone.

Photography was the science of capturing light. As a predator hunted its prey, a photographer hunts and ensnares light in all its forms. He turned to look at his photographs, his collection of prized possessions. He studied them deeply then turned away. Right now he felt they were good, very good, but with a little more vibrancy beneath the glass they would be magical.

It was at this point that his mind turned to Andrea: how her painting had the ability to give soul, feeling, and depth no matter what the subject was, no matter the setting. How talented she was. There had been a few moments yesterday when he wondered whether he would see her again, and that bothered him.

He did not know why -- indeed it bothered him that he allowed himself to care, but right now he had not the energy to decipher his feelings. So in a rare moment of spontaneity he grabbed his coat and set off to the Angel Vaults.

Chapter 22

Surveillance

My, my, thought the old lady whilst peering out of her window, *what a pace he has on today, a purpose to his stride. What was he up to?* She had noticed the bedraggled, wet soul that splattered his way home yesterday. She had never seen Septimus in such a state, looking as if he had fallen in the Thames. Something was afoot, and she knew it. She had been watching him for years through her connection in this world and the next. She knew when he had left the country, and when and where he was when he returned. Surveillance was everything: it always paid to notice. "Notice Everything Always" was her motto.

Her work as a medium required her to have a heightened sensitivity and an acute awareness to the sensibilities of her clients. She tried to take on board every bead of sweat, every stutter and sigh, every move of the hands. She absorbed her clients: the cut and style of their cloth, their scent, mannerisms, even their accent, were all imbibed in the great lakes of her memory.

She didn't see careful observation or cold reading as cheating, so much; it was just useful to have in one's itinerary should the precarious gates into the otherworld be closed. She was always polite when dealing with clients who believed every occurrence in their life was somehow *meant* to be, or that everything was a *sign* of something, even though she was skeptical at best.

Of course, people had sought out this type of consultation since time immemorial, so she accepted their confidence and their money with good grace.

Her skill, though, lay in seeing beyond the veil of mortal life, in contacting those that have passed on to another realm. Not that this path was always an open one: there are times when no matter how perceptive the mind is, fog descends, but more often than not she could engage almost at will.

Landscapes and cityscapes were never dormant to her: the past was never far away. Streets and houses had emotions and commotions echoing through time.

Often she could see faint outlines of where houses used to stand, blurring the angles of avenue and terrace and people from another time, wandering in and out of vision. The only thing that surprised her about this ability was how very few people shared it.

This penetration of the veil was never more apparent than what she sensed when handling an object. She would only have to handle an object for a very short time to feel not only the presence of a past owner, but also the sentiments that were ingrained into it. Gifts, and, more specifically, jewellery, seemed to be particularly potent in storing information about the wearer, past or present.

Indeed, she often recommended that clients brought with them something that had once been worn by the deceased: the more precious in sentiment to the deceased, the easier it was to contact them and make insights about their life and personality.

How she wished she could pass on or at least share these abilities with someone else! She reflected on this whilst watching a spider spinning yet another web on the outside of her dust-ridden window. It was time for her to start weaving her own future. "Mrs Moon, Mrs Moon. Remove this web at once. I need to see that photographer at once. The time has come for a family visit."

Chapter 23

The Italians

The Angel Vaults was its usual vibrant self, loud and full of vigour, smoke, and noise. Sophia was tending the bar as Pigeon collected the glasses. Septimus was surprised to see him here -- was there no pie in London that Pigeon did not have his fingers in? Septimus knew he should not have been surprised, as it was only his enterprising nature that kept the lad alive. Septimus politely touched the brim of his top hat and asked Sophia the whereabouts of Andrea. "She is upstairs, making much mess," Sophia said with a smile.

On reaching the living quarters of the Bianca family, Septimus knocked gently on the door and declared his presence. Mrs Bianca swiftly tidied herself up and greeted Septimus with her usual Italian warmth and grace. "*Ciao Signor* Blackwood, *come stai*? How are you today? Do please take a seat. Drink perhaps?"

"Tea would be most welcome if it's not too much trouble Mrs Bianca," Septimus replied courteously.

Septimus quietly admired Mrs Claudia Bianca, her strength in adversity. "I see you are working on the new design for the back of my new cards Mrs Bianca."

"*Si*, I use an eye glass for the detail. Here, have a look." Claudia passed the draft to Septimus.

"It's fine work indeed. I shall be the envy of all London Mrs Bianca." The beautifully constructed artwork was a fine ink drawing of his premises and studio in Whortleberry Street.

Mrs Bianca had noticed that most of the advertising plates on the back of these photographic cards were usually fairly dull affairs, with the photographer's name and address, a small logo, and a brief description of their work and abilities. So she made sure Septimus' adverts, or as they were more commonly known, "trade plates" were grand affairs, sometimes using ornate flowers, birds, ferns, pillars, and even angels to adorn these small cards. His name, occupation, and prowess as a photographic artist were emblazoned in elaborate scrolls all over the backs of the cards.

There was no small amount of reflected glory on her part. She was proud of her family's role as Septimus' personal artists, and repaid the honour with all of the skill she could muster. Septimus, despite his modest manners and quiet reserve, did enjoy expressions of the grandiose and splendour, and Mrs Bianca was more than happy to oblige in these mini-masterpieces.

Mrs Bianca smiled, "I am glad you like my work *signor* and please call me Claudia."

"Indeed I do Mrs Bianca -- Claudia, I mean."

Informality was not going to sit well with Septimus: he was far happier at a distance, despite his high regard for this woman. He sipped his tea and politely discussed world affairs with Mrs Bianca before placing his now-empty china cup and saucer on the lace tablecloth. Just as Septimus was about to enquire into the whereabouts of Andrea, Mrs Bianca said, "She's in the drawing room." An involuntary smile dared to appear on Septimus' face.

"You obviously have the advantage over me Mrs Bianca."

"It is one of the few gifts old age bestows, young man," Claudia said as she waved her hand at the door.

When Septimus left the room, she contented herself with knowing that her most volatile of daughters had at least found a gentleman. He was, though, a little too deep and reserved for Claudia's tastes, but at thirty-seven Andrea was not getting any younger and her child-bearing days were virtually over. She would never want for money should this be the one for her.

At the very least, their liaison had cemented a semblance of financial stability to this house, which was something they had not enjoyed since she dare not remember.

Andrea smiled generously at Septimus when he entered the room. Septimus never failed to notice how that smile took years off of her appearance. "*Ciao, come stai* Septimus?"

"I am fine Andrea, just fine."

She showed him that her hands were covered in paint, so she could not embrace him as she would have normally done. Septimus nodded, sat beside her, and observed her work. Andrea was expressing her unique vision of the world onto the canvas. Her colours were often deep and vibrant shades of blue, orange, yellow, and green.

The colours of summer, thought Septimus: azure like the summer sky, cloudless from horizon to horizon, yellow like the blazing sun, sumptuous, bold volcanic orange, and a lush fertile green, the mother colour of all life on earth. Such a very different vision of the world from the art of photography, he thought.

Her paintings often portrayed the interconnectedness of the natural world and the universe beyond. The paintings, and indeed the passion with which she approached them, intrigued Septimus to no end. It was as if she grasped the very essence of evolution itself, the encapsulation of the subliminal and subtle links that bind us and every other living thing together. Andrea's paintings were never of what the eye could see, but rather of what the mind could feel. They journeyed way beyond the surface, and into the spirit of the whole, whether it was a painting of a tree, a wave, or of stars in the sky. She unmasked the elusive spark of all being: its birth, its pollination, its death.

Andrea stopped painting for a while and enquired about Septimus' adventures in the tunnels beneath the city, and whether or not he had found what he was looking for. Septimus shook his head and said, "Well my Italian ballerina, I did find something -- whether or not it is what I was looking for, I really could not as yet say."

Septimus often called Andrea "ballerina" because it was something that she had enjoyed in her youth. Unfortunately, due to some kind of family upset or disruption to her life, her lessons had stopped and her aspirations had been dashed. Septimus never could get to the bottom of the exact reason why she had stopped dancing, but even he felt touched by the sadness of her loss and often gave her a dancing ballerina in the shape of a musical box as a gift.

"Was it as horrible below ground as you anticipated?"

"Worse" was his only reply, and he shuddered at the memory.

"When are you going back to discover more?" she enquired, knowing full well that, despite the hardships, he would have to go back down until he found what he was looking for.

"When the tide suits our purpose, I suppose," said Septimus whilst staring emptily at the canvas.

Andrea had come to know the man quite well, though she kept her distance from his work and never understood his motivations. She did not need to. But she did feel a kindred spirit in his ardour in what he was doing, and she did trust him above all others outside of the family.

Later that day, Septimus and Andrea went for a long stroll around the streets and parades and the docks close to their homes. Andrea felt invigorated by taking in the sheer vibrancy of the city: the joy, the sorrow, its scents and the stench, the shouts, the screams, the singing, even the pandemonium created by the drunken pub pianists all brought her joy.

Septimus observed how her chestnut-coloured eyes seemed to widen as they approached the Thames, as if to embrace it whole. Her hair resembled the coils and swell of the waves; unruly, and untamed. Andrea loved the mutable subtlety of the colours in the great river at night, with all its majesty of its boats aglow. Their rich and radiant reflections created a melting mosaic of gold, ochre, and orange, contrasting beautifully with the dark canvas of ivy greens, liquorice black, and bubbling pearl white surrounds.

Septimus also peered into the oily liquid below but his mind had a different focus altogether: the ebb and flow was transporting his mind back into the realms of his quest below – back to the twilight world beneath his feet, the tunnels, the caves, the vast chambers beneath this city. He had found both wonder and dread down there. How many more secrets lay underground -- vaults and rivers abandoned and forgotten?

Were the unsophisticated toshers the sad flotsam and jetsam of a lost underworld society? He recalled how Ocky had told him about his various finds in the underworld: the brooches, the daggers, the jewels. Lucky finds perhaps, deposits discarded by people a long time dead, offerings to the spirits of the river. But what if there was more to it? Septimus was well aware of the ancientness of London and he freely let his mind feed off the potential for a greater knowledge of the deep.

He then recoiled at the stench of it all, the dank, dark, suffocating horror that was the cloaked underground world, a world on the strandline of time and tide.

Andrea cast her eyes further up river. Here the nebulous majesty and seemingly-timeless course of the Thames was interrupted by the intrusion of bridges that defied the river's natural division of land and people.

She remembered how the boy called Pigeon had once told her that his family regularly did moonlight flits to escape paying the rent, and of how they often spent nights sleeping underneath the bridges, jetties, and the hundreds of rope walks that furnished the Thames.

Pigeon knew each bridge and jetty intimately and could describe the conditions under each of them in great detail, so much so that she could not understand the finer points of his observations. Though one thing she was clear about, however, was just how touched she had felt when Pigeon said how he believed that the jetty's wooden pillars were his guardians, and how he would greet them in the morning and give quiet thanks to them for watching over him and his family. He turned each twist and knot of their formation into personalised characteristics, giving each one of them a name and sentience.

He knew that these were his true friends; he could whisper to them long into the night, tell them all his dreams and they would guard them for him, keeping them safe and unbroken.

Andrea brought her gaze back to the water close by. Septimus sensed a downward trend in her demeanour. He surmised that she could well be reflecting on her battered past -- it was, after all, this river that had brought Andrea to these shores, and with the exception of her family, the only link to her native land. He gently but self-consciously put an arm around her.

Septimus had found that attuning oneself to the element of water frequently brought back long distant memories, good ones as well as bad. Water in the shape of seas had always offered him the vast expanses of aspirations and dreams, many too majestic to behold, although far too inspiring to totally let go of. With a slight nod of his head and a slight tightening of his grip around Andrea's waist, the almost mute couple began to walk upstream again, drifting deeper and deeper into the night.

Chapter 24

News

The chemist had temporarily been put in charge of the studio for a day or two while Septimus was on some business in the countryside, or so he said.

Septimus was uncertain as to whether or not it was a good idea, but could not find anyone else at such short notice. He did consider Sophia for the job, as she was usually good with clients, providing they were not younger and prettier than she was. Sadly, her English was not at all good, especially her written English. Bookings needed to be placed and the diary kept up, all of which meant it had to be John.

Septimus had deliberately cancelled shots or meetings with any lone female clients. There were moments when John could be witty and polite, though more often than not he was vulgar or just plain surly, not a good advert for the studio at all.

So it was that John was left to sort out various enquires and the mail left with Angharad at the reception hall. It was not a task he relished, though any time away from Septimus was better than none. Besides that, he was just starting to formulate a plan that could free him from Septimus' bonds for good. John roughly grabbed hold of the various documents and hobbled to the back to the exhibition room, muttering and mumbling all the while about the pain in his legs.

He pulled up a chair and made space to write the diary on the perfectly polished yew table. His mumbling got louder, as he had to push away a display case containing the stuffed remains of a stoat or something or other being strangled by a snake.

A few moments later there was a rapping at the door, which, of course, he duly ignored until Angharad answered it. "Mr Amblewick, it's Pigeon, with some news," Angharad said meekly. John sighed at the presence of the boy. How that boy lived up to his name, he thought, always chirping away, always the annoying fidget.

"Yes boy, what do you want? It had better be important. If it's food you want, forget it!"

"Where is Mr Septimus?" Pigeon asked as his eyes peered around the room.

"Mr Septimus, as you call him, is away on business, so I am in charge of looking after his affairs, and that includes telling you to keep your sticky hands off that glass."

Pigeon's fingers had almost involuntarily moved back and forth over one of the glass cases. He knew the stuffed Giant Eagle was dead, but he still tried to attract its eyes regardless of the fact. "It's dead boy, as you will be if you don't speak your business and fly away, sharpish."

"Yes, I suppose it is. It looks as alive as we do, though, don't it?" Pigeon said dreamily, looking deep into its eyes.

"Well boy, just think how livid it would be if it was not dead, eh boy? As you will be, if you don't state your business and clear off. Well my foul friend? Spit it out before I stuff you and stick you in a glass box."

Pigeon replied absentmindedly, "Oh yes... Melody told me to tell Mr Blackwood that there was a travelling circus coming to Crackwillow Park soon."

"There is always a travelling circus this time of year coming to Crackwillow Park. That's not news boy," John intervened impatiently.

"But this year it is going to be special -- this year the circus is to have one of those freak shows, as well as wonders from around the world."

"Wonders indeed!" coughed John. "The only wonder being, if they are so wonderful, what are they doing coming to this devil's armpit of a place?

"Hmmm! Very well, I suppose I will note it down. His Lordship may be interested I suppose -- sounds like the sort of spectacle his Lordship may be interested in. Go on then, out with it! You obviously have something else to say. Or are you tired out from scratching your fleas and chasing Melody's daughters about?"

Pigeon replied with mock indignation: "Chasing Melody's daughters? Perish the thought Uncle John. They won't leave me alone -- always wanting me to watch 'em dance and sing; it's a trial, it really is."

"Are you sure you mean Melody's daughters and not the fleas?" John grinned sardonically and carried on: "Don't give me that old cobblers, and don't call me uncle. Out with it, what else do you know Bird Boy?"

"As I was about to say Mr Chemist, sir..." Pigeon paused as if to correct John for his rude interruption... "Nonny says there is a couple of blonde fancy pieces treading the boards at Ackroyd's Arcadia -- you know the ballroom down Webb Street?"

"So, what's so special about these so called "fancy pieces" then?" John enquired with a cocked head.

"They say they are heaven-sent -- their beauty is unsurpassable, well that's what Nonny tells me," replied Pigeon.

"That sounds like his words, the big overgrown petticoat that he is. Everything to him is either heavenly or hellish, and nothing is ever mediocre with him, is it? Is that it then boy, you quite finished?" John said with a scowl.

"For the minute Uncle Johnny, yes, I s'pose it is, unless you want to know the winner of the dog fight tonight? Got a good tip, I have."

"Sod the dog fight! Now clear off Bird Boy, and if you call me uncle again you will get the back of my hand. Well, go on then, shift!" The boy still remained, silently looking around the room. "Well, what you waiting for boy? Shift!" John started to raise the point of his stick to the boy.

"It is just that Septimus, being the gent he is, usually gives me a ha'penny for every message I declare."

"Well I ain't no gent, and I ain't even giving you the dew drop off the end of my nose, so take flight Bird Boy."

Pigeon shrugged affably. "Okay Uncle John. I will remind Septimus when he returns." With that last bit of cheek, the Pigeon left in a hurry.

When John had calmed down again, he reflected on the boy's news. He did like the sound of the heaven-sent young ladies very much, even if Nonny was probably exaggerating. His joy was short-lived as there was yet another knock on the door. John ignored it for a while, guessing it was the bird-brained Pigeon boy again. The knocker went again.

Angharad was obviously at the shops or otherwise engaged -- he would have to go. The door was knocked again, much to the annoyance it was giving to his already-aching head.

Mrs Moon inwardly recoiled at the sight of John's scowl as he opened the studio door. She had seen the man skulking about before, but presumed Septimus would have better taste than to employ the man as a receptionist. Typical man, she mused with an almost inaudible tut. The chemist raised his eyebrows enquiringly, as if to silently ask her business. "Good day to you sir. I would like to book an audience with Mr Blackwood, if I may? It's for my mistress." The chemist nodded and gestured for her to enter the reception hall.

Although he felt annoyed at having to book her in, the sooner he knew what she wanted, the sooner he could get on with more pressing matters.

"What is it your mistress would like exactly? We produce small carte, cabinet prints, daguerreotype style, costume prints."

"Actually, it is just as I said -- she simply requires an audience with Mr Blackwood; she has a little business matter to discuss with him."

"Oh, I see. Well Mr Blackwood is not usually in the habit of discussions with folk -- he is usually a very private gentleman, but I will pass the message on to him," John said dismissively, and started to show her the door again.

Mrs Moon was not going to be fobbed off this easily. "Tell him she has news about the old Blackwood estate. I think you will find that he will want that audience then sir."

"As you wish then madam." His eyes scanned the appointment diary.

"I see, shall we say Wednesday at 10.00 am?" said John, intrigued at the mention of the Blackwood estate.

"That will be fine. Wednesday morning at ten o'clock it is then, sir. It's ok, I can see myself out," said Mrs Moon whilst raising her hand to wave off any newly-found civility John may now have been willing to exert, and within the blink of an eye, she was gone. "The Blackwood estate, eh?" John paused for thought.

Chapter 25

The Trouble

Septimus had been spending some time at the home of Professor Walter Savage, the noted London Taxidermist. He lived in Wharton Street, Finsbury WC1, just off the Farringdon Road.

His four-story Regency-period house was as comfortable as it was spacious; its position in the city meant that Savage was not far away from the city's brightest thinkers and questers of the day. Septimus occasionally regretted taking a back step from his more lofty acquaintances with all their talk of their endeavour, explorations, and innovations, but at this present moment he had other fish to fry.

Septimus and Professor Savage went way back with each other. They had become acquaintances whilst studying at Oxford University together. They always seemed to find each other's company stimulating, if nothing else. Septimus always found Savage to be a wonderfully impersonal host, totally aloof with no interest in small talk or the day-to-day social niceties of the world. That said, Septimus did at times find Savage a little too single-minded even for his tastes. His conversation often revolved around some new species of creature found somewhere or other, and what would be the best way of preserving its skin.

Septimus often mused on how Savage would have made a first class embalmer: yes, the funeral trade's loss was taxidermy's gain. Often when their conversations touched on the techniques involved in the ancient Egyptian practice of mummification, Professor Savage's eyes would seem to light up. Savage loved the topic and it almost seemed at times that he was a little regretful that he had missed those glorious days of embalmment and mummification.

Septimus had even half-jokingly asked him if he believed that he might have been an Egyptian priest in a previous life. He asked partly to see Savage's reaction and partly because he, Septimus, was genuinely interested in it as a possibility. Savage's reaction had been predictably dismissive, waffling on about the movement of matter, etc., etc. Septimus himself had always been intrigued by the notion of the transmutation of souls throughout the ages, and it was one he found peculiarly plausible even though his outlook was primarily that of a scientist.

Septimus' carriage was late to arrive.

"Marmaduke is always so reliable -- I wonder what is keeping him," Septimus mused.

"You sure you told him three o'clock old boy?" Professor Savage enquired.

"I did indeed," Septimus replied impatiently.

"Maybe there's been a spot of bother down east again. Can't think what you are doing out that way Septimus; it's a hornet's nest if ever there was one."

Just as the afternoon was merging into evening, Septimus' carriage pulled up outside. Septimus could judge by the huge plumes of warm air emerging from the horses' nostrils that it was close to freezing, and that Marmaduke had been working the horses hard to get here. Septimus bid Walter a good evening and thanked him formally for his stay, whilst Marmaduke jumped down off the carriage and opened the door for him.

Marmaduke apologised for the delay, citing that upon leaving Whortleberry Street, Mortlake had advised him to take a detour from the usual route west, as he had heard there was likely to be trouble along the way. He gently turned the horses before leaping back into the carriage again. It was always a trial turning the horses around on Wharton Street's great slope.

At the bottom of Wharton Street lay Farringdon Road. Septimus could remember Ocky mentioning how the old entombed river fleet ran close by here and how he had found both Saxon and Celtic articles along its course.

Normally Septimus took much pleasure in riding in his own personal carriages, meandering up west, looking at people, searching for specimens and vistas to stimulate him. But tonight's journey was one to be endured rather than enjoyed. It was going to be cold, very cold. The first frosts of the winter had lounged and lingered, and the ghosts of autumn had well and truly been exorcised.

The deeper his carriage ventured east, the more he could sense the agitation rising. Many people were lining the streets -- torches and braziers burned angrily, sparks flew up into the sky as if from metal beaten by hammer on anvil. The London mob was on the rise again: the frosts had been so hard that all work on the docks had virtually stopped -- even the transportation of goods up and down the Thames had ground to a stand-still. Many families were going hungry, and getting more and more desperate by the hour. There was a riot in the air, and Septimus could feel it.

He had heard tell that even the hated workhouses were bursting with willing occupants -- the poor were fighting just to get inside their imposing doors. More and more people were to be found begging in the streets -- the District Unions in charge of spreading the alms to the poor simply could no longer cope: such was the winter of 1860.

Marmaduke was not one to indulge himself often in fear but, due to the tension in the air, he vigorously encouraged the horses to up their pace. Already there were signs of looting -- broken windows, doors kicked in, and angry shopkeepers waving their fists out of first-floor windows. The damage seemed, for the moment anyway, to be reserved for bakers, green grocers, and eateries, but where on earth would it end?

Thankfully there was nothing very much for the people to eat in the studio, thought Septimus. What money he had was well stashed away, where neither the mob nor anybody else could find it. Septimus' main concern was the anger of the mob. He had heard tales of rioting and burning some years ago in Whitechapel district – of how the Thames had frozen over, making tens of thousands of people unemployed.

Many at the time feared it would lead to an organized revolt on the government, even a French-style revolution, but thankfully, after many arrests and considerable discord, Mother Nature had intervened and all was calm again… up until now, of course.

Though many shops had been attacked, others had sensed the danger and boarded themselves up against the mob.

Indeed, even at this hour, Septimus noticed businessmen hastily fixing planking and taut canvas sheeting to the outside of their premises. Thick knots of men congregated in the squares and avenues around the district. Some huddled around a selection of public speakers, who were bawling out their message to anyone who would listen, a disparate and desperate bunch united in anger.

For the great bulk of people, this mayhem was unsettling at best. For others, though, it was a godsend. Nearly every rogue in London had attached themselves to such uprisings, which almost legitimised mugging, burglary, and armed robbery in some areas of the city.

Perhaps because of the speed it was travelling at, or because there was so much chaos already on the debris-strewn streets, Septimus' ostentatious carriage was allowed to carry on its passage unmolested; except, that is, for a few brave and foolish souls who tried to jump onto the front of the carriage, risking life and limb, only to be repelled by the hulking Marmaduke or a quick crack on the reins.

Septimus was pleased to get home to the blazing fire Angharad had set in advance of his return. It had been a long, cold, and unsettling journey, and a reminder to him that he lived right on the edge of the most volatile and combustible area of the city. Rioting had not yet reached Whortleberry Street, but it may …

Septimus pushed his chair closer to the fire and opened the studio's diary with apprehension. He sipped at his brandy, heavily in anticipation of what kind of a muddle he would find there. This time, however, he need not have been that concerned: the chemist's handwriting was legible and up-to-date. He raised his eyebrows at the entry entitled, *Messages from the Bird Boy*: "Travelling circus complete with attached freak show coming soon. Two beautiful actresses that need some photographs taking."

But it was the next entry that really caught Septimus' eye. "Some woman called Mrs Moon wants to arrange a meeting with her employer." Damn the man, he has not even given a name! Septimus sighed at John's ineptitude. "Would like to discuss the old Blackwood Estate." Septimus raised his eyes deep in thought. Who the devil could that be? Anger, suspicion, and outrage flooded through his veins. *Who could possibly know about it? I wonder who has shot their mouth off about it. The toshers? Mortlake? I doubt if it would be the toshers -- they know I am interested in the cellar but why should they want to include another in it? A local resident perhaps? Maybe some chancer has recognized my name and also heard the rumour that all was not destroyed in the fire?*

142

Or maybe it was someone who actually knew them and the estate? Surely not? The fire was in the last century -- no one could possibly still be alive who remembered ... or could they?

Even if they had been in their teens at the time, they would be in their eighties now, and meeting them would not be worth the effort. Of course, it could also be someone bringing news of a will regarding the estate. If so, what had they to gain by declaring it now?

Chapter 26

The Circus at Crackwillow Park

The frost had mercifully lifted just in time for the travelling circus to descend on Crackwillow Park. The park was known locally as the "Dead Elephant's Park," in memory of an elephant that had come over with a circus many years before and died, presumably from the cold or mistreatment. The poor beast had died in the middle of the night, and was allegedly buried at great haste somewhere in the park, but no one quite knew where. As usual, the park was a great mass of caravans, trailers, horses, canvas, flags, and large crowds. Indeed, thousands of people had gathered from all over London, the rich and the poor alike, though the poor greatly outnumbered the rich.

For many folk this was the highlight of their year, a chance to escape, forget all their troubles, to laugh, to sing, to be entertained, to taste exotica. Septimus espied Melody and his twin daughters from afar. The twins were adorned in brightly-coloured pixie outfits, almost assuredly constructed by one of Scarlet Thunderbug's family, Septimus mused.

The girls were gaily dancing around a very unseasonal maypole, which was covered in ribbons and streamers. They were dancing to a reel played by a young fiddler who was dressed up as a medieval minstrel.

Whatever the tune was, it drew folk in to take a closer look at the dancing twins and, in turn, to Melody's ramshackle mobile photographic booth.

As Septimus approached, Melody lent him a smile. Try as he might, Melody could never take to Septimus, and he always felt uneasy in his presence. Despite the greater degree of familiarity, he still felt that there was something baleful about this man. Melody could not put his finger on what exactly it was, but there was something brooding and bubbling beneath Septimus' surface that made Melody keep his distance.

Melody could see he was the focus of Septimus' raptor-like stare, so he had to reluctantly break away from his ever-so-slightly-tipsy photographic client. "Trade is good, I see Melody."

"Yes, quite a crowd sir," Melody replied, whilst tipping his slightly-battered straw hat.

"I trust the fixing paper I gave you for your prints is an improvement?" enquired Septimus, feigning an interest.

"Oh, to be sure it is sir, thanking you. Fixes 'em for good that stuff sir. Fixes 'em for good."

"Good oh," replied Septimus with a nod. Melody was glad to see that Septimus had started to stroll away and was glad it had been only a brief encounter, not just because the further he was away from Septimus the happier he was, but also because he had noticed that his client had started to doze off and was precariously close to falling out of the booth completely.

The rapid rise in temperature had unburdened nearly all of Crackwillow Park of its early morning frost, leaving behind a moisture-rich mixture of mud and horse dung, which made the going sticky at best. Septimus quietly congratulated himself on wearing his long Napoleon leather boots, and bringing along his sturdiest blackthorn cane.

He ignored nearly all of the stalls, sideshows, and merry-go-rounds -- his sole purpose today was to witness, and latterly capture, some of the many so-called *wonders* of which this year's circus did boast. On the whole, Septimus was quite dispassionate about gratuitous voyeurism such as this, but he was not here to poke a stick at the exhibits or jeer at their peculiarities. No, today he was looking for some more interesting specimens to add to his collection, though they had to be genuinely worthy of his collection: only something or someone quite unique would do.

Many of the human marvels on display were in separate tents, ensuring that an individual charge was made for each specimen and each performance. Septimus had arranged in advance via Melody to meet the circus's manager outside a tent of one of the exhibits. The tent in question was that of one "Sagar the Skin-Stretcher." As Septimus approached the tent, he eyed the hulking figure of Vladimir Litvinenko in front of him. He was a darkly-dressed bear of a man, with long, unkempt black hair streaked with vast canals of silver running through it. His voluminous beard was so bushy that it seemed to cover the entirety of his face.

"You must be this famous photographer that Melody told me about," boomed the great Russian whilst holding out his hand.

"Some may describe me as that, yes sir," Septimus replied with false modesty. Septimus' hand was swallowed up in the bear's grip.

"Vladimir Litvinenko, at your service. Now, what exactly do you want from me and my travelling show, Mr Blackwood?" He loosened his grip only to fasten Septimus to the spot with his deep blue eyes, which scorched out of the hairy mass that was his head.

Septimus held his gaze with a well-rehearsed nonchalance. "I seek to make likenesses in the form of photographs from your many marvels. I am a collector of ..." Septimus hesitated for a moment and then continued, "...the wonders of the natural world, as you yourself are, Mr Litvinenko. In return, I will offer you the best photographic likenesses you could wish for. You will get none better in the whole of London sir. Use them as you will."

The circus master scratched his beard in thought, though his eyes betrayed an interest. "We have a deal then Mr Blackwood. On one condition, though -- none of my people leave the park. All the likenesses must be taken here -- my entertainers must never leave the park, is that understood?"

Septimus had hoped to have arranged for a few of the entertainers to come back to his studio: he had no wish to lug all of his precious cameras through this morass, but there was something very insistent in this man's manner -- almost a mania, and it was apparent there was no room for negotiation.

Whatever the circus master's reasons were, this was not the right time to enquire. "You have my word sir, I shall ask none to leave," said Septimus.

The man flashed him a smile and simply said, "Good; we shall talk later," and strode off with due purpose.

Septimus decided to take a closer look at Sagar the Skin-Stretcher -- it all sounded rather repulsive but he was intrigued nonetheless. His wallet was duly lightened of his entrance fee by an olive- skinned, middle-aged woman who bore the weight of a spider monkey upon her left-hand shoulder.

Within the tent there was a booth made up of brightly- painted boards and large panes of glass. Septimus was the last member of the public allowed in to see this particular show. The tent was already heaving with people and a great deal of anticipation. Septimus slid his way over to the middle of the crowd and peered over the heads of a motley group of young men. Suddenly all the eyes were fixed on the man behind the glass as Sagar the Skin-Stretcher appeared from behind a golden curtain.

By now the glass of the booth that confined him was covered with deep condensation on the inside, and a steamy mix of breath and fingerprints on the outside. However, despite this optical infringement, it was still possible to see the man contained within. Sagar was a very tall man, standing at approximately six-feet- four-inches. He was about thirty years of age and as skinny as a hop pole. The exhibit had tightly-cropped mousey brown hair, sunken cheeks, and a huge pair of buck teeth.

Judging by the amount of spare flesh on him, Septimus mused that once upon a time he must have been very corpulent indeed. Sagar's flesh sagged in rolls tumbling down his body. The man walked forward and bowed at the audience shortly before pausing, and then slowly but surely pulling the skin from his neck to completely cover his mouth. The crowd hooted, groaned, and cheered all at once. Some of the ladies present even turned their faces away in disgust, whilst their children mischievously pulled faces back at the man behind the glass.

Not all children were as hardy, however: one little girl screamed and sought sanctuary by burying her head deep into her mother's skirt. The human exhibit followed up his grotesque feat by clipping weights to the outside of his upper arms until his skin hung down like that of a bat's wing. The crowd erupted again, this time with an even louder cacophony, lapping up everything this rubber man seemed to throw at them: the further the show went on, the greater the manipulation.

Sagar rounded up his act by fixing two small metal crocodile clips to each of his cheeks. Upon each clip were attached two large lengths of thick twine, which hung down to his chest. He then prowled around the booth like a wild animal, only stopping now and again to stare at the audience and blow them kisses. Then, with the cries of "Get on with it" and "Show us some more," he started to stick two fingers up at the crowd and hurl insults back at them.

The crowd could not tell whether he meant it or whether it was just part of the act. Whatever the case, it did make for great panto.

Just when the audience had thought it was all over, Sagar leapt up towards them, pushing his face hard against the glass before pulling the string down on both of the clips as hard as he could. The result made him look like some demented human catfish sucking at the side of the glass. This final ghastly contortion made the audience gasp and stand back in horror.

A few responded with nervous laughter but many found it absolutely abhorrent, and it sent them scurrying for the exit. The Skin-Stretcher seemed to relish this part of the act more than any other moment in the show. As if taking some of the audience's departure as a cue, the lady with the monkey on her shoulder entered the tent, pinned back the exit flaps, and shouted, "That's your lot. Show's over. One at time, one at time. Thank you, thank you."

Septimus knew that the more people fled with tales of abomination and horror, the more the crowds would flock to see the outrageous Skin-Stretcher. He mused on what it must be like to be the man behind the glass. Looking out at the audience must be as bizarre and surreal as the spectacle of looking into it; so many eyes, so many expressions to tease and torment the soul. He wondered if the Skin-Stretcher's eyes ever really focused on the crowd outside the glass. Did his eyes glaze over like his glass encasement, filtered and fragmented? At what point does the entertainer become the entertained? Septimus pondered this on his way out, making a mental note that he wanted him in his collection.

The adjacent tent featured the proverbial bearded lady. Septimus had no desire for bearded ladies in his collection, a real beard or otherwise, so he walked on. The next attraction looked far more appealing -- the multi-coloured sign outside bragged: "the Amazing Snake-Boned Girl; half-human, half- snake, the Eighth Wonder of the World."

This lady was obviously one of the circus' star attractions, judging by the large queues and the size of the tent. This act could be worth a look, thought Septimus, so he patiently joined the queue

148

and waited his turn. After paying his entrance fee, Septimus was impressed by brightly coloured glass jars, exotic sculptures, and paintings that furnished the booth within the tent. Many of the glass jars were similar to the type to be found in a science laboratory or an apothecary's shop, except they were much larger. Each of the containers had a slightly different shape than the rest, though all were voluptuous and bright of hue.

Behind the jars was a small wooden stage draped with thick white and grey furs. The scent of incense stung the air -- jasmine and sandalwood burned within the round brass bowls suspended on wires. These vessels were decoratively fashioned with stars and moons, and exuded a perfume that smoked and spun deeply and densely in the cold winter's air.

The canvas door was fastened down as the audience reached its capacity. A young lady appeared from behind a curtain at the back of the stage. Most of her long, dark brown hair was tied back with a red bow made of silk. Her costume was sparse, to say the least -- similar, though more exotic in style, to the new bathing outfits for women on display at the Thunderbug's shop.

Her body was athletic but spare of any heavy muscle. She was fully aware of the spell she was weaving over the audience, and appeared to be in no hurry to start her act, stretching every muscle methodically on the ropes and bars in preparation for the act. Septimus admired her calculated seduction. When she had finished her provocative display of suppleness, and had the audience totally within her thrall, she smiled serenely and bowed gracefully.

With one slow movement she gently arose from her bow, raised her arms above her head, and effortlessly began inching her torso backwards until it formed the shape of an arc.

The audience was captivated by this astounding feat of flexibility. Her legs started to part a little as her torso disappeared from view behind her waist. The crowd waited and watched in silent anticipation, fearful of hearing her backbone snapping in two as her back arched even further downwards.

Little by little the very top of her head became visible between her legs, then her forehead, then her nose, followed by her mouth and chin. The audience watched aghast as she stood with her head peering out from between her legs, facing the crowd. She held the pose unflinchingly for what seemed like an eternity. Then, inch by inch she gracefully uncoiled herself upright again.

Once upright, she smiled demurely and bowed at the applause before gradually sitting down cross-legged in front of the audience. The crowd was enthralled by the actions of this graceful beauty -- they scarcely noticed a moonfaced dwarf dressed as a Harlequin until he was at the very foot of the stage before them. He bowed low to the audience before pointing to the largest of the brightly-coloured bell-shaped jars and then gestured that it was his intent to lower the bright green glass bell on top of the girl on the stage. The dwarf looked at the crowd with wide eyes, as if seeking their permission before performing such an act. And it came as no surprise that the audience yelled, "Yes, do it, do it, do it."

The Harlequin smiled mischievously whilst climbing up the steps towards a strange, crane-type contraption at the side of the stage. From here he pulled a couple of levers and swung the crane around toward the glass bell. Once the crane was above the green jar, he managed to lower the rope and skilfully hook the ring that was on top of the jar. Once it was hooked, the dwarf hoisted the jar high over the head of the girl below and started lowering it gently.

The girl looked up with mock horror at the jar, which was about to encase her. As the jar loomed over her head, it looked impossibly small. The girl crouched down and appeared to be tying herself into a knot, making herself as small as possible in preparation for the encasement. Just as it looked like the bell would never completely cover her, she tugged frantically at her leg. Incredibly the airtight jar slipped over her body, and there she was, completely surrounded by glass. It had seemed truly impossible.

The dwarf then left the crane, ran to the front of the audience, and bowed, taking the applause as if he was the one who had performed the miracle. He then bowed to the left and the right, and again in front of him, totally ignoring the girl encased in the jar. Next he started a ridiculous routine of badly performed acrobatics and dance, always looking to the audience for appreciation. Meanwhile, the jar was starting to mist up with the breath of the imprisoned girl.

There was just enough visibility within the jar to see the girl's head, which was twisting around frantically to attract the dwarf's attention.

The audience had now started to panic and was yelling at the dwarf to lift the jar. The dwarf seemed unconcerned, and carried on with his lunacy, seemingly oblivious to the concerns of the now-frantic crowd. Eventually he looked back at the jar, and a puzzled expression filled his face. He glanced back at the audience and raised his hands to his ears. By this time fine droplets of water had started to trickle down the inside of the jar. The girl inside had become no more than a vague, indefinable, motionless shape within the jar. The dwarf opened his eyes wide with fear: it looked to all intents and purposes as if he had genuinely forgotten the girl entombed in the airtight glass. He raced off to the crane and set about swiftly raising the now-sodden glass surround.

When the jar was raised, the girl was completely still, head bowed, eyes closed. A grim hush filled the tent and the dwarf stared on in horror. The crowd started shouting, "Murderer, murderer" and then the girl opened one eye followed by the other, tilted her head back, and a smile blazed across her pretty face. The audience sighed with relief and clapped furiously as the dwarf held his hand to his brow and mockingly wiped the sweat from upon it.

Even Septimus had begun to believe it may not have been a jest, and had silently applauded the performance for holding the audience in a vice-like thrall. The rest of the act consisted of the snake girl performing various stunts of breathtaking and backbreaking feats on the various assembled ropes and bars within the booth, interspersed with her making herself forever smaller to accommodate two more jars which were successively more impossible than the first.

The last of the jars was unfeasibly tiny and totally transparent, though this time there were small air holes dotted around the top of the jar. Septimus surmised that there was no way a girl her size could fit into such a small container, unless she had rubber for bones. The dwarf looked at the audience as if to gain their permission to continue again. Once more he held his hands to his ears, whipping the crowd up yet further. He kept on shaking his head and then nodding it up and down, milking this pantomime moment for all it was worth. When the din got to fever-pitch, the brightly-coloured dwarf nodded his head in mock reluctant agreement.

The dwarf slowly sauntered over to the crane, glancing back and forth at the audience and shaking his head, as if they were forcing him to do it.

As the jar slowly made its descent towards the girl, she herself rose to her feet and was seductively oiling herself down. Either in anticipation of the tight squeeze ahead of her or, more likely, just to entertain the audience, thought Septimus.

Appearing apprehensive, the dwarf looked towards the audience once more as the glass hovered just above the girl's head. The crowd again roared their approval as the dwarf slowly lowered the jar. The audience gradually descended into silence as the girl visibly seemed to contract before their very eyes. Incredibly, the jar slid all the way over the soft contours of her supple body, which smeared the inside of the jar with oil as it gracefully slithered over her flesh.

The audience could not believe their eyes, and cheered heartily at this wonderful achievement. Unlike the first time, the dwarf released the hook from the jar before bowing to the crowd. As he did so, another dwarf appeared at the back of the stage. This character was carrying a deep wicker basket, and was attired all in black, except for a highly ornate red and white Venetian mask.

The Harlequin dwarf, who was operating the crane, pointed to the back of the stage with disdain, and signalled for the masked dwarf to leave.

The masked dwarf shook his head, strode forward, and placed his basket next to the girl in the glass bell. Alarm spread across the Harlequin dwarf's face as the masked intruder raised the lid of the wicker basket and gazed within.

The audience pressed forward and stood up on tiptoes, noses squashed up against the booth to get a better look. Suddenly the silence was broken by the sound of the high-pitched, hypnotic rhythm of eastern pipe music. The black-robed dwarf had produced a large wooden pipe. This pipe was known to Septimus from his journeys through India - it was called *Pungi* or *Been,* and was made from a hardened gourd and reed then coated with beeswax for protection. The dwarf played it with such a deftness and craft that almost instantaneously he captured the imagination of the crowd. Judging by their faces, he had transported the audience far beyond their natural realms within this dirty, seething city to somewhere unworldly; somewhere far away beckoned, somewhere warm and exotic, a place of magic and enchantment.

All eyes became hypnotically focused on the basket before them. Indeed, such was the allurement of the show that not one of the crowd noticed or felt the odd wallet surreptitiously being removed or pockets being felt; they were completely intoxicated with anticipation.

Slowly but surely the basket gave up its two deadly secrets. The heads of two Indian Pythons emerged from within their willow confines, writhing and swaying with the melody. The masked dwarf reached out tenderly and prized the pythons from their basket lair. He raised them up above his head before looking across at the jar before him. The dwarf let the snakes slide down through his hands until he held the very tips of their tails.

The snakes were a dusky brown colour, which shone liked polished copper when the light kissed their skins. They were also interspersed with creamy lines forming irregular shapes the entire length of their bodies. Each one of them was about six feet in length, which Septimus surmised would either mean they were still partly juveniles or that they were the victims of malnutrition, as the adults were often a good two feet longer than these two.

The audience had naturally assumed that the top of the glass jar was covered with little round holes principally to enable the girl within to breathe, as without them she would surely have passed out by now. But to the spectators' horror, this was not the only reason.

The dwarf lowered one of his hands yet further which was just enough for one of the enquiring pythons to steadily slip his head into the rim of one of the holes in the jar.

Septimus broke away from the spell of the jar to observe the audience: there stood the tanner, the maid, and the undertaker, totally mesmerised with curiosity. Septimus knew that these snakes were not in the least bit venomous but could easily cause death by asphyxiation. One could almost see the crowd's consciences wrestling with the moment but none looked away, not now.

For what the audience could see of the girl's face now, it appeared wary and wide-eyed as the python eased its way around the girl's contorted limbs.

The atmosphere in the tent was now palpably tense. Jaws fastened and lips were chewed as the second python slithered its way into the jar. The sound of the reed pipe seemed to grow forever louder as the second python fought for room between glass and girl. The first python had already wrapped himself fully around the encased girl, but still he kept slithering his way around and around, and in and out. The second python seemed content with coiling itself around the girl's vulnerable neck. In what seemed like no time at all, the second python was completely swallowed by the hungry jar.

It was now almost impossible to distinguish what was girl and what was snake, such was the intensity of the crush within the jar. Some of the audience visibly shuddered at the sight of it.

Slowly and stealthily, all of the second snake's body now rested itself around the girl's neck: they were now cheek to cheek, wrapped in a ghastly embrace. The jar was completely covered in condensation, sweat, and oil. The humidity within the jar looked unbearable to the surrounding audience, who shook their heads in complete wonderment.

There then came a large explosion within the booth and for a few seconds the whole booth was immersed in deeply-hued orange smoke. As the smoke cleared, the piper changed his tune from that of hypnotic seduction to one of shrill urgency.

Although the snakes and the girl remained entwined and as still as stone within the jar, it quite inexplicably started to jerk and rise upwards. The glass swayed from side to side on its slow ascent, as if it were levitating its way skyward. Septimus gazed on, trying to see if the girl was moving it, but it was quite obvious that the snakes robbed her of all movement but for a slight twitch of her eye. There were no strings either – well, not that were visible. *Obviously a very clever deception indeed*, thought he.

The jar was still hovering apparently unaided in the air as the two dwarves sauntered their way over to the girl and gently teased away the pythons from the still-knotted, but now-smiling, girl.

Once the snakes were back in the basket, the dwarves helped the girl back onto her feet. She looked pale and clammy, though other than that was unbowed by her encapsulation. She once again stretched her hands high above her head before taking a long bow in front of the rapturous crowd. On leaving the tent, Septimus was

154

greeted by a blast of cool air, which instantly broke the pungent spell of the snake girl's serpentine abode.

Septimus was rarely impressed, but even he had to admit that the act had style. Obviously the glass jar must have been raised by some sort of fine thread connected to it, which was probably attached speedily when the audience's gaze was momentarily interrupted by the explosion and ensuing orange smoke, but still, it had been admirably choreographed, and the girl showed a remarkable fortitude of mind and body to sustain such feats. He would certainly request the girl and snakes for his collection, and yes, even the dwarves were worthy: he'd not got any of those yet, and really he should have.

One of the largest tents on the site was called The Magical Museum of Marvels. The garishly-painted sign piqued the interest of the cynical yet curious photographer -- that and the fact that the ground outside seemed to be getting more and more squelchy with every passing step. The canvas entrance doors to the tent were guarded by two large coloured gentlemen.

Judging by their attire and skin, Septimus presumed them to be of Greek, Turkish, or Egyptian descent. Both wore high brown leather boots with mud-splattered white trousers, white shirts, red waistcoats and a Fez-type hat with impossibly long tassels that kept blowing into their eyes.

The atmosphere inside this Museum of Marvels was one of pure mayhem. Monkeys swung from ropes overhead, parrots from across the globe squawked and sang. The air was thick and pungent, scents of people, animal, wood smoke, and incense mingled and mutated into uncharted bouquets of miasma. There were musicians from around the world fighting for your attention and fiscal patronage.

The exhibits were scattered around the tent haphazardly. Most were situated around the edges of the tent and many were partitioned off from the others with gaily-painted boarding of duck egg blue, a mustard yellow, and crimson. Although much of the panelling was the reserve of blocks of colour and words, there were also cleverly painted vistas of Chinese emperors, Egyptian pharaohs, desert oases, Indian temples, even vibrant jungles complete with creatures that Septimus knew could never be on the same continent as each other, let alone cheek by jowl. Naïve, yes, but nonetheless, effective and skillful.

The first exhibit that caught Septimus' eye was a glass cabinet displaying a finely preserved skeleton of Siamese twins, supposedly found in deepest Arabia. The next was a huge glass bottle mounted on barrels, and the bottle appeared to be full of liquid that may or may not be water. Contained within this clear solution was what appeared to be a huge swordfish. Septimus had never seen a swordfish that size, not even in books, let alone so perfectly preserved, and he vowed to find out the secrets of such fine preservation.

There was a small arena in the centre of the tent. This seemed to be the reserve of the more chaotic circus attractions: clowns chased each other with nets, and jugglers defied gravity with deft hands.

These were swiftly followed by a young Chinese dancer who moved fleet of foot around avenues of fire, which were laid out in spirals at the centre of the rink. She was being pursued by two men dressed in traditional Chinese dragon outfits. The chase was accompanied by an ever-quickening beat of the drum, the crashing of cymbals, and banging of gongs.

Every so often the dancer would turn and face her hunters, and breathe vast plumes of fire in their direction. The pursuers would then cower down before retreating, and in turn the girl would chase them back around the blazing spiral, ensuring that the hunted then became the hunter.

The young oriental's face and body were covered in blue and ochre paint, which was curiously interspersed with gold oriental letters that sparkled in the flames.

The dance was billed as representing the life-giving Earth Mother being chased by the dark forces of Death and Destruction, locked forever in eternal combat, neither side completely defeating the other. The chase was eventually halted by two ground-shuddering blasts from a massive Tibetan horn, which caused all three of the dancers to look up toward the heavens and fall to the ground.

Septimus turned his head away from the clouds of smoke that tormented his retinas, and noticed a curious booth just to the left of a group of Indian men slumbering on beds of nails. This particular attraction was called *The Ghost Walk of Ecuador*. The *walk* was presumably a set of partitioned passageways, similar to that of a maze with the odd second-rate ghost thrown in for good measure, thought Septimus. Predictable as it was inevitably going to be, Septimus still decided to go in for a quick peep, if only to give himself a break from the plumes of smoke belching from the central arena and the ever-more swampy conditions outside.

Upon entering the *walk*, Septimus was given a small lantern, which contained nothing more than an already-lit white candle and a warning not to drop it.

The first thing that struck Septimus was just how narrow and dark the corridors were -- this and the strange, hollow whistling noises originating from behind the panels. Septimus gazed through the first small window he came to, and to his surprise he saw the most peculiar chess set he had ever laid eyes on. The opposing sides were made up of Spanish Conquistadors and native South Americans. Each piece was approximately eighteen inches in height and skillfully carved.

Even the pawns had very life-like, finely chiselled faces, and all were dressed in strikingly vivid woollen outfits. The blue and red Spanish outfits were marginally less elaborate than the gold and green of the Indians. The native Indians' attire was further decorated with a multitude of feathers and crude, but, nonetheless exquisite, handmade beads. The board itself was about four feet square and made up of two different types of wood to distinguish one square from the other.

The next set of cabinets was filled with large masks with elongated faces. Many of them were human, though there were also wolves, cats, and even pigs. Septimus deduced that given the texture, they were predominantly made of gourds, but some of the human masks looked very heavy and tightly grained, and these were likely to be made from wood.

It was puzzling why these inert objects could conjure up such emotion in the viewer, but Septimus certainly felt it. Maybe it was the lack of surrounding light that seemed to highlight their contorted faces in the candlelight. Or perhaps it was the passion that had been infused into their construction that helped emanate such potency.

Septimus started to become very aware of his breath and it felt as if all his blood was leaving his heart and rushing towards his lower arms and extremities. He fought to undo his tie pin, which held his cravat tight around his neck. He was not really sure if he was hot or cold, though he had become steadily anxious.

Despite his apprehensions, his curiosity led him deeper into the *walk*. Some of the booths had small gas lamps, others mere candles, and it was the latter that furnished the more ghastly of spectacles. Row after row of heads, *real* heads, shrunken heads, some hung by their hair, callously bunched like onions on a stall. However, it was the heads that hung alone that were the most forlorn -- even the dryness of their skin could not conceal the agony of their expression: it was as if in their dying breath they had foreseen the horror of that which awaited them.

It was cold, very cold. Septimus shuddered. His mouth had turned desert-dry and his heart rebelled at the constriction of his chest: the need for air, light, and space seared deep into his mind.

Shafts of air tugged and taunted at the unseen cylindrical instruments out of reach and out of sight. The only time Septimus had witnessed such sounds before was on desolate, wind-swept scarps and moors, places of abandonment and dereliction. The suffocating darkness and the strange feelings brought on by these macabre exhibits and noises sent Septimus scuttling off with undue haste for the exit. Momentarily, he began to think that there was no exit and it was all some sort of ghastly trick. Either that or he was stuck in some sort of nightmare and could not wake up.

How could there be so many passages in such a small area?

Just as Septimus found the exit, the door inexplicably blew open and smashed against the boarding. Septimus was out, at last. He turned back to view the small wooden booth that housed the *walk* and wondered again how could there be so many passages in such a small area.

The elation he felt at being released was short-lived, as a wave of apprehension and shame washed over him.

Much to Septimus' disdain, it would appear that the legacy of fear and panic caused by the frantic clamour to escape the rising water in the sewers still had its grasp on him. This was made all the more worse by the fact that he knew he had to return to the blackness once more.

Once back in the sanctuary of his lair, Septimus forcibly pushed his momentary paranoia back into the distant recesses of his mind.

He sat warming himself by the fire in his study and tried to focus his mind on the potentials of the day. Gradually his acquisitive nature started coursing its way back through his veins.

He set about writing a list of who had inspired him from the circus: the Skin-Stretcher, the Snake Girl, the Dwarves. And why not also try the Dragons and the fiery Earth Mother? He had nothing to lose. He would send Angharad out forthwith to find Pigeon and get a letter to Mr Vladimir Litvinenko, Circus Manager, immediately. He would need to get hold of John too. He searched for his quill.

Chapter 27

Thunderbug's Cloth Emporium

The word had came through Pigeon late last night that John was required by Septimus for a photo session of assorted circus folk in Crackwillow Park on Monday morning. Septimus was going to see Mrs Thunderbug about something or other, and he would pick up John at the Thunderbugs' shop at eleven o'clock. John was not to be late. He was resentful at being at the beck and call of Septimus, but there were a few crumbs of comfort: it meant he would have an excuse to pop round and see Mrs Thunderbug again. How that woman inspired him, despite her haughty, domineering manner. There was something so overwhelmingly enticing about the woman. He was aware that she always tried to avoid him, but who knows, maybe one day his chance would come.

It was a sunny but crisp winter's morning. How John hated the winter -- the cold and the damp air embroiled themselves in his aching joints. The draft invading his bedroom above the chemist shop did little to whet his appetite to venture from his sheets into the wider, and no doubt colder, world outside.

When he did eventually arise, he decided to skip breakfast yet again -- it all seemed like too much effort. Besides, he was running late, so he hurriedly packed his selected chemicals into his battered old work trunk and entered Thunderbug's Cloth Emporium next door.

It was a move he nearly came to regret, since it almost ended in calamity, as two of the Thunderbug children were chasing each other around the shop and nearly knocked him over. The only thing between him and the ground was one of the garment rails situated at the entrance of the shop. His indignity did not end there, though.

"What are you doing amongst my bodices Mr Amblewick?" boomed Mrs Thunderbug.

"Avoiding your feral daughters Mrs Thunderbug. Possessed they are, possessed. They knocked me clean off me feet."

"Hmm," replied a none-too-convinced Mrs Thunderbug. "What do you want? State your business Mr Amblewick, or be off with you. I am very busy at the moment."

John fought for composure, but could not resist leering at Mrs Thunderbug and thinking what a sight the woman was. She was perfect: about forty-five years old, with a pale, creamy complexion. Her hair was a mane of dark brown tight curls. Sadly, like the rest of her, it was rarely allowed the liberty to flow freely -- it was pulled up and held back with much restriction. Her dark chocolate eyes pierced into him. "Your business sir?" She was now pursing hers lips angrily.

"Erm, I need to speak to Herman -- I need him to mind my shop for an hour or two this morning," John replied meekly.

"Well, that is very short notice. An hour or two, you say? More like the rest of the day, I'd say."

"I am not entirely sure but I will pay of course, or else I could always help you out in the shop sometime Scarlet. You know I am always willing to be of service to you my dear," John said with a little more hope than expectance.

"I am not your dear Mr Amblewick, and I wish to be addressed as *Mrs Thunderbug* by you."

"Right you are madam. Right you are. Is Herman around at all?"

"He is in the rag room; hiding, no doubt. You stay here and I'll go and fetch him."

Scarlet was none too keen on John wandering around the shop: bad for trade. God knows where he has been or what people may think. Eventually, a sheepish-looking Herman wandered in and when he saw John, his heavily lined eyes opened eagerly and his mouth stuttered a smile.

He was trying not to look too pleased that he may be out of the domineering clutches of his harridan of a wife.

Within minutes, Septimus walked in with a corresponding draft that announced his entrance before him. John winced at the cold air infiltrating his flesh. Septimus doffed his cap at John and Herman: "Good day to you gentlemen; is Mrs Thunderbug to be found anywhere?"

John piped up with a disgruntled, "You are early. I have not sorted out me store yet." Septimus ignored the remark and his eyes

161

found Scarlet Thunderbug making her way toward him whilst fixing her hair.

"Ah, good day to you Mrs Thunderbug."

"Good day to you Mr Blackwood. Always a pleasure to see you here," Scarlet Thunderbug said as she unleashed a warm and rare smile. John and Herman felt quite sidelined by the attention Mrs Thunderbug gave to Septimus. Herman was glad of it, though John hated to witness her affections bestowed on Septimus in this way.

Mrs Thunderbug was acting like his mother had, all those years ago. John's mood soured and Mr Thunderbug could sense it.

"Right then John, shall we go and sort out your shop?" Herman said in his strong Lancastrian brogue.

"Yes, let's get out of here. The sooner the better," John said bitterly.

"Come now Mr Blackwood, I will show you that coat I mentioned to you the other day," said Scarlet. She took Septimus by the arm and led him to a well-stocked rail at the back of the shop. "Oh, by the way, St Anne's church is having a fete next Saturday morning in the church hall. If you would like to come, you would be made most welcome, I am sure," Scarlet said with a comely smile.

"I shall check my diary Mrs Thunderbug."

"Call me Scarlet, please Septimus -- we are old friends now; no need to stand on ceremony with me my dear."

Septimus found this woman quite perplexing. Outwardly she was one of the holier than thou women; quick to judge the harlot, condemn the thief, and flog the fraudster. However, despite this whiter than white coating, there was a degree of lasciviousness aimed towards him, though only ever displayed to him behind the scenes, which occasionally made him uncomfortable.

Other times, though, well… she was indeed well- proportioned -- not pretty in the usual sense of the word but she did possess a striking, almost angular beauty. Indeed, had it not been for her estuary burr, she could easily have passed off as one of the nobility.

"This is the coat. It's a beauty, isn't it?" Scarlet said enthusiastically. She took the coat off the rail and held it for him. Septimus noticed that she had started to chew gently on her bottom lip. Scarlet always did this when either anxious or excited. Other than her enthusiasm for her trade and certain... *pastimes*, it was the only time she ever (however unwittingly) exposed the girl within the firmly bridled exterior. She looked at Septimus quizzically. "Would you like to try it on for size Septimus? I will hold your coat for you."

"I don't think that will be necessary Mrs Thunderbug. No one is better equipped to know my size more than you are," Septimus said matter-of-factly. Scarlet smiled and nodded politely before turning her face away to avoid revealing a slight blush.

"If you could have it delivered to me as soon as possible Mrs Thunderbug, I'd be much obliged. I would take it now, but I fear we are off to the circus, and goodness knows what type of rogues and blackhearts one shall encounter there."

"Quite so Septimus. You are most wise. I knew you would like it the moment I saw it."

"You are most kind Mrs Thunderbug. Now I must beg your leave. It's imperative I catch the circus as soon as I can."

"Of course Mr Blackwood. You go. Please feel free to call in at your leisure, and don't forget about the fete at the church hall on Saturday," replied Scarlet with a smile.

"I won't. Good day to you Mrs Thunderbug."

Septimus impatiently made his way into John's chemist shop to hurry him on his way. John's shop was as chaotic and disorganized as the man himself. Packets and jars were strewn about the place, many taking refuge on the huge oak counter. Bottles of all shapes and sizes filled the shop. According to the labels there was nothing this man could not cure: *Amblewick's Macassar Oil, prevents hair falling out or turning grey. Amblewick's Tonic Tablets, purify the blood -- tonic for the liver and kidneys, promote vigour. Nurse Amblewick's Baby Soothers, help relieve wind, gripe, whooping cough, and restless nights. Dr Amblewick's Scented Sniffer, relieves asthma, colds, dizziness, and faints.*

"My, my, John, you should have teamed up with that Nightingale woman. Between the pair of you, no one would ever have died in the Crimea," Septimus said sarcastically. John scowled at the rebuke as he refilled one of his huge lozenge jars.

"My remedies are known throughout London. Folk flock from all over the city to sample my wares."

"Yes, so I have heard say. Dame Doxy from the Mermaid Hotel seems to be here very regularly. Is the poor women better yet?" asked Septimus sardonically.

Dame Doxy, whose real name was Rosie Richards, was the owner of an establishment known for offering relief to the not so fair sex at Ginger Lane by the docks. "I dare say she's a regular, yes. There are a lot of ailments about in this city, as well you know," said John defensively.

"Oh yes, I have no doubt whatsoever that there are certainly many things she, and her extended family of girls want to get rid of John, are there not?" John knew what he was implying but resisted the bait.

"I minds me own business, that's what I do Septimus, minds me own."

"That is indeed what we need to do right now, John Amblewick, mind our own business. I am sure Mr Thunderbug can cope with all of your colourful customers, and if he cannot I am sure there is something here he can take to ease the pressure of it all."

John ignored the taunting, and picked up his trunk. He showed Herman a list of instructions and left the shop with little haste. John passed his trunk to Marmaduke, who had been waiting patiently outside the shop, guarding the buggy and equipment stoically. John struggled up into the back of the buggy, grunting and groaning all the while, whilst Septimus hopped aboard with much agility. Marmaduke stirred the horses, and off they trotted with a purpose.

The photoshoot proved to be very successful: all of the people that Septimus had requested were present and willing. Individual photographs in the style of *cartes de visites* were processed and issued to the circus master and each entertainer individually. Some of the shots were taken in the tents, but many in Melody's photographic caravan. Septimus was extremely pleased that it had all worked out fine in the end. Some of the entertainers had been a little unsure about the grooming Sophia had insisted on giving them before the shoot, but they soon warmed to her gentle cajoling and a few more coins in their pocket.

When the time came to leave the circus, Septimus could not resist asking the circus manager about the preservation of the swordfish and the exhibits in the *Ghost Walk of Ecuador*. Vladimir confirmed the provenance of the heads and mentioned that for some strange reason it was always difficult to get the staff to help set up the booth -- they all thought the heads were cursed in one way or another. Regarding the strange whistling noises, Vladimir admitted to using various vents in the back of the booth rigged up to let air in sporadically, which in turn whistled through the large, hollowed out wooden pipes, which were hanging up by the vents.

Chapter 28

The Meeting of Minds

Septimus awoke early and decided to go upstairs to his rooftop studio. The day was just starting to break and the sun was ponderously rising over the horizon. It had just begun to send out precarious beams of light through the huge panes of glass that made up most of the studio surrounds. He surveyed the tireless industry of boatmen, dockers, and warehousemen transhipping, hoisting, and bundling their wares up and down onto a floating forest of jetties below. The torches that illuminated ferries, lighters, and barges alike were slowly being extinguished one by one, thus robbing the Thames of its nocturnal tiara and replacing it with a sun-licked veneer of hammered cooper.

He broke away from the spell of the morning and made his way over to yesterday's photographs. Septimus observed them attentively and briefly allowed himself to bask in his own creations. The clarity and precision of each shot was perfect -- he was indeed the master of his craft. All he needed now was one more flicker of movement behind the glass to convince him that his experiment had worked. Then he would not only be master of photography, he would be master of ....

The potential of his actions giddied him somewhat and he sank into the warm refuge of his easy chair. Since the invention of photography, Septimus had come to believe that, with the exception of the written word, what was not captured by photography or even behind glass, for that matter, may as well not have existed -- it was just dust, gone forever.

How tiresome it was that he should have to break away from his beloved experiments and collection to suffer the mundane tasks of the day. Tuesday morning had come around much too quickly and Septimus had hardly had any time to think about Mrs Moon and her mysterious employer. She was very likely to be a crackpot or a gold-digger, a blackmailer at the very worst. Whatever it was, Septimus did feel obliged to go through the motions of meeting up with them. There was always the remotest possibility that she had something of intrigue about his grandparents and the estate, though it seemed unlikely.

Septimus instructed Angharad to make sure that his study had been set with the best silver tea service and the finest of china in preparation for the meeting. His situation in society as a gentleman meant that he had to at least make some modicum of an effort to entertain these ladies, crackpots or otherwise.

Much as he hated to kill time, he decided to peruse the newspaper until his guests arrived.

Although he received a paper daily, he rarely ever sat down and read it all -- he would on occasion flit in and out of the politics section but usually he just scanned it for news on scientific advancements, explorations, and world news. He loathed the pointless tittle-tattle of the society gossip: the endless banal road of triviality was anathema to his mind. It may sell papers, he thought, but then so did outbreaks of cholera.

Angharad greeted the couple at the door with her doleful but courteous smile. "Good morning to you both. Do come into the reception while I tell Mr Blackwood of your arrival."

"Your guests have arrived Mr Blackwood. Shall I tell them to come in?"

"Yes Angharad, do show them in," said Septimus whilst making a mental note to get back to a story about the engineer Mr Brunel later.

The old lady entered the room first, followed by Mrs Moon. Septimus rose to greet them. "Good day ladies, Septimus Blackwood at your service. I trust you have had a pleasant journey?"

"We reside virtually opposite you sir, on the other side of the street, but yes, our journey was uneventful, thank you," said the older of the two ladies drily. Septimus momentarily felt confused. Had he been watched? This was serious -- who on earth were they?

He tried to appear unmoved by this declaration but replied a little too quickly for it to be believable. "Ah yes, come to think of it your face is of some familiarity to me madam." He looked at Mrs Moon, and she smiled curtly. "Seeing as you two women have the obvious advantage over me and seem to be well acquainted with my affairs, would you do me the honour of furnishing me with your names and your business?" He tried and nearly succeeded in keeping all sense of annoyance out of his tone.

The older of the women stiffened a little on the chair before raising her head and said: "This is Mrs Moon, my housekeeper and companion. My name is Anastasia: Anastasia Blackwood. I am your great-aunt."

Septimus sat frozen and momentarily forgot to breathe. "But that's... it's preposterous. Uncle Augustus never mentioned a sister. You can't be, it's not possible," he retorted, his voice trailing off in disbelief.

"Augustus was indeed my brother," the old lady replied, her voice faltering for a second. "Augustus wanted nothing to do with us, your grandfather and me ..." She looked down for a second before saying, "It was so very long ago now. At the time there were so many reasons for it, but now they all seem very trivial."

Septimus was still unsure whether to believe her or not. "If you are who you say you are, what do you want from me? And why now?"

"There are many things I need to discuss with you Septimus. I have watched your progress and career with interest. You have an enquiring mind and that is to your credit young man, but an enquiring mind must be tempered by wisdom."

"Your purpose madam?" Septimus retorted with growing impatience.

"Very well, there are... sorry, *were* certain books your grandfather had in his possession which could be useful to me."

"What books? How on earth would I know anything about his books? I scarcely know anything at all about the man, or even my father, come to think of it."

"Well Septimus, I think you had better tell me what you do actually know about Cornelius... sorry -- your grandfather.

Then I shall tell you what is truth and what is not." Anastasia looked at Mrs Moon. "Mrs Moon, you can leave us now, if you would be so kind. I am sure my great-nephew means me no harm."

"Very well, if you are sure my lady."

"Quite sure Mrs Moon, quite sure."

"Good day to you Mr Blackwood. Pleased to make your acquaintance," said Mrs Moon as she made her way out of the room.

Septimus' head was still swimming but he managed a courteous, "Likewise Mrs Moon."

When Mrs Moon had taken leave of the room, the two remaining Blackwoods gathered their wits and sat briefly in total silence. Anastasia played with a ring on her finger and watched Septimus and the space around him intently. Septimus' skin prickled and his mind squirmed with both indignation and curiosity. He noticed how her pale blue eyes seemed to momentarily lack focus and emotion, though he was in no doubt that there was a sharp perceptiveness about this woman.

Anastasia held up her hand and showed him the ring. "Do you recognise the seal Septimus?" It had been so long since Septimus had seen this seal -- it was the seal of the Blackwood family, a seal unlike any other he had ever seen. It was of a baby's head with a snake wrapped around its neck. Septimus had thought of it briefly when watching the Snake Girl's act in the park. There were many theories as to what it signified -- some said it was due to one of their ancestors being born with an umbilical cord wrapped around its neck, though others bandied about other more sinister interpretations.

Reluctantly Septimus started to accept this old lady's story: she seemed to know far more about the family heritage than even a learned researcher would ever know. Septimus decided to tell her what he did know about his family, which was not much. He knew that his grandparents were called Cornelius and Morwenna Blackwood. He also knew that the ancestral home was the house that had been lost in the Great Fire of Stepney. He did not know exactly how many generations they went back at his family's seat, though he had heard tell that the family had been there when Stepney was just a small village on the outskirts of London.

"I was told that my father was an only child and that he had trained to be a painter of portraits and landscapes. My parents abandoned me and left me with Great-Uncle Augustus when I was very young.

"Our family was one of the old noble families of England, and they had maintained their finance and status by the importing and exporting of goods."

Septimus continued: "My family's wealth has never been fully accounted for, though it was presumed lost in the fire. There was

169

some intrigue about the final fate of my grandparents, although I think it was largely accepted that they perished in the fire. Because no bodies were found, some believed that they had used the fire as an opportunity to make a run for it.

"Grandfather was apparently embroiled in some type of business of ill repute -- I do not know specifics, though I can surmise it was tax evasion or some such financial skulduggery. One would imagine that it was this that caused the fall out between him and his brother, Great-Uncle Augustus, though I can't be sure. This is about all the information I have been able to attain."

"All?" enquired Anastasia softly, whilst raising her eyebrows.

"More or less, yes," replied Septimus cautiously.

Anastasia had listened intently throughout and her eyelids had slowly fluttered up and down like a shutter on a camera, capturing and storing all of the information offered.

She paused before saying: "Thank you for your candour young man. I think you know a little bit more than you see fit to illuminate me with right now, but, all things considered, I expected no more from you.

"Some of what you say is true. Some, as you say, is nothing more than hearsay. Let us start with your father, my nephew, Dominic." A look of regret came over her face before she continued: "He was a wonderful painter, skilled and imaginative, and could have gone far in the world..." her voice trailed off.

"But for what?" asked Septimus softly but impatiently.

She sighed and continued: "Dominic was tutored at home but all he wanted to do was draw and paint. Butterflies were his favourite. The rest of his education passed him by. He was not what Cornelius had envisaged in a son -- he was sensitive, shy, and at times very anxious and unstable. His father felt he lacked substance and discipline, not that he had much of that himself either, you understand but ..."

Anastasia's face peered briefly out of the sash window. For a short while her attention drifted whilst she tried to find the right words to say to her great-nephew. A horse and cart had pulled up outside with a delivery of sea coal. Angharad had been left holding the horse's reins as the coalman emptied his sacks through the chute into the cellar below. Anastasia's mind focused again.

"Cutting to the chase, your grandfather had very little time for your father and he cut him off and set him adrift while only in his mid-teens, without a penny in his pocket. Looking back, it was not a wise thing to do, given your father's nature. Anyway, Dominic found it difficult to make ends meet here in Britain, and decided to seek his fortune with some other romantically inclined individuals abroad.

"They went to live on one of the Greek islands. I cannot remember which one exactly but they rented an old chateau between them. When he first arrived he wrote to me quite often, but as time went on his correspondence became less and less, until eventually it dried up completely. I sent the word out to various people to take a look out for him, but he'd gone. Vanished. To be honest, we had all given up on him."

The lady looked down and fiddled with her ring a little before continuing. "After about seven years of no contact at all, and at least ten years since he had moved away, Dominic suddenly returned, out of the blue, full of enthusiasm.

"He had apparently moved on again with a few of his friends to Spain and had made quite a name for himself on the continent, selling his paintings for a considerable sum.

"When he came to me first, he had heard nothing of the fire that had consumed the manor house and the fate that had befallen his parents. The news distressed him a great deal, as you can imagine. He had hoped to come back to the country and to stand tall in front of his parents -- his talent had been recognised and his potential fulfilled. Poor Dominic! His emotions were always delicately balanced and the news about his parents troubled him greatly.

"He was telling the truth about his skill with a brush though. He had improved immeasurably -- his work had become incredibly detailed. He could paint straight from his imagination. Dominic still did the odd portraiture but had left landscapes behind and started to …"

For a second Septimus thought his auntie had fallen asleep -- her eyes closed and she sighed. Her hands moved toward the back of her head as if to check if her ashen coloured hair was still securely fastened in its bun, before continuing.

"Dominic had started to paint strange, fantastical scenes. It was almost as if he had gained access into another dimension that was hidden from us mere mortals. The geography of your father's mind was never a flat, clear, open prairie. It was of the deepest lakes and the tallest of mountains. Most of all, it was one of a dark, tangled forest, full of foreboding and fear yet blessed with golden rays of inspiration seeping through the foliage of his mind. Sadly, in time, the foliage of his mind became ever more intense and tangled so that the golden rays of creativity could no longer penetrate through to the gloom. Slowly but surely the finest flower of the forest was lost forever.

"Your father did not disappear into the night, Septimus. Whoever told you that was lying. Maybe they thought it was better for you to think this, I have no idea. Your mother did all she could."

"And what of my mother?" Septimus asked solemnly.

"Sarah, your mother, was the daughter of a shoemaker from Clerkenwell. She did a little modelling for your father in his studio in Whitechapel. Sarah was a fun-loving creature, pretty and uncomplicated, though not lacking in wit and wile. One thing led to another, she fell pregnant, and your father surprised us all by marrying the poor lass.

"The relationship was not always a harmonious one, mainly due to your father's intemperate emotions and lackadaisical attitude towards money.

"They were together for a couple of years, though eventually your father's mental state deteriorated so much that he had to go away. Your mother coped admirably for a while, such a proud girl."

"And?" replied Septimus irritably.

Anastasia cleared her throat and continued. "She took in washing, mended boots, you name it -- anything to get by. She would accept no charity from either me or your Uncle Augustus -- very headstrong."

"What became of her?" Septimus asked quietly.

A cloud passed over Anastasia's face. "The poor girl contracted tuberculosis and died soon after. Of course, Augustus tried his very best to save her but it was no use. The poor girl was worn out. You were about four or five at that time. Augustus and Arianwen took you in and brought you up as their own. They were better situated for children than I, Septimus -- they were married and not blessed

172

with children of their own, although I know they always wished for them."

"And my father, what became of him?"

Anastasia hesitated for a while, then said, "Well, he ... he carried on painting, and produced some magnificent paintings, despite everything."

"Where did he go away to? Why did he not return to help my mother?" Septimus replied sharply.

"Because ... because he was in a hospital. He was ill Septimus; we just could not get through to him. The doctors tried, but sadly in vain."

"Are you saying he was in an asylum Aunt?" Septimus' face flared up with anger.

The old lady pursed her lips before quietly responding. "Yes Septimus, I am... He was allowed to carry on with his art though. I am told he often spent most of the day and night painting. I did go and see him on occasion. I even took you with me once, though I am not sure he knew who we were anymore. When he was not totally absorbed with his work, he would get ... upset ... confused ... his work both consoled and consumed him Septimus. Eventually he started to refuse food and water and just whittled away to nothing. He died in 1821, at the age of forty-seven. I remember this because he was only ten years my junior.

"We were quite close when we were younger -- he was the blond-haired, blue-eyed baby of the family. There was such wonder in his eyes when he was young."

Septimus, who had started to pace around the room, listening to every word his great-aunt said, slowly sank into his chair and stared at the ceiling. His eyes fixed on some ornate plasterwork that surrounded one of the gas lamps. He tried vainly to picture his father and mother. Try as he might, he could not conjure up their faces, though he could vaguely remember a huge corridor immersed in anguish.

It had troubled his dreams for as long as he could remember. The corridor seemed to go on forever and was full of discordant sounds and endless shrieking. Septimus had always wondered where this strange image had come from: perhaps it was from the asylum. Maybe he had even watched his father paint there.

Anastasia and Septimus sat in silence. The only pulse heard or felt in the room was that of the grandfather clock; cold, crass, and insensitive. Septimus' mind sought purchase in the present as he ran his fingers through his heavily oiled hair. When found, he gently lowered his now baleful brown eyes towards the ancient woman before him.

"So Aunt Anastasia," his voice full of bile and frustration, "why did you not make yourself known to me earlier, instead of hiding within the shadows, stalking me like a wolf around London?"

She met his glance impassively.

"Sometimes knowledge can be a dangerous thing, young man. One never knows what the telling of something will lead to, until it is told, and then it is too late. Would it have benefitted you to know about your mother and father earlier? I had very little idea of what you did and did not know. Your Great-Uncle Augustus and I were not close in the end -- we hardly spoke at all after your father died. That said, I believe Augustus provided for you very well. He gave you a home, an education, wealth, and whatever he or his wife told you about Cornelius keeping the family fortune solely for himself is simply not true.

"Our father bought the mansion house in Thame for Augustus when he married Arianwen. It was always known that Cornelius would inherit the house in Stepney and that I would receive a yearly allowance until I married, at which point Cornelius would give me my share of the money.

"It was still, for the most part, my home when the fire engulfed the house. I used to split my time between there and Aunt Louisa's house in Cheyne Walk, Chelsea. I lost nearly everything in that inferno."

"Ah, so it's money you want then Aunt, is it?" Septimus said matter-of-factly.

"Hear me out Septimus," Anastasia said angrily. "No young man, you can keep your money. My motivation for the visit was not fuelled for want of your money. My reason for visiting you today is twofold: firstly, believe it or not, I wanted to see *the man*, Septimus - not my nephew's young son who fell out of an apple tree and cut open his left leg just below the knee: I wanted to see *the man*."

On the mention of the accident, Septimus finally lost even the last remaining tenacious shred of doubt that this woman was any other than who she said she was.

"Yes Septimus, I wanted to see this gentleman photographer and the great collector of life in person."

Septimus raised his eyebrow but said nothing. Anastasia smiled gently at his reaction to her words. Septimus could not help noticing how her face now resembled the bark of a gnarled old oak tree and how her wise old eyes nearly disappeared when she smiled.

"And what is the second reason for your visit?"

"There were many, many books in our old home. People used to joke at how our collection may have rivalled that of the great lost Library of Alexandria in Egypt. The bulk of the books were kept in our library upstairs, though some, I believe, were housed below in the basement. Cornelius was always very protective of them, possibly with good reason. He even kept them from me most of the time, much to my annoyance."

"If you wanted to borrow some reading material, Aunt, feel free to browse my own collection. By the sound of it, it will not rival your old collection, though it is well stocked and I am sure you could find something of interest." Anastasia carried on regardless of the apparent sarcasm in his voice.

"Let's just say that some of those books may offer some intrigue to me, if, of course, they survived the fire."

On hearing this, Septimus rose again, and started walking around the room in a state of mild agitation. "I fail to see what this has to do with me, Aunt -- a few old books in a basement which have probably been burnt to cinders or are now sodden with damp. Or maybe all that is left down there is a nest of well fed, albeit well educated, rats with which to contend," Septimus said coldly.

Unrepentant, Anastasia continued: "Oh, they would be well educated alright... The basement of the old house was far more complex and deeper than you could ever imagine -- there were countless rooms and doors that led this way and that, places no outsider would ever find. You had to live in the house to know it, and I am not sure even if I knew all of it.

"Septimus, I am not going to beat about the bush, time is too short. Your moving here was no coincidence, we both know that.

175

Why else would you be living amongst this rabble? I know you share the same quest -- it's in your blood, you know… I visited the site where the mansion had stood after the fire and I kept going back there for a long while after that. I asked the workmen if they had found anything, but the answer was always no.

"I tried to take the matter higher but all of my father's and brother's so-called friends said it was not worth the bother. It was as if they tried to erase every last fibre of the Blackwoods from the Parish -- after all we had done for the church over the years!"

By this time, her voice had become saturated with emotion. "The foundations to the new lanes and houses were not that deep, Septimus. I saw them being built, you know. Our house had cellars beneath cellars -- the main rooms were huge and had stout, solid ceilings and floors, which is why they never found them. The mansion had almost as many rooms underground as it did above, and contained many secrets. Much of the mansion was medieval Septimus -- you would have loved to have seen it."

"So are you suggesting we knock down the new houses and excavate the entire area?" said Septimus with due incredulity. And maybe with any other person alive he may have got away with it, but not her. She just stared at Septimus impassively. Her gaze both irritated and unnerved him -- the way her eyes probed not only above him, but to his side as well, as if searching for something.

"Do you think I do not know what you are up to? I considered something of the sort myself many years ago but I did not have the resources. *You*, on the other hand …"Anastasia's voice trailed off gently, as if she were taking Septimus with it and into her thoughts.

Septimus had no way of knowing just how much she knew, but at her age she surely was not a threat? If there really were things of value in those chambers, who would be the rightful heir? Him or her? Not that it really mattered; she had no family and she was not going to be around for much longer.

"Your intelligence serves you well, Aunt. I have indeed been formulating plans to search for the cellars. As yet I have not been successful, though I feel I have made progress in the matter."

Anastasia said, "There is more than one entrance to the cellars, Septimus, but of course you are aware of that, are you not?"

"I am aware that there are many possibilities below ground, Aunt. I shall keep you informed of any progress in the project."

"That is very thoughtful of you Septimus. We must speak again before you resume your search. My knowledge of the layout of the house and cellars would be of great use to you young man. Bear that in mind."

"I certainly will," Septimus said politely, though his mind was elsewhere now.

"Good, then we shall meet soon. Now do beg my pardon, young man. I have other business to attend to -- time and tide Septimus, time and tide."

"But of course, Aunt." Septimus had made the word "aunt" sound like a question, though even he now knew it be true.

Septimus made allowances for the unintended slight and declared, "We shall arrange another meeting soon, Aunt. I shall get Angharad to see you home."

"Splendid, and Septimus, do take care. You have many shadows around you. To capture is one thing, to control is another." Anastasia's enigmatic smile was vague and unreadable.

"I shall do my best, Aunt. Good day to you," said Septimus, unconsciously mimicking her expression whilst escorting her to the reception.

"Good day to you young man, and good luck."

Septimus waved Angharad to his aunt and said, "See my great-aunt home, Angharad, if you would. Apparently she lives nearby."

"Certainly sir," said Angharad with surprise shining through her deep-set eyes.

The meeting with his great-aunt had left Septimus numb - so many years had passed with him believing a lie. Why had someone not told him the truth before? What on earth was all this nonsense about shadows and controlling? Old age had obviously addled the woman, hadn't it? Septimus slumped back in the chair, lit a cigar, and sought solace by gazing up at the ceiling.

After a few days without beginnings and nights without endings, Septimus was finally coming to terms with his own past. Instead of weakening his resolve, the news just seemed to have reinforced his craving, vigour, and ambition. He vowed to chase up Jewels and Ocky forthwith to fix a date for the next expedition down into the sewers, even though the very thought of delving into the filthy depths again filled him with dread. He would overcome it -- he *must* overcome it.

Chapter 29

The Vigil

After a busy day in the studio, Septimus decided to spend more time with the fruits of his labour. He would make some time this evening to observe his special photographs at length. He had not had the time of late to observe each one as closely as he would have liked. A second sighting of movement would confirm his belief once and for all that the blend of Dr Zehariah's camera mixed with a living part of an individual's being could either project or contain life. Septimus had not noticed a thing since he had first seen movement behind the glass, and doubt had started to worm its way into his mind. John, too, had said he'd seen movement once before, but he was hardly a reliable witness.

If what he and John thought they had seen turned out to be true, then what they had discovered was not only astonishing, it was truly monumental. If it turned out not to be the case, they would try out other combinations until it worked.

Septimus entered his rooftop glass studio just after a quarter past five as the day was sinking into night. The dark clouds of the afternoon had mingled, mourned, and spat out great droplets of rain onto the glass panels. The wind swarmed and stung Septimus' transparent temple of captured light.

The Thames was at full swell, boiling with the frustration of containment. The creatures that lived, worked, and died on this mighty river were wrestling for purchase on the sodden decks. The masts of the boats were flinching and flaying with discontent.

Septimus had spent many hours gazing at the likenesses behind the framed glass, watching their faces, inert and indisposed. It was at quiet moments like these that pangs of self-doubt seemed to swirl around his consciousness, corroding his resolve. His mind reached out for substance, sending out vast tendrils of thought, seeking safe harbour from the insecurity that lay within him.

The room lay bleak and bemused, eerie contrasts challenged and confused the stillness. Emptiness seemed to fill the room. The decorative gowns hung despondent and dissolute, mourning the meekness of light. The great Grecian backcloths seemed to resonate with despair at the lost glories that had inspired their creation. Vast arrays of cameras stood motionless, icons of stillness and catalysts of static.

After many hours of careful observation, Septimus had eventually fallen asleep, and would have remained in this tranquil state had it not been for the shrieking shards of wind cutting through the room and bringing him back to his senses. The once-sullen oil lamps were now dancing dervishes of delight.

Septimus' entire studio now seemed to be at risk from the unrepentant storm. The huge panes of glass that surrounded him seemed to be bowing under its ferocity. All it needed was one pane of glass to give way now, and his precious glass studio, the envy of every photographer in London, would be torn limb by limb and shredded into the Thames below.

Septimus glanced at the ancient grandfather clock in the corner. The time was five and ten past one o'clock. Septimus decided he would awaken Angharad and get her to send a message to Marmaduke, who was probably asleep in his quarters above the stables across the road. He needed to start a salvage situation as soon as he possibly could. They could move as many of the items as the storm allowed from his beloved rooftop studio to the comparative safety of the rooms below.

As it turned out, Angharad was not in her bed at all, but down in the kitchen, sitting close to the range, knitting away. She had not been able to get to sleep, so had decided to get on with something useful in the warmest room in the house. After Septimus had instructed her to get Marmaduke, he frantically rushed back up the stairs to start rescuing what he could.

He moved swiftly to where his precious collection lay, and then all of a sudden he halted. Eerily, all was now silent: there was no beating of rain, no crying of the wind, just complete tombstone-like silence. If it were not for the glistening beads of water strewn across the glass panels, Septimus could have been forgiven for believing that the storm had just been a figment of his imagination.

Before him was his special collection of people beneath the glass, all perfectly presented and exquisitely framed. He turned this way and that in anticipation of more stabbing rain or damaging gusts, but there were none. His eyes joined with his photographs, and little by little he was becalmed by their serene indolence. His tranquillity was only temporarily broken by the sounds of Marmaduke and Angharad thudding up the staircase. Septimus thanked the pair of them modestly for their troubles, and waved them away again as swiftly as he could.

He was now wide awake and decided to carry on with the vigil he had initially promised himself. He reached over and wound up one of his Swiss musical boxes that Andrea so enjoyed. How pleased he was that the storm had abated -- he had come so close to seeing much of his work ruined. He must see to it that the structure was strengthened and maybe a reduction of glass panels was in order, too -- it would lead to more shadows, but rather that than losing all of his collection ...

The slow waltz emanating from the music box soothed Septimus' spirit almost to the point of sleep again. He ran his tired eyes over the photographs, starting at Miss Fountaine and back again. It was when he returned to Miss Fontaine that he saw a faint flicker of her eyelid -- an eyelid raised. Septimus' heart started to race. "She's moving, she's actually moving," Septimus exclaimed to an empty room. "I have done it." The words echoed slightly in the hollow space of the room. Anna's full lips started to purse, her mouth appeared to open. There was, like the last time, a very slight fogging around the mouth. Septimus' eyes widened grotesquely in triumph and exhilaration.

Anna Fountaine had been quite successful in her bid for fame, though as yet she had not found her fortune. She was now actively sought out for stage roles in the West End of London, and was moving away from the backstreet theatres of the East End. Despite his funny ways, Nonny had turned out to be quite a good choice as theatrical agent for her. Nonny had showed her all of the many taverns, gin palaces, and coffee houses that other actors and actresses frequented. She would never have believed there were so many theatres in London, and Nonny seemed to know them all.

Despite her new-found success, Anna was still happy that all the bookings and payments went through Nonny, even though she was not entirely convinced she got her fair share of the payments all the time.

Nonny too was happy with their arrangement. It had restored his prestige as an agent, having found a young lady with a talent that matched her beauty. Not only did this partnership bring in a few more pounds, shillings, and pennies to Nonny's pocket, but it gave him something else, something he had lost years ago: his self-respect.

He knew that over the last couple of years he had used bravado to cover up his diminishing esteem, but since finding Anna, he had found he didn't need to brag quite so much. Perhaps the most surprising and beneficial thing of all that this union had brought him, though, was that he no longer just cared about himself anymore.

Anna was lodging in an old tenement building not far from Jasper's Cross Marketplace. The house had once been home to a wealthy tea merchant and his family, but his business had collapsed some ten years previously and the house was now owned by one of the many disreputable landlords operating in the Stepney area. Consequently, it had fallen into some disrepair, and now each one of its sixteen rooms was rented out to separate families or individuals. The house was three stories high, with twelve rooms above ground and four below.

The rooms below housed the very poorest with the largest of families. Thankfully, Anna's room was on the second floor and away from some of the noise and chaos below, at least. She was grateful for the fact that it was a fairly large room with a high ceiling and a large, ornately tiled fireplace. And unlike in her last room, which swiftly filled with smoke almost every time she lit the fire, this chimney did at least draw the flames up, saving her the extra job of washing her clothes twice in the cold weather just to get the smell of wood smoke away.

The room was far from perfect though: some of its plaster had fallen away from the wall, exposing the wooden lathing behind, and one of the sash windows would not shut properly when damp. That said, her neighbours were decent enough for the most part -- some were newly arrived immigrants looking for work, others were manual workers and their families, labourers, and dockers. One of the costmonger families downstairs had twelve children, a thought that horrified Anna immensely.

The absentee landlord, a Mr Reid Smith, lived up west, or that's what he told Anna anyway. He had promised her a God- fearing abode and to see that that was the case, he often sent down a rough-looking gentleman, known to the residents as Mr Coshem, to collect the rent and to check all was in order.

Despite the relative stability of her residence, recently Anna had started sleeping fitfully, and woke up in a panic on more than one occasion. Tonight was just one of those nights. All was calm and peaceful at first, but gradually her mouth had become drier and drier and she felt a great deal of agitation. Within the darkness of her dream, Anna saw in the distance a faint glowing of a lamp. Whether this light was inside a room or on the outside, she could not really tell.

Despite the haziness of the illumination, it did offer a strange window -- a window that teased her focus with increasing frustration. For quite some time the nebulous, fidgeting light would not allow enough clarity of vision for her to focus properly on anything recognizable. Whatever life she seemed to believe was there, it was always just outside of her optical grasp.

She felt exposed, yet bound. Anna was used to being the centre of attention, but this was a very different sensation altogether. This was a feeling of entrapment -- Anna could feel her limbs, but they felt rigid, heavy and lifeless, as if they were made of lead. Every time she breathed in, there seemed to be less and less air, and yet, when she breathed out, her vision became more impaired.

Somewhere far off in the distance there was a gentle melody playing, one that she had heard before but could not quite place where or when.

No matter how enticing the tune was, nothing could mask the intense feeling of claustrophobia that swept through her every fibre. Momentarily the fog lifted, and a huge face loomed in front of her. Excited eyes bored into her.

It was much too close, though Anna felt no breath or scent. Anna had forgotten to breathe: she had held her breath too long in mortal terror of her fate. She desperately tried to release some air from her lungs. It was a huge struggle, but she knew her life depended on it. At last she found the will to exhale, albeit in frantic gasps. Throughout all her struggle, the distant melody played on regardless of her fight for life, almost enjoying her anguish.

The face still hung before her, though it had become foggier since she had exhaled. It seemed featureless apart from the intense eyes. Behind the huge face, other eyes peered out into the shadows, but these were not the eyes of a human; these were feral and untamed. All of the moisture in Anna's mouth had now fled with fear -- she could feel her throat starting to close, closing forever faster.

Although Septimus' attention was firmly fixed on Miss Fountaine, he noticed very slight shifts of movement in some of the other photographs nearby. One of Mr Fu Yung's hands had started to tremble, as if a very small pulse was running through it. And it did not stop there either: some of the circus performers were showing signs of life too.

Septimus was awestruck and could not believe his eyes. These were no illusions; these were real people, real life captured behind the glass! This was all he had dreamed of and much more.

Septimus tugged hard on his cigar and mused: *"Why now?"* What was special about now? Why should so many of the special photographs come to life at this ungodly time of night? Was it the atmospheric conditions? Most of the movement was in and around their eyes, though there were subtle changes in expression too. It was as if part of the subject's being was somehow projected into, or through the photographs. Was it that a small part of them had been trapped when the camera had taken the photograph? An echo, a remnant of life entombed in time? Or was it that the inclusion of the living tissue provided in the hair was actually acting as a type of conduit between the photograph and the sitter? In which case, could a type of communication be achieved between him and the sitter? Maybe he could find a way of summoning them? A direct route to their unconscious minds perhaps?

What if they had all been right about Dr Zehariah, and he really had somehow found a way of trapping souls and imprisoning them under glass?

Zehariah had a lust for power and was indeed outstandingly resourceful.

No one doubted that, scientifically, he was years ahead of his time -- it was his dabblings with the mysterious forces and the way he conducted himself that had caused such outrage. Septimus thought long and hard as to what those forces were; he looked skyward as if to seeking guidance from the heavenly bodies, and sure enough it came through in floods. "The moon," he cried out aloud. It may be just a coincidence but he remembered that the last time life erupted behind the glass the moon was fully radiant. Could it be that earth's ancient companion was the true catalyst for such transformations? Ancient man had worked with the moon for thousands of years, hunting, fishing, feasting, why should its brilliance be less potent now than in days gone by?

Septimus had been so embroiled in achieving this magical feat that he had paid little heed as to what to do next. Should he shout it from the rooftops, expose it to the world? He certainly felt like he had the right. This was not only the biggest achievement in photography since the early pioneers had learnt how to fix an image onto glass and metal, this was much more. These were *living photographs*... The possibilities were endless.

Little by little the movement stopped. Anna had been the first to start and the last to finish... Beads of sweat laced Anna's brow.

Her face flushed pink as she awoke, gasping for air. The seductive melody had slowly melted away, and with it the man's face and his ghastly staring eyes.

Septimus briefly mulled over why movement had come to a halt, but it troubled him not. The main thing was that he had proved to himself beyond doubt that he had achieved something magnificent -- no illusion this time, he had captured life itself!

Chapter 30

Upstairs

When he awoke the next morning, Septimus quickly made his way upstairs to see if any of the people in the photographs were still showing signs of life. It came as no surprise or disappointment to him whatsoever that all were dormant. However, what did leave him dumbstruck was the fact that some of the people appeared to have moved position within the photographs. Instead of his usual crisp, well-focused images, some of them had a blurring to them, as if trapped in movement. This blurring seemed to go hand in hand with a grotesque contortion of the face, their mouths open in what appeared to be an agonised, silent scream.

Whether this change was temporary or permanent, who could tell? Struggling altered the fixed image? Perhaps stranger still, when viewed even closer, some of the portrait photographs contained other figures around the sitter, some of whom were dressed in very antiquated attire.

Septimus had seen similar images as this before, though not with the old-fashioned clothing. These were often the result of poor photography, or charlatan photographers working on behalf of quack mediums trying to drum up trade for their dubious séances.

This peculiar distortion was in no way regular in its occurrence within each photograph -- all of the "ghosts" (for want of a better word) were of varying shape and size, many with different degrees of opacity within the photograph.

In all his years of photography, Septimus had never had one of his photographs behave like this. The movements had only occurred in the shots taken with Dr Zehariah's magic camera and the formula found in the old book. The formula was made up of very specific plant extracts and strands of the sitter's hair. The mixture was boiled, then the liquid was passed through a sieve. Once it had cooled down, it was mixed with the fixing chemicals needed to secure the image onto the photographic plate.

Septimus reflected back to the moment when he had first found the peculiar formula in one of his uncle's old books. It had first come to his attention when he was sorting through some of the battered boxes he had left in storage when he went on his travels. It was not the sort of book he had expected to see in his great-uncle's collection and he was surprised he had not spotted it earlier, though the collection was so huge that there was bound to be old tomes yet to be explored.

This particular old book was titled *The Ways of the Wood*. It was a collection of memories, folk tales, spells, and remedies written by a Sylvanus Rycote in 1725. It had a leather cover, which was artfully decorated with tiny roses, oak leaves, and acorns. The decoration was not one of ink or paint, but was embossed into the leather with a hammer and punch. The accuracy of the punch and the patterns this formed were truly sublime. Septimus mused that this work must have been commissioned by somebody wealthy -- whether that was Sylvanus himself or whether he was just a scribe, it was difficult to know. What Septimus could ascertain was that the book was predominantly about the English counties of Oxfordshire and Buckinghamshire, where Septimus had grown up. It mentioned young trees being cleaved open in the centre, and the passing of a sick or injured child through them. Then the tree would be bound together again, and as it healed, so would the child.

Septimus believed this practice of sympathetic healing could still be being practised in the more rural parts of Oxfordshire today. As a boy, he had seen a number of trees with inexplicable seams running up their trunk and with what looked like small horizontal bulges either side. These presumably were the legacy of where the tree had been bound back together again.

Indeed, Septimus could remember the old gamekeeper on the estate, Alfred Howes, talking about shrew ashes and it was not until Septimus had read *The Ways of the Wood* that he truly understood the meaning and significance they held amongst country folk. Apparently, when an animal -- particularly a cow or a sheep -- became ill, people surmised that it must have been touched by a shrew, as these tiny and seemingly harmless creatures were once considered malevolent.

The only cure for such a malady was for the sick animal to be touched by a stick or a wand from a shrew ash. How an ash tree could be transformed into this wonderful, all-healing device was both simple and cruel: a hole would be bored into any mature ash tree with a suitable sized trunk. A shrew would be added into the hole and sealed up alive with a small piece of wood, which acted as cork, thus imbuing the tree with magical healing properties.

Although initially cynical, Septimus had felt himself drawn to the book and its peculiar contents. It was here amongst all of this folklore and superstition that Septimus had stumbled upon the odd formulae for preserving life within an object. This old tome explained how an individual could somehow save their own, or another's, essence by mixing something from a person's living being with the correct amount of plants picked at certain phases of the moon.

Why hadn't Septimus considered this celestial wonder before when looking for a factor behind life behind the glass? The book went on to say that these objects had "warmth" about them, and that it was possible to communicate with the person as if they were standing right next to you.

One of the most remarkable things about this passage in the book was the amount of notes scattered over the original writing. It was obvious that there had been much experimentation undertaken and a need to record its results. Sadly, whoever had added these notes seemed to have little regard for the book's worth, which implied either that it was somebody very ignorant, or somebody with so much wealth that the book itself had little value except for what was written in it.

Septimus deduced it must be the latter -- the notes were written by a well-educated hand, an elaborate copperplate script frustratingly interspersed with a type of ancient shorthand that Septimus had never seen before. Not only was it the clinical vigour and the attention to the smallest of details that had first enthused Septimus, but there was also a small note mentioning some portrait or another that had been painted using the formulae, which was purported to have a sensitivity unlike anything ever witnessed before.

Sadly, the name of the painter and that of the sitter of the portrait remained a mystery, as the scribe had used ancient shorthand when naming them.

Septimus had vowed then to crack the code and seek out this mystery painting, if indeed it was still in existence. At first glance

Septimus had thought that it was nothing more than superstitious nonsense, but, giving the matter a little more thought, why shouldn't a tiny thread of hair or saliva contain the evolutionary individual building blocks of an individual form, and the life contained within it?

It was this same open-minded willingness for experimentation and exploration that had first piqued his interest in Dr Zehariah and his cameras. Septimus had read about the near- fabled work of the mystic, mesmerist, and photographer, Dr Zehariah and he had hungered to see if behind the legend there was a truth. Septimus wanted to take photography to the edge of man's deepest imaginings, as Dr Zehariah had allegedly done before him.

Chapter 31

Dr Zehariah

Septimus had bought up a collection of cameras that were once owned by the mysterious and late Dr Zehariah at an auction house in King's Cross. It came as a surprise to many that Dr Zehariah was in fact a real man -- his antics had blazed a trail through the *Penny Dreadful* magazines: indeed, he was on a par with Spring-Heeled Jack and Sweeny Todd in regards to their notoriety.

Dr Zehariah had been like Septimus in many ways – self-motivated and driven to explore the boundaries of life and perhaps even death. Dr Zehariah had spent a lot of time in the Middle East in the company of mystics and holy men. One of his claims to fame was that he was reputed to be able to mesmerise anybody at a passing glance. It was there, though, that he also gained a reputation for deception, greed, and sacrilege. It was partly for these reasons that he was pursued from country to country by various authorities.

One of the more sinister accusations against him was that he had the ability to steal people's minds. It was said that his cameras were enchanted and that somehow his cameras could also steal away a person's soul. Indeed, there were still people in London who were more than a little fearful that photography was a black art and totally unnatural.

If there was one grain of truth that Dr Zehariah had somehow achieved something new, something momentous with those cameras, Septimus wanted not only to find it but also to apply it and to perfect it even further still. Many years ago, Septimus had seen some photographic plates that had allegedly been taken by Dr Zehariah. They did seem to posses a vibrancy and vivaciousness all of their own, so maybe there was some truth in all the rumours after all.

Chapter 32

An Unholy Alliance

The information given by Septimus' great-aunt had been difficult to digest to say the very least, though Septimus now had a tangible link to his family's past. If he had indeed found the entrance to the cellars of the old mansion house, the old crone's cooperation would be invaluable to him. However, he still had a few nagging doubts as to the old lady's motives for entering his life at such a late stage. Septimus knew it was not sentiment alone which had brought her to his door. No, there was something in one or more of those books that was of great value to her -- maybe it was something of sentimental worth to her? No, having met her, Septimus failed to believe that was likely.

Whatever it was, Septimus' great-aunt's visit had encouraged him somewhat. She really seemed convinced that there may be something in those vaults worth salvaging after all these years. Those cellars must be exceptionally deep, not to mention sturdy if they had been built on top of and unnoticed by the builders. Nonetheless, if there were to have been anything spared by the blaze, it did not necessarily mean it was still there today.

As Septimus had explained to his great-aunt, the voracity of the rats' appetite was one thing, damp was another. Damp, that insidious creeping mistress of the underworld, would certainly have had her say on the matter.

Also, Anastasia could not have been the only other person who had known about the cellars -- there would be others. Perhaps they were looted straight after the blaze. Or if not then, sometime in the years that had followed. So many good reasons for relinquishing himself from the quest, and yet... and yet, his great-aunt was correct: he would still have to know once and for all, and there was no way of knowing for sure unless he saw with his own eyes that it had truly gone. The sooner he met up with his great-aunt again the better.

Septimus was greeted at the door by Mrs Moon, and escorted up the staircase to the rooms she and his great-aunt called home. Upon entering the room, Septimus could not help but notice the grandeur of the surroundings. He had certainly not seen rented rooms such as this, decorated in such a courtly manner, even if it was like taking a step back into the Georgian period. The ruby red walls were graced with exquisite works of art ranging from the landscapes of Capability Brown to portraits and works of supreme fantasy.

"Welcome Septimus. Do be seated. At last I can entertain some family again," the old lady said with a measured degree of warmth.

"It is good to see you, too, Aunt. I trust you are well and enjoying some fortification against this most inclement weather we have been experiencing," Septimus said whilst eyeing up the lingering remains of the ice on the inside of the windows.

"We have had a problem with our chimney of late. We have a sweep coming around later. Anyway dear boy, I am sure you have not arranged this visit to discuss meteorology, or my health, though your concern about the latter has been noted," the old lady replied with a faint smile.

"As you wish Aunt."

Anastasia pointed to a seat and said: "Please do take a seat."

Septimus sat stiffly at the table as Anastasia's gaze briefly swung to the window again. There then followed a short, uneasy pause only broken by the arrival of Mrs Moon with tea and cake.

"Help yourself Mr Blackwood. I hope you like fruitcake."

"Thank you, Mrs Moon. Yes, indeed, you are most kind," Septimus said politely.

"Thank you Mrs Moon. You may leave us now. I will let you know if we require any more refreshment later."

"Right you are madam. If that will be all, I will take my leave of you both."

"Yes, thank you," Anastasia replied.

"Nice to see you again Mr Blackwood. Cheerio for now."

"Yes, cheerio," replied Septimus holding his tea cup up in her direction.

Once she had left the room Septimus immediately continued on with the purpose of his visit. "I plan to have a second attempt at finding the family cellars soon, Aunt. I would be grateful for any information offered."

"Information," the lady repeated the word, and paused. "Information... now let me see, I may be able to furnish you with something, yes. Firstly, may I say that I am glad you have taken me up on my offer and decided to visit me, even though I knew you would. What exactly would you like me to share with you Septimus?"

"Well, that I am looking in the right place would be a start. Am I right in believing that old oak on the roundabout close to St Anne's Church is the same tree that used to stand at the edge of your pleasure garden?"

"Ah, is that still alive? I was of the mind that the smog from this infernal industrialization that we all have had thrust upon us would have seen that off by now. That's right, they did build a roundabout around it. I have not been back there for decades -- brings back so many memories. If only that tree could talk! We were always told that it was planted in the late ninth century to celebrate King Alfred the Great's victory over the Viking leader, Guthrum. True or not, it produced thousands of acorns yearly, some of which Augustus planted in the grounds at Rycote, where you grew up. They must be quite a size now!"

"As I thought, all well and good. I am indebted to you for that alone, Aunt. It means my bearings are correct at the very least. On my last visit below, I was confronted by a huge wooden door that separates the cellars from the tunnel. Do you remember that?"

Anastasia's brow furrowed a little before she replied: "I regret to say I do not remember that, though that does not mean it is not there. It really was like a warren below stairs. I do remember entering one of the cellar rooms from an entrance in the garden once -- Father was not amused."

If Septimus was disappointed by her having no awareness of the door, he refused to show it and continued. "If, and it still is an "if," it is the right place, and we are able to break down the door, any knowledge at all of the vaults, rooms, passageways, and staircases would be much appreciated. Time is of the essence whilst we are below. We are at the mercy of the tides, and a sudden storm could ruin all our plans."

The old lady sat patiently, nodding her head whilst listening to every word Septimus said, biding her time. "Finally, as no doubt you are aware, I cannot do this quest alone. I have had to acquire help, and whilst my colleagues' knowledge and skills are the best there are, these are not the best of men."

"The longer I take to find and excavate the cellar, the more likely they are to talk, or to organize their own gang to excavate the cellars. Fortunately there is immense rivalry between these men of the sewers, so it's unlikely that they would share the knowledge with one of their own. Filthy and uncouth they may be, but they are highly resourceful, and would not be slow to miss an opportunity."

After Septimus had finished talking he sat quietly, awaiting her response.

He had been aware of subtle changes to her mouth and brow as he furnished her with more and more details, how her expression changed from one of vague curiosity to that of total empowerment.

The old lady sighed and said, "You are right Septimus, the chambers below ground are vast, and it may take you a very long time to find all the secrets contained within them. Of course I cannot be sure of what remains below, but I can tell you that the fire engulfed the house suddenly, and nothing, as far as I know, was taken away or moved."

"Do you believe that your brother and his wife died in the fire, Aunt?"

"Do I believe it?" Anastasia pondered for a while before answering: "Most people believed that they had perished in the fire -- there would have been little warning at night. Cornelius only had a few domestic staff, and none of them lived in the house itself; he was most particular about his privacy. Of course, one or two other people suggested that Cornelius and Morwenna had used the fire as a foil to avoid some kind of scandal... As you know, their bodies have never been found, which of course raised some speculation amongst the gossips at the time; though in a fire of that magnitude, what could they hope to find?"

"I said do *you* believe it, Aunt?" Septimus said whilst firming his voice.

"It is possible that they both died in the fire -- as I said, it spread with great voracity, and they could well have been asleep at the time. Personally, I do not think they fled because of any scandal.

193

"Cornelius was undaunted by the opinions of others, and would have held firm if he had been accused of any wrongdoings, regardless of the validity of such accusations. You would have found out by now that I am a medium?"

Septimus nodded nonchalantly, and waved his hand for her to proceed.

"I believe they have slipped in between the worlds," Anastasia said matter-of-factly. Septimus opened his mouth as if to speak, but the old lady raised her stick and continued on with her explanation.

"If they were dead, believe me, I would know about it. I have felt their presence a few times but I have not been able to communicate with them. They hover on the threshold of life and death, being and non-being, neither of this world or the next."

"Surely the pair of them cannot still be alive? They would both be over one hundred years old now if the fire had not killed them -- old age would have killed at least one of them by now," Septimus said incredulously.

"So, you are saying you do not believe they fled the fire on the one hand, yet you also doubt they died in the fire? This really makes no sense at all," Septimus continued, shaking his head.

"Do you believe it possible that you can cheat death in the physical world, Septimus?" the old lady asked calmly. Septimus gazed skywards and silently reflected on the old lady's sanity.

"I do not believe it, Aunt. Then again, I do not disbelieve it either. I believe if one can imagine something, then in time it could well be achieved. We underestimate our own ingenuity -- man is presently at the threshold of many possibilities; why should he rule anything out?"

For a brief moment, Septimus suspected that his aunt knew more about his photographic experiments than he had thought. "This is all most interesting, but what has it got to do with my grandparents' disappearance?"

"It may have a great deal to do with it Septimus. I know for a fact that your grandparents had accumulated a wealth of information on the subject, and I will also surmise that they were engaged in finding out whether or not it could be achieved. I know through my own experience that it is possible to merge minds with another human being, though I am not sure about souls. To be frank, I have never been sure where the mind ends and the soul begins; have you?"

Had it not been for his great-aunt's steady and unflustered delivery of such a revelation, Septimus would have sworn the old lady was losing her mind. He was still not convinced, but answered anyway.

"No... no, I am not sure about that either, though I am intrigued as to what capacity you have shared another's mind. Do you mean that of the dead?"

"I can at times communicate with the dead, but, no, I have not shared their minds or spirits, or whatever you wish to call it," said his aunt.

"How is it possible to share the mind of the living then? I will concede that one could, in some cases, read another man's thoughts and feelings, but to share another's mind? How can that be?"

"Your Grandfather Cornelius called it *Pneumodanism,* as in the sharing or lending of breath or spirit. It is a relatively easy thing to achieve, but there has to be a willingness of both parties to initiate such a connection. One of the participants has to remain physically dormant -- a type of hibernation, I suppose you would say."

"So are you inferring that this unlikely condition of sharing a mind or soul is the one that my grandparents now find themselves in, sharing their minds with another two human beings?"

"It is possible Septimus, though they would have almost certainly been on their own at the time of the fire. So, where would the others have come from with whom to share? I also know that they would have wanted to remain at the mansion at all costs."

"Even at the expense of their lives?" Septimus asked with a raised eyebrow.

"Who can tell?" Anastasia said with a slight shrug.

"Well, not you for one," Septimus said annoyed.

"All I know is that they are not dead, and if there was anybody who could have found a way out of something like that, it would have been Cornelius," Anastasia concluded firmly.

"So, you believe he found a way out of the flames and now lives some sort of half life, neither dead nor alive, trapped between the worlds? Is that what you are saying, Aunt?"

"Like you said earlier, Septimus, it is good to keep an open mind on things, especially when we know so little. I don't know about you, but I would certainly like to get to the bottom of this mystery."

Septimus lowered his gaze and smoothed down his heavily-oiled hair. Right now it did not matter if any of his great-aunt's wild speculations were true or not -- he had decided not to waste any more time on other issues, and to concentrate on the real reason he was here.

"Well, whatever *their* fate, Aunt, I think it is best if we just concern ourselves with finding our way around the wreckage of the house, don't you?"

"As you wish," Anastasia said patiently.

He was as much talking to himself as he was to his great-aunt. Septimus had little concern for his grandparents' wellbeing, especially after what his great-aunt had revealed about the way they had treated his father. However, he was more than a little intrigued by the remote possibility that they could still be alive.

"So, do you propose to draw a layout of the house and cellars for me? I am sure it would be most useful in our quest."

The old lady pondered for a while and lent a curious smile. "I am glad you called it *our* quest, Septimus."

Septimus felt anxious and uneasy at the way she had empathized the word *our* -- he sensed another hand holding the reins now.

"I suppose I could draw you out a little map of some description. I am sure it would be of use to you, but..." Her voice trailed off into another pause for thought.

"But what Aunt, but what?" Septimus enquired with some irritation.

"But it would not be enough, not for you or for me," the old lady replied forcefully. "Time is not on our side, Septimus. You are right to ask others to help you on the quest, but you and I both know that when and if you find the cellars, the secret will be out. As I have mentioned earlier, you cannot hope to retrieve all you want on one or three or four missions underground. The real treasure, if indeed there is any left, is not so much in the way of material wealth, though there may be some of that, too. The real treasure is in the form of knowledge, dear boy. There were huge numbers of books kept below ground, and it is within their pages that the true treasure will be found. Even if your men could keep a secret, and that, by your own admission, is a big if, there are other factors at play here.

"As you know, the new sewer system will soon be making its way through large swaths of underground London, making a lot of the old tunnels and sewers obsolete, maybe even unreachable. And a wretched new underground railway…"

Septimus stopped her in her mid-sentence. "As you mentioned, Aunt, I am more than aware of such developments afoot, and seeing as we are both agreed as to the utmost urgency of this matter, pray, tell me exactly what you are proposing to resolve our dilemma."

The old lady looked straight into Septimus' eyes and paused before continuing, "I propose we do this together, Septimus," she said, still holding his gaze.

"Well of course Aunt, that is the reason I am here," Septimus replied with a hint of exasperation.

"When I say *together*, dear boy, I mean *together*," the old lady said in a steely tone.

"Surely you are not suggesting you come below with us, Aunt? That would be utter madness, preposterous."

The old woman remained totally calm, and continued, "Do you remember what I said about the sharing of minds, Septimus?"

Septimus was stone-faced and wide-eyed. "Surely you cannot be suggesting…"

"I am indeed," said Anastasia, matter-of-factly.

"Sharing a mind with me?" said Septimus, finishing his sentence.

"In a nutshell, yes, I am. Call it a symbiotic relationship, young man. Do not worry Septimus; it is not a painful or a permanent experience," Anastasia said, softening her voice.

"Not permanent, you say? Yet, was it not you who said not ten minutes since that my grandparents may well be suspended in such a nether-world?"

"I said it was unlikely that they were sharing their minds with any other persons, and that I do not believe they are dead. I have reason to think that Cornelius was experimenting with all sorts of ways one could lengthen, shall we say, one's period of hibernation for indefinite periods of time. But I do not know how far advanced he was with this. Sadly, I was not privy to everything he was engaged in -- he was one of the most secretive of creatures.

"You can rest assured, my mind will only be with you for a limited time, and even then it will be intermittent and negligible most of the time. It should be able to last until the end of our journey. My mind can only remain with you while I wish it to be. Sadly, I am losing my ability to sustain myself for any great periods of time outside of my body, as I am not as strong as I was.

"Obviously, the subject who donates the mind has to eat and drink in order to sustain life. It is not as if I am in a coma -- I will eventually need to regain consciousness, and when that happens, the link is broken. It is important that you know that it's not like two minds competing for dominance within one body -- at the end of the day, you, the carrier, will have the last say, and you will still have your own will and sense of purpose to do what you wish. Think of it as a greater awareness, accompanying a broader vision of life, events, and experience."

Again, this woman had succeeded in confusing and dumbfounding Septimus. His mind whistled and whirled like a tornado on a prairie. The idea of sharing his precious thoughts and ideas, let alone his emotions, filled him with utter dread. His initial response was one of complete rejection to the idea. He let out a sound of disbelief as he rose and paced the room, shaking his head. It would be an affront to his intellect; even to give the idea room to fertilize within his mind.

Anastasia's gaze moved back to the window. She stared absently and unfocused. Septimus turned to face her and said, "You are serious, are you not?"

"Deadly," was her response.

"If I was to give this wild idea of yours any credence at all, and go along with your scheme, know you this: the sewers of London are beyond dreadful, and there are many risks. Where would that leave you if I should not make it home?"

The old lady's gaze was still on the world below when she replied, "One can imagine it is vile in the extreme, and as for you not making it home, that would indeed be a pity, for I should experience two deaths in this lifetime."

Septimus had not prepared himself for such a suggestion. How could he have? Surely it was too absurd to be true. The old woman was losing her mind, was she not? Anastasia's face remained largely impassive, though Septimus detected a very subtle trace of triumph around the mouth. Her fingers trawled up and down the arms of her chair, unconsciously revealing either excitement or anxiety -- Septimus could not be sure of which.

The whole idea was deeply disturbing to Septimus. Wave after wave of apprehension lapped the rocky shores of his mind. He felt he really should leave right now. The thought of losing control was utterly repellent to him. There were, however, two good reasons that kept him from drowning in a sea of misgivings. Although unprepared, Septimus could see that if what the old lady was suggesting worked, it would be a much quicker way of discovering his legacy, if not the only way.

The second reason was, of course, Septimus' unbridled curiosity. Despite his initial doubts about this peculiar union his great-aunt was offering, he was naturally curious about what effect it may have on him; if, of course, there was any effect at all. Septimus believed his curiosity sometimes made him vulnerable, insecure, but some risks are worth taking, surely.

"Very well Aunt, we shall see if you have the power you profess to have. I am willing to give it a try, providing that no one shall know about this union of ours. Also, when I... when we return from this expedition, our union will cease until such time, if ever, we need it again."

Anastasia sat expressionless for a while, her gaze far away on some unknown object out of the window. She slowly turned to Septimus and simply said: "How like your grandfather you are. You even look like him, did you know that?"

"No, I did not. So, do we have an agreement then? Mrs Moon will be the only one to know -- I trust her with my life. She will not say a word, I promise you that."

"Very well then, Aunt."

The old lady smiled serenely.

Chapter 33

On the Tramp

After leaving the strange meeting with Great-Aunt Anastasia, Septimus needed a walk to bring things into perspective again. This led him to Andrea's door at the Angel Vaults. Andrea was pleased to accept the distraction, as she had been working on a painting all morning, and, try as she might, nothing seemed to be going right. Andrea and Septimus decided to take a stroll up to Jasper's Cross Market. Septimus was surprised to see just how much traffic there was on the highways and byways now – traffic of all descriptions: buggies, carts, barrows, horses, and livestock, all crammed in tight, cheek by jowl. It was no wonder that some people thought that the only solution to the problem was underground trains, Septimus mused.

Andrea was pleased to be in the open air again, despite the congestion. At times she felt that she had spent her entire life being suffocated by either paint fumes or the tobacco smoke from the inn. Not that she was averse to the odd pipe herself, but it was just being surrounded by it that she objected to. Nonetheless, for Andrea, nothing could beat the scent of a good wine, not so much for the bouquet, or the anticipation of its taste, however, but because it transported her back to her childhood and her father's huge wine cellar in Naples.

As they approached the market, the insentient din of the traffic was replaced by the earthy hollers of the costermen at their barrows. These transient beings had no hanging sign or garish iconic symbols to proudly announce their wares, so they were, in the main, forever oral in their approach.

The market was one of Andrea's favourite places -- she often came here to walk and sell her paintings. Although she did not have a regular pitch on the market, she was well known amongst traders and buyers alike, for her skill as an artist and her fiery temper. She loved perusing her way around the innumerable stalls -- sometimes it seemed as if everything in the entire world could be bought and sold in this one place. Shouts of "Spanish chestnuts,"

"Bologna sausages," "Onions most French, too good for Napoleon," "Garters from Rome, Caesar's own Imperial garters," "Oranges from Spain, orangeeeees," filled the air.

Sellers of every shape, size, and accent vied for dominance of the airwaves with their ingenious poems and prose, spinning webs of intrigue around the punters and shunters of the old Jasper's Cross. They say nothing fuels creativity like hunger, and here it was certainly true.

In amongst the throng, Septimus spotted the statuesque figure of Lilly Whitethorn. Septimus enjoyed the mystery of this fey young lady.

Perhaps it was him, but Septimus always felt that she looked at him as if he was familiar to her, which he was not. Despite her height, Lilly was always graceful and fleet of foot.

When she spoke, it sounded similar to the sound of a harp, as gentle as it was melodious. Septimus surmised that she was only about sixteen or seventeen years of age, though there was something about her that was as old as time itself. She had long, blond hair and sky-blue eyes, which appeared to have a halo of hazel gold surrounding the pupils. Despite wearing simple and often shapeless dresses, there was enough of a woman about her to make her the apple of young Pigeon's eye.

Lilly's family supplied John the chemist with most of the raw natural materials needed to make his potions and lotions for the shop. Andrea approached Lilly and was greeted with the warmest of smiles. Lilly's wicker baskets were brimming over with red valerian, feverfew, rosemary, watercress, penny royal, and hedge mustard, all of which remarkably looked as fresh as if it were still in the ground. It was a total mystery to one and all as to how the family managed to produce such uncannily-fresh produce.

All of the Whitethorn family somehow looked very different from the rest of London folk. Not only did they all look fresh of face, but some of their faces seemed to contain something of the characteristics of the creatures of the woods... no one seemed to know where they lived, though they were always around.

Not that that was anything unique in London -- people often appeared as if from nowhere and vanished back there again, leaving nothing in their wake.

Andrea slipped some coins into the girl's purse and took some feverfew and penny royal from the basket. Lilly nodded and made a smile that could have outshone the sun, had there been one visible to outshine. Septimus touched the brim of his top hat out of politeness to Lilly when she passed him a knowing glance. "Good day to you both," Lilly said in her honeyed tones.

"*E tei*, and you," Andrea replied as the couple strode onwards.

"Eel pies, eel pies," shouted a bearded man balancing a huge tray on his shoulder. The market boasted a fine array of already prepared quick snacks: pickled whelks, pea soup, sheep's trotters, even plum duffs. Andrea tugged sharply at Septimus' arm and pulled him towards the cry of "okay pokey, okay pokey, Neapolitanaaaaaaaaa Neapolitanaaaa ices, penny icessssssss."

Wine was not the only thing from Italy that Andrea bought and enjoyed -- ice cream was another. The seller was Luca Zola, one of a huge Italian family from Whitechapel. They were, according to Andrea, the best makers of ice cream in London. She had told Septimus that some unscrupulous sellers made their ice cream out of pulped root vegetables which were sweetened, coloured, and served so cold that no one could tell the difference between it and the real thing.

Andrea's enjoyment of her ice cream was rudely interrupted by the smell of a passing wheelbarrow full of second-class meat for pet food. A boy with a heavily pockmarked face was selling his chunks of boiled horse, displayed on a skewer. Behind him roamed a ragtag army of dogs and cats of all descriptions and another, younger boy, who was constantly shooing and prodding the beasts away from the barrow with a large stick.

The distraction of the crowd kept Septimus' mind focused on the here and now, and for once he was glad of it. The future held too many possibilities for him to contemplate right now, and for the moment he wanted to lose himself in the chaos of the *now*. He had chosen not to discuss with Andrea this morning's conversation with Great-Aunt Anastasia, and the potential implications it had for his personality, though in all reality the whole idea was probably no more than an illusion dreamt up by a mad old lady, he mused.

In amongst the din of the market place, Septimus heard a familiar sound. It had to be the sound of Melody and his fiddle. Nobody else played that fast. Septimus had heard little from

Melody of late, and had not seen him since the circus at Crackwillow Park. He presumed that Melody had something left of the superior photographic supplies he had given him in return for his reconnaissance, and the mere fact that Melody was still allowed to trade on the market indicated as much.

Skulduggery and shoddy practice were commonplace in the market, but rarely was one trader allowed to cheat or mislead his customers time and time again.

As the afternoon wore on, Septimus and Andrea decided to take their leave of the market and have a look down Shelly's Lane. Shelly's Lane had a reputation as being in the manner of the bohemian -- artists and writers of all abilities and classes gathered here. The lane itself was not considered a poor area when compared to its closest neighbours, though many would say that its residents had poor, or at best negligible, moral standards.

The boutiques and shops that interspersed the living quarters of this fickle and flamboyant place were as audacious and contrasting as its occupants.

Brightly-hued silks from the Orient mixed with seconds from the fashion houses of Milan and Paris. Smut- ridden, dark London brick fused effortlessly with the gaudy paints of the façades of timber and tin.

Hundreds of caged birds swung precariously from hooks on many an upstairs window ledge, teased by freedom and cage alike. These wondrously-plumed exotic creatures had been taken from their native forests, to be sold at ports to passing sailors looking for an investment on their return home. Many of the birds did not survive the weeks and months of the journey at sea.

Those that did survive were often sold for ready cash at the dockside, and then resold as quickly as possible at the marketplace.

Not that it was of any comfort to the birds, but they were not the only outsiders here. Radicals stood side by side with prostitutes, actors, and artists alike – it was a place of poseurs, pimps, and peacocks, drawn like moths to a flame. However, despite (and maybe because of) its somewhat-seedy and slightly- overripe reputation, Shelly's Lane did have a certain appeal to the casual day and night tripper. Some of that appeal was due, in part, to its many theatres. Indeed, many a career started and ended on this lane alone. Many of these so-called theatres were commonly called *penny gaffs*, and their language was as colourful as their costumes. Often these theatres had two to three shows daily, and a full week of the same billing was classed as a big success.

The actors' and actresses' abilities were as varied as the shows they put on -- entertainment to suit nearly every reveller and nearly every pocket. There were plays, downmarket operas, and dance troupes mixed in with ventriloquists, singers, grotesques, dancers, singing dogs, memory men, and bear boxing. One particular *gaff* even advertised a real live unicorn, the only one on the planet.

The entertainment on show at these *penny gaffs* held very little appeal to Septimus, though he liked to watch the thespians and the audience alike, as he would creatures in the zoo. Septimus viewed all life as predominantly alien to him, and that in these theatres was no exception. Septimus particularly liked the late shows, which were especially riotous and chaotic. The later the show, the more rowdy it became, often ending in drunken brawls. Worse-for-wear aristocrats from the west frequently came down to the East End for debauched nights out. They took their chances along with the muggers, cut purses, and whores, who all found their Shangri-Las in and around the Lane of Shelly.

It was not only the children of the night who frequented these places of entertainment -- indeed the audience was largely made up of working folk: costermongers, washerwomen, scavengers, dockers, shop girls, cart drivers, and even *pure (dog shit)* collectors were allowed through the doors.

Such was the tale of the lane in the evening and night-time, but this was the afternoon, and although one could hear the faint tinkling of the ivories and the odd unsavoury holler, it was very subdued in comparison. As Septimus and Andrea passed in front of a gaff, aspirationally called *The Empire Theatre*, who should almost fall out of the doors before them but Nonny, closely followed by Anna Fountaine, the actress from Brittany.

Septimus and Andrea had to step backwards to avoid the staggering Nonny. Nonny leaned heavily and tried to regain focus. "Why, if ain't good old Septimus and Miss Bianca," Nonny proclaimed whilst doffing his slightly crumpled top hat. Anna felt a chill run through her veins.

"Mr Wilding, Miss Fountaine," Septimus replied impassively. Andrea smiled with her mouth, though not with her eyes. She remained silent.

"We have been to see a show, dear fellow, least that's what they call it on this here billboard. Tell you what, though, the wood on the board is less wooden than the performance inside. Bloody amateurs the lot of them, amateurs. Not like this one though, Mr Blackwood, sir. She's going to go far- - far and upwards all the way," Nonny gestured at Anna.

Anna looked beautiful as ever, but tired. "I am afraid *monsieur* and *mademoiselle* that Monsieur Wilding has had one sherry too many today," Miss Fountaine said apologetically, looking at Nonny slightly awkwardly.

Septimus could tell she was a little embarrassed by Nonny's demeanour, but it did little to overshadow the warmth she obviously felt for the old soak.

Though Anna's words and actions towards Nonny were light-hearted, there was something else there in her expression -- a hint of fear. She was deliberately avoiding eye contact with Septimus.

Had she seen him looking through the glass? No, surely not. Impossible. "I trust life is treating you well Miss Fountaine," said Septimus, trying to assess his position with her.

"*Oui*, quite well *monsieur*," her eyes flitted between Nonny and Andrea and then back to the floor. She now knew that this was the face she had seen in her nightmares: it was him, the photographer; that cold, enquiring stare from merciless eyes!

"Come now Nonny, you promised to buy me that dress," Anna said, tugging at Nonny's arm with urgency.

"Did I?" asked Nonny, struggling to adjust his eyes to the daylight.

"Oh come now, Nonny! The dress most *verdi*, the one in Moon and Rabbit Boutique," Anna said, getting a little impatient.

"Oh, yes, I know that boutique. Cannot remember any dress, though, but right you are," said Nonny, still agreeably.

"*Oui*. Well, it's been good to see you both again, but we really must go you understand, before the shutting of the shop," Anna said impatiently.

"Yes, I suppose we must. Very well, then. You take care, old boy, and look after that Miss Bianca, you hear me? Lovely lady that one," said Nonny, his voice trailing off as Anna tugged him up the lane.

Andrea was puzzled by the hastiness of their departure -- she could tell something was troubling the girl. "What do you think was the matter with Miss Fountaine, Septimus?" she enquired.

"I really do not know. Probably wanted to get that dress before the old soak fell over, I suppose," Septimus replied, a little unconvincingly.

Andrea felt a wave of suspicion pass over her, although she remained silent -- it was none of her business. All she needed to know was that Septimus would never hurt her, and that was that.

Septimus could tell Andrea was not totally convinced by his response, but thought no more of it. As for Miss Fountaine's response to him, that was remarkable indeed. She was certainly fearful of him. Could she really have had an awareness of the other night when she had appeared to come alive for him in the frame? He could not be sure. Maybe he should ask her the next time he saw her on her own...

Chapter 34

New Beginnings

Septimus had arranged a meeting with Mortlake, Ocky, and Jewels to confirm the time and date of their next excursion below ground. It was decided that one more pair of hands would be useful -- preferably small ones to get through the tiniest of holes if need be. The pair of hands was going to be Pigeon's. Jewels had first raised concern about taking a boy down below, but Ocky reminded him that both he and Jewels had been mud-larking and toshing since much the same age as Pigeon, if not younger than him, and they had survived to tell the tale.

After the meeting, Septimus made his way to see his great- aunt. Anastasia had assured him that it would be folly to attempt the mission into the sewers too soon after the fusion -- she had warned him that he may feel slightly disoriented and dizzy from time to time, but this would wear off gradually. It was with this in mind that Septimus felt a great sense of foreboding while he waited in the rain, outside the door beneath her apartment at Whortleberry Street.

He was greeted at the door by a bustling Mrs Moon. "Do come in. Miss Blackwood is waiting for you. Don't mind me; I am just about to leave. There is a pot of tea on the table for you," said Mrs Moon, matter-of-factly.

"Thank you Mrs Moon. That's very kind of you."

"Good morning Septimus. It's wretched weather out there, is it not?" Anastasia said warmly.

"The weather is, as you say, wretched. Now it is your turn to be preoccupied with the weather Aunt," Septimus said somewhat drily. Anastasia smiled at his recollection of their last conversation.

"I trust you are well Septimus?"

"Yes, quite well Aunt," Septimus replied, hanging up his damp coat. "And you, Aunt?"

"I still breathe dear boy, I still breathe."

"Well, we should all be grateful for that at least Aunt."

"Indeed *we* should," Anastasia replied, emphasising the "we."

Septimus observed the wrinkled face and liver-spotted hands before him with no small amount of distaste.

He noticed how worn the arms of the chair had become. The rest of the chair was in immaculate condition, but the arms looked greasy and full of scratches. He noticed how the tips of her fingers were worn and blotched, and how her nails were almost non-existent: the result of her either biting them or scratching the chair with boredom. Septimus dare not think of how many hours she had spent scraping and rubbing the arms of her chair -- hour after hour of frustration, gazing out of the smutty glass onto the street below.

"If that will be all, marm, I will leave you in peace," Mrs Moon said casually as she topped up the china teapot with some more hot water.

"Yes, thank you Mrs Moon. No need to rush back, everything will be fine. I have my great nephew here to look out for me now," Anastasia said ominously, smiling at Septimus. "Farewell Mrs Moon. Take care," croaked Anastasia.

"Yes, cheerio Mrs Moon, mind how you go," Septimus said, far too preoccupied to look in her direction. The door closed.

"I must confess I have one or two doubts about this whole business and its validity, but so be it, as needs must," Septimus said as much to himself as to his great-aunt.

"Everything will be fine Septimus, trust me." The furrowed smile returned.

"May I enquire as to what you have told Mrs Moon?"

"Mrs Moon is prepared. She knows what to expect -- that I shall be bedridden and shall appear to be in a state of virtual unconsciousness for some while. I trust Mrs Moon implicitly, something that you really should try yourself sometime. I am now going to retire to my chamber. Please give me a little time to prepare myself. I shall let you know when I am ready."

The time spent waiting to enter Anastasia's chamber allowed Septimus to dwell on the potential effects that this so-called *pneumodanism* would have on him, both in the long and the short term. Was he being made a fool of? Was there anything she was not telling him? Why had his great-uncle not told him about Anastasia's existence? What harm would there have been in him knowing about her? Despite all of these doubts, Septimus was steadfast, and determined to stand his ground.

"You may enter," Anastasia announced regally.

Septimus smiled ironically at this royal summons. The old woman sat upright in her bed, beckoning Septimus to her side.

The bedchamber was airy and light, a product of high ceilings and two large arched windows, and like the other room, it was richly furnished with a distinct feel of Regency about it.

Upon entering the room, Septimus instantly became aware of the strong scent of lavender all around him. Indeed, it was not until he approached the bed itself that he noticed another, more toxic scent present. On the bedside table lay a half-empty glass of what looked like a watered-down milk-type solution. Septimus knew that the lady had recently sipped from the glass, as the milky residue still clung to the inside top edge of the vessel facing the bed. Beside the glass lay a large book, with its yellowing pages left open.

Anastasia already looked close to sleep when she said, "You can close the book for me, if you will Septimus." Septimus nodded and gently took it with both hands to protect its spine. He closed the red, leather-bound book as carefully as he could. "First you must drink this." She pointed to the vile-looking liquid he had noticed just seconds earlier. He looked at the substance with utter distaste. "Then you must kiss me with an open mouth, no matter how repellent this procedure may seem to you. It is vital that you do not flinch or break away until I bid it. Do I make myself clear Septimus?"

"Crystal clear," replied a resigned Septimus.

"I shall transfer my consciousness to you through my mouth."

The thought of such an embrace made Septimus shudder, and bile to rise within his stomach.

"You will experience a slight chill at the back of your throat, but, rest assured, the feeling will wear off quickly. Do not be alarmed if you see what can only be described as fog radiating from around my mouth and nose after our embrace -- it is perfectly natural."

Anastasia raised her hand towards the glass and gestured at Septimus to drink it. Septimus grabbed the still-warm glass and drank the wretched draft as quickly as he possibly could. The taste of the liquid was even more obnoxious than it appeared.

Septimus tried not to wince as he gently pressed his lips on the old lady's already half-opened mouth. Her breath was tainted with a sickly sweet smell that could only be likened to the heavy scent of ivy on a summer's day -- the stench of graveyards and ruins. The old lady's hands pulled her great-nephew's head into an ever tighter embrace. Septimus shut his eyes and prayed he would not be overcome with nausea by the strength and stench of Anastasia's embrace.

The long kiss was interspersed with Anastasia's convulsing wildly. The whole process lasted only a matter of minutes before her grip slackened, and she slumped back on the bed. It may not have lasted long, but it had felt like many lifetimes to the still-nauseated Septimus. As his lips gladly took their leave of Anastasia's, her mouth and nose became engulfed in the wispy white plumes that she had spoken of earlier.

As the old lady was succumbing to sleep, Septimus thought he heard her whisper "Thank you," but he could not be sure. Anastasia was now serene on the bed, her mouth slack and easy. Her eyes were moist, though fully closed. Septimus now felt lightheaded as well as nauseated. The sickly smell that was so reminiscent of ivy still hung heavily in the room, and the vile taste left over from the potion lingered long on his tongue. The old lady lay still, very still -- for one horrific second Septimus thought that she may have died, until eventually her chest rose and fell again.

Septimus pushed himself up off of the chair, only to be accompanied by a debilitating giddiness that valiantly tried to stem his vertical aspirations. He spread out wide, like a tightrope walker trying to restore his balance. Septimus' senses were now totally confused as streaks of light shot past his vision. He then felt hot. Or was it cold? Septimus staggered across the room, arms still splayed wide, groping for equilibrium and purchase.

Thankfully he could just about make out what he knew to be the door handle. The solidity of the cut crystal handle felt reassuring to hold. Septimus took one last glance back at his Great-Aunt Anastasia lying on the bed, and he could not help but notice how much younger she looked whilst asleep.

As a semblance of stability gradually returned to Septimus, he found that he was making his way towards the chair by the window. He resisted the almost-overwhelming urge to sit in it, though he did take a long look out onto the bleak and very wet Whortleberry Street. That had not changed, even if everything else may have. Despite still feeling lightheaded and heavy of limb, Septimus made his way safely out onto the street. He felt liberated to be outside again and for once enjoyed the rain splashing onto his face.

Just before Septimus reached the entrance to his home, he was passed on the street by an oddly-dressed stranger. Septimus turned back and watched him briskly walk up the street until he disappeared into one of the derelict buildings about two hundred yards away from his studio. Uncannily, he could feel a sense of agitation coming from the man, even though he had not seen the expression on his face.

The building the stranger had entered used to be a tavern and was still known locally as Old Neptune's Lantern. The man could not have been more than thirty years old, yet everything about him was of a bygone age. The only time he had seen a tricorn hat like that was on an old tramp he had passed whilst out walking the old footpath between Thame and the hamlet of Moreton when he was a young boy.

Despite the now-incessant rain, Septimus wondered what such a man was up to in that old wreck of a place. He had certainly not heard rumours that the old tavern was to be renovated. Besides, no builder would be wearing such strange apparel as that. Even if that man was an actor, it would be highly unlikely that he would be roaming around in a derelict place such as this whilst in costume. Upon approaching the old tavern, Septimus could see now that there was certainly no way this man could have entered the building, as the doorway was still boarded up. There was even an old railing still in place around the window. Much as this intrigued Septimus, he now had too many other things on his mind for this strange occurrence to trouble him too much.

After an unusually restful sleep, Septimus was trying to come to terms with his union with his Great-Aunt Anastasia. She had told him to expect a certain amount of light-headedness and dizzy spells, but what she had not told him was just how much his senses would be working overtime.

He felt that he now had a greater awareness of the world around him and not just the here and now. No, he was involuntarily tapping into the sentience of place, past and present. Septimus was part in awe and partly frustrated by it, especially when at times it seemed to dominate his thoughts. He no longer felt detached from the life of history -- it was as if he had somehow crossed over a threshold, and now saw and felt history in everything and everyone.

Chapter 35

The Treasure Chest

Another of the side-effects of this fusion was that Septimus no longer felt ever truly alone. It was not his great-aunt's thoughts that were creating this restless and, at times, claustrophobic feeling within him, although he was aware of them now and again. It was the feeling he got inside his own home... Of course he had been aware of it being an old medieval building, and a tavern at that, when he had first bought it. But that was before he had inherited this greater sensitivity. Now he realised just how congested and heavy an old building could become.

It was with this in mind that he had decided to go for a long walk and maybe see if he could track down Ocky. Septimus had not seen or heard from Ocky and Jewels since their last meeting -- not that there was anything rare in that. He just wanted to be sure everything was still going ahead as planned, especially now that he had already joined forces with his great-aunt. Of course this silence may have been due to the favourable tides enabling Pigeon a greater opportunity to go scavenging on the banks of the Thames with the rest of the mud-larks, or maybe Ocky and Jewels were doing their business underground. This last thought made him feel uneasy -- for all he knew, Ocky and Jewels could be down the tunnels right now, trying to steal his inheritance.

Pigeon had reluctantly given him Ocky's address a while back, but Septimus had always given the place a wide berth, as much to avoid the undoubtedly noisome surroundings as to avoid arousing any gossip of their collusion. He hoped he would not live to regret such a liaison, but at this present moment in time Septimus felt driven to seek out this raggedy dweller of the underworld.

Despite the comparable grandeur of Septimus' studio home, the air he breathed was just as rank and putrid as anywhere else in the East End of London. It was made even the more so when the fog descended low, as was the case this morning. Although it was midmorning, the gas lamps were still blazing away inside and outside the shop windows, sleepy beacons of commerce that refused to die in the twilight of the morning.

It was with a grim irony that Septimus' need for wide open spaces now led him to one of the most suffocating areas in the whole of London. It was an unfortunate reality that Septimus had to navigate his way through one of the capital's notorious rookeries to reach Ocky's lair. These rookeries, so called because of the sheer volume of dwellings all crammed together in noisy rickety nests, were a blemish on the face of many of the industrial towns, but especially that of London. Most of these tenement slums were built between the late 17th and 18th centuries when London was expanding at an alarming rate -- far too quickly indeed for its own good.

The sanitation within these places was abysmal. Many had no piped water, and some even shared their dwellings with donkeys, goats, and pigs.

The dense golden fog gave every road, every lane, anonymity it had no right to have. Every step was the same as the last, although no building looked exactly the same – disrepair, it seemed, was always erratic and unpredictable. Raggedly-clad children played amongst the discarded washboards, rotted vegetable peelings, and human waste all around... some of it living, some of it not. Such was the squalor and poverty of the rookeries that few people walked through them out of choice -- even the street-cleaning scavengers often shied away whenever they could.

The haze did nothing to subdue the oppressive nature of this place: with every passing stranger the foreboding just grew and grew. Septimus tightened his grip on his swordstick at every clatter and cry; every new footstep a threat. His ears were pricked back and he primed himself for any sudden movements in his direction. He knew that within the blink of an eye or a flash of a blade his life could be undone. One strike and he would be no more than a scarlet stain on a broken pavement. A sense of doubt about his precise location crept in -- although every house and tenement looked different from the last, they wore the same bleak, malodorous uniform of ruination.

It was then with some relief that Septimus espied a butcher shop in the distance and what looked like a couple of barrow boys outside it. The abrasive sounds of the domestic chaos contained inside the rookery was at last being exchanged for the reassuring din of low commerce. And it was not only the sounds that were changing -- as he approached what appeared to be a crossroads, Septimus could feel the sullen, cloying stench of the rookery rapidly losing its grasp. An avenue of shops opened up before him as the last hanging breath of the maudlin mist fell prey to an almighty gust of wind, sending it silently skyward.

After some initial apprehension, Septimus was gratified to know that, despite the intrusion of the fog, he was heading in the right direction. He had just passed the notorious Green Man Inn, made infamous in days of yore for bawdy ballad singers and riotous goings-on. It was like the whole area had seen better days, but at least he was out of the warren and was now surrounded by cabs and carts and people walking with a purpose, a direction.

After a brief but heartening liaison with a main street, Septimus knew he would temporarily have to go down the less- salubrious thoroughfares once more to reach Ocky's lair. Thankfully, this time the buildings were not so close-knit and the streets were wider and largely free from detritus, human or otherwise.

The putrid fog that had accompanied him virtually all the way had thankfully almost disappeared at ground level, though it still held a tenacious veil over the low-lying winter sun.

In spite of this somewhat sombre embrace, Septimus could actually see colours again, even if they were expressed by the weeds growing defiantly out of the joints in the brickwork and stone. These seeds had been sown partly by the wind and partly by the scavenging birds of the city. These ever-present creatures were everywhere, hiding out amongst the chimney pots and lofty butterfly bushes of old London town -- feral, feathered gargoyles waiting, watching, and shitting their brilliant white deposits on leaden shades of slate and stone.

Upon reaching Ocky's dwelling, Septimus took a step up off the pavement, stopped, and took a long and hard look at the old, dilapidated tenement that was 37 Persephone Place. Just to the right of the double doors in front of him were two poorly painted and sun- blistered signs. One said 37B, the other 37C. Septimus knew that Ocky lived at 37A. He could not see a sign or a number showing that address anywhere. He took a backwards step onto the pavement again and saw that the house next door was number 38, so 37A must be here somewhere ....

Septimus noticed some well-worn steps to the basement, which he just assumed to be the lower level of number 38B. As it turned out, he was right in his assumption, though once below he saw that there was a wooden hatch just to one side of the lower entrance. This door was only a couple of inches proud of the concrete floor. On the wooden hatch there was a rusty metal plate with a barely visible number 37A painted on it. The hatch, or door, as it were, resembled more an entrance to a pub cellar than to a room of human habitation, but, Septimus mused, this was the home of a tosher, after all.

Septimus decided to give the door a couple of thumps with his cane. He paused, and waited for a reply. There wasn't any. This time he decided to beat it a little harder and shout: "Mr Blackwood, are you at home?" Still nothing stirred.

Then a muffled voice from below said, "Who wants him?"

"It's me, Septimus," Septimus said as loudly as he dared.

"What the devil are you doing here?" Ocky replied indignantly.

"I want to speak with you, and I would rather I speak with you below than out here with all and sundry."

The trap door opened. Septimus climbed down the steps into Ocky's subterranean abode. "You're too early for dinner and too late for breakfast, if that's what you're after," said an aggravated Ocky.

"Well, I can live with that," said Septimus wryly, "though I could use a cup of tea."

"Guess that would not be the reason that you are honouring me with you presence your Lordship?"

Septimus was relieved to find Ocky in at least, even though he was well out of his comfort zone -- this was Ocky's den, not his.

"You better take a seat then now you are here. Did you walk or come by carriage?"

"I decided to walk; it's good for my constitution," said Septimus, looking for the cleanest seat.

"Constitution, eh, through the rookery? You are certainly full of surprises Septimus. Well come on then, be seated. Seeing as you have made it your business to come to my home, least you can do is grace one of my chairs," he said sarcastically.

"So what brought you out all this way Septimus?" Ocky said enquiringly.

"As I said, I needed a walk, and as I was in your neck of the woods I decided I would take the opportunity to drop in and discuss the arrangements for our next excursion below." Septimus shifted in his chair, still feeling ill at ease. The chair creaked indignantly. "I have not seen Pigeon for quite a few days, so I thought I would pay you a visit and ask you if there was any further news on our venture."

"Well there ain't been any additional plans really. Providing it don't rain, it is still to be Wednesday. Pigeon and a few others have been busy on the beaches, looking out for what they can find. Me and Jewels seen him there the other day. A couple of boats collided in the fog and one of them went under. Big clipper, it was. Bound to be something floating about or washed up somewhere; usually is."

It was as Ocky stood up to poke the unobliging fire that Septimus became awash with a sense of déjà vu. The reluctant flames sprung back to life and lit up Ocky's distinctive profile. Somehow though, it was not Ocky he was thinking about. Septimus had recognised a face from many, many years previously -- so long ago he could not give it a name or situation, but wherever and whoever it was, he found it reluctantly moving.

"What time on Wednesday suits you then?" asked Septimus, still desperately trying to remember where he had seen that face before.

"We'll meet up Wednesday morning at six. We should have a bit more time than on our last venture; it's one of the lowest tides of the year. We are all sorted. Hopefully we can get past that door -- Mortlake's a dab hand with locks, so I heard," Ocky said with a smile. It was news to Septimus, but it was not a surprise. It felt best just to nod in reply and not get involved in any of Ocky's mind-games.

"If that don't work, which it may not coz of the damp swelling the door an' all, we'll take some jemmies along and prise the bugger open."

"I am glad you have given the matter some thought," said Septimus.

"Ah, I give everything thought Septimus, indeed I do," replied Ocky knowingly.

It had taken Septimus a while, but the heady combination of a warm fire and sweet tea had relieved Septimus of some of his earlier misgivings about this visit -- so much so that he felt relaxed enough to allow his eyes to freely survey the room and take in its squalid delights.

He could not help but notice the sheer volume of tea crates stacked up around the room, many stacks three to four boxes high. "I see you drink a lot of tea, my friend," Septimus said wryly.

"Aw, well, we all have our little collections Septimus, don't we now? The tea has long since been drunk -- in there lays my collection -- call it my mementos if you like. You have your photos of where you have been, I have my little keepsakes," Ocky said proudly whilst cleaning out his clay pipe with a pocket knife.

"From your subterranean safaris, no doubt?" Septimus enquired.

"Aye, that's one way of putting it," proclaimed Ocky as he lifted the lid off one of the boxes. He picked up an object from within the box, and gingerly removed the protective rags that encased it.

Pulling up his stool, he moved to where Septimus was sitting. "This is my memento from the fox hole. Do you like it?" asked Ocky, holding the bracelet close to one of the many tallow dips in his room. Tallow dips were simply a length of burning cloth housed in a bowl of tallow grease or fat. They were much used by the poor. Septimus was amazed by the bracelet's quality and just gazed in wonder.

"Is it of Celtic origin?" Septimus enquired.

"Tshhh no. It's Saxon, possibly Jute. The Saxons were very fond of their garnets. It's largely made of copper but the edging around the wolves and the red jewels there is all gold." The bracelet was about three inches in width and slightly bent, but it was still awe-inspiring.

"There were a few other small trinkets close to where I found it to verify its authenticity. They were also Saxon or Jute, but not as attractive as this piece, though," Ocky said proudly.

Septimus cleared his throat before asking, "Have you any idea of its value?"

Ocky pursed his lips a little before replying, "It is worth what any man is prepared to pay for it, I suppose, though I was offered a handsome sum for it by a dealer a year or so ago. Don't think I'd be sharing such a sight with you if you were not already a rich man, do ya?"

"I appreciate your trust," Septimus replied with mock courtesy.

"I would not go that far Septimus, but at least that makes us even, I reckon. Besides, it ain't very often I get such a distinguished guest as yourself who appreciates such finery as this," Ocky said with feigned meekness.

"Dare I ask how many more trophies you have stored away?"

Ocky grinned his serpent grin. "One or two," he replied. "I know each and every one of them intimately -- where they were found, their provenance so to speak, and, for the most part, which period of time they belonged to -- if one can ever truly say that anything ever belonged to any particular period of time, that is."

Septimus had never had any doubt about this man's intelligence, but it bothered him no end not knowing where it had come from.

"It's an interesting point you make, though I suppose all that matters now is that it belongs to you," Septimus replied pragmatically and offered a brief smile. He held out his hand, hoping to entice Ocky into passing him the object. The hand gesture distracted Ocky's gaze away from the bracelet. He looked at Septimus, raised an eye, and passed the bracelet to him.

"Exquisite, ain't she? Such precision -- masters of their art, the old Saxons."

Septimus' mind was still working overtime, desperately trying to recollect on whom and where he had seen Ocky's profile before. Upon receiving the bracelet, Septimus started to hear voices conversing inside his head. The language sounded harsh and guttural. He could not make out that many words, but he could understand that the male was either scolding the younger female, or giving her instructions and imploring her not to forget.

Distant images and scents now started to occupy the intrusive conversation within Septimus' mind. A young woman with unkempt, braided hair, dressed all in green, was talking to a broad-shouldered man with a blackened face and wild, sweat-stained ginger hair. Above the voices there was another sound. A hammering noise? Metal on metal -- the noise of hammer on anvil.

219

Sparks were flying about everywhere. One soared though the air, and Septimus jerked back his left arm in anticipation of it hitting him.

"What's up with you? You been stung or something?" enquired Ocky. The sound of Ocky's gruff voice sounded far away. "Oi you!" Ocky's voice cut through the vision, banishing all of the other sights and sounds away. As Septimus' senses returned to the present, he realised he was still looking closely at the bracelet. "You ain't having a fit, are you? You're no good to man nor beast down in the sewers if you're a tongue-swallower."

Septimus sighed loudly, shook his head and replied, "It was not a fit, sir, just a shooting pain running up my arm, that's all. Arthritis, I'd expect."

Ocky was not convinced, but let it pass -- it was his life after all. Septimus knew it sounded unconvincing but it was all he could manage, given his state of mind. Septimus now wondered if his newly-acquired, heightened sense of awareness of history had found another conduit in the sense of touch too, for the visions had begun as soon as he had first laid hands on the bracelet. If this were the case, he was obviously going to have his work cut out to control it.

As soon as Septimus gave the bracelet back to Ocky, the whispers stopped. Maybe, Septimus thought, it was not me after all? Maybe this object was in some way enchanted? A catalyst to another era? And Ocky knew all along -- perhaps that is why he chose that particular piece to give to me? To test me out?

Whatever the case may be, Septimus was now bristling with sensory perceptions of all kinds, and was sailing down the vast, unchartered waters of his psyche.

Septimus became aware of the yawning pause in conversation and how the room had become heavy with the burden of unasked questions. "May I enquire as to how long you have lived here?" Septimus dug deep for a sense of the trivial.

Ocky's answer was mercifully swift. "I have been here for just over four years. Before that I moved around a lot. This is the first time I have felt at home somewhere since ..." Ocky's face dropped a little and he turned away momentarily before continuing "...for quite some time." Septimus could tell that whatever Ocky was going to say, but didn't, was regarding a pivotal moment in his life

-- one he either did not wish to dwell on or that he did not see as fodder for conversation.

"My father was a captain of a ship and a merchant too. Never saw him much, but he was a fine man. I can recall him sitting down around the old pine table, playing cards with me mum, sister, and me. He could never sit still -- he was always out making deals when he was not at sea.

"We always knew when he was about to go on his travels again, as the house would start filling up with books for his journey."

"Dare I ask what became of him?" Septimus asked.

"He died. Supposedly an accident on the Thames -- one of the chains snapped on a crane hauling in some bales of cloth. Crushed, so they say. I was only a young'un at the time."

Why did that story sound so familiar? Septimus wondered. He was sure he knew a lot more details about it -- even more than Ocky. "Must have been difficult times for your family?" Septimus surprised himself by asking such a question.

"Blimey, what are you? A copper or summat, all these questions?" Septimus made out to speak, but before he could form his words properly, Ocky continued: "Yes, I s'pose it was. I didn't really think of it at the time. We certainly got to know who our friends really were. All the family pulled together for a while. There was me sis and mum, and one of my grannies was still alive at the time, and she helped a lot. Well, we called her 'Granny' -- truth be told she weren't really blood. My old man was adopted, see. Oh, and there was this old aunt who popped around, a well-heeled, morose sort of woman. I can remember her from way back, though she never ever stopped for long -- just one cup of tea, and then gone. Lord knows where in the family she came from."

"Sounds like you had a house full of women then," said Septimus.

"You're not kidding. I spent most of my time out and about with Tommy Tug. He was a mate of my old man's, and one of his crew. There was not a man in the whole of London who knew the waterways of London better than he did. I suppose you could say he took me under his wing a bit. Some say he was responsible for my father's death, though I never believed it. He showed me all the boats, all of the docks and wharves -- he loved it all. Maybe it was through him I got my love of exploring. Maybe he thought I would somehow carry on in my old man's footsteps or something."

"You chose not to, then?" replied a curious Septimus.

"Well I think maybe life chose it for me... Never liked the idea of working for another, for one thing. There's far too much in this world to find and see to get anchored down somewhere. I used to do a bit of sifting on the shore. That's when I met Jewels. He always was an ugly fucker, even then. We were always running off and ferreting out new places -- forgotten places, hidden places, places where we could do what we liked."

"So a tosher was born," Septimus said wryly.

"If you like. When Mum died, that was it, I was gone. Others had other plans for me, but as far as I was concerned, that was it -- it was my life, I was gone.

"I knew I could survive on my own, see? Didn't need 'em by that time. Me and Jewels started exploring the old tunnels. We could get into places no one else could or even dared to. It was there that we started to find bits of treasure. Of course, Jewels was all for selling everything we found, but not me -- I sell what I need to live on, but if I see something unusual, old, or beautiful, it becomes my treasure, see?"

"Thank you for your candor sir. It is a rare man who is content with his lot," proclaimed Septimus.

"I certainly need no sympathy. I'm a free man and there is precious few who can say that," Ocky replied contentedly.

"Indeed, there was no slight intended. I comprehend you very well," Septimus said calmly.

"Good, because, apart from being one of the aristocracy, there ain't anybody else I want to be. All the rest of 'em are somebody's lackey, and that ain't for me. Anyway, I am sure you have better things to do than sit about here?" said Ocky gruffly, slightly annoyed for giving too much of himself away. It was obviously a cue for Septimus to go.

"I would not put it quite that way, sir, but I shall detain you no longer," Septimus replied matter-of-factly. He had reluctantly felt a strange kind of empathy with Ocky and had surprised himself by being interested in his story, so much so that he had quite forgotten the long walk home and the disturbing incident with the bracelet.

"So I will bid you a good day and see you next week," Septimus said, reaching for his coat.

"Aye, all being well," Ocky replied absent-mindedly as he thrust the grubby poker into the unwilling flames once again. "Shut the hatch on your way out, won't you? Oh, and mind your constitution down them alleyways," exclaimed Ocky, who had obviously reverted back to his confrontational self again.

"You have my word on it," said Septimus, who was already halfway out of the wooden hatch by this time.

Despite the oppressive surroundings of Ocky's hovel, Septimus felt it had been time well spent. He could see that Ocky was not a man motivated by greed alone, which was reassuring in some respects, but not in others. It meant that there was less of a chance that Ocky would organize a search party of his own and plunder the cellars before their proposed venture next week. Juxtaposed to this, though, it also meant that Ocky could not easily be bought, if at all.

Indeed, the man could stop his filthy and dangerous trade tomorrow if he had more items like that bracelet. That alone would fetch a tidy sum at an auction -- there were plenty of collectors of antiquities who would love to acquire such an item. Indeed, even the British Museum would be interested in such a find. Maybe Ocky was saving them all for his retirement. If he lasted that long, that was. Toshing was a very dangerous trade, and certainly not one for the old and infirm.

It was then that Septimus' mind wandered back to what he had seen and heard when he had handled the bracelet. How on earth was it possible for it to take him to another time, if that's what had occurred? On reflection, Ocky had not behaved as a man might have when giving another man a test. Septimus was intrigued as to what the other boxes within Ocky's cavernous lair may contain.

It had seemed inconceivable to Septimus before visiting Ocky's home that anyone could have enjoyed earning a living in that way, but since the meeting, and despite himself, Septimus now believed it possible.

Septimus was so preoccupied with these thoughts that it was not until he had passed the Green Man Inn that his lack of appetite for traversing the abyss of the rookery emerged again. He felt obliged to do the unthinkable -- to get himself a cab. How he hated public transport. It was not the carriages themselves he hated – indeed, he liked few things more than to spy on the city from the comfort of one of his own carriages -- it was the thought of having a driver that was not his own. That and the fact that these cabs were always involved in accidents due to their wheels breaking or coming off and horses bolting. His fears were only eclipsed by his reluctance to endure the sense of foreboding that had so consumed his journey earlier in the day. It was with this in mind that he hailed the first cab he saw, despite its somewhat battered appearance and the horse that looked only a hoof-beat away from the glue factory.

Chapter 36

John's Plan

Whilst looking through the list of appointments at the studio, John had been pleased to see a reminder written at the top of next Wednesday's page saying *"Out all day, tell John I need him."* What's more, there was only one appointment made for that particular day – a Miss Appleby; which meant he could have the whole studio to himself for the rest of the day. John took little interest in Septimus' pursuits outside of the studio, though he was curious as to why he was mixing with some very unlikely characters at the Angel Vaults recently.

Septimus was not the only person to see possibilities in this new way of producing multiple photographic prints onto small cards. For John, it may be the gateway he needed to be out of Septimus' thrall forever. John had slowly and surreptitiously built up a small and growing clientele of his own. He had trusted his more base instincts and knew there was going to be a wide market for so-called exotic images. And his shop gave him the perfect foil to distribute these images.

Septimus' studio was by far the best location, with its vast array of backcloths and outfits and the superb quality of the cameras and the processing area.

John tried to put members of the public off making bookings for when Septimus was away, and then he would fill in the gaps, taking photos of the girls who had come into the studio posing as potential customers wanting to see the studio before making a booking. He knew, however, that he could not do this too often, as that cursed Angharad would surely start to smell a rat and tell Septimus.

With this in mind, John was careful not to spoil a good thing and ended up taking some photo-shoots at the Mermaid, though Dame Doxy was very keen to disguise her interiors as best as she could. John also did the occasional photo-shoot inside various other hotel and lodging-house rooms across the East End. He had found it difficult to find muses for his new idea until he enlisted the help of

Rosie Richards, erstwhile Dame Dolly Doxy. Dame Dolly was the proprietor of the Mermaid Hotel, and also a brothel keeper. But she was not only this -- she was also a keen and successful businesswoman. Unlike many madams, she looked after her girls. She made sure that they were well-clothed and well- fed -- hers was certainly not any ordinary knocking shop. Of course, this expression of tender loving care was not implemented purely on philanthropic grounds alone -- it was good practice if she wanted to attract good, clean, wealthy customers to her premises.

She seemed to relish her "mother to all" pedestal that she had made for herself. She swore she had heard more confessions than the local priest (and that was saying something, given the sheer volume of Irish Catholics in the East End at this time). It never ceased to surprise her: not only the amount of secrets people wanted to share with her but the variety of the content. Indeed, only last week one elderly gentleman had shared how he still felt guilty about how he had ruined a work of art painted by his governess when he was a child.

The painting had been placed on the top shelf of his father's study and his eyes had been drawn to its bright and vivacious strokes. Needless to say, the painting had been placed up high, seemingly out of harm's way, to dry. Evidently, it was not placed high enough to deter the curious boy who wanted a closer look. The boy had not confessed to his sin at the time, and so the blame was firmly placed on one of the young servants within the household.

Quite why that still bothered him today was a mystery, but none of Rosie's concern. Indeed, it was probably her willingness to act as a receptacle to such outpourings and her refusal to judge a person because of them that she found herself in this position anyway. Whatever the reasons behind it, she took great pride in the role. It was to this end that she had unwittingly become a pillar of the community.

Much to the chagrin of others, her newly found sense of pride and status filtered all the way down to her delicately perfumed hair, the cut of her clothes, even the way she walked.

Despite her swank, most of her clientele entered the Mermaid Hotel under the cloak of darkness. It was no coincidence that none of the street lights ever worked in front of the Mermaid. The parish council had repeatedly tried to fix the street lighting around the hotel, but for some inexplicable reason they kept malfunctioning, or in some cases disappearing completely.

Rosie Richards' clientele was not only wealthy; some had knowledge and influence in high places. It was thanks to information passed on by these people that Rosie was always one step ahead of the authorities. Despite highly publicised clean-up campaigns, organized by the self-styled moral majority, Rosie always came up on top, and this was the way she intended to stay.

So it was with deep reservations that she first viewed John the Chemist's idea of producing some exotic likenesses of some of her girls. Firstly, she was not sure she wanted direct evidence of her girls being anything other than residents, helping in the running of her hotel.

Secondly, she had heard tell that he could be boorish and unruly at times, though she herself had never borne witness to such behaviour. So it was after a great deal of reflection that she agreed to go along with John's idea, on her terms.

Her terms were that the girls would be paid individually for each shot, and that Rosie would have a share of the profits for every photograph sold. Each set of prints were to be limited editions -- she would always be told how many were to be processed, and each individual print would have a number. None of the photographs would have any other mark on them other than a number, and most certainly nothing linking them to the Mermaid Hotel.

On no account would any of the girls ever be asked or allowed to have likenesses taken of them without her consent, or without her being present at the photographic session. This latter condition was made primarily for the wellbeing of the girls, rather than down to any mistrust of her girls.

John reluctantly agreed to Rosie's conditions. He knew that, despite all of these restrictions, he would still make a pretty penny under the counter, and be able to sate his appetite for young ladies, albeit at a distance.

It had not taken Rosie long to recognize the potential of these exotic prints either. Despite the disapproval of the moral majority, Rosie was quite a celebrity in the theatre-going community of London. Not only did she revel in the attention given to her, but these were also fertile pastures for finding wealthy clients. She made sure to always have a selection of likenesses and Mermaid Hotel business cards on her person on any one occasion, making very sure that the likenesses of the girls on these cards had not been taken in the actual Mermaid Hotel.

Not only was theatre the best place for her to find new girls looking for work, but also for them to find her. There was no shortage of struggling young actresses and models who would, on occasion, loosen their morals in the right circumstances. These girls were mainly motivated by hunger or the need for a bed for the night, though there were the odd one or two who thought that they could make such an impression that they could improve their lot, either career wise or domestically. Unfortunately, they were often disappointed.

Though on the whole Rosie liked to keep most of her business inside the house to keep it clean and tidy, of course that did not stop her from making the occasional initial arrangement between some of the more high-class street girls and their prospective clients.

There was one peculiarity that had arisen out of this new venture that had surprised Rosie, which was some of the girls' reluctance to be photographed in the nude. Maybe it was that each sexual act had an end to it, unlike the photograph, which could potentially last a lifetime. Whatever the reasoning behind it, Rosie dealt with it compassionately, even though she could never really make sense of it.

Despite all of Rosie's discretion as to who could see the prints and where they would be distributed, John, on the other hand, had no such aspirations. He had never lost his desire to surprise and shock unsuspecting passersby. He delighted in leaving the odd naughtiest shots of all in the most inappropriate of places -- places such as temperance halls and church notice boards.

Another bonus for John was that, although many of the people came to John's Chemist Shop specifically to purchase one or more of these pictures, they often felt duty-bound to buy something else as well, presumably to make it feel like purchasing the photo was just an aside, a by the by to their real reason for entering, which was obviously to buy a packet of throat lozenges.

John had never used any of Septimus' special cameras or fixing formulas for any of the exotic shots. Simply, it was not yet possible to do multiple photographs with these cameras; though even if it were, he was far too lazy to go to all that extra fuss in the processing. Although John had originally shared some of Septimus' curiosity for making living photographs, and was intrigued by Dr Zehariah's cameras, to him it was an interesting experiment and nothing more.

Why bother with that when he could have much more fun taking exotic photographs and making easy money? It was due to the ease and speed with which this new project was making money that he had for the first time in years seen a new beginning, one without Septimus. His plan was to make as much money as possible then move lock, stock, and barrel to the coast.

He would find a place far away -- far from the clutches of Septimus, or anybody else he and his deeds still lingered on in. He could open up a new shop and live out his final years, trying out new potions and working on his beloved contraptions. There would be money, too, for a photographer by the seaside; the rapidly increasing rail network would see to that. There would be young ladies too...

Although Septimus had gained a great deal of satisfaction and pleasure from his collection of living photographs, there was, he felt, something amiss. He had learnt that self-congratulation can only sustain you for so long; eventually you need to reveal, to impress, and gain some sort of recognition for your achievements. It irked him a little that he felt this way, but he did; perhaps it was the impending and potentially hazardous journey deep into the bowels of London that provoked him so. God forbid that if he should die down there, the only person to have known his achievement would be John Amblewick.

It was with this in mind that Septimus had decided the time was right to share his wonderful new collection with a select group of acquaintances. He knew that the moon was at its fullest and he had satisfied himself that, in most cases, his glorious collection burst into life late at night, under the gaze of the full moon.

Professor Savage was first on the list and first to arrive. Septimus knew he could trust him with almost everything; Septimus' endorsement of his skills as a taxidermist and their shared achievements secured Walter's friendship and his tongue. Septimus welcomed the first of his guests in from the cold. "Walter, I am so glad you could make it at this ungodly hour. I trust the journey was none too troublesome; it's a devil of a night out there."

"All quiet, thankfully. Awful night, though; could do with a swift brandy Septimus old boy," said Walter Savage, whilst removing his hat and cloak.

"Angharad, a brandy for the Professor here."

Angharad took the cloak from Professor Savage and made off to get some brandy. "Thank you Angharad," Walter replied courteously.

"So what is this little show you have planned then? You kept it all very quiet I must say," Walter asked curiously.

"All shall be revealed soon," Septimus replied with a twitch of a smile.

The brandy arrived post haste.

"Thank you Angharad. Do help yourself Walter; that's the least I can offer on a night like this."

There was a loud rap at the door. "Ahhh, Sir Edward, good to see you. I've booked you a room at the Bear Hotel. I hear the lodgings are very good, as is the breakfast. I will get Marmaduke to take your luggage straight there."

"Good man Septimus. I must say this is a most irregular hour for a supper. It must be at least two years now; how have you been? Never expected to see you in the East End, but knowing you, you will have very good reason for it."

"I do indeed," Septimus retorted with no elaboration. "Sir Edward Nightingale, this is my friend and arguably the best taxidermist in England, Professor Walter Savage. Walter, this is Sir Edward, antiquarian, occultist, and historian." The two men shook hands warmly but cautiously; neither had expected company.

"How many guests are you expecting Septimus?" Walter asked.

"Just one more, but, please gentlemen, go through to the dining room. I appreciate ten-thirty is a late hour for supper, but your smoked salmon awaits, as does Angharad's cawl. You will not find a better cawl this side of the River Severn.

"Cawl?" Edward enquired curiously.

230

"Cawl is a Welsh broth, usually containing beef or salted bacon, swede, carrots, and potatoes; just the thing for a night such as this."

After the meal, the three men went up to the great glass studio on the top floor. "Now Walter, I know you have been a few times before, so please take a seat, but Sir Edward, do feel free to have a walk around. A large proportion of the creatures here on display are the product of Professor Savage's handiwork. "

"I congratulate you on your handiwork Professor Savage, fine specimens indeed. I have a pair of falcons back home in Somerset. I will let you know when they pass over -- surprising how one gets attached to such things," Sir Edward boomed from the other side of the room.

Septimus had always thought it quite remarkable how someone as diminutive as Edward Nightingale could command such a powerful voice and presence.

Before Walter Savage could reply, the landing door swung open and in walked Septimus' third and final guest. Septimus rose from his chair and said "Dionysus ... I had quite given up on you. I should have known you of all people would be fashionably late."

"I was coerced into amputating some poor wretch's leg this afternoon. She was fixing one of those weaving machines and slipped and fell into the works. That's not the worst of it; she kept waking up all the way through the operation. She must have got through a full bottle of gin by the end of it. It's a shame those weaving girls don't have as much tolerance for pain as they do for gin," Dionysus declared jovially.

"Sir Edward, Walter, let me introduce you to Dionysus MacKay, surgeon and ... and free-thinker. Dionysus let me introduce to my friends Sir Edward Nightingale, historian, and Walter Savage, taxidermist extraordinaire."

"Glad to make your acquaintance, gentlemen," Dionysus said.

Dionysus had long been a puzzle to Septimus; he both intrigued and repulsed Septimus in equal shares. He was undoubtedly a brilliant anatomist: his thoughts and experiments in the field both fascinated and horrified the Royal College of Surgeons, of which he was a notable member. Dionysus could be incredibly compassionate and kind one day, yet callous and cruel the next. He could have been quite the dandy if it was not for his bow legs, sharp, slightly-upturned nose, and questionable personal hygiene. He was prone to fits of frightful melancholia, which were often superseded by bouts of drunken revelry. Septimus knew the man was impervious to scandal; it was all water off a duck's back to Dionysus. However, what he could not brush aside was the fact he had drunkenly confided in Septimus about a very serious matter. He had confessed to Septimus that he was the lover of Lady Dorton; not only her lover, but he had fathered her second son, Alexander. Lord Dorton was an immensely rich and powerful man of ill temperament. Dionysus was all too aware that if Lord Dorton should find out about the affair, not only would his life be in danger but also that of his lover, Lady Dorton. The knowledge of this meant that Dionysus was very much Septimus' man and he could be relied upon to remain silent about tonight's proceedings.

"I am sorry you missed supper Dionysus. If you are hungry I can get Angharad to bring something up for you."

Dionysus helped himself to a large brandy, pulled up a chair, and said, "Thank you Septimus but I am fine, thank you. I knew I was going to be late so I indulged in some pea soup on the way."

Septimus was relieved to know that the provenance of the olive green splashes on Dionysus lower trousers, of which he had just espied, were of leguminous origin.

The same could not be said about the small flakes of sawdust and wood shavings clinging to Dionysus' overly large black shoes, which were evidently leftovers from this afternoon's operation, judging by the flecks of blood contained therein. Repugnant though it was, he was determined not to be distracted from the real reason of tonight's soiree. He swept back his oiled hair and stood up abruptly.

"Gentlemen, thank you for the pleasure of your company. All of us present have sought to keep our fingers, as it were, on the pulse of innovation and exploration, in our own fields and those of the wider world. As far as progress is concerned, nothing can compete with the two greatest tools in our armoury: those of experimentation and imagination. Indeed, it was with this in mind that I endeavoured to achieve something truly momentous within the realms of photography, though outside the realms of accepted scientific thought. I have not invited you here tonight to give you a detailed explanation as to how I have achieved what I have. Moreover, neither have I gathered you here to debate its impact on scientific community or its consequences to the world at large. No gentlemen, my reason for sharing this with you tonight is to inspire and entertain you in equal measures."

Septimus invited them to pull their chairs closer to where he was standing. Behind him was a very large table with some soft sheeting over its top. Gently, Septimus pulled off the sheeting and lit two oil lamps, which had been underneath the cloths. The table top was full of metal, glass, and people. "These, my learned friends, are my little masterpieces," Septimus proclaimed proudly.

"You have certainly attained a huge menagerie of human forms here, really quite exquisite collection. Were it anyone other than you, I would call it a magical collection of likenesses, but I suspect there is more to it than that," exclaimed Sir Edward.

"As ever, your intuition serves you well Sir Edward. There is more to come, one just has to remain patient for just a little while longer," Septimus said reassuringly.

Septimus knew that Sir Edward Nightingale or, "Nightshade," as he was known to his peers, was one of Britain's best known antiquarians, who specialised in excavating and mapping ancient sacred sites up and down the country. What was less well known about Sir Edward was his involvement in a secretive and nefarious group of occultists operating in London.

Sir Edward knew that Septimus (by hook or by crook) had got wind of his involvement in the group, and suspected that was one of the reasons he had been one of the trusted few here tonight.

The blackness of the night sky was broken up by swathes of rain smattering and stippling aggressively at the enormous glass panels. An infernal gust of wind sent a sheet of rain lashing into the side of the great glass studio, causing all of the lamps in the room to shudder wildly. The vast panes of glass should have given a feeling of safe harbour for all those contained within their insentient grasp, but this was far from the case. A feeling of unease crept into the men, causing them to shift nervously in their seats. It seemed as though the whole room was in battle with itself. The dancing blades of light gave rise to grotesque silhouettes.

Septimus grasped the agitation of the others and said, "Gentlemen, please look deep within the photographs and tell me what you see." The men dragged their chairs closer still. Their glances flitted from picture to picture, fleetingly. Septimus' instruction gave them a brief respite from their discomfort, though it was not long before their unease dripped back into their consciousness. Observing the photographs should have given the men a welcome distraction from the tumultuous weather outside and baleful atmosphere within the room, but it did neither.

One by one their confidence and attention seemed to get swallowed up by unseen forces within the room. The flames within the lamps stopped moving from side to side; they shot up and down and spun around the glass in torment, as if they were being agonized by some external malevolence.

An infernal scream shot through the room, causing all to rock back in their seats. For a brief moment the blaze from the lamps was stretched almost to the point of darkness. "Saints preserve us Septimus. I've never heard wind screech like that before," Dionysus said in awe. "Sounds like a harpy's lament to me."

"I cannot say I have been privy to such an event, though, yes, sometimes it can get quite …."

Septimus' reply was cut short by Sir Edward uttering, "My God Septimus. Look at that; it cannot be!" The rain storm had begun to ease, restoring a degree of serenity to the oil lamps, which in turn had provided enough stable light for the gentlemen … light to view the photographs properly. Edward pointed to the photograph of the Sagar the Skin-Stretcher. He noticed that the photograph, along with a few of the others, was just a little blurred, though all of a sudden the figure within it started to move. At first there was a faint misting around the mouth then slight movement of the head. The body twitched as spasmodically as if it were besieged by a mild epileptic seizure.

Movement in this photograph was followed by another, then another.

"Gentlemen, may I present my collection of living photographs," Septimus announced proudly.

Dionysus stared in fascination at a photograph of a beautiful young lady surrounded by vast jars. "This one is simply divine Septimus. Just look at that body, so supple, and not an inch of fat on her, not at all like that wench I operated on earlier."

234

"Ah, yes, I thought that one may interest you Dionysus. Yes, quite a catch… one of the circus folk," declared Septimus.

"Almost worth investing in a big top. Just look at those thighs," Dionysus continued.

It was a cold night in St Giles, near Oxford. Mr Litvinenko's circus had joined the fun fair a day before last. The full moon had at last dazzled its way through stubborn clouds of rain. Susanna, the circus' Snake Girl, had gone through her stretches, and ventured to her bed two or more hours ago. It could be said she was dead to the world, totally dreamless, until little by little she felt as though she was being forced back into one of the great jars of her act. Her limbs felt compressed, her breathing shallow. She could hear the sound of voices; they were deep, though despite being very close, she could not make out what they were saying. In front of her was searing golden light, making it impossible for her to open her eyes fully. Though what she did see was totally terrifying … an enormous, grotesque face peering in at her: eyes aflame, glistening devilishly in the reflected light. Long spindly fingers were heading straight towards her, with nails sharp and uneven. His large mouth began to open; the lips were thin and merciless.

Dionysus grabbed hold of the framed photograph and turned it this way and that, marvelling at the creature contained inside the glass. He reached down and grabbed hold of a monocle from the inside of his jacket.

Susanna felt the need to vomit as she felt herself being thrown about, as if she was little more than a doll made of rags. Gradually her balance returned, though so, too, the menacing glare; this time even more dreadful. One of the monstrous leering eyes was swollen hideously. Despite the dreadful contrasts of light and the prevailing mist, she could clearly see each and every blood vessel in the vast and pallid orb.

Unlike the pawing Dionysus, Walter moved his chair back, stood up, and decided to absorb the full panorama of what lay before him. He likened it to a magnificent collection of butterflies; pinned, framed, and deliciously unique. Unlike the butterflies, though, these were wonderfully animated, a vibrant ensemble of dancing souls. His mind coiled in on itself, trying to fathom out the nature of these beings, if beings they were. They were much more than a trick of the light or the work of a master conjuror, were they not?

Septimus took great delight in observing the expressions upon the men's faces. Each and every one of them was in his thrall, totally mesmerised by his living photographs. Even if it was to be for a brief moment, all present lapsed back into the deepest, darkest recess of their collective unconscious, and believed in magic again. Septimus, the magician, had performed an inexplicable miracle; some outside of this room would undoubtedly call it the work of the devil, but everyone here present knew it was the work of Septimus.

The Snake Girl was not the only unfortunate in the travelling circus to experience a night of unbridled discomfort and terror. Sagar the Skin-Stretcher, the two dwarves, and a host of others writhed with morbid agitation. Dreams of asphyxiation and claustrophobia plagued, taunted, and disturbed.

"Care for a cigar gentlemen?"

"Aye," replied Walter. The other two nodded in agreement, still transfixed by what they were witnessing. Sir Edward pulled out a packet of Lucifer matches and lit his cigar, eyes still glued to the photograph before him. He tugged exuberantly, causing vast plumes of smoke to head skyward.

"Has anybody else seen these?" asked Sir Edward.

"No Sir Edward. My assistant John Amblewick, has witnessed one or two … happenings. Fortunately he is able to keep a secret. Other than that, nobody at all. I have no interest in bringing this into the public domain. Of course I may one day change my mind, but for the foreseeable future it is our little secret."

"Not even any of the people in the likenesses?" enquired a surprised Professor Savage.

"This is my collection Walter. Every sitter here either volunteered to have their likeness taken or was paid. It was not as if I dragged people off of the streets. I do not feel the slightest shred of obligation towards them whatsoever," replied Septimus coldly.

Professor Savage tugged at his silver streaked ginger moustache, weighing Septimus' response, before uttering, "I suppose you have a point. If folk got wind of these, the press would not give you moment's peace."

"Quite so Walter, and I might add that none of these people are friends of mine -- business and pleasure rarely mix well," replied Septimus, his voice softer than the response he gave to Walter's previous question.

"Do you think the people in the photographs are in anyway receptive to their environment? What I mean is do you think they are in any shape or form sentient?"

Dionysus held his cigar up really close to a photograph of a wide-eyed and filthy chimney sweep. "I think they could well be. Look at this!" Dionysus moved his cigar back and forth towards the likeness.

"It's only slight, but look at this chap's face. I swear I can see him wince as the cigar heat gets closer to the glass. Ha ha ha, what fun," Dionysus declared, whilst tossing his head back to remove his long lank black hair away from his vision.

"One can only imagine the long term implications of such a ... I know not whether to describe it as a discovery or an invention Septimus; what say you?" Sir Edward asked.

"Let us just say that ... I have crossed the threshold," Septimus replied enigmatically.

Chapter 37

The Final Descent

Septimus tried valiantly to keep his mind occupied in the days and nights leading up to his forthcoming expedition into the sewers. Mercifully for him, there were some periods of the day he could actually rid himself of the deep anxiety and dread he felt about a return journey down below. Unfortunately these were few and far between: even when he had managed to lose himself in the task of the day, back came the fear in the dead of night; wheedling its way into his dreams like a maggot through cheese.

It was during these bouts of insomnia around the time of the full moon he sought solace watching his collection of living photographs. Septimus would sit hour after hour, transfixed, watching the exhibits writhing and dancing for him under the glass. Sometimes he would hold a candle up to the glass, just as Dionysus had done with his cigar, to provoke and cajole. He loved to experiment with the photographs, arranging them into groups so they all peered in at one another.

Septimus was intrigued, but not overly concerned, with what consequences (if indeed there were any) his experiments were having on the people featured in the living photographs. Most of the action happened at night, causing Septimus to muse if it was because the sitter was relaxed or asleep.

One day Septimus would formulate a plan of enquiry, but for now he was quite content to increase his collection and sit back and admire his handiwork.

Every one of the photographs had, at some time or another, put on a show for him. All, that was, except one…the old lady who Pigeon had given the posy to…how could that be?

Septimus was glad he had shared unique collection of living photographs with the other gentlemen the other night. He was not immune to praise or recognition for that matter; though, despite his feeling of accomplishment, nothing could seem to free his mind from the grim realities he was soon to face again underground. He

238

and the others had ridden their luck last time; this time they may not be so lucky.

So it was after the last of these restless nights that Septimus heard Angharad tap lightly on his bedroom door. Minutes later Pigeon arrived, bright and breezy as ever. Not that Septimus had really needed the knock -- his sleep that night had been predictably fitful at best, and he had been awake for the last two hours at least.

Septimus told Angharad in advance that he would have a long day ahead of him, and to spare nothing at the table when making an early breakfast for him. Angharad had done him proud and, though food was the last thing on his mind, Septimus forced himself to eat what he could. The task of eating was made much worse by Pigeon's hungry eyes fixed on every mouthful he took.

"Angharad, put this boy out of his misery, will you? Feed him too."

"Right you are, sir. He looks like he's in need of a feed." Angharad smiled and gave Pigeon a wink.

"He's in need of something," Septimus replied stiffly.

Angharad had become accustomed to giving the boy a crafty crust or two whenever he knocked, so it was a joy to her that she could watch him sit down and enjoy a proper meal for a change.

Pigeon's eyes widened at the mountain of food in front of him and he made light work of devouring every last morsel. He even finished off what was left on Septimus' plate, which Angharad had taken to the kitchen and put to one side for him.

"There is no filling you up boy, is there?"

"No. Don't know what the matter with you old folk is, leaving food like that," Pigeon replied cheekily.

"Old folk, am I?" She made for Pigeon with her besom brush in mock attack.

"Didn't mean you, did I Miss."

"Be sure you didn't, my lad. I don't know what you're doing today, but take care. I need you to get rid of the scraps."

"I always do Miss. Besides, I have got a farthing on a game of skittles later against Paddy the Patch. It's like taking money from a baby, it is."

There was a distinct chill in the air as the unlikely duo entered the still-darkened streets on their way to meet the others. Septimus had got Pigeon to run over to the coach house and waken the still-slumbering Marmaduke. The gnawing cold brought on by Jack Frost did little to subdue the activity on the banks of the Thames, which seemed more urgent than ever -- no doubt in preparation for the exceptionally low tide expected later.

Pigeon chatted away regardless of the lack of response from either the broodingly-quiet Septimus or the granite-faced Marmaduke. He had so many things to say about each and every one of the docks in London -- about what was unloaded there and the characters that were embroiled within them. Septimus could not help but be envious of the boy's nonchalant regard for the potential dangers ahead of them and his encyclopaedic knowledge of riverside life. Septimus mused on the fact that it was only young Pigeon's gregariousness that would stop him ending up like Ocky; that and the imminent ruination of many of the old sewers and buried rivers by either the new underground railway or the Bazalgette's new, all singing, all dancing super sewer. What is more, Pigeon seemed to view this forthcoming venture below as just another daily escapade; nothing more, nothing less.

Septimus was not bestowed with such an outlook and every now and then a trickle of doubt cascaded into his confidence in the mission. His concern this time was not so much for his own safety, but rather in the thought of breaking down that door below and finding nothing behind it. There surely must be other old cellars and hidden passageways that spilled out into the ancient covered rivers and tunnels of old London town.

Septimus was relived to see Jewels and Ocky already waiting for him by the rickety old water pump in December Court. If ever there was a place well-named, it was this. It was largely a maudlin collection of bleak, crumbling tenements reminiscent of the ones Septimus had encountered on the way to Ocky's dwelling. They were leaden in hue and occupant alike.

Despite the fact that the sun had yet to rise, the whole area still felt shadow-laden. The buildings stood tall but not proud, like swollen, forgotten buboes left over from the time of plague and in need of a lance. Septimus wondered if the sun would ever dare enter such a melancholic place as this. His instincts told him that the sun did not belong here; it would be alien, foreign, and bereft of friends. There were two old men wrapped in a filthy blanket, fast asleep underneath a broken market barrow, patches of vomit and broken glass either side of them.

Septimus surmised that this court needed its own -- the forgotten, the derelict, the desperate. It needed its secrets too, so the voiceless, the nameless, and the mindless could all collude and conspire here together, and drink deep the draught of sweet forgetfulness. Such was the despair that oozed out from the walls of this wretched place. Ironically, it was the sight of a scowling Mortlake in the distance that seemed to lift the gloom. At last they were all here and ready for the off.

After a short briefing from Ocky, they made their way down to Gas Alley to where the manhole lay, pausing only once to pick up their staffs from where Jewels had bundled them up the night before. No matter how much Septimus thought he had become accustomed to the stench below, he still wanted to retch. Ocky led the way with his lantern burning brightly.

"Bloody stinks, this place does. Who would wanna work down here?" Pigeon exclaimed loudly.

"Only those with no noses boy," said Ocky dryly.

"You mean there are people with no noses? What do you call them then?" said asked Pigeon naively.

"Lucky," said Mortlake, ruining Ocky's punchline.

The stench and the intense feeling of claustrophobia often made the first ten minutes belowground the most difficult to endure. These were accompanied by a fear of the unknown and the unknowable, and it was these feelings that seemed not to abate, no matter how long you stayed below ground.

It is a strange truism that what you cannot see or touch holds more menace than what you can, and this was never more the case than when venturing into the vast underbelly of this great city.

Sounds born of the surface could be chaotic and abrasive, but they were usually pacified by the numbing hum of familiarity and form. Contrastingly, the noises spawned belowground seemed stifled and ill at ease with themselves. These base-born infants murmured and babbled inanely on their long, lonely journeys, seeking solace in echoes and anonymity.

Fortunately, the lack of rain and the outgoing tide meant that the filthy water slopping around the gangs' ankles was lower than it had been the last time. This meant that they could wade though inky slime quicker than before, despite the extra weight of the tools.

"I reckon if the Devil exists, this is where they'll find him, don't you?" Pigeon remarked to Mortlake.

"I reckons even the Devil would forsake this place boy. Too bloody cold," Mortlake grumbled. Mortlake was right too -- it was much colder than before, though this had not deterred the rats that were watching their every move.

"Shame the rats ain't forsakin' it too. Hundreds of the little bleeders, ain't there?" said Pigeon. Mortlake replied with a shrug of resignation. Septimus noticed how many smaller inlet tunnels fed this main sewer. Many of them were in poor repair and inaccessible to all, bar a small monkey, or possibly an agile child. Thank goodness they had Pigeon. The thought of what lay beyond each twist and turn of these neglected overflows had piqued Septimus' interest. Since his liaison with Ocky at Persephone Street, Septimus' enthusiasm for exploration and potential excavation of these stinking treasure troves had increased much further than he thought possible.

Despite his dread of confinement and utter hatred of filth, Septimus was now thinking the unthinkable -- that he may actually consider joining Ocky on one of his other escapades… Obviously not for petty, rag-tag, everyday stuff, but for historical artefacts and hidden places. Ocky had spoken to him about Roman rooms under the city, decorated with brightly covered mosaics, and of steps and passageways and forgotten basements.

Ocky's enthusiasm may have sprung forth out of necessity, but, against all the odds, it was infectious. When the time was agreeable to them both, he would talk to Ocky again about such places, but right now they had just arrived at the mysterious archway -- the very same entrance where they had heard the boat's seemingly supernatural shrieks last time.

This time the boat was completely silent -- eerily silent, as if it was conspiring. Septimus found himself being swallowed up by morbid fears, creeping over him like the hushed steps of a spider crawling about in the darkness of his mind. Now the boat did not want to be found -- it sought to trick them, to mislead and to muddle. Its abrasive cries should have acted as a lighthouse, something to reassure in the gloom, but no, now it wished to deceive and dissuade. If it were not for the carved archway, the boat may have won too. Septimus vowed that when he had finally finished here, he would destroy the wretched thing once and for all.

Undeterred by the lack of noise, the group trudged onwards, led by a strident Ocky. Upon reaching the old landing spot, there lay the boat, motionless, secret, and sedate. The lack of rain and low tide had subdued its melancholic motivations, and all, barring Septimus, were glad of it.

"Blimey, what a daft place to keep a boat. Take forever to get her out onto the water from here," said Pigeon.

Jewels replied, "Not if the tide were up. The water level rises high here boy, as high as your chest. Look at the tide stain on the tunnel wall."

The crusty tide line on the wall lay just above the wooden slated jetty. Jewels surmised that it was rare for the tide to completely swallow up this landing point: though decayed, the wooden planking and piles beneath were still fit for purpose. Pigeon stood aghast at the enormity of the height of this natural cave and how it contrasted with the tight, narrow tunnel that led to it. His head became full of notions of smugglers and pirates and excitement, and not until he looked at the wary faces of the men around him did he feel a slight twinge of anxiety.

The largely-silent men heaved themselves onto the jetty and peered in awe at this sunken neverland before them. Jewels just stared in open-mouthed wonder until he found words: "I had thought I had seen it all underground, but this place beggars belief. Just look at those carvings! I don't like it. I don't like it at all!"

"Well, Jewels, no one said this was going to be a pleasure outing, did they? Don't you bottle it now," said Ocky in a slightly mocking manner.

"Oh, I ain't gonna bottle it Ocky. I ain't going all of the way back down them tunnels on my own. But what a queer place, though. Maybe it's full of demons?"

Despite the cold, there were droplets of sweat coursing down Septimus' back. "The only demons down here are your fears, gentlemen. So fear not; we have made it here in one piece and we will make it back in one piece," uttered Septimus. He had had to dig very deep for such reassuring rhetoric, and he said it as much to himself as to the others.

Ever since he had climbed up on the jetty, he had been hearing the whispers again. Not the same ones as before in Ocky's place -- these were dimmer, but all around him. Any sounds below were difficult to ascertain either their province or their provenance, but these whispers were close, very close. Despite the fact that there was only Septimus and his companions here, the passageway felt full of life. The other odd thing about these whispers was that whatever language they were speaking in, it was certainly not English. In spite of their rather vague enunciations and the elusiveness of their tongue, Septimus could detect urgency in their tone. Whether the voices were still speaking now or he had tapped into yet another echo of times past, he could not be sure.

Mortlake and Marmaduke tried to relight some of the wax torches that hung solemnly from the walls of the passage. Their damp wicks seemed hesitant at first, but after much heat were soon aflame again, awakened after countless years of slumber.

The increased light levels and the warmth that the torches bestowed seemed to lift the cloak of grim apprehension from the cold-fingered men. Septimus regained some control over his distractions as the oak door came forever closer. Mortlake shuffled through his pocket for his picklocks as Marmaduke swung down the bag of tools with a sigh of relief.

Septimus was so determined to get the door open this time that he would have clawed it down with his bare hands. Jewels and Marmaduke started to reach into the bag and arm themselves with heavy bars and levers. Witnessing this scrambling about, Septimus said: "Gentlemen, wait. Let us first see if science as opposed to brute force can open this door for us. Mr Mortlake, if you please?" Septimus waved Mortlake through to the front of the door.

Mortlake brought forward two huge rings of keys and small blades. "Blimey, you're a bit of a jailer on the quiet. You would make a right good turnkey with that lot," said an admiring Pigeon.

"He's certainly got the face for it," Ocky jibed.

"If I were, you two would be the first I'd lock up. Out of the way boy," said Mortlake gruffly as he brushed past Pigeon towards the door.

The rest of the gang watched intently as Mortlake set to work on the lock. His ear was pressed tightly against the door, listening to every click his instruments made.

The whole passageway seemed to resound with the sharp clicks of metal on metal as Mortlake used all his senses to find a way in. Mortlake's aptitude reminded Septimus of some surgery he had once witnessed his uncle performing when he was a boy. Fortunately there was no blood here.

Septimus was also reminded of the fact that this man's skill meant he was no stranger to this dark art. Indeed, he had probably acquired it through many years of practice. Jesse Mortlake of course claimed that he had borrowed the picklocks and keys from an acquaintance, but evidently this was almost certainly a lie. Most of the men stood patiently still and in complete silence, willing the door to move. Until, of course, Jewels finally lost his patience.

"Let's break it down! Come on, we'll be here for the night unless he gets a shift on. Let's break it down -- there are enough of us."

At that very moment Mortlake looked at Jewels and smiled. His left hand held a very thin, needle-type implement and his right, a key. There was a faint click, and then what seemed like a procession of cogs and cranks whirled within the lock.

Septimus quickly reached for the circular handle of the door and pushed with all his might. The door moved less than half an inch -- the great lock that held the door had been breached but the door was still too swollen to open fully. The giant Marmaduke threw his shoulder into the door, followed in turn by everybody else's boot. Still no movement. Ocky moved the men to one side and said: "Boys, boys, be patient! Let us give this a try." Ocky plunged one of the huge iron bars that Marmaduke had been carrying underneath the door, and motioned to Pigeon to place one of the wooden staffs beneath it. They now had a lever to work with. Marmaduke stood on the lever and set about rocking it up and down, while Jewels and Ocky rammed their gemmies between the door and the frame. After much hesitancy, the bloated door could not resist the men's efforts any longer and swung open into the blackness.

As the men peered into the deep, dark void, their lungs were greeted by the noisome whiff of stale, damp air combined with the acrid stench of rotting and charred timbers. Needless to say, it was Pigeon who entered the abyss first, swiftly followed by Ocky and Septimus, with lamps and torches ablaze.

Inside the gloom they could just about make out another couple of rowing boats, complete with oars and yard after yard of rope. The cellar was also home to hundreds of storage trunks of all shapes and sizes. Septimus was encouraged by the many different languages he saw expressed over this vast cargo.

Whoever had organised this set-up was obviously receiving goods from across the world. Surely this must have been his grandfather.

Although the oil lamps and torches penetrated through some of the darkness, progress was still slow. The floor was littered with lumps of plaster and masonry partly concealed by a ghostly carpet of both cob and orb webs. Even the rafters supporting the partially ruined ceiling were clothed in the finest weave of this ghostly gauze. Through the torchlight, one could see that this was still the home of a vast array of arachnids. Judging by their size, not all of these webs were of British provenance: they had been made by uninvited guests that had stowed away goodness knows how many years before, surmised an apprehensive Septimus.

Septimus frantically searched for evidence linking this long-forgotten lockup with the semi-mythical cellar of his ancestors. He had half hoped that his mind would be awash with his great-aunt's memories of this place by now, but none had come. Was this in itself evidence of failure? Had he been so blinded by his own curiosity that he had led these men here on a wild goose chase? Septimus knew he should be fascinated by such a find as this, but his intrigue was being soured by doubt. This was, after all, the first cellar they had found. Surely there were others.

He was comforted, though, that this place had been obviously damaged by fire, and it was roughly where his ancestors' home had been. But once underground, all sense of geography was totally lost. Closer inspection of debris beneath his feet exposed remnants of broken statues corresponding to some of the vast holes in the ceiling above. Septimus saw a huge marble column lying broken and idle, surrounded by what at first looked like small pin pricks flashing before the lamps' wanton gaze. He reached down and held the lamp closer to the tiny fragments of light. He discovered them to be splinters of finely cut glass crystal found mainly in chandeliers.

"I was right! Didn't I tell you this was a smuggler's den?" said Pigeon to Jewels gleefully.

"Right enough, boy. Right enough," said a smiling Jewels as they began rummaging through a trunk full of liquor.

Further ahead, Ocky nodded towards Septimus and beckoned him over. In a hushed tone, he said, "Look over there Septimus, a staircase." Ocky surreptitiously lifted up his lantern in the direction of some steps. Sure enough, on the far right-hand side of the room lay an ancient, spiral stone staircase, ascending into the void above.

"Whatever this building was, it's been here for many a year. Worth a few shillings in its day to your Lordship. Maybe this really *is* your lost manor, or what remains of it, anyway."

"And yours too young Thaddy," Septimus whispered out loud, before he had a chance to think about his words. "Of course!" thought Septimus, "This must be Thaddeus' son Octavius!" Thaddeus was Cornelius' son, who was born out of wedlock. "That is where I've seen his face before!" Octavius had always been called Young Thaddy by his mother and other close relatives when he was younger. Septimus knew now that he was seeing through Anastasia's eyes. He was suddenly struck by the realization of not only his words, but his newfound situation too. Ocky, this foetid Prince of the Underworld, was indeed one and the same as Octavius, his cousin. Moreover, he was also a grandson of Cornelius, and, more worryingly, another heir to the estate.

"What did you say? Did you just call me Young Thaddy?" asked a stunned Ocky.

Septimus let the words settle in his head for a while, then calmly but rather unconvincingly replied: "Thaddy? No. Who is Thaddy?" Ocky just glared at him in disbelief. Both men tried to think of something to say, but no words came.

Septimus finally broke the poisonous silence that had brought the two men to a standstill. He turned and shouted to the others: "You men stay here and see what you can find. Ocky and I will explore upstairs." He was careful to avoid Ocky's eyes as he turned.

Jewels looked up momentarily from rummaging and said: "Aye aye, Captain. Plenty of wine here, boys -- reckon it would keep us going until you get back, eh Ocky."

"Reckon as much," said a pensive Ocky, still lost in Septimus' words.

The two men trudged silently up to the top of the soot- stained staircase. Once at the top they were faced with yet another door. Fortunately this was unlocked and dishevelled by flame. To their right lay a landing, to their left yet another staircase going up to another floor. This second staircase was totally impassable due to the amount of debris blocking their way. Septimus and Ocky strode gingerly onto the landing.

Septimus could just about make out remnants of decadence amongst the ruined décor as they made their way across charred rugs and rickety floorboards. Ocky noticed a door slightly ajar to his right. It was barely distinguishable from the darkly-stained and blistered wooden panelling that fought so hard to conceal it. Septimus and Ocky both inexplicably hesitated before entering the room, and felt a sudden drop in temperature when they stepped foot inside its vast embrace.

Chapter 38

The Ballroom

This was it! This must be the grand old ballroom ... Wave after wave of conflicting emotions flooded through Septimus' veins. This was it, surely? The mansion site... ever since Septimus' great-aunt Arianwen had sown the seeds of intrigue so many years ago, the idea of finding the ancestral home of the Blackwoods had gripped him tighter and tighter with every coming year. In amongst joy there lay a deep sadness. At first Septimus thought this was largely due to a sense of regret at these once opulent surroundings rotting silently in resigned ruination.

But, although this was true, it was not the root of the emotion that lay in a far deeper and older sentiment. That sprang from Anastasia's reconciliation with the room -- her youth, her place of dreams, one that she had not seen for nearly seventy years. Her distress poured into the eyes of Septimus. Luckily for him, Ocky had gone off ahead and spared him the embarrassment of seeing the tears trickling down. The rawness of the sentiment chiselled away at Septimus' now-fragile defences. Something altered within the room -- the darkness became light, the lamps were lit, and music filled the air.

Septimus leaned heavily on the tosher's pole he was still carrying. It was as much as he could do to just stand upright.

The dancers paid him no regard as they waltzed and swayed around the room. The sound of their chattering seemed at times elusive and obscure, then suddenly loud and oppressive. He could even taste the wine on their breath. But how cold their breath! Colder than a cemetery on a February morn. Flashes of colour flecked the gowns of the dancing damsels, cajoling and confronting the nebulousness of the immense spinning room.

Faces that had at first seemed so familiar, so comforting, began to melt into obscurity like spent candles in a bowl. The light started to flicker, and deathly silence reigned once more. The once-perfumed air was swiftly replaced with the mustiness of seclusion and sobriety. Septimus could not be sure if he had been visited by the residue of one of Anastasia's distant memories or something much more disconcerting, the memories of the room itself. He ran his fingers through his hair, seeking the sanctuary of his own mortal form, only to find a thin layer of dust was now sticking to his heavily oiled locks.

The floor itself was in an even worse condition than the landing. There were cavernous holes all around, and he was careful not to venture onto the once-impressive rugs for fear of a huge void lying in wait beneath them. Such were the gaps below that Septimus could see the torches and the lamps of the men in the cellar.

He could hear them greedily sorting through what was probably some of the last vestiges of his lost inheritance... well... his and the man he shared this room with.

The plaster on the ballroom's walls was cracked, and stained black with soot and flame. Great chunks of it had crumbled to the floor, leaving the lathe boarding exposed and naked as bone defleshed and devoured. Just as Septimus neared the grand piano, one of the floorboards beneath him gave way and his head hit the floor. Dark became light once more. This time, though, the music was much slower and melancholic. The dancers moved without emotion or joy, mournfully waltzing their way through the dense mounds of rubble and the thicket of spiders' webs under their feet. This time, all of their flashes of gaiety and richness of hue had transformed into a frosted veil of silvery grey.

This veil between the past and the present, the living and the dead, seemed but a kiss away. The fragility of breath seemed to be the only divide; its cold whisper, mocking and malicious. The words spoken by the room were ones of contorted contrasts. Their twisted promise of opulence fell upon dank, deaf, and defeated ears. No majesty in martyrdom, just a fractured folly in the sentence of time.

The broken ornaments and the ruined portraits looked down loftily, weary and worn. The room was suffocating in its own indignant restlessness, and a strange feeling of guilt resonated from its core as if it were somehow responsible for its own demise. Its former grandeur seemed little more than a gilded teardrop, embedded within the sodden fabric of its soul. The few remaining marble pillars which held the ceiling aloft stood isolated and friendless. No pride in their labour, no bravado in their strength, just a begrudging resignation to their destiny.

The sadness one feels when observing statues found no greater stage to unveil the lifeless truth. The statues stared vacantly up at the dancing dead, untouched and untainted by sentiment. Despite their limbs being cracked and their bodies broken, the statues were the only part of this room that was undisturbed and untroubled by their fate.

Note by note, the music dimmed and fled into the darkness again. Septimus' bewildered nausea was only eclipsed by the pain in the back of his head.

"You all right up there?" a concerned Mortlake shouted from below.

"He'll live. He's just getting a bit unsteady in his old age," Ocky joked as he helped Septimus to his feet.

"Lucky you didn't drop that lantern. Last thing we want is another fire, ain't it? Right I reckon we could do with a little more illumination in here, don't you?"

Ocky put down his lamp and relit some of the candlesticks that had remained steadfast upon the tabletops for all these years. Their soft glow seemed to offer some semblance of reality to the situation. Septimus rubbed his head, and, although still in a state of shock, was comforted by the fact that he could very well have been dead now: if any of the other boards had given way, there would be no doubt about it.

The extra light in the room meant they could be more assured of their footing, which gave them both time to marvel at what was still intact in this vast ballroom. It was strange how the coming of the light seemed to rob the room of some of its dignity, as if were happier covering away its shame.

"Amazing how the other half lives, eh Septimus? Or should I say lived? So, do you reckon that this is it then? Is this what remains of your long-lost mansion?" asked Ocky.

Septimus considered his words well before replying laconically, "I am convinced of it."

"Just imagine what this must have looked like in its glory days," Ocky commented, gazing around the entirety of the room.

"Indeed, just imagine," Septimus replied softly.

"Do you want a hand up there Septimus?" Mortlake yelled from below.

"Not yet Mr Mortlake. I will let you know when. Besides, this floor is much too unstable to take any more weight."

Ocky knelt down and peered through one of the holes in the floorboards: "Me and his Lordship are going to have a looksee around the rest of this old tomb. Make sure someone's keeping an eye on the water level -- it didn't feel like rain today but you know what it's like this time of year; things can change mighty quickly."

"Right you are Ocky, though there could be worse places to be trapped. Look at all this booze!" Jewels shouted happily.

"If you think I'm going to carry you out of there later, you got another think coming. Stay sober or I'll let the rats have ya," Ocky replied mischievously.

"Ain't you just the milk of human kindness, Ocky? Nah, you're ok, boy. We are just having a little tasters, that's all," Jewels said unconvincingly.

"You mind that's all you do then," Ocky replied.

Septimus raised his eyebrows enquiringly at Ocky. "It's ok, I know Jewelsy. He's a rake to be sure, but he knows drunken toshers really don't make old bones, or he should do by now." Ocky made his way carefully to the other side of the room and exclaimed: "Blimey, this floor's got more holes in it than that Dutch cheese has."

"It's Emmental, my dear Ocky, and it's actually from Switzerland," Septimus said drily with a hint of a grin.

"Is it really?" Ocky retorted with a sigh of resignation before replying, "Seeing as you are the big cheese and we have finally reached your manorial home, what exactly do you expect us to find besides duty-free wine, cracked plaster, and rising damp? Not that I am besmirching your ancestors' choice of vino -- I have no doubt that it is a more than adequate vintage, but there has to be more to it than that."

Septimus looked Ocky straight in the eyes and replied solemnly, "Personally, I have always found wine to be a wonderful accompaniment to cheese... But I digress."

Ocky rolled his eyes and spat.

"As for what exactly I was expecting to find," Septimus sighed deeply before continuing, "To be honest, I was not entirely sure."

"Not sure?" Ocky enquired. "Don't double-cross me Septimus. I ain't 'ere for the company, you know."

Septimus raised the palm of his hand and said, "Relax yourself my good fellow. You'll get your money, have no fear of that. All I meant was I can't be sure what is here. Of course I have heard rumours of what was here, but as for what is here now…The main thing is that we have found it and I am home again." Septimus said the word *home* without a second thought and it was not until after he had uttered it that a feeling of deep insecurity overcame him. He was starting to wonder just how much of his conscious mind was still his own and how much was Anastasia's.

"I just needed to know that it existed, and now that I know that the rumours are true, this is just the beginning really. Who knows what secrets this place holds in its clammy grasp?"

"Well, let's go see then, Septimus. Standing here mooning about ain't gonna do us any good. Besides, that tide won't wait."

The two men approached the main doors to the ballroom. They were a soot-stained pale cream with gilt edging. The doors surprisingly swung open with the slightest of touches. Behind them was a square landing which housed a wide flight of stairs. "That's the main stairs to the rest of the house. The other flight we noticed led up to the gardens," Septimus said.

"For someone who's never been here before, you seem to be well versed in the geography of this old tomb," Ocky said, raising an eyebrow.

Septimus smiled an unreadable smile before saying: "If I had been here before, I would not have needed your help to find it, now, would I? Cornelius's home burned down nearly a decade before the end of the last century and, contrary to popular belief, I am not that old. I am just being led by family hearsay -- memories of what I was told as a child."

There was something in the tone of Septimus' response that made Ocky suspicious -- he could not think what exactly, but there was definitely something. Ocky often congratulated himself on getting the measure of a person quite quickly, but his assessment of Septimus was altering by the hour.

When Ocky had first met Septimus in the Rope and Anchor he had got him taped: a man not short of resources, neither financially or intellectually; a man that was driven and ruthless; a man who

253

knew his own mind. However, the man in front of him now was a mystery: a man who he swore he had heard refer to him by his childhood name; a man who seemed to speak about this ruined vault as if it were his home -- not just his family's home, *his* home. But that was not the only thing that puzzled him: what were the causes of his bouts of near-trance-like states?

Ocky followed Septimus as he moved cautiously down the hall, which lay to one side of the great stairs. There appeared to be fewer holes in the floorboards here than there had been in the ballroom, but there was still no room for complacency. The floor was littered with fragments of lathe and plaster, and the ceiling looked even less stable than that of the ballroom.

The air in the hall was less cold than that of the ballroom, and not as damp as in the lower cellar, though it shifted anxiously around their exposed skin, which probably meant that somewhere in this labyrinth there must be another opening, cogitated Septimus.

The sheer length of the corridor and the number of doors they passed without even so much as a peep, prompted Ocky to declare, "Your great-aunt must have been very precise about the whereabouts of whatever you reckon may be found here, your Lordship."

"Hmmm. We'll see," Septimus replied absentmindedly. Septimus had heard the words, but paid them little heed as memories of his Great-Aunt Anastasia's youth came seeping back to him as if flowing from the very walls themselves.

Behind each door lay yet another memory. Some were good doors, some were not. "It is my father's... grandfather's (he corrected himself) downstairs library that I am most interested in Octavius. Let us hope it was spared the worst of the blaze. We shall soon be there." Grasping the sheer scale of the building beneath ground, Septimus now knew for certain that he would have wasted hours, maybe days of precious time if he had not made the union with Anastasia.

Even so, he still had huge reservations about this union, as his mind felt like a leaf in the breeze, blowing back and forth throughout time. The visions and voices he had to endure were enough to send a lesser man insane.

As the two men ventured down the corridor, they slowly become more aware of the noises from above. Gone were the ghostly hums and sighs of the tunnels, the unnerving, anonymous moans of the underworld. They had been replaced by the distant sounds of street life, movement and purpose. How far above their heads it actually was, they had not a clue. The sound should have been a comfort, but the ever-present shrill whispers of the rats around them kept them on their guard.

As they approached the door to the underground library, Septimus' heart sank. Most of the other doors they had passed on their way were closed, but the library door was ajar. There was evidence abounding of the fire's tentacles reaching out into these cavernous depths, and a door left open would have been manna from heaven for its greedy grasp.

Septimus tentatively opened the door wide and held up his lamp, almost afraid of what may lie before him. To his great relief, the room had been left virtually unscathed by the fire.

There appeared to be little or no structural harm at all. It still smelt the same as the other rooms – there was still the same acrid odour of burnt timbers and damp decay, which had been with them since entering

The room was far smaller than the ballroom, and consisted of six long rows of bookshelves and what looked like a couple of desks and chairs in the background. "So, this is the treasure you were after, is it? You certainly remembered it very well, didn't ya?" Ocky said almost incredulously.

"It always pays to listen, Octavius, does it not? Do give me a hand to light these candles, please."

Oddly, the room looked completely free of debris, and some parts of the ceiling even looked partially re-plastered, as it lacked any paint and accompanying smoke shadow.

"Blimey, look at all this lot! Amazing how they never went up in the blaze, ain't it? Worth a few quid too, I'd reckon. They certainly liked their books, eh?" Ocky said, hungrily surveying the loot.

"As I am sure you do Octavius," Septimus said knowingly.

"Reckon I do. They answer most of my questions. It's just knowing where to look."

"Quite so Octavius. Knowing where to look is almost as important as knowing what to look for," said Septimus as he thumbed his way through an old tome on toxicology.

"This is nothing compared to the collection in the library upstairs."

"Upstairs?" asked Ocky quizzically.

"Yes, upstairs," Septimus said quietly, silently cursing himself for sounding too familiar with the surroundings. "According to family legend, the library upstairs was one of the largest in Britain. This, so I was led to believe, was a place for Cornelius' personal contemplation, a place where he kept his most private and precious books."

Ocky replied with far-off eyes, "Seeing the age of some of these books makes me think of my old auntie. She always turned up with a load of books for us when I was kid. She was a miserable old woman, didn't say much.

"Bit scared of her when I was very young, but I was always glad of those books. God knows where she got 'em all from. Think she got most of 'em for my father, though some were just for me. Suppose it's in the blood."

"Miserable, you say?" Septimus said with a faint smile.

"Yes, always dressed in black. Me and my sister used to call her The Crow. Never stayed for long, used to turn up every once in a while, always had a faint air of the aristocrat about her. Great-Aunt Anna, that was it. My father used to say we had come from noble origins, though I could never quite work out how she was related, as my father told me he had been adopted. He always said that one day he would tell me who his original parents were."

"And did he?" Septimus asked, feigning nonchalance.

"Nope. That secret died with him, I reckon. Me old mum was not one to talk about the past, and she died years before I ever thought to ask again.

"It was The Crow who tried to make me stay with some uncle or another in the countryside, but that was not for me. I'm a Londoner through and through. You know what they say -- if you are bored with London, you are bored with life."

"I am sure your aunt had your best interests at heart," replied Septimus, blowing the dust off yet another manuscript.

256

"Maybe she did, looking back, but look at me now -- I am a free man, Septimus, and if I had gone off to some toffy-nosed place in the country, I doubt I would have as much liberty as I have now."

Septimus decided to let the conversation wane -- there was no arguing with the man. The thought that he and Ocky could have been brought up in the same house, albeit at slightly different times, was somewhat disturbing.

The bookshelves contained many ancient books and texts. Some were on parchment, some leather-bound. Some of the older scrolls were in Latin and neatly fastened with red ribbon. Other documents had traces of wax seals on them. Goodness knows how many years ago some of these seals were set, Septimus mused. Much to his surprise, some of the scrolls were not just written in Latin or English: some were written in very strange lettering indeed, not dissimilar to the markings on the stone in the churchyard and the entrance to the cavern tunnel. Many of these scrolls were interspersed with what appeared to be creatures chasing one another between the words.

Septimus felt strange to be in Cornelius' private library, almost as if it was an intrusion. Anastasia had rarely been allowed down here as a child, and then not at all when Cornelius had made this his own area of private study. It had been no secret that he was trying to find a way to cheat death, and it was often the primary topic of conversation amongst the family. The longevity of the Blackwoods was already legendary: indeed, much of the fear felt towards their family, Anastasia believed, stemmed from their peculiar ability to live for years longer than any of their contemporaries. Instinctively, she had known that Cornelius was close to achieving his quest because he and his wife were spending more and more time below stairs, indisposed to the rest of the world.

Anastasia now hungered for the same secrets, and if she was going to find a way to sustain this earthly life and finally reveal the true fate of Cornelius and his wife, the answers must lie here: somewhere in this buried chamber was her destiny. There was not time to waste. "Much as I would love to sit down and imbibe all of this entombed knowledge, time is of the essence, and we must get these books to the surface as soon as possible, Octavius."

"Which books would you like us to take back with us?" enquired Ocky.

"All of them," Septimus replied calmly.

"Not possible," Ocky replied, aghast.

"You asked me what I wanted and I told you," said Septimus, matter-of-factly.

"I reckon that would take nigh on ten journeys with the number of men we have here," Ocky retorted pensively.

"I fear you may be right ... unless ..."

"Unless what?" Ocky said, with a raised eyebrow.

"Unless we find another way out."

Ocky shook his head and was just about to voice his objections to this idea, when a thought kicked in. First he hesitated, and then he sighed and surveyed the area some more before announcing, "It does make you wonder, though, doesn't it? I mean, given the location of this place and its geology -- mainly limestone, ain't it?"

"Exactly!" replied Septimus and he continued, "I am convinced there are other ways out of here. It's just a matter of finding the damn things."

"Well, in my experience underground, I've found that there is often more than one route to the same place.

"That said, there are also hundreds of blind alleys, collapsed passageways, and sudden drops that'd take you down in a blink of an eye. There are thousands of lost tunnels and cellarways under this city, all waiting to be rediscovered. But do we have the time?" said Ocky enquiringly.

"It's like you were saying Ocky, about those books; it's all a question of where to look." At that very moment the men were confronted by a blast of fresh air.

"Did you feel that breeze, Octavius?" Septimus asked apprehensively, fearing another spectral visit.

"I did indeed, your Lordship, and judging by the direction that candle is flinching, it is coming from over there." Both men raised their lamps and walked towards the provenance of the draft.

"I don't recall being told this room had another entrance. Maybe it's a crack in the ceiling or something."

"Maybe you weren't told the full story then," Ocky replied with a knowing grin.

As they approached the other end of the room, both men were still baffled by the source of the breeze. Septimus tried to gauge with his lamp the exact height and whereabouts of the draft.

He did this by holding his lamp out at various heights, eyes constantly focusing on the flame. It was during this process that he observed that its flame was most distressed at about knee height, so he sank to his knees. Ocky could not help but notice how his form seemed to resemble that of a bloodhound rather than a man.

Septimus' nose followed his lamp to what seemed like just another oak panel, though the top part of the panelling was obscured by an old rug hanging from a picture rail. The draft seemed to be coming down from the rug above.

Septimus lifted up the bottom of the rug a little and saw that what had first looked like just another piece of panelling was in fact the top of a revolving door, to goodness knows what. Whoever had been the last to use this door had obviously done so in a hurry, and paid no heed to fastening up what had formerly been a concealed entrance.

The door itself must have been about six feet tall and had a metal rod about halfway up the panel on which it revolved. The rug, which hung just above the panel, had hidden the bevel at the top and presumably the old armchair to the left of it was usually pushed in front of the bottom of the panel.

This was new territory even for Anastasia. Clearly old Cornelius Blackwood had been a man of many secrets.

"Well, well, well, your Lordship. Wonder what's behind there then? Maybe it's the place where they stashed all of their filthy lucre."

"I don't know. But whatever it is, we are going to find out. Here, hold the door up for me."

Personally, Septimus did not care that much about what type of licentiousness or skulduggery his ancestors had got up to, but was it something he wanted to share with the others, especially Ocky? He could, of course, reveal to Ocky that this was his legacy too. That may help soften the blow, but it could also make things far more complicated than he had initially envisaged.

Septimus knew from bitter experience that a man could easily plunge to his death by putting his foot in the wrong place, especially in the old ballroom. Indeed, Septimus had sensed that the old ballroom would actually welcome another victim to mourn for. Parts of the ceiling in the hallway looked like they could collapse at any moment. Yes, thought Septimus, yes, the possibilities for silencing any talk were endless.

Chapter 39

Sacred Ground

Septimus pushed the base of the panel, and as the door duly revolved both men crawled through on their hands and knees. This room was infinitely colder than the last, and somewhat similar to where they had earlier encountered the shrieking boat. The room appeared to be virtually empty at first glance, and it was not until both Ocky and Septimus held their lamps aloft that they realised the majesty of their discovery. The cave itself appeared to be a perfect dome, reminiscent, albeit smaller, of the one in St Paul's Cathedral. It was about thirty-feet high in the centre and about the same distance in width. Perhaps the most startling thing of all about it was the smoothness of the surface. The dome and its walls shared the same shamanistic-style hunting scenes and bizarre creatures as the earlier cavern, though here they were more vivid still, both in colour and form.

"What in the name of ...?" Ocky's words trailed off as he explored with amazement. Although Septimus had grown accustomed to his mind being almost enveloped by memories of buildings and landscapes, this had not made the feeling any more comforting to him. Nothing in his past experiences could have prepared him for the torrent of sights, sounds, and emotions that this space contained. This place was truly magnificent, a gateway like no other, and he sank to his knees and stared up at the vast dome above him.

The whole room was alive, truly alive, with whispers, shrieks, and the voices of the forests. All around him was the sound of birds, beasts, and a mourning for things lost.

Septimus felt sunlight and storms, the need for flight and the feeling of flight itself, weightless and free. Septimus knew he needed to be led here and to let go of himself, as it was futile to struggle with something of this magnitude. He soared through the air and felt hunger first, then felt himself burrowing deep into the soil, taking refuge and seeking food. There was the smell of the earth all around him. Deeper and deeper he went amongst the roots

261

of trees, only to emerge once more into the deafening calls of the forest, which greeted the rising of the sun. And what a sun it was! Molten and ablaze. Everything in the forest felt anew, and alive with unending potency. Septimus watched until the sun transformed into a radiant fireball before him.

The centre of the fire drew in his gaze until he saw an image of scores of women, their faces painted violet blue, shrieking curses at an iron-clad foe, and blazing spears thrown at the advancing eagles. Bearded men held aloft huge staffs, which cast shadows over their bone-white, chalk-stained faces. Funeral pyres blended in with round wooden houses, together embraced and encircled by flames. Faces were blackened and streaked with tears.

Septimus watched as a man, whose face was painted with coiled serpents, thrust a vast sword into a river. Behind the painted man was another man, one who was being led forward, arms bound behind his back, gagged and bleeding.

A cold sensation came over Septimus as if it were him in the water, drowning. The man whose face was covered in a mask produced a large knife and cut the inside of his palm, then squeezed it tightly until the scarlet drops of life trickled onto the surface of the river. Septimus watched as the waters took the blood and rode with it downstream, until the river became one with the walls of the cave and the spell was almost lifted.

The thread of time and incidence that was woven into the fabric of this place was never going to be truly silenced -- it was far too potent for that, but for the time being it loosened its grip on the now-nauseated Septimus Blackwood. Septimus was not even sure if his eyes were open or closed when he heard, "Oi, you! What're you up to on the floor? We haven't got time for another one of your fits, you know," said Ocky, his spare frame just about visible on the far side of the room.

Septimus rubbed his eyes and replied, "Pity the man who cannot drink in the majesty of a room such as this."

"I certainly have never seen the like before, your Lordship. Just glad you ain't a tongue-swallower."

Septimus felt faint for a moment but answered with all of the will he could muster, "If you are inferring I may have epilepsy, you are mistaken. Though if I had, I would be sharing it with many a great man." Septimus was pleased that his response had

262

momentarily provoked a pause in the conversation, and had given him time to level his thoughts again. If only he could gain greater control over his newly-acquired sensitivity! Every time he left his outer skin, he brought back to the present greater perceptions and insights into the connectedness of all life and time.

"Do you believe in ghosts Octavius?"

"Ain't given it a lot of thought, really. I could not say for certain that I haven't encountered one, though -- there are so many unnamed noises and movements down here, it's possible that one or more could be some sort of ghost. Some folk swear blind that they have seen 'em, and some of the blokes that are digging that new underground railway reckon that some parts belowground is haunted. I've found deserted crypts and a fair few bones of all descriptions too, but they've found thousands of bones all dumped together -- plague pits, they call 'em.

"Also they have found areas where the mud won't stand still -- moves like it's alive. Never a good idea to disturb the dead, I reckon. Jewelsy is very superstitious. He believes in 'em, won't go below without his lucky coin and a short prayer. Personally, I reckon he may as well pray to Hades itself down here for all the good it's likely to do him. Why? Do you?" Before Ocky could finish his question, he saw something reflecting the light back from his lamp in the far corner of the cave. "What the hell is that?"

Both men held their lamps aloft and made their way to the objects on the far side of the room. "What in the name of...!" Ocky said in amazement. Septimus stood aghast at the sight before his eyes. Never in his wildest imaginings had he thought to find this. Before them lay two caskets. Both were covered with a glass lid, and had what seemed like a pipe protruding out of the top of them. Both men stood speechless at the sight that befell them. "God, there're people inside 'em, look!" Ocky cried out.

Although Septimus was curious, he hesitated to venture his gaze any further.

"They've got pipes coming out of their mouths and out through the glass casing."

Septimus dared to look. "Brother, oh Cornelius, what is going on...?" Septimus whispered to himself, shaking his head in disbelief as he peered closely into one of the caskets. He found himself viewing this stony-faced man with mixed emotions: he felt

Anastasia's warmth for her long-lost brother but he also felt animosity, as here was the man who had disowned his own father, Dominic, in his hour of need.

Neither Cornelius nor Morwenna showed any sign of having aged since the time of the fire in 1796. Septimus took a moment to push any kind of sentiment to one side, and marvelled at this miracle. How had they achieved this?

"The pipe must have been to help 'em breathe. Fear of being buried alive, I reckon. What say you?" Ocky asked in bewilderment.

"There's a lot of dust on top of the glass now. If they weren't dead when they were placed here, they are now." It was all Septimus felt he could say, as he himself could not even be sure as to their condition. He had no wish to stir up any curiosity in Ocky whatsoever.

As if picking up on Septimus' hesitancy, Ocky enquired, "Who on earth are they? They some of your lot?"

"Could not say who they are, or rather were. Besides, we have enough intrigue on our hands getting this library up to the surface, let alone wasting our time here playing who's who," Septimus said, faking little concern.

"Still, I reckon we should go to the police about it, don't you? Maybe they were bumped off?"

"If indeed they were *bumped off,* as you put it, Octavius, I very much doubt that the forces of law would be exactly overawed with witnesses to the fact, do you?"

"Well, no ... but someone may be missing them, somewhere."

"That's as may be, but we cannot bring them back to this mortal coil, now, can we? What is more, it's taken me so long to find this place, I'm damned if I want the whole of the London Constabulary running amuck, rooting through my rightful legacy."

"You're the boss on this one your Lordship, but I still think they should have a rightful burial."

"Don't fret Octavius, I will see to that. Do not trouble yourself anymore on this matter."

How could he possibly tell Octavius that this was his grandfather and grandmother that lay here before him, and that they r may not even be dead? Maybe he should deal with Ocky right now. Get him out of his hair forever. It was the only way out.

After all, he'd served his purpose -- he had helped him find the cellar and he was now surplus to requirements. Yes, he would miss out on another pair of hands to help him get some of this stuff to the surface, but better that than allowing Octavius to blab about this to all and sundry.

Ocky moved over to the large table, which was not far from where the caskets lay. He picked up a jug of white liquid from its remarkably dust-free surface. He could not resist the urge to sniff it. The stench of it brought tears to his eyes. "God, no wonder they died if they had been drinking this. Reckon it's poison?" Ocky walked over and offered the jug up to Septimus. Septimus seemed irritated by the interruption to his train of thought, though he held out his hand nonetheless. Septimus impatiently held the jug to his nose and inhaled. The scent of the potion nearly made him retch.

He quickly thrust the jug back into Ocky's hand, spilling some of the vile substance onto Ocky's moleskin coat. Its noxious scent was not unlike the one he had to endure when his mind merged with that of Anastasia.

"Forgive me Octavius -- please pass it back to me, if you will."

Ocky replied gruffly, "Why bother with the jug -- you can see enough of the stuff on my coat."

"Ah yes, regrettable indeed. If you will be so kind Ocky?" Septimus eyed Ocky sympathetically. Ocky was placated, and passed Septimus the jug back. Septimus was careful to hold the jug at arm's length this time as he held it up to his lantern. Its consistency was very similar to Anastasia's mix -- the same sticky, milky mix, but this was flecked with scarlet and blue. "Some type of berry, perhaps?" mused Septimus.

Septimus hoped that his connection with Anastasia meant that he would automatically recognize its ingredients, but no recognition came. Little by little he was realizing that this union with Anastasia was not one of question and answers -- there was no separation now of her mind and his. Even if her thoughts were not immediately detectable, there were subtle changes in Septimus' reactions and feelings.

Despite the potential benefits of this union, Septimus still resented the lack of control and the intrusions of uninvited spirits into his psyche, not to mention the extra burden of sentimentality.

265

His thoughts returned to the jug before him. How strange it was that there was no sign of any dust. What's more, surely there should be some mould or fungi growing on its surface after all this time. As Septimus peered enquiringly at the jug, Ocky could not resist wiping away some of the dust from the outside of the glass encasement and taking a closer look at the couple entombed within.

"These people look like gentry to me, alright, though I ain't seen gentlemen of his age wearing white silk scarves so high on their neck before. Very old men, yes, when I was a boy but not nowadays."

"Perhaps they hit hard times," Septimus said, attempting to show little interest.

"This is queer, though, look at this, quick."

Septimus reluctantly switched his gaze to where Ocky had wiped the dust off of Cornelius' casket. He closed his eyes in horror. There, to one side of where the pipe ran through the glass lid, was what could only be described as condensation.

"My God, is that breath? They may still be alive!" Ocky shouted out in alarm.

"They can't be, not after all this time," Septimus said, trying to place doubt into his and Ocky's mind.

"Quick, we must do something, Septimus."

Any remote chance of letting this matter rest until Ocky was out of the way had rapidly disappeared. Septimus had no choice but to act now and deal with Ocky later. Ocky had unwittingly sealed his fate.

Septimus was surprised to see that the glass lid had been locked from the outside. Surely nobody else had been involved in this, Septimus mused. Before Septimus had time to see if there was a key in the close vicinity, Ocky had reached in his jacket for the crowbar and was prising frantically at the hinges of the lock. It was not long before the rusted hinges snapped in two.

"Give me a hand with this please Septimus." Septimus duly obliged, albeit with reluctance.

If there had been any shadow of doubt in Septimus' mind that this was his grandfather, it was finally dispelled once and for all as Septimus felt Anastasia's joy in seeing her brother again, be he alive or dead. Septimus checked Cornelius' wrist for a pulse. His flesh was cold but not icy.

In turn Ocky put his forefinger on Cornelius' neck. The men looked up at one another and waited ... and waited. Just as they were about to give up, they felt the tiniest hint of a pulse.

"Christ, they really are alive Septimus! Do you reckon they've been drugged or something?"

"So it would appear. If they have been drugged, it may be dangerous to bring them round too quickly -- the shock may kill them," said Septimus, fighting for time and remembering Anastasia telling him never to wake her whilst she lay in a suspended state.

"Well, we can't just leave 'em lying there, can we?" replied an irritated Ocky, who had already become suspicious of Septimus' nonchalance and lack of urgency.

"My God, you did it, brother, you did it! I knew you were not dead, I just knew it." Septimus could feel Anastasia's warmth and relief swelling up again inside of him. "Let us see if the woman is alive too," urged Septimus, in an attempt to thwart the doubts that were rapidly revealing themselves on Ocky's face. Surely they have not lain here like this for over half a century?

Septimus had always refused to accept limitations – everything, he felt, could be expanded. It was an intrinsic part of evolution. The only boundaries lay in finding the correct methods of application and the limitations of one's own imagination.

However, what was before him now sparked off so many questions all at once. Was this couple indeed partaking in some sort of mind-sharing with others? If not, why sustain your life only to spend it here comatose and entombed in the dark? Maybe Ocky was right -- perhaps there had been foul play. There was certainly another's hand at play here ...

Unbeknownst to the two men lost in the struggle to open Morwenna's casket, somebody was watching them from within the darkness, intrigued.

"Greetings gentlemen. It is rare for us to have visitors down below. In fact, I think you must be the first."

The two men turned, and stood aghast at the presence before them. The same melodic voice continued: "I knew you would come one day. I am pleased to see you ... both of you."

Before them, dressed completely in white, was the almost-spectral form of Lilly Whitethorn, the herb and posy seller from the market. It took Septimus a while to regain his voice. "Why Miss Whitethorn, what on earth brings you to this most desolate and forgotten of places?"

"Ah, well, it may be forgotten by most, but not by my kin." Septimus' gaze lowered to see that Lilly was holding a flagon full of what appeared to be the liquid they had noticed in the jug earlier.

"Forgive me Miss Whitethorn, but would it be rude of me to enquire as to how you entered this cave ... room, call it what you will?"

Lilly smiled serenely, pointed in the opposite direction to which the two men had entered the room, and simply said, "Why, by the door, of course." This door was just about visible in the twilight of the cave.

"Well, you obviously have a better geography of the landscape than even me, dear girl. We are fortunate to have you as a guiding light," said Septimus.

"Guiding light?" the girl repeated, followed by a gentle but unreadable smile.

Ocky looked the girl up and down in awe and disbelief, and enquired, "I see you have no lamp or staff, and nobody in their right mind goes below without a mucker or two. I have heard tell your grandfather used to do some toshing years ago. He should have warned you."

"Come now Octavius, you have a short memory. I know you yourself used to venture out alone regularly, and as for the lamp, I can see well enough down here, thank you. It is true about my grandfather going below, but I assure you he was not toshing," Lilly replied with a good-natured smile.

"Too good for him, was it?" replied an irritated Ocky. "I may have gone below on my tod when I was younger, but that was before I knew better. Besides, you seem to know an awful lot about me, young lady."

"I meant no offence, Octavius. It is a small world and there are not many of us who go belowground now, you know. Besides, our families have had a long association with each other. My family has been searching for something that was lost, and your family searches for things yet to be found. It is, I believe, what men of science refer to as a symbiotic relationship. Our motivations are different, but we all seek the same end," Lilly said enigmatically.

"Families entwined in symbiotic relationships? We haven't got the time to listen to this lunacy, Septimus. The girl is obviously moonshot."

Lilly smiled. "How interesting that you should bring the moon into it. The moon does indeed have great powers: my mother works with it often, though the moon can only reflect what is already there; it has no light of its own."

"Enough of your riddles girl. There're people here that need our help!" Ocky exclaimed, gesturing at the prostrate bodies in the caskets.

"Yes, and one day help will come. They are lost to us at the present, but they will return, of that I am sure," Lilly replied, as if she was discussing a change in the weather.

"Leave her to it, Septimus. She's beyond reason, this one," said Ocky, averting his attention back to opening the second casket.

"Please stop, Octavius," Lilly said calmly, and continued, "Things are not always as they seem, though I am sure they would be touched by your concern."

"How you can talk about people being touched is beyond me; you're the only one touched here, ain't that right Septimus?"

Septimus knew as soon as the words had left his mouth that he should not have said them. "Quiet man! Let the girl have her say."

Lilly smiled, and nodded at Septimus with the utmost grace. "Kind sirs, as you have no doubt become aware, your grandparents are far from dead. It was only a matter of time that the pair of you should return to the nest." Ocky was about to protest. Septimus raised his hand to silence him, resigned to the fact that the damage was already done. "Yes Octavius, they are both yours and Septimus' grandparents. Their spirits have merely... flown... but, as I have said, they will return." Ocky looked at Septimus, aghast. His mouth was wide open but bereft of words. Septimus just gazed up at the reliefs above his head, deep in thought.

Lilly made her way to the pair under the glass. Ocky had sat down on the floor, stunned into silence. Septimus joined Lilly by the side of the caskets. "Please help me get the lid down again so I can reinsert Cornelius' breathing and feeding tube."

"Feeding tube?" Septimus replied inquisitively.

"Yes, I feed him and Morwenna."

"Would they not choke on it, young lady?"

"I'm very careful not to give anything more than a few drops at a time."

"Lilly..." Septimus deliberately softened his voice... "Lilly, what exactly do you *feed* them?"

Lilly's eyes smiled and she said playfully, "Funny-looking jollop, isn't it? My grandfather makes it."

"I see. Pity, as I am intrigued by its contents. Oh well, if you cannot help me on that matter, maybe you could reveal where my bro ... my grandparents are? I see their bodies, but what of their ... what you referred to as spirits?"

Lilly thought on it for a while as she slowly allowed a tiny drop of the liquid down the pipe into first Morwenna's and then Cornelius' mouth.

"I can't really tell," Lilly said serenely. Septimus was starting to get impatient with the girl's vagaries. If it were not for the fact that he believed the girl, he would have given her a good shake or worse. "Careful with those thoughts, Septimus, this room has a life of its own and it would not pay to upset it. As you are no doubt aware, it has memories too," Lilly added.

"At least tell me what happened on the day of the fire; surely you can tell of that."

Lilly looked Septimus in the eyes and said, "Come now, I am sure one of your aunts has already told you much about that day." Septimus shuffled uneasily at her reply. Did she know about Anastasia and him?

"I have heard rumours and hearsay, but never any real details, so if you would be so kind Miss Whitethorn?"

"My grandfather told me that the fire spread from the Thames like a lightning bolt, and many did not have the option to run, Septimus. Many were sleeping – but my grandfather did awaken your grandparents and alert them to the danger."

"But if your grandfather got here in time to wake them, presumably they would have had time to leave with him and escape the inferno."

"There are many ways to awaken people, Septimus. It does not have to be with the spoken word, you know."

"You mentioned earlier that your family was seeking something that was lost, Lilly, and that our families have a common goal. What is it that they sought?"

"Well, I suppose you would call it a language, the language of life."

"I see. I cannot say I am familiar with such a language," replied Septimus, with just about enough of a question in his response to provoke a more detailed answer.

"Oh, but you are Septimus. Every living thing is; it is just that you have lost your connection with it. The language of life is the language of bird, beast, and breath. It's the language that links all living things. Sometimes it cannot be heard -- sometimes it is just felt, experienced, if you wish."

"It certainly sounds an elusive prey. How can one hope to gain such a thing, to comprehend this so-called language of life?" Septimus said with unguarded intrigue.

"One has to truly empathize with the natural world and many of its different creatures before one can truly know it."

"But surely this cannot be possible, to be one with an animal, to feel as a creature of the forest."

"Are you saying you do not know what it is like to be as one with another, Septimus, to see things through another's eyes?"

Unease crept back through Septimus' being; how could this girl know?

"Forgive me, I did not doubt your explanation, I merely wished to comprehend this fascinating language and my family's link to it."

"Yes, go on, enlighten us. I have got to hear this," piped up a still-bewildered Ocky.

Septimus had hoped that Ocky was out of earshot, but all of those years below with his ears pricked had obviously sharpened his senses.

"Very well, though I can only tell what I have been told, no more, no less."

271

"If you will young lady," Septimus said with a courteous nod.

"Many years ago, before the men with eagles came from across the sea -- the sowers of seeds, the keepers of beasts -- even before the building of the great stone rings, the old folk of this land believed that the source of all making and magic came from below the ground.

"Every living thing that has ever existed begins and ends inside the mother. The mother gave us caverns such as this one to feel the single heartbeat that connects all things. In such places the divisions that separate one creature from another are blurred, transient: it is where things are formed.

"The old folk had men and women who were called *the people who know,* who could easily change from one living thing to another and then back again. It was easier then." Lilly's face filled with regret. "They helped us to understand the sounds of the forest, the language of life, to be as one with it, if you like.

"As time went on, more and more invaders came to our land. The forests and other wild places became fewer and fewer and our people became scattered. It is said that some of our kind changed permanently into creatures with the help of our *people who know,* and their descendants still live on in the wild places, waiting to become human again.

"Although the mother beneath our feet is where the places of *making* are to be found, it is not just in caverns where the difference between all living things, past and present, are at their least divided: it is also to be embraced in the mountains, woodlands, river banks, and where the land meets the sea.

"As our wild places became fewer, and our people more dispersed, the language of life became harder and harder for us to hear and more difficult to pass on. This is why these places like the one we are in now are so important to us -- they are the place of our beginnings and where our ancestors still reside."

"I see now why this place is of such importance to you and your kind, but what was my grandfather's involvement?" Septimus asked.

Lilly acknowledged the question with a gentle nod and continued, "As you probably know, the Blackwoods have lived here for generations, though it was not until your great-grandfather, Solomon Blackwood's time that things really changed. Cornelius' father, Solomon, decided to increase the size of his cellars, many years ago. At some time during the excavations they discovered passageways full of primitive markings and icons. These primitive places had been sealed off many years previously. These included the caves, which we are now in, which lead to the brook. Did you know that once upon a time the Brook of Blood had many brightly-coloured fish swimming through its veins?"

Of course, Anastasia had been aware that there were rumours about hidden caves close to the mansion and even her family's involvement in them years ago, though Septimus was not about to reveal such memories to Lilly and Ocky, so he just responded, "No, I was not aware of that particular fact." He then politely nodded at Lilly as a gesture for her to carry on.

Lilly smiled and continued, "According to my family, Solomon had hoped that these pagan places were purely a malicious invention, bandied around by gossipmongers and jealousy. When he saw that this was not the case, he became quite unnerved and had every intention of having them walled up, but he died before he could implement it. As you may be aware, the Blackwood name in those days was not always a good one, and Solomon had deliberately followed a pious path in order to distance himself from unwarranted accusations. So it was after Solomon's death that Cornelius really started venturing into the caverns. That was where he met my grandfather, Rowan. Apparently, it soon became clear to the two men that they could be of great use to one another in realising their respective dreams."

The very mention of Solomon, Anastasia's father, brought a surge of memories back to Anastasia -- of his great beard and kind eyes, and of how he would smell of tobacco everywhere he went. She could even remember the excavation work being carried out and how she used to refer to the workmen as *badgers*.

"Cornelius was a seeker, as were many of the Blackwoods before him. He was fascinated by life and death, and amassed an even greater library than the family had before. It was not only for contraband that he used his trade links across the globe, he also brought back hundreds of esoteric books," Lilly said with a grin. Of course, Anastasia knew that Cornelius was a smuggler, and a huge collector of books, but was happy to listen to the retelling.

"After much research, your grandfather eventually found a formula to allow his spirit to merge with another human being, but he wanted more: he wanted to fly like our *people who know*, to become one with the creatures of the earth."

"And did he succeed, Lilly?" Septimus interrupted.

"We think there is a really good chance of that. Apparently, he spent more and more time experimenting and told my grandfather that he was on the brink of halting the ageing process altogether."

"Judging by the look of them, he succeeded in that at least," Septimus said optimistically.

"Luckily, just before the fire he gave my grandfather the recipe for the elixir, and my family has been giving them small doses ever since the time of the fire."

"I really would like to meet your grandfather some time," said Septimus eagerly.

The girl paused a little before replying, "Yes, that may be possible one day… although the recipe is only half of the process. I know some of the ingredients, but far from all."

"That is truly regrettable, Miss Whitethorn. Tell me this, though, if you will, why does your family go to so much trouble to maintain the life of my grandparents after all these years?"

"As I mentioned earlier, my grandfather and your grandfather regularly talked, and shared ideas and information. Cornelius had the books, you see, and we had the knowledge and the experience that has been passed down since the beginning. It is the curse of our people: we find it nearly impossible to read and write. It is as if we can only understand and interpret sounds."

"There are many folk who cannot read, young lady. Surely if the will is there, it would be possible to learn."

"No, I wish it was that simple. Many of us have tried -- maybe our minds are too close to the other creatures or the forest to comprehend it. Who knows?

"We have lost much of our original knowledge over the centuries, trying to fit into changes of ... this world. In many ways it is surprising that we have as much tradition and lore as we do. Cornelius' books were helping us to piece together these rituals and recipes again, helping us to become whole again, at one with the wildwood. This land has become one senseless mass of smoke and noise, but one day the wildwood will return, and when it does all of the other peoples of the world will need our kind once more."

"These are very noble sentiments young lady," said Septimus respectfully.

"We are a noble kind Septimus. In return for your grandfather's help, my grandfather instructed Cornelius in how to move his spirit into the body of a creature."

"Is this something you can do Lilly?"

Lilly looked up at the dimly-lit but brightly-coloured cave paintings above her. She pondered and then replied, "I do have inclinations towards different creatures at various times, and can easily form a mental and physical bond with different creatures, but my mind, or spirit, call it what you will, has not completely left my body. I think the same could be said of most of our folk, as perhaps, in our hearts, we never left the forest."

Septimus looked at Lilly quizzically and asked, "Do you think your grandfather succeeded in enabling my ... our grandparents' wish to change into another creature? Do you think that is how they, or at least their spirits, escaped the fire?"

"Well Septimus, I couldn't say for certain, but I think it very possible. After all, there are creatures down here far more suited to running and hiding than human beings are. They were not to know that the fire would not reach this place, after all."

Septimus recoiled at the thought of them having to change into one of the beasts of the underworld. "You mean a *rat* Miss Whitethorn?"

"Not necessarily. There are plenty of bats down here if you know where to look for them. That would be a good choice, given their situation."

"How on earth would they have been able to get hold of a bat down here?"

"You are forgetting that they were being taught by my grandfather, who can communicate with most of the familiar and unfamiliar creatures. He would have taught Cornelius and Morwenna to call to them and how to subdue them.

"And if it were to be a rat, the same applies, although they are much more curious and less difficult to catch. There is much to be said about being at one with a rat. Rats know how to survive, how to forage; very adaptable creatures, really."

275

Septimus looked to the floor, as if seeking out any rodents nearby.

"Of course, it need not have been a rat, you know. I have heard said that, like the royal family, your family kept ravens as pets too. Who's to say the ravens were not involved in the change somewhere along the way?"

Anastasia could never forget their hideous cawing sound. She had always thought that it sounded like some old hag being strangled. Her father, Solomon, insisted on keeping up the old family tradition because of some superstition, but never said why.

Ocky at last found his voice. "Much as I have appreciated this family history lesson, missy, I really think we should get a move on. The tide would have turned by now, and I have no intentions of spending the night here."

Lilly looked at Ocky, gave him a warm, sympathetic smile and said, "You are correct Ocky, and our time is indeed precious, would you not agree Septimus? Septimus," Lilly repeated …

"Oh yes, yes quite." Septimus' mind was still totally awash with Anastasia's memories. "Precious indeed," he mumbled, in vague recognition of having heard Lilly's words if nothing else.

"Of course, things would be a jolly sight quicker if you knew of a faster way to reach the surface than we do," Ocky said knowingly.

"There are many ways out. Each has their own individual tales to tell," Lilly replied enigmatically.

"I will settle for the shortest tale on this occasion, though I am sure I will be exploring one or two new chapters soon," replied Ocky with a wink.

"Now I really must be going. I have already stayed here longer than I'd planned," announced Lilly.

Septimus composed himself and said, "You have been a revelation Miss Whitethorn. I will make sure your loyalty to my family does not go unrewarded. Tell your grandfather that I would very much like an audience with him soon, if you would be so kind."

"Why thank you Mr Blackwood. I shall do my best," Lilly replied as she turned to leave.

"Before you go missy!" shouted Ocky.

"Yes Octavius," she replied patiently.

"You said you would show us a quicker way out," Ocky replied suspiciously.

"Of course, I can show you the quickest way I know. Follow me."

Septimus was at last alone with his thoughts -- his and Anastasia's anyway. There was so much to contemplate and so little time. His main priority now was getting the books to the surface and meeting Lilly's grandfather, Rowan, as soon as possible. He knew now exactly why Anastasia had been so very keen on coming below with him -- she knew that somewhere amongst this library was possibly a book to extend her life.

How ironic that a person so immersed in the afterlife should wish to cling so stubbornly to this one. Septimus waited in vain for some sort of recognition from Anastasia, but he knew that was not the way this union worked.

Cornelius and Morwenna had obviously been successful in preserving their outer beings at least, but was that all they had achieved? In cheating death had they wittingly or unwittingly resigned themselves to spend the rest of their lives as beasts?

So many questions needing answers and Septimus still had not recovered fully from having his senses invaded time and time again since entering this place of his ancestors. He found himself stroking back his oiled and now dust-encrusted hair, trying to move all of the fog and gain some stability of thought.

How must he deal with Ocky now? If word of this ever made the outside world, it would soon turn rotten, and all of his grandfather's works would go up in smoke. The rest of them need not know about this secret place beyond the lower library, his grandparents, and the meeting with Lilly. All he really needed Ocky for now was for him to relay Lilly's quicker route to the surface. Once he had that, Septimus could do away with Ocky and tell the others he had met with an accident. Hopefully the quicker route Lilly had mentioned could be accessed from the landing area from which they had first entered the cellars.

That would at least ensure that the rest of them need not go any further than the library in order to get the books and scrolls to the surface.

It was when he heard the sound of footsteps coming from the entrance on the far side of the room that a chilling thought occurred to him. Maybe it was he, Septimus, and not Ocky, that would perish here. There was no reason now why Ocky, knowing that he could well have some stake in the ruined estate, would not wish a similar fate on Septimus. There was no one better prepared to tranship this library back to the surface, and if there was any truth in old Aunt Arianwen's claim that Cornelius had, "sucked the rest of the family dry," maybe there was money down below.

No money of any consequence had been found in the wreckage of the fire. It was presumed to have been swallowed up by the flames. Anastasia had been correct in her supposition that the salvagers had either not "wanted" to explore the cellars underneath the mansion, or more likely, they never knew about them. Great-Uncle Augustus must have also had reason to believe that there could well be much more to be found underground but had kept his suspicions to himself, perhaps fearing what they may find. The fact of the matter was, though, that now that Ocky knew that this place actually existed, nothing on earth would stop him from exploring it further.

Septimus eyed the tosher's staff with ill intent: one swift blow from that would get rid of Ocky once and for all.

As the footsteps grew louder, Septimus made his way to the as yet unexplored far entrance, picking up the staff on the way. The doorway, which Lilly had entered from, was of a similar style to the doorway at the end of the small jetty, which they had discovered at the entrance to the cave. However, this door was not as large, and had an air of insignificance about it, as if it wished to remain anonymous, unobtrusive.

Septimus peered out into the blackness and could see a light approaching along what appeared to be a well-worn path in the rocks. By the side of the path lay a band of water, making its way up towards the oncoming light. Surely this has to be the same stretch of water that leads to the landing area. Looks like I am in luck, Septimus thought malevolently.

"I told you the tide had turned, didn't I?" said Ocky, holding his lantern up to the swollen brook. "This path is a good one, but the brook is deeper than the ones we've encountered before, and judging by the tidemarks on the wall, it comes up well over the path when the tide is at its fullest."

Septimus nodded and backed into the room. As if in anticipation, Ocky held his lantern up higher than was necessary, bedazzling Septimus in the process. "I trust Miss Whitethorn furnished you with a faster route than the one by which we came, Octavius?"

"It would appear so. I didn't follow her far, just enough to get a feel for her directions. Yes, a very articulate girl, that one."

"Was that her sole topic of conversation, or did she enlighten you any further about anything else?" Septimus enquired.

"You mean regarding our estate Septimus?" Ocky quipped sardonically.

It was obvious that both men had now had the time to digest some of Lilly's words at least, and to formulate their next moves.

"She told me many things Septimus ..." Ocky deliberately paused to watch Septimus' reaction before continuing: "Who'd have thought we were cousins, eh? Just goes to show what a small world it is, does it not?"

Septimus could see that Ocky's initial confusion on hearing the revelations had swiftly turned to a sense of empowerment, and the atmosphere in the room had turned even more uncomfortable. "Did you know Septimus, all along, that we were kin and that I also could lay a claim to part of the estate?"

Septimus replied as impassively as he could, "Not an inkling. It would appear that fate has played a trick on us both."

Ocky could not be sure if Septimus was telling the truth, as his face was totally unreadable. "It would appear that my father, Thaddeus, was the son of Cornelius Blackwood of this self-same estate," Ocky replied, measuring his words as best he could, knowing that Septimus had himself been orphaned out into the family at an early age, and may not know as much about his heritage as he made out.

"I have never heard of such a son before. If one had existed, I am sure my great-uncle would have told me. Besides, I have seen the parish registers at St Anne's with my own eyes and have never seen an entry for a Thaddeus, son of Cornelius and Morwenna," Septimus replied dismissively.

"That's because ..." Ocky replied hastily. He then paused and continued hesitantly, "...because he was born out of wedlock."

"Ah, I see," replied Septimus, managing to sound both sympathetic and patronizing at the same time. He'd done well: he had forced Ocky to admit that his father was only the bastard son of Cornelius.

"Well that does explain things then, and also puts pay to any entitlement to the estate. However ..." Septimus needed to think fast. Was he forcing Ocky into a corner, and in doing so placing his own life in jeopardy? He need not take such risk at this moment in time.

"However, what?" Ocky replied impatiently.

"However, I am not a greedy man, and I think there is enough intrigue for the both of us here, Octavius. All the more so if we keep everything we have seen here to ourselves, don't you think? Knowledge is of far more interest to me than money anyway, and much as it irks me to say this, I think we can actually reap far more benefit here as a team."

Ocky took his time before responding. If he took the matter to court, he knew he would not have a leg to stand on against Septimus. If, however, something were to happen to Septimus in the meantime, he may have a chance. But there again, who would believe a tosher claiming to herald from nobility?

Even if that were to be believed, any suspicion regarding Septimus' demise would surely fall on his shoulders.

"I believe we have a deal, sir. Though I do not share your aversion to tosh in itself, just what you have to do to attain it."

"Very well, I will keep all the books and, you, sir, are welcome to all of the other goods, money and wine included, found hereabouts."

"If there is any money," Ocky replied.

"Indeed, if there is any," Septimus repeated his words back to him. "But there's plenty of wine. If your friend, Jewels, leaves you any, that is," said Septimus with his tongue firmly in his cheek.

Ocky pursed his lips. He was confused as to how to respond to this lightening of the subject. "I also want access to all of the books when we reach the surface. And don't think I've forgotten about the money promised to me for helping you find your... *our* estate."

"Fear not Ocky; you and Jewels will get your reward as agreed."

"What do you suppose we should do about these two?" Ocky said in askance, pointing to Cornelius and Morwenna.

"I suggest we leave them in the capable hands of Miss Whitethorn and her elusive grandfather, for the time being at least. Come now, let us go and find the others," Septimus said, making his way to where they had entered the room.

When they found the others, Ocky took Pigeon downstream via the first entrance to see if this really was the same stretch of water that flowed past the other entrance, whilst Septimus organised the transportation of the books and scrolls. He quickly sifted through several of those that had been housed in the library. There were far too many of them to take in one journey alone, and some were in such a fragile condition that they would need to be studied here at a later date.

Thankfully, it was only Jewels who seemed the worse for wear: the temptation of free booze had not been lost on him. Despite the hazards of the return journey and some moaning from Mortlake that they had lost Ocky and Pigeon on some wild goose chase, all went well. Septimus stacked books into small piles that were then carefully placed in the empty chests that had been brought up from the cellar.

By the time the gang had struggled their way across the precarious ballroom and down the steps to the cellar, they were greeted by a wet, smiling Pigeon. "Ocky and I followed the brook along and there's a path alright. Ocky reckons it could lead to the surface."

"That's right, he certainly does," Ocky interjected, as he too entered the cellar.

"Then we are in luck gentlemen. We have not a moment to lose," Septimus said hastily, hoping to dispel any doubts within the ranks.

"Do forgive me for asking," slurred Jewels. "How do we know this path leads to the surface? Wouldn't it be better to go the way we came?" Silence filled the room and all eyes turned to Septimus.

"Because his Lordship and I found an old map in the library, which shows a much quicker way out and if, Jewelsy, you want to go back the long way on your own, feel free, though judging by the state yer in, I don't think you'd make it," Ocky replied swiftly.

"He's right, there. Come on, you old soak, don't be such a milksop," piped up a grinning Pigeon.

"But what if the map is wrong? The water would be too high then to make it back the way we came in," exclaimed Jewels.

"He's got a point Septimus. The tunnel could be blocked or anything. Ain't no point in taking risks," added a cautious Mortlake.

"Yeah, he's right, ain't no point in taking risks," Jewels continued.

"Gentlemen, gentlemen, I don't want to spend any more time here than any of you do, and if it were to be blocked, as you so optimistically put it, Jewels, then we would come back here and wait for the tide to turn and ..." Jewels was just about to respond when Septimus held his hand up and continued ... "and I would personally pay every one of you 30 guineas for the inconvenience of spending the night here with Octavius." Ocky rolled his eyes and could not stop the faintest of smirks from furnishing his face.

"That will do for me Mr Blackwood. Come on, lads." Pigeon mustered the troops and all arguments stopped, for the time being at least.

The water had risen quite considerably since they had found this long-forgotten jetty. None of the gang had any enthusiasm to jump back into the inky slime below. "Make sure you keep the trunks above the water level; I don't want to lose any of these books to the sewers," said a beseeched Septimus.

"I don't know about you boys, but I ain't that keen on working any harder than I have to," Pigeon said with a smile.

"You'll pull your weight boy, or feel the back of my hand," Mortlake gruffly responded.

"What about if we sling some of the trunks into the rowing boat and pull it? The water's high enough. We could take it in turns, save your old backs too," replied a still-smiling Pigeon.

"Aye, lads, he's got something there. It may be on its way out, but look, it's still afloat," Ocky said. "It may just work -- could save a lot of time and effort."

Pigeon's plan worked well -- occasionally the rope would become a little snagged on some protruding rock or debris at the base of the tunnel, but overall it was a blessing. The old, rotting boat that had caused Septimus and Ocky so much consternation had ended up being a godsend rather than a curse.

As they approached the door to the other cavern, Ocky and Septimus made sure that they were the first out of the water and onto the path, in a bid to conceal the door from the others.

None of the others noticed the small doorway, as their attention was fixed on maintaining their footing as they climbed up onto the limestone teeth of the path above. All, that was, except the ever-vigilant Pigeon. "Oi lads, look! Another door! Let's go see what's behind it."

"Already tried it boy. It's stuck fast, I'm afraid," Ocky replied hastily.

"I reckon we could get in okay, lads, don't you?" Pigeon persisted.

"We ain't got time for that boy. Let's just get out of here!" Mortlake yelled back at him.

"Mr Mortlake is right boy. We do not have a moment to spare," Septimus replied, quietly thanking Mortlake's reluctance.

Just past the door there were countless numbers of wax torches hanging on the tunnel wall. Septimus pondered on their age and usage. Their vast numbers spoke of potentially large gatherings … ceremonies perhaps?

"Bridge ahoy!" Pigeon yelled out enthusiastically.

"Looks like something out of a fairy tale, don't it?" Jewels responded with glassy eyes.

Septimus could not help but think that Jewels was right too. It really did look like it had sprung to life within the tunnel itself, such was the confusion and wildness of its construction. In places it was so contorted that it was difficult to believe that it had been made by the hand of man, though its beautiful arch in the centre and the sublime carving of serpents' heads on the handrails laid waste to any supernatural conception.

The bridge was not only beautiful in its own peculiar way, it was also a blessing too, as the path they were walking on was disappearing rapidly under the foetid water. Thankfully, the trunk-laden old rowing boat they were towing along could just about fit underneath the bridge's archway. The new pathway was narrower but mercifully a good eight inches higher than the rising water below.

Concerned by the change in their path, Septimus took Ocky to one side and asked quietly, "I trust Miss Whitethorn mentioned crossing the bridge? I really do not want to be wading through the filth below. It must be at least waist height by now."

"Don't fret, your Lordship. Our course is set fair. We shall soon be at what she called the Adder's Staircase. All we have to do then is climb to the top, and daylight will be ours once more."

Apart from the grumbles of fatigue and Jewels losing his footing on more than one occasion, the journey to the Adder's Staircase proved largely uneventful. Indeed there was barely a shadow of damp upon the old trunks on reaching the maw of the staircase. The literary cargo was unloaded with both speed and care, and it was left for Pigeon to enquire, "What are we going to do with this boat now, then? Shall I let it go or what?"

Mortlake lifted a lazy eye and remarked, "I reckon Pigeon better be a good boy and sail it back to where he found it, don't you boys? It was his idea to bring it."

Following many grunts (withheld smiles) and ayes of agreement from the men, Pigeon (totally unaware his leg was being pulled) momentarily looked wide-eyed and more than a little alarmed at Septimus, who responded to his expression by saying, "I see it is not a voyage you wish to undergo, young man, in which case, tie it tight to one of those posts below, and I mean tightly though, boy; we may need it again one day."

Septimus peered into the blackness of the gouge that was the Adder's Staircase with more than a little foreboding. The light from Ocky's lamp revealed a slow trickle of water sulking down an avenue of algae and roughly-hewn stone.

After a short respite, the men began their ascent to the surface, which was to prove the most arduous part of the entire venture. Hunger had now set in, and the cold was becoming unbearable. Many a time the trunks had to be lowered to the floor for the men to get some feeling back into their icy hands. If this was not bad enough, a little way further up droplets of water had become huge tears on the cheeks of the cave. They ran down onto the steps below, making them even more slippery than they were before, thus causing damage to man and trunk alike.

The overall morale of the men was uncoiling like the twisted passageways of their ascent. The further up they went, the more the girth and height of the cave seemed to shrink and swell. The wet surfaces of the cave had become furnished with a wide variety of gelatinous fungi, and great chasms were opening up on either side of them, leading to some of the men questioning the validity of the route they had embarked upon. Despite the seeds of doubt sown by such gorges, Septimus, Ocky, and Pigeon could not fully withstand the seductive natures of such diversions.

The mystery of each separate opening in the darkness, and its ultimate destination, was a source of great intrigue and fascination for their enquiring minds.

In amongst the fungi and rivulets of water running down the cave's walls were the same primitive carvings, which Septimus had seen on St Anne's Stone and in the caves below. This, though, was becoming the only evidence of man's hand in the fashioning of this subterranean thoroughfare. The subordinate, slippery steps of stone had gradually been superseded by a moist but smooth natural rock face. Paradoxically, the ceiling of the cave had become lined with a profusion of stalactites, hanging like needles of porcelain most pure.

"I've had it. I can't carry these trunks anymore. Why don't we just leave 'em here and come down again tomorrow. You can bet your bottom dollar they will still be here," Jewels said wearily.

"Not far Jewelsy. I reckon we're nearly there now," Ocky replied, raising a hopeful eye to Septimus.

Septimus latched onto the expression and beckoned Pigeon towards him. "Boy, take this lamp and go on ahead. I have no intention of giving up now, so off you go quick as you can. There's a large tot of rum in it for you when we reach the surface."

"Make it two," Pigeon replied, grinning from ear to ear.

"Scarper boy! Go! Run!" Ocky retorted, waving him off impatiently.

Desperation and fatigue had now started to eat away at even Septimus' stoicism. Maybe Jewels was right. Just getting out of here must be the first priority. Surely no one would venture down tonight and steal away their booty.

"Ahoy there!"… The cry came echoing down the cave towards them, along with the sound of pounding feet. "Ahoy! There's light ahead! Light ahead!" Pigeon's voice was unmistakable.

"Praise the Lord," replied the usually mute Marmaduke. He was not alone in breathing a huge sigh of relief.

It was with a renewed sense of vigour and hope that the men marched onwards. It was not long before Septimus first felt the sweet kiss of a breeze on his cheek, in what was otherwise a virtually airless passageway. This was shortly followed by the all-encompassing blackness of the tunnel gradually seeping into grey, so much so that Septimus extinguished his lamp and strode optimistically into the ever-brightening hue.

"There we have it gentlemen! We have light!" Septimus exclaimed, gesturing upward with his arm. The men temporarily lowered the trunks and paused for breath. They ached from top to toe, and many of them had long since lost all feeling in their feet.

All was joyous amongst the men until Septimus espied the ground moving before him.

"Oi, whatcha stopped for?" cried an impatient Mortlake as Septimus came to a grinding halt.

"Look ahead," Septimus said with a whisper. About ten yards ahead of them was a vast knot of serpents blocking their path -- a writhing mass that seemed to boil with venomous vivacity.

Ocky came to the fore and quietly rasped: "So this is what she meant by the Adder's Staircase."

"It looks that way," Septimus replied regretfully before continuing, "I had hoped that when the girl told you that this was called the Adder's Staircase, she was referring to the coiled nature of the passageway, not a home to a nest of vipers!"

"Leave them to me." Ocky lurched forward towards the deadly snakes that blocked their path.

"If there is one thing I cannot stand, it's bleedin' snakes," said a wary Mortlake.

Ocky turned round calmly and exclaimed, "I doubt if they are overly-enamoured by you either, my friend. They have got *some* taste, you know." It was only the threat of the snakes which stopped Mortlake from thumping the mocking grin off of Ocky's face. Ocky turned round again to face the hissing menace blocking their path.

Ocky's only weapons were a small coil of rope, which had been tied around one of the trunks, his tosher's staff, and more than a little guile.

He gently lowered his staff into the centre of the knot of adders and slowly eased them to one side, taking great care not to distress them in any way at all. Once they were away from the middle of the path, he stealthily uncoiled the rope to create a boundary around the circumference of the snakes. He had once overheard an old man at the docks telling a young deckhand about this method years ago. Whether there was any truth in it, or whether it was just part of the age-old game of making a youngster, still wet around the ears, believe anything he was told, he would soon find out.

Ocky had been very careful not to let the rope touch any of the snakes, making sure they had enough room to stretch out unhindered. Hopefully this would allow enough space for the men to sidle their way past the knot without incident.

The rest of the gang watched Octavius Blackwood with awe. "There must be at least twenty adders in that lot," Jewels said anxiously.

"They obviously respond to one of their own," Mortlake muttered.

"Maybe he can charm them too, like the bloke at the fair on Crackwillow Park," Pigeon interjected.

"That would be about the full extent of his charm as far as I am concerned," Mortlake replied sourly.

"Right pick up those trunks and let's move on. Nice and easy now, don't want to rile 'em," said Ocky, as he backed away from the adders, never turning round.

"How do we know they ain't going to cross that rope?" Mortlake said doubtfully.

"We don't, but unless any of you gentlemen have a better plan, I suggest we take that risk," Ocky replied nonchalantly.

Thankfully, for all concerned, Ocky's ruse worked long enough for all the gang to be out of striking range at least.

"I dunno Ocky, you're full of surprises, ain't ya," Jewels said, shaking his head.

"He's certainly full of something," growled Mortlake.

"Well Jewelsy, thankfully you ain't, so let us rejoice," replied Ocky, ignoring Mortlake's unwarranted interjection. Jewels was not sure whether it was a compliment or not, but agreed anyway.

As the men walked up towards the light, they were gratified by the familiar sounds of life on the surface. Just before the forever-meandering tunnel straightened up, they noticed that the natural course of the cave had been blocked up with a huge door with vast, impenetrable iron railings in front of it. This last intrigue was largely ignored, owing to the men's desire to see the surface again. Their path narrowed considerably and the natural curves of the cave had been replaced by stone walls on either side.

Twenty paces later they found their exit back to terra firma. It had been much quicker than their original route, but no less exhausting due to the steepness of their ascent. All that separated them from the world outside was a small metal grid hanging on two huge hinges. Septimus' heart sank when he saw that not only did it have a padlock on it, but it was also touch and go as to whether their cargo could fit through such a small opening.

Pigeon hurried to the door and exclaimed loudly, "It's alright boys, it's not locked. Someone must have forgotten to lock it." Of course, it was only Septimus and Ocky who knew that that certain someone was likely to have been the ethereal Miss Whitethorn.

"Right boy, slip through and see if the coast is clear. It's imperative that no one sees us leaving here," said Septimus, in a hushed but stern tone. Pigeon was delighted that he was going to be the first one out and even more so to be a look-out for the rest of the gang.

Mercifully, nobody saw Pigeon's ascent into the decaying remnants of the day's light. Once out of the small alcove, he eyed up and down the street either side of him. When he turned around and looked back to see where the burrow he had just got out of actually lay, he smiled and said, "You'll never guess where we are, boys!"

"Never mind that boy. Can we get out undetected?" Septimus retorted impatiently.

"All's quiet at present guv'na."

"Good. Come here. Quick about it! Let's see if we can get the trunks out of here in one piece."

Fortunately, Lady Luck smiled on them once more -- all of the cargo passed through the gap with only inches to spare. One by one the last of the men stepped into the small alcove and out onto the road.

Septimus could not believe his eyes to see that the alcove was the old baptistery that lay under the graveyard of St Anne's

Church, the very place that had engaged him so whilst on his way to meet Ocky and Jewels for the first time. The natural course of the tunnel that had been blocked up must have led directly up to the crypt of the old church.

Of course! That must be what the markings on the church's standing stone were all about. In amongst the creatures and the strange archaic lettering there had been engravings of people stepping downwards below an arch and long spirals leading eventually to what looked like a river and then an inner circle. It was all there on the stones after all! No wonder the Christians had felt the need to build a church here.

"Pigeon, go hail down a cab for us, and make it a large one," instructed Septimus. The rest of the gang slumped down on the assorted trunks and waited impatiently for its arrival. When the carriage eventually arrived, the driver was most perturbed by the filthy state of the motley crew.

"You ain't getting in my cab looking like that. Look at the state of ya!" Septimus reached into his now-ragged jacket and pulled out a resplendent wad of notes. "Though I think I may have an old blanket or two which may just about cover the seats," said the driver, changing his tune.

"Please make sure they are clean," replied Septimus dryly.

"They'll be clean," said the cabby as he clambered down out of his seat. "Give me a hand up with these trunks. Ain't loading them all by myself; this ain't Speaker's Corner, you know."

Marmaduke and Mortlake helped the hansom cab driver to load the trunks onto his carriage. "Driver, make sure to rope those poles down well. Don't want to lose me pride and joy now, do I?" Jewels shouted up, enjoying his role as the master for once.

"Hmpfh," the driver retorted, and whispered a few barely audible blasphemies.

The carriage made two stops on its way back to Septimus' studio. The first was to drop off the ever-thirsty Jewels at the Albion Inn and the second was for Mortlake at the corner of October Street near to his home on Darrah Terrace. It was only these brief stops that kept Septimus from falling asleep, soothed as he was by the gentle rhythm of the horse and harness. Indeed, Septimus had not felt so physically and mentally exhausted since his last venture below ground. He was thankful he had not nearly drowned like last time, though nothing could have foreshadowed the amazing discoveries of the day.

Septimus had not only verified all of those tales he had heard long ago but he'd actually found his grandparents alive, if one could call that living. Now he'd found a quicker way to the cellars, it would not be long before he could bring the whole library back to the surface. Maybe he could invest in a house, or a cellar near the baptistery, and burrow his way into one of the existing tunnels for further explorations. He was sure there was much more to find.

Chapter 40

The Unkindness

Septimus' sedate train of thought was interrupted by the guttural shrieks of an unkindness of ravens flying high up above. It was strange to see a group of them this far into the city. He was glad that now he was just seeing an unkindness of ravens, whereas earlier, when seeing through Anastasia's eyes, he had felt nothing but utter revulsion for the creatures.

That was not the only thing that perplexed Septimus, though -- the birds seemed to be flying in amongst what could only be described as a small gathering of mustard-coloured clouds glowing bright and friendless in the otherwise-cloudless night sky. Pigeon's attention had also been alerted to the change of hue on the horizon. "Crickey Moses, reckon another pot of pitch gone southwards again. Either that or a baker, I'll warrant. Those boys never learn."

Soon the sounds of the disturbed birds and the pounding of hooves were accompanied by shouting all around them. The driver of their carriage fought with the horses to find a way through the mass of people running hither and thither. It was not until the carriage turned into Whortleberry Street that they could see the cause of such ado. Septimus' feeling of mild apprehension and curiosity had swiftly turned into his worst nightmare.

A great crowd had gathered around his smoking studio. A scene of utter chaos ensued. Men, women, and dogs were running around in a state of high anxiety. He watched as a group of men jostled their way through a rash of sightseers and residents alike. They were armed with paltry buckets of water that were being pumped up by the members of the London Fire Brigade. Septimus thought he could even see the heavily-whiskered figure of James Braidwood, London's chief fire fighter, at the front of the mob nearest the building.

The carriage soon became hemmed in by the sheer volume of folk lining the street. Septimus bid the driver to wait for him as he leaped down, strode over toward the studio, and watched, transfixed, as the conflagration extended its grip on his home. Such was the intensity of the heat being generated by the blaze that he could only get to within thirty feet of the building. Here he watched in anguish as the hungry flames licked the night's sky. Septimus' magnificent glass house was utterly ravaged -- a tangle of badly woven iron bars remained: a monstrous nest perched high on the twisted pyre of ambition and acquisition.

The sense of loss that Septimus now felt was incomparable. His experiments, his magical cameras, and his wonderful photographs were all gone. Out of the corner of his eye he could see a forlorn creature making its way towards him.

It was Angharad. "Mr Blackwood sir, there was nothing I could do. It was too much for me, too strong," she blurted out, eyes full of tears.

Septimus uncharacteristically reached out towards her. He was still entranced by the magnitude of flames and the loss of his own very private world. He had not given a thought to the human cost of fire. "Was there anyone else in the building? Sophia, Miss Appleby, the ventriloquist girl, one of Nonny's clients ... wasn't she supposed to be in today?" Septimus enquired.

"Thankfully, they left just a little before the fire took hold: Sophia first, followed by the client a little after. Miss Appleby seemed very distressed about something, though I know not what," Angharad replied almost apologetically.

"Distressed?" Septimus asked curiously. Angharad started to weep again. "John!" Septimus exclaimed angrily. He stared at the sky, shaking his head in fury. "Where is he now?"

Angharad tried to speak but the words refused to come. All she could muster as a reply was to turn her head and look up to where the glass house used to be. Her glance seemed to reveal John the Chemist's fate.

Septimus edged his way closer to the building before cold fury overtook his entire body. He yelled up at defiant flames, "You could not resist one last show could you, Spring-Heeled Jack? No more headlines, no more glory, just a sad pitiful excuse of a man, as ever. I hope you burn in hell for this!"

A nearby journalist overheard Septimus' bellowing at the threshold of the raging carcass of his once-great studio. "I do beg your pardon, sir. My name's Rick Best, journalist from *The Star* newspaper. Did my ears deceive me, or did you really shout out the name *Spring-Heeled Jack*? What involvement do you think he had with the fire? Do you know the man? Is he still in the building?"

Septimus slowly turned his face to the over-eager young journalist, and smiled malevolently. Baleful eyes seared into the writer's inquisitive expression. The once-bullish journalist instinctively took a step backwards, uncertain of his fate.

"Sorry, sir, I was only asking, sir. It's just that we've been after him for some time," the young man said apologetically.

Septimus briefly held his tongue, his gaze radiating untold menace at the anxious journalist in front of him. Then he retorted sardonically, "No little man, I think your imagination must have got the better of you. Spring-Heeled Jack is a myth, a bogeyman to scare little children when they've misbehaved. *He* is not responsible for this."

Septimus' face hardened and his jaw set. He continued to glare at the impetuous reporter. The embattled writer backed away slowly saying, "Right you are, sir. Don't s'pose he is, sir. Sorry to trouble you. He's still a wanted man, you know." The last few sheepish words were lost on Septimus. The journalist shrank back into the crowd from whence he had first appeared, fleet of foot and eager for a headline.

Dead or alive, there was no way on earth that Septimus was ever going to give John the Chemist, aka Spring-Heeled Jack, one last front page, one last moment of glory.

Chapter 41

Tinderbox

John the chemist had suffered yet another virtually sleepless night, largely due to the shouts and screams of drunken revellers slopping out and onto the streets at all hours. When sleep had finally arrived, it was fitful and daubed with bittersweet memories of his beloved Juliana. The morning arrived much too soon for the chemist's liking. The exuberant banter of the costermongers on their way to market and the dairy boys deliberately clanging their milk churns down on the hard stone steps sought to drive John to utter despair.

All this, and to cap off his misery, he had remembered that he was supposed to be minding Septimus' studio today.

He had never been keen on Septimus, but now the worm of discontent had truly burrowed its way deep into the core of John's mind. John desperately wanted to spend more time developing new potions and devices. This was supposed to be the age of enterprise and innovation; why should he waste his time aiding Septimus' obsessive desire to make photographs come to life? This frustration, however, was not the only bugbear for the chemist. The constant references to his past and Mrs Thunderbug's increasing infatuation with Septimus really preyed heavily on his mind.

Apart from a few demeaning remarks, the only conversation he could get out of Mrs Thunderbug nowadays was how marvellous Septimus was for improving the reputation of the neighbourhood, and what a gentleman he was. If only John could show her the real Septimus, the self-centred predator that hid behind the lens.

The walk to the studio had done little to shake off John's atrocious hangover, and the cold had played havoc with his sinuses. John had arrived with only minutes to spare before the photo-shoot of Miss Appleby. He was greeted sourly at the door by Septimus' ever-dour housekeeper, Angharad. John had always disliked the way Angharad looked at him -- looks of pity and disdain were not welcome from anyone, let alone from a maudlin, bible-thumping sheep like her. No wonder so many men took to drink with women like that around.

Sophia had been busying herself in the studio with the preparations for the photo-shoot a long time prior to John's arrival. She knew she and John would be working alone together, and the more she could get out of the way before he came in meant the sooner the job would be done and she would be able to leave the vile creature to it. It was not that she feared John -- she knew that she would probably get the better of him in a fight -- it was just everything about him made her skin crawl and she'd certainly never turn her back on him.

She made sure all of the props were in place and that the outfits were neat and tidy and ready for use; not forgetting, of course the hairbrush. Sophia had never questioned the need to get tiny strands of hair from the clients. Septimus' fanatical need to remove and keep every last strand of hair from the brush between users had seemed strange at first, but she soon presumed it was probably required to stop the transportation of lice from one client to the next.

And so it was that Sophia was relieved to see the client swiftly on the heels of John's unwelcome entrance into the room. Sophia enjoyed the company of Miss Appleby, much to the chagrin of John, who seemed to think that he was the butt of their shared mirth. The more the girls giggled, the more aggravated he became, and the more gin he began to swallow.

Needless to say, by the end of the shoot John had become quite abusive to both Sophia and the client. Sophia could not wait to get out of the studio and back to the sanctuary of the Angel Vaults. Knowing what John was like, she insisted that Miss Appleby do the same, but Miss Appleby was having none of it. She had her mind set on perusing through all of Septimus' *amazing* photographs, and that was that. Nothing Sophia could say or do seemed to weaken her resolve or get her to change her mind.

The only crumb of comfort that Sophia could take when leaving the building alone was the fact that John was now so drunk that he could barely put one foot in front of the other, and that Miss Appleby, despite her age and size, was certainly not a young woman to be messed with.

John quickly and rather haphazardly saw to it that all the necessary treatment given to the photographs for development was done before he staggered across the floor towards Miss Appleby. The whole studio arrested Miss Appleby's attention with its beautiful views over the Thames, the sumptuous outfits, and the finely decorated backcloths. Even Septimus' magnificent collection of taxidermy fascinated her, though most of all it was Septimus' photographic collection that she was really overawed with.

"Septimus must be the best photographer in the whole of London I reckons," Miss Appleby exclaimed.

"What you see is both of our work. He'd be nothing without me." How John despised the way that Septimus got all the credit for their work. "You know that your precious Mr Blackwood will probably want to capture you for his collection, young lady?"

"Capture me? What on earth do you mean?" asked Miss Appleby, with little interest. Her eyes and attention were still fixed on the collection, and she refused eye contact with this obnoxious, shambling creature in the background.

John persisted though. "That's why Sophia made such a fuss of your hair -- he needs your hair, you see, to catch ya."

"No offence kind sir, but you are obviously drunk and incapable of rational thought. Catch me indeed!"

"Incapable, am I?" He lit one of the candles from the table and held it up to one of the photographs. "Looky here missy. Watch them squirm! That's what he does, you know." The candle shone bright into the glass. Nothing moved. There was no life, just dead eyes staring into the void.

The girl relented and looked. "There, you see? Absolutely nothing. I had an uncle who started seeing things and making things up, you know. He was certain his backyard was infested with fairies. Fairies, I ask ya. In Whitechapel of all places!"

"Why you ..." John made a lunge for the girl but she was far too quick for him. He hurled the photograph at the wall in a rage. Miss Appleby took flight and ran out of the room and down the stairs as fast as she could, nearly sending an aghast Angharad flying. "Miss Appleby, whatever is the matter?" Angharad shouted after her.

"He's a lunatic, I tell ya. Needs seeing to, he does," the girl shouted, running on to the street without even a backward glance.

John reached for the gin bottle and drank heavily from its moistened neck. He picked up a photograph and stared balefully at its inertia before throwing it at the wall, followed by another, then another. What power he now felt in this wanton destruction of their work. Clumsily, John reached out for the bottle in front of him, losing his balance at the same time. He tried to steady himself with his other hand, but only succeeded in overturning the table and its contents in front of him. Miraculously, he caught hold of the bottle before falling to the floor.

John laughed triumphantly at his ability not to have spilt a drop of gin, despite everything else being in total disarray. At least he'd got his priorities right. He drank deeply, a toast to himself. He carefully put the bottle on the floor, being very cautious not to spill its precious contents. It was at this point that he started to feel a slight stinging pain in the back of his legs. His hand fumbled round to find the back of his leg. His trousers felt strangely sticky to the touch.

John's first thought was that he had not been as successful as he had initially supposed in not spilling any of the liquor. This notion took flight on swift wings as he brought up his hands to see that they were both caked in blood. He realised then that he must have fallen on some shards of glass left over from his wrecking spree, or the contents of the table he had so ignominiously upset seconds before.

His hands clutched at the back of his legs to ease the pain and stem the blood flowing freely from his many wounds. Pain seared up through the rest of his legs, and then relentlessly onward in spiteful waves through the rest of his whole body. The smell of burning paper further assaulted his now-beleaguered senses. He looked over to see that the candle he had lit earlier had been upturned in the crash, and its flame had found liberty amongst Septimus' many notebooks that were now strewn around the glass --ridden floor.

John desperately tried to stand up in order to remove himself as quickly as possible from the intensity of the heat rapidly encircling him. But all was in vain, as both his legs failed. There was only one option left to him -- he would need to slide through the malicious shards to stifle the libertine nature of the ravenous flames. John grimaced in agony as he began making his way closer to the ever-more intense conflagration before him.

Any pain-numbing effects produced by John's consumption of gin had long since been replaced by agony and blind panic. Some of the droplets of sweat had multiplied into rivers, crossing his blistering flesh. The flames flitted and flicked at some of the discarded costumes, like a lover's tongue teasing its prey before erupting into a passion of orange and gold. The rapture embraced one garment, then another, then another. John's earlier devastation had found new disciples of destruction. There seemed no end to the vengeance sought by the studio at John's earlier displays of frustration and rage. He had thrown some of the framed photographs so hard into the great glass panels at the side of the studio that they were now smashed, allowing small but incisive blades of air in to further incite the already-brazen blaze.

As the fire strengthened its grip upon the studio, the victims became many. The silent raptors were set free one by one as their glass cases shattered and cracked in the intense heat.

Their emancipation was short lived as the flames swallowed them up talon by talon. Septimus' special collection of photographs, usually dormant in daylight hours, was being interrupted by the callous inferno. John could just about make out their ghastly grimaces and contorted bodies amongst the buckled frames and the glowing metal plates. How I wish that stupid girl were here now, thought John. She'd see the true monster that was Septimus then, in all his glory. John then closed his eyes, resigned to his fate.

After the fire eventually receded, the spell that had forced Septimus to look deep into the ashes and embers of his dreams departed with it. Now it was fatigue's turn to overwhelm him. It had been the longest day of his life, and now he was happy to see it end. Septimus gave Angharad the money for a hotel room, and instructed her to meet him in his coach house in the morning. It was to that self- same coach house on the opposite side of the street from the studio that he was now heading. The anxious and excited crowd had long since departed; now all that was left to do was to unload the finds of the day and seek the sanctuary and sanity of a warm bed, no matter how humble.

After the last trunk had been safely stashed away, Septimus instructed Pigeon and Marmaduke to take it in turns to stay awake and guard the chests. Septimus had lost more than enough today as it was.

He was going to make quite certain he would not lose any more. "Ocky and I will relieve you of your duties in the morning."

"Will I now?" was Ocky's irritated retort.

"I would hope so. Besides, do you really fancy another walk back through the Rookery tonight when I can get you a warm room at the Angel Vaults?"

"Hmm, I want to be paid for all of this, your Lordship, you know that?"

"Yes, have no fear, you will be paid. Now, I would be much obliged if you could wait here for me for ten minutes. I have one more visit to make before we head off to the inn."

Ocky nodded in agreement and walked over to where Marmaduke and Pigeon were already huddled around a hastily-lit brazier in front of the stables. Despite his exhaustion, Septimus felt an inexplicable compulsion to see Anastasia. He had no intention of waking her or breaking the bond with her tonight, though. He was far too tired for any of that. He just knew he needed to see her. Septimus had not felt her thoughts for a few hours now, so one more night would not trouble him, especially after the day he had had.

Now all Septimus wanted to do was tell Mrs Moon that he had returned safely. His mission had been a success and he wished an audience with Anastasia tomorrow, after lunch. He thought he had caught a glimpse of Mrs Moon earlier watching the fire through the still dirty window, but had been in no mood to talk at that point.

Septimus had not seen Anastasia since their merging of minds, though he had had many intrusions into his consciousness since they had bonded.

Indeed, it seemed like a long time ago since all his thoughts and feelings had been entirely his own. He weighed heavily on the lion-shaped knocker before rapping it hard onto the door -- impatience had overcome discretion.

It was not long before Mrs Moon came to the door and asked who it was. "It is me... Mr Blackwood," Septimus replied eagerly.

Mrs Moon quickly relieved the heavy bolts and opened the door wide.

"Oh Septimus, it *is* you. I was not expecting to see you; please excuse me."

"There is no need to stand on ceremony on my account," Septimus said wearily as he followed her up the stairs.

Once in the room, Mrs Moon continued, "Oh it was not that Mr Blackwood sir, it was ..." Before she could finish her sentence, Septimus had given a couple of taps on Anastasia's bedroom door before swiftly entering her bedchamber.

"Septimus!" Mrs Moon's voice followed him into the chamber. The room was very still. Anastasia lay quietly on the bed, and her expression was one of serenity and ease. Septimus' brow creased and he turned to face Mrs Moon, who had entered the room after him. The smudged powder on her cheeks and a distant, watery glow in her eyes answered every question he had. "I did try to warn you," Mrs Moon said gently.

Septimus replied with a barely audible, "Yes," and turned to face dead Great-Aunt Anastasia one last time.

At first Septimus felt a brief moment of pity, soon to be replaced by anxiety and confusion. *The end, then?* he thought. *Perhaps that is why I had not felt her thoughts or experienced her extrasensory perceptions for a while.* "What time did she go?" Septimus asked Mrs Moon sombrely, eyes still fixed on his great-aunt's body.

"Just after two o'clock. The doctor came this morning and said it was as if she was just closing down."

Septimus bowed his head and reflected on the joy she had felt at reaching her brother. Perhaps it was one of her final thoughts, Septimus mused. Had the old woman known that they may have the book or scroll that could have helped her prolong her life? Did the book matter at all? Had she just been using him to find her sibling? Was he just a receptacle for her soul to go back home to die?

As if seeking answers, Septimus made his way to her bedside, pulled up a chair, and took hold of her hand. She was still wearing the ring bearing the ancient seal of the Blackwoods -- the baby's head with the snake coiled around its neck. "Take it Septimus." The voice seemed to come from inside his head. A wave of panic followed. "Take it Septimus." Thankfully, this time it was the unmistakeable voice of Mrs Moon. "It was her last wish that you should have the ring; my lady told me that Cornelius gave it to her the last time she had seen him alive."

Septimus hesitated and turned his head towards Mrs Moon. "Put the ring on your finger; it is yours." Septimus slowly squeezed the ring between his forefinger and thumb and placed it on his little finger. A warm feeling of recognition coursed though his veins, his psyche becoming full of images. The familiarity he felt when experiencing these visions meant that they were probably memories, though none of which were his own.

For the first time, he could see the Blackwood family mansion as it really was: with its sturdy thatched roof, heavy black timbers, gigantic twisted brick chimneys, and brilliant white plaster. He was certain that this was the house of his ancestors; he felt this was home. The ancient high tower of St Anne's Church stood proudly in the distance, as did the distinctive and gnarled old oak at the bottom of the garden. The mansion seemed bigger than he had seen in the previous drawings and prints of the place, though every time he looked at the mansion it kept changing slightly, as if he was seeing snapshots of it through the ages. The size of the garden never changed, though the plants and the layout did profusely; rising and falling like a verdant wave. Interspersed with these images were half-remembered people, dressed in costumes of almost immeasurable age... family perhaps? Visions of fiery hearths, meal times, parlour games, joyous births, and sorrowful deaths, a kaleidoscope of memories rode through his mind.

Septimus felt a deep sense of empowerment; the ring had given him a direct link to remembrances of the Blackwoods long since passed. Despite the alluring effects of the ring, Septimus could not overcome the feeling of betrayal and anger. In exasperation he sought to pull off the ring as quickly as possible. He was not going to be seduced by the ring's enchantment; although this peculiar band was not a tight fit, he almost felt reluctance within the ring itself to be removed.

Eventually, it yielded to his perseverance and came off his in his hand, along with any remaining gratitude felt for his great-aunt in giving him such a gift.

301

In that simple act of defiance, Septimus, much to his complete and utter abhorrence, realised that Anastasia was not dead. Her physical remains before him were as cold and as dead as granite, though he felt her spirit live on. Septimus may have removed the ring from his finger, but in doing so he felt a great sense of loss. It was not just a vague feeling of detaching himself from his birthright, or the uncanny sense of security it had lent him. Septimus clearly felt a feeling of physical severance at the removal of the ring.

"Are you alright Mr Blackwood? I can understand that it must have come as an awful shock to you," Mrs Moon said, breaking the unbearable intensity that had grasped the room so thoroughly.

Septimus made to turn around and answer her, but words failed him, his gaze finding refuge in the window opposite. He waved his hand abruptly, a gesture to Mrs Moon that he wished to be left alone. She duly slipped out of the room and left Septimus to his thoughts.

Not long after Mrs Moon departed, Septimus lay back on the chair and yawned violently. His eyes watered profusely as fatigue seeped into every fibre of his being. The uneasy calm of the room contrasted wildly with the tumultuous nature of sentiments spinning around within him. They carried on spinning until these words wolfishly crept into the darkest and most anonymous fragment of his mind.

"Use the scrolls, seize the power, you can live forever, the past and the future are both yours."

The words made Septimus sit up with a start; he instinctively peered around the room. There was no one else in the room barring him and a dead Anastasia. He checked her pulse just to make sure there was no lingering malevolence left in her body. He needn't have bothered; it was blatantly obvious she had breathed her last breath in that body at least … Had he spoken the words out aloud? Or was it just a thought? If it was just a thought, how could he know if it was his or not; how could he ever be certain?

Septimus rubbed his weary eyes and whispered defiantly, "Damn you, Aunt; what gave you the right to imprison me?"

He waited … and waited … and waited for her reply…

Septimus had never known a room as silent as this before, or witnessed one so hollow, so devoid of life, imprudently silent. She may be silent now, but he knew she was there, waiting in the shadows.

Despite Septimus' agitation, the day demanded its due, and it was not long before Septimus unwillingly succumbed to a fitful sleep. He dreamt about his collection of living photographs, their faces smudged and grotesque, calling out his name over and over again. Their voracious arms, outstretched, pulling him into the photographs, into the flames.

The End

About the Author

Greg Howes is a genealogist, writer and historical researcher based in Carmarthenshire, South West Wales, UK. Greg has lived in Carmarthenshire for the last twenty-five years, though he originates from Thame in Oxfordshire, England, UK.

Greg's work as a researcher has seen him present (and research for) family history programmes on television for both the BBC and ITV channels. He has taught family history (and horticulture, in his younger days) and featured on national and local radio stations, answering questions and giving advice on family history and the historical landscape.

He has written many articles for various magazines on subjects as diverse as local history, dating and archiving old photographs, and the history of woodland and ancient trees in the landscape.

The idea for the novel was conceived in part when the author's mother, Jennie Howes, asked members of the family to write a short ghostly/supernatural tale for Christmas Eve 2007. Little did she, or indeed the author, know what kind of a monster idea it would turn out to be. As a family history researcher, Greg spent much of his time trawling through the 19th century, so a book seemed a fitting companion to the research. Another source of inspiration came his way back in 1968 when he was taken to see the newly-released film *Oliver Twist* at the tender age of four in London. Greg's grandparents both lived in the centre of London at that time and he expected to see Fagin or the Artful Dodger around every corner. It remains one of his favourite films.

Greg's other great passion is photographic art and design. He has recently released books featuring some of his work, the latest of which is titled *The Dark Room*.

His other pastimes include walking, watching motorcycle speedway, and reading. His favourite authors include Arthur Conan Doyle, Arthur Machen, Peter Ackroyd, David Gemell, Jack

London, Charles Dickens, Bernard Cornwall, Algernon Blackwood, Henry Mayhew, Mary Stewart, Jack Vance, Robin Hobb, Edgar Allan Poe, Oliver Rackham, Marion Zimmer Bradley, H.P Lovecraft, Bram Stoker, Sheridan La Fanu, and Conn Iggulden.

www.themanbehindtheglass.co.uk

www.welshfamilyhistory.co.uk

KING HENRY

Douglas Galbraith

Harvill *Secker*

LONDON

Published by Harvill Secker 2007

2 4 6 8 10 9 7 5 3 1

Copyright © Douglas Galbraith 2007

Douglas Galbraith has asserted his right under the Copyright, Designs
and Patents Act 1988 to be identified as the author of this work

First published in Great Britain in 2007 by
Harvill Secker
Random House, 20 Vauxhall Bridge Road,
London SW1V 2SA

www.randomhouse.co.uk

Addresses for companies within The Random House Group Limited
can be found at: www.randomhouse.co.uk/offices.htm

The Random House Group Limited Reg. No. 954009

A CIP catalogue record for this book is available from the British Library

ISBN 9780436206283

The Random House Group Limited makes every effort to ensure
that the papers used in its books are made from trees that have been
legally sourced from well-managed and credibly certified forests. Our paper
procurement policy can be found at: www.randomhouse.co.uk/paper.htm

Typeset in Bembo by Palimpsest Book Production Limited,
Grangemouth, Stirlingshire

Printed and bound in Great Britain by
Clays Ltd, St Ives PLC

Ray

Billionaires have many friends and it is my privilege to serve Mr Ford by keeping them as far away from him as possible.

For me it started with the five-dollar-a-day business, which anyone could have told him would only lead to trouble. He had his own reasons – and who can say now they didn't turn out to be right? – but there was always going to be a ruckus at the time. It was in the papers one day and every drunk, bum and rif in the state was rattling the gates the next. I could have told him that – if it wasn't for the fact that he hadn't yet exchanged a word with me or learned my name.

You see – it was the five-dollar-a-day business that really made Mr Ford famous. Until then he didn't need me. Or at least he didn't know he needed me. He was just another automobileer and it was getting to seem like there wasn't much else in Detroit. But the five-dollar-a-day business? Well, that changed everything. That was what made him so many friends all of a sudden, and a good few enemies too in among the gentler folks of Detroit. They didn't take kindly to paying five for what they were used to getting for three. These good people had their friends too – some of them police officers. And that's why the crowds in Woodward Avenue and Manchester Street, all cursing and pushing to get through to the employment office, turned into a riot and nobody did much about it. And what with all that the newspapermen got to like him just as much as everybody else.

It was some time in the first week of January and bitter cold when the reporters got the call out to Highland Park to hear the news. I knew because I saw them coming out after the meeting, though I didn't yet know what it was about.

'We're going to lead on the money,' I heard one say.

'Sure – five's the story.'

Well, it turned out later that two dollars and forty-three cents was the story and the rest came in only if you stuck it out for six months or more, were twenty-two years of age (unless already married), did right by your widowed mother, didn't take in too many boarders, swept, tidied and took pride in your backyard, learned English, feared God and used whatever the Sociological Department said was a sufficient quantity of soap on yourself and your children. But that wasn't a story. Like the man said – five was the story.

Well the *Detroit News* carried it that same afternoon. By midnight there was a little bunch of men huddling outside the gates and by the time it was light the next day I'd say there could hardly have been less than ten thousand. The poets of the press gave it their all – 'a magnificent act of generosity', 'a blinding rocket through the dark clouds of depression', 'one of God's own noblemen', 'God bless Henry Ford!' It looked like the whole damned thing was turning into some sort of pilgrimage.

They put out the 'No Hiring' signs right away, but things only got worse. I suppose poor men quickly get used to being lied to and not one of them was willing to turn away just in case there was a job there after all.

So many came in from out of town we must have had fifteen or twenty thousand on our hands by the end of the day. Highland

Park needed one in five of these men and someone – I was against it – had the smart idea of sending company agents out with hiring slips for the better prospects and then telling the rest their chance had gone. Fights broke out at once. If anyone saw you getting one of those slips you had to be a hard and strong man to keep it. Then there was talk of them changing hands for money, and before long the Poles and Italians had more than they ought and the Irish and the Armenians got organised on the other side and then a trolley-load of reds turned up and started to sound off about dignity and the means of production and pulling down the sign off the roof and putting one up saying 'The People'.

That was the day Dreyfus was beaten half to death. He got caught in a corner somewhere with fifty hiring slips and having no more brains than a dog wouldn't give them up and so came back with a busted nose, three broken ribs, one arm kinked halfway up his back and no hiring slips.

'Dreyfus, you moron!' I told him. 'They're numbered, they're all numbered!'

So we gave all those guys jobs and we matched up the numbers and we got their names and their addresses and the names and addresses of their wives and brothers and cousins and their landlords and their creditors and the mothers of their bastard children, and then we called them in like they were going to get their bonus and we took them all out back in a group and we hosed those rats down and kicked them out and not one of them has ever earned a cent in Detroit since that day. Mr Ford likes to run a clean shop.

It was on Monday things really started to go downhill. The men were coming back to work and to watch them go by was, I suppose, just more than fifteen thousand freezing bums could stand. That was when you could really call it a riot and the police stood by with their 'told-you-so' faces and I got all the boys out front and we got ready with every firehose we could find. That

3

was the moment. Mr Ford himself was coming in his automobile through all the shouting and screaming and the air full of whatever a man could throw and he just got through the gates when I heard that voice like some sort of strange angel.

'Mr Ford, Mr Ford sir, is it true you have to pay five dollars because no one can bear to work for you for more than three months? Is it true you want to turn men into machines?'

Ford turned to the voice and it seemed he was looking at me and then I saw the mouth moving and the clean white teeth just the other side of the railings right where I was and I reached through and I turned as I grabbed him and saw Mr Ford's pale eyes looking straight into mine and I felt the shock of that bone coming back through my baton again and again and the warm blood on my hand as I twisted his collar till that red bastard couldn't breathe and all the time Mr Ford looking straight at me.

Then it was over. There was a great *shshsh* as we got all the hoses on them at once and they scattered and ran for whatever homes they had before the clothes froze stiff on their backs. They ripped up all the stalls of the lunch vendors and smashed the cigarette kiosk and trampled everything to pieces and then were gone. The police stamped their feet and folded their hands under their arms. The Captain took out his watch and nodded. The police got into their Ford wagons and then they were gone too.

That's what I remember – and the smell of tobacco trodden into the street, sweet and rich in the wet, cold January air and of the carpets in Mr Ford's office the next day when that runt Liebold showed me in past everyone waiting and them looking at me like I was a bigshot or about to get the sack and Mr Ford himself saying to me – well, never you mind what he said to me.

Since that day I've had a good life and I know who to thank for it.

4

Marquis

The occasion was the first on which I was driven in the back of a chauffeured car into the workplace of my parishioner, Mr Henry Ford. The timing, the place and the manner – a certain imperiousness, shall we say, a whiff of the chancellery, of the state rather than a mere man – all marked it out in my memory.

It was in early January. I was delivered to an obscure rear entrance and guided through the noise and frantic purpose of the factory to a separate office building near the front. I think I must have walked a mile or more before being taken in there. Through successive doors the clangour of metal and machines quickly fell away, and the cold too, as I was led from climate to climate as if through the halls of a hothouse towards its most precious and cosseted specimen. The anteroom was crowded and I experienced a little vainglory as I was shown straight through and ushered directly into Mr Ford's private office. Save for myself, I found the enormous room empty of any life. I took off my coat and fanned myself with my hat, conscious that I would soon be in the presence of a man no more accessible to the greater part of mankind than the Grand Lama of Tibet.

Mr Ford's desk was positioned as a barrier across the remotest corner of the room. I noticed half a dozen of the latest newspapers folded on its top. There was a smaller table in the centre. A chair was placed by it but it was intended for no practical use, the table's surface being taken up entirely by an elegant model car, a barometer in a glass case and a large ship's compass. Another roll-top desk stood against one wall and, at a right angle to this piece, a heavy settee for two persons. An expensive cabinet Victrola stood on its own as if music and dancing might break out on the achievement of the Ford Motor Company's next triumph. The whole arrangement stood on the largest Persian carpet I have seen before or since, extending to within inches of each of the four walls as if made to order for that exact space.

There were two large double windows and an increase in the noise from outside attracted me to them. I looked down on a chaotic scene. Crowds filled the wide space before the factory gates and were increasing still as more men came from both the main avenues. At the front they were pressed against the railings and I recall my fears of a general disaster if no one took control of the situation. Toward the back, where the crowd was less dense, policemen stood in groups waiting for orders. Inside the railings a double row of employees stood looking outwards like soldiers on parade. Their bodies formed a screen, but from my vantage point I could see the water pumps and the coiled hoses behind them. I saw a man struggling to make his way and handing out slips of paper as he went. There was a sudden movement and then papers and hands were all up in the air together and I could no longer tell the clerk from the crowd around him. Immediately beneath me there was shouting, pushing and a few blows as the employees struggled to close the gates behind someone who had just come in.

I remained alone for several more minutes, taking as close an interest in the contents of the office as discretion allowed.

The faint sound of water came through a side door and then Mr Ford entered, drying his hands on a white flannel which he threw casually behind him before closing the door.

I was already beginning to know Henry well in those days, but I had never seen him more excited or pleased with himself. He greeted me warmly and thanked me for coming. I indicated the newspapers on his desk.

'You're a famous man now, Henry. Truly famous.'

'So it seems, so it seems. It's all come as a bit of a surprise, I must say.'

He shot me one of those sharp, humorous glances just to make sure I understood. We both knew that pressmen were some of the most frequent visitors to Highland Park and had been for years. A happy thought made him grin more widely.

'Here, you'll like this. Do you know what Couzens heard from one of the boys?'

'What did he hear?'

'That he meets – the journalist, I mean – that he meets people who think it's just the name of a car, that there is no Mr Ford, nothing human behind it at all. What about that?'

'Well, they won't think that now.'

He tugged up one of the sashes to freshen the air and turned to sit at his desk without, apparently, having noticed the commotion outside. Throughout our interview I saw no evidence that the increasingly riotous noise ever penetrated his consciousness.

'Well, Reverend,' he said to me, eager that I should add further to his pleasure. 'What do you hear? What say my fellow men?'

I nodded towards the open window.

'*They* don't mind, but your own sort – they're not so happy. You double wages in a day and they see their men walking out of their shops and into yours. There are rumblings, Henry, no doubt about it. They'll have to follow suit and they feel the money coming out of their own pockets. I have heard the word "theft". I have even heard the word "red" – though I believe drink had been taken.'

Henry was delighted. He leaned over the newspapers covered in his own name and poked his finger at me.

'A man who doesn't know how to make profits has no right to employ others. If these firms can't afford to live, let them die. Their men can work for me.'

He was in one of his unshakeable moods and I realised that I had been summoned largely to listen. I obliged with a hearty pull on the crank, setting him on his way.

'But five dollars?' I asked. 'A doubling, as near as makes no odds, and all at once?'

I heard at length about the men who made his cars. Who makes them, do you think? Me? No, *they* do – we're giving the men their due, no more and no less. I heard about the dignity of the sweeper who kept the shop a fit place to work, of how his necessity to industry equalled that of the skilled man, of how he must get what was coming to him whatever the harshnesses of the market. I heard of his family's moral condition, of crowded homes, dirty homes, wives forced to work, children neglected, houses crammed with boarders, a short-changed new generation, the working men of tomorrow physically and morally underdeveloped when they came to take their own place in industry. Wrong for one thing, but ineffi-cient too – did anyone really think there wouldn't be a bill to pay?

Phrase after phrase he coined, fell in love with, delivered and forgot. He preached to me, telling me what I already knew with the passion of one who had learned it, or at least who had learned to speak of it, for the first time that day. I told him what I had heard from my other parishioners.

'Some worry,' I said, 'that a doubling of these men's income will ruin as many as it will save.'

He shook his lean, sharp head emphatically.

'We are not afraid of that. Men do not choose their faults. They are imposed upon them by chance. They live the way they do only because they do not have the means to be better. Give them a decent income and they will live decently – will be glad to do so. All they need is the opportunity to do better, and someone to take a little personal interest in them – someone who will show that he has . . . well, faith, I suppose. I don't say a few of them won't need a helping hand, but that's exactly what we're going to give them. We'll walk with them along the way until they can walk by themselves. Men can be trusted to do the right thing, Samuel. That's my gospel, begging your pardon, and I'm going to prove it.'

As I listened to this sermon on industrial Christianity, Henry remained deaf to everything outside. He was on his feet and excitedly developing his theme, striding this way and that across his Persian carpet which, if it had an ear for rhetoric, might very well have lifted from the boards at that moment and carried him directly to his desires. Somewhere in his mental workings, as often happened, a lever was pulled apparently at random and he next treated me to twenty minutes on his new tractor and the revolution it would bring to the world's affairs. I may have wandered a little towards the end of this and Henry caught my inattentive expression.

'You don't believe me,' he said abruptly.

'What?'

'You don't believe a man can change so much, that however low his position he always has the power to get out of it if only there's a helping hand. That's parsons for you – present company excepted of course, Samuel – but I've met a few in my time who had so much faith in God they had nothing left for man.'

'Now that's not fair, Henry. I haven't said a word against you in the last half-hour. I haven't said a word about anything.'

But he insisted all the same that he could see it in my eyes. He stood in the centre of the room near the table with the model car and the compass. The sound of something like a war was coming through the window, but Henry was concentrating on his handkerchief. He folded it into a band.

'I'll show you,' he declared as he tied it about his eyes. 'We'll do it scientific – no cheating.'

As the riot reached its height Henry Ford stood in the middle of his office with a blindfold over his eyes, orating about hope.

'I'll prove it to you,' he told me. 'We can do it right now. Where are you?'

He held out his hands like a blind man.

'Take me down there now into the street. I'll lay my hands by chance on the most worthless and shiftless fellow in the crowd, I'll bring him in here, give him a job with a good wage, I'll give him self-respect and hope for the future. I'll put my trust in him and he won't let me down. I'll show you that same man a year from now and you'll swear he's a different creature entirely. I tell you – we want to make men in this factory as well as automobiles.'

After some effort I persuaded him to abandon the idea of an immediate experiment. I agreed fulsomely with everything he suggested – proof would not be necessary. At last he took the blindfold off.

'This helping hand business, Samuel.'

'Yes?'

'You see, that's why I wanted to talk to you. It's not really something I have time for myself. I need a good man.'

I had many questions but he was reluctant to take them up in any detail. I saw that the subject had suddenly become dull to him. We agreed to talk again at some later date and I understood that the interview was over when he looked at his watch.

We stood together by the windows. It was quiet by this

stage and getting dark. Henry looked down on a cleared and sodden battlefield. I watched a solitary figure struggle to his feet and hoist up a placard that had been trampled in the rush away from the firehoses. Watered ink bled down its face. I could read 'Bread, Brotherhood . . .' but not the third word. A miserable scene to any ordinary man, the great industrialist regarded it with the blank serenity of one who fully expected to see perfection with his own eyes, and very much this side of the grave.

In the six months after the five-dollar-a-day riot, twenty Detroit motor firms and an unknown number of assorted machine shops were priced out of business. Some of their men did come to work for Henry Ford. Of the others, we know nothing. The cars got cheaper and poured from the production lines at an ever faster speed. They paid six dollars a day, and tuned the lines up to a six-dollar speed. The employees could buy their own product. The conundrum of perpetual motion had been solved. Henry sat on top of it all, flying up into the sky on a volcano of dollar bills. No one could touch him now.

Zero

It was six months ago, or maybe a year, when they stopped trying to collect the rent. I was lying right here when a man nailed a plank across the door and then pasted up a notice. Three days later I busted out, but no one seemed to mind. If you don't exist, you don't have to pay. Suits me.

I sleep on rags and old newspapers. There is a roll of the *New York Tribune* beneath my head. I used to read my bed, but now it gives me nightmares. Above, there is a glazed grating. The glass is three inches thick and scuffed by ten thousand feet a day – though only about two hundred on Sundays. You can't see anything but the soles of people's shoes and sometimes just the feet. When the sun shines the pattern cuts me into squares.

Pipes and wires bring me the news and I have given up putting my fingers in my ears. Gas whispers and the telephone sings in my teeth. Greetings from Kaiser Wilhelm dot the air and the day's takings wing through the ether from Wanamaker's Philadelphia to Wanamaker's New York. Autos and trolley-cars drum meanings through the street. Voices come down the tube. It is an old coal chute with the iron cover in the sidewalk long since stolen for scrap. Someone will fall down that, passers-by say once or twice every hour. But they never have yet – or not entirely. Gum wrappers fall down and at night bottles, sometimes whole, sometimes not. Once there was a shoe that came rattling down all on its own, shiny black with a grey silk bow. There was a sweet-sounding, female cry of surprise and then lamentations. I slipped three fingers inside where toes had lately wriggled and could still feel the warmth. A man called a cab and they went off to sue City Hall. But mostly it's words that come down, the words you can say in the space of three paces – four or five if the speaker walks slowly or is unusually short. Countless thousands of little speeches in all the accents and languages there are – the world's newspaper, razored to shreds line by line, an infinity of crossed wires in the Bell Telephone Company's exchange. I hear every one and when there are enough it begins to mean something.

On Sundays, if the street is clear for a moment, boys piss down the chute. The urine gathers in the Sunday bowl and mixes with my own. I stir with a spoon and cast the waters of the city. I know what's coming.

Last week someone hurt me, but I think I'm getting better now. I thought they must have come for the rent at last. Grit caught under the door and I had to drag it open as it scraped a white line across the tiles. I found a young man in a round hat, a brown checked suit, fresh shirt and bright brass pin in his tie. He was already talking as I wondered how he could have made the mistake of coming down here. There was a little hand-cart behind him, a clever folding thing, and a stack of books tied on with a cord. He didn't seem to hear anything I said, and at first I didn't hear him.

'But tell me this, sir – can you afford not to have it? Is it not more necessary than ever in these fast-moving and confusing days when a man's ignorance can so easily embarrass him before friends and colleagues? *The New International All-American Encyclopedia* solves your problem.'

I pointed upwards to the more respectable door he had meant to knock on. He talked like a machine. He forced his way into my mind and the words landed like blows.

'Do you know your *mitrailleuse* from your Maxim, your machine-gun from your mortar from your siege gun from your shrapnel? Can you tell an uhlan from a cuirassier? A Walloon from a muzhik? Can you impress and assist those around you by explaining moratorium, Landsturm, Armageddon, pan-Germanism, balance of power, Reichstag, cataclysm, vodka? Hey, wait a minute! What you doing? You damage those books you gotta pay, mister. Don't touch me. You crazy?'

I chased him up onto the sidewalk and he ran off with his little cart of books at his heels and the truth ringing in his ears as the people walked by smiling and shaking their heads to see me at it again. A hopeless case.

Consider this: land used to be beneath your feet, now it's something you do in an aeroplane.

Louis

I have desires but no power. My desires keep me awake at night. They are the desires of millions and I feel them all inside me, focused on my heart like sunlight through a burning glass. I suffer with them, or at least I feel that I should. I could imagine myself as their instrument – or I could if I was to go completely nuts.

Every minute of the day is filled. I work my fingers to the bone and at night, when I am on the point of sleep, my mind snaps awake with a new thought for tomorrow. I want only for others. What I want is good and right, reason is on my side and still I have no power. There is no connection. Shouldn't there be? In my dreams I run from some danger only to find there is nothing but air beneath my feet. I go nowhere, the dog closes. Only waking holds off the inevitable. How recently did I realise how the world really works? When did I last believe in magic or that prayers are answered, virtue rewarded? Even now I waste time. How many have died since I stopped writing and started to look out of the window? Midnight here and morning in Flanders. The light comes up and the snipers can see again. They at least can see the fruits of their work. In St

Clair Street all is quiet. Just for a moment not even a hog is being butchered in Chicago.

Dear Miss Addams,

I write at the end of a long and most dispiriting evening. I can't help but think back to our work in the spring, how hopeful it was, and how distant now, all spilt and drunk down into the ground like it had never been. Sometimes I want to cry like a child. On my own I don't think I would have the strength to go on. That is when I write to you. It is over a year since I was flattered by the offer to head the Chicago Peace Society, but when I think of what has been achieved in that time I get despondent. I should not allow myself to think of the past, but only of what we must continue to do until sanity has returned to the world. I feel that if only we could . . .

A noise from the bed distracts me. Emmy turns and speaks a word in her sleep. Betty answers with a single treble vowel. The light catches the back of her plump, dimpled hand as it flexes and grasps at the lace of my wife's nightgown where it covers her breast. Betty's face is red with heat and her golden hair dark where it clings damply to her forehead and temples. Very clearly the desire to make love to my wife blocks out everything else. I imagine it perfectly. She is not fully asleep, has no objection to being woken, indeed she has been thinking, feeling just as I have and has been praying for it to become a reality. In truth, my desires have been summoned by hers. Betty turns onto her other side, making space. I lift the nightdress. I am embraced and pulled firmly down. My daughter sleeps on as her brother or sister is beautifully conceived and I, breathlessly, am healed by an enriched future. The muscles in my thigh tense and I almost believe that I am about to get out of my chair, cross the room and, with all simplicity and decision of the man I would like to be, make my wife pregnant. She turns without waking. Betty wriggles closer and whimpers.

> . . . if only we could connect the combatant experience with the mind of the peacetime civilian. Time and again I hear from some decent person, who regularly asks after his neighbours and in his daily life would never think to pass by on the other side that the war is someone else's business and no concern at all of his, as if it were nothing more than a dispute between two anthills. Immediacy is what we need in all our communications. We must penetrate! I am formulating some ideas of this sort that I believe will be of great help and would like your permission to send an outline to you for your comment and . . .

The pen stalls above the paper. I put it down, despising words for their powerlessness. Through the gap in the half-drawn curtains I watch a drunk meander along the sidewalk. He pauses in a shop doorway before moving on. The last eighteen months run through my mind and I recall the International Women's Peace Congress in the Hague – I was there with you, Miss Addams, ghost-writing your daily cables back to the *New York Times*. The resolutions made us feel good. How laughable it seems now that we were going to post them to the governments of Europe and that our ardour would somehow go with them, stir the words into rhetoric and have a . . . Well, have what exactly? An entirely supernatural effect on the human nature of those who read them? That was when Madame Schwimmer stood up.

'Contributions from the floor may be made only through the chairman. Will you respect the chairman?'

'Oh, shut up, you fool!'

She found us, as she seemed instinctively to know, hungry to be led. There would be no 'pusillanimous posting'. Instead, envoys of matrons, statuesque and indomitable, would be sent in person. Officials would be bearded in their lairs and shamed by the invincible advocates of peace. Reporters would be on hand to record the events for all local papers. Darkness would lift from the outraged populations and the church bells ring. Whatever was said subsequently, there was not a single vote against at the time. Direct action was the answer. And when the replies came in it was a glorious vindication. Our ideas would indeed be considered. It would all be over before it had hardly even started. Humanity would do nothing more than frighten itself into peace and reason. What children we were then – we actually thought words meant what they meant.

Memory slips back to the previous summer. Peace still, and Emmy and I together on the boat and our through train tickets to the conference in Vienna. The weather was fine and we were excited and happy. In Paris we even went to the station as if we could have carried on. A man with silver buttons on his tunic and a peaked cap shook his head and expressed his heartfelt regrets. The trains were needed elsewhere – our tickets could not be honoured.

'But we must get to Vienna.'

He tugged at his moustache for inspiration.

'Have you considered joining the Russian army?'

'We are attending a peace conference. We are delegates. It is very important.'

'Ah,' he said, understanding everything in a moment. 'You are Americans? First you must have the war, then the peace conference.'

It was the humour of the day – a necessity through the heat of the afternoon as everyone waited for the evening papers. The city was busy, but hushed as a Sunday. Hour by hour taxis became more scarce and then disappeared altogether. The motor-omnibuses quickly followed. The railway stations sucked in a thickening stream of young men with suitcases and forms in their hands. When we heard that it was not yet hopeless we knew the lying had already started. The next day, too tense to stay at our hotel, we wandered aimlessly, picking up contradictory scraps of conversation. War had become like the weather – it could be neither understood nor averted. Paris had never looked more beautiful. Would it survive? Will it even now?

We left the gardens to watch a socialist demonstration march down the Rue de Rivoli. The flags of France, Austria, Belgium, Germany, Russia and England had been cut up and stitched together in new, blended patterns. Banners proclaimed the universal brotherhood of the working man and a band played the 'Internationale'. A complacent crowd watched them pass. From the street corners policemen looked on with stony faces and attentive camera eyes.

The next day it was a certainty. A small group stood by a noticeboard outside the Ministère de la Marine. A single strip of paper was pinned to the wood – MOBILISATION GÉNÉRALE. Flags spread across the city and here and there a banner about Alsace and Lorraine that made the whole thing seem even stranger, like an inevitability calmly awaited for a whole, vengeful generation. We watched as the mourning cloths were taken from the Strasbourg monument in the Place de la Concorde and replaced with flowers, palm branches and a tricolour sash. The tearful mayor of the *arrondissement* spoke of forty-four years of praying for restoration and justice, of the bugles of the French army sounding the charge. Emmy spoke in my ear, but someone heard her accent and stared. We left before the end.

We ate early at a little restaurant near the hotel but the meal took half the evening to complete. The owner apologised constantly and was in turn constantly congratulated as he explained that half his waiters had already been called up.

Proceedings were further disturbed by the need to stand every few minutes as the band played the 'Marseillaise', 'God Save the King' and the Russian national anthem. The evening ended in a different mood with a mournful rendition of 'La chanson du départ'. An elderly regular leaned over from his table and nodded towards the band.

'And, you know,' he said to me, 'they are all Hungarians!'

He shrugged and made the sign for madness.

We walked back through a confused city, half darkened – Emmy looked up to check for zeppelins – and half gay. We witnessed a celebratory attack on a German-owned china shop. Plates were smashed with great delight and the broken heads and limbs of Dresden figurines were trampled into a bone-white powder. Across the country a violent persecution was launched against the advertisements of a manufacturer of dried soup stock on the grounds – as was explained to me by one patriot in Paris – that they contained treasonous messages so cunningly concealed that only Germans could detect them. At the hotel we were handed police forms and asked with very courteous and regretful formality to fill them in and return them within the next twelve hours if we did not wish to become criminals.

It was not easy to leave Paris. We spent a whole day in the Gare du Nord watching troop trains depart. At seven in the evening we were offered a cattle truck to Le Havre, which rumbled northward through the hot, short night. We were evicted from it just after first light and spent hours on a bench – me sitting, Emmy lengthwise and trying to sleep with her head in my lap – before the first café opened to serve us break-fast. There was no morning sailing and so we found ourselves with the best part of a day in the port. Desperate for anything that might raise our spirits, we consulted our guidebook. Emmy was anxious that we might seem to be trivial at such a terri-ble time. We hid the book behind our menus, but then just made each other laugh with the simultaneous thought that we risked being taken for spies. We found an entry for a church on a hill overlooking the Channel. The traveller was warned not to expect too much, but the view on a fine day was said to make it worth the walk.

The path wound through patches of sea-kale and the pink spots of restharrow. Chalk-blue butterflies rose up at every step and there was the constant sound of larks from overhead. To our right the English Channel was bright, still and empty except for small fishing boats near the coast. 'Can you see the white cliffs?' Emmy asked. We peered northward into the haze, trying to distinguish one summery whiteness from another. After twenty minutes we checked the book again and thought we must have passed our destination. I asked for directions from the only passer-by we encountered. We were sent off in an unlikely direction and happily climbed a hill in an inland direction, not much caring any more whether we found the church or not. I reached the top first. I took my last few steps backward, looking out over the sea before turning to the most extraordinary and sad scene. My French had been at fault and we had been directed not to *l'église* but to *les anglais* – there, in the French countryside, in pristine uniforms amid rows of tents so white and fresh they must have come straight from the laundry, were twenty thousand British soldiers. Emmy arrived by my side and slipped her arm through mine. We said nothing for half a minute and then she asked:

'Is it safe? Perhaps we should go.'

The journalist in me wasn't willing to pass up such a chance. 'I'll talk to them.'

'No, don't – please!'

'It's all right.'

I was already running down the hill. The closest soldiers had seen me and didn't seem to care. They were in a holiday mood.

'Here comes another young man to join us.'

'Steady on. Recruiting office doesn't open till noon.'

I remember catching the smell of an army for the first time – canvas, leather, men, clean, lubricated metal. I can't deny it wasn't attractive, exciting. I felt its call. I was out of breath and realised that I had nothing to say and could not really explain why I was there.

'British Army?' I asked stupidly.

'The very same. Berlin bound – come to give us a hand?'

'I didn't know you were here.'

'We're not. Not till Wednesday – unless Fritz blows the whistle before then and we go for an early kick-off. So we can't let you go until then, I'm afraid. Your good lady coming too?'

The sergeant pointed up the hill to where Emmy was slowly approaching.

'The ladies' facilities aren't quite what they should be, but we'll see what we can do.'

'What? We're getting a boat to England. We're trying to get home. Look, I'm an American.'

I handed over my passport.

'Oh, dear,' said the sergeant, looking sceptically at my surname. 'Whose side are they on then?'

'Neutral – it's nothing to do with us. We were going to a peace conference.'

'Is that so, Herr Lochner? Where was that then?'

'Vienna.'

'Well, I should think it's been cancelled now, wouldn't you?'

The sergeant turned to the small man beside him who seemed to know exactly what was going on.

'Vienna, Harry. Is that good or bad?'

'I think it's bad, Sergeant. I've definitely heard of it and I'm sure someone said it was on the other side.'

'I'd say things are looking pretty black. Who's the Prime Minister of the United States?'

'Wilson.'

'Harry?'

'Common enough name, Sarge. Sounds to me like he's guessing.'

'But it *is* Wilson. I'm a journalist, for heaven's sake.'

'Write things in the papers, do you?'

'Nothing you don't want me to.'

'Still, you can't be too careful.'

He shouted over to another tent.

'Bring those last will and testament forms, will you, Bill – and get another execution squad together.'

I was white and trembling and Emmy beginning to cry when the soldiers burst out laughing. Seeing that they had perhaps gone too far they found us something to sit on and brought tin mugs of tea and asked us about Paris and how we liked London, which seemed to be everyone's home town and of which they were very proud. One asked when America was going to join in while another said it would all be over before we could get there. They were happy to tell everything they knew about their own movements, which wasn't much. Nothing had happened to them yet – they didn't seem to understand war any more than I did. I asked naïve, peaceable questions and they made naïve, peaceable answers. In a lull I suddenly felt the sadness of it all and we were relieved when an officer came by, dismissed everyone but the sergeant and questioned us. My name was taken down and I was searched for a camera. My notebook was read and pages torn from it and put in the fire. Emmy gave her word of honour that she had nothing about her person.

'Say nothing about what you've seen for a week. Not to anyone. Get back to the port and get out quick.'

We ran most of the way back to Le Havre and for half the journey could still hear the officer shouting at his men.

We crossed the Channel then headed straight for Southampton and home, three of us – Emmy, little Elisabeth inside and myself with a bruised, but renewed purpose. I did as I had been asked by the British Army. Emmy and I went beyond the call of duty, not even saying anything to each other, as if all the absurd talk of spies might really be true. I both felt and resented the tug of loyalty. I gave myself over to earnest inner debates in the smoking saloon about breaches of neutrality and taking sides. The ship's Marconi digest was vague. Had the fighting started? Were the men who had threatened to kill us and served us tea still alive? I had never even attended a funeral. By the time we got to New York a week had passed – I ran to the telegraph office and made the most of my scoop. At least I got a story out of it, and then a new job too.

A clock strikes one and I look down at my half-written letter. Deep in the stairwell there is an argument. A door slams and the filament trembles in its vacuum. If I earned more money we would not have to live here.

Abstractions obsess me – purchase, grip, drive. How can it be so easy for one man to seize and move the world, and so hard for another? If I asked such a man could he tell me the answer? I am not wholly lacking. I am a man of ideals, and of passion too. When I speak in public I am moved by my own words. And yet I feel that something fundamental is hidden from me.

I am very tired. I turn out the light and begin to take off my clothes. I look up at the sound of an automobile outside. It slows for the corner and backfires a single shot in my direction before disappearing. A flag on a stick pokes up from the back, suddenly bright as it passes beneath a street lamp.

My mother worries about my career. My prose is purple. My wife says I am more interested in peace than in her. I am a joke.

Clara

I remember the first time Henry made me cry. I was lying there in the dark beside him being sure not to make a sound. When I closed my eyes the tears squeezed out and ran down my temples and into my ears. Something had made him want to talk about his mother. He had tried once or twice before, but had never found the right way. Perhaps it had just come to him then and so he wanted to say it straight out in case he forgot. He put the light out first and then spoke – he said that after she died the house was like a watch that had lost its mainspring. I cried because I thought he wanted me to replace that mainspring and I didn't think I ever could.

It had been a year and a half before that, at the New Year's Ball at the big Martindale house, decked out and bright and the snow around it tram-lined by the runners of the sleighs, that I found out how the skinny, shy Henry Ford danced the polka better than anyone I had ever met. Afterwards he showed me what he had just made and explained how it worked – how the two dials of the watch told standard and railway time and how it could show the days of the week as well. Was there, he wanted to know, any chance of him walking me home after midnight?

Henry was persistent, and I liked his sisters. I do remember thinking that I had hoped for more. Even when his father offered him the loan of eighty acres of timber to clear and build on and farm, it seemed I might be taking on a hard future. But the more I thought about it the more certain I became. I don't say I knew how things were going to turn out twenty – no, let me think now – good heavens, thirty years later, but I saw something and I was the first to see it and I wasn't wrong.

The eighty acres were meant to call Henry back from Detroit where he had been working in the machine shops. He took one look at those trees, cut them down, sawed them up for timber and with me up on top by his side used a huge steam-traction engine to pull out the stumps. When there was nothing left he lost interest and was sad to have to give the traction engine back. It would only have been a few weeks after that, three months before Edsel was born, when he was quieter than usual in the evening and I knew something was on his mind. I had read out a chapter from *Oliver Twist* and was then doing a little sewing when he shifted in his chair and said at last, 'I'm thinking of moving back to Detroit.'

I felt at once how much I had come to like everything about our modest country life. Church and family near, the quiet and the sky and the new house all fresh and smelling of clean new timber and paint and the organ in the parlour that no one, I supposed, would be willing to carry up the stairs to a city apartment. Above all it was where I had imagined my children growing up – my child as it turned out. I remember how nervous Henry looked – we have always been able to read each other's thoughts – and he put his hand up to stop me from speaking.

'Wait. Look.'

He took a sheet from the music rack and drew on the back of it. He talked for hours, but don't ask me now what he said.

In the end I did understand, though not so as I could have said what or how, or explained to anyone else. It was like it is supposed to be when you wade into the river and someone holds you under and everything is quiet for a few seconds. When you come up it really is different and things make sense in a way they never did before. I have always believed in my husband.

When he had finished he looked at me and asked, 'Would you be willing, Callie?' And it scares me now even to think of him asking that question and what the world would have been like if I had said anything other than 'yes'.

Years passed in Detroit. I don't remember how many. John Street was our first place. We unloaded what little we had and I washed the place from top to toe and sang to keep my spirits up. I lived a widow's life, playing with Edsel at home or pushing him round the city when the weather was fine. I looked in on the big houses – one with an iron guard-dog in its garden and another a stag with huge antlers. Fancy Battenberg lace hung behind the tall windows and I liked to think of myself sitting behind that screen talking with friends who lived in houses just like mine, or putting down a book in the afternoon and reaching out for the electric bell to summon whatever I wanted. In winter the George McMillans would swish by in their beautiful cutter behind their two black horses. I remember we were all together so it must have been a Sunday. I was so pleased that Mr McMillan waved to us.

'Aren't they beautiful, Henry?'

'I suppose.'

The next year he bought me a sleigh for the winter, but never the horses to pull it.

I wandered in Hudson's, though more for the company than to buy anything. Sometimes I would get the trolley-car down to the waterfront and watch the ships. Edsel and I went to Canada. I bought him ice-cream and watched him chase the seagulls off the deck. It only cost a nickel if you didn't get off the ferry.

'Tell Daddy what we did today, darling.'

'That's fine,' Henry would say. 'That's just fine. Is dinner ready, Callie? There's a little extra job to do back at the works. The sooner I get back, the sooner it'll be done.'

Often it would be past midnight before I would hear the key in the door downstairs. He would undress as quietly as he could before slipping in beside me. I would pretend to be asleep but wondered for hour after hour, God forgive me, what he had really been doing. In the mornings, before he woke, I would take his long, thin fingers in mine and smell the metal and the gasoline on them and see the black threads of oil pressed deep as engraver's ink into every crevice of his skin.

My evenings were reading alone and mending things that didn't yet need it. I studied Chautauqua courses and tried sometimes to discuss them with Henry in the few hours each week we were together and awake.

Christmas came again. That year we were having my people in from Dearborn. I stood in the kitchen at the end of a long day of preparations, feeling that at last I might take a few minutes' rest when Henry came back early. He struggled through the doorway backwards and as he turned I could see he was carrying something heavy and complicated bolted to a board.

'I'm baking! Don't come in here with that dirty thing while there's food about.'

'I've finished it, Callie,' was all he could say. 'Come over here and help me.'

He pushed a tray of pies out of the way and I had no choice but to hold up one end while he clamped the other to the edge of the kitchen sink and then pulled up the window despite the freezing cold. He was so selfishly excited I very nearly told him what I thought of him for bringing such a thing into my kitchen on Christmas Eve. He took hold of my arms and looked me in the eye, as happy as a boy with a secret.

'It's an engine.'

'Uh-huh.'

'It's going to work, Callie. I know it is. I wanted you to see it. I could have tested it at the works, but I wanted you to see it when it first goes.'

Henry always knew how to win me over. He was clambering on the drying board by this time, taking the bulb out and fixing a wire to the socket.

'I made it with a gas pipe and an old flywheel off something else. It needs a spark too.'

'Careful!'

There was a crackle and a blue flash as he connected the wire to the closed top of the pipe. He took a little oilcan out of his pocket and gave it to me.

'Gasoline,' he said.

'You'll burn the house down.'

'In here when I say go. Not too much, just steady drips. One, two, three, four – like that. Squirt in a bit to start it.'

'Edsel's in the next room.'

Henry stopped for a second and thought about this. Then he asked me:

'Do babies remember things from his age?'

'Well no, not generally.'

'That's fine – we can leave him there then. I'll just have to tell him when he's grown. Ready?'

At arm's length I held the nozzle of the oilcan where I was told, squeezed gently and looked the other way. There was a wheezy cough and a foul-smelling blue haze.

'Oh, really, Henry. This is a kitchen. People are going to have to eat in here.'

'Again.'

I jumped as the damned thing fired.

'Don't move, hold it there, keep dripping it in!'

Everything else was trembling, but I did as I was told and made sure that the oilcan at least held still. The engine went off like a gun four or five times a second, flames came out with every bang and the room was full of smoke as it seemed about to shake the sink to pieces. I could see someone through the window looking up in amazement from the street. There was banging on the walls and when the engine finally stopped Edsel was screaming in fright. Henry took the oilcan from me and threw it in the sink. He took my hands and off we went in the polka again, faster than ever, round and round the kitchen table with Henry singing, 'It works, it works! Didn't I tell you it would work?'

Rosika

*I*t was raining. Passers-by shrugged their shoulders or were in too much of a hurry to stop. I think it was not, in any case, the sort of street where a respectable man could allow himself to talk to a woman he did not know. It was getting dark and colder too as we went up and down, puzzling over numbers that went from eight to twelve and back again. The other side of the street perhaps? There should have been a sign somewhere – we had been promised organisation. I looked about for my own name. Behind me Rebecca spoke with reluctant logic.

'Well, it must be in here.'

I turned to see her disappearing into a narrow, lightless alleyway. A moment later her relentlessly cheerful voice issued from the darkness.

'Here it is.'

She's a sweet thing, really. But how her voice grates on me – shallow, too simple by far to know real suffering. Still, I must make what I can – a poor workman with poor materials in a barbarous age. I followed her into the alleyway.

The place stank. A rat darted for the safety of the trashcans as we walked by. The placard announcing the meeting was on the door where precisely no one could be expected to see it. Inside, though we had paid a dollar extra for heat, the janitor was only then lighting two oil heaters which filled the air with an industrial smell. The place hardly seemed to have been touched for thirty years – the lighting was gas. I put down my bag and gazed disconsolately at the few rows of chairs and two or three pews. There was a stage at the far end and above it an overconfident proscenium with dubious symbols. Rebecca chirruped with all the gaiety of an over-pedalled pianola. I sat as she fussed, shuffling a more precise order into the chairs, coming back from behind the stage with a report of the scullery there and the gas ring she had lit beneath the kettle, taking the placard from the door and moving it out onto the street where it might do some good. I checked to see that the janitor had not stolen my bag. I began to feel a little better.

I found a set of enamelled stacking cups beside the kettle, a medicine bottle full of milk and a packet of sugar and coffee neatly wrapped in a page of the *Utica Observer*. Rebecca's great strength is her ability to turn anything into a picnic. There was a mirror on the wall, spotted and plainly framed and set high up for whatever male performers once frequented that place to make their final adjustments. I shifted a box over from the sink and stood on it so that I could see my whole face. Sounds from the hall suggested that Rebecca had found a broom and was working up a sweat. It would keep her happy for several minutes while I stared, wondered and refused to flinch. Cheated of feature – how true that was – not, indeed, made to court the amorous looking glass. I took off my hat, adjusted my hair and approved, somewhere inside, my long-practised immunity to disappointment. It has been said before – and about most of my associates as well as about me – that we are the sort of women who had no choice. Unmarriageable, by reason of mind as well as body, the nuns of the modern age whose habits are the suffrage sash or the anarcho-syndicalist pamphlet. I can turn my face this way and that, adjust the lamp at the dressing table and find a little something there if I try, but I don't lie any more and I don't regret. Solid, dressed for reason rather than to please and a woman of no country. Married all the same, I'll have you know. Once to a man – poor Paul, I wasn't at all what he wanted – and now to the cause, a happier bond and one from which there will certainly be no divorce. Last year I was in fashion, or at least still a novelty. I had as many speaking engagements as I could manage. I appeared on a dozen platforms with Miss Jane Addams. 'Hungary's Greatest Hebrew' the papers said. I cut that one out and it's in my bag now, beside my steamer ticket – back to Europe in November before the money runs out.

I practised a few gestures then warmed up my expressions – entreaty, righteous anger, the anguish of a martyred continent. The box rumbled beneath my feet and the reflected image became indistinct as a train went by on the El.

'Ready for the show, lady?'

The noise had covered the entrance of the janitor who was looking very pleased with himself.

'What is it? Votes, pay, corset reform?'

I got down from the box and took the kettle off the gas.

'Peace,' I said.

'Peace!'

He shook his head sadly as he sorted through his keys.

'I'll be back to lock up at ten. I suppose you'll be all done by then. Peace – damned Mexicans!'

Rebecca came in from the hall – slightly breathless and with that almost permanent expression of excitement that reminds me of a dog being led towards a park.

'I saw someone reading the sign.'

'Did they come in?'

'No, but people are reading it.'

Simultaneously, we consulted our watches.

'Plenty of time,' said Rebecca.

She began to make some coffee as I caught up with the *New York Times*. I scanned the print, listlessly looking out for something useful. Speaking agents no longer competed for my business – in fact they no longer returned my letters or telephone calls. I had had to make a score of cancellations to go to the Hague for the Women's Peace Party Conference. I made my apologies with full diplomatic courtesy and was assured that I would be re-invited as soon as I returned. They had certainly needed me over there. They had gentility, faith in good intentions and a manner that would not raise its voice to make itself heard across a drawing room in London or Boston. They laboured mightily over their resolutions and decided that the war might end if they dropped them in the post. I stood up at once.

'Infirm of purpose – give me the resolutions!'

That's how I remember it, anyway. It took another hour of debate but in the end it was agreed that we would deliver them in person right across Europe. We would insist on answers – and we got them. Once again I braved the torpedo-infested ocean. Three days back in New York, sitting by a silent telephone, I already knew I had been away too long. I picked up scraps, called in all my debts, presumed on small obligations until my name fell on old friends' ears like news of an illness in the family. I pressed on, the cause justifying all, and so came to be looking at myself in the mirror of a disused masonic hall one rainy evening in New York City.

Rebecca pushed a chipped cup of coffee towards me and smiled.

'The place looks a lot better now.'

There was a sudden coldness in the air and then the sound of the outer door closing. Rebecca looked into the hall hopefully but turned back to me with a dubious expression. Sure enough, the smell of whisky soon reached the scullery. She went out to give him a pamphlet anyway.

By the appointed hour there were a dozen or so – two or three derelicts, a skinny, distracted soul dressed too thinly for the season and with his own placard on a pole, a handful of women of familiar type, Mr Lochner himself in the back row, making good the promise in his telegram, and one smartly turned-out young man with a direct manner I rather liked and the confidence to look me in the eye and touch the brim of his hat when I took my place behind the lectern.

I did the usual thing – the misery and waste of the trenches, the pitiful letters home, the grief of mothers who would never see or hold or hear their sons again. They were a hard lot that night and it was all I could do to get a tear or two from the women. I went quickly through the Hague Peace Conference and the details of the mediation plan – that usually being where I lose them – and then went straight on to the bag routine, testing a few variations for the next real meeting. I explained how it contained the keys of peace, secret papers from the highest functionaries in Europe that would, when known to the world at just the right time and in just the right way, bring a swift end to the horror once and for all. The young man, who kept his hat on and made notes throughout, wanted to know more. I smiled indulgently and let him know of the heavy obligations that limit my work, being, as I am, in the highest confidence of Europe's great empires. I wound up with the outraged motherhood of Europe, my last words inaudible beneath a tremulous and exhausted sob which, though I say so myself, is one of the best in the business.

The drunks snored. That fellow with the placard talked quietly to himself throughout and the women soon became distant when true passion entered my voice. Mr Lochner made the occasional supportive interjection and I can't say, on such a thin night, that I wasn't grateful for his presence. The young man was very attentive. I could see that he followed the argument, making notes at all the most salient points. From halfway,

I began to focus my efforts on him. I realised, as a fisher of peace activists, that here was a real prospect and a chance to redeem an otherwise miserable evening. He was clearly intelligent and energetic too – an excellent recruit. He was the only one to stand up at the end to ask a question. At last he took his hat off and I remember being rather struck by his appearance, as well as his youth – a soldier's age.

'Yes?' I said encouragingly. 'Don't be afraid to speak up.'

His pencil poised over his notebook. He smiled charmingly.

'Swinehart, *Daily News*. Madame Schwimmer, if one of my sources told me you were a German spy, could you really prove otherwise?'

'I am a Hungarian.'

'So, Hungarian spy – is that what you're saying?'

Marion

*D*ust blows through an open window. Through it I can see the dullness of Philadelphia stretching under a bloom of early summer heat. The latest drawings are on my desk. I look through them quickly, pick out one and fan myself with another. 'Ladies' auto coat in oyster linen' – there is a slender model with all her weight on one foot and the other put out to show her sturdy Searle & Baumeister court shoe beneath the hem of the lead product. In this way the costs of the advertisement can be shared. A veil trails from her shoulders and a pair of auto goggles dangle from one finger. It is understood that men will pay, and so she sees a man where I sit and looks out at me with a frank expression that is scarcely decent. This is the one they will choose – a hundred words precisely on a ladies' auto coat in oyster linen.

I watch the nib of my pen above the paper and then look out of the window again.

'Waiting for inspiration?'

It's Lola who asks, sitting across from me on the other side of the wide drawing table. Thirty-five years old and happy to be on double my pay, she has her own apartment and a cat. Lola thinks she is an inspiration. I think she is a warning.

'Auto coat,' I say.

'Dash,' says Lola who is valued above all for her brevity. 'Always something about dash. And then fresh when you take it off at the end. Dash and fresh.'

A fish swims into my mind and refuses to leave when asked. Lola adjusts her glasses and leaves her mouth open in concentration. I laugh.

'What's so funny?'

'Nothing.'

I put myself into the oyster auto coat and the words begin to come. In two minutes what has been impossible is effortlessly completed. I pin the copy sheet to the drawing and prepare to leave, explaining to Lola's frowning face that I have some last-minute preparations for the trip to Chicago.

It was only a week ago that Berton told me *Collier's Magazine* had asked him to cover the races at Chicago. Speedway Park would have its first international one-hundred-mile auto race and Berton had a press pass. Happily, I was going to be in the same city to write up the summer collections for the department stores. An unchaperoned weekend was quickly planned. We would meet on Saturday from our respective hotels and have a day at the races as whoever and whatever we wanted to be. Berton told me he had booked accommodation for that night so we would not have to return until Sunday. As I walk away from the office, I rehearse scenarios where I discover that he has booked a) two rooms, one for himself and one for his sister or b) one room for the fictional married couple. I give the question up as hopeless and realise with excitement that I cannot predict my own behaviour. I tell myself this is good because it means I won't really be to blame for whatever happens. I tell myself also that this is a very bad argument, but it will just have to do.

I can't concentrate on the show and decide to be nice to everyone rather than pay any attention to the clothes. About a third of the way through I've already finished my piece in my head, bestowing general and safely vague praise alike on the Kuppenheimer peach-basket hats (a little passé in fact), the Hart Schaffner and Marx light woollens and the assured victory of the long coat over last summer's tunic. I warmly recommend the rust-proof Goodwin girdle long before I see it and concur that Russian lines will be 'in' next year as parasols and coloured ostrich feathers blur before my eyes. The advertisers will be pleased. I join a scatter of applause, offer excuses and head for the door.

At the hotel there's half an hour's work with the portable and I'm done. I sit alone in the dining room and decline an offer of company from an older gentleman. I spend the rest of the evening in my room, debating going down to the lobby to telephone and hoping that every passing footfall is a bell-boy come with a message. In the end, neither side weakens and I suppose it's a good thing we're about as proud as each other. I flick through the ads in an old copy of *McClure's*. I think of tomorrow as offers pass before me, silent as a picture play – Professor Hubert's Malvina Cream; Why Sigh for Freedom? 9 a.m. and the day's work done with the Fritz Premier Electric Cleaner $25 ($27.50 west of the Rockies); Write for the Moving Pictures – no talent or experience required; put music in your home with the Angel Player Piano; Do You Have Power of Will?; Gossamer Powder; A Good Judge of Men? – Let Me Make you Better. I go to bed and read a few pages of a serial story. 'Jenny-tired-of-her-husband' slips from my hands and I sleep.

There are a dozen men in for breakfast the next morning – two with wives dressed about 1909. I say No, thank you to a waiter's offer of a newspaper and explain that I am not waiting for Mr Rubincam and will order immediately. The exchange attracts some attention so I take a magazine from the rack and pretend to be absorbed through a quick and nervous meal.

Berton and I are to meet at the station. I have to stand still in the bustle for five minutes before I hear his voice. I turn and there he is, beautifully turned out too, in cream flannel, linen waistcoat with this year's large tortoisehell buttons and one of the lovely new panama hats.

'Marion!'

We kiss and then he looks crestfallen.

'What is it?'

'The trains – it's hopeless. Everything is completely booked up. They've closed the ticket office.'

'They can't have.'

He has his hand on my arm and is guiding me round to the side of the station, talking all the time about how he should have got tickets in advance and how the whole weekend was ruined and it was all his fault. He's leading me, so I can't see his face until he stops and turns to me, excited and slightly scared and trying not to laugh all at once.

'So,' says Berton, with a flourish towards the street. 'We'll just have to take this.'

I look with amazement at a bright, new open tourer. Smart leather straps curve over a green hood, the seats are of scarlet leather and everywhere the brasswork is polished to perfection so that the whole thing looks unreal, like a gold and ruby beetle taken from a jeweller's window.

'What – it's yours?'

'Ours,' says Berton. 'For the weekend, anyway. The Model C King – "The Car of No Regrets", or so they tell me.'

'Oh dear, I could have done better than that.'

'I'll tell them. All I have to do is mention it five times in my piece.'

'Can you drive it?'

He reaches inside and comes up with a booklet bearing a picture of the car on the front.

'How hard can it be?'

There's a noisy fracas in the street. A horse is shying and men shouting. Another King Tourer rushes by in a cloud of smoke and honking like a giant goose. The driver waves at Berton and yells happily – 'Eat dust, losers!' as he veers away from a trolley-car at the last instant.

'That's Harry,' Berton explains. '*Scribner's* – great guy.'

'They've all got one?'

'Marion, they're practically giving them away. Every journalist at the races will be in a new car. Look, I got everything we need.'

He takes my case and puts it in the back. Everyone seems to be watching as he pulls out from the trunk a long linen auto coat, a hat with a veil –

'It can be a sort of scarf till we get out of town.'

'I know what to do with it, Berton.'

– and an enormous pair of goggles. We both dress for our parts and then laugh at each other with our strange saucer eyes, unrecognisable and barely human.

'Great – let's go.'

There's a tingle of fear as Berton pushes the starter and the car trembles beneath us. I cry out as it twitches backwards.

'Hey, hey!' someone shouts. 'Stick to a horse if you can't handle it.'

'Hold on.'

He works a lever and the car startles, coughs to a halt, jumps again.

'Damn it.'

The engine races and then we surge forward down the street, scattering lesser beings to left and right. As we pick up speed my scarf trails straight out behind me and I grab my hat just in time.

'Careful!'

I can't see Berton's eyes through the goggles. Whatever he is feeling comes to me only through his wrestler's grip on the wheel and the tense, fixed exhilaration of his mouth and jaw. A poster flashes by, advertising the races. The hunched autonaut glares ahead and looks so exactly like Berton there is a moment of confusion and I almost expect to see white blazes of speed shooting backwards from his shoulder and cap.

'We'll catch Harry,' he shouts through the din. 'I'll be damned if a *Scribner's* man'll get there first.'

The city is soon left behind and on the dirt roads we speed along like a little green and gold comet at the head of its own trail of dust. The air ahead gets hazy and Berton goads the car on. We round a bend and see another a quarter-mile in front.

'There he is!'

I put my hand on Berton's arm but he doesn't notice and we get faster and faster down the straight and then the corner is coming up like something I've never seen before, like we are falling towards it. Everything changes. I'm pushed forward and things rise up to one side and we tip into the corner and some very large trees appear from nowhere. I hang on with all my strength. For a moment I'm looking down on the outside of the car. I see the wheel not turning but quite still as the tyre scuffs sideways across the grit with a ripping noise. There's nothing beneath me. Car, road and posterior reconnect with a bump and off we fly along the new straight.

We never catch the other car. At Speedway Park we turn in and are marshalled to our spot by men in armbands. As the engine rattles to a stop I stand up and then climb up on the seat to get a better view. In the distance Lake Michigan is a glittering line on the horizon. Closer in there is nothing but cars, an amazing acreage of them drawn up in neat rows, a huge field of cars just like they had grown where they were and there had never been anything else before. From one direction there is an unnatural haze and a steady mechanical growl.

'You hear?' Berton asks. 'The big sixes.'

The smell of gasoline is in the air. Berton takes a deep breath, says it is in our blood now and declares it the perfume of the future. He makes a note in his little book. I shake a cloud of road dust from my coat and veil, take them off and get down onto the grass.

Berton puts his hands on my shoulders.

'Did I frighten you?'

I shake my head and say no.

'I'm sorry. It was stupid.'

'No, really – I wasn't scared.'

He looks a little sceptical.

'Really you weren't?'

'Not a bit. It was fun.'

He seems very serious and happy at the same time. I think he is about to say something. I am sure this is it. Then he looks about and a passing car sounds its horn and there's another obliterating wave of noise from the track.

'Come on. Let's get on the stands.'

Rickety, wedge-shaped ranks of benches line the track. Some look as if they have been put up just for this race. We climb up high to the back of the only one with any space left. It shakes with every movement of the crowd, its timbers catch the voice of the racers as they pass. The supports at one end have sunk into the ground so that the whole thing tilts and apples roll along the benches as if we were at sea. At my back I feel the pressure of a single strip of timber behind which there is a twenty-foot drop. Two cars rush by side by side. The crowd yells and a man waves a flag.

'Now it's the real thing.'

Berton explains in detail as the day becomes uncomfortably warm.

'These monsters can go a hundred miles an hour.'

The main event starts. The cars are lined up inert on one side of the track and their drivers on the other. There's a pistol shot and in a chaos of running and clambering they come together. Mechanics shove from behind, engines catch and they're away with a roar so loud you could shout with all you have and still not hear your own voice. One team pushes their car a hundred yards before it comes to life. As the smoke clears we see another unmoved from its starting spot. There is a minute of frantic efforts before hope is given up. The driver gets out and walks away, throwing off a mechanic's hand with a violent shrug. In no time the cars are there again, tearing by in a stormcloud of speed as the first lap ends.

The afternoon settles down. The pack of cars stretches out until only two or three pass us at a time. Later solitary racers rush past and I get confused.

'Is he winning?'

'I think he's last.'

The crowd cheers anyway and the drivers don't seem to care, flying round the bends as recklessly as if they were neck and neck, as if gravity itself were the enemy. Sometimes I have my fingers in my ears, sometimes I can hear larks and there is only a distant thunder from the far side of the track. The heat rises and I alternate between wearing my hat and fanning myself with it. Vendors with trays hanging from their necks balance on the springing benches like tightrope walkers and sell us cups of lemonade. Several times a car passes us never to be seen again. I have a strange notion of them getting lost, or just going straight on for ever as fast as they can. I try to ignore the smoke rising in the distance against the brightness of the water.

'Engine fire,' says Berton. 'He'll be fine.'

Another hour passes and the race becomes a mystery. For Berton's sake I try to stifle a yawn and it is then I wake up as something different and appalling slides in from the right. The noise is in the crowd at first – a surge of alarm that runs with the rising wave of people that hits and lifts us too so we can see a car which seems at first still to be in the race except that

44

it is on its side. It moves across the surface of the track like it must be ice, hardly slowing at all, but there's a shrieking and a yellow-gold trail of light from where the metal tears at the ground. I can see the head and shoulders of the driver and the blank gleam of his goggles. His hands are on the wheel. He's stretching up to keep his head from the track. He's still trying to turn the wheel, but there's nothing he can do now. The car catches on something, spins and stops right in front of where we're sitting. Men run forward and there's shouting as one is almost cut down by another racer. I smell gasoline and see figures struggle in a thickening white cloud. The driver is moving, but there is brightness too. It's small at first and for a moment I don't understand before the whole car is engulfed in a gust of heat and the rescuers reel back. Berton's hand is over my eyes, but I push it away and stand on my toes. Men are running into the flames. Everything seems hopeless when the driver himself rolls out, still burning. Mechanics tip buckets of sand and they try to beat out the flames as someone even throws a cup of lemonade from the front row. There's a moment of stillness when everyone stands back and smoke drifts from the body and another car goes by, though no one sees it now, and it all seems for nothing. Then – do you know those machines at the fairs, the ones you put your hand on and they make your hair stand up on end? – well that's how it is and not just for me; the man in front's hat rises up a good half-inch. The driver moves. Even with the smoke still coming off him he begins to move his arms and legs, and then he gets to his knees and then stands up. A mechanic goes to help him but can't because he's too hot to touch. There he stands, black and smouldering like he's just been cast in a furnace. He's dazed and moves slowly. His hands, trailing smoke, go to his eyes and he takes off his goggles and there's the white skin beneath, the only white thing about him, so white it makes him look like he has two huge pale eyes. He sees the crowd. Everyone begins to cheer and he raises his arms and we scream ourselves hoarse and shout and stamp and no one cares that the stand's about to collapse. I feel so happy. Not just relieved, but happier than before, happier than if it hadn't happened at all. The smouldering driver stands in triumph, like he always knew he'd live, like it was just a trick, Houdini's latest sensation.

Eventually someone wins. Berton drives steadily on the way back. I get drowsy, wrap myself up against the dust and lean my head on his shoulder. The noise of the car travels from bone to bone. I fold my hands over my front and curl up. Berton plants a kiss on my forehead and it's like I am inside a warm, humming engine that keeps me safe and lulls me to sleep. Some time later he wakes me with a question.

'Can you read a map?'

I am surprised to be in the city already. I take the street plan Berton holds out to me and look around, but there's nothing I recognise. I see a sign for Clark Street and there's a bridge too. The car stops as I'm looking down, trying to find where we are. When I put my head up again I see that Berton has taken his hat and goggles off. He's getting out of the car, looking at something down the street and not answering me. Then I see the ambulances, and other vans too of all sorts blocking all the roads. There are exhausted fire crews resting and police officers everywhere. On some of the vans there are large red crosses and it all looks like a newspaper picture from Europe.

Berton goes towards them and I have no choice but to follow. I smell river water. Nurses guide women by, blankets about their shoulders and water dripping from their clothes. There's something strange at the end of the street, like a new, windowless building right across it where it shouldn't be. Propellers stick out at one end and there are sparks where men are cutting holes in the upturned steel. The Chicago River is full of small boats and empty life vests and picnic baskets and other things I won't look at. From the boats men fish with

46

long poles. From somewhere in the crowd grief is suddenly loud. Priests and a rabbi walk among those who wait.

For almost an hour I am alone and then Berton comes back with 'the story'. I can't listen to anything he says. From where I stand I can see the edge of the quay. I see the backs of strong men straining as they lift from the boats below. Berton is talking about himself now and me and the future. He is walking very fast up and down. 'I don't know,' he says to himself over and again. 'I don't know, I don't know.' He stops and stands in front of me. He is pale and breathing hard.

'Marion . . .'

Over his shoulder I watch a man straighten slowly. His hands go under the arms of a girl and are clasped in front over her chest. He pulls her up and I see the water draining from her dress. I recognise it. I know the store and what she paid for it when it was new last summer.

'Marion Rubincam, will you . . .'

Her hair is long and fair and hangs down like a mask over her face. Water trickles from the end of her hair and the heels of her best shoes drag on the cobbles. A newsman takes a picture with a camera. Berton has stopped talking.

'No. No, Berton. No. Never!'

Clara

*L*ife moved steadily after that smoky, noisy evening in the kitchen. Henry did well and we moved up to a place in Bagley Avenue. He was then the chief engineer at the Edison Illuminating Company. He explained to me more than once how the dynamos were driven by a steam engine. At home from the works he would sit quietly in his chair, sometimes for an hour or two at a time without saying a single word while I sewed or read a novel.

'Shall I read aloud, my dear?'

He would shake his head and go on staring at the electric lamp as it glowed with the current made by the machines he tended. It was as if he expected the steam to follow him down the wires, somehow to hold him back even in his own home.

'A steam engine was the most exciting thing I ever saw as a boy,' he said to me one evening. 'I hate them now. I hate everything about them.'

Once, out in the town with Edsel, I saw one of the first horseless carriages putter by. I said nothing about it to Henry. But soon the great families of Detroit made a fashion of them and there were two or three, then half a dozen and I could almost rely on seeing one every other week. I began to learn these French and German names and took care never to utter them in Henry's presence. Second-hand surreys were advertised for sale in the newspaper, and the price of horses fell. The great new ambition was to turn one's stables into a garage. The Van Heerdens subscribed to *The Horseless Age* and left it about their drawing room on Saturday mornings for guests to see. Then the circus came to town and Barnum and Bailey paraded down Main Street headed by an American car, steered crazily from side to side by a clown waving to the crowds.

Henry worked harder. I fed him and slept unnoticed beside his exhausted body for the three or four hours each night he allowed himself. Meals would be snatched on returning from the plant and then it would be straight out to the shed in the back yard until the early hours of the morning. He borrowed tools from the Edison plant and spent all our money on more. I would fall asleep to the sound of the lathe turning in the shed. Once I awoke in early light to find him sitting on the edge of the bed still in his clothes. He jumped as I touched him. I watched him undress. He has always been lean, but he seemed starved then like an old picture of a saint in a desert, or a pilgrim wasted by his journey. He wrapped himself around me and held me tight – like a spanner on a nut is what he says. That was the morning I said Edsel was lonely, that a little brother would be good for him, or a little sister. There was only silence, then a slackening of his grip and snoring.

I got out of bed one night and looked down from the back window to see the shed doors open and Henry outlined against the light. He had an axe in his hand and was breathing heavily. I recognised Jim Bishop from the Edison works and even old Mr Julien from next door. Mr Bishop had a sledgehammer and I understood the noise that had woken me when he and Henry starting up again attacking the shed. Splinters of wood flew everywhere and when the door frame was done

49

they started to knock the bricks out too, like they were going to knock down the whole thing.

'That'll do it.'

Something like two bicycles hitched together or a giant's perambulator was wheeled out through the widened gap. I went down in my dressing gown, one ear listening for Edsel. It was two o'clock in the morning.

'You're just in time, Callie.'

I followed them out to the alley at the back. I remember light rain. I think I had an umbrella with me and I held it over Mr Julien as we watched. The night was still and slightly humid. The smell of gasoline hung in the air. A light appeared at a window across the way and the sash was pulled up by a wary onlooker.

Henry turned something and the engine started. He and Jim Bishop looked at each other. Henry clambered on and I half expected the flimsy thing to collapse beneath him. Jim handed him his hat. A lever was pushed and the contraption juddered and began to move forward slowly, Jim walking with it and then beginning to trot at its side as it picked up speed.

'Callie,' Henry shouted to me as he trundled down the alley to the main road, 'This thing has no reverse and no brake!'

He let out a noise the like of which I've never heard before or since. Jim was running to keep up.

'Try the other gear.'

The thing shot forward and left him standing. Away it went, careering out of sight into Grand River Avenue and down to Washington Boulevard. There was an electric doorbell on the front to warn people he was coming. Jim and I and Mr Julien stood together in silence. We could hear it – tring-tring, trrrrinnng! – sounding across the city ever more faintly.

I went inside. I kissed Edsel. I think I cried a little before I fell asleep.

★   ★   ★

More years passed. Certainly, no one could say we were at any risk of being spoiled by early success. A second car was built and I continued to sleep alone for half of every night. The *Maine* blew up in Havana harbour. There was a sort of war, but just as anyone was starting to pay attention it was over. In the streets people whistled the tune to *In My Merry Oldsmobile*. In August '99 I found Henry home in the afternoon.

'Callie,' he said, 'I've resigned.'

There were backers, stockholders and a new plan. In the winter I met my first journalist and got the Sunday papers early to read all about it − I think it's still in my album.

SWIFTER THAN A RACEHORSE, IT FLEW OVER THE ICY STREETS − flying along at eight miles an hour, twenty-five on asphalt, dreamlike smoothness, infinite rapidity, Whiz! Hold on! Whew! Perfect safety; spice of peril; what more could you ask? First the lion's roar, then the voice of man. Next the voice of wind in sails, the report of gunpowder and the shrill steam whistle. And now, the long, quick, mellow, not harsh, not unmusical not distressing note that falls on the ear as civilisation's newest voice.

I believe that young gentleman writes poems now.

There were delays. The stockholders wanted sales, Henry wanted a better car. $86,000 later a halt was called. They changed their name to the Cadillac Company and Henry was sacked.

'What do we live on now, Henry?'

'Callie, you have nothing to fear. Not in that department.'

We moved in with Henry's father and sister to save money and Henry rented a workshop on Cass Avenue, down by the railroad tracks. For a while I made almost all of Edsel's clothes myself. I got fatter and Henry thinner.

The answer was a racing car. In September somebody shot

the President and in October the Judge closed the Court in the afternoon so that he and the attorneys along with everyone else in Detroit could troop down Jefferson Avenue and out to the tracks at Grosse Pointe to cheer the hometown entry. Vanderbilt had put in for it, and Murray from Pittsburgh, but the man to beat was Winton, a mustachioed Scotsman and ex-bicycle-maker who was already making and selling thirty cars a month. No one could remember the last time he had not won a race.

I spent the evening before begging Henry not to drive the car himself. Nothing I said made any difference. Well before the end, I was talking to myself as Henry just sat there, silent and grim and not even looking at me.

The afternoon of the race Edsel and I got seats high on a bleacher by the first corner. Vanderbilt had pulled out. Murray had engine trouble and was pushed off the starting line. Only Henry and Winton were left. Don't ask me what happened next. I spent the worst thirteen minutes, twenty-three and three quarter seconds of my married life with my eyes closed and my fingers in my ears. At the end I supposed the cheering must have been for someone and when I opened my eyes I saw it was for Henry. He was covered from head to foot in oil and dust, but I hugged him anyway.

'Never again. Please, Henry – never again.'

For a second time the money came in. For a second time the arguments started. Everyone in those days thought the car was for rich men and that it could never be otherwise. There was an order to things, something invisible but very strong. Men of sense understood it and respected it, fools came to grief trying to break it. Henry, they said, was trying to break the order of things.

'I know something they don't,' he told me one evening. 'I know it in my bones, I can see it everywhere and I've told them time and again but they don't understand. They think the car is just a machine, but it isn't – it's a new life, a revolution, it changes everything. It's not the car, you see? – it's what the car does to the man and it will do a thousand times more for the poor man than for the rich.'

Well, that was one thing, but there was another too – since leaving the Edison Illuminating Company Henry's nightmare was having to go back. He could no longer tolerate the thought of anyone above him. Equals hurt him almost as much. Within a few months he was out again with nothing but nine hundred dollars and his name. More racing cars followed. The 'Arrow' was wrecked on a time trial in Milwaukee. But the '999' won everything in sight and Henry himself drove it to the mile world record over the ice of Anchor Bay.

'Well, it's not a race, Callie,' he said to me. 'I only said I wouldn't race again.'

Once more the money came in. These were different men. They understood Henry better, above all they understood how to keep out of his way. A new, cheap car was built and this time they got the words right as well as the machine. A man called LeRoy Pelletier was taken on. A colourful describer of Klondike shoot-outs for the *New York Times,* he turned the Model A into the Fordmobile, the Latest and Best, the Boss of the Road – no novelties, no tricks, no furbelows or fangles, no experiments, no mechanical hallucinations, no surprises and all at an exceedingly reasonable price within the reach of many thousands.

'The reader of an advertisement, Mr Ford, is a lock to be picked. If you cannot turn the last lever he remains as closed as if you had achieved nothing at all. "Reach" is the key here. "Reach" is the soul of the auto-buyer. Put this word, or its spirit, in everything you address to the American public and you will not fail.'

The cars got made and sat in the factory yard waiting to be sold. More were made and the yard was full.

'That's it,' Henry said to me one Friday. 'That's the last time we can pay the salaries.'

The change was as undramatic and senseless as a throw of the dice. We received a letter on 15 July 1903. A Dr Pfennig wanted to buy a car and enclosed his payment accordingly. Three months later I was going through the pockets of a pair of pants Henry had left out for cleaning. I felt something and took out a cheque for twenty thousand dollars. When he came home that evening he whistled the first phrase of our tune and I whistled the last. He kissed me on the cheek.

'Henry, I found this.'

He took the cheque and put it away in another pocket.

'Thank you, Callie. I wondered where I'd left that.'

Theodore

*D*isaster has been good to me. She first turned up my cards when Seth Sicherman stepped on ice while making his way out of Molloy's. That left me in the office on Friday night more or less on my own when Mrs Sicherman called.

'What?' I said to her. 'Again?'

I heard this injured, indignant noise from the other end and thought I'd got myself in trouble. I started to apologise but she was already talking.

'I call that a very unkind remark. Mr Sicherman was in a state of complete sobriety, just as he was the last time it happened. A man can be unfortunate can't he?'

I reassured her that this was certainly possible, indeed in some cases it was more than likely.

'That's right,' said Mrs Sicherman. 'That's exactly what I was saying.'

She went on with some details I can't remember now and hoped I would be able to let Mr Pipp, my and her husband's mutual superior, know about this mishap in a suitable manner. I swore a melodramatic oath that I would give an account of complete accuracy.

Another telephone started to ring.

'I gotta go, Mrs Sicherman. Yes I will, I'll manage fine.'

Two were ringing at once and then a boy came running in, his hand full of radiograms.

'It's war! War!'

'Mrs Sicherman? I really do have to go.'

The news had jumped from ship to ship by Marconi and from what I could work out it seemed only to have happened a few hours before. For all I knew, it was at one and same moment that the heel of sober Seth Sicherman's shoe came into contact with a chunk of ice and, four thousand miles away, a torpedo slashed through the Irish sea right into the side of the *Lusitania*. Anyway, it was one hell of a piece of luck.

I had often dreamed of pronouncing those greatest of words. I thought it might happen in twenty or thirty years if everything went well, but I never imagined it could come so soon. But there I was shouting into the telephone and feeling that I must be on a stage somewhere and not still in the real world. A voice had already said 'Printing House' and I could hear the clatter in the background. I took a deep breath.

'*Hold the front page!*'

'Oh, yeah?' said the voice. 'And who the hell are you?'

I explained. There was a shout and I heard the power of the pure, crystalline historical moment in action as the presses slowed and then fell silent. The voice came on again, changed.

'Really?'

I hung up, made some calls, read all the radiograms and everything coming off the wires. Pretty soon the boys started coming in and through the night the office was crowded, but I'd stolen an early march on all of them and when Seth Sicherman called up at three in the morning and tried to dictate something through groans of pain from his orthopaedic bed the copy somehow got lost. Anyway, by the time our new front page appeared at dawn Sicherman's name was still at the head of the column, but the words were mine. Second-Coming type took up near a third of the page – Piracy and Murder: World Waits for Wilson to Act. Below I gave them everything I'd got – the cowardliness of the U-boat, the shuddering blast of the torpedo, heroism and dignity in the evacuation, the cold, cold water and lovers' weakened hands slipping from each other's grasp moments before the end. Inside, Mr Pipp waxed indignant – world aghast at horror, can this be the twentieth century? Above, a cartoon Kaiser, swarthy and hook-nosed, held an infant Civilisation beneath the waters with his own hands. Teddy Roosevelt thundered about humanity and national self-respect and 'saddling up'. The President was calm. In the basement bars of Hoboken the resting crew members of the *Vaterland* toasted victory. The dachshund kicker appeared in syndicated cartoons across the nation. In short, it was a pretty good time to be starting out in the news business.

Well, there was no war. There was an exchange of telegrams, the *Lusitania* widows dried their eyes and the world moved on. I got my reward a few weeks later.

'We've got to do something on this exposition,' Pipp told me one morning. 'No one else will spend two straight days on a train so it has to be you. You got three days there and when you get back I'd better believe you haven't just read the brochures.'

He threw down tickets and a hotel reservation.

'Go see America, young man.'

I did, and there was nothing there. Plains spooled endlessly by. When I slept it was impossible to say for how long. I would awake to precisely identical scenes and could only guess as to whether I had drowsed for a minute or an hour. Mountains intervened and after them the dullness of plains was refreshed with the dullness of deserts. The window seemed like a moving picture when the projector freezes – your mind insists it must still be moving, but the eye contradicts. From time to time there were arbitrary halts at places with names stranger than those in the most remote of foreign countries. It felt like a true adventure and I understood for the first time how much I am a city boy, at home only in that coastal fringe of cities, stretched tight and thin as the skin of a balloon around a huge and absolute nothingness. I remembered that story where someone goes right through the centre of the earth in a machine and for days on end it seems hopeless and then, just in time, they break through to the other side and there's air again and light. I think they must have got the train from Detroit to San Francisco before they wrote that. At last the Sierras broke the monotony. We snaked down the far side, pushed gently forward as Mr Westinghouse's air brakes squeezed the speed from the train, wafting it to a halt in the station as smoothly as a magic carpet.

Just where the newest houses start there are two billboards, each three storeys high. The first says Panama–Pacific International Exposition 1915. On the other something like an oriole is launched into the sky with the help of friendly, finger-like flames. The wording beneath fascinated me and I turned my head as it flashed by – First the Earthquake, then the Fire and Now . . . I looked out eagerly for signs of biblical destruction, the black remains of incineration perhaps or jagged chasms where the earth had opened for the unworthy and conducted them down to their just deserts. I was disappointed – except that everything was a little newer and neater than I was used to, there was no sign that anything had ever happened. My first sight of San Francisco put me in a sombre mood. I felt diminished by such a display of recuperative powers. It lacked drama and suggested that there could be no disaster in human affairs, however great, that could not be quickly wiped away.

A Japanese taxi driver made a furious passage through the city. I was thrown off my seat at one point by a near collision with another cab. There was a spectacular exchange of oriental abuse – neither man, it seemed, in the least concerned about the impossibility of being understood by the other.

'No good,' explained my driver. 'Chinese dirty. Why don't you send them home?'

At the hotel I lay down on a motionless bed and instantly fell asleep.

In the morning, in bright sunlight, I flowed helplessly toward turnstiles. I showed my press pass and with a click was admitted to the future. The Tower of Jewels stood before me, Novagems of coloured glass glittering with promise as they drifted in the breeze. Everywhere there was evidence of a war on normality. The only buildings permissible were palaces – the Palace of the Liberal Arts, the Palace of Transportation and the Palace of Social Economy. I thought I would leave that one till later and took a right down the crowded Avenue of Palms. The Court of Flowers gave onto the Court of Abundance and the Court of Abundance delivered me to the Palace of Machines where a crowd stood mesmerised by the clattering rhythms of a folding machine. Paper shot in at one end and appeared at the other as an endless stream of gummed envelopes. An attendant gathered them into boxes and stacked them on the floor, the machine doing, so the sign explained, the work of twenty skilled men every hour. Six hundred boxes of envelopes were produced every day – for demonstration purposes. Further down the aisle a Hearst colour press ran out a blurring stream of magazine covers – teeth and eyes and the highlighted pearl in one ear rushed by like the face of a passenger in a train. I turned a corner and found that I had been shrunk to one thousandth of my size as I looked up at a fourteen-ton Underwood typewriter as big as a house. A dozen vestal typists catered to its every need. All of a young woman's strength was required to depress a single key, two at once strained to turn the cylinder. To return the carriage the whole team organised themselves on the end of a rope and heaved like galley slaves. Line by line the day's headlines appeared on the starched bedsheet of paper in six-inch type – Bryan's Statement Amazes Officials; Teutons Assail Foes; England's Heavy Loss; Say Frank Should Die – Prison Commission Advises no Clemency; Reply to Germany Firm but Friendly. The girls wound the paper up another two feet and were applauded for their efforts. A sign hung down from the roof beams. I heard the words spoken in the voice of a monstrous typewriter – 'Exact Reproduction of the Machine You Will Eventually Buy'.

I passed the display of the Cyclops Iron Works and a device that ate wire and threatened, at the other end, to bury the world beneath an infinite mound of hairpins. Girls delved into the hopper and helped themselves to handfuls which now, presumably, they would have no need to buy. Outside, between the Water Gate and the North Gardens, a crowd of men and boys pressed around the edges of a swimming pool in which a submarine dived, bubbled and resurfaced over and again. For a quarter you could go down in it and watch the water rise over the windows. On a stand nearby a polished torpedo exerted a magnetic fascination. A boy repeatedly banged the heel of his hand on its bronze tip. His father dragged him away to some fresh attraction. He followed happily enough, exploding as he went with enthusiastic noises and wide, scattering gestures.

Something began to oppress me and I followed a sign to the marina, believing that a sight of the sea was what I needed. The esplanade was busy but I found a spot at the railing at which I could look outward and be less aware of the crowds. Here was something new – my first sight of the Pacific Ocean. I imagined a line being drawn straight out from between my shoes and not stopping until it reached Japan. Was there a counterpart there, looking eastward? I tried to think of this person – in a vague way I could see that she was young and female and very beautiful. I struggled to make the picture clearer but someone jostled me and I was back with the toy submarine and the tyrant typewriter. I scanned the nearer waters of the bay, half hoping that I might be the one to spot the hostile periscope amongst the steam yachts and the visiting dreadnoughts.

A whiff of the farmyard came to me on the sea breeze. I turned to watch a fancy dress cavalcade trot down to the marina's edge. A man in pasteboard cuirasse brandished a sword, praised the sea and gave it its name on behalf of free peoples everywhere. With his three followers he rode out of sight. Balboa had discovered the Pacific Ocean as he would every hour on the hour for the next three months.

Such were the preliminaries or the mere frame, if you like, for the picture I really remember from my first day at the World's Fair. There was a disturbance in the crowd, a parting. Some way ahead there was a man cranking a moving-picture camera. Everyone understood that they must make way for three tall men. They say this country is a republic, but I doubted it at that moment when the unspoken instruction spread and the people pressed themselves to the sides to let pass this little procession which could so easily, if re-dressed in purple and ermine, have taken place in the most antique of European capitals. The older man was in the centre. In bow tie and wing collar, the others deferred to him – the man on his right in elegant grey flannels listening carefully to what he was saying, his other companion walking half a pace behind as he toyed with his cane or adjusted the flower in his button-hole until he should be called to rejoin the conversation. From my schoolbooks I recognised Thomas Edison. I soon learned that at his right hand the aquiline man in grey, with a hundred times more wealth at his command, was my first view of Mr Henry Ford. On the left, the dapper, modest attendant to these two gods was Mr Harvey Firestone. The machines of the future fascinated, but at the appearance of the men who made them there was something new, closer to reverence as if the cloth had just been pulled from the icons of a new religion. I followed and watched them stop before the camera. I must be in those pictures – hesitant with notebook in hand, failing utterly as a journalist as I let the moment pass. A child was pushed out to collect autographs. He bowed very solemnly and made people laugh before being gathered in again. America's industrial trinity moved onto a landing stage and boarded a yacht. There were other journalists there. We chatted and traded rumours until someone ran up and told us Fatty Arbuckle was filming somewhere. He had fallen down the stairs and ended up on top of Mabel Normand. There was said to be a photograph. The new hunt started at once, but I went my own way.

That night in the hotel I finished my thousand words for the *Detroit Free Press* in an hour. I smoked too many cigarettes, went out, drank a beer in a bar, spoke to no one and got my head down early. The two days left to me I spent more as a tourist and it was a tiring business. Every display I looked at seemed to draw something out of me. If there were credits they never matched the debits. I left the working model of the Panama Canal or the miniature Grand Canyon or the Japanese Village or the Court of Abundance feeling that someone had slyly picked my pocket of what little was left in it. I refreshed myself in the Marine Café or the Bowls of Joy and went out again grimly to do battle with an invisible enemy. I craned my neck up to the Column of Progress. A bowman stood on the top loosing an arrow (so said the brochure) into the future. I tried hard not to feel that if it found its mark and went straight through the heart I would only be relieved. I accosted a guide and asked him where the English pavilion was, or the palace of Germany. He shrugged his shoulders – 'I guess they didn't come'. I had a headache on the Arc of Progress, my feet hurt on Olympian Way.

I stayed late on the last day, reasoning that if I was tired enough in the morning I might sleep better on the train. The biplane curved in over the bay and landed with its last fare-paying passenger. Night fell – or would have done had the General Electric Company not prevented it. I have never seen such illumination, a true artificial day generated by the Exposition's own power plant. The Tower of Jewels glittered more brilliantly. From out in the bay the Scintillator, a coal barge for the rest of the year, lit up the sky with forty-eight gaudy searchlights. The night was as tiring as the day and my dejection increased. Others seemed to feel it too – a paleness, a shortness of temper, a flinching in the eyes of an animal unnaturally deprived of darkness. From Administration Avenue I turned down Sunset Court where the light was less piercing. There was one thing I wanted to see again and I soon found her – the Star Maiden, standing on her pedestal in the Court of the Universe, looking out to sea with her head slightly upward, homeward I suppose. In the welcome dimness her features were no longer clear, but I remembered them from when I first saw her. Her arms were held upwards framing her head, the fingers straight and palms together at the top. From her head-dress beams of starlight filled this space. Her eyes were serenely half closed. There was cloth, a garment of some sort around her shoulders. Hanging down a little way it described her breasts but did not cover them. Below was a lean, naked abdomen with a subtle, central indented line between the stretched muscles punctuated two thirds of the way down by a deep navel from which, no doubt, she had been umbilically attached to the heavens themselves. Slung in descending curves from hip to hip, sheer silk draped down to ankles. Feet balanced on the world and held it firmly with a wide spread of toes which had never known the confines of a shoe. The cloth was damp and pressed against her intimately as if she faced into the breeze. It flowed round hips and thighs and between the thighs, hardly less precise than the skin beneath. I thought of the model who must have stood in the studio, shivering perhaps and complaining every ten minutes that no one could be expected to stand like that for long. I could see her getting down from her stool, being rude and sulky with the artist, arguing about money, smoking a cigarette.

A woman approached from the direction of the Manufacturer's Palace. She gave every sign of recognising me and perhaps it seemed as if I recognised her too as I smiled back, only too ready for a chance meeting with an acquaintance. She said some things about the Expo and the warmth of the evening. When I apologised and asked if she would remind me where we had met before she just laughed. She looked up at the Star Maiden and then, slyly, at me.

'It's me, you know. Don't you recognise me?'

I hesitated, as if it might be true. She put her hand lightly on my arm.

'Well, almost. Are you here on your own?'

We walked together down Florentine Way and into the darkness between two candy stalls closed for the night.

On the way back the train could not go fast enough. I revised my copy, tried to interest myself in *The Pentecost of Calamity* – it went downhill after the title – and slept impatiently. I told myself that I was well and truly launched and that a happy prospect opened before me. I was a journalist, a real newspaperman, my apprenticeship served and my press pass to the future firmly in my pocket. I looked forward to a life that would combine, rather cleverly I thought, the excitement of events with the safety, physical as well as psychological, of the scribe's detatchment. These views did not last long – in particular they did not survive my third and final initiation into the journalistic mysteries.

I few weeks later I was sent to Chicago to do an easy piece on the city's newest and tallest building. There had been little of interest in the job and I had put together about as much as I could bear by the early afternoon. I misread a timetable and on account of filling the extra hour with a couple of beers, missed the next train too. I now had two hours to kill and drifted out of the station in a poor mood and with nothing particular in mind. A crowd in North La Salle Street attracted my attention. I pushed through to the front and found a police line holding everyone back. I gave a fancy name and lied about being from the *Tribune*. When I got through I expected to find nothing more than an auto accident and perhaps pick up two or three extra paragraphs to take back to Detroit if I was lucky. At first I couldn't see what the problem was – just a wide empty space leading down to the intersection and the bridge and the river. The people there moved slowly and were quiet, they moved like priests in a church. The upturned bulk of a Lake Michigan excursion steamer confused me, as did the emotionless face of the fireman coming towards the police line. He held something small in his arms. It was wrapped in a woman's coat. Plump infant feet stuck out at one end, but when I looked to see the child's face it was covered. I went down to the quayside and stood under the monumental shadow of the *Eastland*. Covered stretchers lay in rows – feet protruding from blankets or hands that had slipped from the side lying lightly on the ground. Only then was the connection made and that odd, easy dullness I had half been aware of for the last two months finally cleared, as if something had been taken from my ears, a mist wiped clean from before my eyes. For me, you see, the *Eastland* was the *Lusitania* and a reproach for everything I had felt through that happy, excited night in the offices of the *Free Press*. Only at that moment, in the middle of Chicago, and in the middle too of my third stroke of luck, did the *Lusitania* emerge at last to become something more than words. I steadied myself, then took out my notebook and went to work.

The boys from the *Daily News* were there, and the real journalists from the *Tribune* too. I talked to all of them and soon had everything together. Then I ran into Braley from *Collier's* whom I knew a little.

'I was out covering the races at Speedway Park.'

'Some crummy tall building story.'

We stood side by side, dazed at the scene before us.

'You know I just saw a man crash his car and it burst into flames and then they just put him out and he walked away.'

'Is that so?'

We compared and exchanged. It was what you already know, what you read in the papers that Monday morning. The employees of the Western Electric Company had come together early to set out for their annual summer picnic. They had crowded onto the *Eastland*, preferring the upper decks where the air was fresh and they could wave to their friends and family on the quay. The work of the Jenks Ship Building Company and more accustomed to the accommodation of freight than of passengers, the *Eastland* had a troubled history. Its owners knew this well, though its passengers did not. It was top heavy and its ballast system old-fashioned and hard to control. After several near accidents its owners met their responsibilities by adding more lifeboats and rafts to the top deck. Twenty-two days later it was this extra fourteen tons of safety equipment that caused it to capsize. In four minutes eight hundred people lost their lives.

'Death by lifeboat, then,' I said.

'I guess.'

Braley looked back up the street. A young woman was standing on her own in a hat with a lifted muslin veil and a dusty auto coat.

'I gotta go,' he said, looking so white I thought he was about to faint. 'I got my girl here.'

'Sure.'

Soldiers appeared and began removing bodies to a temporary mortuary in the barracks nearby. Stretchers were carried past me with numbers pinned to grey blankets. A man cranking a movie camera waved me out of his shot. I stepped forward almost to the edge of the quay. Hard by the top deck of the *Eastland*, now vertical and mostly submerged, a grimy salvage barge was at work. A cable ran down from its crane and vanished into the oil and water of the river. In the darkness below Arthur Loeb, king of the bell divers, blindly laid his hand on another ankle and swam back to his iron bubble of air.

I grew up at the *Eastland*. I connected words and things and began to see how many did not. I learned too that I really was the sort of man who could savour an irony, even as he stood among the dead.

Lloyd

*O*verdressed, I scout the street from a window table of the Powhatan Restaurant and do my best to ignore the attention I am attracting. I toy with the newspaper and count the change in my pocket by touch. Outside a gathering of police officers tells me that things are about to start. I get a refill as she goes by, and a hurtful smile.

'Cheer up, soldier. It's not your funeral.'

I say nothing and look away, hoping all the same that she'll forgive me and stop again next time around. I compose a little scene for myself – her shift ends (so what if it is the middle of the morning? it ends) and she comes and sits down opposite, she props her chin on her hand, smiles once more, determined to get it out of me, and says exactly what I need her to say.

'Go on, then. Tell me your story.'

And as I start she is sometimes herself and sometimes you, Amelia. At the happier, more distant moments, the ones we might still recall together one day, her features change, become a little fuller as the eyes turn to that rich brown and the movements take on that stage-trained finesse by which I could always find you in a crowd.

'I found her in Hicksville,' I say. 'No, really – that's what the place is called. I suppose it started a pattern – you see, my dear, my life has always been dogged by the illusion of meaning. It would be nearly twenty years ago now – I had just finished three nights at the Huber Theatre and was staying at the Swilley Hotel across the road. They were used to actors there and had laid on a late breakfast for me. I was leaving town that day and had plenty of time for my train. Well, I was served by a young lady I hadn't seen before and from the very start I couldn't take my eyes off her. I watched her carefully as she carried things to and from my table, her style all the way from the walk to her fingers uncoiling from around a cream jug. I came up with reasons to call her back and it was clear that she saw my interest and did not in the least shy away from it. I sensed that this was what she intended, a frank playing up to my one-man audience. I was excited and began to believe I had found that most precious of treasures – a natural. I ordered a fourth egg. She came with it and struggled to find a place on the overcrowded table. She spoke to me.

'You're having quite a . . . well, a titanic breakfast I would say.'

My ear caught on that word right away and I became more certain that I had stumbled on a pearl nestling in the, as it were, sty of Hicksville.

'No god, madam,' I demurred. 'A mere man – Lloyd Bingham, an actor by profession. Actor-manager to be precise. You may have seen the show last night?'

'I was not at liberty to see it, sir.'

'A pity. I would have acted better if I had seen you there, Miss . . . ?'

She laughed and did modesty in that way – oh, you know – that way no man but a fool can misread, even if he is half drunk and looking on from the back row of a poorly lit provincial playhouse. Hate me for it if you will, but that was the moment my pearl turned golden.

'Swilley,' she said. 'Amelia Swilley.'

She theatrically presented her hand and I theatrically kissed it. I was a little dizzy with the pace of it all. Just who was the spider here and who the fly? Miss Swilley observed that I had not eaten my fourth egg.

'Alas,' said I, 'I am discovered. I ordered it only to bring you closer.'

'Not worth the price of an egg, I'm sure.'

'But is not my hostess of the tavern a most sweet wench?' I asked.

The shutters opened on the limelight, the beam flooded down and I could see nothing but her, Amelia, as she replied at once and greatly to my surprise –

'As the honey of Hybla, my old lad of the castle.'

'You know it?'

She made a face – disdainful, impatient.

'It's my vacation assignment – I'm at Wesleyan. I was supposed to be staying with a friend, but her mother died unexpectedly so it was no longer convenient.'

'You're the daughter of the house, then?'

She cast a dejected eye about the gloomy dining room.

'I am afraid so.'

I pushed the egg across the table and suggested it would be a sin to waste it. She sat down and with two neat movements crushed its skull and exposed its innards. I watched her eat and asked how long the vacation would keep her in Hicksville. She looked at me for a while, thoughtfully.

'Well, I don't really know, Mr Bingham. Why don't you tell me all about the theatre?'

I did so, and effectively too, for within half an hour Miss Amelia Swilley had decided on a new life. We agreed on a simple ruse freely adapted from *The Desperations of Dolores*, with which the company had had a good success the year before. I would leave something of great importance in my room,

Amelia would discover it and feel obliged to take it personally to the station. She would deliver herself as well as my
watch and telegraph her intentions back to Hicksville from the
next station, thus escaping the 'the triple-locked deep dungeon
darkness of my life' as Dolores so feelingly refers to it in Act
III as she topples from the upstage dais beneath the charging
wheels of the Pittsburgh express.

That very night, scantily protected by the curtain on a second-
class sleeping berth, Amelia pressed her maidenhead upon me.
Her cheek lay against mine, hot and damp. Her breath was fast
in my ear.

'Oh, Lloyd. I may call you Lloyd?'

'My darling.'

And hidden within the rhythm of the train I heard no word
of warning as she confessed to me – 'Lloyd, I want *everything*.'

What followed need not be recounted in detail. Suffice it
to say that the fatal verities of magazine fiction were confirmed
in ghastly detail. The proprieties were quickly observed, Amelia
consenting to become Mrs Lloyd Bingham. The first act
unfolded in spotless sunshine. Amelia excelled at minor parts
and quickly graduated to the leading roles. She needed only
to read her lines once to learn them and quickly became frustrated as she waited for others to catch up. At the curtain calls
she was given more and accepted it all without question. The
flowers were for her, the press notices and the stage-door loiter-
ers. Within a year envy broke up the Bingham Stock Company
and we were on our own. Breakfasting in her hotel bed, Amelia
received the news calmly.

'We must be free, Lloyd. We must shake the dust from our
feet.'

She took a card from her night-stand and held it out to me.

'Last night I conversed with a gentleman from San Francisco.
You might care to have a word with him.'

Before the day was out we had signed for a ten-venue West

Coast tour. I played Butler, Chauffeur, Fishmonger [Voice Offstage], Cyclist Passing Upstage Left to Right and the Queen of Sheba's Footstool. I counted the money and made up the accounts. Every time I caught sight of my name in the newspaper it turned out to be hers and not mine at all.

'Oh, Lloyd,' said Amelia after a year. 'It's so unfair – I get three times more money than you for only half the work and it's making me feel bad.'

You can't say she wasn't a considerate woman.

'Why don't you just give up? You can be my full-time agent.'

I travelled at her heels, was tolerated, was broken to the sound of 'my husband'. I watched the clocks in railway stations, then stood alone on a platform once the crowd had gone. There was a message at the telegraph office:

Dearest,
New engagement Kansas City. Stand by.
Ever Your Pearl.

I stood by. Years passed. I followed you, Amelia, in all the theatrical columns I could get. I watched your name change from Mrs Lloyd Bingham to Mrs Amelia Bingham to Miss Amelia Bingham. I read your notices for *The Power of Gold*, *Hearts are Trumps*, *The Charlatan*, *The Leash of Love* and felt proud. In Oshkosh I knocked a salesman down for saying he was a good friend of yours. I lay in wait for Acton Davies after he had made a beast of himself in the *Evening Sun*. I tracked him to the Hoffman Café and dealt out correction blow for blow. For you, Amelia, I damned near bit his finger off – 'Lloyd the Loyal', 'Cannibal Lloyd'. You must have seen those stories, surely? What should I have done Amelia? The faster I ran towards you, the further away you got. We nearly met in Washington. I had heard you were at the Garden Theatre, but the gods were ahead of me – I was arrested for exceeding the speed limit on Pennsylvania Avenue in the open Winton Six bought with your money.

She started her own company, became a producer in a small way. I began to pick up the odd little part again. They called them top-and-tail bills – one Bingham at the top and another at the bottom. I had hopes for a while and we were always together once a year to go back to Hicksville, the slate of her parents' disapproval long since wiped clean. They liked to see me driving the latest model and carrying the valises up the path. It didn't last long.

'Good news, dear. Look!'

A letter from Charles Frohman, Mr Broadway himself.

'An offer, Lloyd. And look at these figures. My goodness, Lloyd, just look at them. You won't have to do anything now.'

I saw even less of her after that. I heard from a smirking acquaintance that divorce had been advised against on grounds of cost, 'reputational risks' and because there didn't seem much point. She sent more money and I sent back flowers, though without ever learning if she could tell mine from the scores of others her dresser gathered up every night, stuffed into a cab and had sent to the nearest hospital. It was all New York then, and even London. Beautiful American Leading Lady fills Palace Theatre with *Big Moments from Great Plays*. I worried when the war started – I never knew if she was at sea, or on which ship. I still read the passenger lists when there's a sinking.

My spurned waitress passes, but I am unforgiven. I summon her hazy likeness all the same and make her lean her elbows on the table and rest chin in palm with that way she has and raise an encouraging eyebrow.

'It could all have been so different, Pearl. I could have been something. I met Mack Sennett in a bar once. He knew who I was.'

Outside everything has gone quiet. The traffic has stopped

on Broadway and the black-plumed cortège gathers before a line of police officers. Amelia is close. I shake my head at the thought and turn back to the empty chair on the other side of my table.

'You know – I could have been a Keystone Kop.'

I let the enormity of the misfortune sink in and direct that a heavy, glycerine-bright, advertisement tear should gather in the corner of her eye. It's irresistibly real and I reach across to wipe it away. People look up as I put my arm out in front of me and gesture against thin air. I find the flesh-and-blood waitress standing nearby with a question on her face. I nudge the coffee cup and she slops it full of steaming black before moving on without a word.

And then what happens? What brought me here? The big news day a couple of weeks ago and I find I'm one of that ten, maybe twenty thousand in the world for whom it's also personal. I'm looking for my name again, rushing in a panic up and down the double column of First Cabin Passengers – Battersby, Bilicke, Bistio, Bloomfield, Braithwaite. She's not there, but before any calm can come to me I'm gripped by a thought so obvious, so right that I'm sure it's true. She's not a Bingham at all now, she's gone back all the way to Amelia Swilley. My eyes move right and down – Shymer, Sonneborn, Stockhouse, van Straaten, Tiberghien, Twenlo, Vanderbilt and valet. She's alive! I'm shaking and start to walk to disguise it. I get a drink at a bar, read the reports and go over the list again. And that's when I see it.

'Another whisky.'

'Someone you know?'

I read the name half a dozen times, but it doesn't change. Charles Frohman, Frohman the showman, star-maker Charlie. Well, well, well. How should I feel, am I bereaved, have I lost the manager of my wife?

Wounded By Torpedoes
Appeals for Help Made
No Word of Prominent Men

I settle down at the bar and wait for the late edition. I'm the first to snatch a copy from the boy when he comes. I scan the bread-warm pages and there it is –

Frohman Lost, Theatre Mourns

And he made a good job of it too, made all his old clients proud of him at the end and left a little something for the newspaper boys as he went down. Swimming around in the waters off Kinsale with that charming little Rita Jolivet, struggling until he found the right words.

'Rita, my sweetness, take this down, won't you? Ahem! Why fear death? It is the most beautiful adventure that life gives us.'

The buoyancy of inflated sentiment left him and down he went. Professional to the last. She of course survived – well they do, don't they? In the following days I read of the arrangements for the return of the sunken hero (he had bobbed up again somewhere else – I don't criticise; I've always had a weakness for the second curtain call myself). You read that too, Amelia, how could you not? I knew you would be here, not half a mile from this spot, I'm sure – this is one rendezvous not even you could break. I look out the window, sift the mourners. No, not yet – but somewhere close.

I tried to get in touch, Amelia – I mean, more persistently than usual. I got a card from your secretary – 'Miss Bingham has received your communication and is grateful for your interest in her work.' Perhaps you neglected to tell your secretary that you have a husband? If I embarrass you I'll change – just tell me how.

Did you read this – as you prepared over a late breakfast? I can see it. You make even black beautiful, Amelia. And your beautiful laugh as you read in your morning paper, the same one I have here, of Mrs S. R. Meissner of 1524 Thirty-First Street, Georgetown, recipient of the wisdom of Mr Charles Frohman from beyond the grave. 'It is I, Charles Frohman, speaking. I want to tell everyone in the world there is no such thing as death. I called out for help and someone took my hand and they said to me "It is the greatest adventure in life." I asked what they meant and they said "Only what you have already said yourself." I said I had spoken of death but my helper said to me "Why, this is death," and I could hardly believe he was speaking the truth.'

Should I give her a go, Amelia? Should I cross the widow Meissner's palm with silver and ask her for a few words from my wife? I suppose she'd ask me how and when you died. Tricky.

I can see that things are about to start. I leave some coins on the table, fold up my paper and leave.

The ears of the mourners, and of the horses await the signal. To the tap of a muffled drum the cortège steps out. The face I'm looking for isn't there and so I begin to make my way through the crowds down to the Temple Emanu-El at Fifth and Forty-Third. I get there in good time. Grief-featured, I am admitted to the synagogue gloom and make a search of the early arrivals. There is no one I know. All well and good – Amelia, I can be sure, would not waste her entrance by arriving too soon. I go out again and position myself carefully in the swelling audience, a spot just right to see the cars as they draw up to the steps. There is a steady stream, a few unknown faces, acquaintances mostly, a good show of my more fortunate colleagues. Now and then a famous face appears and a frisson runs through the onlookers. When it's a moving picture actor they strain forward and make a noise – urgent and inarticulate like a response at Mass. Mr Roscoe 'Fatty' Arbuckle eases himself from a covered sedan and labours up the steps with the help of an ebony cane with a black bombazine rosette. The comedian is impeccably dressed and dignified as a statesman, but habit still overwhelms someone in the crowd and they laugh crudely.

The hearse arrives and the undead remains of Charles Frohman are borne into the synagogue chattering away, for all I know, to the enterprising Mrs Meissner of Georgetown. An automobile is hard on its heels. Anytime now it could be her – my heart quickens and I feel a little sick as my hatband moistens and tightens around my head in the heat. A woman emerges from the car and the crowd reacts quietly. She is followed closely by a man. They look about themselves, count to three and slowly ascend. I am excited too – it is Rita Jolivet, Rita the survivor, the bearer of the great man's last words (from this side of the divide at least). The story of the *Lusitania* made flesh pauses by the elaborate portal. I've heard that the offers are coming in and a star is never at rest these days. Accordingly, she makes a *distrait* quarter-turn to the audience and looks down to signal that the emotion is about to go to her knees. She slumps onto the well-timed support of what will tomorrow be described as her 'unknown gentleman friend'. There is a low 'Oohh' of sympathy. It seems to restore her. From somewhere deep within she finds the strength to go on and steps inside. Nicely done, Rita, you hard-hearted bitch.

I'm looking back up the street to get the first sight of every car that might still come. There are a few more and each one is a torment. Then there's a lull and I become certain that this is the moment. The minor cast members are out of the way, the pause is dramatic, in my head drums roll as I push my way closer to the front. Everything is right, every term of the incantation has been pronounced and must, surely, summon her. When a man looks at me strangely I realise I am saying her name out loud. At the top of the steps men take pocket-watches from their waistcoats. The doors of the synagogue are closed and the crowd goes slack and dilutes itself back into the city.

I go too, vacantly, and drift into the park to find myself a bench over which the last, brown-edged blossom of a cherry tree scatters with every turn of the breeze. It is the edge of summer, the moment at which trees are in new and immaculate leaf. Strollers and their children abound. Connections are everywhere on display – marriages, offspring, friendships. I have to take care not to turn and talk to the absence at my side.

So, Amelia – I was wrong again. And you too, Charlie. Can you see her from up there, do your files tell you where she's working tonight? Hundreds of miles away, I'm sure – maybe thousands. I feel her distance now, as intensely as I felt her closeness half an hour ago. I thought she would turn up for you, Charlie, I really did. But she didn't, no more for you than for me – ah, well. A brotherly tear for the late Mr Charles Frohman surprises me and I unfold my newspaper – President Expects Germans to Agree; Spain Opens Doors to Jews; Greeks Vote for War; Few Americans in London – smallest consumption of cocktails and least use of ice ever recorded, but fewer spoons stolen, say hoteliers.

I turn a page now and again like I'm really reading it and so come back to that absurd column on Mrs Meissner and the dead impresario. For the first time I catch the last paragraph. In the background the trees and the sunlight, the birds and the people all come together like those bits in symphonies that change everything you feel just at the end. And exactly what was it that the dead Frohman whispered to the clairvoyant, what was the message? 'I want people to understand that everything depends on the way they have tried to live, not on the way they have lived, but on the way they have most tried to live, because we cannot all attain to what we would most wish to do. I thank God for letting me write this down.'

For a while I have to keep the paper steady in front of my

face. When at last I can put it down, words and setting mingle – on the stage it would be the cue for the next musical number and the summer strollers would step into a pattern and dance. My heart lifts as I too receive a message – that the world is not indifferent, that the invisible hand that guides it cannot tolerate too much unfairness and must turn the fortunes of this or that man when long-delayed justice demands it. I am made a promise, an offer on easy, though admittedly uncertain, terms. A law of nature reveals itself to me, its certain operation guarantees my future. This cannot last, my life will get better – and soon.

Marquis

$\mathcal{I}$ must have seen Henry Ford many times before he was rich, but not once did I notice him. Henry, Clara and the growing Edsel would have been regular attenders at St Paul's long before I was able to pick them out from their fellow worshippers. It was one of my own who first drew them to my attention. The more progressive members of the Detroit clergy came together regularly in those days to disburse some modest charitable funds of which we had the trust. I believe it was at the end of one of our Monday meetings, probably on the steps of the deanery, that I felt a hand on my elbow and a discreet, envious voice in my ear.

'So, Samuel – I hear you've bagged the Fords. Play those cards right and you'll not be wanting to spend any more time with us arguing over ten dollars here or twenty there.'

When I asked what he meant I received only a knowing look and a tap of the finger on the side of his nose.

'The automobile man?' I asked. 'He comes to St Paul's?'

'You really don't know?'

I listened to a description of the tall, angular industrialist, the dowdy sheet-anchor wife and the neat, bright son and heir.

'Ah, yes,' I said. 'Now I know who you mean. So that's him, is it?'

'Be careful, Samuel. You know what they say – money is to the modern clergyman as the incense of Noah to the nostrils of God, a sweet smell indeed. If you won't have him someone else will.'

My fellow pastor smiled at me, tipped his hat and went on his way with a virtuous spring in his step.

It was, however, by an entire coincidence that I received an invitation from the Fords not more than a week after this conversation. Henry was already a wealthy man, but not yet one of those half-dozen or so extreme exceptions that chance or genius throws up in every generation. He was well-rooted in his middle years and had known just enough of hard work and poverty not to have become wholly detached from his fellow human beings. That day, talking and drinking punch in the garden at Edison Avenue, I met characters in brighter plumage and more heavily freighted by far with their own self-regard. I heard the established old merchant names of the city, the senior partners of the leading law firms, the farming famil-ies whose land had become the rentable parcels of Detroit and the old French aristocrats who had first survived and then been borne up by the regrettable Anglo-Saxon flood. They seemed to be conscious of the favour they had done Henry by accept-ing his invitation, and also baffled and a little amused by the fact that Henry, with his easy manners and his out-of-town accent, was not at all conscious of this favour and did not even seem to be aware of who they were.

I, a poor man in such company, was the only one thinking of money that day – and then only because of what my colleague had said to me. I don't believe a single one of those guests could have imagined that within a short space of time their economic relation to their host would be so dramatically reversed. None of them, save for Henry himself, had any abil-ity at all to see into the future. Within a year of that encounter Henry Ford would have been able to dispose of the entire wealth of one of those men with a cheque from his personal account and not notice the difference. Within three years you could have bought and sold that gathering for less than a month's interest on his capital. I can't tell you what lies at the heart of Henry Ford – that is as obscure to me now as when I first shook his hand and gave him my name – but I will say that he is the same with several hundreds of millions beneath him as he was with ten thousand and I doubt that any man in history has been less changed, for good or ill, by incalculable wealth.

I talked little to Henry on that first social occasion – I was merely introduced, complimented on the 'good sound practicality' of my preaching and passed on into the throng. I exchanged pleasantries with this or that leading member of Detroit society and two or three times drifted on the edges of Henry's own conversations. I watched the shifting circles of listeners silently communicate their bemusement, eye to eye, as Henry explained the transforming power of the machine and how his gasoline tractor would extend the revolution from town to country. When they began to believe him they became uncomfortable. These were men who already had the world the way they wanted it, whereas for Henry staying still was the sin of sins – plant him in Paradise and he would go to Hell for the sake of the journey.

The afternoon would have been inconsequential had I not found myself becalmed by a bed of roses. The buds were breaking – enough for the first colours to show, but still several days from blooming. A short, rather plain woman in early middle years had just crossed the lawn to join me. I gestured over the roses with an empty punch cup.

'On the edge of glory – I think that's when I like them best.'

Her face lit up. I thought at the time, though quite wrongly, that it was a little exaggerated.

'What a lovely phrase – and I'm *so* pleased you like roses.'
She held out her hand.

'Clara Ford, and I'm sorry I missed you earlier – kitchen
panic. Tell me, which one do you like most?'

It was apparent from the outset that I knew little of roses
and my hostess a great deal. What I clumsily described by
colour and size she would name with poetic relish as the Agnes,
the Reine de Violettes, the Blush Damask and the Belle
Poitevine, the Baltimore Belle and Shakespeare's Eglantine. She
turned and pointed to something reddish clambering aggressively around the porch colums.

'My Zéphirine Drouhin. Henry didn't notice it when he
bought the house, but I would have bought it just for that.'

I hesitated, fearing that it might seem insincere to agree too
readily with such an improbable statement.

'You must come back in a fortnight, Reverend Marquis.'

'Samuel, please.'

'I will show it to you then and you will understand. In fact
I will show it to you blindfolded. Have you noticed that? –
you only tell me what they look like. The best conversation I
ever had about roses was with a blind man. He could name
them by scent and was never wrong.'

From such auspicious beginnings we had a long and excellent talk. The subject of the rose in literature put me on surer
ground and showed how willing Mrs Ford was to be taught
as well as teacher. She claimed a great love of reading and a
nostalgia for those first schoolday encounters with lines she
still loved. We found we were at one on the pleasures and high
importance of reading and I mentioned a school in a poor
quarter of the city I had long been associated with and had
struggled to improve.

'Such industry! Such hope! And yet so little chance of any
of it being fulfilled.'

With keen interest and gentle tact, Mrs Ford obtained the

name and address of this school and the name of its principal teacher, all without the slightest suggestion that anything was being asked for, or granted.

Within three weeks I had indeed returned for my further education in the matter of roses. I had also returned to my pet elementary school and found there, as I had hoped, a scene of transformation. New glass replaced the old cracked panes, bright pictures were on the walls, new books on every desk and outside in the cramped yard, a border freshly dug and planted with roses. The children too were changed – awoken by the revelation that they really were provided for by an invisible power. I stood at the back of the class. Thirty bright-green copies of the Reverend McGuffey's *Eclectic Reader* were open at the same page – the very book for which Clara and Henry particularly had such feeling, the book which had done most to form that small part of the magnate's brain not wholly possessed with matters mechanical.

'Now, children,' asked the teacher. 'Who can tell me about Shylock?'

Thirty hands go up as one. Small bodies squirm with anxiety to be the first to answer.

As her husband rose, Clara Ford also became prominent in Detroit society. Her house has never quite been a salon, but what figures Detroit had to muster would often be there and what they had to say would be said. I became a part of this and the Episcopalian Church and my own causes did not suffer as a result. Henry was often absent and even when he was there, on some evenings and the occasional weekend, it was usually for a short time only. We understood that he was an active part of what the rest of us were fated passively to observe. We suspected at some simple level that like a projectionist in a picture playhouse, if he failed in his work the story would stop or the next day's newspaper be blank. Sometimes I would stay on after a worthy talk in the Ford drawing room or a summer garden party that had strayed long into the evening. When she was unsure of what to think of them, Clara would raise the issues of the day or hint at her worries about Edsel or how she wished Henry would not work so hard. Her devotion to Henry was absolute and had about it something of the martyr, unwilling ever to acknowledge needs for which her husband did not provide. We knew each other well by the time she turned to me in the garden and stopped in the middle of a sentence.

'Samuel, I would like to think of you as my spiritual adviser. I already do, but I realise I haven't asked and it seems presumptious. May I use that phrase, just to myself?'

If I hesitated it was only because I was so moved. I declared that it was an honour and hoped from that day on there would be some true service she could ask of me, that I could say 'yes' to and be happy.

The years passed steadily, news of other lives our only landmarks. Roosevelt went and Taft came, pulled in the presidential victoria between high, shovelled mounds of March snow. Suffragettes paraded on the same day, led by a young woman with a sword all in white on a tall white horse. After him, Wilson, waving from the back seat of an automobile. A Frenchman flew across the English Channel. Talk of war meant prohibition, then Mexico. Harriman, the great railroad man, died. Henry read the obituaries and was gloomy for a week while on the Pennsylvania Railroad the locomotives went ninety-nine miles in an hour. In May the next year we gathered out at Dearborn where the new mansion was to be built. We looked up at Halley's comet and drank to the future as we passed through its tail at 2,500 miles a minute while farmers out west locked themselves in cyclone cellars and workers stayed home to spend their last day on earth with their families. The Standard Oil Company was broken up and the *Mona Lisa* stolen. Mark Twain died – Clara and I reread his books –

the *Los Angeles Times* building blew up. A Norwegian stood at the South Pole and Mrs Alice Longworth smoked a cigarette. Henry visited a slaughterhouse. He watched and calculated as the butchers stood still and the carcasses moved past them on hooks. He went to his factory and shook his head as he looked down on the wastefulness of movement. Waste was immoral. From then on the cars moved and the men who made them stood still. The price went down again and the model letter ticked up to T. Expansion gave way to explosion.

China became a republic, its Manchu dynasty living on in the opera house alone. The *Titanic* and John Jacob Astor met their end as the band played on – one of my own particular favourites which the Fords and the rest of the congregation sang in St Paul's the following Sunday.

> *Hold me up, mighty waters,*
> *Keep my eye on things above.*

Germany increased her naval budget and automobiles could now be started with the touch of a button. Women, for whom wrestling with the starting handle had been considered a gross immodesty, became customers in their own right. The American Suffrage Union wrote Henry to thank him for the physical emancipation of their sex and asked him for money to help finish the job. They were not the only petitioners – it was from this year that the gates of the Ford residence were closed and guarded every hour of the day. Herman Rosenthal found his death beneath a streetlight in New York. The seven police officers standing nearby saw nothing, caught no one and obtained no evidence. John Schrank took a shot at Theodore Roosevelt, only the thickness of the manuscript of the speech the great hunter was about to give saving his life.

The Ford businesses abroad were growing fast. Because Henry could call it work, this made Clara's longed-for trip to England possible at last. Edsel went too – nineteen years old in 1912 and with no more independence of thought than a be-medalled and feather-hatted crown prince awaiting his inheritance. Long Island friends saw them off on the ship and gave Clara a seal-bound *Record of My Trip* for the great adventure. She wrote in it assiduously – extracts became letters, some of them to me. I heard of the Rolls-Royce in which they were driven round the country, of Bristol and Bath, Windsor Castle, the Piccadilly Hotel, Buckingham Palace and shopping in London as the men clubbed together on their own for the sacred rites of 'business'. I heard of Warwick and of finding the house in Linen Street where Clara's mother had lived as a girl. A photograph was taken on the step and the sexton disturbed to show the parish records. Warwick Castle diverted them on their return. A piece of Chinese porcelain in the great hall got under Clara's skin – she yearned for it, thought of how finely it would set off her peonies and idly mentioned to Henry how nice it would be if they could find another like it. I heard of offers being made, refused, repeated and refused again. The story went quiet and I cheered inwardly for the old powers of resistance, of decency. I told myself that it must have been Clara who had called a halt to the vulgar game. And yet, a month after the Fords' return, at a charitable reception, there was the Earl of Warwick's porcelain and Clara herself making me feel a little sad as she called it a punch bowl and asked if I didn't think it was fine.

There were great floods in Indiana and Ohio. Men rowed boats in Dayton like Venetians. Three thousand were said to have died, but the waters receded before the universal cleansing some anticipated. Our time, it seemed, had not yet come. Mr J. Pierpont Morgan died, thus moving Henry a step closer to being the richest man in the world and stimulating in him another week of reflection and discontent. The President threw a switch and sent across a continent of wires the spark that would detonate beneath the Gamboa dyke, over the remains of which the Pacific and Atlantic waters would mingle in the Panama Canal. Mary Pickford was the Queen of the Movies, her name known even to those who had never seen such an entertainment. The appearance of Broncho Billy on the streets of Cleveland caused a riot and out on the plains the cattle-men went short-handed as their cowboys rode off to find better wages in front of the camera.

It had been a good year for Ford. That Christmas the aston-ishing figures in the company accounts, the spirit of the season, and perhaps also a little problem with staff turnover combined to bring on the idea of the five-dollar day. Henry became a public man as never before and I sat in his office with the sound of a riot coming through the windows as I listened to a machine-shop boy's explanation of the world.

'There's something called sociology, Samuel. It's new and scientific and gets right to the heart of people. It tells you just what they're like and what you have to do to change them. If someone was starting religion today all over again this is what it would be.'

The offer, as you know, was made but not at first accepted. The Ford Sociological Department came into being without me and I continued my life in the Church. I heard tell of its works, read of them in the newspapers, endured reminders from Henry and sometimes, less directly, from Clara too.

The year wound on in innocence. The news was all of things getting bigger and faster. George Westinghouse, who had quite a hand in this aspect of our history, died.

'He was only sixty-eight,' I remember Henry telling me. He shook his head and looked distant as he did the alarming arith-metic in his head.

Kaiser Wilhelm radio-telegraphed his greetings straight to President Wilson. The newspapers told us of the amiable German's latest entertainment – Live Targets, a cinematographic device of some sort which allowed the user to shoot at moving projections. In one May afternoon the Kaiser destroyed three hundred aeroplanes, animals and human beings and declared himself highly delighted. He ordered the machine installed in various cadet schools and the same pleasure was soon available here at the larger travelling funfairs. Cartoonists enjoyed a great boost to their income as Josephus Daniels decided we should have a 'dry' navy. The General Federation of Women's Clubs took up the prohibition fashion and pronounced a solemn ban on the tango and the hesitation waltz.

An assassination in Europe attracted little attention. The war itself unfolded slowly in the minds of most Americans. For the men at the top it arrived dramatically on the last day of July as the New York Stock Exchange was forced to close by an avalanche of sell orders from Europe, where every other means of turning paper back into gold had already been used up. The conflict was baffling, antique. Maps and tables of dates and photographs in the newspapers of men in brass helmets, swords and operatic uniforms had no meaning in our progressive republic. American business boomed, but Henry Ford was one of the few not to entertain the purchasing agents of the belligerent powers. Henry did not approve of war. It upset him. Dead men did not buy cars. In the greatest industrial plants in America there was no war.

Socially, the only change to his life was a further swelling of the ranks of petitioners. To utopianists, perpetual motioneers, paper-money nuts, workshy geniuses in need of annuities, respectable cadgers for church and college, dog doctors and the proponents of the artificial cow were now added the peace campaigners. To a few of these, the most persistent, the secrets so long withheld from the rest of humanity had been vouchsafed – they not only disapproved of war, they knew how to stop it once and for all. There were schemes of such arcane delicacy their full detail could not be revealed until funding was in place; occult elixirs of peace waiting to be stirred to life and efficacy with a liberal admixture of dollars. Against them all Henry hardened his heart. It was his conviction that no one wished to tell him anything he did not already know, or discuss any problem to which he did not already have the solution.

'I know how to stop the war, Samuel,' he revealed to me one day. 'Men aren't fools – give a man a car and let him drive a hundred miles this way or that whenever he pleases and he'll see for himself that men in one place are no different from men in another. If he's been told otherwise it's lies and he'll see for himself it's nothing but lies. There's nothing I could teach the great manufacturer in the sky about standardised production – humanity is a one-model range. Have people never asked themselves why you can take two people from the opposite sides of the world and still fit them together just like they were made for it? Piston and cylinder, just like they should be. Understand that and war makes no sense. When there are enough cars in the world, Samuel, there'll be no more wars.'

No employee or would-be recipient of his charity could ever contradict him. His peace of mind was the particular care of twenty men, at their head the saturnine form of his private secretary Mr Ernest G. Liebold, who lay course upon course of mortar and brick between Henry and the world.

The calm that came from ignoring everything outside himself became one of Henry's chief characteristics at this time. I recall when he accepted my invitation to the most important church reception of the year. There I was, shepherding him through the press of dignitaries, when someone took my arm and drew me away for an urgent word with a colleague. When I returned I found that a line had formed in front of Henry as it might on Easter Sunday before the Holy Father himself. Each supplicant explained their case in half a minute and left calling cards with sums of money written on the back and the number and type of motor vehicles they could best use. I myself was besieged with enquiries about the nature of Mr Ford, how to ingratiate oneself with him, the flatteries to which he was most susceptible, the weak points in the vaults and strongrooms of his goodwill. Ray drove us back that evening and Henry and I sat in silence for half the journey. I was in deep embarrassment and barely articulate as I stammered out my apology – that I had not foreseen such a crude display, there had been no improper motive in my invitation, that he must not, above all, think there was any league or compact between myself and my fellow clergy. Henry smiled and said nothing.

I learned later that not one of the supplicants from that evening received a single dollar. By various means I was let known that for me, the friend of his wife, the discusser of roses, it would be different – the offer that had been made still stood and could be accepted at any time. As I worked hard with other rich men for fifty dollars for a school or a slum clinic, I knew that the head of the Ford Sociological Department was equipped with a company chequebook on which his signature alone was good for up to a hundred times as much. My religion and Henry Ford's resources – was there anything to be said against such a marriage? It was in the drawing room of the Ford residence on Edison Avenue with the Earl of Warwick's vase gracing the window sill that I finally made my decision. So it was that I walked with the employees of Henry Ford, indeed became one of them and gave the others the helping hand he had spoken of. I became the designated conduit of their employer's personal interest, the love of Ford made flesh.

'Samuel,' said Clara as she leaned forward that day and patted me on the back of the hand, 'I am so pleased.'

The war in Europe settled down and apart from a few cranks most people lost interest. The news repeated itself, changing little from month to month. There would be sudden flare-ups

– panicky sightings of submarines in the Hudson, lurid talk of Germano-Mexican plots and angry knock-down debates on neutrality, 'preparedness' and being too proud to fight.

Alexander Graham Bell spoke into a telephone the exact same words he had spoken thirty-nine years before. Only this time he spoke in New York and was heard in San Francisco. Wireless experiments were an even greater sensation – the voice of the American Telephone and Telegraph Company President waving out from New York and halfway across the ocean to Honolulu and into the ears of Lloyd Espenchied as he crouched in a hut on the shores of Pearl Harbor. A loyal German tried to blow up a bridge with dynamite. Charlie Chaplin walked into Mack Sennett's office and asked to be given a chance. Within six months few people did not know his name. Lincoln Beachy, famous for flying his plane under the Steel Arch bridge at Niagara and appearing through the mists as if from nothing, flew in circles over the San Francisco Exposition, crashed and was killed. The *Eastland* cast off and capsized in Chicago. Eight hundred and forty-four lives ended more quickly than on any battlefield.

It was a busy time for me, doing the Lord's work and not just preaching it. Once Henry had got his way and installed me at the head of his new project I saw much less of him than before. A distant master suited me well and I was able to get on according to my own ideas as much as Henry's. It pleased me to become a well-known figure in the poorer parts of the city and it is no exaggeration to say that soon there were not many streets in Detroit I could walk down without exchanging a few words with a Ford man of one rank or another. I found myself a sort of bishop presiding over seventy-seven parishes, each containing an average of five hundred and twenty-three communicants with the Ford faith. The investigators were their priests, connecting them to the bounty of the Company or threatening excommunication if they should fall by the wayside once too often. The newspapers were gloomy, but I looked forward to days of uplift, living the parable of the talents, doing what we could to ensure that every Ford dollar was spent the Ford way. We distributed *Helpful Hints for Ford Employees*. From the back cover Joe Polianski, his wife and three clean and neatly dressed children smiled at the camera and held up the banner – We Bless the Day the Investigators Entered Our House. The English language advanced across the Polish and German quarters, new furniture was bought and the sidewalks piled with the old and dirty, books appeared on shelves and new shoes on young feet, the stairwells of tenements smelled more of soap than whisky. Back at the great Highland Park plant these new men would enter shift after shift, machined to engage in the great common enterprise, turning smoothly in their allotted place as the profits of philanthropy piled ever higher.

The Sociological Department was friend and pastor to all Ford men on $200 a month or less. Thus we covered a wide range, from the simple-minded shop sweeper to the skilled men, foremen, white-collar clerks and draughtsmen. It was our job to guide and foster these ranks in the steady life of the Ford family. Less officially, I worked to protect them and repair the damage whenever there was a change in the weather. 'Reorganisation' was a rumour which put anxiety, or downright fear, into everyone who heard it. Things would start with an uneasy feeling. There would be a darkening of the sky, a pitched tightness in the mind such as epileptics speak of before a fit. Henry himself would appear more deeply lined. Normally taciturn, he would become secretive, almost entirely silent and his gaze would be sharper, exhausted. The storm would certainly follow, as fearsome and arbitrary as thunder and lightning to the ancients. Policies would be changed, rules turned inside-out, men transferred from what they knew to what they did not know or discharged without warning or explanation. When the chaos died down I and a few others would man the ambulances. The sacked would be quietly re-hired, the transferred edged back to the jobs they did best and abolished departments reconstructed under the disguise of a new name.

We were in the midst of one such convulsion when I found myself in Henry's office. It was not clear why I had been summoned and in the end I never did find out, or not exactly. I found him seated behind his desk in the corner, pale and worn as he was at these times and distracted by great events elsewhere. He greeted me and waved at the chair where I should sit. He pushed the newspaper away and rubbed his eyes.

'Who was Frohman?'

I explained that he was a man of the theatre, the country's biggest Broadway producer. The information had no effect. He folded the paper and dropped it in the waste basket.

'Vanderbilt too. You know it says in there, Samuel, that it cost three million dollars to build her and only four thousand for the torpedo that sank her.'

For three seconds he concentrated on the remote corner of the room.

'That's two fifteenths of one per cent. One hell of a margin – if you'll excuse me.'

I agreed briefly and waited for him to get to the point. Henry looked past me, played with a pencil, pinched the bridge of his nose and screwed his eyes tight shut like it was too long since he had last slept.

'You'll have been hearing things, I expect.'

I said the men were confused, that they didn't know what was coming next. The plant was full of talk.

'You must tell them there are reasons for it.'

I waited.

'Just tell them there are good reasons for it. A man can't argue against a good reason, can he?'

There was a pause, a familiar vagueness in the eyes as he turned inward for what he needed.

'It's in the nature of some things to stand still, Samuel, and for others always to be moving. Change is good. Change is what made all this. What you have to understand, Samuel, is that . . . well, that in our world stillness is death. We have to . . .'

And with that borrowed phrase there followed one of those lengthy statements that collectively express the obscurity of Henry Ford's mind. It was of the times – as discordant and fragmentary as the new music, the connections between one clause and the next twisted, tenuous or, even to the most subtle thinker, wholly absent. This particular essay on inevitable progress, the greatest good for the greatest number, the best of all possible worlds and the breaking of eggs to make omelettes was still in its early stages when I became aware of other voices coming from the anteroom. Henry seemed nervous, but continued speaking. Outside, Liebold was suddenly loud and there was a bump against the panels of the double doors, though they did not open. Henry paused and shifted his position. He looked down and fiddled with the edge of his cuffs. He mumbled something about the drawing office before returning to his theme. The disturbance grew and as the situation threatened to become ridiculous I stood up and excused myself for a minute to deal with it.

'You do that,' said Henry, getting out of his chair as if to come with me.

I found Liebold nose to nose with a man I knew well – the mild-mannered Mr Perlmann, chief clerk of the drawing office. I had never seen him in such a state before. His hands trembled and he was rigid with anger. Liebold was sweating and had his back to the door. It seemed certain that any second the dispute must go beyond words. The usual anteroom crew looked on in eager fascination.

'Well?' demanded Perlmann. 'I'll not leave without an answer. I have thirty men waiting to hear what this means. Are they transferred? How are they to do their work? Where? Why are they being treated like this? When Mr Ford hears about this . . .'

He turned to me as I slipped out from Henry's office.

'Dr Marquis – your meeting has finished?'

Liebold edged to the left to block Perlmann's way. I managed to get the two men into Liebold's tiny side office and closed the door behind us. The secretary staunchly refused to say anything and Perlmann could never quite bring himself to the heart of the matter. I began to see that it would have humiliated him even to mention it. He kept repeating that Henry could know nothing about it, that he would be very angry when he found out and that a personal interview with his employer would put everything straight. At a loss for what to do, I hoped that he might be right and promised to get him his chance. I went back into Henry's office but found it as empty as when I had first been there and the side door open, the one that led to the private washroom and through that to the fire stairs beyond.

I soon learned the story of the drawing office from other sources, and then played my part in reconstructing it. In the end I don't believe there was a single man who was not re-hired. The truth was the company couldn't work without them. Outwardly nothing tangible had been lost, but tomorrow was never a certainty again for those men and that must have been the purpose of the whole affair, or it had no purpose at all. Between Henry and myself the episode was never mentioned in so many words. But the preacher in me had not quite died and on a social occasion when I had him to myself for a moment I spoke a few words as if they had been said to me by someone else, not as if I agreed or approved them in the slightest but merely as a fact, and a humorous one at that, about what could be heard around the lower depths of the Ford world. I let him know how it was said that a man in the Ford organisation had but a short time to live and is full of care, that he cometh up and is cut down like a flower, that he never continueth long on the job. Henry's eyes narrowed. He looked at me sideways, played with the glass of soda water in his hands. He said nothing as that distant, calculating expression returned to his features. The burden of his wealth became clear and I saw that I was suspected, weighed sadly as nothing but another traitor in waiting. Clara came up. She chatted cheerfully but then stopped and frowned as she caught the chill between us. She smiled uncertainly. The Ford marriage is a curiosity. They are very different people, but when together there are times when they hardly seem to be individuals at all. I did not believe that Clara either could, or would, save me from another of Henry's reorganisations.

Ray

*B*ack in the winter of '14 I roomed with Ledenev and his wife. Ledenev was an aristocrat, a fully skilled machinist earning twice what I did. It meant the apartment was better than most and I was lucky to have a place there. I made sure I got on well with them.

Sometimes we would see little of each other, at others our shifts would coincide and we went and came back from Highland Park together and ate and slept at the same hours. Going up and down the stairs of that tenement with Ledenev I learned five languages just to say 'good morning' to the others in the building. In that part of town there was no fire under the melting pot – two words of each language was all I ever learned.

That winter was a hard one. Ledenev and I took all the extra work we could find and it was on account of this that his apartment was the only one never to fall short of coal. On Sundays the place would fill with eastern Jews – Russians, Germans, a few Poles. The place was full of pamphlets, newspapers and books. They piled up and we had to move round them like the place was a library. Whenever one of these books was brushed to the floor Ledenev would wince and make a show of picking it up and dusting it off. His worst fights with Shula were over which newspapers they could burn and which they must keep. Making parts for cars was a stage in Ledenev's journey. He always let you know that your paths might be crossing for a while, but that his would soon take him elsewhere.

On Sundays, the visitors would wave the pamphlets, newspapers and books at each other and the talk would become riotous, with Ledenev in the thick of it. I would sit in the corner like a child, too dead-tired from the week's work to pay any attention. He gave me things and told me I should read them. 'Go on,' he would say, 'it's in English.' But it wasn't for me. To be honest I don't know where they got the energy or why they were bothering. Two or three languages were on the go at once, but they seemed to understand each other well enough. Sometimes I got the idea they were plotting something, but they never minded me being there. I picked up only a few words that were the same or little changed in each language. For a while I thought of cracking their code, but never got very far. Of the words they had in common, 'Ford' is the only one I still remember. When the noise got too much Shula would shush them down and they would all wave their hands and say sorry and start again quieter, but not for long. She would smile at me then, as if to say, 'Yes, it is all nonsense. Noisy, hopeless nonsense – but it keeps them happy.'

She would be sewing aprons for a little extra money, or just lying back looking up at the grimy ceiling with her hands knitted over her belly, waiting for her baby in the spring. I sat near her by the window that looked out over the back courts. The other side of the building was close and as the winter afternoons drew in the lights would come on one by one. Dim vertical stripes showed the stairwells and brighter patches on either side were the rooms. They would flicker as figures moved in front of the bulbs. The sculleries looked onto the back as well and there was one, a couple of floors down from the top, where a woman was in the habit of standing in her stone sink and washing herself from head to toe. Maybe one time in five I was lucky enough to catch her and that was a good weekend for me. Then the Jews were complaining they couldn't read in the afternoon gloom and Shula put her lights on a few minutes earlier. My picture frame lit up and my sink bather saw me looking down on her and that was the end of that.

When I came back from the riot I still had a streak of blood on my face, though it wasn't mine. Shula fussed about me as I cleaned up and kept asking about Ledenev who hadn't come back yet. I said he must be fine, that he had been inside working his lathe, that he had what the others wanted and that was why there was a riot. I told her then that I had seen Mr Ford, actually seen him. I told her the sight of him had stopped me cold and that he was a strange-looking man, but I didn't say what I was doing at the time. Then I was summoned the next morning and you know about that. Within a week I had twice the money and within a month three times more than before. I got a place of my own and packed my bag and said goodbye to the Ledenevs. They didn't pretend much that they were sad to see me go. They had the new five-dollar wage and the baby coming and the books piling up and all that, so I understood.

Now the more you have, the more some people will take from you, and that's what made so much work for me and the boys. We patrolled the perimeter as before and we kept our ears open for union talk and dealt with that too. We got friendly with the scrap-metal dealers in the city and found out who was stealing all that copper wire. We visited homes to check in tool boxes for anything that shouldn't be there and when the men stole from each other, we helped them out there as well. The old coatracks went and were replaced with pulleys. The bell rang at the start of the shift and the coats and lunch pails were hauled up to the ceiling way out of reach. Mr Ford was very pleased. 'The perfect industrial solution to human nature,' he called it – 'if you can't fly you can't steal.' The men worked the first half of the shift getting hungrier and hungrier just thinking of those lunch pails hanging above their heads. Then the bell would ring for the lunch hour and the pulleys would come down. 'Manna from heaven!' one guy always joked. Thirty minutes later everything had to be back on its hook and the bell would ring again and up it went, out of the way for another four hours. It was better really – you weren't worrying who was at your things and it cut down on the ugly rumours. No one was suspected, because no one was trusted.

Mr Ford liked to walk around the plant himself to see that things were going right. In those days things were getting so much bigger so much faster it was like a completely different place every month. He used to stop by the lathes and talk to the skilled men about their work. Sometimes the men would clam up if he talked to them, wondering what it was all about really, frightened in case something wasn't right. He got used to my company and from then on whenever he walked the shop floors I was with him. It felt good walking there by his side. We passed Ledenev one day, working at his lathe. He gave me quite a look, but I didn't care. That's my advice – arrange things so a great man gets used to you being there. I'd say that's the best an ordinary Joe can get in this life.

They taught me how to drive and life speeded up. Sometimes I drove Mr Ford himself when he was going to a function in the evenings or at the weekends and he didn't want to have to bother about anything himself. That's how I met Mrs Ford who's a real lady and has always treated me well. I'd do anything for her, just as I would for her husband. They gave me money for a suit of clothes so I wouldn't look out of place and I began to see things I never thought I would and learn how to handle myself with all sorts of people. I even had Mr Thomas

Edison in the back of my car once, though not everyone believes me.

There has never been a name for my job. I do what is required and whatever doesn't fit neatly with the other men. Mr Ford always likes to say he can rely on me and when he needs some special sort of reliability that's my job. One way or another I've ended up seeing most of the Ford Motor Company, and in the end that included the Sociological Department. Everyone talked about it and no one liked it and things certainly didn't get any better when the Reverend took over. According to the grapevine he was some sort of favourite of Mrs Ford but to the men he was just Slimy Sam, always poking his nose in where it didn't belong. Me – I ended up in the middle and did my best to say nothing to no one.

For a long time the Sociological men looked after themselves. Then one of their moral uplifters woke a drunken polack at the wrong time and got his hair mussed. They all ran for their new Model Ts and drove back to Highland Park. They had a conference in their office and someone took a crayon and coloured in the map on the wall. Red was those parts of the city where folks were less passionate about self-improvement. Whenever one of Slimy Sam's college boys had to take his clipboard out to a red block either me or one of my men had to go with him.

That's how I found myself back at Ledenev's a year and a half after I'd left. The Sociological Department had long since lost the element of surprise. People would know in advance which area they were heading for on any particular day, and even if they didn't whole blocks would swing into action as soon as their cars were seen pulling up at the sidewalk. Clean clothes would be placed in the top of laundry baskets, lodgers would brush themselves down, pomade their hair and rehearse their stories about being blood relatives from out of town just come on a visit. Windows would open all at once and cough dust into the air like this too was a factory and every part of it running off the same powertrain. Bibles and schoolbooks from the Ford English School would be placed on tables and opened to show how piety had been interrupted. The contents of ashtrays were tipped into drawers and water dripped from the overflow pipes as whisky bottles were lowered into lavatory cisterns. That was the deal – the investigators treated the employees like children, and the employees made fools of the investigators.

Usually I had little to do except hang around the cars in the street while the questions were being asked and the forms filled. But being in that neighbourhood made me feel kind of uneasy. I recognised some of the faces in the street and a couple of folk nodded back at me uncertainly. The word had gone out that there was a reorganisation on and it made everyone tense. Anyway, after a quarter of an hour I went in and climbed the stairs to the top apartment. The door was open. I heard Shula's voice giving short answers, and a man who spoke much more than she did. Between questions he talked on with a stagey casualness like a dentist who knew he was about to hurt you. I rapped my knuckles on the door frame and went in. There was a moment of non-recognition in Shula's face and then a look of relief. She turned her back on the investigator as we greeted each other and asked about the usual things. The other man was younger than me. You could see the care he took over his appearance. He had a sort of marble face that looked like he must have shaved it every two hours and he held a clipboard and the green fountain pen his mother gave him for his birthday. He knew who I was, of course, and it wasn't easy for him to ask me to leave. He looked sternly at his clipboard all the same, at the questions that remained to be asked and then looked straight at me and raised an eyebrow like some high-handed society doctor asking to be left alone with his patient. Shula reacted at once.

'You'll stay, won't you?'

'Sure,' I said. 'There's a lot to catch up on.'

I glared back at the young investigator, pleased with my victory, and let him know that he should carry on without worrying about me.

The apartment had changed. A new shelf had been clumsily attached to the wall where it supported a small Chinese jar and a dozen books which were now the only ones to be seen. Prominent at the end of this short row was the Ford pamphlet *Helpful Hints*. Its advice on light and airiness had been ruthlessly followed. The stacks of newspapers had all gone. The place smelled of paint and new rose-patterned curtains hung at the window. I looked out and down two floors to see the white square of the sink I used to watch so keenly all Sunday afternoon. There was a fat armchair and a soft red rug on the floor. In the corner, in a wooden pen, a sturdy eighteen-month-old girl dropped a red wooden brick onto a green one. We eyed each other cautiously as she picked up the brick and tried to fit it into her mouth.

'Getting enough sleep? Yes? And your husband? That's good.'

Shula and the investigator were just out of sight, but I could hear everything they said. He talked like he was reading out of a book, all about how the Ford way was to see factory and home as part of the same big picture, how they often found that a man who did less than his share in the factory had troubles at home. Did Mrs Ledenev have anything she wanted the investigators to know?

I moved round to where I could see them – the questioner with his back to me and Shula just visible over his shoulder. He must have been younger than her by a good few years and it grated on me to hear his worldly-wise tone and how he worked hard on her to get in where he had no right to be. Shula's answers got shorter and sometimes she said nothing at all, but I guess he thought he could get away with anything.

'You know the Ford Motor Company pays top dollar. They pay the best in the industry, Mrs Ledenev, and they feel that's what they should get from their men in return. If a man starts his day on the line and he's already tired wouldn't you say that's a problem? Another baby coming? No, no – of course. I was just wondering. So it's no, then?'

He makes a mark on his clipboard.

'And this little beauty here, she must keep you both pretty busy at home. Enough for anyone, I expect. And Mr Ledenev, he has interests? I mean things outside the home, things that take up his time and energy. Have you ever seen your husband drunk, Mrs Ledenev? Well, I'll take that as a no. I have to ask, you understand.'

He makes another mark on his clipboard and writes a few words.

'So you're doing something to stop another baby coming?'
Silence. I take a step forward.

'Do you need advice on that? We've got people who can talk to you about it. The Ford Motor Company feels that a man who takes top dollar for his work should be fresh when he starts. If you think of it from our point of view, Mrs Ledenev, it's really not fair if . . .'

He moves towards her and gives an odd sort of laugh under his breath.

'Well, I mean . . . if it's all been taken out of a man before . . .'
She used the flat of her hand, but otherwise did it like a man, turning her whole body, putting everything into it and catching him square on the side of the face. His head jerked sideways and cracked off the door frame. He dropped his clipboard and stumbled backwards, nearly falling into Ledenev's armchair. After a few seconds with no one saying anything he asked if I saw what happened. I just told him it was better he should go. The best he could do was to pick up his clipboard and tick a box in as threatening a way as he could manage.

We listened to his steps as he retreated down the stairwell. When there was silence Shula spoke.

'Skid row – is that how you say it? Back on skid row again.'

She looked at the armchair and the patch of carpet and the rose-patterned curtains and started to cry and then the baby started too. She went to pick her up.

'What if he tells the police?' she asked me.

'He won't. Anyway, it's easily dealt with – you just tell them he put his hand where he shouldn't've and got what he deserved. Give them my name, if you like. I'll back you up.'

For a moment I thought she hadn't really understood, and it was then the whole thing started to get to me as I saw that what bothered her most was telling a lie. I remembered how it was for me before I had some cash in the bank and I told her straight.

'You can't play fair with these people, Shula – you'll always lose if you do.'

She had a desperate look and I guessed she was wondering what she would say to Ledenev when he got home.

When I got down to the street I nearly jumped out of my skin when I saw the man himself coming back after an early shift. I must have looked guilty and I started to feel it. He didn't look too happy to see me and I think he would have walked right by if I hadn't spoken to him. He was cool, but I tried to keep it going until most of the investigators got into their cars and headed off back to Highland Park. I was wondering all the time if I should tell him what happened or leave it to Shula to decide what to say. When there was no one left in the street he suddenly said I should come round some time and that he was sorry if he had seemed unfriendly. A man had to take what he could get in America and no one should hold it against him.

'The truth is, Ray – if I'm seen talking to you these days I lose friends. I'm sorry, but that's how it is.'

I made my own excuses, saying I was not really a part of it but just come along with my boys for safety's sake. Then I felt even more I should tell him about the investigator and I was about to when he took me by the arm, strong enough like he was about to throw me out of a bar and giving me a look that put the hair up on the back of my neck.

His daughter's voice, harsh and angry, sounded down the stairwell.

'You know what this is, don't you?' he says to me. 'You know what it all amounts to?'

He nods upwards to his apartment.

'When I'm awake at night and she's sleeping, sometimes she used to say my name – now she says his.'

There was nothing to say after that. I got my boys together and we went back to the plant directly. I described the investigator in Ledenev's apartment and one of them knew him by name. I told them how Shula had damned near floored him and they all thought that pretty funny and were keen to get a closer look. So we made up something as soon as we got back and we got him apart from the rest in a vacant shed. We couldn't touch him of course, but we backed him up in a corner till he looked real scared and couldn't get away. We asked him how many of the employees' wives he had touched up, why he had gone too far with Mrs Ledenev, and if he hadn't why she had laid that big red mark down one side of his face. I knew what would hurt him most and as I got my money out I could see I was right. It was like a blow in the belly when he saw what I had in my hand – a guy like me with money like that. He could see what I was worth to Mr Ford, and I guess he knew what he was worth. Well, maybe he had some troubles at home of his own, because that bastard college boy took my money and for that I got the Ledenev Sociological Report and the pleasure of throwing it in the fire myself.

The reorganisation went on and for a while I got as jumpy as everyone else – I'd stuck my neck out pretty far, after all. When it was about a week later and I got in to find a note calling me to Mr Ford's office, I thought that was the end. Now Mr Ford doesn't always say what he means like other people and as I stood there and listened to him and wondered what he was on about I still thought I was finished. You see, you just have to wait for a few clear words among all the others and hold on tight to those words when they come.

Well they did come – somewhere in among a lot of talk about efficiency and keeping things moving and people getting too comfortable and taking advantage and some detail that passed me by about the drawing office. I told him I'd be right on it, that he could be sure I'd do a good job. I got the boys together and we went to the drawing office and before anyone else was there took all the desks and the chairs and the drawing tables out back. Then I handed out some axes and took one myself and in half an hour we had the whole lot in pieces. Perlmann turned up before we were through. He watched us and had a look on his face like he was getting fit to cry like a baby. I put my back into it then and every time I swung that axe and let it bite into the wood I just felt so happy it was him and not me.

Theodore

*T*hings got quiet that summer. 'Stalemate' was the only news from Europe and after being told of the great advances on the Western Front for the fiftieth time and still nothing happening, the story slipped back to the second and then the third pages, giving way to unexpected baseball results and local automobile accidents. When Seth Sicherman limped back into the office with a cane and a grievance things got even quieter for me. I was kicked down a few rungs to the apprentice stories – *demi-monde* weddings, arrests for drunkenness among the moderately well-known, the ready-to-wear clothing debate or being sent to hang around Windsor docks all day, asking every young man who got off the ferry if he was deserting his country in disgust to join up with the Canadians to save civilisation. Two of them said they were and that I should do the same, and one threatened to knock me down.

Our own war of words settled down in its rhetorical trenches. Pacifists were 'milk-faced grubs' and the preachers of preparedness nothing but 'jingoes' and 'warmongers'. Anxiety pitched up to hysteria when the snoozing and conspicuously sabre-slashed Dr Heinrich Albert had his briefcase stolen by a Secret Service man at the 50th Street elevated and saw its contents splashed all over the front of the New York *World*, proving that everyone's worst fears were as nothing compared to the awful truth. Mr William Jennings Bryan packed up his troublesome conscience and flounced out of President Wilson's cabinet. He got up on the stump before his fellow Americans and asked them the same question ten times a day – why should they live in a pistol-toting nation if they were not going to live by a pistol-toter's ideas? Well, that was the end of him.

With Sicherman back in harness these plums all fell on his side of the fence. That put me back on local news and it just so happened that one of the most constant sources of local news in Detroit, ever since he doubled the pay in his factory and started to preach the gospel of industrial salvation, was Mr Henry Ford. Since 1905 Sicherman had held to the view that the horseless carriage had no future, it was nothing more than a symptom of a futile and disordered restlessness, the mechanical expression of the same illness that made fools prattle on about conservation, rational dress and votes for women. By 1915 the matter had become too painful to discuss and he had decided to revenge himself on Henry Ford by ignoring him and all his works. It had become an article of faith for him that nothing of interest or importance could come from that quarter and so for me, the field was clear.

Mr Ford was known for getting on well with newspapermen. He was good copy and they listened to him the way he liked to be listened to. Because he rarely read any newspapers they could write anything they wanted and still be welcomed back a month later. During quieter periods they would go to him and, if they could get through, ask him what he thought of the great issues of the day. He would explain how an increase in the export of cars to Mexico or of tractors to Russia would make these problems evaporate like a bad dream. Like the cars themselves, it was all a bit of a joke. But somehow Ford got into people's heads. No one could quite say how it happened

– America woke up one day and found that Henry Ford was, well, kind of ubiquitous I guess.

The war got beneath Mr Ford's skin and this put the whole newspaper game into a new gear. As a manufacturer he made a big thing of not supplying any of the countries involved. He started to get mail from all sorts of pacifists and cranks. I heard he never read a single letter of that sort, but he liked to make his voice heard all the same and it was heard, louder and louder through the second half of 1915. The word was that Henry Ford was bored with making cars, that he had his eye on higher things, that he was in need of a new cause, an adventure perhaps, something to soak up all that money. You can be sure there were plenty of newspapermen who lay awake long into the night trying to work out how they could arrange it for him.

As 'accidental' sinkings of American ships went on Mr Ford waded into the preparedness debate. He took the view that if Belgium hadn't been prepared for war she wouldn't have, as he put it, 'got her nose punched'. The newspapers asked if that were so then why should people even bother to lock their doors or pay for a police force to catch thieves or, for that matter, to stop someone bigger and stronger taking Mr Ford's factory away from him? It was suggested that he would be as happy making cars under a foreign government as under one of his own countrymen. I don't suppose he was troubled by any of this, or even much aware of it. And as for the fuss caused when he pointed out that the Ford Motor Company did indeed have a factory in Germany and that the German people needed cars and tractors as much as anyone else, I truly believe he didn't even understand it. As I got closer to him I saw how he spoke to the world as if through a telephone that only worked one way. It was his privilege to use such a rare machine, for his words to be carried to the people and yet for no troubling echo ever to come back. He never heard the fury of his opponents, or their arguments. Maybe he was just bored, maybe it was just a game, but it didn't seem so to me as I happily became part of Henry Ford's one-way telephone and thrilled to see my words printed under his name.

So there I was, being sent out on slow news days to hang around the offices in the Highland Park plant hoping for a Ford quote. I got to see how the whole set-up worked and was filled in by a fellow named Swinehart who'd been there longer than anyone. There were three people who mattered, collectively known as the pack; the bull terrier, the poodle and the retriever. The first was a big guy called Ray who'd come from nowhere and was supposedly the chauffeur, though he was really a lot more than that; then there was Liebold, the personal secretary, a poisonous, hairless German who prided himself on not having a friend in the world; and finally Marquis, Mr Respectable, head of the Sociological Department and said to be the keeper of Clara Ford's secrets.

'Look out for Marquis,' Swinehart told me. 'Ex man of God.'

'You don't say?'

This judgement turned out to be a little unfair, but it woke me up at the time, it being an axiom of our trade that the affairs of fallen clergymen are happy hunting grounds. And so I started to pay particular attention to Dean Marquis whenever he passed me in the anteroom and we soon got on a nodding acquaintance.

The anteroom was so big it was really more of a hall. Pictures of cars hung on the walls, along with six or seven clocks. Rows of chairs went down either side and there was a desk at the far end, just to one side of the large double doors that led to Mr Ford's office. Liebold worked in a small side room and also from this desk which allowed him a schoolmaster's view of everyone waiting. More than once I watched him play with people, keeping them there all day, moving them to a more hopeful chair closer to the great doors just when they seemed about to despair and head for home. That was his joke and we, as observers, soon learned that the poor fool who had worked his way up to chair two or three by five in the afternoon had only a few minutes left before being dismissed. Liebold was always impassive as he gave them the bad news – no sympathy, no joy either. But I noticed that he would always go into his private room immediately afterwards. What he liked to do in there, I'll never be sure – but from the sound of it he was either running on the spot to keep fit, or dancing.

I asked Swinehart about the clocks and learned that this was one of Mr Ford's great enthusiasms, that he had dismantled them and taught himself how to repair them as a child. I made sure to spend my next Sunday afternoon in the Detroit City Library and when Mr Ford was next passing me in the anteroom at Highland Park I happened to remark in his hearing:

'Is that not a particularly rare three-weight Chauncey Jerome of the mid-1850s hanging on the wall over there?'

Swinehart gave me a deadly look and Liebold, dogging his master's steps at the time, smirked but then looked crestfallen as Mr Ford's face came alive and he took me by the arm and guided me about the room telling me of the peculiarities of each clock and how he had acquired it. What a pleasure it was, he said, to meet a young man who takes an interest in these things. He asked my name and acknowledged me after that and when he had nothing to tell us at the end of the day his cheery, 'Nothing for you today, boys' always seemed more in my direction than towards the others.

'You snake,' Swinehart said to me later, 'You slimy snake, Delavigne.'

Through the summer and into the fall things got nowhere fast for me. The hopes for a big Ford story faded. It was agony for us – all the volatile elements were there, all that was needed was a little good luck or a touch of the newsman's art to bring them together. But 'the pack' were every bit as smart as we were, and smarter than all the peacettes in the whole damned country put together. For all the truck-loads of mail Mr Ford got every week, they made sure that nothing got through to him that might set off the explosion we were all hoping for. They were good at what they did, no doubt about that – they kept Mr Ford wrapped up like a baby. People started to give up. I was assigned to other stories and by the time the starting gun finally went off I wasn't even there to hear it.

From what I could work out there was nothing unusual that day and no warning of what was about to happen. We knew the front pages of all the big papers but they weren't a lot different from what they always were around that time. That's kind of what I like about the news – sometimes things just go off for no reason at all. For a newsman, there's always hope.

The first thing anyone noticed was this voice coming from Mr Ford's office, even though there was no one in there but Ford himself. It got louder and kept repeating the same thing and so everyone was looking at Liebold as he got up and went nervously to the doors only for them to burst open right in his face and Mr Ford to be there in his shirtsleeves with a copy of the *New York Times* in his hand.

Well, according to the version I got he just walked right out into the middle and shouted in front of all those people – 'Twenty thousand! Good God in heaven, twenty thousand in one day! I can't even make cars as fast as that!' and then went straight back in again without saying another word. Everyone just stared at everyone else, apart from the newspapermen – they were already running for the stairs. And that's how the gun went off – that's how all the fun started.

Soon every paper in the area was calling in and next day those from out east as well. It was all Liebold could do to keep them off. Mr Ford was determined to have his say and my guess is – don't ask me to prove it – that Liebold hoped he could satisfy him with a piece in a local paper and would then just pray the story wouldn't go much further. Well that was one thing and the other was that my boss, Mr Pipp, and Ford had some history. I never got to the bottom of it, but they went back quite a way, to before Mr Ford got to what he is now. Anyway, it was enough to put the *Detroit Free Press* at the head of the queue.

I was in the office finishing off something I don't remember now when Mr Pipp came out, swinging his spectacles around his fingers like he does. He had that sort of sly, fat look and a good lunch inside him.

'You're thick with Ford, aren't you Teddy?'

'I wouldn't say that.'

Two desks away Sicherman brutalised his typewriter, but refused to look up.

'Sure you are. He likes you. You can talk clocks with each other or whatever it is he likes to go on about these days. Anyway, you'll get more out of him than most so why don't you do it? It's fixed – tomorrow at eleven. A man from the works will pick you up here. You know the sort of thing we're looking for.'

So I was collected the next morning from our city offices and chauffeured through the streets of Detroit in a bright Pierce-Arrows like an important man. It was big Ray himself at the wheel. He said I would have half an hour for the interview and that he was sorry the car was not a Ford. He told me how competitors' products were bought for assessment and at busy times you had to take what you could get if you needed a vehicle in a hurry. I was excited and enjoyed being looked at by all the people on the sidewalks.

'No need to apologise.'

We got into the country in no time and then swung onto a rough road that took us into the Fords' Dearborn estate. It seemed an odd, semi-wild place for a mechanic to want to live in. We passed a new building on a river that would be the powerhouse, and then the great Fair Lane mansion itself. It was half built then, covered in scaffolding and with piles of uncut timber still lying about. Beyond it was Ten Eyck Farm where the Fords were living until Fair Lane was ready. The Pierce-Arrows scudded to a stop in the dust. I was reaching for the handle when Ray opened the door for me and I got out and stood before a large, old-style farmhouse.

I tugged the bell-pull and was ushered in by the Fords' Japanese butler. Hat in hand, I waited in the hallway as instructed. Two or three minutes passed and in the end I was caught out examining myself in the hat-rack mirror.

'How're you looking today, Mr Delavigne?'

I can't say why, but it still seems extraordinary to me – there he was in the hallway, coming towards me with his hand out, just like anybody in his $20 suit and his silver watch-chain and so skinny it was like there was nothing inside but a few canes holding his pants and jacket up in a shop window somewhere. Mr Ford has an easy manner even in his office, but there in his home he made me feel like I'd known him for years. He even asked about my mother's health. I said, 'Fine, thank you sir' and then right away wondered how he knew to ask. He reached for his own hat.

'Walk with me, young man. I think better on the move. How did you take to the Pierce?'

I hesitated and Mr Ford smiled.

'Isn't she smart? – A dandy little car for a young man like you.'

We enthused together over this luxurious and powerful automobile.

'Did you see what was wrong with her?' he asked me.

'Well I'm no engineer, sir.'

'The price, Mr Delavigne, that's what's wrong with her. Not one American in ten thousand will ever own a car like that.

The men who make that car have no ambition. That car will not change the world, mine will. Let's go this way.'

We turned to the left and started to walk up through the woods. I listened to him talk about how much his father had wanted to keep him on the land and had brought his son back from Detroit for a while with some new acreage to look after.

'But all I did was cut down all the lumber and when that was gone I went back to the machine shops where I'd been happy before. That was home for me. I didn't think I'd ever need this again.'

We walked on, deeper into the woods. He was pleased to tell me the names of the plants and of some of the birds we saw. He talked about his good friend John Burroughs the naturalist and the pleasure he had gained from giving the old man a car so he could more easily get out to wild places. All the time I thought of the questions I had prepared, about the war and pacifism, the rumours of his political ambitions, but there never seemed to be a right moment to speak up. Mr Ford stopped all of a sudden, filled his lungs and looked up at the trees.

'You know I fought in the civil war?'

I wasn't sure I'd heard him correctly.

'Sir?'

'That's right. I mean, of course, in an earlier life – the one immediately before this one. I was born, as you may know, in 1863. A bullet hit a Union soldier fighting Freedom's fight, and I was born. That's the way it happened. Sometimes I see it like I was there myself.'

'And you were,' I coaxed, excited by the scent of a scoop yet anxious not to scare it away.

'I was indeed. I dream of it sometimes, you know? There are details I never read in any book – how else could you explain it?'

'Makes sense to me.'

He started off again, and though he must be more than twenty years my senior I struggled to keep up with his long stride.

'I worked very hard as a young man, Mr Delavigne.'

'Yes, sir.'

'Then I got what I deserved, then I got so much I thought I must be lucky. But now I wonder if it wasn't all meant to be.'

'May I quote you on that, Mr Ford?'

'Of course. I'm not a politician, Mr Delavigne. I'm not ashamed of my private opinions. You put it all in the way you think best. You'll have heard for yourself I'm not a words man.'

I reassured him on this point, but was interrupted.

'Goldfinch! There – you see it?'

'Eh, I think . . .'

'Now, isn't that beautiful? I always want to write a poem when I see a goldfinch.'

'Have you written a poem, Mr Ford?'

'Not yet. I do keep a notebook with me now, just to be ready for when there's something worth preserving. I have a dozen or so at home all full up. It happens more and more these days, something worth preserving I mean. Time of life, I suppose.'

I trotted along by his side as he wandered randomly through his enthusiasms – how he had bought an old farm and would preserve it just as it had been, his passion for old carts and carriages and pieces of horse harness which were already becoming hard to find, the old-time music and the dances folks were already forgetting, the school readers he had learned from and still enjoyed today and even the hard bench seats of the country schoolroom which he had rescued from the bankrupt stock sale of the company that made them. Bone by bone he exhumed that whole life of forty years ago and talked of how he was storing the pieces and would one day assemble them and bring back to life everything that had been lost. Then he stopped and leaned a hand on one of the trees and put his head down as if feeling faint.

'Mr Ford?'

He looked at me blankly until I thought he was about to ask who I was and what my business might be walking through his woods. I laughed nervously and reached for the first thing I could think of to say.

'So you're ready for that poem, sir?'

'Mm?'

'In your notebook, sir. You'll be ready for that poem when it comes to you?'

To my relief he seemed to understand again, as if something loose had suddenly been re-engaged.

'I am, Mr Delavigne, you're absolutely right. I'm ready for it whenever it comes. Dammit, there was something else. The thing I really wanted to tell you.'

He pinched the bridge of his nose and assumed an expression of great effort. I got my pencil ready and sent up a newsman's prayer. A shudder shook his bony shoulders and he started off again, striding quickly through the woods. He began to speak and I stayed with him, scribbling page after page of jolted, broken script.

'What you've got to understand, Mr Delavigne, what you've got to make our people see, is that New York wants war, the moneylenders, the arms makers, all those fancy folks in the east, they want war. They know there's money in it for them. Fighting over there is none of America's business, but there are people, elements, interests, powers we can't see clearly who want to make it America's business just because of what's in it for them.

'I don't want to make guns, Mr Delavigne, I want to make cars and tractors – ploughshares and pruning hooks – and I'm going to and you can't have the gasoline tractor and war in the same world at the same time. You see, if you let people stay home and make a good living then that's what they'll do. It won't matter any more who comes round banging a drum and telling them they got to stick their noses into someone else's affairs the other side of the world. Do you know why we call the Ford the Universal Car, Mr Delavigne? Because it shows people they're all the same. The affordable car and warfare just won't go together. Try starting a war when the common man can drive into his neighbour's country any time he feels like it and take a look for himself – I tell you, the days when men only travel in an army are gone. And that's what I want you to tell your readers, Mr Delavigne. I say I would rather burn a factory down than let it be used for arms. You are the first to know that I'm going to give a million dollars for a worldwide campaign for universal peace. I'll do more – I'll give everything I possess to stop the war and the stockpiling of weapons in this country. Every last cent I've got! This is the new work of my life – Universal Car, Universal Peace.'

My prayers had been answered – more than that, I had had such a cornucopia of front-page copy emptied over my head in the space of two minutes I was momentarily speechless.

'Mr Ford, sir, do you really mean that?'

He didn't hesitate.

'Yes sir, in heaven's name, I do.'

He put his long hand on my shoulder and pinned me eye to eye.

'This is what I want you to tell the people, Mr Delavigne – there may be money in war, but there's money in peace too and it's a hundred times more. And this is just for you, son – for now, I'd bet I'm the only man in the world who has any idea how big it's really going to be. This isn't just a new century, it's a new age and it doesn't have time for wars. Who can tell me what's new about war? Come on, young man – this way.'

By the time I could start after him he was almost out of

sight. I felt light, unsteady even, as I sensed a lifetime of scepticism being pulled from under my feet. Could all this talk mean anything – universal man, permanent peace somehow worked by the strange magic of the affordable automobile? Nonsense, surely – mere childishness. But I couldn't entirely shake it off.

I was still a little dazed when we came out of the woods and I saw that he had guided us in a loop so that we returned precisely to our starting point. The Pierce-Arrows was rolling majestically up the driveway and I understood that my interview was coming to an end.

When I took my leave Mr Ford held me by the arm and I could hardly believe it when I heard:

'Say, Mr Delavigne, you know I've been thinking lately how important it is for the modern company to be clearly understood. You know how once a man gets a wrong idea in his head it's a tough business to get it out. It's always cheaper to stop it getting in there in the first place. To my way of thinking a bad idea in a man's head is like sand in his gasoline – the cost is out of all proportion to the size. There's a good future for people who can stop wrong ideas getting around and you and I seem pretty much of one mind – why don't you work for me?'

Of one mind did he say? Whose? I was sure I hadn't said anything all day.

'Well, Mr Ford, that's a remarkable offer, it really is, but . . .'

'But . . . ?'

He was opening the door to the car and ushering me in. I was conscious of looking down on him for the first time. Ray had never left the driver's seat and his bulky head and shoulders seemed to hem me in.

'You see, Mr Ford sir, I'm rather fond of the *Free Press*.'

'And why not? It's a fine little paper, perhaps I'll buy it. Promise me you'll think about it, won't you?'

'Yes sir. I will.'

'I need a man like you and I pay a man his worth. You married?'

I said I wasn't married.

'Marry!' said Mr Ford. 'Marry, have children, work for me.'

Ray put the car in gear and as it moved off I looked back through the rear window at the shrinking image of the great industrialist. His peculiar parting words were all I could think of. They swirled round in my mind till I got scared I would forget everything else and have nothing to write when I got back to the office. I made notes as best I could in the car. Ray drove fast and violently, shaking me about. It seemed that every time I looked up all I saw were his eyes in the mirror. And then he asked me:

'So you're going to be one of us, huh?'

His tone was far from welcoming.

'Maybe.'

I said no more, but started to write my piece in my head. I knew it was the best I'd ever done and I couldn't wait to get back to the office. When the car finally stopped Ray jumped out, keeping to his chauffeur role, though opening the door this time with a rather heavy irony. I believe I caught the gleam of metal under his jacket. He saw me react, but only moved his lapel very slightly before stepping back.

I ran up the stairs and went straight to my desk. I grabbed a sheet of paper and set the keys flying. It was like I was standing up there and giving a speech to a great crowd and I wanted to write it just as fast as I was speaking it.

'Look at him go!' someone shouted.

They all laughed and when Mr Pipp read it he came out of his office right over to my desk with everyone watching on account of the smile on his face and he asked me:

'So Teddy, that old witch doctor has cast a spell on you too.'

I told him straight Mr Ford was a great man. Well, I don't

really know what that look on his face meant, but he printed it anyway just as I had written it, even the poem I did for Mr Ford about the goldfinch.

I went back to him three days later and said that piece on Ford was the last work I would do for the *Free Press*. I regretfully informed him of my new position and he told me with that queer smile of his that he was always happy to see a young man succeed. A handful of my colleagues came down to the street to see me off. They stood there on the steps, openmouthed as I walked towards the polished Pierce-Arrows, fired up its huge engine and took off in the direction of Highland Park.

Rosika

*T*ime was short, money shorter still. The tide flowed strongly against us. The voices of men grew louder while the frail female voice of sanity struggled to be heard at all. Zeppelins rained bombs on London while in New York J. P. Morgan & Co. loaned $500,000,000 to the British and French governments. Not a cent of it ever left America – it all went straight to the arms makers. Somehow humanity had to raise its voice against $500,000,000. Seeing the weakness of all others, I came progressively to understand that I alone, the mother and conscience of a bleeding continent, was fit for such a task.

'Preparedness' was the weasel word of the day. It was debated in cafés, saloons and railway carriages. It filled the newspapers. In the mouths of hypocrites and ranting demagogues it lent decency to every evil. Prepare for security, prepare for safety, prepare for slaughter, prepare to get rich. Preparedness meant dreadnoughts and submarines, it meant three-shift, seven-day working in the Bethlehem, du Pont, Remington and Winchester factories. On Sundays America went to church and got down on its knees to give thanks for the work it had just done – O, Lord, give us this day our daily munitions orders from friend and foe alike. And so what did peace come to mean? It meant an end to this plenty, it meant dashing the bottle from the drunkard's lips. Good men who loved money saw it all too clearly – 'Yes', they said, 'let me be peaceable, let me be sober, but not yet'. President Wilson heard and spoke no more of being too proud to fight. Even our own maternal sex had its traitors. Women's Navy Leagues sprang up, Security Sororities with badges of crossed cannons pinned to their clothes. Their campaigns reached the summit of madness with a sinister pledge to be imposed on every child at the start of the school day. They would chant that they were the slaves of the state, heart, mind and body, that they stood ready to be spent in the fires of war whenever their superiors thought fit. Military parades increased. Women lined the streets, urging their sons on to death. Any lesser soul would have despaired. Happily, I do not permit myself despair.

My anxieties were practical too – I had once, briefly, the uncomfortable experience of being an enemy alien in England. A declaration of war by the United States would return me to such a condition, a wanderer perforce, the natural state, as some say, of my people.

I had two dates in Detroit. Little was expected of them and I knew they might well be my last in America. My friends in Hungary wanted me back. They told me of the work to do there, how they thought they were close to winning the vote for women. They asked me if that was not the best way to peace, what government elected by women would ever give itself over to such cruelty again? I told them that if we could not stop the present war there would be no one left to vote but women.

From the slowing train I looked down on acre after acre of small factories and workshops. There was metal in the air and the occasional flash of fire as unionless labourers sweated for their bread and beer. Miss Rebecca Shelly, sitting opposite, gave me a smile of vacant cheerfulness – she had already told me that Detroit was her home town.

125

'Do you remember it?' I asked her.

'Oh, no – not this bit.'

The train slowed more sharply, a platform appeared, then a Negro porter running – backwards it seemed at first, then level with our window and finally moving ahead as we came to a halt. I held tightly to my bag, heavy with the confidences of statesmen, treasures greater than any bank bill, promises on which the fate of millions hung. In the midst of the rushing, crowded concourse I stopped. From some hidden source a new strength suffused me. I felt refreshed, as if taking up the cause for the first time. An unreasoning hope, one might almost say a new faith, re-entered my heart. I stood still and straight. I held my arms out wide.

'Detroit!' I declared, causing no little astonishment in those around me. 'Detroit, graveyard of organisers. Detroit, my Calvary!'

Rebecca caught up. Having failed to attract the attention of a porter, she laboured, red-faced and breathless, under the weight of our baggage.

'Are you all right?' she asked.

Can you believe it? I, who feel the pierce of every bullet and bayonet with my own skin, who feels as keenly as if my own life were being taken ten thousand times a day, was asked if I was all right.

'Where can we find a taxi?'

Rebecca pointed to the main exit of the station and I set off smartly. My sweet simple companion bounded after as best she could.

'Oh well,' I could just hear her say. 'Home sweet home.'

Economy compelled us to occupy a single apartment in the Pontchartrain Rooming House. It was to this cheerless shelter that we returned after our first and particularly unrewarding meeting. Even the journalists I had contacted could no longer be bothered to come and sneer. Reviewing my scanty audience, I was forced to wonder at one point whether I was the only *compos mentis* person in the room. There were no questions at the end, only the canvassing of a number of supposed solutions to the world's moral crisis to which my own ideas were, by implication, irrelevant. These included, from what I can recall, pelmanism for all, theosophy, Christian Science, the abolition of the slavery of marriage in favour of free love, anarchism, matriarchy, the expropriation of the Jews and the annexation of Mexico. What strength had been given to me in the station seemed just as quickly to leak away, to exhaust me as violently as if I were losing my own literal lifeblood. I was quiet during our return. I considered gloomily that everyone who had attended our meeting did so merely as a preamble before moving on to other, and perhaps even more absurd, gatherings. Were these people my true fellows? When I looked down on them with – and I shan't deny it – contempt, was I looking in a mirror without realising it? I knew in my heart that the world would go mad before I did, but to carry the burden of one's certain truth is so much harder at some times than at others. I looked through a rainy window at a dark, strange city.

'Courage, my friend,' said Rebecca. 'Courage.'

The taxi drew up at the rooming house. It was a dispiriting place indeed. Two narrow beds stood on bare boards. A pair of rugs covered the floor in part, but a creeping mange had so eaten away at their pattern that one hesitated to put one's feet on them. A finger drawn across the window glass came away black and left a thin streak of clarity. No joint in any item of furniture was quite true or sound. Table, chair and bed would lean and creak agedly whenever put to use. On the mattress an ancient stain showed through the worn translucence of the sheet. Tobacco and sour whisky breathed from the curtains and the wallpaper so that I had the uneasy feeling that the previous tenant had not entirely left. The darkened cork tips of his cigarettes lay by the bed, in a saucer commemorating the 1904 World's Fair.

Rebecca let the cases fall noisily to the floor.

'Oh, well. It'll do.'

She seemed to rejoice in these circumstances, so much so that I wondered if she had chosen them deliberately. She started on a series of witless anecdotes about her life as a pupil in a boarding school where the dormitories had closely resembled the Pontchartrain Rooming House. Unpacking a case, she showed that she was indeed better adapted than I by producing a sturdy flannel dressing gown and a pair of slippers to protect her feet from the rough wood of the floor. Thus attired like a character from her own comfortable past, she padded happily down the corridor to the communal washroom. I lay back on my bed and looked up at the ceiling from which old cobwebs hung, grey with dust and hardly moving in the stagnant air. The plumbing vibrated as Rebecca made use of the facilities. I thought of home, of a ship crossing the ocean back to everything I knew. I would be returning in failure. Everyone would deny it for my sake, but it wouldn't make any difference. The old demons started to debate with me, to lay out alluringly the compensations for accepting failure, to whisper lovingly that it couldn't be half so bad as I imagined. Budapest became clear in my mind. I could smell its cafés and almost spoke aloud as I joined in the talk of good friends.

'Water's hot. Get it while you can.'

Rebecca burst back into the room. She unwrapped her bathrobe and let it hang over the back of a chair then jumped into her bed with girlish athleticism and pulled the covers up to her chin. For half a minute she held her eyes tight shut like a child at prayer. When she was finished she turned to look at me and found, for a brief moment, some solemnity.

'We're right. You're right, Rosika, and they have to see it. They will see it, if only we can keep going long enough.'

'Thank you, Rebecca.'

She was asleep when I returned to the room. She lay on her back, her thumbs tucked under the sheet, her fingers straight and flat against the white surface, as neat as two paper clips. Her mouth was slightly open and her large front teeth just visible in a manner that suggested sharing the room with an enormous rodent. She snored very slightly. The sound would not disturb me and might, one day, be essential to the rest of a child or a husband. She had not been able to turn off her bedside lamp before falling asleep. I did it for her, hesitating with my finger on the switch, sharply caught off guard as I saw the daughter I had decided never to have. I brushed the hair from her forehead, very lightly and with fear, as if testing the delicate mechanism of a trap. I might have kissed her had I not been held back by a vision of how absurd it would be if she were to wake and question me. I climbed into my own bed and settled to read Emma Goldman's article in the latest *Mother Earth* with my spectacles on and the magazine held close in the dingy light. The scene shifted to a sad parody of marriage, and a confirmation too that my course was the right one. I concentrated on the article, marking a few phrases fit for plunder, turning over in my mind how I might arrange for myself a short and useful spell of imprisonment. At ten o'clock a noise I had not previously noticed fell silent. The room became cold. After another half-hour, and without any intervention on my part, the lights went out. The cause wrapped its arms tight around me.

In the morning we breakfasted with the single other guest – a commercial traveller in novelty cutlery who made his way noisily through a bowl of Dr Kellogg's cereal with a banana-handled spoon.

'People need a boost in the morning, a little sunshine to send them on their way. Business is good. Gotta go, ladies.'

Rebecca had been out early and had returned with half a

dozen newspapers. I drifted through the war news and searched automatically for any hopeful sign of change in Washington. Silently, I rehearsed passages of rhetoric for our meeting at seven o'clock that evening. Even at such a low ebb the words stirred me. Their power and humanity had always seemed to me irresistible – if only they could be properly heard. I was in search of the heart – the heart of the great neutral republic. I thought of it as a pearl locked in a safe, as a princess charmed into an age-long sleep, as a fabled city hidden behind high walls. On that particular morning I don't think I could have offered any evidence for the existence of this treasure, but I still believed in it with a perfect certainty. I was sure there was some way of opening that safe or of waking that princess. If only I could find the right way, the right words, those walls would come down quicker than anyone might think. I saw myself being received by President Wilson. 'No, no!' I have to say to him, 'Please, Mr President, do not apologise – only now promise that you will do the right thing.' Once again, he regrets that he had not listened to me sooner. The reverie fades. I fold the paper and place it on the table. I wipe the ink from my fingers on the edge of the cloth.

For the next two minutes there was a silence of mounting awkwardness as I looked at the crown of Rebecca's head. She seemed even to have stopped reading, to have become completely frozen. I wondered what could have so wholly absorbed her and was close to making some disobliging remark about the latest celebrity murder or the new winter fashions when she looked up and stopped me. Had she read of the death of some acquaintance or perhaps, as she looked too astonished even for that, of some miraculous recovery? She folded the *Detroit Free Press* and passed it to me across the table. There, at the top of the page in two-inch type I read the words **Ford Repeats Pledge – *All I Have For Peace***. Below, set out by Our Staff Reporter, were the words I had never dared to hope for.

His opinions seemed to be my own – there was little to choose between the soldier and the murderer, war was a folly that left nothing but high taxes and crêpe at the door, take away the capitalists and you will sweep war from the world, only through misapprehension do men fight each other, it's the men sitting around the table not the men dying in the trenches who finally settle the differences. And then towards the end and perhaps most hopefully of all – 'I don't read history. That's all in the past.'

Here was a human decency and a courage to speak out that reminded me of nothing so much as myself – a true fellow spirit, only in this case a fellow spirit attached to a practical infinity of money. At that stage I knew little about Henry Ford but had heard it said more than once that he was no ordinary manufacturer. On that morning, over the breakfast table, I was ready to believe it when I came to the end of the article and found there a most affecting expression of compassion for all living things in the form of a beautiful poem by the great man himself. Here, I felt sure, was a man I could do business with.

Rebecca leaned across the table and tapped her finger on the newsprint.

'I know this man. I used to go to his church.'

Everything seemed possible at such a moment – 'Henry Ford has his own church?'

'No, no. Look – there.'

I looked more precisely. There was a passing mention of Ford's wife and a dubious character described as her 'spiritual adviser'.

'I was in his congregation for ten years. I think he'll remember me. He'll certainly remember my parents.'

As one we were struck by the same alarming thought – how many people were reading that newspaper, how many were already ahead of us in the race? We jumped from our seats and ran down the corridor to the outside door. Fortune smiled on us in the form of two taxis which immediately answered our call. We went down the steps with a grimy hall porter following and threatening to sell our baggage if we didn't come back. I was obliged to inform him that as the fate of countless millions was in our hands at that very moment we could hardly be expected to care about our baggage. I shouted to Rebecca.

'You take Svengali, I'll take Ford.'

Doors slammed. I ordered my driver to take his vehicle back to its maker with all possible speed.

Louis

I never quite worked out how she did it. I asked, of course,
but Madame Schwimmer was not the sort of woman
who felt much obliged always to give the same answer to the
same question. Her explanations varied with her mood.
Occasionally she admitted to luck but would then, in more
confident passages, revert to hints involving the mastery of dark
arts and deeper matters still, matters that honour would never
allow her to disclose. Others had their own versions. Many just
shrugged their shoulders. A muckraker by the name of Swinehart
told me the credit was all his. Madame Schwimmer had gone
to the offices of the *Detroit Free Press* in the hope of finding
the author of the article that had set things off. It turned out
the young man had resigned only a few days previously to take
Henry Ford's dollar and had become as hard to find as his
employer. Swinehart was on the same trail and there was an
encounter on the sidewalk – a literal collision, as he has it, a
contest for a cab.

'A strange old maid, kind of sad. Anyway, I'd been to one
of her meetings a while back and she recognised me – we
hadn't exactly been friendly. I guessed what she was there for
– there was quite a pack about town that day, I kept running

into them everywhere. I was looking for someone to put my money on. It had to be someone just right – not too loopy and none too sober either. Someone who would get through, but who would set the fireworks off when he got there – you know what Ford is like. Well, I picked her. And boy, did she come home!'

Swinehart knew one thing the others didn't. He had a telephone number and he knew that at the end of that line was Mr Anderson, and that Mr Anderson hated Mr Liebold. He made the call, came back with a time and a place and handed them on a card to Rosika Schwimmer.

'Thlouis –' It was years later and he was slopping his tenth whisky on the floor of some basement bar. 'I tell you I was the one that got her through. That whole damned party would never have started without me. I got her through – I damned near got her a red carpet right up to his door. People forget that.'

Things hadn't gone well for Swinehart after the war, but he still told a good story.

When all this was happening I was in Chicago and knew nothing about it. That changed with Rosika's mystifying telegram – 'Why are you not coming to keep your appointment with Mr Ford?' At that time I was not a great believer in tycoons. Carnegie had talked peace, but had done nothing to make it real. I had been to see John Wanamaker, the department store king, but received nothing from him but platitudes and a copy of *Pollyanna*. My work with the Chicago Peace Society had taught me to recognise a false dawn when I saw one and I knew also that Ford had a liking for making headlines and had good men around him to protect him from the consequences of his enthusiasms. This was not the first time he had shown a rhetorical hatred of war, and it had never come to anything in the past. Added to all that was the fact that the telegram came from Schwimmer – I admired her energy but

134

not her judgement, and her name at the bottom of that strange message did nothing to allay my doubts. What appointment, who had made it, did it exist at all?

In the peace business it was normal to receive a good deal of unreliable correspondence. In our case this included a sheaf of letters from a crank in New York who discerned meanings in the rattling of auto engines and offered to arrange a rendezvous with the notoriously inaccessible Ford. We had recently tried to put him off by wiring that such a meeting had already been arranged through other channels – thank you and don't write, telephone, cable or call in person ever again. Had it not been for Schwimmer's signature I would have added this new telegram to the pile and thought no more of it. Instead, I read it a dozen times and wondered. Had she really done it, had she somehow got through? I looked at my desk diary – the afternoon appointments did not excite. Outside was a dusky November morning with rain starting to streak windows the Society could not afford to have cleaned. On top of that, the arrival of the telegram fell on one of our monthly Sacrifice Days – an initiative of our treasurer which meant there would be no heating. The story began to seem more plausible. A feather of self-indulgence settled on the scales and tipped them. I declared a possible breakthrough to the secretaries in the outer office, consulted a railway timetable, drew thirty dollars from petty cash and left in a guilty rush.

The train was a welcome asylum. I kept my coat on and enjoyed the warmth as the chilly scenes passed outside. I dozed for much of the first long stretch, going back over the hopeful but unproductive days of the year and a half since Emmy and I had been stopped on a Paris station platform and told it was too late to go to a peace conference. I recalled the English soldiers near the coast – as I did every time I read a newspaper – and knew they could not all still be alive. When wakeful I had the company of my book, *The Great Illusion*, which I had snatched from the shelf at home and thrown in my bag as I gave a breathless half-explanation to Emmy before running back to the cab waiting for me in the street. Angell's phrases lifted me as they always did – obedience to primitive instincts, enslavement by catchwords, indolence before the necessary revision of old ideas. The robust, invincible logic momentarily refreshed my hopes before I turned back to the title page and the miserable date I knew I would find there – 1913. The old, needle-sharp argument followed – if they had not listened to him, what chance did I have? I returned to my obsession – power and its cryptic sources, more practically the question of where it was to be found, by what force, exactly, might our horseless carriage be coaxed into motion? The features of someone rather like Henry Ford coalesced in my mind, borrowed uncertainly from an advertisement photograph. I struggled to make the picture clearer, worrying foolishly that I might suffer the embarrassment of failing to recognise him. The face remained general – human, certainly, but too remote to name. A fellow passenger noticed the title of my book. He guessed wrongly and bored me with an anecdote about Harry Houdini. I feigned sleep.

After the change at Toledo I had about an hour more of travelling. The approach of Detroit disturbed my concentration and I frittered away the time looking out the window or with my eyes closed, enacting a variety of scenarios, some hopeful, others more useful as preparations for disappointment, or excuses for the waste of money when I got back to the office in Chicago. As we hit the suburbs I reached out for an old magazine someone had left behind. There was the usual young woman on the coloured cover – implausible perfection, indiscriminate smile. I spent a few seconds betraying my wife in her imaginary company before moving on to the inside pages. Their cheerful trivia depressed me. Here was that stubborn, leaden resistance to anxiety that I and all my colleagues were struggling against. As a record of the world the magazine had swept reality from its bright halls with an almost perfect cleanness. If it alone survives the fire, historians will have no choice but to conclude there was no war. It strengthened my suspicion that existence consists of only two types. One, and by far the largest, is wholly absorbed in the prosecution of a loud and hilarious party. The other, a rarer and less happy breed, includes myelf – and there I am, standing on the steps of this house of fun as the music beats out through the open windows and the warm night air is barley-rich with beer and whisky. I knock on the door, not to gain entrance, but only to ask, very politely, that the merrymakers look at the horror I hold in my hands and perhaps hold down the noise a little. It is no surprise that I and my kind are never welcome guests.

Beside the cover girl, I recall only a single detail from that abandoned *McClure's* – an advertisement containing one of those lines that pull you up as sharply as a fish-hook in the mouth.

Is Your Will Dormant?

Look back upon your life. Once upon a time no doubt, you weaved great dreams of what you were going to make of yourself. Are they accomplished now? Is it not because you lacked a strong, powerful, inflexible, dominating **WILL**?

You too can be Indomitable

Send no money now

It was Frank Channing Haddock, PhD, MS, who offered these services and whose masterful features scowled from a small oval portrait beside the text. Dr Haddock could show a man, through simple exercises anyone could do, how to seize control of his own life, how to trample on the caprices of Fortune and relentlessly bend the world to his own purposes. I wondered how many could be entirely deaf to such a call – it seemed certain that Dr Haddock enjoyed a steady business.

I might have thought no more about this fraud were it not for the eerie experience of seeing the same features staring back at me through the window enlarged a hundred times. The Haddock enterprise clearly had enough turnover to engage in billboard advertising as well and there he was, repeatedly through the last mile before the station, looking down on me with a calculated blend of contempt and blandishment. Through the flickering darkness of steel girders and in the gaps between tightly packed warehouses and the newer office buildings the question repeated itself with a mesmerising rhythm – *Is Your Will Dormant?* I thought of dreams and the discouraging question of their accomplishment. I thought of my wife and daughter. I thought too of Henry Ford and the matter, unexpectedly, became hilarious. Walls veered closer, this time bearing a vast image of an automobile that seemed about to collide with our train. Beneath it I recognised, without reading, the flowing lines of the Ford Motor Company's trademark. There were four words – Ford, the Universal Car. We rumbled over an elevated section and I found myself looking down on a congested street, jam-packed with Ford cars, vans and light trucks. Fresher posters appeared, in brighter colours and with enticing pictures of the newest model. Without a break they lined the wall all the way into the station so that it was impossible not to see them. Watch the Fords Go By; Watch the Fords Go By; Watch the Fords, Go Buy. The refrain worked simply on my appetites so that I almost felt hungry looking at them. The instruction was impossible to resist. When the train finally came to a halt I had become convinced that Detroit was his city, personally. I felt that I was arriving as the ambassador from a remote and impoverished province, an unknown and unregarded man who would have to jostle to present his credentials at the court of the most stupendous power. I put on my hat and took my case down from the rack. I realised I had made a decision. I would give it all up and join the party. This would be my last effort – it would be Mr Ford, or Dr Haddock.

That evening I felt it was too late to have any useful conversation with the Ford works. I checked into a better hotel than I had any right to and dined in genial commercial company. The next morning, in one of the telephone cabins in the lobby, I got through easily to a young woman at the Highland Park factory but had barely started on my explanation before instinct told me to hang up. I still had no confidence in the reality of this appointment and calculated, though without any great delusion about the physical presence of Louis Lochner, that I might be a little harder to reject in the flesh than as a voice over the telephone. So it was that, after a short taxi ride, I found myself in the crowded anteroom with its clocks and its pictures of birds, its huddles of press men and campaigners and a handful of bewildered salesmen who had come to talk car parts but found themselves instead at something very like the temporary centre of the world. I strained to get a glimpse over all these heads of my first goal, the private secretary, just as he was turning a dishevelled character by the shoulders and pointing him in the direction of the exit with the words 'You again!' I reached the worn carpet in front of his desk.

'Louis Lochner to see Mr Ford.'

The man looked up with an unexpectedly amiable expression.

'Do you have your letter with you, Mr Lochner?'

A rapt silence settled behind me. There was a sense of movement as twenty faces turned in my direction.

'Letter?'

'Mr Ford's appointments are always confirmed by letter.'

I confessed I had no letter. The secretary gave a world-weary and rather disappointed sigh as if, by this late stage in the game, the very least a charlatan could do was entertain him with a more painstaking deception than this.

'Well, I'm afraid . . .'

'I'm the secretary of the Chicago Peace Society.'

There was laughter at my back. No doubt an indomitable alumnus of Haddock would have found a way through, but I was already turning to leave.

'Ah,' said the secretary. 'A Peace Society?'

Voices could be heard through stout double doors. Mr Anderson cocked an ear in their direction, the press men leaned closer, like a row of pins pulled about by a magnet.

'I would be sorry to have to turn you away. Let me make quite sure.'

We entered a small side office and I watched as Mr Anderson made a sympathetic show of consulting a diary the size of a ledger.

'My senior colleague is away, you see. I should know, really, but perhaps you made an arrangement with him? He might have failed to pass the information on? Not everyone is always perfect.'

Mr Anderson paused for a moment to enjoy some private joke, then raised his eyebrow at me to repeat the question.

'I have a telegram.'

'A telegram, Mr Lochner?'

I unfolded it and handed it over.

'I see,' said the second secretary. 'From Madame Schwimmer. Well, then – perhaps that dispels a little of the mystery. You were meant to come together. We have nothing more here than a misunderstanding as to times.'

I watched his finger come to a halt in the middle of the huge page and could just make out, upside-down, a capital S followed by some less distinct letters.

'But I'm sorry,' he was forced to admit. 'I can't find you. You're just not here at all.'

The book took on a fateful significance and I was embarrassed by my own plaintive tone as I insisted – 'But I've come all the way from Chicago.'

'That really is too bad. It is a shame that you seem to have made such a long journey for nothing.'

A disturbance in the anteroom attracted our attention. Voices from within were suddenly louder. They had the rhythm and tone of leavetaking. Sure enough one of the doors opened abruptly – the left-hand one, blocking completely my view of who was coming out. The press went into noisy action and I thought I must be mistaken as I heard the flat, emphatic vowels of middle Europe cut through the chorus of questions. Mr Anderson took me by the arm and moved me forward. There indeed, at the centre of chaos, was the sturdy, bespectacled form of Rosika Schwimmer. Over her head I got a glimpse of the interior of Mr Ford's private office. Three men remained seated at a table strewn with papers. One of them rose from his seat and approached me only to close the door in my face and restore the privacy of these grim advisers.

'Louis!' Rosika exclaimed disapprovingly. 'So you decided to come?'

The lean, angular man in his early fifties by her side could only be Ford. For the moment he ignored Mrs Schwimmer and his secretary and enjoyed a teasing exchange with the newspapermen. It was only when I got to know Swinehart later that I realised his features had been in the midst of the crush. He was smiling hopefully in the direction of his Hungarian secret weapon. He was the one who called out in his strong New York accent:

'Are you going to stop the war, Mr Ford?'

The auto king seemed not to hear. He turned to speak to Mr Anderson who, in a gap between one word and another from his employer, indicated my presence by his side and attempted an introduction. I was standing before Henry Ford, my case was being made to him, I appeared to be the sole object of his attention and felt as if I was about to faint.

'This man is a victim of circumstances,' explained Mr Anderson. 'He . . .'

'A victim, are you?'

I stumbled over a few meaningless syllables and appeared, indeed, to have been thoroughly victimised. Mr Ford turned to the journalists.

'What do you say to that, boys? We have a victim in our midst. Well, we can't have that.'

He indicated Rosika Schwimmer whose anxious features signalled to me that now was not the time to speak. Ford must have missed Rosika's earlier remark and presented her to me as a fresh acquaintance.

'This is Madame Schwimmer. I have asked her to come out to our home tomorrow. I want her to meet Mrs Ford. Won't you come out with her? I'll arrange to have you both taken out there. Mr Anderson . . .'

Mr Anderson stepped forward.

'Arrange to have these good people taken out to Fair Lane tomorrow morning. And tell these other gentlemen they can go home. I'll have nothing for them today.'

Mr Ford turned his eyes toward the exit. A path cleared before him and he took it.

I did not see Rosika again until the next morning when I found her already installed in the car sent to collect me from my hotel.

'You're Mr Ford's chauffeur?'

The large, slightly swaggering man holding open the door had not introduced himself but seemed to know who I was.

'You can just call me Ray.'

Inside, Rosika was tightly wrapped in a heavy coat and flicking energetically through the pages of a small notebook.

'Good morning,' I said, only to be told there was no time for pleasantries when the lives and happiness of millions weighed on our shoulders. She spoke with terse command, her heavy Central European accent making unfortunate connections in my mind with the broad comedy of the vaudeville houses.

'We have an even chance,' she declared. 'No better than that. If we get him, we get everything. If we don't, I go back to Hungary.'

The stakes could not be higher. She closed her notebook for a moment and scowled out at the November dullness of Detroit as at the features of a personal enemy. I received a report of the meeting with Ford the day before.

'I had hoped to speak to him alone, but as you saw that was not to be. Instead I found myself in the lion's den. The lawyer was the worst. I have met that sort before – a man who would not save an infant from drowning without writing a ten-page brief on the implications of such a rash action, then charging the bereaved mother a hundred dollars for his wisdom. There was a retired banker, an old friend of Ford's I understand, and a most peculiar clergyman, a useless, mumbling old social gospeller who is said to have some sort of connection with Mrs Ford on the precise nature of which I couldn't possibly speculate. They are the "do nothing" party. They wish Mr Ford only to make cars and money. They want to keep him within their reach. He is in thrall to these wreckers, these dwarfs. They are the Lilliputians to his Gulliver, the Delilahs to his Samson!'

I watched as her knuckles tensed about the clasps of a large, black, leather bag. She clutched it more passionately to her bosom.

'They doubted me. They questioned my integrity, my documents! I wanted to show them to Mr Ford, but of course I couldn't – not with *them* there.'

'You all right, lady?'

Ray was turning slightly in his seat to get a sideways glance at his strange passenger.

'Entirely, thank you. Are we there yet?'

'Not nearly. Forty minutes without hold-ups.'

Rosika placed a kid-gloved and confidential hand on my arm.

'We have time to plan, Louis. If they are there, the jailers of his greatness, I fear there will be nothing we can do. But if we can talk to him on his own we may yet win through. There is greatness in Mr Ford – from what I saw yesterday I have no doubt of that. He is a man in chains, a Prometheus on his rock, a chosen people groaning under the yoke of modern tyranny. What he needs is . . . is . . .'

Ray shifted again in his seat, eager to hear more clearly as the concept of his employer as slave came to his ears.

'A Moses?' I suggested.

'Yes!' pounced Rosika. 'Or, in more modern terms, Louis – what Mr Ford needs is me.'

She told me more of her meeting with the gilded slave of industry. The enemies of peace were precisely characterised and complex stratagems laid while I gave an impression of attentiveness as downtown shrank to suburb and the suburbs gave way to the wintry countryside of Michigan. We moved out of rain and into a sunny, sharp morning.

I remembered the telegram and took it from my pocket.

'Why did you send me this?'

Rosika plucked it from my fingers and read the single line.

'Why did I have to? Why get an appointment with Ford and then not come to keep it? That's what I can't understand.'

'But what appointment? I hadn't made one. I assumed you had on my behalf, though when I got there no one had heard of me. Even now I don't think Mr Ford has much idea who I am.'

'Nonsense. You told me yourself you had been given an appointment.'

'Now, Mrs Schwimmer,' I said very calmly, 'you just know that isn't true.'

'Then what's this?'

She snapped open the clasps on her bag and opened it narrowly. Just visible in its capacious, shadowy depths was the folded whiteness of secrets. She leaned away from me, a child jealously shielding a schoolroom slate, before finding the letter she was searching for.

'But this isn't from me,' I protested.

'As good as.'

'It's no such thing.'

I recognised the name at the bottom of the ardent, but incoherent text. This was the very same character who sent to us in Chicago two or three times a week; the one we had recently tried to shake off with the innocent fiction of a real appointment.

'This man is a crank. He's not well.'

'Who you associate with, Louis, is your business. You told him you had made an appointment with Mr Ford.'

'Only to get rid of him.'

'Nevertheless. The Goddess of Peace moves in mysterious ways her wonders to perform, my dear Louis. That is what you told him, he told me and I told you. I really don't see how you can object. If you were misled it was only by your own words.'

Rosika was finished with the matter. When Madame Schwimmer is finished with a subject of conversation she is most emphatically finished with it. She does not end topics, she guillotines them with a stroke of the open hand and from this fate I have never known any to return.

'Mrs Ford,' she asserted.

Ray's ears and the back of his head, if such a thing is possible, seemed to become more alert. I held back from too much talk and tried to give a cautious expression as the driver was surely listening to every word.

'Do you know her?'

'No,' I said. 'Of course not.'

'That priest or whatever he is – Samuel Marquis – I have a young helper who knows him and takes to him but I most decidedly do not. If he represents her way of thinking then we have a problem. Yes, I fear Clara Ford.'

'Really?'

'I understand her. Of course I do. She married a man – I have been busy in the newsaper offices; I have found out a lot, you know. Yes indeed, she married a man but now finds herself the consort of a great power, one that may be on the brink of waking to its responsibilities, of espousing the great cause. She wishes to keep him close to her, small and comfortable like he was when they were young. Ah, Louis – so often it is those we love who most keep us back from fulfilment.'

A handkerchief was produced. Her glasses were slightly adjusted and there was a barely necessary dab at one eye.

'Love can be such a selfish thing, but the heart must give way to the greater good. I too have lived through these dilemmas. I must find some way of letting her know, I must commune with Clara. Leave that to me.'

I assured her I would not interfere. We passed more slowly over rougher roads. I felt my chest tighten as I realised we were only minutes from arriving.

'There are some things you must know about Mr Ford. He is a great genius, no doubt, but of a particular sort. He has no taste for abstractions. I spent some time explaining our continuous mediation plan. I thought I made allowances for the fact that he is largely of a mechanical nature, but I'm still not sure he followed me. No single concept can detain him for long and the connections he makes between one topic and another are not necessarily those that would occur to a more conventionally schooled intellect. You should show no surprise when he jumps tracks, just follow a little way then give him a nudge at the next set of points. He believes he has prospered solely as result of his personal qualities. His wealth is the proof of his wisdom and it is a long time since he was contradicted by anyone. Do not smoke in his presence – he considers it witty to refer to cigarettes as "white slavers" and believes that the products of paper combustion rust the nerves. He will explain at length how the petrol-engined tractor will end once and for all the griefs of rural humanity. You must pretend to be convinced of this. If necessary, point out that he could sell more tractors in Flanders if it was not currently a battlefield. He idolises women and is advanced on female suffrage. He will want to tell you how working in a Ford factory is all that is required to reform the character of countless inmates of Sing Sing. You will refrain from pointing out that such a life leaves a man too exhausted to commit a crime. He is a bookish man – two books from what I have been able to discover.'

Rosika handed me a sheet of paper and I looked down at half a dozen lines of poetry.

'For today at least, we will admire what he admires. I'll do Emerson, you do *Locksley Hall*. Reason, I suspect, has limited power over him, Louis, but sympathy may win the day. Some of his opinions are embarrassing – you will know what I mean if that particular topic comes up. Do not react. Do not feel any obligation to defend me or my people. In any case, I heard it all yesterday. His moral conception of America is essentially geographical – east is evil, west is virtuous. You will try to sound more Chicago than New York, won't you? You will discover that you have been under a complete delusion as to the causes of the European war. It is in fact a conspiracy of New York bankers who maintain the conflict for commercial reasons only – nothing swells one's loan book like a war. All bankers are Jews. Ah, I think we've arrived.'

We turned through gateposts. I learned my lines from Henry Ford's favourite poem as we bumped over a rough track through trees and then into a wide open space. The great mansion was to the right, nearly finished. Ahead of us was the building it would replace, a white timber farmhouse of pioneer simplicity, with a tall thin man already standing on the porch. Rosika leaned closer and for the first time lowered her voice.

'In short, Mr Ford is a well-intentioned simpleton. Remember, Louis, we have only one purpose here; to hitch his money to our minds – the perfect combination.'

It was Mr Ford himself who opened the door of the car. He smiled warmly, held out his hand and greeted me.

'My victim!'

We found our host dressed like a character from a Fenimore Cooper novel and I feared I would be expected to tramp the Michigan countryside with him and perhaps bring down our own lunch with a musket-shot. To my relief, Mr Ford explained that he had just finished his daily walk through the woods – a practice he enthusiastically recommended to me, along with the works of his good friend John Burroughs.

'I'll send you a set – profitable reading, wonderful man. I give him a car every year.'

'That's very generous of you, Mr Ford,' said Rosika.

The man of business sensed a premature start to the proceedings. Rosika's eyes connected meaningfully with mine. Ford shrugged bony shoulders.

'It's nothing to me. The old fellow says it scares the birds and the deer away, but if it wasn't for that vehicle he'd just have to remember the countryside.'

Clara Ford emerged and we were introduced. As we shook hands and exchanged a few words about our journey and the weather I couldn't help being reminded of my mother. Although for the rest of the day, and on a few later occasions, I was constantly expecting her ordinariness to slip, and for us both suddenly to laugh with each other and enjoy the quality of her disguise, it never happened.

'And this is Mr Delavigne, one of my latest acquisitions. He'll be helping me handle the press from now on.'

A young man in a new suit of clothes shook Rosika's hand and mine and treated us both to a penetrating, though not unfriendly, top-to-toe examination. Mr Ford's voice sounded confidentially in my ear – 'Let's leave the girls to gab on. I've got something more exciting to show you.'

While Rosika Schwimmer and Mrs Ford got acquainted I endured the tractor factory. With Delavigne at the wheel of some extraordinary vehicle of the sort I was sure Mr Ford would never manufacture, all three of us made the drive to the new plant nearby. I was constantly on the look-out for openings on the matter of the peace campaign but the subject never came up, nor anything remotely like it. I agreed with my host that a world without intoxicating liquors would be a much better place, that the spread of the cigarette habit threatened the moral health of young men and that the latest dance fashions were distasteful foreign imports, gravely inferior to the styles of Mr Ford's youth and, what is more, shot through with secret significances that could only end in the triumph of bolshevism. I enthused, as best I could, over countless engineers' drawings and admired the sample machines that had already been put together. Before one of these we stood in a line of three. For quite a time Mr Ford fell silent and it seemed our role was simply to revere this object as a new golden calf. I became convinced that a long line of petitioners had gone that way before me, been treated to the same solipsistic tour, and been sent on their way empty-handed. I began to think of train timetables and whether it was still possible for me to be back home with Emma and Elizabeth before the end of the day. Mr Ford turned abruptly to his new press secretary.

'When was the plough invented, do you think?'

'Long time ago, sir.'

'But when exactly?'

He turned to me and accused me of having an education.

'You must know – how long ago.'

'Five thousand,' I guessed. 'Maybe six thousand years. It's not my field.'

Delavigne reacted politely to the unintended pun.

'Six thousand years. Men pulled them first – brothers, or fathers and sons labouring like beasts just to survive. Thousands of years passed, then they harnessed bullocks, water buffalo, horses and thousands more passed. The steam engine raised hopes, but it was too heavy and costly. I ploughed behind horses when I was a boy, the same way others had for thousands of years. I was no good – furrows all squint as my mind wandered to other things.'

He planted his feet more widely and put his fists on his hips. We redoubled the intensity of our gaze at this strange and revolutionary device.

'Just think – six thousand years. Then I put my hand to the problem and in twenty more years it'll all be over. Gentlemen, the muscle-powered plough will be in its grave before I am. Six thousand years of nothing and then, Henry Ford.'

Delavigne fumbled in his pockets, then urgently made a note in a little book. Ford clapped him on the shoulder.

'Good man – there's a whole article in that. Write one up for me.'

We moved on through the vast factory and I began to despair of ever getting to my business when Mr Ford diverted Delavigne onto some other task and I found myself in a room with him alone. He sat on a drawing table, and commended me for my patience.

'So what do you think of this Schwimmer's ideas? Will they work?'

I went through it carefully – the stalemate in the war, the desire for peace and the paralysing fear of weakness that held men back from admitting it. I told him of all our contacts in the neutral countries, of their willingness to help, how I believed that men's minds were ready, that the sides could slowly be led towards more moderate positions, that there could be peace without victory and without defeat, a peace that no one need fear. Help had to come from outside, and from where else could it come other than the great, neutral, peace-loving republic herself, from America? All it needed was . . . was . . . My speech faltered. I went through the truth in my mind – money, a figurehead, a headline-grabber, a public face and name. My eye settled coyly on the drawings on the table.

'To be thrown into gear – that's what it needs. Yes, that's it. All the parts are there – it just needs to be assembled and turned over and thrown into gear.'

'Thrown into gear, eh?'

It seemed a masterstroke. I was sure the moment had come.

'That's right,' I rushed on, the goal in sight. 'Think of the plough, Mr Ford. For how many thousands of years has there been warfare? Put your hand to this problem and perhaps you can end war too – maybe for ever.'

I received a sharp look and an unnerving, worldly smile. Mr Ford stepped out of the room and I followed.

'I wouldn't put too much faith in what Mr Delavigne writes for the newspapers. Let me show you the transmission assembly line.'

That day, and through all my later dealings with Henry Ford, I found no trace of Rosika's well-intentioned simpleton.

When we returned to the house I discovered my colleague still hard at work on the business of communing with Mrs Ford.

'And you cook the cherries in a skillet with brown sugar and butter? And for the layers of bread in the casserole tin – any special type?'

'Well,' said Clara, hesitantly, 'just bread.'

Rosika looked round and frowned to find me within earshot.

'Louis,' she continued smoothly, 'Mrs Ford has agreed to fund our telegraphic peace message campaign. We can send thousands of peace messages to the White House. We think $10,000 should suffice.'

The figure seemed to land on Clara's consciousness like a bucket of ice water, but she had hardly begun her first word of protest when her husband waved the figure away and declared he was hungry.

At lunch we were joined by Edsel, a pale, dominated youth and the only child of the Ford union. We listened to Mr Ford's theories about the justice of poverty and wealth — how the first is an incentive to self-improvement and, failing that, a reasonable punishment for idleness and incompetence. The second is never more than fair reward for ingenuity and effort. Rosika glared at me fiercely when I debated with him on these issues. She should not have worried — Mr Ford was not at all perturbed by or even interested in any of my criticisms.

The lunch ended bizarrely when an Edison Phonograph was started and a reluctant Edsel chivvied into accompanying the music on a set of drums. We applauded his modest talent as Rosika kicked me beneath the table and mouthed the word 'poem'. I remained silent and left the matter to her.

'Ah — the war drums throb no longer and the battle flags are furled.'

An affronted Edsel muttered something about ragtime and left the room.

'Tennyson, I think,' Rosika prompted the embarrassed millionaires, 'but I forget the title.'

Mr Ford obligingly supplied it and confirmed it was one of their favourites. For several seconds my colleague's eyes did not leave mine. She turned at last to Clara.

'Such a fine boy, Edsel. Has he ever thought of joining the army?'

It was Mr Ford who answered abruptly.

'Edsel's future is decided.'

From somewhere a clock ticked more loudly. Upstairs, a door slammed and the drapes shuddered in sympathy. I had a vision of myself with cards in hand. Call? Raise? Give the whole thing up as hopeless? I had never been much good at gambling. I began to sweat as I went over the things I would have said had I been another, better man. The war seemed very distant and our pretensions to affect its course nothing less than ludicrous. Ford sat still and silent at the head of the table. A week's interest on his capital would meet our needs several times over and yet to me it seemed an outrageous demand. This is how we misunderstand the rich – there is a scale to human lives, first it is a matter of propriety and then a tightness around the mind that forever holds back a ten-dollar man from placing fifty-dollar bets. We tremble to ask our worth, but in the end only disappoint with the smallness of our ambition. I think he wanted to be asked then. That was where we so nearly lost it, because we simply could not think as he did.

'You must see the new house before you go,' said Mrs Ford. 'It's too cold for me to come – I hope you understand. Henry, will you . . . ?'

In the failing light we toured the magnificent shell.

'We'll have our own power plant,' Mr Ford explained. 'Turbines'll run in the river. They're not there yet.' He idly worked an electrical switch.

We explored the place like children in a ruin, our eyes following the weak light of a battery lamp. A towering pipe organ appeared in the beam.

'Do you play?' asked Rosika.

'No.'

His manner became perfunctory, absorbed. I know now that

he is often this way, but at the time I was sure we had offended him and because of that lost our cause. We made our way back outside, stepping over cut timber and boxes of nails. I had resigned myself to failure, but Rosika began again on our case as we shivered our way through the gardens. We walked through a gap in some bushes and found ourselves by an empty swimming pool. The tiling had just been finished and tools still lay about the edges.

'The builders said we should have one,' explained Ford. 'But I don't suppose it'll see much use.'

It was the only bright thing – a giant porcelain bowl holding all that was left of the light.

'Perhaps I could put fish in it?'

Rosika, who had been talking all this time about diplomacy, mediation, neutrality, borders, attrition, war aims, finally ground to a halt, accepting that Mr Ford had not heard a single word. We stared gloomily into the pristine, frivolous absurdity of the swimming pool.

'A ship,' said Rosika.

'You spoke, Mrs Schwimmer?'

'A ship. That's what we need – a peace *ship.*'

A hefty tonnage of steel and coal, of pistons, connecting rods, boilers, screws, funnels, smoke and hooting steam-whistles coalesced before the tiled blankness and planted a stirring kiss on Henry Ford's mind.

'A ship?'

'A peace ship. *The* Peace Ship – to take all the delegates to a mediation conference. And journalists too, to cover the story.'

'Journalists, eh?' mused Mr Ford. 'A peace ship, you say.'

'The Henry Ford Peace Ship,' I chipped in shamelessly.

Mr Ford tried the words out to see how they fitted.

'The Henry Ford Peace Ship.'

Have you seen an express train pick up a mail bag? They hang it out below a wide iron hoop, like a keyring but twenty times the size. Then they hang the hoop on a pole right by the track and when the train comes it scoops it up at a hundred miles an hour and carries it off. You can never quite see how it happens. One second it's there, and the next it's gone, disappeared as if the fast and the slow are too different to live in the same world. I stood in the hall of the Ford farmhouse like one of those mail bags waiting passively for its train. Mr Ford was speaking on the telephone. Clara looked worried as she searched for a warm coat for her husband. Ray was getting the car ready out front. I would not see my wife and daughter that day, or the next day or for many months, each hour of which would be lived at the dizzying, foreign pace of money.

'You work for me now, Mr Lochner. I've annexed you.'

Rosika danced before the frowning Mrs Ford. She kissed me on the cheek and delivered her belated line of Emerson – 'Things are in the saddle, ride mankind!'

Within an hour I was on a train to New York with Henry Ford. He talked expansively about *our* peace campaign and it was strange to hear those words that could only be prayers or mere whimsy for other men, but for him could all be turned into realities in a moment with a telephone call or a signature. Power had been hitched to our wagon, and money in abundance too. As the night rushed by I understood that if we still failed it would have to be for some other, less excusable reason.

On the seat beside my new employer his bag lay open, stuffed tight as a mattress with unread telegrams.

Marquis

*I*t was my fault. The young lady who came to my door unannounced was charming, perhaps cleverly so. I know her parents and respect them. I remembered her from when she was a child and had no reason to be suspicious. She stated her business plainly and was not, I am sure, insincere. In the space of a few minutes' conversation we found that we had many common views on the European war. Unfortunately, I was pressed for time that day and embarrassed that I could not spend longer with her. That is why, hat in hand, I passed Miss Shelly innocently on to my wife. When I left there had not yet been any mention of Henry Ford, money or the relentless Madame Rosika Schwimmer. I gave no instruction or warning to Mrs Marquis. When I returned in the afternoon and found that the delightful visitor had obtained a passport straight to my wife's good friend Clara Ford there was no one else to blame. It was, I fear to say, the first chink in the Ford armour.

To be charitable to myself, that is not the whole story. There were other lines of attack – ones I was in no position to block. Even chance seemed on the side of this doubtful adventure. Mr Ford is a great believer in destiny. His attraction to the idea forms one of the many shallows of his mind. As a pastor it is my duty to discourage such nonsense, nevertheless, such has been the profusion and the ordering of coincidences over the last two weeks that I also have been musing on invisible forces. For one thing, it all happened when Liebold was on vacation. A man with an infinity of money and a weakness for sudden enthusiasms must be protected against himself and Mr Liebold has long been recognised as the most reliable defence against mishaps of this sort. For this very reason all Ford's intimates take great care not to let it be known when Liebold is absent or, as it was once put to me, when the lid is off the honey pot. From what I hear some journalist got wind of it anyway and passed the tip onto the Schwimmer woman. This, I am to believe, resulted from a chance encounter in the street. No doubt the truth will come out in the end.

Even at this stage nothing would have happened had Mr Anderson not proved to be another happy throw of the dice for the peacettes. Anderson has groaned under Liebold's tyranny for years. Liebold despises him and greatly fears being replaced by him. Mr Anderson greatly fears that he will not replace Liebold. Anderson would have had no difficulty in repelling the advances of Rosika Schwimmer and Rebecca Shelly – after all, he did exactly that for a dozen other petitioners on the very same day Schwimmer turned up. No indeed – it was his ambition to present Liebold on his return with a changed situation, a change of his own authorship, and what better than a new and captivating cause that would carry Mr Ford beyond the recall of his squat, balding, Germanic and – let us be frank – decidedly unpleasant personal secretary? So it was that Madame Schwimmer was ushered into the Ford presence in his office at Highland Park. Aside from the two principals, the meeting was attended by Charles Brownell, the Ford Motor Company's advertising director, Mr Ford's attorney, Alfred Lucking and myself.

Everything went well. Madame Schwimmer's case was fluent,

nuanced, complex and passionate and Mr Ford's eyes quickly glazed over. After a few minutes he became absorbed in drawing a clutch plate on a notepad. The danger of a new project receded and Schwimmer finally stopped, no longer able to pretend that she was not being rudely ignored by the man she had come to see. Ford looked up then turned to Brownell.

'What do you say, Charlie?'

'No sale. Now I know I've said this before, but ambulances are the thing. Do you collect for ambulances, Mrs Schwimmer?'

Madame swelled with indignation.

'Let's face it – they gotta need 'em and we can make 'em. Ambulances is a game we can't lose.'

The advertising director's eyes took on a visionary remoteness as his hands sketched the dimensions of a new poster.

'Ford First on Flanders Field, Ford to the Rescue, and then one on the way to the dressing station – Thank God it's a Ford, nurses standing by with white aprons and red crosses on them. Nurses are good.'

Mr Ford showed Brownell the back of his hand – it's a gesture of his, the hand held up to the temple as if to shield the eye from a disturbing light. It means 'enough' and must be instantly obeyed. Brownell sat back in his chair, accepting that the time was not yet right. The magnate turned to face his petitioner.

'I know who caused the war.'

Madame Schwimmer cleared the disconsolate look from her face while the rest of us stiffened for the awkwardness to come.

'I know who's under the whole rotten business and I know who's keeping it going.'

You should understand that Mr Ford has very definite opinions about the Jews. From time to time he will get relief from whatever ails him by sharing these views with anyone willing to listen and of course, when you are Henry Ford, everyone is willing to listen. His concept of Jewry is abstract and no less primitive than the evil eye or some minor deity of inconvenience who must be named and cursed whenever an engine will not start or the interest rate rises. Real men of flesh and blood do not impinge on the matter in the slightest – he sends a Christmas card and a new car every year to his good friend Rabbi Franklin. Indeed, such is the purity of his views in this field, their pristine isolation from the world of realities, that I doubt he could reliably point out a Jew in a crowded synagogue. So it was that while Brownell, Lucking and myself could all accurately interpret Madame Schwimmer's name, background, appearance, manner, accent and cast of mind, these things meant nothing to Mr Ford. The poor woman – I did not want her to succeed, but I felt for her deeply as she sat through a quarter-hour explanation of how, as a matter of scientific fact, her own people were at the root of all the world's problems, not least the war she so foolishly dreamed of stopping. I looked on with mounting discomfort as her eyes brightened and brimmed behind the heavy lenses of her spectacles and I prayed that the tear would not drop.

There the story of Henry Ford and the great peace campaign would certainly have ended had it not been for the most extraordinary mischance of all. Clara would have had her husband by her side for Christmas, hopes would not cruelly have been raised and the world's great industrialist would have done what he can instead of what he cannot. The meeting was over. Madame Schwimmer got to her feet and collected her bag, ponderous with secrets, from where it had sat beside her on its own chair throughout. She gathered herself bravely.

'Ah, well. It seems my quest is not yet over.'

We did not respond when she talked of an imminent voyage back home to Hungary. I and my colleagues returned to our seats and exchanged glances of mutual satisfaction and relief. Mr Ford ushered Madame Schwimmer to the door, all danger surely passed. But as it opened, apparently against some resistance, the sound of excitement and disorder came from the anteroom. The word 'Louis' was exclaimed by Schwimmer. The press men fell silent and as I looked, from where I sat, at a shadowy jostle of shoulders and the backs of heads I heard Mr Anderson's voice introduce a new actor to the drama. Whether thoughtlessly, or through a genius intuition into the mysteries of his employer's heart, he used the only word in the language that could have had such a transforming effect on the fortunes of this 'victim of circumstance'. Brownell, Lucking and I stared at each other with amazement and some alarm as we heard of a private invitation to Mr Ford's new home at Fair Lane, an invitation that had certainly never been mentioned before.

It was there, the next day and in the less protected surroundings of his own home, that the deed was done. Cleverly, they lured him out to the freezing grounds and away from Clara's good common sense. It was in the garden, by a swimming pool no less, that Madame Rosika Schwimmer, the quintessence of old Europe, subtle and opaque, sinfully persuasive, a refined oratorical disease to which the infant Henry had no more resistance than an Inca to smallpox, took the last steps of her long, iceberg way and convinced – oh dear, oh dear – convinced Henry Ford that he could stop the war.

The newly engaged Mr Delavigne waxed hyperbolical on the peace scheme, but did his master little good by putting the phrase 'Out of the trenches by Christmas, never to return' into his mouth. We were already deep into November, and the newspapers already laughing.

'You're going to stop the war in a month, Mr Ford?'

'Well,' shrugged the engineer, 'there's always Easter.'

His next suggestion – that Christmas Day on the European battlefields would see a general strike of fighting men 'taking the business of peace into their own hands' caused panic among the foreign delegations in Washington and briefly promoted

Mr Ford to the front ranks of international revolutionary Marxism. Someone asked him if this was his new creed and the tragedy was up and running when he replied, 'If it stops the war, maybe it is.'

These fragments, and others still more lurid, we received at a distance, trying to interpret them as best we could. I stayed in Detroit, as did Clara, while Henry dashed from New York to Washington and back with his fresh new friends. They generated headline after headline and cartoons too, which I had to look at over my breakfast, hoping unreasonably that no one else would see them, above all that Clara would not see them. Mr Ford had had enthusiasms before and no one who knew him well believed this would come to anything. Even Liebold, who extended his vacation in Colorado to view some local plants, read the Denver newspapers without concern, certain that he could dampen his employer's ardour as soon as he got back to Detroit. A nameless inside source passed this morsel on to the local papers and there he was the Tuesday after his return – drawn as a dwarfish uniformed Prussian with a Kaiser moustache, spiked helmet and the 1915 Ford price-list poking out of his tunic pocket. He held a small fire-bucket of sand as he stood disconsolately by the edge of the blazing forest of Henry's moral passions.

It was only during my last ten days on dry land that I began to take the idea of an actual peace voyage to Europe seriously. There were reports of shipping agents brawling in the lobby of the Biltmore Hotel and then a photograph of an actual ship. A destination was announced only as 'a certain central point at which delegates will congregate'. Flocks of invitations flew across the land, darkening the skies. Declarations were made, so definite that even Henry Ford would have found them hard to back out of. I prayed that it would end well and, even as the telephone rang, thanked the Lord that I would have nothing to do with it myself.

Clara summoned me. On a cloudy late November morning the lamps were still lit in the main parlour at Edison Avenue. Some of the furniture had already been removed to the new house at Fair Lane and these unfamiliar spaces left us sitting in a stage-set atmosphere of disaster. Edsel was brought in for a few minutes of small-talk then sent on his way, his mother looking after her minimal family with anxious intensity. I waited for an accusation and perhaps received it when she handed me a terse letter from her husband. It talked of the packing of bags and her immediate travel to New York and embarkation.

'He really means it, then?' I said.

I felt the cold formality of her speech.

'It would appear so.'

She looked again to the door through which young Edsel had just left.

'Since my marriage day I have never left my husband's side. I hoped never to do so but you will understand, Samuel, that as a mother I could never do anything that might leave Edsel an orphan.'

The unworthy thought rose up in my mind – how dreadful it would be to inherit the Ford Motor Company at an early age.

'Two more ships lost last week,' Clara continued. 'Both of them neutral. Germany apologises and says they can't be expected to see through fog, but does anyone believe them? If you can't see and shoot anyway what difference does it make? Have we forgotten the *Lusitania*?'

Her voice rose with the anger of abandonment. Why only one son? I found myself wondering. Why this sudden foreign love of Henry's, the only cause that could take him physically so far from his wife?

'It won't come to anything, Clara, surely. You know how he is. If any ship goes anywhere Henry won't be on it. A few days before departure he'll send someone else in his place and it'll be better for everyone.'

'I'm not so sure, Samuel. I don't know these people, I don't understand them, I don't know what they want. Why does he need to be with them? Can't he just give them some money?'

I had never seen her so shaken or so heedless of anyone's problems but her own. For Clara, a brush with the world's great problems had brought none of that uplift the campaigners so loved to speak of and she seemed truly to have worked herself into the belief that she might never see Henry again. Her anxiety was real and drew from me a thoughtless gesture.

'If there's anything I can do, Clara. Anything at all . . .'

She reached to her sewing basket and took the letter from where it had lain in wait behind pincushions and hanks of coloured yarn. She softened, brightened as my words brought her instant relief.

'I knew I wouldn't have to ask, Samuel. I knew I could rely on you.'

I took the envelope, sternly addressed to 'Henry Ford, my husband' in the disciplined, country school hand I remembered well from my first invitation to the Ford residence. It was only then, holding that weighty document, that I understood how right Clara was – that this was no mere jaunt but could, quite literally, be a matter of life and death. Why not another torpedo in the night? The ghastly scene dramatised itself until Clara's words recalled me.

'You must go to him.'

For an awful moment it seemed she was suggesting I share Mr Ford's madness and go with him to Europe.

'But, Clara, what could I do? And to leave you here at a time like this . . .'

It was a misjudgement and she did not spare me.

'What can you do here, Samuel? No, you must go to him at once – please. He will listen to you. That is what I ask him to do in the letter. You can stop all this nonsense before it is too late, I am sure. I would not ask anyone else. I don't even know where he is. Sometimes I read New York, sometimes Washington, sometimes both on the same day. I telephone the Biltmore Hotel and I can't get connected. *I* can't get through. Look.'

She handed me a scrap of newspaper which advertised a 'Mother's Day' Peace Rally to be held at the Belasco Theatre in Washington before the presentation of peace resolutions to President Wilson. Rosika Schwimmer was among the attractions as, in rather larger type, was the new, escaped Henry Ford.

'Bring him back to me, Samuel. Back to those who truly care for him.'

Relieved of all thought of steaming to Europe, this was an embassy I was happy to accept. I slipped into the daily stream of my fellow citizens as Clara Ford's confidential agent, rubbing shoulders, if the newspapers are to be believed, with the spies and secret procurers of a dozen other powers all engaged on equally clandestine work. For the first time these fantasies seemed plausible to me. In trains and station waiting rooms I became self-consciously unobtrusive, avoiding eyes and anxiously questioning the motives of the most innocent glance. Faces around me turned to images from magazine stories. I became convinced I was being followed and so intimidated an elderly gentleman by turning on him and asking him his business that he actually told me, taking a worn shoe from a bag to show me as evidence of his journey to a repair shop. In the event, I proved to have some talent for the work, slipping the nets of my unseen enemies and arriving unharmed on the morning of 26 November at a scene of histrionic chaos only a few blocks from the White House itself.

The amazons of peace milled densely outside the theatre doors, my employer's lean grey head nowhere visible above the press of bonnets and the umbrellas opening as rain began to fall. Large posters proclaimed the event – Schwimmer's name in skyscraper letters and then 'Henry Ford' with a generous second billing, and lower still Mrs Ethel Snowden, an obscure Englishwoman with whom I was never to exchange a word. I had not announced my arrival to the organisers, fearing they could make difficulties in my obtaining a personal interview with Mr Ford, or that they would coach him with arguments against me. Mine was to be a surprise attack and I slipped past the crowd and down an alleyway to the stage door.

Once inside, my presence was detected as quickly as that of a fox in a hen-house. The charming Miss Shelly appeared at my side and told me how delighted she was to see me. She asserted that I must have come to support their cause and I did not contradict her. When I said I had a message for Mr Ford she said, 'Of course,' and asked if I would like her to take it to him. When I said I must speak to him in person and that I believed he was somewhere in the building she said, 'Of course,' and offered to be my guide. It was some twenty minutes later and after frequent apologies for her failure to find him that we found ourselves in a sub-basement. Under the light of a single dingy bulb I looked round at the heaped costumes of harlequins, clowns, pirates, waifs, angels, imperilled princesses and pasteboard kings. Miss Shelly shrugged.

'He doesn't seem to be here either. I really am sorry – everything is a bit chaotic.'

'Miss Shelly, shall we end this now? It's beneath you.'

She straightened and became severe.

'Dean Marquis, I believe in what I am doing. I draw no stipend or salary for my work. We aim to succeed and will do whatever we honestly can to reach that goal.'

'Honestly? Have you honestly brought me down here?'

'There is a higher honesty.'

I moved some wooden swords from the top of a property basket, took off my hat and coat and sat down.

'Miss Shelly, I pray that you will succeed, as earnestly as I have ever prayed for anything.'

'But you don't think we will, do you? You are not with us.'

'I . . .'

I felt a sudden heaviness, as I had once before in my life in the last instant before telling a lie. I raised my hands emptily as I waited for something to say.

'I am not against you.'

'That's not enough. You have come to dissuade him.'

'I have come to give him a letter from his wife.'

'And to talk to him.'

'Yes. I have to care for Mr Ford too, and for Mrs Ford — she needs him.'

'So do we. She can come with us. I know she has the invitation.'

'That's impossible.'

'It's her choice.'

'You are harsh, Miss Shelly.'

'Yes, I am. People don't understand that about us. I suppose it's because we want peace — it's a common mistake.'

'He is here, isn't he?'

'Yes, he's here.'

'Will you take me to him, please.'

'Why don't *you* speak?'

'To whom?'

'To the meeting. To everyone. You say you are not against us. You are respected, Dr Marquis. Just say a few words at the start, then you can talk to Mr Ford.'

'Are you bargaining with me, Miss Shelly?'

She smiled.

'But how could I? I'm powerless.'

From above, a sound like distant thunder penetrated the floors. Miss Shelly consulted the little watch pinned to her blouse.

166

'Come on, we're about to start.'

Perspiring in the heat, I was led quickly up several flights of stairs, the noise growing all the time, then through another door and into the bustling excitement of the wings, crowded with figures indistinct in silhouette or starkly half-lit by the brilliance from the stage. Although I couldn't see her, Madame Schwimmer's voice sounded clearly above the fray, the one sharp, irrepressible instrument no orchestra could drown. Someone was already speaking and the sound from the auditorium surged through the offbeats of their rhetoric. A confusion of excitement and panic took hold of me. As in a dream of frustration, endless stumbling blocks appeared from all around. I thought I saw something and stepped forward only to collide with Mr Lochner, late of the Chicago Peace Society. He shook my hand and congratulated me on my conversion to the cause. I shouted in his ear.

'Where's Mr Ford?'

He turned and I followed the direction of his gaze. There, on the threshold of the stage, black against its limelight was the tall, pauper-thin and unmistakable outline of Henry Ford. A stranger asked to find the odd one out would have had no difficulty. There was a poignant foreignness to his movements, the timid if hungry leaning forward to see and the quick step back to avoid being seen. Here was no actor, unless a very skilful one already in character. With an odd, barely controlled sense of urgency I felt I had to speak to him that instant – not merely that, but to get a hand on him too as if he were a child on the point of being stolen away.

'Mr Ford!'

I found Madame Schwimmer in my path. She stood very close and spoke too rapidly to be understood. My view was filled with her broad, ecstatic face, her wide, full bloom of wiry hair and, where the dark eyes should have been, only the moist obscurity of clouded lenses. A huge wave of noise came from the stage.

167

'Mr Ford!'

My words drowned. The glare made it hard to see. There was someone standing by Ford's side. She had her hand on his arm and just as I called a second time she stepped out with him into the light which was so intense he seemed to switch all at once from black to white. Schwimmer too went out on stage and took her seat behind the long table, skirted with the banner of the Women's International Peace Committee. She polished her pince-nez and calmly reached for a pitcher of water. Mid-stage, Ford hesitated, abruptly discovered in the stage lights. He looked to his left and I felt for him as he gauchely shielded his eyes in an attempt to see the audience. One chair behind the table was left unoccupied. As he looked longingly in its direction the cheering of the crowd resolved into a chant.

'We want Henry! We want Henry! We want Henry!'

Slowly he was drawn to the front of the stage. As the noise abated I heard a few words of the anxious exchange.

'Say it for me.'

'*I* can't say it. It must be you.'

Mr Ford pleaded but was inexorably moved forward. The silence became profound. Halting and weakly he spoke his fatal line.

'Out of the trenches by Christmas – never to return.'

A deafening response came out of the darkness. Feet stamped and the whole building vibrated. The mystified and slightly trembling engineer was led to his place. From where she sat by his side, Madame Schwimmer raised her glass in my direction and stood to begin her work. With her hands she calmed the storm.

'The Dean of the Episcopal Cathedral of Detroit, the Reverend Dr Samuel Marquis, will start us off with a short prayer.'

★   ★   ★

Late that afternoon, as the peace campaigners stood in silent vigil outside the White House while Madame Schwimmer delivered the conference resolutions, Henry Ford and I wrestled in the warmth of the New Willard Hotel. Victory often seemed close, but at times the noise and stage light of the Belasco Theatre came back into his mind and to these arguments – whatever they were – I had no answer. I persuaded him at least to return to Detroit and to Clara, and was sure, as I rode with him on the train, that she would prevail where I could not. Man and wife talked, and in an earlier age that would certainly have been enough but Lochner and Schwimmer and all that buzzed in New York came down the wires of the long-distance telephone and fought for his soul. Under Clara's eyes he spoke uncertainly into the ether.

'Do you think I really have to go?'

The other voice orated at length and we could hear its sharp crackle as it got louder. I detected Madame Schwimmer's slightly alien rhythms. Mr Ford hooked the receiver and turned to give us his decision.

'I'll talk to them,' he said. 'Maybe I'll just see them off.'

So he went back east and for a second time I was sent after him and found myself in his room at the Biltmore at two in the morning on the day of departure. Travel-soiled and exhausted, I lay slumped in my chair, staring out at the city. The long note of a tugboat sounded from where it worked on the Hudson. Mr Ford had had a busy day with the peace campaigners. At that moment he sat opposite, as lively and restored as the winner of a bare-knuckle fight.

'So that's that.'

I had nothing more to give. Over two hours all my sermons had revolted and turned against me. 'You said' became Ford's refrain. 'You said . . . you said . . .'

'But . . .'

'I've got it right, haven't I, Samuel? Word for word. That *is* what you said.'

That was true. The parts he did remember, he remembered perfectly. They had become drawings in his mind. The parts he had forgotten, he had forgotten with equal perfection.

'Didn't you tell me that what is right cannot fail?'

'That's what I believe.'

'And is it not right to try to stop the war?'

'Of course, but . . .'

'Then that's that. I got a hunch, Samuel, and I'm going through with it. I'm going to stick by these people. I'm going the whole way with them, soup to nuts and that's that.'

He stood up and pushed open the window. Even at that hour, the rumble from his countless products echoed up from the streets. Lights flowed like blood around the great monuments of the moneylenders, the capitols of the unseen empire that so obsessed him. Mr Ford had come amongst them, he had set up his camp in the very heart of that hidden power that plotted relentlessly to drag his country into a foreign war. Somewhere down there Baruch, Goldman, Warburg and Rothschild were whispering together in a cryptic tongue. For a moment I wondered if he even thought of Europe at all.

'Will you look at that? The first car I ever travelled in, Samuel, was one I made with my own hands and when I drove it, it was the only one on the road. In ten days the millionth will roll off the line at Highland Park. In little more than a year another million will follow. I just . . .'

He told me these things with the tone of one announcing a bereavement and as he faltered I hoped for one last chance to reason with him.

'Surely you can help them here – direct the campaign at home while they are away?'

He seemed not to hear me.

'I just wish I could make you understand how sad money is. Show me a rich man and I'll show you a disappointed man. I think there must be some law about it – there are delays, but

in the end the result is always the same. I don't know how to
. . .'

He turned to me, suddenly cheered by a thought.

'Do you like this hotel, Samuel?'

I was used to his mental jumps, but this was one I couldn't
follow. I shrugged and gave him a questioning look.

'Do you want it?'

'What do you mean?'

'Just that – do you want it? We can wrap it up in a few
days. We'll wire the proprietors, have it valued, offer three times
as much, call the lawyers in – by the end of next week it's
yours. Look, there's another one over there. Why not have two?
It'd make no difference to me. You just say the word, Samuel.'

Any man could say these things, but when Henry Ford says
this to you it is very different. There is no fantasy in such an
exchange and the hair rises on the back of your neck as you
grasp the power of your response. Just say the word. One says
'No', of course. One says it quickly, or dismissively – whatever
one needs to cover the hesitation as one brushes by that other,
radically changed life, yours for the price of a single syllable.

'Do you follow me, Samuel? I am in a peculiar position.
No one can give me anything. There is nothing I want I cannot
have, but I do not want the things money can buy. Neither
the making nor the use of money means anything to me as
far as I am personally concerned. I want to live a life, to make
the world a little better for having lived in it. You know, the
trouble with people is that they do not think. I want to do
and say things that will make them think.'

The homespun school of philosophy is Mr Ford's last and
most impregnable fortress. When he retires behind its walls and
pulls up its drawbridge only a fool does not admit defeat.

'Well,' I relented. 'Busy day tomorrow – best get some sleep.'

'Goodnight, Samuel.'

'Goodnight, Mr Ford.'

Anticipating failure, Clara had come through from Detroit two days before. If necessary she would see her husband off, but had firmly refused to go further. She had her own room two floors down, away from the disturbance and indiscretion of the campaign headquarters. Past muffled snores and a sleepy bellboy carrying a glass of whisky on a tray, I trod the thick crimson carpet as it snaked over the veined marble of the stairs – the Biltmore's advertisements talked of Italian palaces, of the luxury of experiencing Europe without ever leaving home. I knocked lightly on Clara's door – perhaps she would not hear, perhaps it could all be put off till the morning? But it opened promptly and I went in. I said at once that it was hopeless and she thanked me for trying.

Preparations for the morning were still being made, a selection of furs lying on the bed or draped over the back of the dressing-table chair. In only a few hours she would go to Hoboken with her husband, be seen by the press and the public and make a good show sending him off on the *Oscar II*. I would return with her to Detroit.

'Go with him, Samuel.'

'What?'

She put her hands on my arms and drew me towards her.

'Who else can I trust? Who else can I ask? I want you to bring him back to me, whatever happens.'

I made my excuses, and they were not trivial – my job, my engagements, my wife.

'This one thing, Samuel, please. If I never ask for anything again? Samuel – for me.'

Is it that some women know how to be unrefusable, or that money knows how to command? I have given the question up and recline here, quite pleasantly for the moment, on the first-class promenade deck of a Danish liner that has seen better days. I am flanked by new friends. Mr Bingham on my left, a gentleman of the theatre. And on my right young Berton

Braley, reporter and syndicated poet of the people, still a little dazed by the freshness of his matrimony. We are not good sailors and the swell makes it unwise for us to stand too long. By contrast, Miss Inez Milholland walks steadily by, as untroubled as a mermaid, and spares us a glance of scant respect. Helplessly, our three married heads turn to watch her pass. Inspired, poet Braley takes out a pencil and makes a note on the back of a menu card.

Theodore

*O*h, sure – Ford was a dream job. In the days between my first piece in the *Free Press* and that riot on Hoboken pier you couldn't shift a spotlight fast enough to keep him out of it. The old man was as generous with his name as he was with his money – he didn't care at all how I used it and it became the biggest and best megaphone anyone could have wished for. Articles by 'Henry Ford' appeared everywhere and the whole country was reading my words – *Millions Murdered by Military Parasites*; *Cannon and Slaughter No Part of Patriotism*; *Sloths and Lunatics in Military Cliques*; *World Cries Out Against War – Ford Takes the Lead*. Everyone was talking about it. Under other names I could syndicate inside stories about the Peace Ship right across the country. What Mr Ford paid me was maybe half of what I made in those few weeks. I did a good job for him.

I was really supposed to be back in Detroit, but I got out of that as quickly as I could and decamped to New York where everything was happening. The seventh floor of the Biltmore Hotel was an inferno and for the week before the *Oscar* slipped out of Hoboken it must have been the most exciting place in the world. The Ford office on Long Island was thrown into chaos and then just as quickly re-tooled for the new task of promoting world peace. Omnibuses arrived and decanted scores of bewildered staff – stenographers, typists, clerks, messengers, translators and cashiers who swarmed all over the place.

'Hey, buddy – you'd think there's a war on!'

No one seemed really sure what was going on, but everyone knew it was important. You could see from their faces they just knew nothing like this would ever happen to them again, however long they lived.

Mr Ford's a natural for good copy, but I learned early on he's better with one or two people at a time than he is with groups. This is, after all, the man who addressed the prisoners in Sing Sing with the phrase 'Hope to meet you all here again soon.' There was, accordingly, no little anxiety on the morning of the big anouncement. Forty reporters crowded round in the lobby of the hotel, their eyes focused on a dry-mouthed Mr Ford, myself, Mr Louis 'the victim' Lochner, and Mr Oswald Garrison Villard of the *Evening Post* who had come at Mr Ford's invitation to lend his expertise in press matters. As it turned out, it's just as well he was there.

'We're going to try to get the boys out of the trenches by Christmas,' he started. 'I've chartered a ship and some of us are going to Europe.'

The reporters scribbled then looked up again and waited in silence.

'You see we . . . The main idea is to crush militarism and to . . . Well, to get the boys out of the trenches. Our object is to stop war for all times, and also preparedness. War is nothing but preparedness. Those who talk of preparedness in America are nothing but warmongers, profiteers. There are hidden forces in . . .'

Mr Villard gave him a sharp nudge.

'No boy would ever kill a bird if he didn't first have a slingshot or a gun. That's what I say.'

There was another pause, and when it seemed that was the end of the statement the man from the *Tribune* put up his hand.

'Mr Ford, sir. What *exactly* do you plan to do once you're over there?'

'I'll leave that to the experts.'

Mr Lochner explained the international neutral commission of mediation and enquiry while Ford looked vaguely into the middle distance. When the questions came they were all for him. Mr Ford answered by saying how the ship would be armed with the Marconi equipment, 'the longest gun in the world', that would keep everyone in touch with the movement. He then repeated his desire to get the boys out of the trenches.

'They don't want to fight. I know they don't. They'd be just as happy to shake hands with each other. That's what we're going to do over there, gentlemen. We're going to do the greatest good to the greatest number. Thank you.'

With that he reached behind himself, found the handle of a door, and disappeared. The newsmen had plenty more to ask and we stayed on a few minutes trying to limit the damage as best we could. I got on the telephone straight after and bought a lot of drinks that evening. The next morning it was clear I had squared some of the papers, but not others. According to one yellow rag we had kidnapped Mr Ford and had him hypnotised by Madame Bolshevatsky (Rosika Schwimmer's secret sister) so he no longer knew he was an American. The *Times* thundered harmlessly above the heads of the people by calling him 'a callow utilitarian'.

'Now tell me, Theodore, is that a good thing or a bad thing to be?'

I reassured him on that point. He liked the *Trib* headline best of all: GREAT WAR ENDS CHRISTMAS DAY – Ford to Stop It – *Best of all Christmases Less Than a Month Away*. I got pretty nervous when he picked that up, but he read the whole thing without getting it and no one saw the need to put him right. If Mr Ford was happy, we were happy. To tell the truth, the cartoons were more of a problem than the reports. Mr Ford didn't read much but he would look at any number of pictures. In the end they started to come so thick and fast Lochner took on a boy just to cut them out and hide them first thing in the morning. 'Cuttings for the archives' was the answer if anyone ever asked us. No one did, not even Mr Ford, who just looked through the holes and never gave them a second thought.

With the great industrialist installed and his purse-strings loosened, the Biltmore did a land-office business in hucksters and charlatans. Beside the herds of reporters, photographers and publicity agents there was a steady stream of vaporous enthusiasts who came to tell us we were getting this peace thing all wrong and how, by following their plan, we could get it all right. Others came to denounce the German plot they believed us to be. Some of the newspapers had fun hiring sabre-slashed Prussians from whatever Broadway theatre or moving-picture concern could spare one and sneaking them in in the hope getting a photograph of their 'spy' beside Ford, Lochner or Schwimmer. Half the crowd had nothing to do with the peace campaign. Promoters of useless accessories for the Model T descended in plague proportions only to flutter hopelessly against Ray's impenetrable screen. Amongst them, failed vaudevillians not yet engaged for the Christmas season offered at a discount their morale-raising talents.

These were the souls, hopeful or sneering by turns, who populated the outer circles of the Biltmore headquarters. At the centre of the storm sat Rosika Schwimmer doing all the real work. It was her job to select the delegates who would bring peace to Europe. Thousands volunteered every day by letter or telegram and while these were all conscientiously sifted, few, I think, ever got through to the lady herself. She had other names in mind – the sort who had to be pursued rather than fended off. After long debate a text was settled on and this is what the invitees received:

> Will you come as my guest aboard the *Oscar II* of the Scandinavian-American Line, sailing from New York December 4th for Christiania, Stockholm and Copenhagen? I am cabling the leading men and women of the European nations to join us *en route* and at some central point, to be determined later, to establish an international conference to lead to a just settlement of the War.
>
> One hundred representative Americans are being invited, among whom Jane Addams, Thomas Edison and John Wanamaker have accepted today.
>
> With 20,000 men killed every twenty-four hours, tens of thousands maimed, homes ruined and another winter begun the time has come for women and men of courage and energy to free the goodwill of Europe that it may assert itself for peace and justice.
>
> HENRY FORD

Changes were soon necessary on account of the fact that none of the three named persons had accepted. Mr Ford, being admirably plain in his own use of language, had not heard the silent 'but' at the end of John Wanamaker's response – 'I would go to the ends of the earth with you to halt the war . . .' As for the Edisons, Ford had shared the Thanksgiving turkey with them but had returned crestfallen. It was painful to see how long he held to the hope that his great mentor and model would go with him. And the great Miss Jane Addams? Well, let's just say the truth of that one remains unclear.

Madame Schwimmer was undaunted. All signs were good, if only they were correctly interpreted, and she declared it was for the best if lily-livered, torpedo-fearing fainthearts stayed at home. These were not people any true peace-campaigner would care to share a cabin with. There were plenty more willing to take up their place, and as the image of a Peace Ark became commonplace Rosika rose magnificently to her role of the new Noah, parading through the corridors of the Biltmore with an ominous list in her hand. Early each morning I looked over the shoulder of our boy censor as he cut the caricatures of our ample, bespectacled, bun-haired leader from the papers. There she was, standing by the gangplank with list and goose-feather quill at the ready, saving friends and damning enemies to extinction as the patient line of delegates snaked away to the vanishing point. In another, the *Oscar* was already at sea (her name crossed out and replaced with *Ship of Fools*) while behind her the United States themselves were sinking. 'The Good Lord be thanked!' burbled the Statue of Liberty as she went beneath the waves, 'The best of America is saved'. On the other side of the ocean the British Army organised a welcoming honour guard, a mustachioed sergeant shouting the order 'Squad – present straitjackets!'

'I don't fear criticism,' Mr Ford liked to say. 'I learn from it.'

The lesson many learned from their morning papers was that the Peace Ship was fast becoming untouchable. Cardinal Gibbons down in Baltimore had started off by calling it the finest and best gift for Christmas. Mr Ford received his personal blessing and sent a cablegram to the Holy Father himself, detailing the project. A confusion over some roman numerals didn't help (not my fault), and it ended up being addressed to someone who had been dead for six hundred years. Anyway, the next we heard at the Biltmore was talk of caution and 'rocks ahead' and fears that Mr Ford's sincere wishes might be prevented by unspecified obstacles. Mr William Jennings Bryan, recently departed from President Wilson's cabinet on account of preparedness, had been associated with our campaign from its earliest days. He came to see us at the hotel and spoke for an hour with Mr Ford. After, I admired the skill with which he handled the reporters:

'I have seen Mr Ford and am in hearty sympathy with the effort he is making, and hope to join the party later once it is established in Europe. Only those who want the war to continue ridicule the effort. This was to be expected. Ridicule is the favoured weapon of those who desire to oppose any movement against which they can find no rational argument. If any of the persons on the Ark had been making money out of the Flood, they would have ridiculed Noah for sending out the dove. Success to Mr Ford and his companions. May they return with an olive leaf.'

In other words – I will come with you to the end of the pier, but no further.

With one exception, all the Governors of the States found excuses or were frankly opposed. Ida Tarbell came in person to give her regrets to Mr Ford. Minor ailments and 'personal reasons' were reported from all quarters. Just before we were due to sail Clara Ford herself came to the Biltmore with Edsel, her son. Their presence was felt two floors above in the Stop the War Suite, and made flesh in the person of Clara's suave, creeping agent, Reverend Samuel Marquis. There were fears that Mr Ford himself would not go and it was in the middle of this anxiety that Louis Lochner put down a report on Madame Schwimmer's desk:

JANE ADDAMS IN HOSPITAL – BUT ONLY FOR OBSERVATION
Jane Addams, settlement worker and peace advocate, was taken to the Presbyterian hospital today for 'observation'.

Dr James Herrick said that her illness is not serious.

Miss Addams has not been feeling well for several days.

Whether her condition will prevent her from accompanying the Ford peace party abroad depends on developments.

Schwimmer immediately headed for the lobby. At the height of her energy she drove in a taxi-cab round every hospital in the city and returned three hours later. One third furious, two thirds triumphant, she declared to Louis and me – 'Just as I thought. Nowhere to be found – the rat!'

We threw our net pretty widely in this business of gathering delegates. Former presidents were by no means beyond our ambition. Theodore Roosevelt was not polite, but when we heard that Mr Taft was coming through town Schwimmer sent a messenger to catch him up and ask for his answer. This enterprising boy finally got hold of Taft and had a broad smile on his face by the time he got back to the Biltmore, still with our message in hand, though it had clearly been opened and resealed.

'Well?' demanded Schwimmer.

'I wish I knew what was in it, lady. When Mr Taft read your letter he laughed so hard he set the whole Twenty-third Street Ferry rocking.'

It was about this time I started to think. I was getting to dream about ships, and most usually things didn't go too well and I'd wake up in a sweat. Maybe the rocking Twenty-third Street Ferry was a sign too.

Clergymen were easier – we had no shortage of them. Men of middling rank and advanced opinions were also bolder. Judge Ben B. Lindsey of Colorado, the fashionable juvenile judge and apostle of free love said 'yes' and stayed true to his word. The old warhorse of the muckracking days S. S. McClure also found some space in his diary now that his business partners had thrown him off his own magazine. Those with no reputation at all were never a problem. Journalists we had to stave off like drowning men from a lifeboat – this was a story everyone wanted a part of, and no need to worry about expenses neither.

We had guys from the *Times* (New York and Brooklyn), the *Eagle, The Day,* the *World,* the *Tribune* (New York and Chicago), *Harper's Weekly* and *Collier's Magazine,* the St Louis *Globe Democrat* and the *Jewish Daily News* all the way down to *Staats Zeitung* and the Spartanburg *Herald.* A quartet of photographers and three cinematograph men completed the press corps.

One other species had to be gathered together and loaded before the *Oscar* was ready for the off. Being a great despiser of education, Mr Ford felt that students would be better off going to Europe than wasting time in the classroom.

'I want fellows with sand,' he explained. 'Young men and women who'll quit their colleges if need be to go on the expedition.'

It turned out that a very large number of students felt exactly the same way about their education, and had no lack of 'sand'. We soon had more than we could use and were forced to impose a quota. Struggle broke out across the most gilded campuses of the land. In the end some twenty-five Athletic Union Presidents and all-round habitual participators elbowed their way to the front and received their accreditation. A small but exquisite contingent from Vassar and Brown added greatly to the aesthetic quality of the passenger list and there was a new and more salacious outbreak of Ark metaphors. Mrs Ada Morse Clark, personal secretary to the Chancellor of Stanford, was sent precisely to put an end to all such talk. A good job had been done disinforming this formidable lady about train timetables, sailing times and the new passport regulations. Nevertheless, the chaperone cleared all obstacles and arrived from California with papers in order and five minutes to spare, only to be booed from the rail of the second-class deck by her disappointed charges and immediately christened 'Policeman Clark'.

Being bound for a war-torn continent, it was decided that this peace army should carry all its materiel with it and be as independent as possible. Accordingly, the name of Rexford Holmes was added to the payroll, an energetic character who relished the task of provisioning such a mighty expeditionary force.

'Yes, sir!' he told me. 'It's a ripsnorter and no doubt about it.'

Twenty thousand large envelopes were ordered, six hundred reams of paper and three hundred boxes of carbon paper, two thousand pencils, forty jars of paste and, with admirable realism, five gross of erasers. A set of rustproof Navy typewriters was acquired and a team of staff to use them. Whatever was going to happen would certainly be well recorded.

Money washed out across the city. Much of it went to the Biltmore, which provided luxury after luxury without ever being asked, or being told not to. Madame Schwimmer found the ship itself not quite fit for the noble cause of peace and ordered a $1,000 freshen-up from Wanamaker's. The lounge and cabin furnishings were redone and the drapes and lampshades changed to match. Six score of new cushions were strewn about the place to support the delegates in their post-debate exhaustion. A hot-house of palms and flowers appeared. Pigeons vanished from the public parks, were stuffed and bleached and equipped with olive branches and wired to the branches of frosted Christmas trees. A hedge of decency grew up across the corner bar in the grand saloon – prohibitionists on one side, journalists on the other.

Many of the delegates had little or no money and no one thought it reasonable that they should equip themselves for a sea voyage and European diplomacy at their own expense. Purchase orders from the Ford Motor Company became as good as banknotes. The mere mention of the Peace Expedition was enough to make a customer creditworthy. Shop assistants put away the serge and flannel in favour of *peau de soie*. Astrakhan and skunkskin gave way to seal. The merchants of life-vests, waterproof trunks and sea-sickness remedies had never known a year like it. The comedians at the Hippodrome sang that Santa Ford had come to town. In the audience, delegates, students and journalists laughed and charged their tickets to the company.

On the grounds that Peace should not go threadbare, Rosika Schwimmer herself was forced to impose upon the generosity of her patron. The pawning of her jewels for the cause was an oft-told tale and whenever we heard it we knew we were in for two hours of calm as she headed for the department stores to gather a few more items for her 'peace wardrobe'. This also mattered because on her return from these trips she was, for a short while, in her most malleable mood. The time to strike was as she struggled from the elevator, momentarily balanced between an equal weight of purchases in each hand. That was the moment when ideas that had been folly in the morning, or persons who had been proscribed on account of some ancient offence, might be slipped past her guard. That was how that fool Bingham got his ticket. There were all sorts of theories, but it really was just as simple as that. I was there by Lochner's side as she puffed down the corridor towards us.

'What about these fellows?' he asked her, waving a handful of letters and telegrams and decade-old signed photographs of made-up faces. 'We've been talking about it in the office – maybe it makes sense after all. We could call them Entertainments Officer, or something. There are going to be a lot of opinions on that ship, a lot of very different people. It might be wise to think about the lighter side.'

She took the applications and shuffled through them, quick as a card sharp, before handing them back. Surrounded by parcels and bags, economy was one objection she could not raise.

'I don't see the point of it myself, but if you like. Pick the most hopeless, the one who really needs it. At least then it'll do some good.'

Rosika went into her private office and returned a few minutes later to provide us with the day's other memorable moment. She held in her hand a large, flat jeweller's case. She opened it to display a spectacular necklace of pearls.

'What do you think?'

Minor extravagance, the sort that everyone felt was too vanishingly small to trouble the Fords, had become the order of the day – people even joked about it – but this was something different. Louis and I stared stiffly at the pearls and said nothing. Rosika reacted with shock at the failure of her gesture.

'You think . . . ? I don't believe it. You think I bought them for *myself*?'

Louis and I shrugged and waited to be told otherwise.

'They are a gift,' Rosika nearly shouted. 'A gift for Mrs Ford, for all her support.'

'You're going to give those to Mrs Ford?'

'But you . . .' Louis looked at me for some hint of how best to go on. 'You bought them with . . . Oh, forget it. Whatever you think best.'

Rich or poor, most of us understand there is an etiquette to money, a way of handling oneself in its presence. Madame Rosika Schwimmer has never learned those rules. Where and how she lived before getting in with Henry Ford I don't know, but she seemed not even to suspect that such things existed. Perhaps she had some theory that explained why she alone, with the privilege of her cause, was exempt. That would have been in character, but I don't know – I never heard her say it. Like the laughter of President Taft on the Twenty-third Street Ferry, the incident sounded once again the warning bell. If the torpedoes didn't get her, then the money surely would.

The day dawned. There had been worry the night before as we lost sight of Marquis and guessed what he was up to.

But it all started well – not only had he failed to detatch our chief from the expedition, the net he had been sent to cut trawled him up too and we hastily arranged one more first-class cabin. I encountered him in one of the corridors as he struggled towards Madame Schwimmer's office.

'Well done, Reverend!'

He had his funeral face on and ignored me as he pushed on by.

With our leading man still in place I went down to the lobby to release copies of Mr Ford's departing statement to the press. Like the others, a work of Schwimmer and Lochner, it talked of the carnage depopulating Europe and the terrible slaughter of young manhood, of the secret assurances of thirteen envoys of belligerent and neutral governments, of the certain and universal desire for peace. Hardened hacks scanned it briefly before thrusting it into their raincoat pockets.

'So where's the boss?'

'All in good time. We don't sail till two.'

I checked out. Outside, the black five-car caravan that would take Mr Ford and his staff and family across the river to New Jersey had already assembled. The newsmen were gathering round it, trying to pump the drivers for information, and I had the satisfaction of having my Pierce-Arrows brought round and seeing them all follow me with their eyes as I motored off to Hoboken.

There was the *Oscar II*, her name painted in huge white letters against the middle of her black hull. White crosses were at the bow and stern and between them DANMARK in letters high as houses – visible, one hoped, through a distant periscope. Someone had already boarded and their peace banner hung over the rail showing the white knight of civilisation pacifically lancing the dragon of militarism. A red pennant fluttered from a mast with the word 'Peace' in white letters. Early delegates harassed the tourist conductors hired to bring order to the embarkation, and these in turn fretted over huge mounds of luggage. The first three stowaways had been detected and were being menaced in a corner by the harbour police. The smallest had been revealed when a dropped trunk cried out in pain. A tearful ten-year-old with a German accent explained he had been given ten dollars to hide in the trunk and say he was a spy when he got out.

'He told me he was a magician,' sniffed the boy.

I recognised the style.

'Sure he did, Hansel. His name's Prescott Schumacher and he works for the *Morning Herald*. You see him again you run away – got that? Here.'

Overtaken by the mood of the occasion, I gave him ten more and told him to get lost before someone made him a mascot.

The crowd swelled steadily until a carnival of five to six thousand persons was in full swing. The twin spirits of Ziegfeld and Barnum hovered invisibly over the chaos and took fleshly form in Lloyd Bingham, jester and energetic MC. In beret, smock and canary yellow spats he enjoyed to the full his greatest ever success, leading the cheers for every identifiable delegate as they came up the gangway, clowning the Kaiser, shadow-boxing the monster of war and conducting the band in endless repetitions of 'I didn't raise my boy to be a soldier'. Wielding an enormous megaphone, he made announcements of escalating grandeur as the minutes were counted down to the moment of departure:

'The Reverend Jenkin Lloyd Jones! Hurray for Reverend Jones!'

A man with a large white beard attempted to lead a prayer for peace, but was quickly drowned out by a chorus of Santa Claus jokes.

'Mr Louis B. Hanna, Governor of the great state of North Dakota!'

Governor Hanna, grim-faced and plodding as he ascended to the ship, brightened as he saw a friend in the crowd. He cupped his hands to his mouth and shouted down – 'What can I do? I've got relatives in Sweden I haven't seen for years!'

Again Bingham raised the megaphone to his lips.

'Mrs Inez Milholland Boissevain.'

A tall figure seized the instrument, causing Bingham to step back in amazement. As the band fell silent a powerful female voice sounded out across the seething quay. There was a passionate response – low, masculine booing and shrill female cheers. The speaker seemed highly satisfied and handed back the bright cone of metal with a flourish.

I shook off a panic-stricken squirrel as it ran up my leg. A number of the reporters had decided to add colour to the event by bringing their own props and these included squirrels, on the ground that Hoboken was where the 'nuts' were. A score of these hapless animals had been released and darted here and there, giving rise to shrieks of alarm when they tried to climb whatever dress or lady's coat most resembled a tree trunk. A dog set off in violent pursuit of one, others sped up the ropes and promptly infested the ship. A dozen remained incarcerated in bird-cages, awaiting the leading figures of the voyage. The menagerie was completed as a cloud of white doves emerged from a laundry basket only to escape the scene as fast as they were able. Women became hysterical. An epileptic had a fit.

'Mr S. S. McClure. Hurray for Samuel McClure!'

The fallen titan of the magazine business acknowledged a largely generous reception. Behind him, a brawl threatened to break out over whether 'Onward Christian Soldiers' was a suitable number. The first punch was about to be thrown when an electric tremor ran through the crowd. Heads turned, a way was made. Madame Schwimmer herself appeared, borne forward on a wave of noise and excitement, holding aloft the famous black shagreen bag as she made the only entrance of the day to be reported in the fashion as well as the news pages – 'Carrying her beaver-trimmed coat over her arm despite the chill and the commencing rain, Madame Schwimmer proved a model for the older woman of refinement, with a full skirt of black satin moire with a pleasing velvet ornamentation, the whole cut simply with two front gores and a plain French-gathered waist that was perhaps only a little too tight beneath the ribbon belt in the suffrage colours of yellow and white. A dove-grey blouse with a deep yoke collar of fine batiste and insets of real valenciennes completed an outfit of authority. The whole was highlighted with much passementerie of tarnished gold.' Male eyes saw it differently. One thought she had come as a magpie. Another recorded that '. . . the rotund Hungarian idealist entered into the costume party spirit and came as Lady Macbeth on her way to a free lunch'.

Bingham gave her the star treatment. She disappeared on stepping off the gangway, and then was seen a minute later, higher up at the rail of the first-class deck. To a storm of cheering and hooting and a certain quantity of laughter, she brandished her famous bag of secrets. Briefly, she invoked an ocean of blood and misery and the essential goodness of mankind before asking to be excused so that she could begin her work.

'The Reverend Samuel S. Marquis. Hurray for Reverend Marquis!'

Carrying in his hand a small, hastily packed valise, the joyless episcopalian climbed to the ship as tragically as to his own execution. Bingham stepped aside and presented him to the crowd with an impresario's sweep of the hand. Pilgrim Marquis was not tempted and passed on without saying a word. He spotted me and hesitated, glowering down to where I stood on the quayside, perhaps surprised and a little envious to see me still on dry land. Up to the last two or three days I had thought I would travel too. But then enthusiasm – or was it courage, or conviction? – started to slip away under cover of darkness. Each morning I awoke with diminished forces and began to wonder if I should not join the deserters myself. A more honourable course became possible when I found myself alone with Mr Ford on the last Wednesday at the Biltmore.

'You need a good man to stay behind, sir. Someone to direct the campaign at home while you're away.'

There was a lengthy silence while he considered the idea.

'You don't want to turn your back on Congress, sir. You know what they're like – someone should stay back to keep things on the boil.'

He began to tell me something about himself, stopped, shook his head and said, 'No, no – it's too late now. Fair enough, Mr Delavigne; you stay, I'll go.'

With the suggestion that my title be adjusted to Homeland Peace Secretary, the deal was done. Something deep down told me I had used up my luck with ships. The quayside was where I wanted to be and I was happy there, as the mercury plunged and the rain strengthened, as Lloyd Bingham clowned on and as Dean Marquis raised his hat to me from where he stood by the rail with his worldly, and rather sad smile. I wonder if we weren't the only two who had much of an idea what was going on. The Peace Campaign offered Henry greatness – that was its purpose – and it was Marquis's mission to take him home to his factory and make him small again. Of all the snakes in the grass they took with them on that ship, Marquis was the most dangerous and it came as no surprise to me that he was also, ultimately, the most successful.

'Mr Berton Braley, America's great popular poet. Hurray for the hayseed Homer!'

Berton scampered up the gangway, pulling after him a girl who vaguely resembled the one I had seen at the *Eastland* disaster back in the summer. He was going as correspondent for his magazine, but had just enough fame to be greeted as a delegate.

'Poem! Poem! Poem! Poem!' demanded the crowd.

The people's laureate chose his spot by the ship's rail, took a sheet of paper from inside his coat and unfolded it momentously.

> *From Europe we came to make a good New World.*
> *Now our old home groans with war's banners unfurled.*
>
> *We brought the best of Man to this land of peace,*
> *And now we return like well-intentioned geese.*

'Boo! Rubbish! Drown him for his bad verses!' shouted the envious newsmen on the pier. Berton held up his hand and managed a modicum of quiet.

> *Henry Ford's our leader, getting mankind on the move;*
> *He knows how the car and the human heart to improve.*
>
> *Off on the* Oscar *we go, to snowy Christiania*
> *Peace and love to bring by Christmas and New Yeeah.*

'Boooo!'

'Hurray! Out of the trenches by Christmas!'

Berton adjusted the arctic fox stole about the neck of his young companion, then embraced her passionately, eliciting a more general cheer.

From the pier, where he sat enthroned on his own small mountain of luggage, Dr Charles Giffin Pease looked on with a sharpened sense of injustice. He had boarded half an hour before with much hoopla from Bingham, but had now been forced to return to dry land. A pale, dominated woman stood by his side. She shivered and was occasionally tearful as Dr Pease gave the truth of the story to the clustered reporters.

'Personal reasons have frustrated my plans.'

Dr Pease was well liked in the news business. The nation's leading opponent of fumimania he appeared regularly as he rode the trains and trolley-cars of New York, plucking cigarettes from the lips of startled tobacco inebriates and dancing on the ashes as he delivered another lecture on the evils of tobacco, alcohol, coffee, tea, ginger ale, corsets, vinegar, meat, cocoa, chocolate, vaccination, excessive condiment intake, and the licking of artificially flavoured lollipops. Mr Ford is a believer in the Pease gospel and his invitation was one of the few he insisted on personally. Dr Pease was dressed as a cigar. Smoke drifted weakly from the crown of his brown plush top hat which emitted a hissing sound every time a raindrop scored a direct hit. It was discovered too late in the day that the good doctor did have one vice – her name was Annette Hazelton and she was snivelling and saying she wanted to go home. At the mention of personal reasons all eyes turned in her direction.

'Is Miss Hazelton your personal reason, Dr Pease?'

'I resent that. Miss Hazelton is my private secretary. A man of such extensive affairs as myself could not possibly do without assistance.'

'Would you still be sailing, sir, if you were married to Miss Hazelton?'

'You are a cocoa degenerate, young man. It has poisoned your sense of propriety. No man with a healthy mind and body would have asked such a question. Read this pamphlet before it is too late – and if you want to be useful call me a taxi cab.'

Purged of immorality, the *Oscar* was now fit to receive Mr Ford. He arrived half an hour before sailing when everything was complete and waiting only for him. From where I stood it was impossible to see the line of cars from the Biltmore draw up, or Mr Ford himself getting out. I knew it had happened because of the roar from the crowd – a huge, unanimous earthquake of noise that swept everyone together, whatever their real views of the Ford–Schwimmer project. Two minutes passed before, through a canyon of cheering people, Mr Ford appeared, blithely carrying the caged squirrel that had just been thrust into his hand. The noise grew and grew. At once solemn, ecstatic and humble, my employer's face showed what it meant to him. The joke of the squirrel failed utterly. Not only that – it was inverted, changing Mr Ford into a new St Francis. He paused obligingly for a photographer, holding up the cage to give him a better shot and peering in at the terrified animal. I looked again at the photographer as he thanked Mr Ford and moved away. It was true – there were tears in his eyes and suddenly the emotion was everywhere. Even the newsmen joined in, overwhelmed by the moment. Mr Ford shyly acknowledged the crowd. He seemed like a man reprieved, a man whose every need and prayer had been answered all at once. By his side, a disregarded and fearful Mrs Ford concentrated her attention on the squirrel. A bemused Edsel supported his mother by the arm. Behind these three Ray followed closely, with Louis Lochner two steps further back, dapper in his own new peace wardrobe and with authoritative attaché case in hand.

The Ford party embarked and took their place by the rail of the first-class deck. Rosika Schwimmer came out to join them. Reverend Marquis's hat was just visible in the background of the group. From another disturbance on the quayside an elderly Thomas Edison slowly emerged, leaning on the arm of the Great Commoner himself, the champion of neutrality, Mr William Jennings Bryan. Mr Ford seemed greatly relieved to see them and waved vigorously. After several minutes they appeared by his side on the deck, a trio of great Americans buoyed up on a new surge of acclaim. All at once

I saw the *Oscar* arriving rather than departing, the buildings different and the clothes of the same huge crowd slightly strange on the other side of the ocean. This Hoboken scene was a mirror image of how the Peace Ship would arrive in Europe. I made a sudden, exhilarating discovery, like a piece of maths I had struggled and struggled with and could now see as clear as day – success was guaranteed, it really would work and – who knows? – maybe even by Christmas too. Fireworks went off, paper streamers rained down from the ship. It all made sense.

Bryan made a booming, gesture-filled speech of which little could be understood. The sailing bell rang and the call went out – 'All ashore that's going ashore!' Mr Ford kissed his wife. Soon the well-wishers, a trembling Mrs Ford and the son were back on the quay. The gangway was rolled back, the hawsers cast off. A thick cone of breath shot into the air as the steam whistle shrieked, making some leap for joy and others cover their ears. The waters churned, and as the band played 'America the Beautiful' the gap between the *Oscar* and the pier slowly widened. Tugs nudged in at bow and stern and started to push her further out. Mr Ford threw American Beauty roses down to his wife, the last handful of blooms falling short and floating brilliantly on the murky water. It seemed that everyone on the ship, all the delegates, the students and the journalists too, was pressing against the shore-side rail and waving and shouting down to everyone below. Lloyd Bingham held to his post, miming limp and harpoon and the sighting of distant whales as a comic Ahab set out to catch and pull in his elusive obsession. Mr Ford moved to the stern from where he could be more easily seen as the ship turned to the sea. He stood there quite still, except for occasionally raising his hat and saluting his supporters. I took my eyes from him only once when distracted by a last caprice of the crowd.

'Jump! Jump! Jump! Jump!'

A bizarrely dressed figure whirled his arms and fell into the water, paper wings torn from his shoulders by the impact. Sounds of alarm and ridicule mingled as a harbour police boat turned and lazily rowed in his direction.

The *Oscar* slipped away down Ambrose Channel and the sounds of her excited, happy cargo became faint. A hazy bar of smoke rose from the single stack, drifting slowly southward in the calm air. Above, a weakness in the clouds cast down a brighter almost-sunlight on the ship. Mr Ford stood motionless by the stern rail, picked out in an electroplated gleam, an affordable altarpiece for the Age of Innocence, shrinking away in the direction of Europe.

Zero

I sensed that something was about to happen. And I sensed too – oh, terrible thought! – that it might not happen, that the smallest part of the mechanism was also the most essential, that if it failed, if I failed, humanity would fail. But what to do? How to prophesy in the very heart of Mammon?

Messages filled the air more thickly than ever. The cars in the street chattered to me as they passed. At night, above my head, the gun-barrel apparatus of the Milholland & Batcheller Pneumatic Despatch Tube Co. hissed and thumped without a moment's rest. At last the Word came to me. It was a cold night and I was stuffing a newspaper up my vest by the Forty-Second Street soup kitchen. I reached for another sheet and then, as lightning flickered in the cloudless sky, I saw the headline – *Ford Pledges All for Peace* – and I knew that he would achieve nothing without my help.

'Talk to Henry.'

'Excuse me?'

Another auto went by.

'Talk to Henry. Talk to Henry. Talk to Henry.'

I got straight down to work. I danced around my hat in Central Park, I learned new tunes on my squeeze-box, I swept the stoops of the idle rich, I made a new sign – Blessed are the Peace Makers – and held out a tin cup beneath it all hours of the day and many of the night. Before long I had enough for paper, envelopes, a box of steel nibs, a bottle of ink and a sheet of two-cent stamps. As the man said – give me a lever and I'll move the world. I wrote to the names I picked out of the papers. Theodore Delavigne seemed the most hopeful at first, though I was wrong about him. I wrote to Mr Lochner many times explaining how I had been invited to bring him together with the only man who could make peace. I wrote to Mrs Schwimmer, that wonderful, good woman, that great soul, and told her the door was open. I had cleared the way for them and if only she and her friend from Chicago would ask, they would receive. Three days later – it was cold and I was on the hunt for more insulation – I read the news that all my hopes had been fulfilled.

So you see, this is my doing, whatever anyone else might tell you. I go now to give it my blessing, winged as Victorious Peace, edging through the people who smile and cheer and clap me on the shoulders and urge me on because they understand. I step aside for a man dressed as a cigar coming the other way – these events often attract the benighted. I press on, anxious that I am too late. The whistle sounds and a great shout goes up. I hear the water thrash and the engines turn. The tugs sound their horns, the bands play. At last I am at the edge. There is the ship, there the man. It is the first time I have seen him – in the flesh, that is. Everything is perfect. The people cheer me on. Hope is on every face as they chant. Through a furled newspaper I address them –

My name is Mr Zero,
A thoroughly modern hero.
To swim for peace I go.
Splash! Cheerio!

I take a great run at it, clearing people out the way. One, two, three, four, faster and faster. Too fast now. Too late. Good! And a great jump from the edge and the water's far beneath me and the nuts are falling into it from all around, a brown hail-storm of nuts from them that know not Peace, and everyone's shouting and screaming and the squirrels are running all over the place and the newspapermen are laughing, but oh! let them, 'cos they're thinking too, they're writing in their heads and it will be in all the papers tomorrow, I know it will as I spread my arms and feel the wind beneath them, I know I've done it, it's working, Zero Stops the War! And then I'm flying and the gulls are beside me and I see the *Oscar* and it's all so right as I knew it would be and the *Oscar*'s upside-down and . . .

Ouff!

Cold! Cold! Cold!

But no! I'm swimming, slapping down the holy oil and water of Hoboken, and there's Henry at the rail, Saint Henry, King Henry, the sun is on him and I'm hailing him and he turns and I give him my all and he's going to take it to that poor dark place and it's going to be all right because I know it is now because it can't not be, and the water's getting thicker and I'm kneeling on it, I'm getting up on it as it helps me because the sun is on it too now and I know what that means. I'm going to stand on this water and run across these waves, I'm going to lay my hands on the *Oscar*, on her sainted iron that from this day forth will know no rust. I'm getting to my knees on this oil and water, I'm going to stride across these waters, peace beneath my feet and put it all in the *Oscar* and up to the deck plates and up through the shoes, feet and very bones of the sainted Mr Henry Ford, automobileer of the age, and into his dollars green as leaves and I'm standing now, Peace raises up her servant and the little boats are rowing after to cheer me on and Hey! lemmygo, lemmygo I'm gonna stop the war!

Inez

The first floor of a brownstone two blocks from Washington Square, and at a rent we might not be able to afford for much longer – a domestic scene of the espoused at breakfast in a quiet, childless household. I check the papers for my own name and pretend to be relieved when it is not there. *Germans Mass 500,000 Troops on Bulgarian Frontier; Carranza Nearer to Power in Mexico; Duma Members Arrested – Plans to Forestall Popular Demonstrations; British 'Blacklist' US Commerce; 10,000 Turks Wiped Out, p.2.*

'Have you read this, dear?'

'Mm?'

'A German submarine disguised itself as a British submarine and was then torpedoed by one of its own. Blew up and sank. Off Denmark.'

'How do you disguise a submarine?'

'It doesn't say, flags or something I suppose.'

'Under water?'

'Oh, Eugen – that's not the point. It's just terrible, appalling!'

'They certainly don't seem to have thought it through.'

'Can you imagine women doing that? Can you? It just couldn't *ever* happen!'

Half a minute of silence passes. I contemplate my husband – a cheerful, dark-haired Dutchman caught and reeled in two years ago while crossing on the *Mauretania*. My father thought I had taken leave of my senses – 'enamoured of an ass' was his first comment – but parents come round to these things in the end. I tell Eugen, calmly, that I will shortly be forced to throw something at him. I explain that it is probably already too late to avoid this incident, that I hope it won't do him too much harm and that when it does happen he should remember that it is really his fault. The mantel clock chimes the quarter hour and rouses him to sudden energy.

'I have to go. I'm seeing a man uptown about the coffee business. If he buys it we'll be on easy street – for a while anyway. We must go away somewhere – rest after all your excitement.'

He kisses me as he shakes himself into his coat and clips a good fountain pen to his inside pocket. On leaving the room he stops abruptly.

'No, that won't do. I'll run out halfway through the afternoon and not be able to think of anything else.'

He comes back and kisses me hard, pushing me until the chair tilts on its two hind legs. I put my fingers behind his head and stroke his ear with my thumb. I feel his hand on my breast, running slowly down to my waist and then over my thigh to burrow like a puppy into the warmth between. Suddenly, I'm weightless. I give a smothered cry of warning and throw my arm out to catch the edge of the table with enough force to make the knives rattle on their plates. I pull myself level as Eugen regains his balance.

'That's better. You won't make love to anyone else while I'm gone?'

'Not today,' I tell him.

'Promise? I won't be any longer than I'll have to be. I think Peter's coming soon. I'm sure of it.'

'Yes,' I say. 'Or Eugenie. Perhaps she'll come first.'

'Or Eugenie.'

He presses his lips to my cheek and leaves. Martha, who has been listening all the time, hears the sound of the door closing, comes in and asks if she may clear the table.

'Will there be visitors today, Mrs Boissevain?'

'No, Martha.'

I settle by the window and put my feet up. I take something to read but leave it closed in my lap, preferring to look outside. In the street people hurry and hold together the lapels of their coats. The clouds are paper white and threaten early snow. I think of Eugen, somewhere out there. I have been so lucky sometimes I can cry thinking about it, and I know it is wrong not to be happier than I am. It is my time to be unwell for a few days and a cavernous, echoing mood of review settles on me – my life becomes a space I can stand in and see all at once, the house that takes shape as its first great timbers are joined. My dear parents have a cuttings file that is already Bible-thick, but what does it all amount to really?

For years now you've known my name, perhaps even my face – the ardent child activist of the International Sunshine Society who grew up to be the Gibson Girl of radical politics. The convictions, like the features, were inherited – a provincial newspaper proprietor for a father, the title sold at a profit before moving on to dabble in the progressive wing of Republican politics. Once the Napoleon of the Manhattan Eleventh Assembly District, old men pushed him aside for conservatives, forgetting that he had been the first to organise behind McKinley's candidacy. Instead, it was Police Commissioner Roosevelt who made the headlines and then, with the help of an assassin's bullet, the White House. Later, when he had made something of himself, Father recalled standing by a young Henry Ford at the presidential funeral service. He shared a train with him until the change at Philly. He said the future hero of the five-dollar day was a strange man with little to say for himself. He spent much of the time reading a three-cent pamphlet called *A Short View on Great Questions* and making notes in the margins with a pencil. He said you wouldn't have guessed the way it turned out. It could have been different, Father always said – very different.

He left the front line of politics, but kept some of his friends. One of them was honest John Wanamaker, the inventor of the department store and former postmaster-general under Harrison. Father and Uncle John had a talk about the pneumatic tubes that blew the cash takings from Wanamaker's store here and there beneath the streets of Philadelphia. He said he'd have a go and in October 1897 the Milholland family Bible, wrapped in the Stars and Stripes, whooshed from the central post office to Produce Exchange, New York City in forty seconds, rather than a messenger boy's more usual seventeen minutes. In a few years fifty-four miles of mail tubes sucked and blew half a million letters around New York every day and I was the daughter of a very wealthy family.

The family farm was bought back. And then the old country made its call and life became transatlantic. From when I was thirteen you could show me a photograph taken inside any of the better liners and I would name the ship and tell you when I had last sailed on her and in which cabin. For a year I was Daisy Miller – *the* American girl in Budapest, Vienna, Berlin, Antwerp, Paris, Edinburgh, London. We settled in 4 Prince of Wales Terrace from where I walked to the Kensington High School for Girls and played with my brother and sister in Kensington Gardens. We went to see *The Mikado* and *Pirates of Penzance* and sang the songs at home as my mother played the piano and little Vida discovered she had a voice. We nodded to Mr Barrie in the park at the weekends and were there on the first night for Charles Frohman's production of *Peter Pan*.

Billy Marconi we met on the *Lucania* from New York to

London one fall. In the middle of the ocean he could send messages to Europe and North America at the same time. He showed us how it worked and the next morning my mother and I found a message from Father back in New York pinned to the ship's bulletin board. It is a Milholland family tradition that this was the world's first Marconi-gram. For the rest of the trip we treated the wireless like a private toy.

Billy became a regular visitor to our London home. He was a frequent faller-in-love and proposed marriage when I was seventeen and he a sumptuously established thirty. I accepted as lightly as the offer was made, our engagement lasting a year until I heard that he had married an Irish baroness and gone off to sell wireless sets to the generals of the Russo-Japanese war. I learned what silliness it is to talk of broken hearts and how much better to keep on old lovers as friends.

School ended, but Cambridge was stuffy and full of old maids too abjectly grateful to be there at all. Besides, they refused Miss Pankhurst the right to make a speech there so it would have been totally impossible for me. I got back on the boat and went to Vassar, where people listened to my mid-Atlantic accent and asked which part of England I was from. Captain of hockey, record-holder for the shot put, Romeo to another girl's Juliet, I was praised in the college magazine for my passionate balcony scene. Real passion came in the last year when President Taylor banned a suffrage meeting in college and it fell to me to lead the women of the new century across the road and into the cemetery where he had no authority. There we made the speeches among the graves of those who had lived and died in a man's world, without ever once having their voices heard. My romance with the press began the very next day – *Vassar Invaded!* – *Boadicea of the Ballot Brigade Leads the Way*, and a rather nice photograph underneath. I had found my cause.

That summer in London I marched with the suffragettes

on Women's Sunday and we filled the whole of Hyde Park. Back in New York I stepped off the *Lusitania* into a crowd of eager journalists.

'Were you not afraid in such an enormous demonstration, Miss Milholland?'

'Not me, but I think some men were pretty scared. Here we come, boys, ready or not!'

It was noticed that I had a certain effect on people and I was soon put to work in the movement. I observed the pickets in the shirtwaist strike and when the women were arrested I went with them to Night Court and told them their rights and gave evidence against the police. I collected money so they could eat and keep themselves warm during the lockout, and when they were put in prison Vida and I put ladders up against the wall and sang the suffragettes' 'Marseillaise' so they could hear it in the cells. In the end the employers gave in and I and my friends got all our cars together and the workers got in and we paraded through the garment district in triumph. WOMEN TAKE THE WHEEL, said the *Times*. The girls in my little 28 h.p. graduation present said it was the first time they had been in one. Only the Triangle Shirtwaist Company held out – the one that had started all the trouble in the first place. That was the one that burned down the next year, one hundred and forty six women and girls dying behind its barred windows and locked doors. In the papers I graduated again and became 'the well-known socialist agitator'.

Journalism seemed an obvious second string and I covered the 1912 Women's Suffrage Association for *McClure's* Magazine, writing an account of Jane Addams speaking. All the boys were in love with me and, which was more important, the cameras too. And so when it came to choosing a leader for the suffrage parade on the eve of President Wilson's inauguration everyone was kind enough to think of me. I was dressed all in white – 'the beautifullest suffragist in town' – and mounted on Grey

Dawn, stallion or gelding according to the sympathies of the newspapers. I carried the suffrage banner – Forward through the darkness! Forward into light!

The parade was to go from the Capitol to the Treasury where we would perform our allegory of the suffrage struggle. Almost at once it degenerated into a riot. The crowds for the inauguration the next day were huge and we could see hardly any police. There was a strong smell of drink in the air and within a hundred yards we were pushed together almost into single file and then stopped altogether. The abuse got louder, the gestures more vulgar. I understood when I saw a police officer looking the other way. I dug my heels in and Grey Dawn leapt forward scattering the cowards to left and right.

'Shame on you! Shame on you men!'

I don't think I'd ever had such excitement. I kicked away the hands that grabbed at my ankles and rode down the drunks to clear a way for the parade behind me. In two hours of battle we had still only made half the distance. Ambulances queued to remove the wounded, the overcome and the intoxicated. At last, a troop of cavalry came from Fort Myers across the river and cleared the avenue with a single magnificent charge. As I watched them, I wondered for the first time in my life if it wouldn't also be rather nice to be a boy. Then I arrived at the Treasury and dismounted and saw the flanks of my poor horse, slick with human spittle and the ash marks where the lighted cigarettes and cigar butts had found their target.

It was a few months later, in the summer of 1913, that I walked into the dining room of Holland House in the company of my good friend and onetime fiancé Marconi and his wife, Beatrice. It was there that I was first seen by my husband, Eugen Boissevain. Billy turned out to be a mutual friend. We were introduced and sat down to share the same table. It was thunder and lightning, or so Eugen told me. This Dutch-Irish businessman, coffee planter, big game hunter and former patient of Carl Jung (he was quick to reassure me that he was completely uncured) listened to me talk over plans for a trip to England and immediately abandoned everything that had brought him to America.

'I must come with you. I will come with you! Which ship? When does she sail?'

Before we set foot in England I had proposed to him, more than once. We went with the Marconis to their estate at Eaglehurst and there, in the topmost room of the tower, in sight and sound of the sea, we made love for the first time.

'It's yes, then?'

'Yes,' he said. 'Yes, my wife.'

We promised never to own each other, always to keep each other free. The newspapers back home were delighted – *World's Prettiest Suffragette Succumbs to Tyrant Man*.

Some sort of independence was in order and it took the form of a little two-bed flat at 35 East Thirtieth Street. Father still helped, and it was always possible to have someone come in to do my hair and nails for the evening, even though he grumbled at the bills. From there I tried to make my way as a laywer and Eugen worked hard to breathe some life into the struggling coffee business.

'We could go to Java,' he suggested one morning. 'Live on my family's plantations. Life is easy there.'

'Easy? For whom?'

We didn't talk about it again. Eugen told me I could do anything and I think I still almost believe him.

'You know,' he told me once after making love in the afternoon, 'I always wanted to look up to my wife, to admire her. When people say "This is the husband of Inez Milholland" I am very happy.'

I don't think I could have made a better choice.

The suffrage work continued – we mobbed Senator

O'Gorman's office on Wall Street, and danced the turkey trot all night at the victory party of the new pro-suffrage mayor. Freedom of the press was another front. I battled the Comstock laws for novels honest about human nature and some not very good moving pictures about the so-called white slave trade. I got myself nearly shouted down in a meeting of the NAACP when I told them that freedom for *The House of Bondage* also meant freedom for the likes of Mr Griffiths and his poisonous history of our nation. I began to feel quite grown-up, except for one thing – although I lectured on birth control I did not practise it and still no Peter and no Eugenie to join us.

I read the newspapers closer than most, but still the war was a shock. At the time I could not have been more surprised if the Black Death had broken out again, or if a dinosaur had hauled himself out of the East River and lumbered down Broadway. Jane Addams founded the Women's Peace Party and the new cause left me busier than ever. It became clear to me that war was only to be expected in a world where the women did not vote. The male was morally obsolete and incapable of restoring himself to health without help. Now, the ghastlier things get, the more desperately they need their women.

Personally, the war has cut my life in two and for now I have to live wholly as an American, stranded on one side of my transatlantic home. When it started it was the occasion of the saddest letter I hope ever to receive from Father. He wrote to me from London and explained why we had to give up our home there. He described the men loading the vans with furniture and the servants closing the shutters before being paid off and the young soldiers at drill among the daisies in Kensington Gardens.

I spoke from more platforms, marched on more parades, pressed on in the courtrooms against the prejudices of my own profession. Before, slow progress seemed better than none, but since the war started I can no longer tell myself that is enough.

I could not be busier and yet I get very low sometimes and ask if there is anything a woman can do to make a difference. I must have been in that sort of mood when I thought of my little Italian adventure.

In the spring I was still hopeful that Italy would stay out of the madness. I made a reassuring story for myself about such a culture never succumbing to barbarism and was very sad indeed when this proved to be just another delusion. I tried to cheer myself up by accepting a dinner invitation from Billy and it was then he told me that 'the call' had come and he was returning to direct the wireless operations of the Italian forces. As I had had a few successes in *McClure's* and *Harper's* I knew how little there was to being a journalist and I decided there and then to go with him and report the war. Eugen was wonderful – would one husband in a thousand have loved me enough to let me go just like that?

'Yes, you must go. You must fulfil your heart's desires! But I think I had better stay here and look after business.'

Money was tight, but I promised to get an exclusive, an interview with a king or a prime minister. A friend had told me I could get two thousand dollars for a piece like that and I saw no reason why I shouldn't. If Mary Roberts Rhinehart could make a living writing about night patrols in no-man's-land for the *Saturday Evening Post,* I could certainly do the same. Surely, there could be nothing more modern than that. On 22 May, Eugen and my tearful mother saw me off on the *St Paul.* Inez, *correspondante de guerre* – I was as excited as a child.

Although the papers had covered his voyage, the Marconi name appeared nowhere on the passenger list and Billy gave me all his personal papers for the duration just in case. Our captain thought it entirely likely that the Germans would stop the ship and take him off if they could. He personally censored every outgoing radiogram and assured us at dinner of his thoroughness.

'You will not be betrayed by your own invention, Signor Marconi – forgive me – Mr Smith. Not on my ship.'

Off Ireland we slowed. There was a service and wreaths were laid on the water where the *Lusitania* had gone down only a fortnight before. A steward told me how the *St Paul* had nosed through wreckage for an hour on her outward journey. He had seen a life-raft carrying a dead woman with her arms around a dead child. Only once we were safely in Liverpool did the Captain tell us we had been followed by a U-boat. I cabled the story to the *Tribune* and made the front page.

When we entered France the first struggle was to get press credentials from the authorities. I was a little embarrassed to discover that half of America had come with me. Seasoned veterans stood back and exchanged disobliging remarks as a younger crew of sports editors, baseball reporters, drama critics, book reviewers, gossip columnists and cartoonists waved their passports and posed dashingly in new riding breeches.

'Let me through,' drawled one of the onlookers to his friend, 'I'm from the *Philadelphia Ladies' Home Journal*.'

'Perhaps she's researching a piece on bandages.'

I asked if they were referring to me, but they just smiled, tipped their hats and walked away.

Billy, of course, knew everyone and he had agreed that we should meet up with Will Irwin as soon as the formalities were over. It was in his car that we were chauffeured all the way to Paris. My skin tingled all over as we pushed our way out of the port through fleets of ambulances and strange armoured cars. My first sight of injured soldiers lying on stretchers and the thrilling brightness of blood did something almost sensual for me and I regretted Eugen wasn't there to share it. I began to compose in my mind the passionate letter I would send him that night. We bumped over railway tracks and I looked out at the train that had just arrived. Red Cross nurses were lined up and being held back until the officers had all got off – the female repairers waiting on the male destroyers.

In the first hour we were stopped by so many sentries we nearly ran out of cigarettes to bribe them with. After that the military traffic thinned out and we passed through a succession of half-deserted villages where old men sat together on benches and young girls peered out like portraits frozen in window frames, bracing themselves for news, or hoping for life to start again in the form of a handsome German soldier. Paris was unutterably sad, hunkered down and only half alive, like an animal in winter. The streets had been thrown back to the eighteen-nineties with horses everywhere and only the occasional official or staff-officer in a car. At the sound of a motor people looked up, fearing a Zeppelin rather than an automobile. We lunched the next day at the American Embassy and coincided with a tetchy Jane Addams who had come straight from the Hague where the Women's Peace Party had just broken up. She was attempting to deliver the conference's resolution to the French government.

'We were going to post them,' she complained. 'A simple device allowing for both thrift and tact. The matter was nearly concluded when a brassy, rather eastern voice sounded from the back of the hall. Schwimmer is her name. I have had dealings with her before. All heart and rhetoric, I am sorry to say, and in two minutes she persuaded the conference to make personal embassies across the whole of Europe. A costly way of being ignored, I say. That is why I am in Paris, Mrs Boissevain. I am a postwoman. An emotional woman, Frau Schwimmer. Very emotional.'

I commiserated and tried not to smile. There is an age for adventure and Miss Addams has passed it.

The next day a slow, halting train took us south to where Billy and I would part – he to the business of war, I to record it. In Rome my opponent was the Ministry of the Interior on whose silence I waited as they considered my letters of introduction and my commissions from the *Tribune, Collier's* and others. I wasted my time in the Grand Hotel, typing pieces on charity kitchens and the courageous efforts of the American ambassador's wife between shaking my sheets from the balcony, counting the flea-bites on my skin and slowly falling out of love with Italy.

Frustrated, I helped myself to a seat in a train of officers going north. I toured the hospitals, passed round more cigarettes, admired the pieces of shrapnel the soldiers showed me and their X-ray photographs with the sharp, white shapes inside their ghostly bodies. I hated everything I saw of the war and wrote voluminously every night about its cruel stupidity. In Vicenza I met a mother of three sons. Not one of them is able-bodied and she was angry and humiliated that they cannot go to the war. She haunts the recruiting office and harangues the officials there, spitting on their enrolment forms when they reject her offer. Patriotic demonstrations are common and are fuelled by impossible quantities of wine.

I got closer to the *zona di guerra*. Fresher casualties were carried back from the front and sometimes the sound of artillery could just be heard. I pressed on – what right did I have to protect myself from what I might see there? I felt that I had to see it and, if I could, to bear witness to the very moment at which a life is violently lost. That would be something to come home with – new passion, new words on the stump. After doing my articles I wrote to Eugen every night, how what I sought was coming close, how it would make us both safe. 'Let me love myself first, Eugen. Then I will bring a child into the world.'

Nearer the fighting the army controls journalists more tightly. I found myself corralled in a farmhouse with half a dozen boorish newsmen and Guido, a charming army press officer who censored our despatches and promised an escorted trip to the trenches. I had to listen to anecdotes about 'correspondentesses' like the English girl supposedly found in sodden Flanders with sleeping bag, six pencils and a powder puff. I endured being told I wanted to see a battle the way a child wanted to see a pantomime. I filled my despatches with loathing for war and compliments for the gallantry of certain young Italian officers, men one would so easily fall in love with if one were not a married woman. Guido read, smiled and applied his rubber stamp before passing them on to the telegraph office.

When the day came for the trip to the front line the men squeezed themselves excitedly into two staff cars and then gleefully told me that regulations forbade women from attending the war zone. The next day notification came from Rome that I was immediately to return to the capital.

'Too bad, Sugar-Plum.'

The 'boys' contained their disappointment and played another hand. Guido obtained a forty-eight-hour extension for me over the weekend on which he was also due some leave. On my last night in the north, more comfortably quartered in the Hotel Vicenza, I opened my door to him and we spent a long and delicious night together. He was very beautiful, and sweetly conventional – we were already standing in each other's arms and quite naked when he stopped and took his hands off me and asked about 'Mr Boissevain'.

'You must not worry, Guido. I will tell him everything.'

'That is all right in America? What a wonderful country.'

I received a letter from him just before I was expelled – more gratitude than love and all the better for that. Briefly, the war seemed a little smaller. He says he will come to live here as soon as there is peace, if he is still alive.

In Rome the Minister of the Interior frowned at me over a stupendous desk. I accused him of conspiracy.

'It was the other journalists, wasn't it? The men put you up to it and you were happy to go along with them. Why not?

Men do not want us to see what they are doing. They want to war in secret and still be welcomed home by their women. I have seen why they want to keep it a secret, and I will tell the truth. That is why you have recalled me.'

The Minister pushed an extract from a *Tribune* article across his desk. I read it.

'So?'

'You tell the people of New York the only brave Italian is a drunk Italian.'

'No – I tell them the drunker they are the braver they are.'

'A nicety.'

'You can't say you haven't seen it for yourself. Don't you ever tell the truth? Look – we're alone. Tell me now you know it is true. Who would ever know?'

'The readers of your newspaper. Signora, I have a war to fight. Let us meet again when the world is a happier place. For now, I regret that I must compel you to go home.'

He stood, kissed my hand and returned my passport with ten thousand regrets and a cancelled visa.

'This will be good for you, yes? This little adventure.'

He was not entirely wrong. But there was unpleasantness too – a letter from Irwin blaming me for Italy banning all correspondents from neutral countries, and another from Eugen which I read on the ship back. 'Dearest Nan, I know I should be more modern. I am. I believe in it, but sometimes it is too hard. Damn that stinking Latin macaroni monkey! Damn him for taking what is mine! I see myself shooting him. And if I ever met him and really did it, I know I would be proud. I am sad and frightened. What of Peter, of Eugenie? Are they safe? Will they be mine?' The answer to that was clear before the end of the voyage – he had nothing to fear, or hope for.

So there I was, back in New York in the last week of September, walking down the West Thirty-fourth Street pier and getting more than my fair share of the scavenging newsmen. The Minister's prediction was abundantly proven – being expelled from Italy was my best ad yet. Everyone was so excited it would have been selfish to talk of failure.

'Miss Milholland!' (They still call me that here.) 'Inez, Inez! Over here!'

I turn into the flashes and answer the question.

'Because men fear to make peace more than they fear war, that's why. Give me supreme command of the press of Italy, or of any warring country, and I will guarantee to turn the sentiment of that country for peace inside a month.'

How desolate I felt as they wrote it down. And it was no help the next day to be back on the front pages under someone else's byline, still emptily making the news rather than reporting it.

So this is what I am, the plant that grows in this easy soil. And these are the 'adventures' from which I must rest as Eugen goes uptown to sell a failing coffee-import business and I sit here with my feet up by the window, watching the first white flakes fall. Of course, there has been no end of friends to welcome me back, and when they say how good it is of me to be here for the suffrage referendum I go along with them and pretend it was all planned. I speak tonight at Cooper Union – back up on my soapbox and banging away at the forces of evil. I'll put on a good show for the cause and never let on to anyone that it is no substitute for war.

The doorbell rings and Martha goes to answer it. I feel a cold draught of outside air as I listen to the exchange and try to make out what is being said. The cadence of her words is repeated more forcefully.

'Martha?'

She comes into the room.

'Some crazy man wanting to sweep the steps for a nickel.' She raises her hand to the side of her head and makes that uncharitable gesture. 'I told him I keep them clean enough, thank you, and I wouldn't want him touching them anyhow.'

'Give him a quarter, Martha.'

She looks at me as if I must be every bit as mad as the vagrant shivering out on the stoop.

'If you say so.'

I hear the outer door close and then see the man on the sidewalk. Dressed in ragpicker's motley he looks up to the window and doffs a green lady's hat with the quill end of a feather just poking above the band. I return the salute as he walks out of sight.

Berton

Queen of *Herland*

Inez, Inez, newest of New Women!
Amazon, Androgyne, Outdoor Pal;

To all your smilings
We are as iron filings;

Under your powers magnetic
Slaves quite pathetic.

Inez, Inez, you were loved by Marconi,
But his love was too tele-phoney.

You gave your heart to suffrage,
But it wasn't enoughrage.

Then, my dear, you married a Dutchman
And the hearts of your lovers turned to Edam;

Happiness for you, I hope, and a life of ease.
But for us — hard cheese!

One of my better ones, I think — beauty brings out the best in me. Not a payer, though, not the versified World's Series or the right charm at last to crack that long dry spell at *Vanity Fair*. One for the locked cabinet. I close my notebook and slip it back into my pocket, leaving my hand in there to protect it from the cold.

A grey, steady, medium swell extends to the horizon and above it a blank sky save for one patch of half-hearted brightness where the sun is concealed. I look out on this scene, the middle of three muffled statues — a trilby-hatted padre from Detroit on one side and one of the guys who's organising this whole thing on the other. I would ask his name if he hadn't told me three times already.

'Better weather today,' says one of the statues. The other two make affirmative noises.

Twenty feet along the deck Inez Milholland — or is it Mrs Boissevain? — leans on the rail and frames her profile against the western sky. Unhusbanded, fiercely suffragettical and emphatically anti-prohibition (also rumoured to be radical in matters of the heart), she has only enemies and admirers and nothing at all in between. Another glass of champagne, which she early declared to be the only effective remedy for *mal de mer*, is in her hand.

'It's still working, then?' I ask her. She smiles but says nothing. I feel foolish and look back at the sea.

A door bursts open and there appears on deck a large man making gestures as if he has just entered from the wings of a stage to the accompaniment of a drum roll and a few notes on a trombone. He is dressed to resemble a college football coach and has a stopwatch hanging from a lanyard around his neck. Despite his considerable bulk he runs energetically on the spot.

'What! Not laughing? That's not allowed. Captain Bingham's order of the day. Here.'

He hands out menu cards with the shipping line's crest at the top, but the word 'Entertainments' printed just below.

'Deck quoits at two – second round of the tournament. It's gonna be a hot one. Will the sophomores win a clean sweep, will wisdom prevail over youth? Charades in the smoking lounge after dinner. Plenty of time to work on your acts, gentlemen. Everyone loves charades. Say, did you hear?'

He looks behind, then leans towards us with his hand shielding one side of his mouth.

'We're off course – Miss Beautiful back there was standing too close to the compass.'

He plucks my menu card from my hand and turns it over.

'Submarine competition – first one to see Fritz poking his nose out of the water, you note it down. Win a life preserver – it's the only one we got! No prizes for torpedoes. Hup, hup! Gotta go!'

He explodes with a messy sneeze, says 'Oh, my' to himself and trots off, wiping his hand on his jersey.

The intervention leaves us speechless and my two companions more morose than before. The younger man checks his watch and says he has a meeting to prepare for. As he leaves, I notice that under cover of Bingham's tirade of cheerfulness someone else has arrived to take the air. The lean, life-worn figure of Samuel McClure surveys the sea from a position by Miss Milholland's elbow. They talk together too quietly to be understood, the movement of the ship moving the thick merino cloth of their coat sleeves together and apart in slow rhythm. Inez laughs and throws her empty champagne glass into the sea. Together they go inside, McClure guiding her through the narrow doorway with a fatherly hand between her shoulders. Five years ago he was a man I wouldn't have let out of my sight – one good word from McClure could make a man's career – but now I am merely curious.

I turn to the autoville bishop and nod at the empty recliner.

'That man – I can't let him tell me again – what *is* his name?'

'Lochner – La Schwimmer's second fiddle.'

'That's the one. Seems a nice guy, if a little nervous.'

He says nothing to this, but instead looks at the spot newly vacated by Inez and then at my pocket. He asks, and with a tone I don't quite like: 'Was that inspiration you experienced a moment ago, Mr Braley?'

'Pardon me?'

'When I saw you writing in your notebook.'

'Even a married man can be a poet.'

'I don't doubt it. How is Mrs Braley?'

'It's the swell – it doesn't agree with her. To be honest she doesn't take to ships at all.'

'That's too bad – especially on a honeymoon.'

Unexpectedly, he takes a hip flask from his coat and offers it to me.

'Will you take something for the cold?'

A mouthful of good brandy slips down and starts to fan out towards my fingers and toes, and that other extremity too.

'And Mr Ford?' I ask, as if out of politeness and wishing also to avoid the question of whether there is a spouse I should be asking about.

'Well enough, last time I saw him.'

I'd like to press him, maybe get a bit of a scoop here (the word is that this Marquis fellow is one of the few who really knows what's going on), but there's a warning in his tone and a fixed stare at the horizon. I should give him something.

'You know that Inez girl?'

'We were introduced yesterday.'

'Rotten journalist.'

'Mm?'

'Shocking. She sent pieces in to my magazine. We had to wring the tears out of every despatch before we could read them. Then we laughed so much they got wet all over again. Editor spiked every last one of them. Don't get me wrong – lovely girl, looks great on a horse. But, you know – enthusiastic.'

He tells me he used to be enthusiastic and keeps on looking at the sea.

'Bet I know what you're thinking,' I say.

'Slug of brandy says you don't.'

I look out on the same queasy grey and think of what's to come and of what lies two decks down, waiting for me.

'You're thinking "What in God's name am I doing here?" – if you'll excuse the expression.'

He hands me his flask. I drink and join him in the same line of thought.

Well, I suppose Mr Henry Ford had quite a lot to do with it, and pure chance too, and a war and a lack of dollars and a timid heart that needed something big to set it working the way it should. Perhaps you know that old story about John Barrymore and the San Francisco earthquake? John came to with the pieces that used to be his hotel collapsing around him. Somehow he got out alive and was wandering the streets in his nightshirt when some troopers conscripted him for a clearing gang. On hearing all about it his uncle remarked – 'Just like John. It took a convulsion of nature to get him up in the morning and the United States Army to put him to work.' Well, it was kind of like that with me and marriage – it took a European war and a rich man's scruples to make it happen.

I'd made a false start on the business back in the summer and ever since stammering to a halt in Chicago with the upturned hull of the *Eastland* as a backdrop I had never ceased to carry that ring with me. I had learned something about timing, but also something about myself that made me realise it might never happen without a little outside help. Nothing in the intervening months made a difference. I was still selling six or seven verses a week and getting a little more reporting work on the back of the *Eastland* story, but was nowhere near what any respectable father would consider a 'prospect' for his daughter. I liked Marion just as much, and she still seemed to like me. And so along we went, smoothly enough one weekend in two.

Late in the fall the Ford story began to break and I saw my old friend's name up there on the front page of the Detroit papers. 'Good for you, Theodore,' I said to myself. 'Nice to see someone making a living.' At that time there was no reason why it should have anything to do with me and I thought no more about it. It was a good few weeks later, just after the last of the charming Inez's hymns to suffering humanity had come in over the wires from Italy and been put out of its misery, that the story seemed to catch fire in a whole new way. It wasn't clear to me exactly what had happened, but somehow someone had got through and the talk turned to money. That was interesting enough, but then the whole ship business started and the telegrams of invitation. Now there have been many 'hottest tickets of the century' over the last fourteen years and eleven months – most of them heavyweight boxing bouts – but here was one that really deserved the name. As human nature is not at its best in proximity to a hot ticket, I lost out to a lesser man as far as the *Collier's Magazine* berth went. My first thought was to call my old friend Bill Hawkins at UP and remind him how much he owed me.

'Berton,' he said to me, 'the whole world has gone mad and I've decided to join them. As far as I can see it makes about as much sense sending a poet over there as anyone else on that damned fool ship. Good luck to you, my friend.'

No dice with Bill. It was then I saw that Delavigne had done the wise thing and ditched journalism for being Henry Ford's Peace Secretary, whatever that was. I put in a call for old times' sake.

'Theo, you old devil! How you do land on your feet. What's the secret? Berton. Berton Braley. *Collier's Magazine*. Used to be staff poet for *The American Machinist*. Course you do! Oh, you had me going there for a moment.'

We caught up on the last six months.

'Listen, Berton,' he said to me. 'It's about the ship, isn't it? It's the peace thing?'

'Glad you raised it, Theodore. Get me on and you'll always be in my prayers.'

Three long seconds of silence.

'You really think it's a good idea for you to go, Berton?'

My turn to pause – translating silences can be tricky.

'You know something about this, Theo? There's something you know and I don't?'

'Nothing. It's what it seems. You've read it all already.'

'U-boats? The Germans?'

'Berton – '

'You're going?'

'Absolutely. Safest ship on the ocean. You want to get over there, it's the only way to go.'

'You can do it for me? To tell the truth I need this. It's the poem business – I don't know, maybe it's the war or something, but the bottom's fallen out of the light-verse market. There are other things too.'

'You still got that girl?'

'Sweet as ever.'

'You're not trying to escape from her, are you?'

'No, no – that's not it at all.'

'So what about two tickets?'

'It's possible? You can really do it?'

'All I need is an address – oh, and her name.'

The next weekend was a married weekend. We met at a little place in New Jersey and booked in as Mr and Mrs Trenton. It was there, in room 13, behind curtains half drawn on a view of the back lot and the gloom of a late November afternoon, that I moved my hand over her shoulder and down the long, sweeping dip of her back – that line of lines that she hid so very slightly under the muslins and taffetas of her fashion drawings. Over that rolling fleshscape I looked with one eye at a bleak room – my pants crumpled on the threadbare rug, my jacket hanging from the chairback with the lump in one pocket where the weight of a boxed ring was slowly wearing through the lining.

'I might be going on a trip.'

'Mm?'

'You could come with me.'

'Is it the weekend after next?'

'It could be several weeks, maybe months – who knows? We might never come back, Marion.'

'Where?'

'Europe.'

She turned over on her side before wriggling back into me. We waited while a train went by.

'Where in Europe?' she asked sleepily.

'At a location to be decided.'

'Have you done something wrong, Berton? Do you have police trouble?'

'Don't be silly. It's the Ford Peace Ship, the campaign to stop the . . .'

'That thing! The *Enquirer* says they're a bunch of nuts.'

'Well, there you go – you've already read about them. Nuts make good copy. It's an opportunity, Marion.'

'But weeks?'

'Think of it as an adventure. Come with me on an adventure, Marion.'

I kissed the back of her neck persuasively.

'You must be thinking of your other girl.'

'What?'

'I have a job, Berton. I work for a living – have you forgotten that?'

'You're good at your job, aren't you?'

'Yes, I am.'

'So get another when you get back.'

There was a pause. She turned to face me, arranged my hair with her fingers, hooked one leg over me and squeezed.

'Will I need one?'

I looked straight into her eyes and she looked into mine with a steady, competitive stare. Had she been through my pockets? Did she know what was in there? I backtracked through our movements since we booked in. It was possible – there had been unguarded moments.

'I want you to come with me, Marion.'

'Do you, Berton?'

'I do.'

'I will.'

'You have a passport?'

'You think I should?'

Two weeks later we paid off our cab on the edge of a huge carnival of chaos in Hoboken. Marion got into the spirit of it, delighted to have so many people to admire her. She pushed ahead and I followed on, pursuing the brilliant white flash of her fur like one rabbit on the heels of another. I'd say it took a good twenty minutes for us to fight our way through to the ship and when we got there it was no more organised. As we waited to show someone our invitations a shadow passed over us and we looked up.

'Oh, look Berton! Look! I can see one of ours.'

An enormous pile of suitcases and steamer trunks was being hauled up in a rope net.

'We're going Berton, we're going. It's really happening.'

She kissed me as if we were the only people there. Everyone was looking and she enjoyed that. I noticed for the first time that the whole thing was as much a fashion show as a peace campaign. Everywhere was the newest and the best and I couldn't help wondering if we were to be the poorest people on the ship. Where had all this money come from? I picked out Theodore Delavigne from the crowd. He was further away from the ship and standing on something that put him two or three feet above the other heads. I waved.

'Hey, Theo. Theo!'

He turned and saw us.

'We always meet on quaysides. D'you think there's something in it? How are you?'

He gave me the thumbs up.

'We'll see you on board,' I shouted.

He smiled and brandished his hat.

We climbed up most of the gangway to where we had to wait behind a group of students as they had their invitations checked and were given directions to their cabins. They were steadily sorted by gender, the young ladies being sent forward and the men aft. It was our turn to present our credentials.

'Braley. We're together.'

'Good afternoon, Mr Braley.'

The strong Scandinavian accent seemed to confirm that an adventure was about to begin. Marion was behind me looking the other way and happily waving to the crowd which responded as if it knew who she was.

'This is incredible,' she laughed.

I jumped as a booming voice announced my name through an enormous red megaphone. There was another indiscriminate cheer from below.

'But we have just a single cabin here. There is a mistake?'

The official was showing me a piece of paper with names

handwritten in among printed Danish. I noticed his peaked cap and the single line of gold along the top of the eye-shade.

'No mistake. That's us.'

I held out my hand for the return of our documents, but it wasn't going to be that easy. The man examined Marion's new passport.

'You have been married recently, perhaps. Since 23 November, yes?'

Well, sometimes a very small last push is all that's needed and that happened to be it. I got down on one knee. I felt the cold dampness of the deck seeping through my trousers as I fumbled for the ring. There really couldn't be any going back, certainly not after Marion turned around from waving at the crowd and saw me there, looking up at her with God only knows what sort of an expression on my face.

'Berton?'

'Marion Rubincam, you are indispensable to my happiness and I . . . well . . .'

I coughed and felt like I'd swallowed a hair.

'I'll do my damnedest not to disappoint you, Marion.'

She pushed her finger through the ring while down on the pier one of the bands segued into the wedding march. And that was that. I have revisited the moment a good few times over the last two days. I tend to change some things – my own part, mostly, and I like to remember Marion as more surprised than she really was.

The chief steward, or whoever he was, was only partly satisfied.

'This is progress, Mr Braley, but it is not yet marriage, I think.'

'Look, bud, neither were Adam and Eve – it's the thought that counts, right? Anyway, what does it matter to you? You're not telling me you haven't seen a bit of life on this ship.'

'It matters nothing to me. In fact, sir, my staff would rather

not have to clean the bridal cabin, but there are unusual char-
ter conditions. Our . . .'

He flicked through his papers a trifle self-consciously.

'Yes, here we are. Mr Henry Ford wishes to run, as I believe
it is said in English, a "very tight ship". Two passengers have
already been asked to leave.'

The man nodded toward the pier and I looked down on
the ludicrously attired Dr Pease and the sulky young woman
by his side and the hungry journalists all around them.

'He threw them off?'

'Mr Ford's bodyguard escorted them ashore.'

'Oh, well – at least we'll be able to have a smoke in peace.
What do you say, Marion, could there be a better start than
this? Shall we go the whole hog?'

'The whole damned hog, Berton!'

She threw herself into my arms and I held her tight, pressing my cheek into the warmth of her neck as I stared into the
beady black eyes of an arctic fox. From that point on I knew
nothing of the remaining speeches or the last stages of the
send-off or how the *Oscar* made her way out of port. Marion
and I were inside, the subjects of a marriage arranged as summar-
ily as a frontier hanging, but very strange and delightful and
highly auspicious for all that.

It being a peace expedition there was no shortage of clergymen aboard. A conclave was held and a white-bearded
unitarian found who was willing to do the job. The Reverend
Jenkin Lloyd Jones presided over the dearly beloved who
crammed tight as immigrants into the main saloon. Mr William
Jennings Bryan was there, smiling on the proceedings exactly
as he does from all those countless newspaper photographs.
And at the last moment, just before the crucial words were
pronounced, I saw the face I was looking for, the lean, American
features of Mr Ford himself as he slipped in and joined the
back row of the congregation. Like a child confronted with

the reality of a monument after years of revering it in a school-book, it was all I could do not to point and exclaim and interrupt Reverend Jones in a way that could never have been forgiven. Ford was there nevertheless, his presence was with us, and his benediction.

'By the power vested in me by the states of New York and Illinois . . .'

There was a loud whisper from someone I couldn't see.

'Hey, aren't we in New Jersey?'

'Shut up for Christ's sake or we'll never get out of here.'

'. . . I now pronounce you man and wife.'

I kissed my bride. Marion had been persuaded to part with her fox fur for the duration of the ceremony and had left it on a bench at the side of the saloon. Mercifully, she could not see it at that culminating moment. I could, and was forced to observe a squirrel, inspired perhaps by the epithalamial spirit, crouch low over the soft white fur and knead the stuff with accelerating urgency before pressing down its trembling squirrel loins. The creature's tail reached a pitch of ecstatic vibration in the moment before it was swept from its partner's back by someone wielding a large hat.

'Shoo! Get away, you filthy little thing!' commanded an outraged Bostonian matron.

It ran up the curtains and disappeared. I quickly kissed Marion again to prevent her from turning around and because my own mind was turning hungrily to the next stage in the drama.

There was some debate about the legitimacy of our union and I feared a further delay. A harassed Captain Hempel looked at his watch and said that if anyone was worried he could do the whole thing again as soon as we passed out of territorial waters. Mr Bryan had a more practical argument – namely that the 'all ashore' was being sounded and that if Marion was no legal bride he would miss the chance to kiss her before getting back to dry land. This won the day and we were man and wife by common consent whether or not in the eyes of the Lord. Mr Bryan got his kiss, but Mr Ford had already left the scene.

We were declared to be good omens, the lucky charms of the expedition. A tumultuous escort accompanied us to the bridal cabin and the key was ceremoniously handed over. Once in, we locked the door and lost no time in consummating what must be the most modern and American marriage ever made. I got an answer to a question that had been bothering me – is it different when a man makes love to a woman who has just become his wife, I mean a woman he already knows in that way? Well the answer is, surprisingly – yes.

'Well, Mrs Braley?'

'Very well, thank you, Mr Braley.'

'Did you see Mr Ford there?'

'Not knowingly.'

'Oh, come on, Marion.'

'What do you mean – how would I know what he looks like?'

'Well, he was there. He came in specially, just at the right moment. Marion, we were damned near married by Henry Ford himself!'

Time passed, the porthole went black. Now and again there were sounds of considerable excitement from other parts of the ship, but neither of us was at all curious to know what was happening there. Eventually we were disturbed by a tentative knock. Marion put on her new silk kimono (an unreturned sample from a department store), answered the door and came back with a brown derby hat. We sat together on the bed and looked inside. There was a note that said 'From the Ford Peace Delegates and Press with all best wishes for the future'. We unwrapped the red-spotted handkerchief and found inside enough five-, ten- and twenty-dollar gold pieces to fill Marion's cupped hands. She picked them up and let them tumble musically back into the hat.

'How kind people are.'

Marion let the kimono slip down around her ankles and got back into bed. I started at once to curl myself around the warmth of my new wife but she moved away suddenly, put her hand flat over her navel and looked up at the ceiling. There was an anxious expression on her face, as if she was asking herself a difficult question.

'Are we moving? Do you feel right, Berton?'

'It's love, gorgeous. The power of love.'

I took an ear-lobe between my lips and paid no attention at all to the rising sound of the wind. She pushed me away, raised her hand to cover her mouth and groaned.

'Need a rest?'

She nodded silently.

That was two days ago and in that time I've explored everything there is to explore on this ship, human and mechanical. I've endured all manner of barely decent enquiries about the first night of my marriage, met up with a few old friends, made plenty of new ones, and a handful of enemies too. I've even radiogrammed a few reports to my employers back home. And now here I am in the company of a gloomy Dean Marquis of Detroit, somewhere in the middle of the Atlantic ocean. Lloyd Bingham's absurd talk comes back to me and I find myself squinting at a patch of sea I don't like the look of, as if a submarine really could be just beneath the surface.

'I'd be pleased if you would call me Samuel, Berton. There doesn't seem much point in talk of "Reverend" or "Doctor" or whatever out here.'

'All in the same boat, eh?' I say lamely.

'That's one way of putting it.'

'This whole thing going to work, d'you think? D'you

really think anyone will listen, that the war'll stop?'

'I suppose it will have to some day.'

Another mouthful of brandy goes down before I speak again.

'That marriage — was it really kosher?'

I get worried as Samuel thinks about this for a long time, like he's going through a whole list of problems in his mind.

'Well, Berton, you're here now. You really want my advice?'

'Yes sir, I do.'

'Don't ever ask. You had more clergy there than a royal wedding and everyone heard you say yes. Let that be enough. Question it and all you'll do is make a lot of lawyers even richer. And good luck.'

'Thank you, sir. I appreciate that. Wind's getting up again. Will I see you at dinner this evening?'

'It doesn't seem to affect me.'

'Until then, Samuel.'

I take his words with me down below and let myself quietly into the bridal cabin. With the shade drawn over the porthole and a single dim night light burning, Marion's sleeping form, stretched face down on the marriage bed, stops me quite still and tells me something new about beauty. I sit down by her side and peel back the sheet. The shoulders, the line of the back rising to spread in perfect buttocks — if there is one thing in the life of a man he can never tire of, this wondrous shape must surely be it, God's never-failing covenant against boredom. I put my hand there and press gently. Warmth, softness. Marion wakes and makes a noise like a cat with its tail in the door. She waves one arm violently behind herself and slaps me away.

'You're made of ice! Are you *trying* to kill me? Is this terrible ship not enough?'

I say I'm sorry. She fumbles for an empty bottle of patent medicine on the night table and it drops to the floor. She pulls up the sheet and turns to look at me. Her face is nausea-white and snake-framed in unwashed hair. But it's the voice that is more strangely changed, straight from twenty years into a spoiled future.

'Have you been drinking, Berton Braley?'

Ray

Mr Ford often sees something in a newspaperman I don't and I've never come to like that particular breed. When I first came across Mr Theodore Delavigne he wasn't much to look at or listen to. Then in no time he's going round in a fancy car and with more money than he's worth and I start to hear about his qualities from Mr Ford himself. Well, I suppose he'd crossed the line and come over to our side and so I tried to like him, but it still kind of rankled when he was the one sent to tell me.

'Ray,' he said, right of the blue. 'You're going to Europe.'

'What? But I ain't done nothing.'

'Mr Ford needs you.'

'In Europe? Why? I can't even speak the language. What use . . .'

'It's all right, Ray. Mr Ford's going too. You'll be with him.'

'Mr Ford's going to Europe?'

'That's right and Mrs Ford would like you to go with him.'

'Oh yeah? How would you know?'

'Well now, Ray, I just heard — that's all.'

'To the factory in England?'

'No, not to England.'

'In France?'

'Don't think so, not at the moment anyway.'

'Then where?'

'Well, we don't know yet, but it will be somewhere in Europe. He's going to stop the war.'

Then it all came out and I can't say I was pleased.

'Listen,' I said to him, 'is that a good idea?'

Delavigne didn't seem too sure himself. In fact, he wasn't at all sure. Then I find out later that he's the one behind most of those pieces in the papers, that he writes the words, words I never heard Mr Ford use, and makes him say all those big things like he can really do it any time he wants. That's what I mean about newspapermen.

'One other thing,' he tells me before he goes back into the Biltmore. He taps me on the side of my jacket. 'They don't like guns.'

'What're you talking about?'

'Those Europeans over there – they don't like guns.'

'*They* don't like guns. Tell me it's a joke.'

'I mean off the battlefield, Ray. I'm not telling you your business, just be discreet that's all I'm saying. Mr Ford shouldn't be embarrassed.'

'Well it won't be *me* who does that.'

And so in no time I find myself on the deck of this rust-bucket having just fought my way through something that looks for all the world like a revival in a lunatic asylum. The papers say it's a nut house and guess what? – you get here and they don't even have the half of it. Mr Ford is out front where he can be seen and I feel better now I've got him on the ship. Young Edsel is at his side looking pretty happy at the prospect of getting out from under his father for a few weeks, or months, or – who knows? – maybe for ever. Mrs Ford is on the other side preparing to go ashore. She has an expression on her face like she's about to put her husband over her knee and spank him and the only thing stopping her is other people. I look around to see what we've got. Schwimmer is there, close enough to be intruding on the family group. Mr Lochner holds back at a more respectful distance. Then there's Dean Marquis, spotless, giving nothing away. I concentrate on Mr Ford, but can see Marquis looking at me all the time. When I look back he turns away after a fraction of a second. Delegates I don't know are everywhere, and I'm trying to keep an eye on all of them at once. Photographers start pushing over the best spot and journalists are muscling in from the lower deck – men whose luggage consists largely of hot-water bottles filled with whisky.

The whistle blows for the last time. Mrs Ford has to go and I make sure I'm by her side. Schwimmer comes forward with a simple-minded smile on her face like she's about to hand out a Bible tract. She almost stands right in her way, but Mrs Ford just goes on by without seeing her and I follow close behind.

'I'm relying on you, Ray,' she tells me just before stepping off the ship. 'I'm relying on you and Dr Marquis.'

'Yes, Mrs Ford,' I say, though without really knowing what she means.

She and Edsel walk down to the pier and almost as soon as their feet touch the ground I feel the engines start. The *Oscar* eases out from the pier and I think 'Oh, Christ! It's really happening after all.'

What's left of the first day goes quickly. It's hard to think of Dr Marquis and myself as a team but things seem to work out all right. He tails Mr Ford around the upper decks while I sort out the problems below and start studying the passenger list and putting faces to names. I take time to learn where the wireless operator lives and find a good-humoured American who tells me his story about how he was taken on in New Jersey at the last minute and is as surprised to be here as I am.

Some joker in charge of the cabin allocation puts Marquis above the coal bunker at the far end of the ship from Mr Ford, who also has to change on account of a wedding breaking out and the use of the bridal suite messing everything up. I eventually find three cabins together at the end of a corridor and kick out a bunch of old maids and one looker who seems happy enough to move on. Now no one can get to Mr Ford without passing me and Marquis. By nine everyone's exhausted or seasick and the ship starts to quieten down, apart from the newspapermen around the bar of the second-class saloon. I go through Mr Ford's luggage with the Dean and find a miniature Model T car someone's given him. It has a little tank at the back and smells of gasoline so we drop it over the side just in case. I lay out Mr Ford's nightshirt on the bed and put the old school reader he's brought with him under the lamp. When I'm sure he wants nothing more I close the door and set my chair outside and stretch my legs out across the way. After a few minutes Dr Marquis steps over my legs, nods goodnight and double locks himself into his own cabin.

I know it's still there – the weight under my arm – but I have to put my hand inside and touch it just to get that feeling, like a shot of whisky after hours of wanting one. There's no movement anywhere and I drift off trying to work out how many hours there will be in our passage and, if somehow we can come back straight away, how many hours that will be before I put my feet back on American soil. By the time I come to an answer – I make it five hundred and twenty-eight – it's time to take one off. Five hundred and twenty-seven hours then. In another forty minutes it'll be closer to a mere five hundred and twenty-six.

This number and the roll of the ship make me sleepy and I'm caught with my chin on my chest by a young woman walking round the corner who stops sharply as soon as she sees me. I've seen her before, always in the company of Mrs

Schwimmer, but I don't know her name yet. She carries an envelope and holds it like she'd rather it would disappear. I'm getting up and about to ask if she has something there for Mr Ford but she just makes a little noise, flaps a hand and runs off. Twenty minutes later her head and shoulders appear for a second and dart away again. This time I follow her to the other side of the ship and down the long corridor that gives access to the starboard first-class cabins. There she is, halfway down, sitting on her own chair just like mine, with a tray at her feet with a cup and a pot of coffee I can smell from where I'm standing. She glances at me and there's the trace of a smile before she turns to look straight ahead to concentrate on the task of guarding her leader. From inside Rosika Schwimmer's cabin comes the irregular tick of a typewriter at one o'clock in the morning.

I return to my station and find Mr Ford standing in the corridor in his nightshirt. He takes my arm nervously.

'Ray, where have you been?'

'Just checking on something, Mr Ford. Everything's fine. Is there something I can get you?'

He puts his finger to his lips and looks up and down both ways. Then he whispers – 'The Dean!'

'Mr Ford?'

'Get me some dirt on the Dean.'

'Yes, Mr Ford.'

He goes back into his cabin. I can't stay awake for much longer and so I take the key from my pocket and quietly lock him in before going to my own bed.

Louis

*O*ne of the most extraordinary consequences of my annexation by Henry Ford was that I became for the first, and no doubt last time in my life, a *habitué* of the White House.

The first occasion had nothing to do with Mr Ford, but without him it would have remained my only experience of presidential interviews. I gained admission as the companion of Dr David Starr Jordan, illustrious peace campaigner, president of Stanford University and our nation's greatest expert on fish. Given the background and character of our current President, it was thought that Dr Jordan would be able to talk to him as one college man to another and thereby achieve better results.

We were received at ten-thirty in the morning. I noticed at once how the President and Dr Jordan, once equals, are now very far apart indeed. Mr Wilson was affable and calm and spoke in the whole meeting one or two words to our ten. Dr Jordan, constrained in a stern Prince Albert coat, was nervous and perhaps embarrassed by the great change in their relative positions. He was so painfully conscious of the situation that he began his explanations while still standing and had to start all over again after he had been asked to sit down.

A peace conference had recently been concluded in San

Francisco and the resolutions sent to the President. We learned that he had read them and were encouraged to hear that he had '. . . revolved them carefully in my mind a dozen times or more'. The scheme was explained – neutral mediation led by America, the world's great new power for peace, the only country that could lead, Wilson the only man who could do it. A conference in Europe when the parties were ready, Wilson in the boulevards of Paris or the great palaces of Berlin, directing the groundwork for a new and better world.

'And do they want it, Dr Jordan? Will the powers you talk of have this peace?'

The weariness of the combatants was set out, reports gained through private channels relayed. The President's objections were considered and subtle, but Dr Jordan, as he forgot where he was, became more fluent and met them all with mounting eloquence, the President himself acknowledging the force of our arguments with little noises of assent and nods of the head. Our hour was over and I was convinced that we had triumphed and that no man of reason and goodwill could withhold his agreement from what we were proposing. Success was at hand – a success which, as one of its smaller consequences, would have kept me away from Henry Ford and this ship. I spoke up confidently:

'Then, Mr President, may we take the message with us that you will act?'

The President's manner changed suddenly.

'No. That is for me to say when the right moment, in my judgement, arrives.'

It was my first lesson in power.

Then a telegram, a confusion, a stroke of luck, a conversation by an empty swimming pool and holding out my hand as an express train rushed by and carried me straight back into the White House ten days later. As the President greeted me very civilly Mr Ford made his choice of armchair, sat in it before being asked and let a long, thin leg hang over one arm and swing back and forth.

'You are looking very well, Mr President – better than I have ever seen you before. You must tell me what you do to keep yourself in such good trim.'

The President explained that he liked to forget about business outside business hours and always enjoyed a good joke. Mr Ford told him one and the President responded with one of his favourite limericks. These preliminaries over, Mr Ford started briskly in the same manner, I suppose, in which he orders half a million tyres or some inconceivable tonnage of iron ore.

'I don't think I need say much about the plan I favour. I have decided to back the proposal for neutral mediation. If you will take the steps to appoint a mediation commission with all the authority of your office, I will offer unlimited financial backing for the undertaking. Failure would be impossible.'

'Hmm,' said the President.

He went on to explain, so far as I could understand it (and heaven knows what Mr Ford made of this), that he was not necessarily of the opinion that the plan was not quite possibly the best one that had yet been offered. Commendable though this was, he had to give full regard to his position as head of a neutral country and, more particularly, to the need to retain the United States' full freedom of action in the event that a better plan might be proposed at some later date.

For a brief moment Mr Ford's expression resembled that of a dog to which someone had just read Hamlet's soliloquy – a very brief moment.

'Mr President, tomorrow morning in New York at ten o'clock precisely representatives of every newspaper in the country worth a damn will come to my apartment for a story. I will tell them I have chartered a steamship and offered it to you to send delegates to Europe. If you don't act, I will. I will tell the newspapermen I'll do it myself. One way or another, I will put an end to this obscenity in Europe.'

The President blinked. He seemed about to laugh but then stopped himself, doubtless recalling that the man before him had a treasury for a bank account and no Congress to tell him how to spend it.

That was not quite the end of my second encounter with President Wilson, but as to what was said or done between that moment and me finding myself once again on the steps outside the White House, my memory is indistinct. Mr Ford pressed his hat firmly back on before shaking his head slowly from side to side in disappointment.

'Louis,' he said to me, 'Mr Woodrow Wilson is a small man.'

The following ten days was a sort of fever. The thought of it is almost as exhausting as the events themselves. I became the passive, hollowed-out instrument of the cause and by the end, when I was looking forward to boarding the *Oscar* as my only chance of salvation, I felt something less than human. Finally resentful of these demands, I left the Biltmore hotel on the last afternoon before sailing, Schwimmer's imperious voice calling my name as the elevator doors closed and I was carried down to a few hours of freedom.

I had not picked a good hour. The city seemed to be in a state of hysteria, the streets seething with vehicles which bellowed at and threatened each other like they must be more than mere machines. Only a passing horse seemed calm, pulling a truck loaded with half a dozen iron stoves and living surely, behind its blinkers, in some remote, resigned horse world far from the city. I walked aimlessly. Was I about to embark on one of the greatest humanitarian triumphs, or on something quite stupid and futile? There were good and thoughtful people on both sides. I tired myself trying to come to a decision and felt I must be betraying my friends even to think about it that way. Madame Schwimmer never weakened – what was her secret?

New York is loud to the eye as well as to the ear. Almost every convenient surface seems to have been hired to impose some profitable idea on the passer-by – Thermos, Kodak, Waterman, Colgate all blare out. Side by side, two peeling posters recommend the 'Allah' Christmas card and Pebeco dentifrice – a third insisted that I should learn to stuff birds for a rewarding hobby. Higher, brighter and more costly, the Aetna Insurance Company issued its fiery warning – 'One man in seven is accidentally killed or injured each year. You may be the one.' I tried to keep that information out of my mind but couldn't stop myself from wondering if their actuaries had included the risks of being torpedoed in the western approaches. Perhaps my chances were not even as good as one in seven. Illuminated every few seconds, an angel descended onto a piano stool. Its hands remained rigid while a mechansim out of sight caused it to vigorously pedal the Angel Player Piano. After a while I came to a halt under an enormous gilded revolver that hung over an ironmonger's shop-front. Behind the glass and a steel security grille guns were laid out in careful display –

The Colt Automatic Pistol
Fire the first shot first!
Trust Colt for the Protection of Home and Family.

A cheaper model was still more sensationally advertised. The prospective buyers of the Ivor Johnson Safety Automatic Revolver were encouraged to envisage themselves confronting a crouching, distorted form in which a commercial artist had just about managed to combine the feline with the human.

Is a cruel, lurking, murderous beast any less a beast because it is human? If your business takes you into bad or lonely

242

neighbourhoods, there is but one way to guard against the possibility of a crushed skull and a broken body – keep your distance and cow others into keeping theirs.

$6.00

I stared through the glass, mesmerised by the guns and the picture of the crouching man-beast. Another wanderer did likewise and we became aware of each other at the same time as the only two figures standing against the flow of the sidewalk. I tried to get a look at him without moving my head, only to find that he was doing exactly the same to me. I caught a jaundiced, wary eye and easily imagined us both running into the shop in a desperate hurry to be the first to buy a safety revolver.

I walked on until I found myself outside the faded Lincoln Vaudeville theatre, reading an offer that would keep me away from the Biltmore for half the evening. I bought a ticket and sat in the semi-darkness with maybe a dozen others. At length curtains parted to reveal a large white screen obscuring the disused stage. The darkness deepened. A whirring started and a hot, chemical smell as a narrow triangle of light shot through the theatre. A boy pressed a chord on a piano as the letters DG appeared on the screen along with a stern guarantee of the authenticity of what we were about to see. Words appeared advising me to consult the printed programme (absent), and then some pomposity about the liberty to show the dark side of wrong in order to better illuminate the bright side of virtue. The freedom of the written word was invoked, along with Shakespeare and the Bible – then slaves cringing in a marketplace before the pianist picked up the tempo as we were shown the domestic happiness of the Stoneman family prior to its destruction by the evils of war. In a very short time I found what I really needed – two hours of uninterrupted sleep.

After a restless night in the hotel I rose early and struggled for over an hour to find the right words for a letter to Emmy and Elizabeth. I put myself in a state of high anxiety with the thought that these might be the last words my little girl would have from her father. From 5 a.m. the noise of preparation rose beyond my door and I let two people knock and call my name and go away before giving up and sealing into its envelope a letter that was sometimes too plain and sometimes too mawkish. I decided that if I got back I would find the letter at the bottom of Emmy's drawer and secretly burn it to celebrate my return.

With no breakfast, save for the taste of stamp glue on my tongue, I was pulled back into the fray and in a few hours found myself on the deck of the *Oscar* beside my chief and his great friend Mr Thomas Edison. Mr Bryan, the recently resigned Secretary of State, was also there and communicated with the crowd with a politician's skill. Rosika placed herself carefully where she could best see all the players at once. She had a distant, visionary smile on her face and held her now famous bag high against her chest. From time to time Mr Ford would make observations to Mr Edison and would point things out among the holiday crowd on the pier. The old man would smile and nod and lift his hat to the people below. Mr Ford put his hand on the arm of his mentor and onetime employer and spoke a few words that I believe only I could have heard.

'Come with me, Thomas. Don't go ashore. I'll give you a million dollars to come with me to Europe.'

Mr Edison raised his hat and received once again the gratitude of the nation of electric light and recorded music. The fringe of white hair around his head blew in the icy wind, as fine as a baby's. At nearly seventy years of age he is a little deaf and was spared the embarrassment of responding.

The well-wishers returned to shore and as the whistle blew Mr Ford was sent on his way with a storm of cheers and handclapping and hurrahs. He bowed again and again and had a calm, certain smile on his face that I had not seen before any time in my short acquaintance with him. There were not a few tears of emotion.

Delegates installed themselves in their cabins and quickly reappeared in the smoking rooms and lounges in high excitement and with their names pinned to their clothes. Hardened social uplifters – mostly women of a certain age – greeted each other familiarly and separated into hunting parties to track down and shake by the hand the greatest celebrities on board. Mr Ford was the most valuable prize of all and by the end of that first evening he had charmed everyone on board with his modesty and openness. It was universally agreed that as great industrialists go, Mr Ford is the best you can get.

As might have been expected, the arrangements made so meticulously on paper did not long survive their first brush with reality. Cabin arrangements decreed by Mrs Ford herself for the protection of her husband had been overturned by Rosika Schwimmer.

'The King must be accessible to his court!' declared Rosika to a twitching and highly coloured Dr Marquis.

'If you wish to be a Queen, Madame, you may be accessible! *We* will inform you of Mr Ford's arrangements.'

She lost that one.

An impromptu and farcical wedding further upset the allocation of cabins. A youthful Marion Penn was quartered with three female students. In the spirit of the voyage a debate was held in which Mr Penn argued for a pioneering attack on the outmoded taboos of the older generation.

'Rational dress for our minds as well as bodies, girls. We must take the corsets from our thoughts as well as our waists.'

The girls applauded, but said they could not possibly share a cabin with a man who wore a corset. He lost the vote three to one and was sent off to find the chief purser and more suitable bachelor accommodation. Thus a line of dominoes was set tumbling which resulted in me standing at nine in the evening before a door with four names behind its isinglass cover, one of them Mrs Inez Milholland. She answered the door herself, venting an incongruous cloud of camphor and naphthalene. Her expression softened into a tired smile.

'Louis Lochner.'

'Oh, yes,' she said. 'I know.'

Inez moved out into the narrow gangway and almost closed the door behind her. She was forced to stand very close and I was struck by how the pupils of her eyes in that low light seemed as wide as coat buttons. I mumbled my explanation and wondered if she could possibly accept moving cabins even at that late hour.

'Oh, thank God!'

There was a noise from within and then, in another voice, an emphatic 'Good riddance, I say!'

Inez went back into the cabin, slammed shut a suitcase and seized her fur-collared wrap and hat.

'Ladies, I must leave you. Louis – I may call you that? – can someone send these flowers on to my new cabin? They do not agree with my friends.'

There was a loud sneeze from one of the three more mature residents.

Inez's new address was twice the size of the old and reserved for her sole occupation.

'But this is wonderful!'

I tried to explain that it was also accidental. She dropped her things on the bed and kissed me on the cheek.

'Thank you.'

'It's all been a bit of a mess, that's all.'

'I never sleep on boats,' she declared firmly. 'Not properly, anyway. And I certainly won't on this one with everything being so exciting and all these fascinating people here. I just want to talk and talk and talk. I want you to come and talk

246

to me any time, Louis. Absolutely any time at all – except just now.'

The newspapermen scented their way to the bar from the off and were delighted to find it was to be free for the duration. A handful of prohibitionists started the first debate of the voyage, insisting that a peace mission was no place for strong drink. The journalists held a vote and unanimously found the prohibitionists to be 'boring'. The latter stormed off to Mr Ford who sternly disapproved of liquor but was unwilling to tell grown men what to do, especially men who wrote for the newspapers.

Although we have a captain – Hempel by name – his authority largely evaporated as soon as Mr Ford stepped on board. All cases are taken to him for judgement in the ancient manner and the next on the court list, after the burning issue of wet or dry, was the first great human interest story of the expedition. One Jacob 'Squint' Greenberg emerged after seven hours in a lavatory cubicle and declared himself a stowaway. He had gained access to the ship with the help of an American District Telegraph uniform and a bogus, but all too plausible, *bon voyage* message for Inez Milholland. He baffled Mr Ford by enthusiastically spouting Tom Paine and Walt Whitman and spoke with confusion and sincerity about our mission. There was talk of a long sentence of potato peeling in the galley. Mr Ford took a quite different view, commending Greenberg for his determination and appointing him to the expedition staff as his personal messenger. With the addition of much colour and imaginative detail the story was quickly wired back to New York for the Sunday papers in a dozen competing versions. As soon as the wireless office got free I slipped in and spent a useful twenty minutes making the acquaintance of Robert Bastian, the wireless operator. I quickly got the story of his last-minute appointment, of the wife and two children back in New Jersey, of his love for the job and his bright-eyed enthusiasm for the future of the wireless.

'It's only just started. You wait. In ten years everyone will have their own. You'll be able to hear your baby cry from the other side of the world.'

He admits the money isn't good.

'Look,' I said. 'You know what we're trying to do here? You know this isn't the voyage you signed on for any more?'

He's articulate – more than most in his position – and knows a lot about our campaign. He tells me very definitely that he is with us.

'I'd like to help you out.'

He hesitated just short of taking the two ten-dollar bills.

'It's Mr Ford's money,' I told him. 'It's all right. Official. Not everyone thinks the way we do and I need to know what's being said – to know everything that goes out over the wires.'

'Wire*less*.'

'Sure. I mean from the journalists. You understand?'

'Yeah, I get it. You know the captain has to censor all the messages – to keep within the neutrality regulations.'

'I want to know before he does. And other things too, things that might not bother him. And not just the journalists – the delegates too.'

He smiled and took the money. He said he wanted to help, but I got the feeling it would soon cost me another twenty dollars.

'Which delegates?'

I shrugged and began to feel a little grubby. Bastian was keen to play the secret agent. 'Any names I should be looking out for? Who are the suspects? Makes it easy for me – that's all.'

'Anything unhelpful.'

Late at night I make a last round of the ship. Ray dozes on his chair outside Mr Ford's cabin while the young Rebecca Shelly mimics him on the other side of the ship. William Bullitt of the *Philadelphia Public Ledger* emerges from Rosika's cabin with notebook and heads wearily for the press room. In the lounges the other newspapermen are red-faced, unsteady and loud. Elsewhere, in a quiet corner Inez, true to her claims of insomnia, has emerged in a silk dressing gown and gives her rapt attention to an anecdote from the debonair and inexhaustible Samuel McClure. I can't match him and go below in search of my bed – or is it 'bunk' now? I pass doors that emit whisky, snores, astringent life-preserving embrocations and from Lloyd Bingham's cabin, coughing.

In darkness and solitude at last, my mind plays over its old theme of power, of how to make things happen. I'm in the middle of it now, at the very heart of the mechanism that turns the world to its own beat. I've heard tell that Mr Ford, as a boy, once looked at a watch and then made one himself merely from that single glance at its workings. That is something I shall never do.

The ship's band woke us this morning with a Sunday hymn. The weather has worsened and only a handful have appeared for breakfast. The students are holding up well and Reverend Charles Aked has also joined us. An Englishman, he has some experience of peace work – his church and home having been wrecked by a mob in Liverpool when he spoke out against the Boer War. He improved his circumstances by crossing the Atlantic and ministering to the spiritual needs of John D. Rockefeller, before being dispensed with and moving on to San Francisco. As Dr Jones made a lengthy speech at Hoboken yesterday, it is Dr Aked's turn this morning. A sense of occasion has been added by the information that his entire sermon will be telegraphed back to New York. Someone has calculated the cost – in an hour's time I shall be listening to an eight-hundred-dollar, world-record-breaking radiogram.

McClure comes in, bouncy as a new puppy. He orders an enormous, high-smelling Scandinavian breakfast and begins to look over some notes ostentatiously as he eats. I catch his eye and he responds with an ambiguous wink. I know he has not always been a friend of the peace movement and decide to check his telegrams after breakfast. Other delegates and the odd hung-over journalist wander by in search of another spoonful of Mothersill's Seasick Panacæa. Some have the verdigris skin colour of the Statue of Liberty, a picture of which has been posted on the wall, redrawn as a suffering Belgium. Through the dining-room window the horizon shows, vanishes, shows again in a deep, oily rhythm. I have to look away and for a moment I fear I am about to embarrass myself. I hold the edge of the table and half rise from my chair as I stare down at the unhelpful sight of a gnawed brioche and the black circle of coffee in a cup, the scent of which is now nauseatingly powerful. My stomach contracts, I poise to run before, just as quickly as it came, the sensation passes. All this time I have been under the amused observation of Samuel McClure as he relishes his pickled herring.

My morning promises to improve as Mr Ford enters and joins me. A steward is instantly in attendance and takes an order for stewed fruit, toast and coffee. I see the thin, black lines of oil worked under his fingernails. A smell of coal diffuses from his clothes. He is in an excellent mood and explains in copious detail the workings of the steam engines down below, where he has already spent two happy hours.

'I don't suppose you can make them go any faster?' I ask.

'Not these ones. It's quite a museum down there, though don't tell the second engineer I said that – a charming fellow. You know – if this business comes to anything I might buy this ship. People can pay a dime to see the ship that brought peace to the world, and how engines used to be.'

I ask him, now that he has had the opportunity to meet everyone, what he makes of his motley crew.

'They suit me exactly. It's like a community – some old,

some very pretty young ones, rich and poor, men and women, prominent and obscure, able and less able. It's as though I had scooped up an average American community and transferred it straight to this ship. I like this crowd. It's representative. You see, Louis, this is what I do. I scoop up America and set it to making cars, or whatever else I want it to make. I don't care what a man knows when he walks through the gates of Highland Park. I teach him all he needs to know. Now we'll make peace instead of cars. Say – that's rather good, isn't it? Write it down for me and we'll send it out over that Marconi thing.'

He talks on volubly on the subject of progress, which he ascribes to animals as well as machines, explaining how biology keeps up with engineering through the transmigration of souls. His proof is an observation on the behaviour of chickens.

'You see – when I first drove a car on America's roads most creatures, men and beasts, had never seen such a thing before. Chickens would run straight in front of me, right along the road, and would often get hit. Now, you watch next time you go driving out in the country – when you come round a corner and find yourself nearly running over a chicken you'll see it'll go left or right and save itself more often than not. And why is that? Chickens don't read history any more than I do. They don't talk to each other. There's only one explanation – that chicken was hit in the ass in a previous life and that's how it learned its lesson.'

I feel a little faint as I look down at my abandoned meal. Hunger and nerves make my fingers tremble. McClure's unsympathetic gaze is upon me from across the tables. Like a bullying parent Mr Ford urges me to eat. I decide that the best I can do is to dose my coffee generously with sugar. I reach for the bowl only to be intercepted by Mr Ford's firm grip across my wrist. The most self-made of all America's great self-made men shakes his head in sombre warning.

'Don't do it, Louis.'

I return an uncomprehending look.

'Have you ever examined granulated sugar beneath the microscope? I thought not. Razors! The edges of those crystals on an empty stomach have sent many a good man to his grave before now. Let me get you some honey.'

'Thank you, Mr Ford.'

McClure

*A*h, well – even with a passenger list like this, S. S. McClure is still the biggest name here, that's always something. Then again, when you think about all those who turned the old man down maybe being here isn't such a good thing after all. At least Bryan didn't come – in his human form, anyway. God's own windbag – he really would have made me sick.

The third day out. Weather even worse, but folk are beginning to get their sea legs and be a little more sociable in the evenings. The students are delightful, though whether they are much good for the self-regard of the delegates is harder to judge. They walk about with an exaggerated respect for everyone five years older than they are, convinced they must be dignitaries of the highest order. Then, as soon as they are a few paces past one invariably asks the other 'Who was that?' It's a fair question – there are some luminaries here even I don't know.

The scribes I am all more or less familiar with. I have given most of them work in my time, and sacked one of them on three separate occasions. At the moment they are gathered round the bar, loudly celebrating the birth of their new fraternity, the Vacillating Sons of St Vitus. Behind the leafy barrier a contest is in train to decide on the Vacillating Sons' anthem. Ugly looks are piercing the palm fronds as college club voices get rough:

It's a long way to Copenhagen,
It's a long way to go.
It's a long way to Copenhagen,
We're going on Henry's dough!

Actually we're going to Christiania – but that doesn't quite fit and these aren't men to let an extra syllable, let alone the truth, get in their way.

'Ruffians!' declares someone. Or did they just sneeze? I'm not sure – *la grippe* is making its way through the *Oscar* on the heels of *mal de mer*. Meanwhile, Mrs Morse Clark keeps such a tight rein on her student charges that I doubt any other French diseases will get much of a chance.

It's a curious scene, to be sure. Herman Bernstein gives me a nod as he goes by – publisher of *The Day*, translator of Tolstoy and Chekhov and Foreman of the Brotherhood of American Yeomen. He still has enough Russian in his accent for Madame Schwimmer to have taken a shine to him – gossips are marrying them off. If benevolence, culture and sincerity can do anything, he's a good man to have with you.

The southern tones of Colonel Robert Henry remain clear, even when voices are raised. The Grand Commander of the Mississippi Masons is here because his master, the Governor of Mississippi, had a change of mind late in the day but felt he shouldn't be entirely unrepresented. I listen to him explaining why it is a woman's privilege to remain unsullied by politics, why no true Southern gentleman would foist the indignity of voting on her. His astonished interlocutor, John Jones of the Anti-War Society, sounds like just the sort of man who should be here, but I know for a fact he solicited his invitation. Estelle, his wife, has been stashed down below in case they appear too flagrantly to be a couple in search of a free ticket to Europe.

Governor Hanna of North Dakota is broadcasting through the ship, and through the ether, his intention of visiting the battlefields as soon as landfall permits. Someone has told him that pacifism is not much use in gathering votes. He has turned the Ford Peace Ship into 'Hanna Heads for the War!' A neat piece of work from a man who clearly still has some ambition. He chats amiably with a colleague of South Carolina whose command of English reached its height at Hoboken when he declared to the crowd that departing the United States with Henry Ford was 'an unspeakable blessing to mankind'.

There is an entire synod of padres of one stripe or another and a quantity of women in La Schwimmer's image – widows or spinsters beyond marriageable age, a quartet of teachers on furlough. One presented a children's peace petition to the State Department two miles long, another thunders with the full authority of the Oregon Federation of Women's Clubs. Helen Ring Robinson, our nation's first female state senator, is here as well as the stately Mary Fels. Mistress of the Fels Naphtha soap concern, she has perhaps a half of one per cent of Henry Ford's capital and is, therefore, a very wealthy woman indeed. She is the party's second tycoon and emits, as if a living advertisement, a reassuring odour. A pair of bewildered Finns talk only to each other. The older woman, another associate of the Hungarian, enjoys the cachet of having been exiled from her homeland by the Russian bear and, in the absence of any Belgians, holds the trump card for suffering and subject peoples. Her charming young friend, Miss Eriksson, wears her national costume this evening. With a rod of braided ash-blonde hair extending down her back she seems to have been freshly animated from the pages of Hans Christian Andersen, or some other fairy tale.

In the corner a pretty co-ed, still in her fur coat, attempts to interest the former Secretary of State in an anchovy canapé. She mashes the pastry through the bars of the cage and asks the trembling rodent in her sweet Bennington accent whether it too gets sea sick. This is William Jennings Bryan, the squirrel. Beside him in another cage, Squirrel Ford has listlessly turned his face to the corner and is talking to no one. There was a fracas the evening before and the two cages had to be moved apart in the interests of inter-squirrel peace and security. There is now a small card between the cages which reads 'Buffer Zone – Do Not Cross' and there has been much earnest talk on whether the theories of international relations can be made more scientific if they are tested first on small but suitably aggressive animals. Reporters have sent another $200 of radiograms declaring the Ford Peace Expedition's first success.

Across the room, through a gap between two shoulders, I glimpse the five-foot-five frame of my old friend Ben Lindsey, the juvenile court judge the newspapers apostrophise as the man who puts a little love back in the law; the second biggest thing in Colorado after Pike's Peak, and last year's eighth greatest living American, tying for the honour with Andrew Carnegie and Billy Sunday. He seems to have pestered one of the stewards for a glass of carrot juice which he brandishes in my direction.

'Still on the wagon, Ben?'

'Clean as a whistle, inside and out!'

We last met a year and a half ago at the Battle Creek Sanitarium. We put the world to rights over a bowl of oatmeal soup and he read the galleys of my autobiography. That was before my recent difficulties which, by chance, also originated while under the care of the good Doctor Kellogg.

There are prominent absentees. The Braleys remain below. There are conflicting reports – according to one of the younger newsmen much of the ship's uncomfortable motion can be attributed to their activities; according to the Braleys' neighbours, separated from them by the thinnest of partitions, there is already trouble in paradise. From the music room comes the umpteenth performance of 'Alexander's Ragtime Band' followed by the stagey booming of Lloyd Bingham, our tireless court jester who is enjoying an unparalleled success with the students and those newsmen young enough to find some novelty in a vaudeville act of the 1890s.

Madame Schwimmer's heavy responsibilities confine her to her cabin and we have seen little of our guiding genius except for a few contributions to discussion groups and a teasing presentation on the contents of her infamous bag. The earnest Mr Lochner is more in evidence. On the subject of neutral mediation plans he is endlessly informative and seems to know no doubt. One would think there is nothing more to him until the conversation finally flags and he shows you a photograph of his infant daughter and coyly mentions the expected sibling and his hopes for him or her to be born into a peaceful world. He apologises and puts the photograph away and then is at a loss for what else to say and is greatly relieved when a note comes from Schwimmer and he dashes off to her cabin.

As for Mr Ford himself, he was seen at dinner this evening – entrance to 'Stars and Stripes Forever' courtesy of the ship's band – but seemed to me a little greyer and more sunken than before. He sat with only his bodyguard and Dean Marquis of Detroit who talked incessantly, but too discreetly to be overheard. Ford appeared to listen to every word with the fixed attentiveness of a mesmeriser's patient. The conversation in the dining saloon nearly stopped at one point as everyone had their eyes on this pair and was paying no attention at all to what their companions were saying. No doubt a report will already be in Madame Schwimmer's hands.

I would have listed Inez Milholland high amongst these absentees if she had not come in just this moment. A woman mostly known from newspaper photographs of a goddess on a white horse, she does not disappoint in the flesh. The beauty is unconventional – a sensuously ambiguous face, eyes pale as a husky's and a nose that would not disgrace the bust of a Roman senator; a smile that is warm and yet sufficiently reserved never to seem easy. It's a face countless thousands have turned to take a second look at without quite knowing why. She carries with her the unspoken electric thrill of scandal, a hint that a moment of guiltless and thoroughly up-to-date happiness might for once be more than fantasy. Inez is the future. When I watch our half-dozen female students I feel only fatherly, but when I see Inez, my fifty-six years become desolate. She wears a black silk gown loosely wrapped around and belted at the waist with a simple strip of the same material. A white lace bodice shows between the broad lapels, and if she did not move with such confidence it would seem that Miss Milholland had taken to walking the ship in her night clothes. She goes straight to the screened bar, jokes with the newsmen who are at once charmed and chastened by her appearance among them. She emerges with a glass of stomach-settling champagne, sees me, approaches and sits down.

'I was hoping to have such an opportunity, Mr McClure.'

She laughs quietly as I kiss her hand.

'Would it be too awkward for you to call me Samuel?'

'But I have a bone to pick with you first. Why do you never print my journalism?'

'Did you send it to me?'

'I thought so – you rejected it without even reading it, all my reports from Italy, I sent them to your magazine.'

'That is easy to explain – it is edited by imbeciles and no longer mine.'

'Alibi,' declares Inez, attorney-at-law. 'The complete defence. Perhaps I shall just have to like you after all. Talk to me about anything other than politics, peace or war. Otherwise I shall go mad, I shall run to the lifeboats and cast myself adrift.'

And so the question can no longer be avoided — why am I here? I am the only member of this strange crew, other than Ford himself and just possibly the soap widow, whose name is a household word. But now it runs off the presses with no trace of my mind or hand in its pages. My own name disturbs my sleep, mocking me as letters on a magazine cover and a signature on a lapsed insurance policy.

'But someone tells me you have written your autobiography,' declares Inez. 'Too soon, surely. Can that really be true?'

'Almost true.'

'I'm fascinated — really. But oh no, I can't read at sea. Never could — even as a girl it made me just too sick.'

I acquiesce and save Inez the inconvenience of having to wait for dry land before learning the life story of Samuel S. McClure. I pass briefly over the remoter episodes — the simple childhood in rural Ireland, crucible of the McClure myth; the start of school which was the start also of memory from my fifth year, the mile walk along the meandering road shut in between the blossoming high hawthorn hedges. Later in the year the whin bushes were yellow and the flax fields beyond as blue as the sky. I tell how I was kept in that school for six hours a day, fifty weeks of the year and resented only that it could not be longer. When new readers came from Dublin once a year and the box was opened and I saw the bright colours and smelled the fresh ink I could not have been happier. I rose at six each morning to study before breakfast. Ever since, I have hated rest and been a martyr to my interests. I have never derived any pleasure from putting my occupations aside even for a day or two, as so many others seem to.

Two tall monuments stand over those early years and both are stories of death. On the first occasion I was eight years old and walked into McKeever's store one evening on an errand for my mother. A group of men stood close together in the candlelight. They talked excitedly and I soon understood that President Lincoln had been assassinated. Years later, when I published Ida Tarbell's *Life of Lincoln* in *McClure's Magazine*, I talked to many people about when they first heard the news and every one recalled the circumstances with complete precision. That's how it was for me too. It was the first time the outside world had cast a shadow over my own life and I can see McKeever's store now, as perfectly as a photograph.

The second event was altogether different. Lately it has been clearer than for years – the war I suppose, and too much time on ships.

You see, I say to Inez, a warship killed my father. It was the end of the shift and the men were walking off, half blind with exhaustion. My father stepped into an uncovered hatch and fell the depth of five decks through the empty shell of steel to be broken and killed on the keel. It took a week for the news to make its way home to Ireland from the Clyde. My friends and I were stealing sweet turnips and Daniel called over the wall to me.

'Your da's dead.'

That night I thought of the last week and how it had been no different from any other. I hadn't known I had no father. Then the coffin came back with his wages and we buried him. He was thirty-two years old. I began to dream of a country where such things could not happen.

My younger brother was born, my father's posthumous son. Our little farm was sold and I began to understand what poverty was. We took to reading steamship circulars and railway maps of the United States and before long made our passage on the *Mongolia*. I remember the scene of parting at Glarryford railway station. The old women wept as bitterly as at the graveside and no doubt many did not see their children again.

We landed at Quebec on 26 June 1866. The journey by rail

from there to Valparaiso, Indiana, where my mother's married sister lived, took seven days. Time and again our immigrant train was laid up in sidings while passenger and even freight trains were allowed to pass ahead of us. I remember nothing of our arrival, but recall clearly the next day when we were driven to Hebron, a few miles away, where I celebrated my first Fourth of July, watched my first firecrackers explode and tasted my first lemonade. The Democratic candidate made a speech. He talked of a young country ripe for the ambitions of Youth. I suppose it seemed true in those days. I thrilled to that message, but took a dislike to the man who delivered it. I could already guess that I felt what he wanted me to feel. For no better reason than that I became a Republican that day.

There were hard times ahead and, more for money than love, my mother married again. Mr Simpson became my step-father and I was put to work on his farm, snatching a few hours of schooling a week when the chores were done. There was nothing to read in the house but the *Agricultural Reports* and the *Farmstead Catalogue*. Later, when I was on the point of making my fortune with the newspaper syndicate, I remembered those years and the emptiness of young boys' minds all across the prairies. I put Stevenson and Kipling and Stephen Crane and Conan Doyle into their newspapers, and pieces on how to collect fossils or butterflies; all those things of which I was most starved as a child.

The debt on the farm never got any smaller and one day, when I was fourteen years old, my mother called me to her and told me to leave for the new High School in Valparaiso or I would never make anything of myself. I left with the new clothes she had made for me, a dollar in one pocket, and a great sheltering ignorance of the world. Between working as a chore-boy and as a country schoolteacher, and tramping the roads as a pedlar in the summer and with the help of the occasional act of kindness, an education was finally obtained. What defects remained were made good at Knox College, Illinois. There I completed my young mind and lost my heart to Harriet Hurd, Professor Hurd's daughter, who was promptly instructed not to see such a worthless fellow again and sent out of harm's way to a Protestant girls' school on the banks of the St Lawrence. By eavesdropping – or journalism as I would later call it – I obtained the address of this place. I wrote at once, but she was an obedient girl and I received no reply.

On graduation I found myself no taller or more decisive than before and with no great cause in view. I sternly judged my features in the mirror and could not conceive of them ever being set up in marble or bronze on a public plinth. I had one great anxiety – that Harriet's letters (which had been secretly re-established after our first break) had once again stopped. I knew that she was staying with a friend near Utica, New York. With not the slightest plan in mind I packed my bag and left the West for the last time. I located my love, but only received from her a painful dismissal which I accepted as final. I walked back to the station at Marcy and asked how soon there would be another train out. I bought a ticket without asking where it went.

I might have starved in Boston, but instead found the direction of my life. It was while wandering in that city that I discovered my one remaining asset – my connection with the Pope Manufacturing Company, makers of the ubiquitous Columbia bicycle. I say 'connection' – in fact there was nothing more than the fact that I had once sold this company some advertising space in our college newspaper. On this slender pretext I presented myself at their offices at 597 Washington Street on 3 July and requested to see Colonel Pope himself. Colonel Pope explained that he did not wish to buy any more advertising that season. I replied that I wanted work, but he told me he was laying off hands. I persisted and in the end was given a position scrubbing floors at the downtown bicycle rink. Colonel Pope observed his employees closely and when he wished to start the *Wheelman,* his own cycling magazine, he called me into his office and asked me if I thought I could edit it. By this chance I found my vocation.

The new venture prospered and I liked the work well. You are too young, Inez, to recall the importance of the bicycle in those days. For people in cities, the world beyond the end of the trolley-car tracks was stranger and more exciting then than it is today – less spoiled too. The bicycle opened it up. Attorney's clerks and doctors riding for their health would send us stories of adventures that went on for days or weeks and hundreds of miles. They would read Mark Twain, then mount a Columbia bicycle and live it. I remembered my time as a pedlar in the long vacations away from college. It's only thirty-five years ago and yet, away from the railway tracks, I could spend the best part of a summer and never hear the sound of a machine.

We grew quickly and then Colonel Pope decided to take over another magazine and merge it with the *Wheelman.* He presented me one day with a co-editor acquired from this other publication. I don't doubt he was an excellent man, but I found it was no longer in my nature to have an equal. I understood that I could never be happy except as my own man. Under this impulse I sat down one day and set out every last detail of a simple idea that would give me my freedom and, for a while, no little fortune by the standards of ordinary men. I would enlist newspapers and periodicals of every sort across the continent and promise them good articles and stories on a weekly basis. I would then go to writers and tell them they could have their work published not once, but a hundred times or more from New York to San Francisco if only they would put it exclusively into my hands. It started slowly, as all new things do. I managed it from a desk in the corner of one room in our small apartment, working all the hours I could, taking papers to the library when the baby cried too much. Oh, yes

– Harriet. I wore her down in the end – and her father too. After five months there still seemed no end to the losses. Would it ever work? I wandered on my own in the summer evenings and knew some of the worst days of discouragement I have ever experienced. It was a six-storey city in those days (at most). You see how old I am? The Upper West Side was still largely empty and Harlem was a country district. It was lit by gas and every car was drawn by horses, or by the little steam-engines that pulled the elevated trains. Mr Henry Ford was out there somewhere in the western darkness and there was nothing to suggest it would ever change. The city seemed complete to me, as if everything had been done and there were no further possibilities.

Well, you know what happened. Within a very few years I could offer my good friend Mr Robert Louis Stevenson $8,000 for the American serial rights to his next story. I was the one who gave him enough money to charter that yacht and sail off to the South Seas. I bought Rider Haggard, I bought the Sherlock Holmes stories for $60 a piece, I paid Rudyard Kipling $25,000 for *Kim* and still made a profit on it. The magazine was added to the syndicate. We serialised the life of Lincoln. Circulation went from 120,000 to 175,000 to 250,000 in December 1895. *McClure's Magazine* was soon bigger than *Century*, *Harper's* and *Scribner's* put together. We became a power in the land and myself the chief of the 'muckrakers'. Important men began to fear us as we ran the Standard Oil articles, and then Steffens' pieces on municipal corruption. We were the first of our kind to take science seriously, covering Drummond on evolution, the excavation of dinosaurs, Marconi's wireless telegraph and the Wright brothers' first flight. On the last two occasions we received many letters from professors in mid-western colleges telling us sternly that we had been imposed upon by practical jokers. Because of all this a million minds a month were less empty than they might have been.

'There you are, Mrs Inez Milholland Boissevain – the contents of my autobiography. I have done myself out of a sale. Very unprofessional.'

She covers a yawn with her hand and asks if it is true that Miss Willa Cather wrote my life story for me. She says she is a great admirer of Willa Cather and I must tell all about her. The thread of our conversation goes slack. There are only a few of us left up. The ship's band disperses from the music room as Lloyd Bingham's revels melt away. And yet, neither of us seems quite ready to be alone. I almost laugh at myself as I feel the strength of my need to impress this young woman. She looks at me intently and with a very slight and inviting smile. I choose to find some compassion there, woven through the unspoken question – 'That's all very well, Samuel McClure, but you're here, aren't you? Why would you be here at all if it were not for these more recent, unwritten chapters – the ones your tame Miss Cather could never have mentioned?'

'Of course,' I say, 'things have changed a lot since then. You see, I slaved to feed those minds and in the end it broke my health. I began to spend more time away from the office. The old restlessness came back and I wandered for months each year in Europe. At first I pretended that I was looking for new material for the magazine and the syndicate, but in truth I was in flight from something I could never quite name. The steady repetition of success wore me down as much as any routine ever did. I began to feel like I was back teaching in a country school, always planning my escape before the end of term. This was when I became a good customer of the Battle Creek Sanitarium.

'I left good men in charge of my business, but editing is personal, the impress of one man's mental thumb-print on the final product. No one else can do it quite the same way and every time I came back *McClure's Magazine* was a little less my own. Can you understand how painful that is, Miss Milholland?

It is like seeing your own child run to a stranger for comfort. I would set things right, only to flee again as soon as the dust had settled. Our competitors learnt our tricks, our better writers began to look elsewhere. One day I found my business partners all on one side of the table and myself alone on the other. They offered me ten thousand dollars a year for the use of my name and a promise never to interfere again in the magazine I had created. These are the men who turned down your excellent journalism.

'And so I was unhorsed, or liberated as I prefer to think of it. I travelled, adding from time to time another lecture to my repertoire. I found myself in London for the thirteen days between the ultimatum to Serbia and the British declaration of war. All my old friends were running to the colours – Wells, Bennett, Conan Doyle, Kipling. My energy came flooding back. I wanted to work again, like a young man. But through what instrument, with what voice? Circumstance had silenced me.

'I went home and lectured for the money, struggling grimly way out in Kansas and Nebraska with audiences who shouted me down as anti-German. I wrote my life story and saw it serialised by my former colleagues in *McClure's Magazine*. People said it was the only good thing in it any more and, sadly, they were right. I proposed a biography of Henry Ford but received a terse reply telling me the project was already in hand. I went down to Mexico to cover the revolution. I got sick of staying in hotels where everyone was a journalist half my age. I went back to New York and I suppose it all ended well when . . .'

I open my hands expansively to indicate everything around us, and to include most particularly Inez herself.

'When I found myself free to say yes to a new adventure.'

Inez puts her hand over mine and tells me she is very, very pleased to find me aboard.

'You know,' she says, 'I believe that for the first time in my

266

life I might be about to get a good night's sleep on a ship. And I haven't felt sick for hours. You are better than champagne, Samuel McClure.'

She gives me her cabin number and an open invitation adding at the end 'and I really mean that.' She asks if she will see me at the preparedness debate tomorrow evening. I tell her she can be sure of it and then pat my inside jacket pocket and let her know I have something special for the occasion, a little bomb to throw, something she will not want to miss. She smiles with that appetite for trouble I recognise so well and that is so indispensable for anyone who would change the world.

'Goodnight, then.'

'Goodnight, Inez.'

It is a quarter to two in the morning. Drunken newsmen watch her as she goes. They turn to look at me and shake their heads in disbelief.

There was no need to tell her the rest – she must know it anyway, or all the most fatal parts that have appeared in the newspapers. That one last piece in the story started in the Battle Creek Sanitarium to which dejection and a general malaise had once again drawn me. It was in one of the cleansing suites, where I lay face down preparing for that deep relaxation I so value when the attendant eases in his instrument, that I turned my head to one side to find, being similarly treated, a young acquaintance by the name of Dr Edward Rumely. He had made a little money for himself through the manufacture of farm equipment and had asked me a year before if I would print a neutral article on how the British blockade of Germany was damaging American business, not least his own contract for the supply of diesel-engined tractors. I could not oblige, but found him nevertheless a moderate and sympathetic man whose frustrations in his business life I could understand all too easily. In the intervening period he had acquired some powerful associates and, as he explained to me over a week at the Sanitarium, they were now in a position to make an offer to buy the *New York Evening Mail* and to run it as a neutral paper propagandising neither for the Germans nor the Allies. In Rumely's own phrase, he and his partners could not believe their luck when they heard that a man of my stature was free to take the helm of their new venture. We talked about editorial policy. I made my loyalties clear, but they were no obstacle – if they could get McClure editing their newspaper, they would have him. I was back in the saddle.

It was on Saturday 24 July that Albert Heinrich, *Geheimrat* of the German Reich, and his friend Sylvester Viereck, editor of the pro-German weekly *The Fatherland*, boarded the northbound elevated at the Sixth Avenue Station. Viereck got off after a few stops, but Heinrich travelled on, drowsing in the summer heat. He nearly missed his stop, and in his hurry to get off the train momentarily forgot his briefcase. He ran back to get it, but it was already gone, carried off into the crowd by the Secret Service agent who had been dogging his every move for days. By some unknown route these papers, which contained my name in several innocent passages, quickly made their way from the hands of the government to those of the editor of *The World* who had little love for me. The first I knew of the affair was when a journalist from that paper came to ask if it was true that secret German money backed the purchase of the *Evening Mail*, that it was a propaganda front for the Kaiser, that I had been recommended by nameless persons as a useful instrument for promoting an embargo on American arms to the Allies?

'No', I said. 'None of it is true. No, I do not want Germany to win the war.'

But it was too late for the truth. As I left my office that evening old friends cut me dead in the street. A few days later I was informed that my unrestricted passport had been withdrawn at the request of the British authorities. And so when

I opened that unlooked-for telegram and read the high-flown rhetoric of the invitation and saw Henry Ford's name at the bottom of it, I might have laughed if only I'd had anywhere else to go.

With this all swirling in my mind I step out for a little cool air before turning in. I lean on the rail and look out on the heavy, lightless swell. Uneasily, I sense the trajectory of life, that ever steepening downward curve and the cold mathematical laws that make it so and from which there is no appeal. I tell myself, with a violent shudder, that it is just a metaphor, that it might describe quite perfectly a thrown ball falling to earth without saying anything at all about life. And yet, if it is a universal law, truly universal –

Ahead of us, where nothing else is visible and first light still many hours away, an eerie hazing of the air puzzles me. Thinking of what I have read in the newspapers, I prepare myself for the stink of chlorine. In a moment of tragic indulgence I reflect that this innovation in war has come, for me, at the right time. I will breathe deeply and cut off only a last act for which I have no great appetite. But instead, soft descending curtains of grey approach and then cover the ship. I look up and experience the dizzying illusion of moving vertically upwards through a shower of soft hail. It falls faster than snow, slower than rain. It collects in the palm of the hand before melting, as regular as ball bearings or shot from a gun, like miniature snowballs, each moulded from a single flake. In the heart of the shower the fall is so dense that every flat surface is soon covered. In fifty-six years of life and a hundred crossings I have never quite seen anything like it. We move out of the shower and the harmless, charming transformation is already over. The strangeness of the scene evokes old magazine illustrations of Ancient Mariners, Flying Dutchmen, explorers' ships trapped in Arctic ice. It quickens something in me and this, together with the conviction that I am alone, licenses a

grand, confessional gesture towards the discreet blackness of
the sea. I step towards imaginary footlights and strike an orator's
pose.

'You clutch at straws and sink a little faster, pulled down by
the weight of one more straw.'

I turn to the sound of a solitary, slow handclap and become
aware of the whisky-scented bulk of Lloyd Bingham no more
than ten feet away and now picked out with crown and
epaulettes of white.

'Sounds familiar,' he says hoarsely. 'Remind me.'

I tell him I just made it up, but he shakes his head firmly.

'No, no – some old play. I was in it once.'

Inez

*T*he coffee business didn't sell and the suffrage meetings palled. The same old arguments, the same old people, the same excess of chiefs trying too hard to make everyone else a mere indian. It's coming for sure – we'll get there soon – but just for now I think the cause can do without me. There was something about the Italian fiasco as well – an unsatisfactory breaking off, something very like an unfair eviction that had to be reversed. There hadn't been enough of an adventure and I knew, as I looked across the breakfast table at my dear Eugen, that an unsatisfied desire for adventure was a dangerous thing in a marriage. I waved the telegram casually over my coffee, looked at the back of it, re-read the text on the front.

'You know, I've half a mind to go.'

He spoke without looking up.

'Do you think it will work? Has any war ever ended just because people asked that it should end?'

'Lots, I'm sure.'

'After they got tired of killing each other.'

'It's your continent, Eugen. Don't you think you should take a little more interest?'

'I know them better than you, my dear.'

'Well just because you're depressed doesn't mean others can't do something worthwhile. Why shouldn't good people talking plain common sense make a difference?'

'It sounds to me like you have a whole mind to go.'

He put down the letter he had been reading, placing it near the middle of the table so I could clearly see it was another bill. Keeping his eyes closed, he let his head drop back. He sighed heavily and made, all in all, a typically pathetic male appeal. I closed the door to the hall, got him to move his chair away from the table and sat on his lap. He put his head on my shoulder and I smoothed his hair and planted a kiss on his forehead. He moaned about money as I contemplated his hairline and tried to remember exactly where it had been six months before – quite the same place, or had the tide already turned?

'Why don't you go in with Father? You know he'd be happy to have you.'

'*He'd* be happy.'

'Don't be so proud.'

'You would really prefer me not to be?'

'I'm sorry.'

I told him all would be well and talked vaguely about him needing a clear run at the problem, about darkness before the dawn, about me only being in his way. By spring next year everything would look different.

'And just how will this happen?'

'You'll see. And it's all expenses paid – or at least I suppose it is.'

'What is?'

'The trip. The Henry Ford Peace Ship. It does say "guest" – look. So you see, I'll be one less mouth to feed. And I can write for the newspapers. This is the start of better things. And what if it really works – you wouldn't want me not to be there, would you? I'll miss you so much.'

'Go, then,' he said sulkily. 'Go and do whatever it is *you* want to do.'

I slipped one hand beneath myself and wriggled my fingers until they had burrowed between his thighs.

'I'll miss Simon, too. I'll have to dream of him every night in my lonely little cabin.'

'Simon will miss you.'

'Just think – I might be away for months. When I get back we'll be strangers. It will be like the first time again. Could anything be more exciting?'

Over the next week Eugen cheered up and was perfectly sweet on the day of departure – vigorous in bed, attentive and organised through the morning, and gallantly agreeing that I had made the right decision after all. Hoboken was frantic and it made no sense for him to come all the way to the ship with me. We parted by a brass band – intimate in the privacy of the crowd and his breath warm in my ear.

'Come back safely, Nan. That's all I ask.'

I'm not so sure now, but I thought I could still see him when I reached the top of the gangway. I seized a megaphone from the outlandish figure announcing my arrival and turned back to search the crowd. What last words should Eugen hear from me if it all ended in delicious tragedy?

'Votes for Women!'

There was a gratifying response, divided about half and half, which is a lot better than we usually get.

At first I was unlucky in the cabin allocation, finding myself closely quartered with three well-seasoned followers of causes. The first presented an ample chest to the world, so densely covered in badges declaring her various loyalties that she seemed to be wearing a suit of armour. She talked too much, had unrealistic views of our expedition, and embarrassed me by repeating how excited she was to be sharing a cabin with the 'famous' Inez Milholland. The other, a Mrs Neuhaus, was no less committed, venturing forth on a winter voyage despite a keen sense of danger. She quaffed Sanatogen like an addict and offered us the protection of germ-killing Formamint throat pastilles in case we should be assailed in the night by 'one of the old mistakes of Creation'.

'Caruso uses them, you know. And Mr Bernard Shaw.'

'No, thank you.'

'Be it on your own head.'

On my account the tiny cabin began to fill with flowers – another threat to the survival of Mrs Neuhaus, it seemed, as she began to wheeze and waft away imaginary toxins.

'I can't wait to get to Norway,' she said eagerly. 'I hear it's so clean.'

At the end of the evening when we were making our cramped preparations for sleep, I watched in mounting amazement as she opened her Indestructo steamer trunk and donned a Neversink life-vest over her voluminous nightshirt. She turned her back to me.

'Tie me up my dear, if you would please. You didn't bring one yourself?'

The ritual was completed with the lighting of a tiny, stinking spirit lamp. This, explained Mrs Neuhaus, was the Vapo-Cresolene night guard – it would protect us from whooping cough, sore throat, asthma, bronchitis, catarrh and spasmodic croup as well as mitigating the effects of diphtheria should that demonic condition catch hold of our fragile souls before dawn.

'Well you can't stop a war if you don't get there first,' reasoned Mrs Neuhaus, pulling a thick stocking over her head and falling asleep as instantly as a parrot in a draped cage.

There was an apologetic knock on the door. I opened it to find a harrassed Louis Lochner – one of the expedition's organisers. I had spoken to him earlier on the subject of accommodation and he had now come, as it appeared from his anxious expression and stumbling words, to disappoint me.

I was so tired myself that I was hardly able to understand him and when at last I grasped that he had come to escort me to my own stateroom I fear I made my relief a little too obvious. I and my first-night companions parted coldly.

'Make her take the flowers,' demanded Mrs Neuhaus, resentful at being woken and now with her stocking over one eye like a pantomime pirate.

My new quarters were very superior and have already proved convenient. I wrote to Eugen with the last of my strength before settling for a night of that sleepless rest which is the best I ever get at sea.

The next day I discovered a strange assemblage indeed. Ardour was everywhere, poured out in a ceaseless intensity of conversation — the single tax, women's suffrage, the solution to youthful delinquency, prohibition, free love, the outlawing of war, the removal of everything red from elementary schools. A group of female students created a wide, empty space about themselves in the first-class lounge by discussing contraception with commendable frankness. Even the war was discussed.

'Agendas for sale! Who'll buy my sweet agendas? Agenda, madam?'

'Get away from me, you stupid oaf.'

Poor Lloyd Bingham made few friends with that one, though my heart began to go out to him as I discovered just how humourless many of my fellow travellers are. In four days I have changed my mind on his inclusion which I now see as very necessary indeed.

Just at the moment we are a little sore and shy with each other after last night's explosions. In the time leading up to what is already referred to as the Great Preparedness Debate we have talked and been talked at on a heroic scale. I have listened to Miss Rebecca Shelly's account of her spiritual rebirth, Reverend Dr Aked tell me I was on a journey no less significant than that of St Paul himself, a Miss Wales describe the detail and theory of neutral mediation and the splendid Dr Lloyd Jones lecture on the perfectibility of mankind and the modern battleship. On Monday evening I got my first sight and sound of Madame Schwimmer as she addressed us stirringly on The Purpose of this Journey. She is a small, energetic and passionately sexless woman who has whittled away her existence to nothing but the doing of good. Her speech is vigorous and full of imperatives and high moral seriousness, her manner enthralling to those apt to be enthralled. She is the finished version of a type I know well. They can be effective, no doubt, whenever simplicity and relentlessness can win the day. She seems but narrowly to have missed the masculine gender and would, I think, in other circumstances have made an excellent general. Actor and politician complete her portfolio and in both she does exceedingly well. She achieved quite an effect with her locked black bag and was adept at avoiding the issue of its precise contents.

'Friends, these documents were given to me only because I was trusted. Can I not ask you to trust me the same way? In time of war there are things men can only say to women. With each other they are paralysed by the fear of weakness, but to me they told the truth, to me they opened the better, feminine heart of humanity . . .'

'Hear, hear!'

'*What* did she say?'

There was a snort from among the newsmen.

'What these men dared not say to foreign ambassadors, or to heads of government and ministers of war they dared say to me. And yet, if these secrets are exposed to the harsh light of day before their time they will only be disowned and our chance lost.'

She gestured airily, a slight fluttering of raised fingers, the hand's hopeless dying away suggesting the evaporation of a volatile diplomatic opportunity. There was a sudden silence.

Needle stares fixed on the great mystery of the bag. She held it high and for a moment it seemed to be the only thing in the room. We looked like bears, stupidly gazing up at a meat-safe dangling from the branch of a tree. I can't say I know quite what to make of her, but the next time I speak in public I'm sure there will be a few changes.

Through all this Mr Ford passes serenely, taking no part in the debates himself. At his approach the students and more impressionable delegates fall silent and make way. For his own part, Mr Ford seems not to have the slightest consciousness of rank. He is affable with everyone and pleasingly ordinary. If one was not forewarned of his name or did not recognise that much-photographed face, one would not at all suspect the extraordinary truth of his life. According to one anecdote he makes good use of this plainness when on motoring trips through country districts. When he finds one of his cars that needs repair he talks with the owner about the weather or the price of corn that year before moving on. A few days later a team of Ford factory mechanics appear from nowhere. Some, it is said, awake to find shining new automobiles in place of the old and are never quite sure what disguised god has blessed them. He has spoken with me twice, remarking on both occasions how pleased he was to meet me. Neither then nor any other time in my hearing has he mentioned the war and it is impossible to say whether he is uninterested in the subject or merely reticent. His opinions generally are a mystery and at times his face suggests an oriental detachment from the affairs of the lower world. I half expect to discover him cross-legged in an attitude of meditation. If he died the engines would stop and we would drift endlessly and never be heard of again.

One thing counters this image and reminds the casual observer what Mr Ford really is. He is accompanied every-where by two other men. The first is his bodyguard, a large and unreflective character who is known only as Ray and who frequently puts his right hand inside his coat. The other is usually a few paces behind and it is not clear, at first sight, whether the Reverend Samuel Marquis is a retainer or a pursuer. His features suggest permanent anxiety and he has the look of a detective from an English magazine story, hot on the heels of his quarry. It is his habit never to let Mr Ford dine alone and while at table he talks and talks but gets little in the way of answers from the great engineer, who seems either to ignore him or winces as if suffering some sharp discomfort. The newsmen tease with rumours of Marquis's sinister hold over Mrs Ford back home, or of her hold over him – she is the true director of the whole show, he is her secret agent, her *eminence grise* and perhaps even more than that. None of which, I suppose, contains a single word of truth.

For the rest I must say I am a little disappointed, though I have been lucky to find something of a soul-mate in Samuel 'SS' McClure, the big magazine publisher of ten or twenty years ago. He talks too much about himself (the students say his initials stand for Seldom Silent) but it is not an uninteresting story and he keeps me up late enough to give me some chance of rest in the small hours of the morning. He has his own rather pressing reasons for being here. Poor man – toward the end of one evening I thought he was about to propose some business venture or even solicit a loan of money. There are differences in our politics which I ought to care about more than I do, but they never seem to matter much when we talk. We share an appetite for trouble and in the last few hours he has certainly made some, as he warned me he would. I should say he is a few years short of sixty, an age in men I find more interesting the more I experience it.

It is now five o'clock in the morning and about half an hour since Samuel and I agreed it was safe for him to go back to his own cabin. We are, I would guess, some 50 degrees west or thereabouts. That is to say, in the middle of the Atlantic Ocean and as far away from settled humanity as any modern person ever gets. Since girlhood it has been for me the most philosophical of locations. Drowsing to the beat of engines, unimaginably far from anywhere, the great questions at last came within reach, preoccupations shrank to nothing, impossibilities unravelled like slipknots leaving life brilliant and simple. All my most passionate diary entries were written in the middle of the ocean. There were nights when everything became clear and I thought I would be President by now, and there would be nothing more to do in a perfected world.

Not much became clear last night, though it was certainly one of the more memorable I have ever spent at sea. It was the preparedness debate that put an end to our harmony. The delegates packed the first-class dining room, and as we had calm water even those laid low by sea-sickness were able to join us. Everyone seemed happy and excited by the prospect of the rousing rhetorical exercises to come, the joyful affirmation of self-evident truths. Men and women of good will would come together.

'I see the snakes have left the garden,' remarked Mrs Clark.

It was true. Meyer Block of the *Jewish Morning Journal* had drawn the short straw and was the only journalist present to cover the meeting – controversy was not expected. I looked round for a glimpse of Mr Ford but couldn't find him, or either of his two constant companions.

Reverend Jones opened proceedings with a homily, advising that when Cain raised up his hoe in the field and slew his brother this was the first instance of the great preparedness lie. Ever after, no peace-loving man or nation went prepared for conflict without the mark of Cain on his heart. The proof of America's closeness to God was that she bore no arms worth mentioning. General murmurs of approval, except among the students where a discussion started on whether a hoe, having a dual purpose and being arguably essential for life, was the equivalent in modern international law of the armed merchant-man and therefore subject to special rules. Someone hissed angrily and the future Supreme Court Justice fell silent.

Madame Schwimmer ascended the dais, her head becoming visible above the throng for the first time. She adjusted her spectacles.

'I can spare only a few minutes to be with you before returning to our diplomatic preparations.'

Suppressed laughter from an unknown quarter. Disapproving scowls. She recounted her odyssey – the struggle up from the depths of *mitteleuropa*; ceaseless, predestined wandering in the cause; her work for women's labour unions and universal suffrage. She sketched for us the groaning, enslaved nations of Austria-Hungary, how their hearts and minds were kept dull by endlessly fretting over ancient wrongs. And yet, even as they wandered on the dark seas of moral confusion (signs from some of returning nausea here), they looked outward to the light that was America, to the twin beams of peace and reason – 'I refer, of course, to the hopeful voices radiating from that tower of American enlightenment, President Woodrow Wilson, and his good friend Mr Henry Ford.'

Cheers here, and an abortive chorus of 'For He's a Jolly Good Fellow'. A perspiring Lloyd Bingham blew a rhythm on his whistle before quickly running out of breath. A shadow came over Schwimmer's face. Her audience fell silent. A sudden pain struck at her, or perhaps a memory of some deep grief.

'And what is this light that is now so threatened? Yes! – threatened I tell you. Is it the light that comes from more dreadnoughts, from more guns, from poisoned gas and the submarine? Some would have the Great Republic equip itself with these things – preparedness they call it, and who could doubt they mean preparedness for war? It'll never happen, they say. Or if it does it won't be our fault. And when it does we should be ready for whatever comes. But think, my friends – what approaching menace could this be? Will we poor, squabbling Europeans drain the Atlantic and attack North America ourselves one night? Will the waves of the Pacific turn warlike, or Canada's polar bears cast a covetous eye on the plains of Illinois? Perhaps the Mexicans will stop fighting each other for long enough to notice their neighbour to the north? Not likely, I think. And yet, those who talk of preparedness push and push for America to spend money on arms even though she has no enemies, no part, as President Wilson says, in this war. No war, say the preparers – but let us prepare for war. Do you believe them?'

Boos and loud denial from all sides. Calls of 'warmongers' and 'jingoes'. Block begins to make some notes as two or three more journalists come in from the smoking room. The heat rises from the press of bodies. As I look across the heads, packed as close as in the morning train, I see where Sam McClure finds something to stand on and suddenly appears above the rest. There is a look in his eye as he slips his hand inside his jacket. I can see the white corner of the paper he lightly touches with his fingers, the promised apple of discord. On the dais Madame Schwimmer, eyes closed, mouth slightly open, head upturned, awaits a message from beyond, from something greater than herself.

'What is America to be? A man who leaves his own safe and lawful home at night to go abroad with a knife in one pocket, a gun in the other, a bludgeon in his pants and lock-picks in his vest, all bought and paid for from the public purse? One who looks at you straight and tells you, "No, Sir, you mistake me. I go equipped for burglary and robbery not to do these things, but only so that the town may be safer." It *can't* be true. I speak as a woman, as the suffering sex, as one of the age-old onlookers to human violence. Take it from me, gentlemen, from your wives, lovers, daughters, sisters, from those who know your nature better than you know it yourselves – give a man a sword and he *will* use it, as sure as a dog is given teeth to bite.

'This is not the America war-torn Europe looks to. You may have heard that the preachers of preparedness have an English accent, or sometimes French. Perhaps it is so, but all these siren voices can do is drag America down into their own hell. They say America must defend herself, but what they mean is that America must come to their defence. And when they talk of defence, they mean war. This is not what the peoples of Europe want. Europe wants peace. I know – she has told me . . .'

The bag is held forth, a capacious envelope of black shagreen with two long, looped handles of the same material. They hang down like ears as Madame Schwimmer cradles the treasure from beneath.

'I have her deepest desires here, close to my chest. Peace! she cries out. Peace, oh peace, won't you lead me to peace! It is the America of peace that Europe needs – the vision of Henry Ford and the wisdom of President Wilson. If the preachers of military preparedness carry the day, the light of America, which is the light of peace, will go out. My friends, true America is here, on this brave ship in the middle of the ocean. True America has heard and sends, in us, her new pilgrims. We come not with any avenging army, but pure of heart and with the greater power of empty, harmless hands.'

A storm of cheering and clapping, of waving of arms, of *God Bless America*, of fainting – one near, one actual. Collars were loosened and menu cards waved as fans. Down the glass of the little windows moisture beaded and ran. Madame Schwimmer regretted that she had already taken too much time away from her duties. She begged to be excused and left triumphant, detained briefly by an applauding Louis Lochner who bent down to give his congratulations intimately into her ear.

'Stay on, please, Mr Lochner, and report to me later every word that is said.'

There were half a dozen more speeches, none of which can have given Madame Schwimmer any concern. They were orthodox and loyal and not very brilliant. One got the sense that the professional musician had left her instruments on the stage and that we were now being entertained by a succession of children and apprentices getting whatever sound out of them they could. Someone attempted too literal a demonstration of his argument when he produced a meat cleaver and brandished it menacingly at the audience.

'Don't worry – I'm only "preparing" for diplomacy and international law.'

Meyer Block scribbled rapidly in his notebook as a steward impassively relieved the speaker of his prop and returned it to the galley. All that was needed was a comic turn from Lloyd Bingham, and he seemed about to oblige when a heavier pitch toppled him into a well-placed chair and he thought better of it, his supporters flapping at his pale, sweat-sheened face as if he were an exhausted boxer sticking to his corner.

Lesser figures had their moment, adding to the warm glow of consensus. The preponderance of Americans steered the gathering in a patriotic direction and President Wilson came in for much praise as the man who would always keep us out of the war, the man who taught his people that there was such a thing as being 'too proud to fight'. Louis Lochner stepped forward and spoke of his personal acquaintance with the President and of his complete faith in his judgement and moral strength. There was another hearty cheer and a ragged chant of 'Peace! Peace!', in the dying away of which Samuel McClure unfolded the paper I had glimpsed two nights before. He held it up and waited for silence.

'It might interest you all to know what is in the President's State of the Union address to Congress.'

A pause to let this phrase have its full effect as he hooked out his reading spectacles from his vest pocket and put them on.

'I received my usual advance copy and . . .'

An artful consultation of his pocket watch.

'As the President is probably about halfway through his remarks by now, I think the embargo can fairly be said to have lifted. I will summarise.'

Newsmen gathered more thickly from the smoking room and soon there was a dozen of them clustered together by the door. It started well, with Sam putting on Wilson's rhetoric like a costume and beginning to swagger in its grand style. You could see the hope in everyone's eyes. Surely he would mention us, out here on the darkness of the sea doing something about the peace he so loved to talk about. Something oblique would do – we listened intently for the coded phrase, the word of half-approval that would strengthen our hand with the chancelleries of Europe. He was our man, and we knew that only discretion held him back from saying so.

'We have stood apart, studiously neutral. It was our manifest duty to do so . . . no part or interest in the causes that have brought the conflict on . . . neutrality, to which we were bidden by our habitual detachment from the politics of Europe and a clear perception of international duty . . . moral partnership . . . common sympathies. Ah, thank you.'

The Voice of the Republic accepted a glass of water, tendered ceremoniously by Reverend Lloyd Jones.

'Where was I? Yes, he goes on – United States as guardian of the republics to the south of her against encroachments from the other side of the water; disinterested enthusiasm for freedom; unmolested self-government of independent peoples; misconceptions of our motives put behind us; unabated spirit of President Monroe; common cause of national independence and political liberty in America; no selfish purpose or taking

284

of advantage. All governments of America on a footing of genuine equality; been put to the test by Mexico and have passed that test; no imposition on her; drinking at the true fountains of principle and tradition; Virginia Bill of Rights dum de dum de dum . . .'

'A little more respect, if you please,' interjected Governor Hanna.

'Just getting to the juice, Governor. Now I've lost my place. Here we are. Pan-Americanism, no spirit of empire but law, independence and mutual service; bonds of honourable partnership and common advantage. Americas destined to play part together in the adjustments of the next generation before peace resumes its healthful tasks – blah, blah, blah. Ah, yes – here we are. Good Lord, the man has clearly never worked for a newspaper. Climb aboard this sentence and hold on to your hats, ladies and gentlemen – "I am interested to fix your attention on this prospect now because unless you take it within your view and permit the full significance of it to command your thought I cannot find the right light in which to set forth the particular matter that lies at the very front of my whole thought as I address you today. I mean . . ."'

A pause here, with exaggerated breathlessness, a gulp of water, a visible straightening of the spine and expansion of the chest and, in my direction, a distinctly mischievous hint of a smile.

'. . . "national defence."'

There was a rustle through the tightly packed audience, the wave of alertness that ripples out from the leading edge of a storm.

There was first a brief nod to not maintaining a standing army beyond peacetime needs, but only as a preamble to the right of the people to bear arms and the farmers at Lexington rising to take care of themselves. What patriot could object to that? Things moved swiftly on, McClure so enjoying his presidential performance that it was hard to believe he hadn't once nurtured hopes in that direction, or at least dreams.

'"To fight effectively upon a sudden summons; to play the great role in the world for which we are qualified by principle and chastened ambition."'

Anxiety remained within bounds and pacifist hopes just alive so long as it was nothing more than words. The presidential stand-in pressed on.

'"These seem to me the essential first steps – an increase in the standing force of the regular army of fifty-two companies of coast artillery, fifteen companies of engineers, ten regiments of infantry, four regiments of field artillery, and four aero squadrons. In addition, by way of making the country ready to assert its real power promptly and on a larger scale the plan contemplates supplementing the army by a force of four hundred thousand disciplined citizens . . ."'

The murmuring had started right away, but that last, monstrous figure was too much. The spectre of a nation permanently in arms, poised for violence, struck the listeners as a sickening physical blow. A high, female voice rang out.

'Treason! Nothing less than treason!'

'Hey, it's Mrs Wilkes Booth. Get that good lady a gun.'

'Who said that? How dare you! Show yourself if you're a gentleman.'

Our little family began to divide. Half began to chatter about universal humanity, those deepest calls of nature that go beyond the lesser loyalties of tribe, class and country. Others, either in their hearts or in their more calculating brains, felt and answered that little twitch on the thread of nationhood. Whatever their opinions might have been half an hour before, they could not now knowingly go against their leader in a time of danger. Gloomy silence returned as McClure read on.

'"The programme which will be laid before you by the Secretary of the Navy is similarly conceived. It contemplates the construction within the first year of two battleships, two battlecruisers, three scout cruisers, fifteen destroyers, five fleet submarines, twenty-five coast submarines, two gunboats and one hospital ship; the second year two battleships, one scout cruiser, ten destroyers, four fleet submarines, fifteen coast submarines, one gun boat and one fuel oil ship; the third year . . ."'

'Stop! Stop, for pity's sake.'

I couldn't see who was shouting. Sam was only encouraged.

'Oh, but there's more.' He fanned through the pages of the speech. 'Don't you want to hear it all?'

Someone must have jumped – I could see the hand, high and isolated just before the crumpling noise and the swift disappearance of the speech as it was snatched away. Confusion broke out from all quarters. The newsmen looked like children at Christmas.

'Hey, I've got it,' declared one. 'Wilson only let these nuts out here so they couldn't cause any trouble.'

He turned to an outraged Mrs Morse Clark who looked as if she might abandon her principles for the pleasure of hitting him over the head with her evening bag.

'Try lobbying your senator now, lady.'

He threw his head back and laughed delightedly. He called to one of his colleagues who was already sidling towards the exit, notebook in hand.

'Hey, Hirsch! You better get 'em to make this boat go a little faster or they'll turn you into a soldier before we even get there. First ashore and straight *into* the trenches by Christmas. There's your story.'

Louis Lochner, pale with the shock of a personal betrayal, tried to quell the disorder.

'Please. Ladies and gentlemen, please be calm.'

They began to pay attention as he proposed that the expedition leaders would draft a resolution condemning military preparedness and that everyone who still wanted to be associated with the aims of the Henry Ford Peace Ship would sign it. Internationalists cheered, patriots growled. Lochner's temper deserted him.

'Anyone who doesn't put their name to the resolution has come on this voyage as nothing more than an enormous joyride.'

Uproar resumed. Lochner waved his arms in despair.

'German!'

He turned as if someone had slapped his face – only to find the insult was directed at someone else.

'A mouthpiece for the Kaiser, a propagandist – have you given the Kaiser his money back yet, McClure?'

As an accusation it made no sense, but as the dirtiest thing within reach I suppose it had a certain inevitability. Sam had no chance to reply before being confronted by a more immediate danger – Jenkin Lloyd Jones in an extremity of passion.

'You have misled the young people on this ship. You have preached armament and war from the outset.'

Reverend Jones' face was a festive scarlet and his beard more snowy white than ever. He seemed almost literally to burn as he held his features inches away from McClure's and shook his fist at him. For the space of a few words he became incoherent. I feared a fatal apoplexy.

'Go to bed, sir!' was what he ended up with. 'Go to bed!'

The newsmen beamed with joy. I watched as Max Swain of the *Herald* played that old trick with one of his cronies. His friend smashed his knuckles hard into the palm of his hand while Max shouted 'Fight!' The word made it so – in the news reports at least – and it was already too late for Lochner as he climbed on a serving table and made a last-ditch attempt to rescue the situation.

'Delegates of the Ford Peace Expedition – let us remember why we are here!'

He rapped a wine glass with a knife, only to smash it in his eagerness and then drop both to the floor. The knife skittered and span across the polished wood. The glass crunched under milling heels.

What happened next was a little unclear. The newspapermen and a trio of photographers bolted for the door with a single mind. I would not like to suggest that Mr Lochner deliberately tripped one of them up, but one way or another the formidable and loudly complaining bulk of Theophilus E. Montgomery of the Union Press Association found itself flat on the floor, blocking the progress of his colleagues. Lochner nimbly cleared the barrier and got a head start. The news posse briefly tugged at Theophilus' heels, then gave up all thought of moving him in preference for trampling him flat as they got after Lochner. I followed, guessing where they were going and determined to get every last detail for the feature story that would re-launch me as a journalist. We tumbled down steep stairs and then dashed back along a lower corridor. Lochner's voice sounded from ahead.

'Mr Bastian! Will you lock the door, Mr Bastian!'

We ran into each other in an excited, jostling heap. I was at the back and had to jump to see what was happening. There, in the brief instants in which I could keep my head above the others, was poor Louis Lochner, crucified across the entrance to the wireless telegraph office.

'Censorship!'

Lochner appealed for calm.

'You're dealing with the press, Lochner!' shouted someone in a strong New York accent. 'Patience is unconstitootional.'

Our little community was so stirred up that half the long night had gone before there was any peace. Lochner instilled some order in the newsmen by reminding them that regulations for neutral shipping required all messages to be cleared with the captain first. They agreed to wait while he went for consultations, but by the time he returned Mr Bastian had sold his command and many of their dispatches had already been sent, hopping from ship to ship all the way back to New York in time for the next day's evening editions.

Lochner went to bed in despair, the journalists to the bar in the first-class lounge. There they celebrated the fulfilment of their hopes and gave themselves energetically to a mock trial of the absent Samuel McClure on a charge of corrupting the morals of youth. Lloyd Bingham presided, it being agreed that he would be asleep throughout the proceedings and therefore even-handedly deaf to all submissions. The trial was called to order by the banging of a stuffed dove on the whisky-spattered bar and the witnesses' hands placed solemnly on a tobacco tin as they swore to tell nothing but lies. The star prosecution witness, Reverend Jones, was dismissed as incompetent on the grounds that he was indeed Santa Claus and so did not exist. A journalist spoke for the defence, testifying that McClure could take years to pay for a manuscript and was therefore a stranger to preparedness of any sort, military or otherwise. The jury pronounced the bar closed and brought in a verdict of not guilty just as Bingham finally toppled from his stool.

These details I heard later, but I was there in the gangway of the first-class deck as the fallen actor was carried past – two straining newsmen under his shoulders and another in front, holding his legs like the poles of a stretcher. He was given a stateroom of his own, much to the relief of his former cabin-mate who had complained widely of Bingham's coughing and snoring through the night. I passed that way half an hour later and saw, drawn round the number on the door with a finger dipped in borrowed rouge, a star and beneath it the words – 'at last'.

There were huddles of debaters throughout the ship and much coming and going from cabin to the Schwimmer staff stateroom as opinions were lobbied, votes firmed up, divisions solidified. Mr Ford slept on, so far as anyone knew, at the far end of the upper passenger deck, beyond the double barrier of the light-sleeping Dean Marquis and the taciturn Ray, ever watchful on his chair with his long legs stretched out across the way and his toes touching the opposite wall.

McClure survived his mock trial only to be summoned to a real one before Madame Schwimmer. Delegates loitered outside, pretending to converse with each other or to be waiting for their own interviews. No one quite had the effrontery to put their ear to the door, but they were all too curious to move on. Much of what passed between the two remained inaudible, but at the end the eavesdroppers were satisfied.

'I never trusted you – never! I've seen your type at work before. What have you ever made, Mr McClure? We all know what you've destroyed in your life, but tell me one thing you have built, just one thing.'

'Listen Schwimmer, I've known a good few martyrs in my time and last I heard they were all doing pretty good business and so far I don't see that you're any . . .'

'Why don't you destroy yourself?'

'Oh, that's nice. You're a real piece of work, aren't you? You know what I think? I think if you hadn't led such an unnatural life maybe you could tell the difference between a rational argument and a fit of hysteria.'

'Men and war, men and war – it never changes. No men, no war – that's what I say.'

'Tell that to the new Mrs Braley, you frozen old bat.'

'Get out!'

'I'm going, don't worry. Just remember this – you were born in your country and you left it. I chose my country and I'm sticking by it.'

Then the door opened and there was Samuel standing in the corridor pursued by Madame Schwimmer's voice in its full stage volume.

'And that's why I'm better than you are, you ... you ... *follower!*'

He walked towards me, away from the astonished audience. I made sure our eyes met. He seemed tired, as we all were then, and a little unsure of his triumph.

'Well, Samuel,' I said to him. 'You certainly had an effect.'

He looked over his shoulder. An even number of supporters and enemies returned his gaze. Sam had a more dramatic assessment, though it was not one that displeased him.

'I'm a hunted man, Inez.'

I moved aside and held open the door to my cabin.

'Asylum?'

He hesitated – his old-fashioned, gallant concern making me smile.

'Oh, don't worry about that,' I told him. 'I already have a reputation and I'm perfectly happy with it.'

I don't how long we spent together before that strange night was finally over. I broke the seal on my special brandy, telling the story of its acquisition in Paris and how I liked to think of myself as taking it home, preserving it for the victory celebration.

'Victory?'

'You think it's as well we should drink it now?'

We talked over the Wilson speech and I heard about the other parts there had been no time to read out. Scarcely conceivable sums of money were demanded to pay for these grand plans. Hundreds of millions loomed in my mind as I thought miserably on all the better things they could not now buy. There was polished rhetoric – for a moment it was almost like Schwimmer talking – about threats from within, citizens born under other flags, the poison of disloyalty in the very arteries of national life, how we would once have been ashamed to suspect our neighbours but must now prepare to crush out such creatures of passion and disloyalty.

Sam performed these solid phrases with a flourish and then a wistful dying away.

'And they can cast that net pretty wide. As wide as they want to.'

'Is that why you're for it?' I asked him. 'Because of what people will go on saying about you if you're not?'

'Inez, you do me an injustice. I never held a position for selfish motives and I won't now. No, it's worse than that. I believe the President is right. He is choosing the lesser of two evils.'

I told him how I hated war, the ease with which men fell into it, the slickness of their endless excuses, not one of which through the whole of history I had ever believed.

'I suppose I should hate you too.'

'Do you? Can you?'

I refilled our glasses, holding the little bottle upside-down for the last drop before pushing back the cork and letting it slip into the waste-paper basket.

'Maybe it's just as he says,' I offered hopefully – 'a precaution for something that will never happen.'

'No, your lot are right – don't give that up now. It's war. It's a certainty. They'll lie and lie and lie all the way down to the last week before the mobilisation orders. Then they'll tell you they changed their minds last Tuesday for whatever reason they feel like and that everything's different now. America is arming for war. The decision has been made and whatever else is said or done we'll all look back and say this was the day. Schwimmer's not all mad, you know.'

'I never thought she was.'

'She's right about the dog and its teeth. The dog is not an animal to make idle threats. America, in peacetime, is arming for war. But I'll stick with her.'

He raised his glass to the invisible object of his loyalties, then emptied it.

'I just don't know if she'll ever find her way back.'

For a long time we were still. No voices, no sounds of argument or debate came from without and even poor Mr Bingham appeared at last to have found some peace. I felt there was a moment when something might be said. I tensed, primed for something meaningful, either word or movement. The silent crisis passed and a deep common sadness settled on us both.

Sam exhaled heavily, stretched the tiredness out of his spine and ran his palms over his face.

'Well, I suppose . . .'

He stood up.

'I should go now.'

I kissed a rough cheek.

'Goodnight, Sam.'

Rosika

*S*pies are everywhere, perhaps assassins too. Rebecca herself brought me confirmation of this within the first twelve hours of our voyage, referring breathlessly to our patron.

'There's a man outside his door. It looks like he's going to stay there all night and . . .'

The last part of her report was whispered as though the walls themselves were not to be trusted.

'. . . they say he has a gun.'

I remarked on the irony.

'You laugh in the face of danger, Madame Schwimmer, but if Mr Ford's life is in danger, think how much you must be at risk – you without whom we could not go on.'

I bowed to the logic of this argument and an arrangement was soon in place by which Rebecca and Elli Eriksson, companion to the exiled Madame Malmberg, now share the duties of night-watchwomen. As I permit myself only four hours sleep a night, four guilty hours through which the hideous slaughter continues, their sacrifice is not too great. That we carry our enemies with us is an excellent sign – they take us seriously, they know we are on our way to achieving something. As for what Rebecca or the charming little Elli with her white linen cap and her embroidered bodice, her china-blue eyes and spun-gold pigtails, would do to preserve my life against a determined opponent I can't say. Neither do I fret much over the issue, being at that free and happy point in a leader's life where she knows that martyrdom can only speed the day. I expect my enemies know this too. Indeed, they think they are being clever by letting me live and I might be safer now than I have been for years. I did not explain this to Rebecca. She is too earnest, too passionate. It is kinder to let her serve. In a few minutes I will hear some quiet words outside my door and the slight shifting of a chair as the guard changes. It is strange, but in only a few days this has gained the force of a lifelong habit. I must stay awake for it, like they say children must for a parent's kiss. Only then, and almost at once, is there sleep.

The early histories of great causes have a regularity that comes very near to being a law of nature. Sometimes these seasons unravel over years, or even decades. We, vanguard of the century of speed, have rushed through the first few phases in a matter of days. One starts with the cheerful, thoughtless send-off. So it was at the pier at Hoboken. My detractors say I am part of this; that I share the optimisim of the crowd, the simple conviction that whatever they set themselves to has already been achieved, that it is never too early to celebrate a victory which will come as surely as tomorrow. They are wrong. I was carried back from that moment to another crowd with the same gestures, shouts, faces. It was London, not quite eighteen months ago. The people were happy then too – it was the start of the war.

On the deck of the *Oscar* I touched Mr Ford's elbow and he overcame his shyness, stepping forward to where everyone could see him. Was there a tremor in that narrow, thrifty body as he met the hopeful roar of thousands? He turned a little to his side, indicating that I should come forward to stand beside him. There we stood, the twin pillars of the world's best hope

– he the gold, I the genius without which nothing much can ever be achieved. I saw how powerfully Mr Ford was moved by the acclaim that surged up from the pier.

From even earlier, that day at the Belasco theatre, I had begun to guess what the great assembler needed and why this was such a secret desire, how he could reach out for it only haltingly and with a fear that few would ever guess at. Mr Ford needed to have cars taken out of his life. He needed them to be replaced with men and women, but was powerless to bring this about, paralysed. Who could deliver him? Not even Mrs Ford, evidently. She stood behind us, glum with her own small thoughts. I understood her homely worries, but can only be relieved that I am not weighed down by such distractions myself. In times like these it is nothing less than a humiliation for the thinking person to care too much about individuals. As I waved at the excited mass of well-wishers it was clear to me that I had grasped something about Mr Ford not even his wife had seen. There are great men who have everything they need to fulfil themselves, while others are held back by some obscure want that leaves only a latency of greatness which might never come to fruition. Mr Ford is of the latter sort – he has been, until now, a seed in a dry desert. I recall his features as the steam whistle sounded and as the ropes were cast off. Our eyes met and he conveyed to me as certainly as through the simplest spoken declaration – 'Madame Schwimmer, you have changed my life as much as I have changed yours.'

It is true – I have rained on Henry Ford.

In such high spirits we set off. An office was organised at once. Daily bulletins were issued, instructional and uplift programmes organised hour by hour. All was harmony and optimism. I, naturally, held myself apart. Accustomed to the solitude of leadership, I observed these first innocent forty-eight hours from afar, preparing myself for the troubles that would come. I received and collated reports on the journalists and began to work out which of them were not quite what they seemed. At that time they were still humorous rather than poisonous, but I know their nature well and was determined to be ready for the change. I puzzled over the presence of the mysterious Dr Marquis, watching closely as he followed Ford and as Mr Ford's valet followed him. I sorted the faithful from the self-seeking and the merely accidental. Who is Lloyd Bingham, why is he here? Louis Lochner tells me I made the decision myself but I'm sure I'd never heard of the man before he was introduced to me on board. Surprisingly, Mr Ford finds him acceptable and I have seen them talking together more than once. That young man, supposed to be a poet and who very nearly turned our departure into a farce, has also been given more than his due. Untaxing company I suppose, and a barrier to keep the relentless Marquis at bay.

There are other types sure to fall by the wayside at an early stage – earnest doers of God's work, disappointed politicians giving it one last try, energetic burnishers of their own conscience. I wondered about Mrs Boissevain (I gather she is styling herself Miss Milholland for the duration of the trip), but in the end have been disappointed. I can almost hear the words aloud when she passes me – 'I polish and polish and polish. Look! Is my heart not now as beautiful as I am?' That old fool McClure certainly thinks so. Anyway, I've put a stop to him. Rebecca brought me a report of his lecture this afternoon – audience much diminished. And then there's young Mr Louis Lochner himself, with his commitment and his peace pedigree and his education and yet – how much really do I know about him? All the history books tell us that intimates make the best assassins. You can win the war (I mean metaphorically of course) and return in triumph, but when it's Clytemnestra lurking at home it all comes to nothing in the end. I was reflecting on these lessons while making an early visit to the wireless room only to find that Louis had got there first. He was just leaving and seemed very pleased with what he had achieved.

'Everything's fine,' he smiled a conspiratorial smile. 'Shall we have a word about it later?'

I went in myself on the pretext of sending a personal message. I found the operator to be an engaging young man employed, I would say, rather below his station. He was of sound views and surprisingly well informed, explaining that his late father had inculcated the habit of reading a good newspaper every day and that this took the place of the education his family had never been able to afford.

'And I hardly ever need pay for them neither. There's not much worth knowing you can't find in the bins of any decent railway station or steamer quay. All you need is the curiosity. I even read about you and seen a big picture too. First time I've met a news story. Can you really do it, mam?'

'If goodwill and sanity prevail.'

'Yes, mam.'

'Was Mr Lochner sending a message?'

There was a pause and a sly look I rather respected. I explained that I had no objection to Louis sending messages, or to him reading over other people's.

'He said he wants his finger on the pulse, that's how he put it. I'm with you. Said I'd do anything to help.'

I felt inside the hidden pocket of my purse and eased out a ten-dollar gold piece.

'Can you see that I get everything first? A separate copy, mind you.'

'And Mr Lochner's own messages?'

And so I sit at night going through the endless magnetic chatter, the yellow journalism and the self-promotion and the broadcast billet-doux of Louis Lochner who, after a day of following Mrs Boissevain around the ship, sends sparks of love back to Emmeline and little morse-coded kisses for the baby. Sometimes it's hard to understand why he came. A continent in flames and still his heart is elsewhere – perhaps our work can never be completed until we have a world without men.

And so we moved on to the next stage – the first testing storm. I admit the particular provocateur who stirred it up came as a slight surprise. On the first night when I addressed the delegates it was McClure who jumped forward and declared 'I'm with you there, Madame Schwimmer. I have seen those documents and they convinced me.' I can't say I recall ever showing them to him, but I let it pass at the time. There he was again at the preparedness debate. I made my speech and he had no objection to it as long as I was in the room. Not half an hour later, as I was in my cabin composing another of Mr Ford's wireless bulletins to the press, Rebecca burst in to report that chaos had broken out. There was wild talk of mutiny and even the suggestion that we should turn right around and return to New York before America 'stabbed peace in the back'. I calmed her down and understood the situation as soon as I could get some sense out of her. Having made it my business to know all about Mr McClure's recent difficulties I realised an antidote was close to hand. Rebecca was sweetly uncomprehending.

'But what do you mean? I don't understand.'

'Just say it – others will understand.'

I sent her up all the same, carrying her one-word message to be delivered in perfect innocence. I got her report about midnight, which was highly satisfactory – perhaps it made things a little worse at first, but when it comes to catharsis there must be no half measures. If it is necessary to portray McClure as a German sympathiser, he is the one who has made it necessary. Later I received a sheaf of the latest telegrams. Years of police court sensationalism had gone into them and they made colourful reading – 'War on the Peace Ship'; 'Mutiny on the Oscar'

– 'Pistol Shots Believed Fired'; 'Ford Locked in Room – Chained to Bed by "Secretary"'. There was a message from a westbound liner – 'Do you need assistance?' Captain Hempel's reply came next; an apology and terse explanation that the 'mutiny' was metaphorical. All in all it was not good, but the news was flying to New York and Washington, not to Europe where our business is now. It can do no harm. Besides, I was sure at the time, and have been proved entirely right, that within twenty-four hours of this upset we would know who is truly with us and who against. The immediate affair ended with me being intruded upon by McClure in the early hours. He came, so he said, to 'state his position'. The interview quickly deteriorated into him storming about reputation and integrity. He demanded that I should enquire into who had so direly insulted him. I asked if he cared about his reputation more than about the war. Like all his sex, he considers righteous anger a virtue and regrettable things were said before the door finally slammed shut. To give him his due, I received an apology before breakfast the next day, though not a recantation.

It is always better to get such unpleasantness over sooner rather than later. When we land in Christiania we can now be more certain of success than ever. Some of those same guns that fire in brutish cruelty will be melted and cast into statues to be set up in the public squares of every city in Europe. Children will come with flowers in spring and lay them by the peace memorial steps as doves flutter up from their cages. I now know the faces that will be on those statues, and the faces that will not; the names of the peacebringers carved on the plinths below, and the names of the forgotten.

Mr Ford's name, I suppose, will have to be there. Those in the future who can ever find out the truth of this adventure will note it as one of the minor ironies of history. In reality our manufacturer slept through these debates and reacted to reports of them the next morning with such calm as usually comes only from not understanding what has been said. Copies were made of President Wilson's speech and distributed throughout the ship. One was sent to Mr Ford with his breakfast, carried by Dean Marquis. I should add that Marquis has taken the precaution of sending no telegrams on any subject at all and will discuss nothing other than opera and novels, leaving me in ignorance of his true beliefs. If he took the opportunity to influence Mr Ford against us, the situation could have been distinctly awkward. Both Louis and I asked to see Ford early but were sternly repulsed by his bodyguard, a man who discusses nothing with anyone. We waited anxiously for a response and it was Marquis himself who brought and read out a brief note. Firstly, the auto-maker forbore under any circumstances to censor 'my friends in the press'. Then the note drew attention to a sentence late in Wilson's speech which no one had yet noticed. It was proposed that his monstrous list of weapons be paid for by taxing gasoline at the rate of one cent per gallon. Mr Ford deplored this suggestion as an attack on the freedom of the American road and mused as to whether a country that taxed movement itself would truly be worth defending.

'And, eh . . .' concluded Dr Marquis, folding the paper and replacing it in his pocket, 'that's it.'

Since departing the United States this is the first statement issued by Ford not written either by myself or Mr Lochner. It was almost a surprise to hear his voice. I would not for the world let anyone hear me say it, but it seemed to me very plain that he makes a better puppet than a man.

I am exhausted. I lie back and let my papers slip to the floor. I hear a snatch of drunken male song and recognise two of the journalists. Their emptiness is almost enviable at times. At its extreme it reaches to a sort of invulnerability – quite simply there is nothing there to hurt. But think of their deaths – I don't envy them that. Think of being conscious at the last and having nothing more to look back on than the ephemera of having been a newsman. Not life, but a report on life. Not this great peace we will make, but merely a record of what others did to achieve it. Death for them will be a crumpled sheet of newspaper blowing down an empty street.

The coloured cabin night light glows dimly as a candle. I have explained what will happen. Tomorrow, in the afternoon, we will approach the Orkney Islands. Once in territorial waters we will come under Britannia's sway and must satisfy her navy before going on. We will then steam through the war zone under our flag of peace and begin our mission at Christiania. Norway worries me – still no response to my messages. Mr Bastian in the wireless room tells me the atmosphere is bad. I will ask again first thing in the morning. I check my father's pocket-watch, holding it close to the night light so that I can read the face. I begin to sink down sweetly to sleep. I can just hear the quiet, caring voices outside my door. It is that time – the changing of the guard, for myself just as it is for Mr Ford. Rebecca has come for the late watch. One guard gently hushes the other. I have enough strength only to raise my head and see the handle of my door turn, the lock tested and safe. The cares of leadership, the cares! The loneliness! But now, all the lead in my life turns to feathers, to breath. My fingers loosen from around the handle of my bag. Weightless in sunlight, I walk in the dream of my life where my work is done and the world is as it should be.

Louis

The sick list grows. Lloyd Bingham is said to be giving some concern and now Mr Ford has a worsening cold. The ship's nurse (a formidable and highly Scandinavian woman) bossed him into accepting a rub down with alcohol and pronounced the matter trivial. He appeared early in the afternoon and whispered hoarsely in my ear.

'Lochner, swear to me on your life you will never let that woman near me again. If I am revived it was only because of the need to defend myself. I'm going to get some heat in my bones. Don't give me away, will you?'

Off he went, down to the engine room where he spends endless contented hours watching things rise and fall and needles tremble on the faces of pressure gauges. He talks to the men about steam engines, the machine whose empire he did more than anyone to destroy. There is a story among the journalists that one of them was stopped by a stoker up for air one evening and asked, 'That man — who is he?'

The cause of Mr Ford's indisposition is supposedly dramatic, but was witnessed only by Berton Braley. Our ardent bard alleges that he alone was strolling outside the principal stateroom when Ford emerged for an early-morning constitutional only to be engulfed by a freak wave. It is already an oft-recounted incident, with Berton casting his pen and notebook to the savage flood as he sprang into action to save the struggling titan. We are to believe that Mr Ford was in the process of being swept away as the waters drained from the deck and it is certainly true that his lean frame would easily slip between the railings and the lifeboat davits. Berton conjures an image of himself fighting through the billows, able to see nothing but a brown derby hat and the gleam of Ford's gold-topped walking cane.

'Oh sure – *now* I believe him,' opines Tom Seltzer of *The Call*. 'He was going for the cane and got old Henry's ankle by mistake.'

'There's a Model T waiting for you when you get home, Berton.'

'You think?'

General laughter.

We are promised a versified Saving of Henry – a work of perfect poetic equipoise, says its excited author, somewhere between Hokusai's *Great Wave*, *Moby Dick* and Sherlock Holmes's headlong flight down the Reichenbach Falls, although with a happier ending.

There appears to be some truth in the story, though only some. Mr Ford is reluctant to enter into details (the image of frailty cannot appeal), but has explained that he has been forced to change to his second-favourite hat on account of a white crust of salt developing around the ribbon of the first. I have not yet found an opportunity to ask, but am madly curious to know whether the proprietor of one of the world's greatest industrial concerns has brought with him only two hats – which would be considerably fewer than Rosika Schwimmer, I might add. Knowing the man, as I am slowly beginning to do, I think it is only too likely – quite charming, really. More significantly, he confirms that his cold is on the wane and that he looks forward to landfall in Norway as keenly as the rest of us.

With respect to our internal dissensions some sort of truce has finally been declared. Rosika claims it as a victory for her methods but I wonder if there was not an easier way. I admire her as much as ever – her tenacity, her courage against the odds, but I think my feelings for her will not go beyond admiration. On one thing I remain quite clear in my mind – I could not play her role and she is as essential to this effort as Mr Ford himself.

President Wilson's speech on preparedness – let me call it what it is – on the arming of America, came as a heavy blow to me. As McClure droned on through that horrible list of weapons I was aware that I was the only one in the room who had actually spoken with Wilson, who had sat and talked peace with him twice in the last few weeks. Now I know what he was thinking as he listened to us and nodded and said so little in reply. He must have been writing that speech at the very same time!

'Yes, gentlemen, how wise you are – *two battlecruisers or three?*'

'Indeed, Mr Lochner, I have often thought so myself – *two hundred thousand for the citizen militia, or four hundred thousand?*'

And then my foolish question at the end and his laconic 'No, that is for me to decide', except that he already had decided.

I have made altogether too much of my meetings with the President. I spoke of them several times to Miss Miholland and then, when McClure was relishing the worst of the speech and could still be heard and the riot had not yet started, I suffered all the more when I found her eyes on me and that entrancing, transatlantic smile which said, surely – 'The more fool you, Louis, for ever believing him in the first place.'

My own loyalties are comfortably undivided. I hardly know how properly to express the strength of my feelings on this.

There is a strangeness to it, a slightly feverish sense of remoteness, as if my own country had all at once become foreign to me. It is as if I had awoken to find myself speaking with an outsider's accent and struggling to make myself understood to people who are now, though faultlessly polite, a little more formal than before and stand six inches further away. I have read the President's message over many times. It is a deep disturbance in American tradition, all the more so as we are asked to arm ourselves against no specified enemy and to defend against a threat of no certain reality. It is Mr Wilson himself who has described the European conflict as 'a war with which we have nothing to do, whose causes cannot touch us'. And yet the question must be asked – if we are now at peace and with no enemy in sight and even so are asked to live and spend as warriors, shall we ever be farmers again?

While I am entirely with Rosika in putting peace before everything, other Americans feel differently and she finds this hard to understand. She is harsh on all matters of national sentiment, insisting that it is a sort of intellectual failure, a purely emotional excuse for abandoning principle. She trusts too much to reason. I have raised the subject with her several times in quiet moments and tried to steer her gently away from making things worse, but with little success. She now holds herself out to be a perpetual wanderer, a citizen of no country, unencumbered by any of these loyalties she dismisses as 'all flags, anthems and hatred'. She cannot see that while she promotes this rootlessness (objectivity is her word for it) as a great modern virtue, a good part of her audience, and most particularly Americans, on the hook of Wilson's rhetoric, see it as the most ghastly and unnatural of defects. For them it is as if Rosika is a child proudly declaring its lack of love for its parents. Governor Hanna, his mind on elections back home and drink having been taken, recommended pregnancy as the cure for her ills and pronounced expertly on 'having seen this

sort of thing before'. Others in the patriotic camp do not hesitate to diagnose the envy of the Jews for those who have a
country of their own and say so frankly in front of me, as if
I also should not be offended. She is now reputed to be a
ceaseless plotter applying her shadowy 'Dual Monarchy' mind
to the destruction of whoever disagrees with her.

'It is nothing, Louis, nothing at all. I have borne it all my
life. It has never much harmed me before and it certainly won't
now. Remember, Louis, that everything really important is
simple. One must not let the small-minded confuse things
unnecessarily. I am a partisan of humanity and whoever cannot
say the same has no business being here. You mustn't worry –
as soon as we land the dross will take care of itself. I expect
that Milholland woman will disappear into the nearest department store and never be seen again.'

All very forthright, all very clear – admirable qualities in a
field marshal, but she wins few friends and, worryingly for one
on an expedition such as this, she is no diplomat. Besides myself
only one American shares the open grandeur of her vision –
Mr Ford.

'She's right, Louis. She's ahead of them all. In a hundred
years there won't be any countries left. All there'll be is
customers and they'll be the same all over the world. Our
problems will be over then.'

It was Mr Ford who came up with the method for calm-
ing the upset caused by the preparedness debate. He proposed
a moratorium on taking firm positions and suggested instead
that working parties be set up to consider all the issues before
coming together in three days to settle on a common platform
everyone could accept. For these three days there was peace
as the delegation settled down to what it does best – talk. The
Oscar became a floating university of peace. We put war under
a powerful collective microscope, we defined its structures,
designed and prescribed the vaccine that will permanently

remove it from our world. I smile a little, it is true, but I believe it all the same. In the future war will be a crime just as murder is today. When diplomacy fails, the peaceful blockade will be as far as any country will be allowed to go in pursuit of its own ends. A growing, and finally world federation of nations will teach everyone their common interest and make war seem as antique and barbarous as the Colosseum games of Rome. Briefly, in our cockleshell upon the seas, we became the prototype of that future world of reason.

This grace period ended Friday when a more general meeting was called in the evening finally to heal the rift. Rosika had been busy in the meantime, inventing a Resolutions Committee and packing it with her most pliable friends. This produced a document that boldly declared opposition to the growth in American arms and called on the citizens of every state of the Union to unite against it. I put my own name to it without difficulty, but was not surprised when several of my older countrymen were outraged. Worse was to come when it became clear that the new resolution was intended to be a test of faith and a ticket for the rest of the journey – signatories would continue as accredited members of the peace delegation, dissenters would be excluded.

It was Reverend Aked who announced the new arrangements, his English accent suddenly more prominent and less tolerable than before.

'If there is anybody who cannot sign the resolution we are very sorry. Copies are being distributed for signature by those who are with us.'

A forlorn attempt was made to adjourn the meeting. McClure – who else? – was instantly on his feet. Everyone supported the peace mission, he explained, and everyone hoped it would lead to international disarmament in due time. But to oppose the weapons of his own country, to 'impugn the course laid out by the President' – that he could not do. He stuck his

thumb in his vest pocket and looked upwards before conclud-
ing with some plangent line on conscience and martyrdom
that might almost have come from Rosika. He sat down with
that look of self-loving sternness by which a man says 'Of these
things I have spoken, I shall never speak again' – though of
course he did, and at inexhaustible length.

There was plenty of support. Judge Ben Lindsey ruled that
accepting an invitation did not mean accepting the host's opinions. Governor Hanna declared that he would return by the
first available boat so that he could be with his country in its
hour of need. Inez Milholland said the whole thing was un-
democratic. Others talked of railroading, while our leading
prohibitionist deposed an oath that he would not sign the
Golden Rule-itself if it were presented in such a way. Thus
Rosika's old-world methods reignited the issue and made it
burn more fiercely than before.

'The situation is positively European,' one wit wirelessed
back to his paper.

The weekend, pencilled in for reconciliation, was given over
to more preaching and bickering. Some two dozen signed right
away and got the name 'Rosika's people'. Many of the rest
tumbled all the way back down the hill to wallow in loud talk
of the 'my country right or wrong' type. Once everyone had
argued themselves to a standstill it was accepted that only authority could break the deadlock. The matter was carried up to
Mr Ford, our silent idol. Pale and weary, swaddled in two coats
and muffler in his over-heated stateroom, the tycoon sat
vacantly through lengthy presentations. Dean Samuel Marquis
took care always to be present, observing the suffering of his
employer with no sign of sympathy. In the end Mr Ford turned
to me, almost pathetically.

'But what difference does it make? They came on a peace
expedition, the resolution is against war – let them sign it.'

I explained again that no one questioned the support for a

negotiated peace, or the call for general disarmament in the future.

'It's just the last clause, Mr Ford – the one deploring America's new weapons. The American delegates – they feel . . .'

'A gun's a gun. What does it matter who's holding it? If you're against them, you're against them. I'm against them.'

This is what some call his saintliness, others his mere ignorance of all things not connected with the automobile, others again his fitful genius for cutting through to what is hidden from more cluttered minds. Mr Ford shuddered and blew his nose.

'I can see where this is going. Those bastard Dodge brothers and that bastard Walter Chrysler will make the guns and their Jew bastard bankers in New York'll give them the money to do it. Why not? They're already giving it to England and Germany and France.'

I glanced at Marquis. We three were alone in the room. With something between a weak smile and a twinge of physical discomfort he looked away to the sluggish, grey heave of the Atlantic through which we churned with unbearable slowness.

'The Ford Motor Company is not a democracy,' Mr Ford added unnecessarily.

He began to ramble about tractors again, indulging a new whim about travelling to Moscow to sell them to the Russians.

'Put the Russian steppe under the plough with Fordson tractors – that'll solve their problems. Why do they want to be mixed up in this anyway? Oh, Louis – can you ask the ship's nurse to call on me again?'

On Saturday, then, Mr Ford was immovable and I was sent back to make a futile plea for obedience. Rosika was delighted and chattered that evening in her cabin about future schemes to which she could hitch the willing Ford engine after the war.

'Captive Greece has captured Rome. It's for the best, Louis. Many a time in history great powers have been misdirected or left idle, unquickened by any directing vitality. An unused power is no power at all – for a generation the cause of humanity drifts simply because brain and muscle have not come together in the right way.'

She lay back on the narrow cabin bed and arranged the folds of her kimono. She sipped a glass of schnapps she had just had brought to her by one of the stewards.

'Have you ever wondered what would have become of Henry Ford if he had not met me?'

She paused to work up her *aperçu* – a line, no doubt, in an autobiography.

'The engine would race, Louis, but the wheels would not turn. What would be left in the end but a name enamelled on a radiator grille?'

Elsewhere, stubborn resisters bustled from meeting to meeting, determined to dig their heels in against anything that would put them on the wrong side of their own government as the war drums began to sound. At the worst we risked leaving America as a peace expedition only to arrive in Europe talking half about peace, half about war and making little sense about either. Impending farce made my thoughts turn timidly back on myself – what of my reputation, my career? Should I scurry home and issue Petrine denials – 'The Ford Peace Ship? No, no – you must have someone else in mind. I never had anything to do with it.' I have a long letter to Emmy ready for posting at Kirkwall (a Marconigram would be seen by too many eyes). I try to explain what is happening and tell her not to read the newspapers.

There was no point in talking to Rosika any more about compromise. I did what I could on my own, spending Sunday making the best of quiet moments of conversation alone with our newly inflamed patriots. Without an audience McClure was reasoned and patient. In half an hour I felt him draw me in to his own way of seeing things. Only the thought of the pleasure he would gain from making a convert held me back.

'You know,' he told me with a confidential air, 'Inez Milholland thinks just the same way I do. Wouldn't a little compromise be so much easier?'

'Mr Ford's concern is what is right, not what is easy.'

He almost derided the mention of Ford's name and suggested casually that I could talk him round to anything I wanted.

'After all,' he claimed archly, 'that's how this whole thing got started, isn't it?'

I said he might be underestimating our patron.

'You see,' I explained, 'Mr Ford tells me his motor company is not a democracy. He is very firm on that point. He has a way of doing things which, we have to admit, has done pretty well so far.'

McClure objected that we were hardly his employees and that such an idea could only make relations with the delegates worse.

'Maybe so, but he does rather see you as on the payroll. He gets the bills, you understand. It colours his viewpoint.'

'*You're* on the payroll, Lochner. Look, don't get me wrong. I want this thing to work, as much as it can, but don't you see how what Wilson's said to Congress changes things? I don't know what's going to happen, but signing up against preparedness could be a millstone around these people's necks. Most of the people on this boat are going to have to go home and earn a living after this. Not Ford or Mrs Fels with her soap factories, but the rest will – opinion matters to them, they're not so free. Why don't you try telling him that? Make it a matter of money rather than principle – easier for him to understand.'

I objected to that last remark and he withdrew it with an easy smile.

'Just change a few words,' he pressed. 'Just take out anything about Wilson, preparedness, anything about America. I'm sorry, but I can't stay with it otherwise.'

'Don't the words matter, or at least the meaning?'

It sounded jejune as soon as I had said it and it certainly amused McClure.

'Listen, Louis – words are my business, my life. When I was your age I used to think as you do. Now I'm a little older things are clearer. So why don't you benefit from my advice and wise up a few decades before your time? Write anything you like to keep people on board – just keep them on board. It's what people do that matters.'

'And Madame Schwimmer?'

'Ah', said McClure, 'Madame Schwimmer.'

He ran his thumb to and fro through the greying wire of his moustache, looked distant and frowned.

'Well, she's your problem.'

Resignations were threatened and through the day the rumoured list of names grew longer. McClure came first with Inez Milholland, taking a stand on democratic methods, close behind. Newsmen paired them and hummed wedding tunes whenever Inez passed by on deck or in the smoking lounge. Before long their political consciences were worked up to a scandalous elopement, the lurid details of which I could read in Mr Bastian's copy telegrams.

I saw Mr Ford again that afternoon with the intention of telling him the peace expedition was about to split, that President Wilson's blast on the trumpet had left too few Americans still willing to sign up to a universal principle. His stateroom is on the upper deck and second only in scale and elaboration to that of the Braleys. A triple window looks out to the front and allows the same view of the bow and the featureless direction of travel as that enjoyed by Captain Hempel from the bridge immediately above. I found him sitting by this window, his narrow legs pressed together and covered with a plaid travelling blanket, an illustrated magazine unregarded in his lap. The wicker chair creaked with his every slight movement and a silver spoon tinkled in a glass as Ray stirred powder into a steaming cold remedy, handing it to his employer before going out to stand guard in the corridor. Marquis, in a leather easy chair, looked up from a sheaf of papers and offered a brief, consoling smile.

'I'm better,' said Mr Ford. 'My guests must think me a very poor host to shut myself away like this. You can tell them I'll be fully recovered tomorrow.'

I was not so sure. There was a darkness around his eyes and a tremor in his hands I had not seen before. For the first time it occurred to me that his condition might be dangerous and an appalling prospect opened before me. He coughed several times, each dry hack connected to the next by a long, convulsive wheeze that pressed all the breath from his body. He waved dismissively when I expressed concern.

'I know my own mechanism, Louis. Tell me about yourself. How is my victim? How goes the world outside?'

I explained the situation, though he seemed to hear none of it as he gazed down at the ocean and endlessly worried at the corner of a page in his magazine.

'Well, just make them sign it,' he said at length. 'People have to be in step, to work to the same beat. There's always some that don't like it at first, but they come round when they see what it can do – I learned that early on.'

I looked at Marquis with a silent question – was there a fever, was his understanding affected? The Dean's eyebrows rose very slightly, but with no hint of an answer. I started to list the delegates likely to resign.

'You see,' Mr Ford interrupted, 'nothing much good ever went down the stream of life without a ripple.'

He worked his theme erratically, finding links to the

prohibition of alcohol, the health-giving effects of old-style dancing and the corrosion of the will accruing from too much education. He mused on his likely future adoption of vegetarianism, recommended a study of the habits of birds as a more reliable guide to life than that available from any human philosopher and regretted that the boys – by which he meant the journalists – drank too much and were thus apt to uncharitable opinions contrary to their better natures. They were all good fellows really.

Marquis attempted to interrupt but was run down by a vertiginous tour of the Ford plans for world improvement after the 'European business' had been dealt with.

'The book-learned tell you there are civilised societies and primitive ones – the poorest and most benighted they call "unspoiled". Well, they're going to have to write their books all over again because in the future the two societies will be motorised and unmotorised. Maybe *I* should write a book. Louis, would you like to write a book? You could do it for me, I'll tell you what to say. Yes, that's the problem of the world today – how to motorise the unmotorised. The men who do that will change the world more than presidents and kings. Perhaps I'll stop over in Europe a while once we're done. My German agents tell me Poland is the place to look – the market's bound to be good once this war business is over. And then further east too – did you know, Louis, there are whole continents with hardly a mile of road fit for good Firestone rubber? My Cairo concessionaire writes a letter four times a year telling me to look south. In Africa, where there is no railroad and no river for boats to ply, there is no trade. Men live in a perpetual prison, the cells of which are measured by how far they may carry a load in a day on their own feet. I will throw them the key to their prison. Have you ever operated an automobile tractor, Louis?'

'You were good enough to show me the factory, Mr Ford.'

'A child can master it in an hour and be taught to maintain it in five. Your Hottentot with the latest Fordson tractor beneath him will bow to no man. Africa will burgeon, her displaced sons and daughters will abandon their cotton sacks and their shoe-shine stands and take ship again, returning to fulfil their homeland's promise, ending a historic injustice.'

The theme was pursued until all the world was covered and the mechanically assisted perfection of man complete. Only Australia was excepted (all sand) and Japan (all mountains). Antarctica he forgot.

Dr Marquis, who showed no surprise at any of this, put aside his papers and leaned forward to speak.

'Best, don't you think, to put the present war behind us first?'

Mr Ford drank the last of his cold remedy and returned his attention to the sea. He spoke quietly to himself – 'Get the boys out of the trenches by Christmas.'

I was unsure of what to expect from Marquis. He is not a delegate on the peace expedition and no one seems quite sure what he is. His conversations with me have been courteous but restrained, as if he were a diplomat from an opposing power, a gentleman to his glove-tips but careful all the same not to give away the slightest detail of policy. I know from Mr Bastian's reports that the newsmen have cast him as the urbane Rasputin of the Ford Empire and Mr Ford has frankly described him to me as 'a disappointment'. I believe he is a thorough sceptic on the matter of our mission, privately he may even find it laughable. What remains a particular mystery is the nature of the bond between Marquis and Mr Ford, who seems obliged to accept his company for almost every waking hour, though it clearly brings him no pleasure. Ordinarily, I would have preferred him not to be there but on this occasion, whatever his intention, he was not unhelpful.

'This statement,' continued the Dean, 'does it have to be so specific – I mean, to single out a particular country, the policy of a particular man? If we raise the tone to a more general level?'

'There are no generalities!' snapped Mr Ford. 'I don't make general cars, my customers don't generally buy them and young men in Flanders aren't generally killed. Men who talk like that are the problem. We must cut through them.'

He gestured incisively. The glass was knocked from the arm of the chair and shattered on the floor. Thoughtlessly, I moved forward but was curtly ordered not to. I sat down unhappily, like a schoolboy who had failed to ingratiate himself with a master.

'Mr Woodrow Wilson does not generally intend to waste the American people's money on battleships. I didn't take to the man – I wouldn't give him a job neither.'

'I'm sure you're right,' smoothed Marquis. 'Perhaps it's just a matter of how people see things, of perspective?'

Mr Ford's eyes narrowed, his nose wrinkled as if he were about to sneeze. Marquis, glancing in another direction, pressed on.

'It is hardly surprising if a man whose whole life takes place in a single region of a single country has a narrower, let us say, a more simply patriotic view of things than a man who manufactures in a dozen countries and under a dozen governments. To see and feel equally about the whole map of the world at one time is given to few men. Practically speaking, one has to make allowances for the smallness of the ordinary man.'

'Dr Marquis, I will say you have a remarkable way with words. You could describe one of my own cars to me so that even I would not buy it. The fact is I always feel insulted when a man tries to flatter me. I thought you would know that by now.'

Marquis was unperturbed. He had the air of one who knew how to handle a familiar situation.

'I'm worried – and not just about you. Think of Clara . . . of Mrs Ford.'

'What does *any* of this have to do with my wife?'

'I mean what Mrs Ford will have to read in the newspapers.'

'She's seen worse.'

'Are you sure? And more than that – your own position once you return. If the United States should end up fighting in this war you will be the most prominent person to have been against her preparing for such an ordeal.'

'You take our failure for granted?'

'Not at all. I just mean that . . . Well, to put your own name to such a bald statement might make no difference in the end and do you some harm.'

'Harm? Speaking the truth does no harm. War is harm. Putting your taxes up and giving you back your son in a coffin is harm. Say, Louis – make a note of that one, will you?'

I patted my pockets in search of a pen and in the end accepted a pencil stub held out by Marquis. Mr Ford became enjoyably agitated. The orator, so deeply hidden at the Belasco Theatre, began to rise to the surface. In time, we might make quite a fine campaigner out of him.

'Wilson will do harm and I aim to stop him. And as for me, Samuel Marquis, do you think I am the sort of man to fold up his principles and pack them away as soon as someone runs a flag up a pole?'

He suppressed another fit of coughing while signalling enthusiastically that I should record this too.

'Damn! I make such good sense when I'm angry.'

Marquis jumped to his feet.

'But Mr Ford, please – to go against your President?'

There was a hesitation in the older man, an attentive stillness as if better to hear his inner voice. Marquis seemed hopeful of a breakthrough. I looked on as Mr Ford's expression changed into that hard, distant grandeur all his intimates know and that I had first seen in the winter gloom by the edge of an empty swimming pool. Henry Ford was thinking, not in any ordinary way (even for him), but labouring intensely to bring forth a precise and novel conception, perhaps even a new turn on his life's road.

'You know,' he said quite simply, 'I think you might be right. Presidents come and go after all, and I don't think the American people should have to tolerate a man in the White House who would tax gasoline.'

At that moment I believe Mr Ford could clearly see the outline of the Supreme Court Chief Justice before him, and hear the murmuring reverence of the crowd as he spoke the oath of office. And why not? Why not, indeed? Marquis turned pale. His eyes flickered upwards as if truly about to faint and he looked just as a man should look the moment after he has committed the most fatal and irreversible error of his life. He said no more.

My problem remained and as the awesome quality of the silence ebbed away I returned to it as gently as I could. It was hard to regain Mr Ford's attention and I'm not sure I ever quite succeeded. He did not look at me for the rest of the interview, but continued staring at the sea and the gradually lightening sky. At length I arrived back at the issue of resignations.

'Miss Milholland, I fear, will also go. She would be a particular loss, I feel.'

The patient, hollow-cheeked and with his steel-grey hair now seeming white and thin, drifted in his own thoughts and gave no sign of having heard.

'Such a small, indeed a barely noticeable change of wording would solve the whole problem.'

I went on to explain how these resignations from the peace delegation would not be like dismissing an employee.

'There would be consequences, sir. These people will talk to the press. Whatever the truth, the delegation will be seen to be divided. Our enemies will make mischief.'

He stirred at the word 'enemies', but was not sufficiently roused to speak.

'If only the platform was voluntary – if no one actually *had* to sign it.'

It seemed barely honest to ask for the abandonment of everything Mr Ford had insisted on over the last five days. If I had been speaking to Rosika there would have been shouting, statuesque poses, grand phrases and the slamming of doors. The facts had not changed, neither had the arguments and neither, I suppose, had anyone's principles. And so I was slow to understand when Mr Ford, shifting to relieve some slight discomfort and still not looking at me, spoke a few quiet words.

'Well, what does it matter in the end?'

The phrase was discouragingly close to the one he had used five days before to insist on the opposite position. But the tone now – the actions, the sense, the feel of it, everything but the actual, dictionary-defined words was so different that it had the effect of a sudden, unexpected insertion of a foreign language. The whole grounds and foundation of the fight were now being given up as if they had never mattered in the first place, as if all that had been gone through might just as well not have happened. What did it mean?

I was speaking – saying something irrelevant no doubt, something hesitant and puzzled, when Marquis caught my attention and gave me that look that so clearly urges 'Go on, do it now, take your chance.'

'Delegates *don't* need to sign the resolution, then?'

I worried that I had made it too much of a question, or that I had sounded astonished. Mr Ford continued to look out of the window. The bow dipped and rose gently against the wintry sea. I rose slowly from my chair and began to edge towards the door, stealthy as a burglar, or as an exhausted parent creeping from a sleeping child's bedroom. My nerve could not quite hold and I spoke again.

'I'll let everyone know, shall I?'

My hand was on the door – he had another chance to stop me or, as in fact happened, to let me take his silence as an instruction and to slip out without another word being said.

Thus Atlas shrugged and what had mattered so much no longer mattered at all. The Ford Peace Expedition platform was voluntary – you could sign it if you wanted to, or ignore it completely without the slightest consequence. By the end of the day thirty-five had signed. Inez refused but conceded that 'as the demands of conscience are now being respected' she could stay with us and lend her weight to bringing peace to Europe. McClure, having won what he had fought for, resigned anyway, immediately appointing himself to the press corps as an ordinary newsman and announcing that he could still come with us in this more neutral role. Whether anyone has noticed a difference I can't say.

The sense of relaxation throughout the ship was enjoyed by everyone. The dissolution of the dispute was so complete there was not even any sense of victory or defeat to disturb the newly restored peace. Rosika alone held back from the general rejoicing. She has kept more than ever to her stateroom, claiming that arrangements for our arrival in Norway are taking all her time. When we are together there have been no openly harsh words, but a new coolness and a miserliness with information. She feels herself undermined. Miss Rebecca Shelly's loyalty to her mistress has remained absolute and she also now looks on me with a suspicious eye. Our outbreak of peace has had one other effect – the working of a small healing miracle. Lloyd Bingham rallied that evening and was seen outside his cabin and on his feet for the first time in two days. He demonstrated his recovery by drawing deep, athletic breaths and declaring that the air was much improved. It would be fair to say that he has not always been to everyone's taste, but on that peace-making evening he brought off an unmitigated success. All the talents were marshalled for the Bingham Follies, the ship's band was roped in and, after a certain hour, no one was above making a fool of himself for the general good, myself included. With Lloyd's comic songs and ten-year-old jokes the night ended with laughing until it hurt and abandonment and empty bottles rolling in the gangways.

It was timely. The *Argosy*, our little shipboard news-sheet, was pushed under our doors in the early hours. We awoke with sore heads and swung our feet down from our bunks to place them on the fresh ink of its four gossipy pages. There was an outline map of the Atlantic, a little cartoon *Oscar* and a dotted line tracing our passage from New York. We approached Scotland's Orkney Islands and were at the point of intersecting another line that bulged around them, a line neatly labelled with two words in a bold black box – WAR ZONE.

It is midnight now, or a little past. A while ago, just as in olden days, the bell rang to change the watch, though now the sound has a less musical, electric trill to it. On either side there is the North Sea – flat as a new shop window, mirror-bright under a three-quarters moon. The *Oscar* makes her steady, purposeful way while on her back is played out a scene of unutterable strangeness, something one could only believe on the stage, a swirling musical interlude in a faery play, a midwinter night's dream of romance and transformation. We are there, everyone says to themselves, so very nearly there.

Only a few hours ago we were released from our three days' captivity at the hands of the British navy. It was on Monday last that war became real for many of us for the first time. Captain Hempel, though no alarmist, issued orders that sobered everyone and frightened quite a few. The watch was doubled, and these men no longer wandered about their posts or chatted with each other or tried to charm the female students as before but worked hard, staring through large binoculars for a trace of a periscope or the turbulent wake of a torpedo. Steel brackets with electric lights were extended over either side so that the *Oscar's* name and country of origin and her large Danish flag would be unmistakably clear in the eye of any U-boat commander. The lifeboats were swung out on their davits, ready to be lowered. We watched excitedly as teams of crew members went from boat to boat loosening the tarpaulins that covered them and equipping each with extra drinking water, food, flares, storm lanterns and gallon tins of paraffin fuel.

'Hey, Sven,' called out the man from the Brooklyn *Eagle*, 'which one has the whisky in it? There are fates worse than death, you know.'

'Never mind that,' says his friend, 'which one's Schwimmer in?'

'Now you're really spooking me. Can you imagine? A hundred days adrift and then a committee to decide who gets to drink whose blood and that Rosika dame in the chair. Hell already!'

Soon everyone was a gallows joker. The inhabitants of lower cabins moved above the waterline to squeeze in with top-deck friends. The more nervous ladies risked pneumonia by living almost permanently on the promenade deck benches. I would pass rows of them perching there, almost unchanged in their order and aspect from morning to afternoon. Squeezed in the middle, the mature Miss Severine Mylecraine of the San Francisco Women's Peace League explained that she was wearing her new rubber-soled easy walkers to protect against the effects of lightning and so that she might benefit, in case of an even greater misfortune, from their superior buoyancy in salt water. Determined not to go silently to the deep, Miss Mylecraine rolled up her political testament and sealed it in an empty champagne bottle which she then hurled a quite remarkable distance over the side.

'School discus champion,' she responded to the heartfelt applause, 'eighteen ninety-two.'

Along the deck, resting on a steamer chair under a blanket and ready for a quick escape, Berton Braley furrowed his brow and scribbled all afternoon in search of the deathless lines the occasion demanded. Elsewhere a brief religious revival was experienced with excellent attendances at contrasting services of prayer and song. Traditionalists favoured Reverend Lloyd Jones, looking for all the world as if he had just been peeled from one of the more Old Testament panels of the Sistine Chapel ceiling. A narrow victory, nevertheless, was said to have been scored by Reverend Charles Aked, a brilliantined entrepreneur of God as modern and simply effective in his field as one of Mr Ford's automobiles. A handful of the most pious were seen at both events and were duly teased by their fellow travellers. Rosika kept to her cabin, drafting speeches and growling about the opium of the people.

The first excitement of the day was caused by the appearance of a vast battlecruiser about half a mile off our left-hand side. Some were for immediately abandoning ship before word got round that the monster was British and should have no more sinister intention than enforcing the blockade regulations. We were followed for some two hours in the afternoon. The newsmen were thrilled. Those with moving-picture cameras set themselves up and eagerly cranked away at this authentic image of Europe. Others took their drinks from the bar and stood by the rail. They gestured and called out pointlessly to the warship and engaged in boyish arguments about the size of her guns and the effortlessness with which she could destroy us. Mr Ford joined us briefly. He scowled at the bristling outline and called it a waste of good steel before pulling his collar tight about his neck and hurrying back to the warmth.

I was there among the other watchers late in the afternoon when we were all caught off guard and made to jump out of our skins. A rib-shaking crack of thunder rolled over us out of a clear sky. Here was the traditional shot across the bows. Captain Hempel stopped the engines and we rolled in the swell, feebly awaiting capture. I looked eastwards, hoping to get some sight of land through the gloom. At first there was nothing I could make out and then a few points of light that indicated another approaching ship. A liner appeared, converted for war. She circled us then let down a boat with ten men, four of whom worked the oars to bring themselves across the short gap of sea to bump against our plates and climb aboard. A middle-aged reserve Lieutenant Trevithick was in command. Without any order being given six of his men lined up and shouldered their rifles. Lieutenant Trevithick adjusted his bearing better to convey the authority of the British Empire. He swept us with a look of stern regret – the peace delegates, the newsmen, Lloyd Bingham who resembled him somewhat in his roundness and the touch of feverish colour in his cheeks, the short, dark, bespectacled and bun-haired intensity of Rosika Schwimmer and myself. He shook his head sadly before pronouncing his judgement.

'They're a villainous lot, Wilhelm, to be sure. It's a wonder you're still alive at all. Are all these the mutineers?'

The Captain offered a brief explanation which Lieutenant Trevithick accepted with no great show of interest.

'Ah well then,' he said equably, 'here was me and my lads getting all excited and it was nothing but a lot of newspaper talk after all. There you go.'

He extended a cigarette to his friend and the two men chatted for a while about what the sea-going life had brought them since the last of their regular encounters. The butts were thrown over the side and the Lieutenant gave a lackadaisical order.

'Righto lads, let's get on with it. Too cold to hang about here.'

It is a war, I suppose, but very much the edge of one.

Trevithick's men sealed the wireless transmitter and installed a pilot on the bridge to guide us in to Kirkwall. Just before leaving us they pulled down the Danish flag and hoisted in its place the Union Jack. No one was pleased to see it – a fact not lost on Trevithick as he took his leave.

'Don't worry, ladies – you've got the Empire with you now.'

There were dark looks in reply as our captor turned to the journalists.

'Oh and you gentlemen of the press – it won't be so funny next time. I wouldn't send any more messages like that if you don't want to go swimming.'

The fourth estate shifted guiltily and mumbled their promises of better behaviour.

'Jesus!' exclaimed one of them as soon as it was safe. 'Makes you wonder if they're worth saving.'

Our engines turned for forty minutes and then stopped again as we reached our anchorage outside the harbour, invisible in the darkness and guarded for the night by its gate of mines. Judge Ben Lindsey lectured on the law of the sea and found much to interest him in the issue of whether we could now, temporarily under a belligerent flag, be lawfully killed by a declared combatant. He thought it an uncertain area, lacking in any clear precedent. Otherwise, it was a dull evening and most retired early with thoughts of the morning and the first sight of land in ten days.

Orkney is a low range of grass-covered hills populated largely by sheep and devoid of interest as a landscape. At one point in its past all the trees were removed the better to allow the uninterrupted passage of the winds over its surface and no one has since thought to put them back, preferring instead to weigh down the roofs of their houses with stones so they do not blow off quite so often. The houses of Kirkwall are low and tenacious in appearance and seem to have no purpose other than the mere sheltering of their inhabitants who, presumably, have such long winters and short days that they care little what they look like from the outside. Frankly, on my first morning in Orkney harbour, land seemed less exciting than I remembered it.

The authorities – a combination of the Royal Navy and the amiable but determined Kirkwall harbourmaster – proved ingenious at coming up with excuses for searching, questioning and delaying us. It wasn't long before the word 'incarceration' was being used freely. There were compensations, nevertheless, and the first of these was the delivery of a large packet of newspapers on our first morning. We fell upon them like starved animals and breakfast was a wordless affair as we scanned them with that special intensity readers reserve for when they are the news.

'There's nothing here.'

'This can't be right. How old are these papers?'

I looked through my own copy of *The Times* – Slander Action: Butcher Called 'German' by Fishmonger; Horatio Bottomley says No Peace Piffle!; See how it becomes new again with the correct use of Fels-Naphtha Soap, give your Family the Fels-Naphtha smile! Below the soap ad a young man with a steel plate strapped to his chest smiled at the reader:

Send at Once a
DAYField Body Shield
to Father, Brother, Son or Friend
to save his Life

Sir Hiram Maxim heartily endorsed the product which could be sent directly to the front for twenty-two shillings and sixpence.

'Censorship!' declared someone. 'Not a word and it's nothing but downright censorship.'

328

'Hold on – here's something. Bottom of page five. "Ford Peace Party at Kirkwall, arrived yesterday. Understood that faddists will not be allowed to land."'

'Faddists!'

'What else?'

'I think that's it.'

'Just as I told you – naked censorship.'

A thorough search revealed a second mention of our project deep in a parliamentary report. A certain Lord Rosebery had amused the upper house with talk of a ship fraught with peace, financed by an American gentleman believed to be a manufacturer of perambulators. A statement from Rosika's office welcomed this evidence of our growing success – 'My fellow humanitarians – if we did not have the power to stop the war, governments would not feel the need to ignore us. A true peacemaker must have the courage to have the right enemies as well as the right friends. Mr Ford and I are in possession of information we cannot yet share with you. All is well.'

'Louis,' he said to me later.

'Yes, Mr Ford?'

'What is it I know that I mustn't tell you?'

'I couldn't say, sir.'

'You'll be sure and stop me if I'm going to say something I shouldn't, won't you Louis?'

'You can rely on me, Mr Ford.'

The newsmen rattled off dispatches to their papers back home all about the spinelessness and the low moral standards of their English colleagues – U-boats Torpedo English Liberty; Sufferings of a Hoodwinked Europe – Where Ignorant Armies Clash by Night.

'Hey, nice one, Schulzy – your own?'

'Sure is, my friend. You're talking here to the muse of the news.'

Such creativity may not have travelled far. These dispatches and the sack-loads of other mail that was hurriedly written had to be collected unsealed by the harbourmaster and rowed back to his office on the quayside. There was grumbling from the British and talk of further censors being taken on just for us, and the great expense to His Majesty's Government. On the first night after our arrival, as I walked round the *Oscar's* tight circumference, I could see the lights in that office burning late into the night as bleary-eyed and yawning censors waded through all our hopes, boasts, lies, reassurances, uncertainties, yearnings and declarations of love, searching for the least trace of hidden enmity.

The ship was examined as thoroughly as our correspondence. Suitcases of unwashed clothes were rifled for secrets or the material of war. Uniformed men and guns were everywhere. I came upon three rifles propped in a corner, apparently forgotten by their owners as they searched a hold. Newsmen harried the young sailors with questions, but they held loyally to their orders to say nothing. They did have one area of weakness and that was their curiosity about the great man himself. They had seen his name on motor cars and vans and on advertisements in newspapers and magazines – was he real, what did he look like, sound like, could he really do it? These are the men whose lives Mr Ford, and all of us, have come to save and he was every bit as keen to meet them. Several interviews were held while officers were looking the other way and I was at one of these, watching as three ratings stood in a line with their hats in their hands. Mr Ford asked their names, where they were from and how they liked their work. He learned of brothers and fathers serving elsewhere and was pleased to hear that none of them had yet lost a family member. There was a short silence before one of them spoke up.

'We're all with you, sir. The boys all agreed to tell you, everyone here and at home too. We know what you're doing and everyone's with you.'

Mr Ford smiled serenely.

'I appreciate that, son, I really do.'

'It's hard, sir, you see with a wife and kiddies back home you haven't seen for six months and no end to it. We hate it, to tell the truth. Can you do it, sir? Do you really think you can do it?'

Here was a tonic straight to the heart of my chief. His eyes filled with brightness and the colour came back to his cheeks.

'Now I want you boys to trust me and all the good people on this ship. Whatever humanity and common sense, brain-power and a good deal of money can do, we're going to do and we won't stop till you get those orders to go home where you're needed.'

In that moment his enthusiasm and faith in our journey were fully revived.

'We must let everyone know about this, Louis. Put it in a press release and get it straight out as soon as those limeys have given us our radio transmitter back. You'll know what to say – the full hundred horsepower!'

Outside, a frustrated mob of newsmen lay in wait.

'Hey, bud, how come you get an interview and we don't? Cigarette? What did he say? Did he tell you not to obey orders – isn't that what he said, huh? Could you use five dollars, my friend?'

The newsmen were to receive a much greater blow on the morning of our last day in Kirkwall harbour. The alarm was raised, very calmly at first, when it became clear that one of our number was indeed going ashore, whatever the blockade regulations said. Bob Doman of the *Morning Telegraph* was the first to notice.

'Aw – are we losing our radio man? He was a really nice guy.'

There was the personable and ever helpful Robert Bastian sitting in the bow of a tiny dinghy, looking back at us over the shoulder of another man who rowed vigorously in the direction of an iron ladder set in the wall of the harbour. At the rower's feet lay two large sacks and something shiny.

'What's he got there? Is he turning mailman?'

More people gathered to wave at Mr Bastian – he had done them all favours, including favours of a highly confidential nature. The other man picked up the pace with the oars and they both turned to look at the ladder and up to the little Hotchkiss car that waited above it.

'What *is* he doing?'

The newsmen fell quiet and concentrated anxiously on the diminishing figures. The dinghy bumped the ladder and there was an ungainly scramble as the two men made their way up with their various items of cargo. A bright metallic flash signalled back to us through the chilly sunlight. Lloyd Bingham had pushed his way to the front and was standing beside me. His shoulders began to shake and I could hear the beginnings of rumbling, phlegmatic laughter.

'It can't be!' said someone.

Speechless journalists began to gape like fish. On the quay Bastian's friend cranked the little car into life and got behind the wheel. Bastian himself struck a triumphant pose and held up two gleaming, round mirrors – cans of movie film.

'The bastard!'

His voice travelled to us across the water, weak and half-strange as in a phonograph recording. There was a new and unfamiliar accent.

'My name is James Joseph Cooper and you won't ever forget it! I was born and raised in London and in ten hours' time I'll be back there. I'll be walking down Fleet Street with copies of every message you've ever sent and photographs of everything you've ever done and I'll be the richest and most famous journalist in the whole of Europe!'

'Shoot that man! God damn it – shoot both of them!'

Two startled sailors broke off from their leisurely search for contraband.

'Those men in the car, sir?'

'Yes, those men in the car! Quick, they're getting away. In the name of the freedom of the press shoot them now! For Christ's sake can't you at least shoot the car?'

The sailors looked thoughtfully at the disappearing Hotchkiss.

'If you was an officer, sir, we could oblige. But seeing as you aren't I don't think we can help. I'm sorry you're upset.'

Hats were thrown on the deck and trampled in impotent rage. The car vanished, leaving only a trail of blue smoke dissipating slowly in the winter air. Bingham was convulsing with delight.

'You know what that was?' he asked me. 'That was the first half-decent piece of organisation I've seen since I fought my way out of the lobby of the Biltmore Hotel.'

Doman was alone among the journalists in seeing the funny side. He shook his head slowly and smiled.

'Shall I tell you a better joke, boys? A bigger one? That crumb gets to Fleet Street, he walks up and down all day, in and out of every office he can think of and when it's over he can't sell the whole damned lot for a dime – now *that's* funny!'

A movie cameraman was unconsoled. He put his head in his hands and groaned.

'Oh, Jesus! This was my first foreign assignment. What am I going to tell my boss?'

McClure stepped up and put a fatherly arm around his shoulders.

'Don't worry about it, young fellow – there's plenty better ways of making a living. Gentlemen, I believe the bar has been restocked.'

The search of the *Oscar* finally came to an end. The whole procedure ended with a pleasing farce. Three hundred sacks of parcel post had been discovered in Hold no. 5. These consisted for the most part of brightly wrapped Christmas presents brought by the delegates and Mr Ford for the children of Norway. The very innocence of these packages aroused the suspicions of the customs officers and the outrage they provoked when some were found knee-deep in brown plush bears and wooden aeroplanes and china dolls and clockwork racing cars was all the confirmation they needed that hidden somewhere in that huge mound of good will there must lurk something harmful.

'That's it, lads – it'll all have to go.'

The journalists, the delegates and even members of the *Oscar*'s crew gathered by the side of the ship to witness the crime and abuse the perpetrators. The *Pax Vobiscum* and the *Good Shepherd*, two elderly steam-powered tenders, puttered away through the early northern gloom. Uniformed men stood guard over the sacks of presents – a cartoon of war's evil, humourless Santas stealing Christmas itself.

'Thieves!' shouted our most fiery co-ed.

Someone urged caution but Inez, looking on happily at one of the next generation's fighters, nudged her with an elbow and whispered encouragement.

'Common thieves!'

'Remember the Boston Tea Party!' shouted another.

One sailor turned to make an indecent gesture before being ordered to ignore us.

The *Oscar* received her licence to proceed and these strange theatricals somehow came together. The sea is as Captain Hempel has never seen it before. His first officer tells me it is because we are tiptoeing our way across a graveyard. He says I should listen for a scraping sound – the wrecks of our predecessors clutching at our still living hull. Tonight no one could hear it. We are crowded together on what, for other latitudes and seasons, is known as the sun deck. Hats and thick coats are our evening dress, our breaths whiten in the icy air as we dance, the ladies are buxom in their life-vests and the unfaded stars above as new to my city eyes as to a child. Stewards weave through us and as we pick glasses of champagne from the salvers they seem to come down from the moon itself. The band plays lustily to keep itself warm. We swirl to up-tempo renditions of 'By the Beautiful Sea', 'They Didn't Believe Me' and 'Roamin' in the Gloamin''. Mr and Mrs Berton Braley are seen in each other's arms for the first time in three days. The white fox is about Marion's shoulders, brilliant under the white light of the moon. As they turn I see first Berton's peaceful features and then Marion's and then the black button nose and glinting glass eyes of the fox as it crouches by the warmth of her neck. The music changes. Marion spins away to deliver herself to a delighted Samuel McClure.

'Poem! Poem!'

Berton feigns reluctance then jumps onto a life-raft and silences the band. He fumbles with three slips of paper, re-arranging them in different pockets before finding the right one.

Hail, Argonauts of Peace Sailing from America's golden
    Hesperides!
We come, we come to raise despairing Europe from her
    knees.

There to seek and find the gleaming secret of Peace,
Humanity's hyperborean gilded Fleece.

Henry of the Fjords labours at our oars,
Soon to triumph over the war god, floored.

Together in the Oscar, *brimful with benevolence,*
We come to drive all that is evil from men's hearts thence.

Hurray for the Oscar! *Hurray for Henry Ford!*
We fight on till war be universally deplored!

'Drivel, did he say? We come to drivel?'

'Genius! Hurray, carve it in stone!'

Everyone cheers wildly and claps. Marion is about to burst with pride. Her husband bows a dozen times and then, quite overcome, is helped to make a shaky descent from his platform. Mr Ford, sitting to the side in two coats, a lady's sable muffler and a quantity of travelling blankets around his knees, orders the verses to be sent out over the wireless. At the very same moment Rosika Schwimmer comes upon us in high excitement. She has been working our new wireless operator hard. She is breathless as she gains the sweating, gyrating sun deck. She carves a route through the dancers, holding a white sheet of paper as high as her stature permits. She ascends a bench and signals for the music to stop. As 'The Aba Daba Honeymoon' crashes to disorder Rosika stands there quite still, darkly clothed as ever, her dark arm held up against the cloudless night and at the end of it, bright as fire, the moonlit and slightly fluttering brilliance of her sheet of paper.

'The Prime Minister of England will discuss serious peace terms. Asquith is with us, the English are with us. My friends – it's peace!'

Delirium, ecstasy, a deluge of champagne. The stars spin round, the band plays 'For He's a Jolly Good Fellow', the notes thumping through the *Oscar's* hull, snaking away through the deep dark waters to hum, mysterious and hallucinatory, in the ears of homesick submariners. I turn from partner to partner, hoping, sure that it must be. Here is Inez, her left hand falling into my right as neatly as a well-caught ball, her right hand on my shoulder, pressing firmly. Her features, marble-pale, are those of a quizzical female Antinous, her grey eyes more arresting than ever.

'A polka!' demands someone. 'A polka to warm us up.'

The band begins at once and we are off at a gallop. Everything is colour and movement – black sky, swirling winter coats, cold air and warm breath, faces champagne-bright. Inez is my compass point, the only clarity.

Captain Hempel climbs up to see the strangest thing ever to happen in the long years of his command. He stands by Mr Ford, whose face is very white and serene. He presides over the magical, impossible scene like the Prospero of the industrial age, sustaining everything he sees by his will alone. The polka comes to an end and we slow to a breathless halt beside the two old men. Mr Ford is applauding, his face beaming with delight.

'The old dances are the best,' he shouts. 'You young folks don't have as much fun as we used to.'

Inez pulls me close and kisses me on the cheek. With eyes, the turn of her head and fingers moving around my waist she communicates, with no possible ambiguity, the scandalous offer that is her heart's creed. Statuesque, exquisite, scented, she smiles down at the seated Mr Ford.

'We're going to do it. By heaven, I'll wager the *Oscar* to a penny we're going to get those boys out of the trenches by Christmas! I'll buy her and set her up as a museum in Detroit. People will come from all over the world to see where war was ended. What do you say to that, Captain?'

Lloyd

*a*melia, Amelia – I am with you in spirit. At least I think I am, it's just that I don't know where to send my spirit at the moment. In all the excitement of departure I did a foolish thing – I told myself over and again to pack your engagements list, but forgot it in the end all the same. I went through my valise and all my pockets a dozen times before giving up and then kicked the wall of my cabin hard enough to break a hole in it. And so, my dear, I don't know where you are. I while away the hours as I lie here trying to remember the theatres and the dates. I try to unfold in my mind that maddening sheet of paper – is this an engagements list I see before me, the words towards my eyes? Come, that I may clutch thee. I have thee not . . . dum, de-dum, de-dum. How does it go? I'm wandering.

Where are you, Amelia? I get as far as the words – I know I'm on the right track because I recognise your secretary's typing mistakes. Then they start to move around and I get so frustrated it tires me out. Is it Philly tonight, or Frisco? Are you charming the roughnecks out in Bismarck or Cheyenne, or have you flown south for the winter to Mobile or to that new vaudeville in Galveston, relaxing on the balcony, looking out over the Gulf? Are you back in the Bijou where you first made it big in the east? I can smell that place. I don't know what it was but the Bijou always had its own smell, like no other theatre. I breathe it in now and I'm there. You are too, your face flickering from limelight to shadow as you run into the wings, flowers falling as you open your arms – 'Oh Lloyd, Lloyd, thank you. I could never have done it without . . .' Amelia, my darling, perhaps you are closer, perhaps you are in London – why not? If the call came just after I left you would have crossed quicker than we did in that rusting old cockleshell Ford hired. You could be here in two days, or I could come to you – what does this gloomy Swedish sawbones know? The Lyceum is it, Wyndhams?

So you see, my dear, because of my forgetfulness all I can do is guess. I must broadcast. That's what they call it now – scatter in all directions, though whether I can make myself heard through the babble from all these Marconi machines these days, I don't know. Sometimes I think the world will never be quiet again. At least you know where I am. When was the last time my name was in print more often than yours, my dear? Twenty years ago or more, I should think. Now you will be reading about me every day – or at least about my new friends. I can't tell you what a complete triumph everything has been. The great days are come again, and it's true after all what they say about talent – you can misplace it, but you can never lose it. Just wait till I get home – this thing is the greatest comedy in fifty years. I've thought it all through – you and me together again. The parts are perfect – I swear no one in the world can do them better than we can. We're going to pack the houses from coast to coast, and then they'll make a moving picture of it. You'll be Clara Ford and Rosika Schwimmer. Don't worry – I'll explain everything and no quick changes needed. So keep the faith, my dear, for our reward is coming. Pick my love from the air and send your thoughts back to me, Mr Lloyd Bingham, room 317, Grand Hotel, Christiania, Norway. Oh, oh – here comes Dr Grimgloom. I'll pretend to sleep. Amelia . . . are you there? I don't want to frighten you, my girl, but if things don't work out you'll receive a letter from Mrs S. R. Meissner of 1524 Thirty-First Street, Georgetown – she specialises in our sort.

Better today. I outlasted old Sawbones and got some peace in the end. You know I think he doubles as the undertaker. Normally I'd call that a conflict of interest, but this place is none too big a town. The hotel is pretty fine – colossal room, big picture window all winter clouds where I can see through and green above where the blind is pulled half down. The light makes me look jaundiced. It snows most of the time. The furniture is classy, little bits on it everywhere, very European. There's everything here for a historical drama. I can see you now, stopping by that fancy table under the window to deliver your lines. There's heavy paper with the letterhead stamped on so thick you could read it blindfold, and a pen tray with a big crystal inkwell. I think I ask for these things, but either they don't understand or that Swedish quack has got some idea about writing being bad for my health. They don't seem to get the heat right – always too hot or too cold. Strange that – with everything else just so.

Sad news, my dear, which I doubt the newspapers will bother to inform you of – Henry Ford is dead. He was poorly much of the way, but very nearly made it across. I witnessed a most affecting burial at sea when we were already within sight of land. None of the clergy aboard were willing to officiate, but Berton composed a delightful funeral ode. At the words 'nearer my hazelnut to thee' the little chopping board was tipped up and the furry peacemaker slipped from beneath a handkerchief to his eternal rest. Unsure whether this was a squirrel of the Christian persuasion, Poseidon was also offered a few glasses of whisky to ease the passing of this toothy soul. An evergreen corsage was plucked from a lady's breast and thrown on the waters. You'll call me a fool, but there was quite a tear in my eye by the end. William Jennings Bryan remains in robust health and now gets twice the attention and twice the food. There has been talk of foul play – but on a peace ship? The human Ford is still with us and I'm sure has no intention of ascending to the great dealership in the sky any time soon. Like me, he has had a little seasickness, a slight cold, but that is all. I hear someone coughing in the room above – that could be him.

So this letter – I shall think you a letter. It's barely two weeks since I ambled downstairs after a late breakfast to tackle the mail. You know how it's been lately – for me at least. It's getting so I like a bit of lunch too before taking the first blows of the day. Bill, bill, first reminder, second reminder, final demand, Dear Mr Bingham, The commencement of proceedings in the District Court of . . . Oh, by the way, did I get your cheque last month, my dear? I suppose I must have done. This time, in amongst all the threats and the ingratitude, a telegram too. I fortified myself and tore it open with a flourish – do your worst, telegram! Some sort of joke, obviously. One of my old friends trying to make a laughing stock of me. Even after I confirmed by telephone I was still a little suspicious. The *what* expedition? Henry Ford – *the* Henry Ford? I certainly hadn't volunteered for this – in fact, it would be no exaggeration to say I hadn't heard anything about it. Then I realised. Amelia, my darling, my guardian angel – you had been looking after me all the time. You called them – or, more likely, they called you.

'Mrs Bingham, I wonder if you would be so good as to advise us. We need an exceptional man for a most unusual position. We appreciate of course that you could not do it yourself, but . . .'

What else could you say? How things turn, my dear, how they turn. I was a good agent for you and now you return the favour. You know, I'm still a little unclear about the fees for this job, but I suppose you've wrapped all that up. But don't you think it a bit strange that no one has mentioned money? A lot of these folks seem to be giving up their time for nothing and I'm just hoping there hasn't been some dreadful misunderstanding. Perhaps I shouldn't complain – I haven't spent a dollar of my own since leaving Hoboken.

Oh, you should have seen me that day. Perhaps you did? If I missed you in the crowd, my dear, I can only apologise – it *was* the biggest I had ever had. Nothing could have done me more good. So there I was – the new Noah welcoming these strange creatures aboard. How they lapped it up! Apparently it was raining, apparently it was freezing cold – I stayed out there to the end and didn't notice a thing. The theatre, my dear one, is the only miracle cure I ever believed in and it didn't let me down. You know, part of my audience was so enthusiastic he came swimming after me. How's that for a review?

I guess you'll have read a fair bit about the characters on this jaunt. Among the women there is more than the usual quota of twitchers and blinkers. One is never seen in daylight and jumps out of her shoes whenever you meet her coming round a corner. Another is on her honeymoon and is never seen outside her cabin. The queen of them all is Madame Schwimmer. She looks just like she sounds – you half expect her to ask for a quarter to tell your fortune – sort of cross between Pandora, Lady Bracknell and a serio-comic middle-aged Hedda Gabler. She's a scream – one hundred per cent pure comic potential. Do you remember a girl on a white horse causing a riot at some suffragette thing a few years back? Well she's here too! She's the honey – think Cleopatra ten years before she had that last fling. Amelia, my darling, by the time we've put this farce on stage where it belongs it'll be as big a success for you as it's already been for me. Good parts for the boys, too. We brim with padres of every conceivable hue – one is an Englishman with a hidden past and looks like a salesman, another has clearly been abducted from a department store grotto and finds it impossible to get himself taken seriously. A third, Marquis by name, personally attends the great man himself, though whether he conveys messages from God to Henry Ford or from Henry Ford to God, no one is entirely sure. The newsmen swell the cast and chorus drunken prophecies of doom. A sprinkling of ingénues from the best colleges look on wide-eyed and agonisingly untouchable. Oh, you know me, my darling – nothing to worry about there. Not these days, anyway. Not now.

I shall play Henry Ford myself. Sacrifices will be required – the man doesn't eat much. You'd think with all that money he'd enjoy himself more but he looks like a few rags on a broomstick. Amelia, is that you? 'You could lose a few pounds, Lloyd, you know you could. You look puffy in the mornings.' Ah, sweetness, you could be here in this room! Well, you got me a job, my guardian agent, and now it's payday for both of us – I tell you, this is a hit. I got the whole thing in my head. Hire a stenographer, my dear, when I get home I'll talk for three days solid and we'll have a script by the weekend. Charlie Frohman will come back to life to produce this one.

I suppose you'll have heard about some disagreements. What the papers might not have told you is who set it right, who the hero of the hour was. Yes indeed, my dear – yours truly, the only tried and tested, bona fide peacemaker on this here expedition to date. Don't ask me what it was all about – half the folks on this ship talk like a convention of college professors and no sane man would go near them without ear plugs. Whatever it was, in the space of a few hours one evening they worked themselves into a powerful hatred of each other. At the time I was laid up, but they came and knocked on my door anyway and begged for help. What else could they do? It was nothing really – the Muse cured me in an instant and, though I say so myself, I improvised a pretty fine cabaret. Peace was restored and I was the toast of the ship. Mr Ford acknowledged me the next day. I have a new theory, Amelia – that if anyone is going to stop this war it's as likely to be people like you and me as anyone else. All the same, I'm getting to like these people. They sort of belong together and in ten short days I've come to feel at home with them.

Then we got captured by the British Navy and taken to some island and searched high and low like we were smugglers. Are you following this, my dear? It's important – I want you to know how it was. There must have been another argument about that time – things were a little worse with me and I was in my cabin for much of the day, but I could hear raised voices and doors banging. The next thing was music and laughing and rounds of applause as I drowsed and woke, and the feet drumming on the deck above as everyone was dancing. Well what happened next was a peach, a juicy, fat, sweet peach. You know, I've been called a genius before and I will be again, but sometimes all a man needs to do is sit under the tree of life and let the good things fall into his lap. This was one such occasion and I tell you, Amelia, when I think of what you're going to do with material like this I get sore laughing. No doubt about it – this scene is a show-stopper.

It's all about the bag. I did explain the bag, didn't I? – no matter. The bag's the whole damn thing, that's all you need to know. Get the bag and you've got the whole chase and the thing you've got to know about the bag is how it got under the skin of the newsboys before anyone even cast off from Hoboken. Whatever was in it, the public had a right to know and they were determined to get it any way they could. It wasn't easy – Schwimmer was rarely seen without it, two girls guarded her cabin day and night and on the few occasions when they were able to try the door in the early hours of the morning it was always firmly locked. But everyone dancing under the moonlight and Schwimmer up there too vapouring about some message from the Prime Minister of England was just what they had been waiting for. Picture the scene, my dear – there I am, a little revived by the sound of all this merry-making and wondering if I should go up myself to join in when a distinctly suspicious noise comes to my ears. There is a rattling in the corridor, the sound of effort and the self-conscious attempts of three or four strong men to stay quiet. The very sounds, put another way, that would make a police-man's ears prick up and all of them coming from the direction of the boss-woman's cabin. There was a grunt, a hushed demand to be careful and then the bang of something being forcibly opened. By the time I was decent and in the corridor the boys were coming the other way, young Hirsch holding up the bag itself like a captured standard.

'Why, Lloyd!' exclaimed another. 'How are you? You catch us at a glorious moment – rescuing the truth from its abductors.'

The prospect of a little fun did wonders for my head and in no time we were all together in the smoking room crowd-ing round as someone forced the bag lock with a knife. Pop! – it opened, cavernous and black. Did we fear to look inside? Who was the man for the job? The place was full of news-men by this stage and some instinct made them all turn to me. So I got straight into character and there I was, balancing belly-down on a barstool 'schwimming' an Atlantic of tears.

'Don't panic, don't panic!'

Heavy garment-district accent.

'Ich kommt to make ze peas. I eff everyzing vee need right eear!'

I stir around inside, averting my eyes until my hand falls upon one of those all-important secret dispatches. The boys get the idea, but they're tense too. Like me, they can't quite shake the idea that there might really be something there, that if everything they know about the world and everything they believe turns out, just this once, to be wrong that'll be the bigger story. They want to be wrong. For a second, they're all leaning toward me and the bag, hoping for a revelation.

Crash goes the cymbal – and there's the first piece. I wave it in the air.

'A lady's handkerchief, embroidered RS, lightly soiled.'

'Something to wipe away her tears with.'

'No way – she's going to rip it in two and each side's going to use it to surrender to the other.'

We're a double act, we get a rhythm going. Oh, Amelia – is anything better? Throw physic to the dogs; I'll none of it.

'A small powder compact – a very dainty piece, gentlemen.'

'To make the human animal look better than it really is – essential rainbow-chasers' kit.'

'Get on with it, fat boy. Where's the beef?'

Ah, to be heckled again – how it did my heart good. More averting of the eyes, more stirring of the hand in the stygian darkness of the bag.

'Here it is – something on paper anyway.'

I pull out a scarlet notebook, closed with a bronze clasp.

'Now we're getting there.'

'An address book? A blackmail list?'

'Recipes for putting spells on elderly auto-makers,' suggests another.

'No,' says a third, 'it's her secret diary. Who's she in love with? Toss it here, Bingham.'

The book flies, is caught and violated.

'It's in foreign. Hey, Hirsch, you read this stuff, don't you?'

There is a moment's hush as the pages are quickly gone through.

'What you got there, hot-shot? Don't you dare hold anything back.'

Hirsch is already at the end and is flicking back for another look. He shrugs.

'It's nothing.'

'What! No Asquith, no Lloyd George, no Clemenceau, no Bethmann Hollweg?'

'Personal stuff. Nothing at all.'

The book is snatched away.

'Hey, dopey – you missed a bit. My dearest little Austro-Hungarian Rose, how I recall your words from last summer. I see now you are right. War is silly and together we will stop it at once. Oh, how I yearn to be in your short, thick arms again. Your ever loving Paul von Hindendindenburg, your cuddly Prussian bear and general of the Imperial German forces – kiss, kiss. What do you know, she does have some charms!'

'Shut up, Hiram – you're not funny. Lloyd – get on with it. Is there anything in there or are we wasting our time?'

I go fishing again. She can't have lied completely – surely there's got to be something.

'Hold on. Here's another book.'

I bring out a tiny English–Hungarian dictionary. The boys start to hook up.

'Oh, Grandma,' says one, 'what a large vocabulary you have.'

'All the better to fool you with, my dear.'

'Here's another one – "Travel and Accommodation Guide to Northern Europe With Railway Timetables".'

'Give it here. Maybe there are some notes in it. There might be clues.'

'Check out the timetables for secret codes.'

I bring out, one after the other, a near-empty bottle of sea-sickness pills, a magnifying vanity mirror, a lipstick and a small tortoiseshell jewel case which, when opened, reveals a single gleaming false tooth. Schwimmer is successively accused of hoarding essentials, having a distorted view of the world, trying to paint over the truth and disguising her true identity.

That seems to be it, but I'm back in the bag for a last check. I dive in there.

'Oh, can this be all?' I moan. 'Tell me it's not true.'

I straighten up. The bag is stuck on my head. I'm half man, half bag-monster and I do the blind schtick – arms out, blundering around, carefully knocking into all the things I've memorised. It started out fine and then there was that sublime moment when there's only one guy on stage who doesn't hear the silence – really we couldn't have rehearsed it better. I plough on for a few seconds, still working for the next laugh. Then I realise it hasn't just gone quiet out there, it's a damned funeral. I take the bag off my head and there she is – Schwimmer herself, towering, outraged, basilisk eyes, bust poised for attack. The audience can't contain themselves and the scene is held until their applause dies away. Meanwhile, the newsboys have been struck dumb and are all looking at each other and then at me – me, who they dragged in and put up to the whole thing! But get this. Here's the clever bit – she brandishes . . . yes, you guessed it – THE BAG! We look from bag to identical bag. It's the comedy of errors with bags rather than people. Are we being fooled, is there real treasure anywhere? Schwimmer triumphant.

'You faithless imbeciles, you cynics, you hypocrites. Not even a decent thief among you.'

'Hey, easy, lady – we're just doing our job.'

You storm magnificently.

'Infants – not knowing right from wrong, not knowing what you do!'

No comeback from the boys this time – just a conceding droop of the shoulders. Only one has the spunk to speak up.

'Say, Rosika, how many of those bags you got?'

'Ha!' replies the idealist. 'One more than you could ever steal. That's all *you* need to know.'

Amelia Bingham's dazzling portrayal of Madame Schwimmer

gathers herself for a magisterial departure. And then . . . Ah, my dear, something we really didn't expect at all. Something that was entirely, shockingly unnecessary. She stops, turns, sweeps us with a baleful, contemptuous gaze – the gaze of the microscopist on the squirming forms of her infinitely insignificant subjects. She inhales. We wait. We are all ears.

'And one other thing, gentlemen, before I go – Henry Ford and I are *not* lovers.'

Well, this was new – and I tell you, Amelia, when the Israelites watched the waters part and looked down on whalebones and shipwrecks and the snarled nets of their grandfathers, they could only have had an expression of the mildest surprise by comparison with the look on those newsboys' faces. No one had ever suggested such a thing. I would guess that no one had conceived of it other than Schwimmer herself. A shudder started somewhere and ran through the whole group as if they had, with a single appalled sense, sucked on a whole barrel-load of pickled limes. Schwimmer had already swept out and got no idea of the full catastrophe of her mistake.

'Oh well,' said J. J. O'Neill, lighting another cigarette. 'If you've gotta deny it, it's gotta be a story.'

I suppose I blotted my copy-book with Madame with that little performance, but I'll say one thing for her – she's no bearer of grudges. I had a visit this morning and she spoke as if nothing had ever happened. No, sir – whatever you read, my dear, there is no smallness of heart in Rosika Schwimmer. The flowers on my side table are hers too – the bill, as ever, Henry's. Reverend Marquis has been as well. After a few minutes he forgets the obligations of the sick-room visitor and drones on about his own problems. I have had some surprising confidences, Amelia, and will be very popular with the newsboys once I am on my feet again. The man is a puzzle. Of all the great excess of clergymen we brought with us I sometimes wonder if it isn't Marquis who has most completely mistaken his vocation. He hasn't got the bedside thing at all and always seems a little sadder after seeing me – and I certainly feel a little sicker. Dr Glumsmussen is here. I asked him just now if that was a tape-measure sticking out of his pocket in place of his stethoscope, but he is a humourless man. He stands by the window, a frock-coated silhouette of mourning paper, casting my dark water against a bleak light. I think the damned furnace has broken again. Amelia, my dearest, I fear the snowball fight was a mistake.

Next morning we saw beautiful, snow-capped land. The *Oscar* coasted northward all that day and through the following night. The students shouted at fishermen and waved their banner. Schwimmer practically camped in the radio office, sending out dozens of messages to all her pre-war friends and making a big deal out of the few replies. As the early darkness fell we met up with the Norwegian coastguard and took on their pilot. There was great excitement in the dining room. Appetites were off and we all hurried away to pack and to look out the one clean set of clothes we had been saving for disembarkation. The newsboys made their final attack on the bar and swore a fraternal oath never to set foot on European soil before they had drunk it dry.

'I was overcharged for a replacement drive-belt in 1911,' swayed Teddy Pockman of the *Tribune*. 'If I don't get myself a full refund tonight I never will. Hey there, Lloyd, you're looking better. How's that famous wife of yours doing?'

Trunks and suitcases began to stack up in the gangways. Matrons twittered and ran from cabin to cabin brandishing passports hours before they were needed.

'Grace, Edith – call me at once if anything happens. I'll not be sleeping.'

At four in the morning we gathered before the approaching lights of a harbour. The *Oscar* crept into her berth, a team of her own crew climbing down to secure the cables. The scene lifted our shivering spirits – the homes and workshops of land-living creatures, the smell of it, steep roofs thick with snow and all the charm and strangeness of a department-store window at Christmas. An annunciation painted on a stolen bedsheet was unrolled over the side while a student played a hymn on a trumpet.

'Hey – there's someone. Ask him.'

A man packing fish in wooden boxes was, beside ourselves, the only life to be seen. One of the newsboys spoke up.

'*Entschuldigung*, Bud – you know anything about these fruits? Peace Ship, Henry Ford, mediation, stopping the war, anything at all?'

There was a shrug and a reply of several words in the middle of which only a heavily accented 'Ford' stood out as meaningful. We looked to Madame Malmberg, our stately and many-tongued Finnish exile.

'He says he used to have one and it was all right although sometimes it wouldn't start in the winter. He now drives a Renault. You can get more fish in a Renault.'

'That's all?' asked Rosika.

'That's all.'

'Well,' explained someone, 'it *is* four in the morning.'

'And it *is* twelve degrees below zero.'

'And he *is* only a fisherman.'

'And it's Sunday, too.'

All would still be well. Five hours later, as the Norwegian day struggled out of darkness, we were indeed welcomed by a small delegation of local campaigners. The women all looked like Schwimmer's long-lost sisters and the handful of men bore a discouraging likeness to our various padres. Some local journalists came with them and, after asking forlornly if they could see Mr Ford, were guided away by their American colleagues to the discretion of the palm-screened bar and a great deluge of advice as to what they should put in their papers. There was talk of a reception in the evening – arrangements were in hand, the students of the university were highly excited and the townspeople agog for their first sight of the great man. The manager of the Grand Hotel plucked the dust sheets from his fifty best rooms, the occupation of which he had not hoped to see again before the end of the war. Spring came early to the hearts of high-class provisioners, tip-starved waiters and general vendors of the unnecessary. In short, as the sun rose over a cloudless, crystalline scene and we put our feet on the salted stones of the quayside, the circus had come to town.

'No, no, no.'

Ford waved away the taxi Marquis had summoned for him. The curate of industrial souls looked worried. He went aside with the impassive bodyguard and had a few words with him. Their mutual master would not be moved.

'Nonsense! A walk is exactly what I need. Walking is a powerful medicine. Walking is what I haven't had enough of these last ten days.'

It's a strange thing, my dear, but I have come to feel oddly connected to Henry Ford. When he weakens, I too weaken. When he is up, the same energy surges through me. There are times when he seems to have more than any one man can contain and it spills out to everyone around him. People sort of tune up with him – they feel like him, think like him, they fall into step by his side and are carried along that bit faster as they get a little of what it must be like to be Henry Ford. So you see, Amelia – you really mustn't worry. Even if I should not write or wire for a few days you only have to look in the paper to see how I am. If our Henry is doing well, you'll know that I'm just fine.

'Here's one, girls!'

Schwimmer invaded the taxi Ford had just turned down. She summoned Madame Malmberg, Mrs Fels and Rebecca

Shelly to join her. The magnetic Miss Inez Milholland took a step in their direction, then looked elsewhere as the door on the inner sisterhood slammed shut. We heard an umbrella being stoutly rapped on the roof and the words 'Grand Hotel!' falling on the driver like the stroke of a whip. The car jumped and made off with a spurt of slush from its hobnailed tyres.

'It must be this way.'

The miraculously refuelled Ford followed in its tracks with an entourage of people half his age struggling after. Around me there gathered a jam of taxis and luggage sleds drawn by shaggy, steaming ponies. No Hoboken this – no freaks, bands, fainters, thieves, swimmers after publicity, self-seekers, chaos or squirrels, with the single honourable exception of little William Jennings Bryan shivering in his cage as he dangled from the lilac-gloved hand of the new Mrs Braley.

'This was your idea, Berton. *All* yours. Where the hell is this place, anyway?'

Instead, the calm tagging and loading of luggage, the steady bearing away of the Ford Peace Party by taxi-loads of threes and fours as if our sort arrived from America twice a week and had done for as long as anyone could recall. I squeezed into a horse-drawn sled beside the Braleys and a heap of suit-cases. Off we went, jingling through snow-banked streets, gaps cut in the white walls wherever there was a door. Halfway, we ran up behind Ford, Marquis, the bodyguard, a ruddy Louis Lochner, a dozen of the newsboys and the magic bearded Reverend Jones. Ahead of them McClure strode out, his perpetually overwound mechanism stamping into the snow. The intrepid Inez Milholland straggled between the two, skipping every third step to keep up with the fallen magazine king. Braley stood up and cracked an imaginary whip between the ears of our plodding, one-horsepower engine.

'Huzzah! Clear the way there.'

An elated, humorous Ford shook his fist at us.

'Roadhogs.'

'Come on!' shouted Inez.

She picked up her skirts and ran, quickly outpacing McClure and very nearly us too. The whole thing descended into a preposterous race to the hotel and I laughed until I couldn't breathe.

By the time we arrived at the hotel a couple of dozen had got there before us and the local press made up the numbers until the lobby was crammed with bodies and shouting. Ford's arrival, as usual, set a match to the whole thing. The warmth sort of got to me all of a sudden and I toppled into the nearest chair as the journalists threw questions and a happy Ford fired out all the grand phrases he had been saving, ten to the dozen. Lochner waved his hands and tried to get some order in it all.

'No, he didn't mean that. Mr Ford is very tired. Interviews later, please – there'll be plenty of time for everyone. Interview requests to the Peace Party Staff, please.'

Only no one was paying the blindest bit of attention and the local reporters started to fight each other for the three telephone cabins. While this entertainment developed nicely a worried young man with brass on his tunic tried to explain that I had tumbled by sacriligious mischance into the ever-to-be-empty chair of the late Henrik Ibsen, onetime habitué of the Christiania Grand Hotel. This no doubt accounted for the sensation of a thread breaking beneath my ample rump as I restored some human warmth to the great playwright's station.

'Ah, Ibsen,' I declared. 'The source, you know, of some of my wife's finest triumphs.'

I went on, of course. I gave him your full due, my dear, you may be sure of that, but it required more English than he had at his disposal and I soon settled for being moved to a leather sofa closer to the fire.

Keys flew through the air and just failed to blind me.

'Hey, Lloydy-boy! Room 102 – the best in the west. Come on.'

I struggled to the edge of the sofa and failed to stand – tremulous, hamstrung.

'Give me a hand here.'

So there I was – half dragged to the elevator between two uncaring pillars of health.

'You need a rest, Lloyd, a good long rest – that's all.'

Everyone around me is a doctor now. Ah, my dear, what a scene it was – affecting would not be too strong a word. And yet my hopes now are brighter than for years. I am on the very threshold of my late, great phase. I ripen into the full measure of good John Falstaff's costume. Amelia, my love, just wait till I get home – what a terror it will be. For a genera- tion no one will dare play the part after me – if only I can shake this thing, escape this bed and this damned Norwedish coffin-carver coming at me with his stolen stethoscope. At least this will be something for you to savour, Amelia. The irony will not be lost – ready for Falstaff, trapped instead in some interminable Scandinavian stage-wake any sane man would take poison not to have to sit through. Pay no atten- tion, Amelia. I talk nonsense, I fumble with the sheets and play with flowers.

Two days ago I still had strength. After a half-hour's rest on this bed I was up again and in the flow. The corridors filled with laundry bags, steam billowed from bathrooms as we washed away the voyage. We mobbed the dining room, devas- tated the larders. At least the young people did. We older ones were still queasy and my own long-suffering stomach would take nothing more than a few crackers, a horse-trough of coffee and a balloon of best French brandy.

'Put that on my bill, Olga.'

Everyone agreed it was not the time to start skimping on universal peace. The man with his name on the world's biggest hotel bill sat at a round table in the middle of us all, serene in the sunlight, objecting to nothing. Then Lochner was on his feet calling for quiet. Some nonsense about refreshing hearts and minds, rebuilding harmony, clearing metaphorically cluttered metaphorical desks for the great task ahead. What it all amounted to was that before getting down to work there would be an expedition up a mountain and a chance for everyone to get their land legs back.

The idea seemed a little less ridiculous once I learned we were to take an electric railway to the top. A festival atmosphere quickened to near hysteria as we gathered outside the hotel.

'Has someone read the papers today?'

Fingers were jammed childishly into ears.

'Not listening, not listening, not listening, not listening!'

No one had.

'We'll miss the train.'

The train, chartered just as the *Oscar* had been, was waiting for us. Like factory workers on their annual day of forgetting, we jammed into this elaborate toy. Its electric motors hummed, the air filled with ozone and lightning crackled from the power rail. Up front, Mr Ford leaned from a window, charmed by the mechanism and talking all the time to himself about its good and bad points and what he would improve and what would never catch on. Gears meshed and slowly we began to move. We ticked and whirred our way up an impossibly sugar-white mountain, past the gingerbread Holmenkollen church and on into a perfect, Christmas-card blue. At the top, a Norwegian Sunday – everything white and blue and the deep green-blackness of the trees, everyone young and beautiful and impossibly healthy, blond hair whizzing by on skis, girls exotic in tinted snow goggles, and ourselves, the Ford Peace Expedition on our improving mission, out of place, unequipped, skittish as the snowballs started to fly. Was the air too thin, Amelia? Should I have eaten more for breakfast, or have I been away too long from you, my strength? Was it the well-aimed shot from – from who knows? – that finally tipped my balance, setting off that private earthquake beneath my feet as I bent to scoop up a retaliatory handful only for the world to turn sideways and the blue sky to fill everything and a dark circle of heads to gather round and talk in distant voices.

'Jeez! His face is the same colour as the snow.'

'You're going to be all right, Lloyd. You're going to be just fine.'

Shifting, grunting, cracks about my weight. Then I'm shoulder high and being borne down to the boardwalk halt where the train waits to unwind itself back down the mountain. A taxi, the welcome, blessed heat of the hotel, a practised commotion among the staff as the doctor is summoned. I find my tongue and tell everyone not to bother, not to make such a fuss. The diamond-patterned grill of the elevator gates closes across my face. There is movement, but my legs feel light.

'He's going,' says someone right in my ear. 'He's going.'

I found myself here, in this soft bed, in this hot and cold Scandinavian room so very far away from the only thing that could bring me comfort. I'm sorry, my dear, I was about to break our old rule – whatever happens, definitely no self-pity. And for how long in this room which now bores me more than I have ever been bored before? I can't count. Is it day or night?

Marquis was here a while ago – to do his duty. I spoke to him the two words I most wanted to say in the world. I beckoned with a finger, with the expression on my face and he leant close and turned his ear to my dry mouth. Marquis, you should know, is a proud and a dull, dull man. He doesn't think anyone like me can tell him anything. But I did. Oh, my dear Amelia, I did.

I wonder what time it is with you. Is it evening yet? Are

357

the house lights dimming, is the curtain about to rise? I think it must be that time again, for here comes our comedy doctor with a mirror in his hands. Not so close – how can I see?

My dear, it's the strangest thing – I don't believe I even have the strength to close my eyes.

Marquis

*M*y mind worries endlessly at a scene I dread, but that must come soon. I am home in America, on the train to Detroit travelling to that painful meeting. Will it be in the town house, or out at Dearborn with me splashing across the track to the half-built mansion, Clara standing in the cold to greet me? Inside everything is proper, dignified exactly as I would expect. Edsel is there, of course, standing throughout as the man of the house. He is weighed down but shows no emotion. Clara is the strongest of the three.

'I don't blame you, Samuel,' I have her say to me. 'There was nothing more you could have done.'

There, with such an unsatisfactory self-acquittal, my imagination fails.

The truth is, if it goes badly I will be more to blame than it appears from the outside. I have known for some time that one of Mr Ford's axioms is to do the perfect opposite of whatever I suggest to him. I believe he is attempting to escape something in his own life, and it is my misfortune to remind him of whatever that thing is. And so when I urged him on the freezing quayside to take a taxi to the hotel it was decided that he must walk. When the others prepared for their winter train-ride and I pleaded with him to stay behind and regain his strength, I might as well have pushed him up that mountain myself.

Two days here and I already look back on the crossing as a period of relative sanity. With a fresh infusion of local press and Madame Schwimmer perched recklessly in the driving seat we have returned to the near-continuous frenzy of Hoboken pier and the Biltmore Hotel. After the unnecessary walk to the Grand Hotel things deteriorated further with an impromptu press conference by the check-in desk. Unfortunately, Mr Ford had been thinking up some new phrases.

'If we can save just one boy it will all have been worth while.'

'One by Christmas, Mr Ford?'

Louis Lochner tried to limit the damage, but it did little good. The least sympathetic of the Norwegian newspapers distributed lottery tickets with its morning edition, advising readers to send them to the front so the lucky Ford soldier could be fairly chosen. An accompanying cartoon showed the winner of life returning to a Carl Larsson family on Christmas morning in his complimentary Model T while the fire and smoke of war still billowed over a distant horizon.

While Schwimmer got down to the business of organising the first publicity events a stupendous landfall breakfast took place, by the end of which I had suffered my second failure of the day. I don't know how the project started, but by the time any reasonable advice could be given it had gained a juvenile momentum of its own and was impossible to stop. Mr Ford showed little interest in the mountain trip until he learned that it involved an electric train. Then, in my efforts to dissuade him from going, I made a mistake in risking too bold a use of Mrs Ford's name. When he was at his weakest on the ship he was amenable and willing to listen, but with the excitement of arrival and the prospect of new mechanical experiences he drifted once again back into the world of Schwimmer and young Lochner. I confessed to him my secret purpose — that I had not come out of any belief at all in the prospects of success, but solely because his wife had asked me, charging me, at all costs, with bringing him home alive and well.

'It is all she cares about, Henry, and right now it is all I care about too.'

I compounded my mistake by referring to his son. As we waited in the lobby of the hotel I had to endure his response, certainly loud enough to be overheard.

'You won't tell me what is good for me, Dr Marquis, and by God you won't tell me what is good for my wife.'

Patience was needed, as well as what the generals far to the south of us might call a tactical withdrawal. Mr Ford boarded the train at the front, I at the back. There we were — as harshly exposed in that too-brilliant northern light as at any time since the whole miserable idea was planted in Mr Ford's mind. Our leader lectured us on why electric power had no future and instructed the fawning Lochner to arrange meetings with local manufacturers. Mr Bingham, sporting something like an engine-driver's cap, pulled an imaginary cord and made chesty impressions of a steam whistle. Off we went, to a destination no one had ever heard of and for an obscure purpose on which none of us could agree. No one mentioned the war. My depression deepened when I remarked obliquely on this fact to Samuel McClure and even he seemed not to have the slightest idea of what I was talking about. The old campaigner has found his own way to make a fool of himself. He has become inseparable from his new companion Miss Milholland, a woman already assumed by the hotel staff to be his daughter and one who, according to the journalists' gleeful rumour, is prepared to pay more than just a financial price to get into print.

So there I was, as solitary and joyless as the one sober man in a party of drunkards, silent and sullen and adding, no doubt, to the overall comedy of the scene. At the top, I should think no more than fifteen minutes passed before poor Mr Bingham collapsed. After another short delay while it was established that this was not a joke, disordered attempts at rescue began. I watched these from a distance (there were already too many hands), and thought more about my own light-headed unconcern than the events themselves. They struck me as disasters must have struck the ancients, unforeseen to be sure, but always vindicating prophecy.

The journalists formed a team and gave orders and pushed the others away as they got beneath their helpless friend. I followed them down to the train station, dawdling to let Mr Ford go ahead so that I could keep him constantly in sight. I thought of home and all that would have to be done to get back there, and what story I would have to tell. Was Mr Ford paler than usual, was that a stumble, was that cough sinister? My nerves frayed. Mentally, I worded telegrams I prayed I would never have to send.

By the time we regained the hotel Bingham had rallied and there was jocular talk of too much whisky at breakfast. His legs moved weakly as two of the newsmen held his weight and guided him towards the elevator. He rambled through a mixture of jokes and apologies, making little sense in either vein. I concentrated on Mr Ford and found him, as he cast his own fearful eye on the stricken entertainer, willing to be shepherded up to his room and straight to bed.

I was reassured to make the acquaintance of Dr Rasmussen, the hotel's excellent physician. He moved quickly from one sickroom to the other, drawing me aside in the corridor for a confidential word on Bingham before attending to Mr Ford.

'I have concerns, sir, I will not conceal them from you – but perhaps we may yet avert a crisis. I am glad you did not wait any longer before consulting me. Can I ask you, is there money for a nurse?'

A nurse was engaged immediately and two others retained in preparation for the night and early shifts.

Dr Rasmussen is a perfect dictator in medical matters and he cleared Mr Ford's room of all unnecessary persons with a few words and an emphatic gesture. He scowled at me as I lingered in closing the door, looking past him to where his patient lay on the bed, very pale and ready, it seemed to me, to be under another man's authority if only for a few minutes. A large and indecently curious crowd assembled in the corridor outside. The journalists shifted like runners waiting for the gun. They consulted their watches, never changed from New York time, and calculated distances to the telephones – some loitered by the stairs, others put their money on the elevator. Anecdotes of newsworthy deaths were exchanged – how that old fox J. P. Morgan had scooped them from beyond the grave, his mortal remains cooling in a Roman hotel bedroom long past the evening deadline on the other side of the world. They looked suspiciously at the door to Mr Ford's room – what story was breaking on the other side of it, what dastardly plot being cooked up to deny the newspaper readers of the world their rights? Dr Rasmussen emerged and cast an expressionless eye over us all before finally settling on me.

'You are in authority here?'

He drew me apart and gave a brief résumé of what he had found before handing over a note of his fees and heading for the stairs.

'He's fine,' I said to the journalists. 'It's nothing but a cold and the chest is clear. There is no cause for concern.'

There was a general exodus in the direction of the bar, where death would no doubt draw a line under their credit as well as Mr Ford's life.

Lochner and I went in to find the bed empty and steam drifting through the open doorway of the bathroom. Mr Ford gave instructions to his bodyguard, who had clearly been admitted also to the intimacies of the valet, while we sat outside in the main room of the suite. From my position, the narrow neck and greying head could just be seen in misty outline above the rim of the bath.

'What did I tell you?' he demanded. 'Nothing to worry about.'

'Dr Rasmussen told me you must rest. He said it was absolutely essential.'

'I knew he was a charlatan. What doctor ever says you don't need him?'

'He recommended a sanatorium. A few days would put you right.'

'Small men always think great men are mad. You know you're on the right track when small men say you're mad.'

'A *sanatorium*, Mr Ford – for your health. It's in the mountains.'

'Jesus Christ! Have I not just come down from a mountain? Does he think I didn't spend enough time up there?

There was vigorous splashing and a terse order for a towel. I looked away just too slowly to avoid seeing the naked billionaire standing in his bath before gingerly stepping out and into the enveloping whiteness held out for him by Ray. A moment later he emerged tying the belt of a blue silk dressing gown just as young Lochner finished noting down his thoughts on madness.

'Whose fool idea was that anyway – the mountain thing?'
Neither of us knew.

'Well, it doesn't matter now. I expect Rasmussen owns the sanatorium. I expect it's the Rasmussinovitch sanatorium, the Rabinovitch sanatorium more likely. You've got to be on your guard against these things. Anyway, I'm better now.'

At that moment, still pink from the heat of his bath, it seemed true.

Lochner started on a report of what he and Madame

Schwimmer had arranged with their local supporters. The first great public event was only hours away. The Ford Peace Party was to be the guest of the university students' association — the biggest hall in town had been hired and tickets were selling fast. Everyone of substance in Christiania was certain to be there and they had all been promised sight of the famous Mr Henry Ford. I interrupted at once, before Lochner could say another word.

'It's impossible. You can't, you absolutely can't — at night, in these temperatures, in an unheated hall. Listen to Dr Rasmussen if not to me.'

I glared at Lochner, forbidding him to suggest anything that might lead Mr Ford to put himself in danger. He lay on the bed and extended his neat, bath-softened, dancer's feet to Ray, who covered them with a pair of slippers.

'It doesn't look good,' he told me. 'You know there's nothing I hate more than disappointing people.'

Lochner jumped in with the solution.

'People will understand, Mr Ford.'

'You think so?'

'Oh, yes — there's great good will towards you, sir. No one would want you to risk your health.'

'You might be right. But all the same . . .'

'A day's rest, Mr Ford sir . . .'

'Two days,' I interjected.

'Yes, just two days, it's all we ask. No one could ask for more than you have already given.'

Lochner had quickly learned the ways of his employer. With these and a handful of similar phrases he worked like a masseur on the needs and fears of Henry Ford. The maker of three hundred thousand cars a year lay back on his pillows and allowed surrender momentarily to ease his features. Lochner persisted.

'It's all a matter of how it's handled. With the right words it's no problem at all. You must send the people a message, Mr Ford. Tell them – well, tell them you will look the people of Norway in the eye and talk to them of peace before you move on.'

'That's good. Yes, tell them I said that.'

His words became vague at the end and he seemed suddenly to be very tired.

'Square it with the boys downstairs, won't you, Louis? No misunderstandings.'

Lochner was leaving when he was given one further instruction – to get the desk clerk to send up the Wall Street closing prices from the wires.

When the door closed I was entirely alone with Henry for the first time since the night before our departure from New York. I had failed then to put any doubt in his mind and he now gave me a look that conveyed how ashamed I should feel for finally having run him to ground. I decided to be ruthless.

'Do you think you should send a telegram to Mrs Ford? I know you get on well with the reporters but they are apt to exaggerate. I'm concerned that she shouldn't read something unduly worrying in the papers. Perhaps if I found the right words . . . ?'

'Sure,' he said to me. 'Say something fancy so she knows it comes from you.'

'I really think it would be a good idea – for Edsel too. For the company.'

'Well, do it! Where is this damned war, anyway? Did someone make it up?'

'The papers are full of Turkey, Baghdad.'

'Why? Why don't they report the war? I know why they don't report the war – it's too profitable, that's why – and you know who for, don't you?'

My hopes rose. I knew from occasions in the past how he

would return to harping on old themes and how these oubursts would often precede moments of weakness or, as others saw it, of reluctant reasonableness. I saw how he suffered from the sudden, chilly withdrawal of romance, from the intrusion of questions too long held at bay by excitement and novelty and thoughtless optimism – what was he *really* doing here, just how many miles was he from home and how in God's name had this whole cockeyed thing happened at all?

The day had clouded over and the light was already dying. From the window I looked down on a scene of blue-grey bleakness and people hurrying away to shelter. From its damp edges, crystals of ice had started to grow across the glass. I switched on another table lamp, the effect of which was only to give the impression that night had fallen with the abruptness of the close of an eye. Mr Ford gathered his robe around his shoulders and gloomily regarded his surroundings.

'You go ahead and do that telegram home. Sign it for me.'

I was about to leave when he started on a question, then halted after the first word and said at once that it was nothing.

'There's something else I can do for you?'

He glared at me resentfully, accused me of enjoying the situation and then asked, 'How is Gingham?'

'Mr Bingham? He's . . .'

I recalled Dr Rasmussen's words and decided that their blandness, their hint of encouragement were not at all what was needed. Some embellishment was in order – for the common good. I shook my head in grim resignation.

'Very grave, I'm sorry to say, very grave indeed. It's a sad state of affairs – he is hardly older than I am, a few years younger than yourself. Still a young man, some would say, and then comes a sudden chill on the chest and what can be done . . . ? Sad indeed – but I must let you rest.'

I left my employer to stew in mortality.

As there seemed, in truth, nothing about the condition of

either man to keep me at the hotel, I wrapped myself in half the clothing I had and joined the others tramping through the streets of Christiania to the first great public announcement of the plan to end the war. Madame Schwimmer had begun her work earlier in the afternoon, returning from a private meeting with the Norwegian chapter of the Women's International Peace League bearing tidings that would have made the angel of the annunciation a miserable pessimist by comparison. Reason had returned to Europe the moment her own dainty, Ford-funded foot had stepped off the *Oscar*. A new light shone from the heavens and was already doing its humane work. The evening meeting was to be an altogether larger affair and, I assumed, a tougher test. I was keen to witness it for myself and to make sure that Mr Ford received my version of events as well as others.

In the company of a sombre Reverend Lloyd Jones (he claimed to have some knowledge of the next morning's newspapers), I followed the flow, turning the last corner to find the place already full and a crowd of mostly young people milling around outside. The advent of Mr Ford had not failed to bring with it an entrepreneurial spirit and we had to part with two kroner to be allowed in. The better sections of Christiania society packed the interior. It may have been true that there was nothing much on at the theatre that evening, but the turnout was impressive all the same and the audience just dense enough to bring a little warmth to the air. Standing in a side aisle I recognised the American Minister to Norway, looking apprehensive and perhaps a little bemused by how his obscure office had been so suddenly thrust into activity. I regarded him with sympathy as he endured his own minor case of what can only be described as the Ford effect. He had brought his stenographer to make a record of this private diplomacy and would no doubt be exchanging more telegrams with Washington over the next week than in all the last six months together.

His account of what followed will have caused no great anxiety in the State Department. Things started badly when Lochner explained Mr Ford's absence. There was politeness and concern and unconcealed disappointment. Ford was the image they had come to gaze on and without him the price of admission weighed more heavily on the audience's mind. The affair deteriorated further as Reverend Jones led prayers in a manner suspiciously unfamiliar. An earnest lecture on the Christian duty to be a peacemaker recovered no ground at all. Miss Wales followed with a technical account of continuous mediation. May I be forgiven for recording it, but the truth is she is a woman of rare dullness and the translator clearly did an excellent job in conveying this to her listeners. There was a steady crescendo of shifting and sighing. There was folding of the arms and glances over shoulders towards the exit. There was thought, no doubt, of the many small and necessary tasks that remained to be done at home, of the warm beds that are man's supreme pleasure on a winter's night. I looked across at the American Minister. All anxiety had left his face and his stenographer had ceased to write. The Ford peace expedition looked set to be the most complete and untroubling failure. I do believe he even smiled as he contemplated the phrases with which he would fill out his confidental report. Perhaps he would get Paris next time, or Berlin? Some reward would be in order for these good tidings, surely.

It was left to Madame Schwimmer to turn the tide. She laboured mightily and had a certain effect, there's no denying. But even she struggled, nearly losing her poise altogether as she stood with arms outstretched, breathing heavily in a moment of pregnant silence only for the gap to be filled by a burst of laughter from the back. You would have thought that Schwimmer alone had not heard this disastrous interruption so smoothly did she carry on, but I was close enough to see the sweat run down her face and the heart-racing tremor in her hand. She and her sort are not for me – all the same, as I watched her work to pull back everything she had lost in that savage moment and make the whole hopeless dream seem possible again, she forced no little admiration from me and I willingly joined the applause at the end.

It was Lochner who saved the day. Tempering passion with reason, he found the right tone for his sceptical Scandinavian audience. His explanations were credible without being tediously detailed. He did not shed tears, clutch at his heart or contort his features with a personal agony. He frightened no one and could just about be imagined sitting in a foreign ministry conducting a conversation with men of power and being listened to. The people of Christiania concluded there was only one Rosika Schwimmer in the Ford Peace Party and gave it their blessing.

At the end, those who had spoken came to the front of the stage, joined hands and bowed like actors. The applause swelled, the students shouted and cheered. People were already leaving when Schwimmer called for quiet and astonished everybody, not least those in the inner circle of the Peace Party, by declaring that Mr Ford had decided to donate ten thousand dollars to good causes in every city they visited and the students could do with this money whatever they thought best. Then came a bizarre coda to the evening's events. Singing broke out and the spaces left by the older members of the audience were filled as the young crowd pushed in from where it had been waiting in the cold for the last two hours. The smell of strong drink suffused the air. Chanting started as there emerged from the back of the hall the gilded effigy of an enormous pig carried on poles by four students. The bearers made the pig dance as the chanting and the clapping and the stamping grew louder. The golden pig approached the stage and bowed in gratitude for Henry Ford's ten thousand dollars. Madame Schwimmer bowed to the pig. For a few moments the war, if not stopped, had at least been forgotten.

At the hotel I found a solemn Dr Rasmussen waiting for me in the lobby. Upstairs in Bingham's room the transformation to hospital was complete. The air was stifling and pungent with antiseptic. White-uniformed nurses were changing shift and moved about their work with an ominous, studied quiet. Bingham lay on his back, his face and neck very red and with a sheen of perspiration. He snored, but strangely.

'He is asleep,' I said hopefully.

'No, he is unconscious.'

Dr Rasmussen applied his stethoscope.

'I am sorry, but there is an infection in your friend's lungs. In both of them. Listen.'

He tapped Bingham's chest in several places, so firmly that I was sure his patient would wake up and object.

'You hear that?'

'I don't . . . I know nothing about medicine.'

'You know an empty bottle sounds different from a full one – it's the same. There should be air under here, but there is fluid. When I first examined Mr Bingham there was fluid only here, but now it is here and in a few hours . . .'

His hand moved further up Bingham's chest and then he shrugged and turned to look at me to make sure I understood.

'It was already serious a few hours ago, but little is certain, even in science, Reverend Marquis, and I have seen strong men survive such things. You understand why I said less than I might have done? But now, with weakness, with other illnesses . . .'

'Other illnesses?'

'Your friend has not been well for a long time. Did he not tell you that?'

'I don't know Mr Bingham well.'

'I see.'

'There's no chance?'

Dr Rasmussen glanced briefly at his patient to check, I suppose, that he had not regained consciousness.

'Oh, no – none at all. This man has been dying for the last week. Is it true, what I heard – that he was up at Holmenkollen this morning? Now *that* is remarkable. His case is typical in other respects, but to be on a mountain when it is already so advanced is something I have never heard of before.'

I stared at the rotund and seemingly peaceful form on the bed. My mind turned to practicalities.

'How long?'

'I would say twelve to twenty hours, not likely more than a full day, though I am often wrong about these things. There could still be periods of consciousness, but they will be shorter and more widely spaced as time goes on. The breathing will become shallower and more rapid. The lungs will progressively lose their function and so it is the lack of oxygen in the blood that will be the specific cause of death. If he is aware near the end there will nothing more than a little dizziness. It is like, well perhaps it is like how you feel if you stand up too quickly in the morning – you know?'

I nodded.

'Nothing more than that. A quarter to half an hour later death will follow. But I don't need to explain – as a clergyman you have seen this many times.'

'Well, actually . . .'

'Then perhaps you will see it now, if you wish to.'

He snapped his bag shut and spoke briefly to the nurse before turning back to me.

'I will look in from time to time. Your friend will not be neglected.'

I followed him into the corridor and put the question that really worried me.

'And Mr Ford?'

'Ah, yes,' asked the doctor. 'How is he?'

For an hour I was the only member of the Peace Party to know of Bingham's certain death. I was disturbed by the conviction, however unfounded, that there must be some connection between his fate and Mr Ford's. At first I wanted to reassure myself by visiting him at once – but what if there was some contagion, or I disturbed his rest and weakened him? Was that possible, or mere nonsense? As Dr Rasmussen no doubt meant to convey, a minister of religion is not always a very useful thing to be. I had lurid thoughts of Lloyd Bingham as a dead body, weirdly multiplied in size and weight. What on earth was one to do? Who was to be informed of a dead American entertainer in a Norwegian hotel room? I had some vague notion that his wife was an actress but knew no more than that. Where was she, what would this mean to her? How, more strangely still, had he come to be involved in this? I paced my room and steeled myself for a meeting with Rosika Schwimmer.

In a suite of rooms two floors up the arrangement mimicked that of a government office. Outer chambers were filled with secretarial activity, the salt-proof typewriters already unpacked and ticking away at innumerable reports and press releases. There were new faces – young, local staff, serious as they worked on translations or reports of the Scandinavian and other continental press, the less interesting parts of which lay ankle-deep in shreds about the floor. Six telephones had been installed but perhaps not yet connected – in any case none of them rang when I was there. Room service came and went, feeding and watering those who had no right to a moment's rest. Someone I had not seen before signed for an elaborately garnished lobster. Further in, the more domestic pieces of furniture had been stacked to one side with the peremptoriness of an occupying army. Through this clutter one approached the former master bedroom, now the cabinet of Madame Schwimmer. The door was ajar and her voice could be heard in the steady rhythm of dictation. There was a pause, a thud, a flash and a curl of white smoke drifting into the outer room as the words started again. I stepped aside to let pass a pair of photographers with their bulky equipment.

'Reverend Marquis – come in, come in. Thank you, Rebecca, we'll finish this later.'

Schwimmer strode rapidly to and fro before her desk. She wrung her hands energetically and looked in a vague upward direction, though not at anything in particular.

'What a triumph – a triumph! Let the doubters fly.'

I asked her when Mr Ford had agreed to make his very generous donation. The question seemed trivial to her, quite without implication.

'Mr Ford is a great man. But I have more news for you – it gets better. We have momentum – what all struggling causes need, what transforms them from hopeless to unstoppable in a single day – momentum. Mr Ford has an appointment to meet the Norwegian Foreign Minister tomorrow. There is talk of a meeting with the Prime Minister, perhaps even the King. Interest is growing in Copenhagen – I have excellent reports from our friends there. Peace is coming. It is close.'

She held out her hands to beckon the timid, invisible creature that hovered just out of reach.

'I am negotiating our passage through Germany as we speak. Dr Marquis – we are Europe's new dawn come from the west.'

A telephone rang.

'Excuse me, that must be Berlin now.'

She returned a minute later, only a little crestfallen but with no visible loss of momentum. I didn't ask about the telephone call.

'We must get into the German newspapers and the French – we must speak to the people directly. I will handle Hungary myself, of course. Do you know people in Russia? We must have Russia!'

Madame Schwimmer had ascended to her destiny – the Napoleon of peace.

'There is something you should know.'

In her elation, all news was good news and she was eager to hear it.

'Lloyd Bingham is dying.'

She seemed not to have understood and I started on an explanation.

'So,' she interrupted, 'our vaudevillian is leaving us. I am sorry.'

We were, of course, talking about the man who had ridiculed her, the man who had collaborated in the journalists' theft and rifling of her bag, the identical twin of which stood on the table at our side. A warm response was hardly to be expected.

'He must have his due and I will make sure he gets it. Peace has its casualties as well as war. Let me see now – does he know, has he said anything?'

'He's sleeping. He might not wake again.'

'Then he must trust to us. I shall prepare press releases immediately. Something along the lines of – "I die in a foreign land, far from home but with hope in my heart. I die for the greatest cause possible. I die in joy on the eve of Peace."'

'It doesn't sound like him.'

'People can change. And quite frankly, Dr Marquis, they can also be useful. A dying man should be happy to be made use of – what other compensations can he have for his condition? I think there's a wife somewhere. I'm sure a good collection of press cuttings will ease the pain. They say she is an actress, after all.'

'That's what I wanted to ask you about. Where do we send the telegram, how do we ask her for instructions? I mean – does she want him back? You must have an address.'

The bureaucracy over which Madame Schwimmer presided had been concentrating on other things and she thought it unlikely there was any information.

'But why was he here at all? I've never quite understood

that. What was the connection, how did it happen? If it's going to end this way I just feel I should understand something.'

'You know – there's something strange there. He told me once his wife had arranged it.'

'Is that true?'

'No. I never heard of her before he went on and on about her. He had been drinking.'

'He always seemed out of place.'

'You saw yourself how it was in New York. There was a score of them or more. Mr Bingham was chosen at . . .'

She stopped and looked upwards again, vaguely scanning the cornice.

'He was drafted. Yes, that's it – a soldier for peace. Do you think he would object to being photographed?'

It all happened exactly as Dr Rasmussen had predicted. Bingham did wake from time to time and he talked good clear sense as late as four or five in the morning of his last day. Then there were ramblings and the tiring frustration with others who were too slow-witted to understand him.

'Say, Reverend – you haven't come to give me my last rites, have you? Tell the truth, I don't much hold with that sort of thing.'

I denied any such intention and agreed entirely when he said he might be unwell for quite a while. I don't believe the poor man ever understood his situation and I'm glad of that. I was with him frequently, sometimes for a quarter-hour, sometimes for just a few minutes. A nurse was always there and Rasmussen kept his promise, calling in several times and making sure that he was present at the end. Reverend Lloyd Jones proved stalwart. Miss Milholland came with flowers she had found at a most unsociable hour and talked on cheeringly for a good long time, though without a word of response.

When the morning came and the hotel began to stir I was surprised that we were so completely left alone. The reason was soon clear – the rest of the party was in the dining room and the lounges downstairs already mourning Lloyd Bingham. The translated digest of the local press brought them the news that Madame Schwimmer had not been able to wait for her first martyr. An unknown Bingham was described, his passing the close of one of the great humanitarian careers of the last fifty years. The return of his corpse to the United States, it was confidently predicted, would be the occasion of national grief on a quite unprecedented scale. The temptation was understandable – who in Norway knew anything about any of us? With the exception of Mr Ford we can be whatever we please. In the last hours of Madame Schwimmer's happiness I saw no point in raising the issue with her. I was sure I knew already what her position would be. She would retreat to the possibility of shortening the war by a single day. She would ask how mere honesty could compare with the saving of one, two or five thousand young lives or whatever the last day's toll would be. Who could begrudge anything to the bearer of such an infallible moral pass-key as that? Besides, I also had my uses for the unfortunate Mr Bingham.

I spent the day busy with my own preparations, breaking off whenever I could to check in on Bingham and on my employer too. Mr Ford's physical condition improved steadily and I began to put my most exaggerated fears behind me. His mind remained dark, however, and it was no part of my plan to cheer him up. I kept him closely informed of Bingham's decline and of our difficulties in finding any relative to contact. I firmly approved the cancellation of his appointment with the Foreign Minister and generally remarked as often as I could on all matters relating to cold, dullness and discomfort. I allowed myself the occasional positive note about how well the peace campaign seemed to be doing – how well, that is, without his active participation. In spare moments I studied railway timetables and steamer schedules. I pumped the desk clerks for advice on the availability of taxis at all hours and bribed them handsomely to say nothing to anyone. I left a note for the senior night porter who, I was told, possessed the only key to the hotel safe between the hours of midnight and five a.m.

When it was learned that the entertainer still lived, his sick room became the social centre of the Peace Party. The newsmen were the most frequent visitors, each offering lame jokes about surviving one's own obituary as if they might have the power of a spell, or what seemed to them the only sort of prayer that might work where all earthly power had failed. Several of these new acquaintances wept. All promised him an honourable mention in despatches and I feel sure that if any comfort is to be had for the widow, it will be from these brief lines wired back to the American papers rather than anything Schwimmer has had a hand in. Another public meeting in the town drew them away and so it was quiet in the afternoon when I received what were, for all I know, Lloyd Bingham's last words. I could see from the nurse that nothing more had been expected. She was surprised and quickly active about her patient as soon as there was movement in one arm, a noise in the throat and an opening of clear blue eyes. She spoke in her own language, then asked in English if he was in pain. Bingham made no response but instead, with a vast effort raised a hand from the sheet and laid it on my arm. He turned his head towards me as slowly as if it were made of lead. I believe there was recognition.

'What is it, my friend – is there something we can do for you?'

He started to speak and I leant closer to hear the words . . .

'More clowns. If only you had brought more clowns.'

His hand slipped back and his eyes closed.

The nurse thought there were still some hours to go. I spent the time packing, at one point standing immobile before a half-filled suitcase as someone knocked on my door. How could I explain it if they came in? It was, undoubtedly, a crime scene and I waited until they left before silently turning the lock.

I envisaged what might happen – going though each of the possible obstacles and adjusting my plan point by point until they were all smoothed away. I practised glib answers to awkward questions. Where mere ambiguities would not do, I crafted lies in advance so they would be ready for immediate use. I rehearsed them to a mirror, my ears sharp for the over-eager intonation or the unnatural cadence of deceit. I drilled myself until there was no danger of stopping for a conscience-stricken swallow between one syllable and the next. I would eat with the pacifists in the evening and take an interest in what they thought tomorrow would bring. Perhaps I would add how much I was looking forward to our journey to Stockholm and then to The Hague where we would settle to our task of ending the war, turning the moral force of Henry Ford's billions on the great mystery of human self-destruction. I would drink with the newsmen in the saloon bar, share their worn opinions and agree that the best of the comedy was yet to come. To keep them all blind for another few hours was the essential thing. All that was required was a little organisation, a taxi and ten unwitnessed minutes just after four in the morning. It would be best for everyone.

I called in on Mr Ford again just to make sure there was no change in his mood. All seemed well – other appointments had been cancelled and he blew his nose frequently and complained of every little thing. He rambled on about great mechanical projects and told me he had, in the last half-hour, decided that he would start to make aeroplanes as soon as he got home.

'Aeroplanes are the future, Samuel. There will be a great demand for aeroplanes in the future. Mechanical man ascends through the elements – from land to air to . . . whatever. With the right machines man can be at home anywhere. In ten years I'll make them as cheap as cars. In thirty you'll be able to drive all the way up to heaven just for the weekend and be back in time for work on Monday morning. What do you say to that?'

The old love was reasserting itself, and in Henry Ford's heart there is only room for one at a time.

'How's that man whose name I can never remember? Is he dead yet? Are there children?'

I said I didn't know.

'Well, find out. Tell someone to find out. Is there a widow? I mean, will there be . . . ?'

'A famous actress, they say.'

'I'm going to do right by these people. Remind me of that, Samuel. Don't let me forget.'

'They say she earns the money.'

'I'll send her a car. A car is always acceptable.'

I glanced again at the railway and steamer timetable I had brought in with me. Mr Ford had looked at it pointedly several times, but I had said nothing and there was now an under-standing that neither of us would. I had marked it in pencil – slightly vague marks and certainly without words. They were marks one could interpret any way one pleased. They might not have any meaning at all. I laid the timetable down at the foot of the bed and forgot about it.

'You'll let me know when . . . When it's over?'

I stepped outside to find Ray close by. He confirmed that through the afternoon he had kept everyone away, twice telling Lochner that Mr Ford was asleep and once fending off Samuel McClure's demands for an interview.

'No one must see him now, do you understand? Mr Ford will be fine, but he does not want to speak to anyone – is that clear?'

'Clear enough for me.'

'Just you and me, Ray – no one else.'

He nodded definitely, but had no curiosity as to the purpose of these instructions.

'Tell me, Ray – are you a sound sleeper?'

'You'll have no trouble waking me, sir – any time you need me.'

'I would try to get some rest early tonight. Try to get a couple of hours before twelve.'

I waited for a second or two before leaving him. Surely he must have a question now, I thought, and for a moment I desperately wanted him to ask it. But, no – nothing but another nod of assent and silence. Whatever happened, Ray would be sharing none of the blame.

For half an hour I went over things in my room and listened to the soft tread of feet in the corridor outside and the dulled, recriminatory voices of the Braleys from the floor above. I paced and checked my watch and made primitive attempts to catch some hint of death in the air. What if Bingham survived against all the odds? What if he rose from his bed and told a joke and danced a jig and was taken for a sign and the life flooded back into Mr Ford too and the whole pointless cavalcade rolled on to Stockholm, Copenhagen, Berlin or the trenches on the Somme or whatever damn fool plan she had? Did such things ever happen? I prayed like a child – Oh God, why can't people just see things the way they are?

It was five o'clock. I splashed a little water on my face and stood before the mirror to straighten what needed straightening. I stepped out and turned left toward Lloyd Bingham's room, detecting the disturbing scents of illness long before arriving and finding the door open by a few inches. Inside, there was only Bingham, Dr Rasmussen and the nurse. Rasmussen leaned over his patient with a stethoscope in his ears. I hoped it was over, but as I came further into the room I could hear the faint rasping of breath and see the rise and fall of the chest. This survival exhausted me, and as there was nothing that remained to be done anywhere else I found a chair and sat down, determined to stay till the end. Dr Rasmussen sympathised with my tiredness and told me, in tones proper for the delivery of good news, that it would not be long. Checks were made every few minutes. Breathing diminished to the barely visible, then the invisible. The nurse moistened his staring eyes and closed the lids with her fingers, but still the breath laboured on.

'Has he said anything?'

The doctor smiled at my foolishness and shook his head.

Rasmussen sat at the writing table and opened his bag. He took out a form, a traveller's inkwell and an old-fashioned pen. He took his pocket-watch from where it hung at his black waistcoat and set it, face open, on the table. He sat down to write. If there was a moment, I missed it. Whether I slept or daydreamed I can't say and the next time I was aware of the room nothing seemed to have changed. Bingham lay peacefully on the bed, the whiteness of the sheets and pillow the only bright thing to be seen. Dr Rasmussen continued to fill in his form until the nurse called him over. I too went slowly to the bedside, approaching as the pulse was checked, the stethoscope applied to the rash-red skin of the chest and the eyes, once again open, closely examined. The doctor returned to his bag and took out a metal mirror which he polished on his sleeve. He held it above Bingham's face, flashing its bright reflection in his eyes before holding it steady above his nose and mouth.

'You see?' he asked as he turned its unmisted surface towards me. 'It is over.'

The nurse pulled up the sheet. Rasmussen checked his watch and completed his form before pushing it towards me and indicating the last blank.

'If you would be a witness, please.'

I signed.

'You will need this if you wish to remove the body from the country. If you permit me, I will talk to the manager of the hotel. I know him well – he is an excellent man in these matters and will make whatever arrangements you wish. If there is property of value a notarised inventory can be useful – I have known customs officials to be difficult, particularly these days.'

We both looked at the bedside table. There was an old leather pocketbook and the nickel wristwatch he had shown me on the ship. I heard his voice telling me 'I'm mad for anything new.'

'Well,' said the doctor as he packed up, 'I will leave these things to you.'

The problem of where to send the telegram bothered me again and I hoped something in the pocketbook might provide an answer. I opened it, all too conscious of the intrusion, but found nothing save a single crisp five-dollar bill and, tucked in an inside pocket where it had pressed its shape into the leather over the years, a picture card. My heart felt the shock as I eased it out and held it under the light. There was a young woman in a short brocade jacket with cuffs and lapels trimmed in white fur, a very full lace blouse and a voluminous black bodice skirt very tight about the waist. She held herself carefully in three-quarter profile with her face turned further to the right, darkening one cheek and eye which she directed coquettishly at the camera lens. Tight curls were crowned with the most extravagant millinery. In her gloved hands a parasol was opening. At her feet was the name 'Amelia Bingham' and beneath, in gold cursive against the black frame – *Ogden's Guinea Gold Cigarettes*. I turned it over hoping for an address. There were only a few words handwritten over the print and a date nearly twenty years in the past.

Madame Schwimmer hoped that good things would come of Bingham's demise and I had the same intention as I carried news of it up the stairs and along the corridor, past the ever-watchful Ray and into Mr Ford's room. My parishioner has little taste for religion, being guided in his observances more by a sense of social propriety than by belief. It is not a subject he discusses, but if prompted he would explain to me how my convictions are an outmoded machine, a tangle of old horse harness in an age of automotive miracles. He would tell me how much he had created – more than any man naturally could – how his name was on every street in the civilised world, whatever gods they prayed to, how his workers eat or starve according to what he decides and how he will stop the war. In Mr Ford's religion death is never seeing his factory again, and of this he has an immeasurable fear. I found him in bed, five-day-old American newspapers scattered about and a mess of ticker-tape on the floor.

'Well?'

'Mr Bingham passed away a few moments ago. It was a very peaceful end.'

He had nothing to say about this, but observed instead that the hotel was quiet and asked what he was missing.

'Another public meeting. The town hall this time – some local councillors are attending and professors from the university, I hear.'

Mr Ford particularly deplores professors. He removed the spectacles he usually pretends not to need and let them drop on the coverlet.

'Were they told I would be there?'

'They know not to expect you. Your illness is in all the papers – everyone is concerned.'

I was holding Lloyd Bingham's death certificate – just a piece of paper which I folded at that moment and discreetly put away. Mr Ford's eyes were rimmed with darkness, his narrow features depleted. I looked for the steamer timetable and saw a corner of it beneath one of the newspapers. There was an understanding, but would that be enough? I agonised over whether I should risk another word. Mr Ford greatly values the belief that he is the author of his own life and I have seen before how the most persuasive case comes to nothing only because it is tainted with the opinions and will of another man. Any hint that a return to America was more my idea than his would condemn us both to weeks or even months in Europe, and possibly to no return at all. I waited. I prayed. I felt for him as I watched the long, boyish adventure of not being himself slowly drain away.

'Samuel,' he said to me, 'I guess it's time to go home to mother.'

Ray

I got this theory about men of religion. Think how it is when you're in sight or earshot of one of these characters – there are things you don't say, words you don't use, things you don't do until you're round the corner. Well, after a few years of that your average padre must end up with a pretty partial view of what folks really are. I never did yet meet one without gaps in his knowledge, or who didn't hold to notions a half-witted child would long since have given up on. Now a man in my line of work sees all the things they never catch sight of, and to my mind that gives me no little advantage in the judgement of situations. This Marquis fellow dresses well and talks even better – whatever the subject it's never long before you know about the books Reverend Marquis has read and the operas he's been to. When he says something you don't understand he seems to like it, as if he never meant you to get his drift in the first place or doesn't much care whether you do or not. But I started to wonder if he was any different from the others I've known and I guessed pretty soon he wasn't. And then he came out of Mr Ford's room not twelve hours ago and said to me, 'Ray, I can trust you, can't I? It's tonight – everything's arranged, it'll all go smoothly. Just be ready for when Mr Ford needs you.'

Well, then I knew there must be gaps in his knowledge too – and on more than one count. You see, it's just not in the nature of these things to go smoothly and I wouldn't have bet you a cent to a dollar it had any chance of doing so. There are contrary passions in the world, and they just are what they are. Well-meaning folk can talk them away as long as they like, but it never makes any difference that I can see. There they still are, as hot and senseless as ever. And sometimes they come together, and then there has to be a fight and all you can do is be ready for it. Marquis thought he could get round all that. He thought sneaking away in the middle of the night would be the better way. The whole thing must have been his idea – it had Sunday and sermons and 'God bless you, mam' written all over it, but it ain't my gospel. Now I'm not saying that I can tell the future – it's just that I knew what was going to happen because I was the one that went and told Madame Schwimmer all about it.

'Yes, sir,' I said to Reverend Dr Marquis of the Detroit Episcopal Church. 'You can trust me.'

But to do what? I don't believe the question ever entered his mind.

When I went to see the lady herself I cleared everyone else out of the room and shut the door and sat down without being asked and folded my arms so she couldn't see me shaking.

'Oh!' she says – I had interrupted her in the middle of making up another speech. 'Oh! It's poor Mr Bingham, isn't it. Tell me the worst.'

'Bingham's problems were over three hours ago – half a day after you buried him in the newspapers, from what I hear.'

'That's unkind, Ray. Excuse me – I don't think I ever learned your surname. You must understand that I have always acted for the best. There are bigger things at stake and I am one of those whose role in life is to be burdened by bigger things.'

'That's as may be, lady, but it's not Bingham I've come to talk about. It's Mr Ford.'

'Not Mr Ford too! Oh, monstrous war – are you never satisfied?'

'Mr Ford is going to be just fine. In fact, I'd say that within a week or so he'll be back to normal.'

'I thank God for it. I must talk to him, I want to tell him how well everything is going.'

'Listen, Schwimmer – you're never going to talk to Henry Ford again. You're never going to get within five secretaries of him again, your calls will never be returned, your letters will come back unopened and if anyone catches you anywhere near his home without a damned good explanation you're going to end up in a police station because that's what happens to people Henry Ford doesn't want to see any more.'

What followed was the longest period of silence I ever heard from Madame Schwimmer. She felt her way round the huge desk and slumped into a chair where she seemed, just for a moment, very small and beaten. Perhaps I hadn't said any of it. Perhaps the things you didn't like about the world could be made to go away if only you were good enough at ignoring them. That was the rule all along with these people, and for Schwimmer I guess it had to be worth one last try.

'But what are you saying? I don't understand.'

'I want you to get this first – what I am about to do is give you the power to destroy me. When I walk out of here all it'll take from you is one word and I'll be back where I was ten years ago just as if nothing had happened. I'll be back on the docks at four-thirty in the morning pushing old men out of the way to get a day's work at thirty cents an hour, but I'm going to do it anyway. It's simple – he's doing a runner. Marquis has arranged the whole thing. Four o'clock tomorrow morning they flit for the early boat train to Bergen. No looking the people of Norway in the eye, no spending his fortune to stop the war, no nothing. It's over.'

It just wouldn't go in.

'It's not true. You hate him, I can see that. You don't care about what we're trying to do. I know him – he is a good man.'

'Listen, Rosika. When Henry Ford doesn't feel like talking to his marketing director he climbs out the window of his own goddamned office. And don't tell me it isn't true – I'm the guy who sits in his car all day at the bottom of the fire escape to take him home. That's my job and in a few hours I'm going to do it again.'

'It's a misunderstanding. Let me talk to him, let me give him a little strength. Someone has poisoned his mind, but when I tell him how close we are . . .'

'It's too late. He's lost interest in you, he's lost interest in the war. This is how it always is. Don't you see? None of this was ever supposed to happen. There are men whose whole purpose in life is to stop people like you getting anywhere near Henry Ford – not because they're 'small people', but because they know what he's like. Normally they're pretty good at it, then someone messes up or a crank gets lucky and we all go on a jaunt. There were others, now there's this one and there'll be more in the future. He doesn't care, Rosika – he just gets bored.'

There's one thing you can't take away from Rosika Schwimmer – she can take a blow as good as any eighteen-stone bare-knuckle prizefighter and press on through to the bell like it was nothing. I saw that when she picked herself up after Bingham ridiculed her in front of all those newsmen, and I saw it again just then as she got her breath back and her mind right on the job.

'So,' she says to me, 'what about the money?'

I shrugged, said I knew nothing about it, that I kept away from all that. She pressed me, asking if I had heard anything at all about it, had it been mentioned, would Mr Ford really cut off the cause of world peace without a cent?

'You really want my advice? Say nothing about the money. There's an even chance that whatever you're getting now you'll still be getting in six months' time, if only because no one back in Detroit notices the cost of half a dozen cars a day out of a couple of thousand. Let him forget about you and he'll forget about the money too. People don't get the money, Rosika. They think it's commitment, but that's not it at all. To Mr Ford it simply isn't worth anything.'

We were standing together by the door. She asked one more time if she could speak to him but showed no surprise when I refused. I began to make my excuses, telling her it would be better for everyone if I got back before questions were asked. She half opened the door and then closed it again and took a step closer so that I had to look straight down on her small, unnerving form. She put her hand on my arm.

'You believe in us, don't you, Ray? You believe we can make peace. Why don't you come with us?'

'You really want to know why I'm here? It wasn't part of my plan, but you asked so I'll tell you. It's got nothing to do with you or your rainbow-chasing peace project. I came here because you and I are a pair. Before Henry Ford took me up I was nothing and when he's finished with me I'll be nothing again, just like you. What he's going to do to you tomorrow morning, he'll do to me one day, sure as death. When that happens I'll want to tell myself there was five minutes in the whole damned ride when I wasn't owned. Well, that was my five minutes.'

'Come with us, Ray. It can be more than five minutes.'

That's another thing about Rosika Schwimmer – she can deal out the blows just as well as she can take them. I guess that was how she got her whole strange crew together in the first place, Mr Ford included – stirring them up, then promising each one she had the balm for what ailed them. I tried to look as if it hadn't got through, but I reckon everyone who's lived a bit has got that spot – that special place so that however cleverly you say it isn't there, the words still come out like a cry of pain.

'You can't afford my services, Rosika. You don't need them neither – you'll never be important enough for anyone to assassinate. Goodnight.'

I spent time in my room, counting off the minutes until the journey home could start. Dulled voices came through the wall – Marquis mostly, and the occasional word from the captive Mr Ford. I got to thinking – why did it have to be this way, why not a speech to everyone, thanks, a big fat cheque and best wishes for the future? Why not in daylight? Then again, why does he still climb out of his window rather than call through to his secretary and cancel the appointment? Things way back, I suppose – the things that make folk as they are. You need more than a billion dollars to change that.

I slept a little and tried to forget Rosika's words and that look on her face as she said them – '. . . more than five minutes'. You got to ask yourself – who else but Rosika Schwimmer could have brought us here, to this? The woman's got qualities. What you would call them exactly, I don't know – but she's got them. Was it so impossible – going with them and making peace, or at least feeling good while we tried? I started to see the moment. The taxi door would slam with me still on the outside and I make some big-sounding speech through the window.

'Mr Ford, sir – you may have all the money in the world but I've got what you ain't – principles, a heart, love for my fellow man and I'm staying.'

People love that stuff. I could look real serious and wag my finger at him and then someone would hold the words up on a board and everyone would cheer. I started to think maybe I should go west and get a job in the pictures – they say all you have to do is look human. How hard can that be? My mind wandered to places it hadn't been for ten years and I found myself again and again pulled back to the moment it all changed. There are the railings and the batons, the fire-hoses and the rank steam rising from the crowd of men on the other side. There is the face of that scrawny guy I've got by the collar – not pushing him away any more like the others but pulling him towards me, dragging his miserable features hard up against the iron of the railings till we're damn near skin to skin as I swing at him and he's calling me everything evil he can think of and I turn to see why they're opening the gates and there, in that fixed, powder-flash clarity is all I can remember of my first sight of Mr Henry Ford. What did I think then, and what did I think a day later when I came out of his office feeling like . . . , well I don't know – something like what those big tent preachers go on about when God has been talking to them? I felt like I would never be on the wrong side of those railings again. And that, I suppose, is the heart of it. Own myself for more than five minutes? I like to talk that stuff, but the truth is I owned myself for thirty years up till that day. I just didn't make anything of it – not like Mr Ford has.

I awoke stiff and seedy from sleeping in my clothes and thinking I must have heard something. There was another timid knock at the door and the sound of Marquis hissing my name. I checked the time – twenty after three. The door handle turned furtively and there he was with his coat buttoned up and his hat and gloves on and an unhappy Mr Ford by his side, clutching his lapels around his neck and starting to shiver with nerves.

'Ray, are you ready?'

He froze for a few seconds, testing the silence.

'Come on, everything's fine,' he told me. 'The taxi should be waiting. We'll be at the station in no time.'

He reached out to call the elevator, pushed the button a second and then a third time and swore. A few minutes passed as we retreated into Mr Ford's room and Marquis summoned night porters and organised an eight-man baggage train down the main staircase. They were hardly clumsy, but Marquis made things worse by loudly shushing them and wincing with every tiny noise.

There was something comical about it as I watched them creep down. What was waiting for Mr Ford and his friend in the lobby? I couldn't be sure and didn't even know what to hope for – an easy end to it, or the full melodramatic works. What would Rosika Schwimmer choose?

Either way there was another thing Marquis didn't know. His habits always took him early to bed and he never understood that the Ford Peace Party had quite a night life, whether it be in the form of newsmen drinking and arguing, political and social debaters who never knew when to stop, or the young folks sneaking from room to room when there was no one but me around to see. All in all I reckoned his chances of getting clean away were no better than zero.

'You go on,' I said to them both. 'I'll give the room one last check.'

They went out of sight around the turn of the stairs, inching down a step at a time behind two porters with a steamer trunk. I leaned back, lit a cigarette and waited. What would the first sound be? The farce of a trunk falling down the stairs and sleepy people coming from all directions to see what was up? Or would it be the opening phrases of Rosika's great speech as she put some steel into the boss and changed his mind for him? It turned out a little different in the end.

It was Marion Braley who set the fireworks off. Everyone knew the first few days of married life had been a disappointment to this young lady. Her voice was shrill and often carried beyond the walls of cabin or hotel room as she made her complaints. Even at four in the morning it was not unusual to hear her, and so I paid no attention at first. Then I realised she was really letting it rip and if there had ever been a chance of a clean getaway Marion was about to ruin it. I start to go down and I'm just getting to the first floor when the Braleys' door bursts open. There's Marion in her nightdress not giving a damn about anything. She's crying and screaming all at once and I duck as a shoe flies by and bounces off the wall.

'You bastard, Berton Braley! Ten days – ten days married and *this*, you bastard.'

I try to get past her, but she doesn't even see me and wanders in my way as she tears this piece of paper to shreds and throws them back towards the room. Berton shouts something I don't catch, but it only makes Marion more mad.

'It is *not* a work of art, Berton Braley. It's not even a poem, you bastard – it's a love letter!'

Berton comes stumbling out, half tripping over himself as he stuffs his shirt tails into his pants.

'For Christ's sake, Marion, do you want to wake the whole damned . . .'

He sees me and freezes. Doors are opening everywhere, lights are coming on, ordinary folks coming out and asking questions or complaining in several languages. Half a flight of stairs down Marquis is shouting, 'Go on, go on.' Someone stumbles over a valise and for a few seconds they go nowhere. Berton notices them for the first time and walks past his new wife to look over the bannister. Twenty other assorted guests of the Christiania Grand Hotel do the same. They find the Reverend Dr Marquis of Detroit and Mr Henry Ford in a jam of baggage, dressed for escape and looking back up at them with two of the worst poker faces in the whole history of the world, caught like they were no more than a couple of bums who couldn't pay the bill. Berton forgets all about his domestic troubles and tries instead for a career-making story.

'Would you say something to the readers of *Collier's Magazine* before you go, Mr Ford? Have you changed your mind about peace? Were your critics right all along? Should America join the war?'

Foreigners mill about trying to find out what's going on, Marion speechifies about her louse husband and the worst mistake of her life, Berton hustles for a quote from the boss as Marquis bullies the porters.

'Pick it up, get a move on!'

They do exactly that and go down out of my sight, turning to the last flight of stairs where they can be seen from the lobby. There's an ambush of noise and camera flashes. Rosika has elected for the big scene and it's her voice that cuts through the chaos.

'Be strong, Mr Ford. Be all you can be – don't be dragged down by the little people!'

Lochner's voice is in there somewhere too and I can pick out six or seven of the newsmen all shouting questions at once. The bearded reverend starts to sing. Pretty much the whole damned expedition has been lying in wait – thanks to me. Marquis's voice is suddenly loud – he's losing his grip.

'Get away from him you stupid woman – haven't you done enough harm already? Ray, Ray where the hell are you?'

I can hear the panic and go down to be with the old man. I push the newsmen out of the way and tell Marquis to go ahead. I get such a hold on Mr Ford I nearly lift him clean off the floor and drag him to the door. The Hungarian gets there first and plants herself in our way.

'Oh, Mr Ford, don't do this, I beg you. We're so close to success. We *can* stop the war, we really can, and there'll never be another, and it'll be the greatest thing anyone has ever done. The future of mankind is a future of peace. Mr Ford, you can put your name on it for ever!'

Well, that Rosika Schwimmer is one smart lady and she knows just what Mr Ford likes to hear. And the strangest thing is it almost worked. No one else will ever know it, but I felt his skinny arm stiffen and his body push back against mine and for half a second I feared he might stop and say – 'Just wait a minute, Ray, maybe this whole thing isn't so stupid after all.'

Rosika might have learned something about Mr Ford, but she'd got me all wrong. I tell her to get out the way and before she has the chance to think about it I lay a hand on her and yank her aside so hard she falls over. She shrieks with alarm, little feet kicking out the end of her petticoat as her glasses go sliding over the polished floor and find their end somewhere under the feet of a photographer. She makes a meal of it, of course, and gentlemanly types come running to help.

'Outrageous! How dare you!'

But I don't give a damn for any of them. And just at that moment, working at what I know best, I didn't give a damn for Rosika either. She had had her chance, Marquis was getting his punishment and I had my job to do. I step over her and drag a trembling Mr Ford out of the hotel. The cold drops on us like an anvil. It's snowing heavily – everything is thick white and I can see from the lack of tracks that there have been few visitors to the hotel in the last hours. It's not even clear where the driveway is and I think for a nightmarish moment there just isn't one there at all, this is all there is of the world and we'll be re-running this farce night after night for ever.

The only marks in this field of snow curve round to a large laundry truck which has just pulled up. Two guys are getting out and starting to ask questions I can't understand. There's no sign of the taxi Marquis promised, but then I hear his voice from the other side of the truck and I go round with Mr Ford to see him picking his way through the snow towards oncoming lights.

'Here it is,' he calls back to us.

The taxi slithers to a halt as soon as it meets Marquis, thirty yards or more from the doorway of the hotel. Mr Ford's hat and shoulders are already white with snow. His face is bluish and he's shivering violently as I rush him towards the taxi. All the time the scene is getting brighter as the last few people asleep in the hotel wake up, turn on their lights and pull back the curtains to see what's happening. We have stage shadows as we run about, Marquis now going back the other way as he remembers the baggage and the porters at whom he shouts and waves a handful of banknotes. I get Mr Ford into the back of the cab. He's dazed, listless – he doesn't seem to know where he is. I bellow, 'Station, train station, railway,' until there's some sign of understanding from the driver. What has he been told, has anything been organised at all? The man clearly has no experience of emergency getaways and starts to help with the bags. Two suitcases are bundled in the back beside a rigid Mr Ford, another is slammed on the roof. A luggage rack overhangs the back of the vehicle and here there is a confused struggle involving hotel porters, Marquis, a steamer trunk and too many leather straps. It's all bad news, and I realise just how bad as I look back towards the hotel and see the posse coming our way. All the hard cases are there – Lochner, Fels the soap widow, Madame Malmberg the Finnish exile and her tasty pig-tailed sidekick, Judge Ben Lindsey, State Senator Robinson, a whole pack of reverends, two comedians off to one side who fight and fall over as they try to set up a moving-picture camera, even Berton Braley has found some more clothes and is heading our way with a notebook and pencil. To the fore is Rebecca Shelly and at the head of them all the dumpy relentless darkness of Rosika Schwimmer herself, wrapped up in her new fur coat.

Someone is shouting from a hotel window and I guess 'politi' must be Norwegian for the cops. I make a quick count of the peacettes and realise we're in serious trouble. I get the notion they're going to surround the car. Marquis will crack for sure and the whole idea of a breakout will fall apart. At this moment he's concentrating on a second trunk.

'Leave it,' I yell at him. 'For Christ's sake, leave the damned thing and get in the car!'

He turns to see Schwimmer and the gang advancing on him. Marquis isn't made for this. His thinking gets stuck on the trunk and he goes back to the straps and tells me just another second or two and it'll be fine, like we're all off on a goddamned picnic.

It's an emergency. I put my hand to my inside jacket pocket. Marquis lets the trunk fall on his toes and then jumps in front of me, holding his arms out wide and shouting like a madman.

'Oh, God – not that, Ray. For pity's sake, don't let it come to that!'

People get the strangest ideas. I take it out anyway – what Mr Ford gave me in the Biltmore Hotel. 'Now you keep that out of sight, Ray. That's just a little reserve for you and me in case we should need it.' It's given me a queer feeling all along, a man like me carrying a thing like that and having to put my fingers in there to touch it all the time to see that it's not vanished somehow, as if it could. It's the same for the others – they stare intently as though a curtain has just risen on something they've never seen before. Only Mr Ford, shivering in the car, pays no attention to the neat block of two hundred fifty dollar bills still in their cashier's wrapper fresh from the bank – a lifetime's work for Joe, in the palm of one man's hand. I yell again at Marquis to get in the car and at last he does what he's told. The trunk and the other cases are left where they lie. I peel off a thickness of money and hand it out to the nearest hotel porter.

'You send these on, understand? Mr Henry Ford, United States of America – they'll get there.'

The man hesitates and I let the bills flutter down to the snow. I catch myself despising him, almost as if the money is mine, then there's no time to think of anything.

Marquis is in the front seat. Mr Ford is in the back at the

right-hand side and I jump in at the left. We might have made it just then, had anyone been behind the wheel. There's an outburst of profanities and shouting and the driver gives up on the bags and runs for his cab. It's too late. Rosika catches us and starts banging on the window and screaming and crying like someone's stealing her baby. She does all this six inches from Mr Ford's face, but he looks ahead so still and pale and like he's frozen solid there I wonder if it's all for nothing.

'Drive, drive!' shouts Marquis.

The engine sings, the wheels spin against the snow and we go nowhere. People are trying to haul Rosika back, but she's losing control. She grabs for the door handle and gets it half open before I can lean across and slam it shut again. She's got a new tune to sing, all about how much she cares for Mr Ford.

'Don't do this. Mr Ford, don't let them take you – you're too ill to travel. Stay with us until you're stronger.'

She goes for broke.

'Murder! Kidnap! Somebody stop them.'

Now I'm yelling at the driver too, praying he can find some grip. Rosika is coming round to the other side and the cab lurches forward just as she's behind it. I can't quite see what happens – maybe she stumbles, maybe she reaches for it, I don't suppose I'll ever know. The cab jumps again then picks up some speed, slewing this way and that across the soft snow. Marquis thanks God and urges the driver on. I look back through the tiny rear window. The Peace Party delegates, the newsboys, the hotel, the laundry truck and the moving cameramen shooting the night all get smaller – only Rosika's panic-stricken face stays the same.

I look down and see her white hands paralysed on the luggage straps. Her feet draw tramlines within the cab's wider tracks as she's pulled along.

'Can't you go any faster?' asks Marquis, who is looking ahead and thinking of home.

The driver says something angry but opens the throttle all the same. Mr Ford is still a statue and even a strangulated shriek from Rosika doesn't shake him. Marquis looks back at the noise just as I say, 'Brake, brake!' The driver does his best, but we glide on over the snow, twisting sideways. Marquis is saying she must be mad. Rosika, now pressed up against the rear glass by the loss of momentum, is yammering away in her mother tongue. It occurs to me that this white, soft-edged world we are escaping through is padded, momentarily safe for the insane.

'Give it some gas, Mac. Shake her off.'

The driver lifts from the brake and steers into the slide. We pick up speed and Rosika is plucked from the luggage straps and deposited as a dark, furry mound in the middle of the snowbound driveway. We slide to a halt. Except for Mr Ford we're all looking backwards. The driver and I hold our breath. Marquis laments – 'We've killed her. Oh, my God. Oh, Jesus, we've killed her.'

But the helpers come running and there is movement. The scene freezes in my mind as Rosika is helped to her feet and, deeper in the lit background, the laundry truck stands with its wing doors open as it receives, discreetly as they must have thought at this godforsaken hour, the mortal remains of Lloyd Bingham. Lochner dusts the snow from the standing, unharmed conscience of the world. I follow his gaze upward and see that in all this we have barely gone beyond the length of the hotel itself. Directly above, through a bright open window, cut out against the darkness, there tolls over us all, as unanswerable as Cinderella's midnight bell, the beautiful laughter of Inez Milholland.

Clara

*O*ne afternoon, when Henry was still away, I remembered who I was – Clara Bryant of Dearborn, Michigan, daughter of farming folk, sister to two sisters and seven brothers, descendant of Warwickshire stock, good at baking and with a neat quilting stitch. What more was there to know about me? I was like the others and can look back on four or five young men who might have been my husband. I'm sure Henry can do the same and think of half a dozen from our small field of friends and acquaintances who might have done well enough had a dance, or a glance, been different. We married, we had few choices – good enough was good enough. I wonder what those other brides would have become – changed versions of themselves or just me, the Mrs Henry Ford, slightly different raw materials in at one end but the same reliable product out the other?

Sometimes I want to ask him how much he foresaw. Did he know what a long, strange journey he would take, and me with him, dragged along farther and faster than I could ever have imagined? I don't say I was ever reluctant, but there are days when I wonder if less might have been happier. The invoice from Altman's has come. I look over the list of carpets and rugs I have ordered for Fair Lane and write a cheque for fifty-seven thousand one hundred and five dollars and eighty-one cents. I carefully transfer the number into my account book, never failing to hear my mother's advice on the importance of looking after the cents. Two people look at the number – one still astonished, but the other unstirred by anything except perhaps a sense of unlooked-for responsibility and a guilty sadness.

I quickly learned that it is the vocation of Mrs Henry Ford to be alone – alone across the dinner table from her husband, alone in the same bed, alone with our lonely only son, alone when reading to him by the fire only to discover that he has been somewhere else for the last five pages. Twenty years ago, I secretly tried to teach myself engineering. I hid a primer beneath the mattress for fear that he should find it and laugh at me. I felt it like the princess felt her pea as I lay awake and listened to the sound of machinery coming from his workshop through half the night. I planned to ask him a question one evening about vanadium alloys – the words are all I can remember now. I imagined we could talk together for hour after hour like he did with the men, but I never had the courage to start that conversation.

I contented myself with the things I understood, all the things Henry does not outwardly care for or know about, or even much notice, as long as they are still there when he comes home, whistling his little tune in the hallway. I built my own machine – until recently it has turned my husband's world so smoothly he has never suspected its existence. This domestic machine does many things, but the most important of all has been to keep my Henry safe from himself and from all the cunning and cleverness of the world that a man who only knows one thing could easily fall prey to. The worst times when he was away were when I thought of him not coming back at all. When I learned that one delegate had indeed died, the idea of widowhood grew in my mind almost to a certainty as if it had already happened. With it came the thought that it would be my fault, the result of a breakdown in my machine. I don't believe I have ever been more miserable than when I returned from New York and that disaster on the Hoboken pier. Edsel stayed with me for a couple of days and I went on as if nothing had happened. Then he went golfing in Virginia and I sent the staff away and wept from morning till night. Who were these strangers Henry was so keen to follow, why was my house suddenly so empty? This was a new way of being alone, and in the middle of the winter too. I heard bird calls as voices and when the wind blew and the timbers creaked it was the sound of a car pulling up and Henry opening the door, just as they say it is when you know someone is never coming back. I am still angry with him for that.

There are, of course, expectations of the Mrs Henry Ford. Her married name rolls down every Main Street in the country and proclaims itself from every fourth billboard in the world – or at least in all those parts of the world I have visited. She is durable and easily repaired. She is never off the road for long. I busied myself with completing the house, choosing the fabric for the curtains and sorting through the player rolls that had been sent for the organ, deciding which to keep and which to send back. I endured a visit from Mr Liebold, such an unsympathetic man. He pestered me for an invitation and I was forced to find half an hour for him in town. He wanted to talk about his concerns for me at this worrying time, but quickly moved on to an explanation of where he had been when Madame Schwimmer and Mr Lochner first came to call on my husband. He repeated how firmly he had been against the whole peace scheme. I fell quiet before the end of his visit and allowed the maid to show him out. I really don't know what Henry sees in him.

I thought ahead to spring and drew and redrew plans for

the new gardens. Hours could pass this way almost entirely without anxiety. The men from Willens came to review the construction of the glasshouses and then Mr Jensen himself from Chicago. We wrapped up warm and walked the grounds for a whole afternoon until I could see exactly how it would be.

'In ten years,' he told me, 'it will be exquisite.'

We understood each other so well and he described every-thing so beautifully that it became quite real to me. I could see and smell the summer even as we stood among the drip-ping trees and the dreary, melting snow. But in my daydreams it was only myself I could see walking by the brilliant banks of peonies.

Back at the house the hall table groaned under letters and newspapers and telegrams too terrible in my imagination for me even to touch. I opened a parcel one morning – it was the day the *Oscar* steamed into the restricted zone where the U-boats hunt. Inside was a jeweller's case, and inside that a string of pearls paid for with my husband's money. I would like to forget that day.

The newspapers have been a burden and one, surely, that no earlier generation has had to bear in quite this way. Young Mr Delavigne has been scathing about his former colleagues and tells me I mustn't pay attention to a single thing they say. He says he knows for a fact that a full two thirds of every-thing in the papers is just plain made up, but I suppose he is just trying to be kind. It is strangely hard to keep away from what people write about you and your family, and what others read all over the country in their hundreds of thousands, in their millions I suppose. Privacy is wrecked, a single harsh word withers the day and yet one is drawn back to it again and again, peace as much spoiled by ignorance as by knowledge. Friends send consoling notes – dreadful, they say, outright lies, rise above it all. And yet, their well-meaning letter is the first one hears of it – gunfire in the dining room, my husband a deranged prisoner in his own cabin, a Pittsburgh steel-worker's dream of the *Oscar* torpedoed and sinking in mid-Atlantic. At such times everyone is a bearer of bad news. Henry knows nothing of these things. It is against his principles to notice backward steps. When he talks of the future, and I love it when he does, all is progress and improvement and I'm sure that part of the picture he sees will come together exactly as he says. But I think we make new pains for ourselves too. The newspapers are a new pain, and the tar on the country roads that kills the fish when it rains. We get what we want faster and easier, and electric trains crash into stalled automobiles and Victor Nicholson, returning from an orphanage outing, dies at five years of age and is forgotten as I fold his name out of sight. Something always holds us back.

I would not go to New York when Henry came home. My experience of the Biltmore Hotel and the departure from Hoboken is something I swore I would never repeat. I read of my husband's return in the newspapers, but let him and his companions take the train to Detroit from where Samuel and Mr Delavigne brought him out here to Dearborn. It was near a month since I had last seen him, our longest ever separation, but at first sight it could have been ten years and I had to try hard not to let him see how worried I was. At first all I wanted was to keep everyone away from him, the whole bruising world if I could. I managed it for a while, intercepting letters and telegrams, fending off the company's managers and secretaries and even lying to Mr Liebold on the telephone about all his messages I had not, in fact, passed on. Henry never questioned it – he seemed to believe everything I told him and for a while there was peace such as we have not enjoyed for many years.

I should not have been so anxious about his physical condition. Within a few days it was clear that it was nothing more than his usual winter cold made worse by tiredness and nerves.

But he suffers still in his mind, his thoughts endlessly returning to the events of his misadventure, redrawing them a thousand
times as if they are a puzzle or a machine that can finally be
made to work.

I talk to him of ordinary things, the domestic tasks of the
day, nothing that is not within sight or reach. We oversee the
work on Fair Lane, settling the last details of the design and
choosing the furniture from the catalogues and pattern-books
the tradesmen bring. Mostly I make suggestions and Henry
distractedly agrees. It is good for him not to make decisions.
We still live in the old farmhouse and in the evenings when
the staff have finished and we are alone we sit either side of
the fireplace like a picture of our parents from forty years ago.
I read *Good Housekeeping* while Henry looks through *Scientific
American* before falling asleep. These are happy moments for
me and I can imagine that the last few weeks never happened.
I think of a future of twenty years or more just the same –
the company sold, the newspapers read only for recipes or the
latest fashions, grandchildren, being no one but ourselves. I
conduct imaginary conversations in which Henry gradually
comes to understand me and lays down these pointless burdens
that have made him so pale and lined. But this was never more
than a private game, and one I treasured as I watched him
recover, knowing that every day he strengthened and cleared
his mind was a day closer to it starting all over again.

The first room to be habitable in the new house is our
wonderful sun parlour facing the river. On good days it gets
as warm as a greenhouse and Henry is happy to be planted
there for hours on end. He sets himself up with his telescope
and keeps his eye on the bird boxes in the woods. Three years
ago, when we were travelling in a peaceful Europe, Henry
stopped suddenly one morning and said, 'Listen – don't you
think these birds sing more sweetly than the ones at home?' I
suggested they might just be different, but he was very sure

and found an aviary in London to put six hundred thrushes, finches, skylarks, linnets, warblers and nuthatches into cages and ship them across to America. The survivors were released here the following April. From time to time Henry still thinks he sees one of them or hears a foreign call, but to me the birds in Dearborn seem just as they always did.

It was in the sun parlour that I found him a fortnight ago drowsing in a recliner, happy for having seen a grey jay, but with the outside world washed up around him in a litter of newspaper pages. I put the tray down on the table and sat beside him. He took my hand and we were quiet for a long time.

'Callie,' he said at last. 'Who was King Canute?'

'I don't know, dear.'

'Don Quixote?'

'I don't know dear, I really don't. You shouldn't be reading those terrible things. What good can it do?'

King Midas he does know, the story recalled in every detail from one of his old school readers. He nudges one of the newspaper sheets with his foot.

'It's true what they say about me here – I have been a failure at everything except making money.'

I tell him right away I don't like to hear such talk. For a moment he seems distant and shocked and infinitely regretful as if he suspects that money, gold if you will, and any amount of it, can do no good so long as it is in his faulty hands. I refuse to talk about this. I refuse to be interested in any of it and say the only thing in my mind.

'You married me, Henry.'

I watch the sun inch across the new carpets as the long, slow thought forms.

'Callie, if I were to die and come back to another life I would change everything except my wife.'

We have reached the middle of March and the early signs

of spring are certain. There are as many difficulties as before, but we are stronger in bearing them. There now seems to be no subject of discussion other than preparedness for this terrible conflict. Mr Wilson speaks of little else, Congress votes money, some say it was always going to be this way, there was never anything anyone could have done. The people ask, 'How can we be safe?' A man on Brooklyn Bridge is arrested with a bomb in his suitcase. It is hard for Henry to see all this. He shouts at the newspapers and there is hardly a single page he can now read without some upset – health tonics to make you fighting fit, boots good for marching, corsets that promise a shape that will please embarking soldiers. The flag is everywhere and he has come to hate it – 'Flags are for fools,' he tells me. 'What are they but something to rally round? I'll pull the flag down from the factory and never raise it again. Why should I not? Men born in fifty countries go to work there every day.' I spoke to Samuel and Mr Delavigne and they dissuaded him, for now at least. Somehow his opinions reached the press and there are those who openly call him a traitor. For others he is a hero and his name has appeared on the Republican presidential nomination, though only in Nebraska. Henry will not admit to knowing how this has happened, but I have told my dear husband that if he runs for President I will divorce him. He smiled.

Fair Lane is now fit for guests, on the ground floor at least. Henry has decided it is fit for business too. He has had a long table set up in the sun parlour and he is there now, alone after a tiring day. Outside, men are talking and engines starting. Henry is in his recliner holding his field glasses to his eyes. I stroke his hair and ask him if he has seen anything interesting. In reply he puts his finger to his lips and says – 'Not a word, Callie. Not a single word.'

I sit with him and together we look out across the river. I see the bright blue of Mr Delavigne's automobile as it splashes down the half-made road towards town. In the back sit the men from the War Office. They hold their briefcases on their laps. In one of them there is my husband's contract for ten thousand ambulances.